A Ransom of Shadow and Souls

J.L. Tomlinson

A RANSOM OF SHADOW AND SOULS

First edition. November 2, 2025.

Copyright © 2025 J.L. Tomlinson.

Written by J.L. Tomlinson.

ISBN: 978-0-473-76762-4

To all those who made it clear every day how special
these characters were, who supporeted me dispite the delays.
I thank you for your kindness.

In a world where you can be anything, be kind.

Unless you can be Beyonce. Then be Beyonce.

JOR'THALAS

MOR'THRAVAR

THAL'MORVEN

EYR'DROGUL

FYN'ROTHAR

BAEV'KALATH
HOUSE MORDORIN

PARISETH

GRYN'VELCOR

THE UNTOLD SEA

CYRATH
HOUSE ITHRANOR

THE SUNDERED
KINGDOMS

KALE HARBOR

VALORNE
HOUSE MALEDANNAN

LORTHYS
HOUSE CAELITHAR

THE GROVE

RETHMAR
HOUSE VALASTRAL

THYROS
HOUSE TARAMETHOS

CHAPTER 1
DAED

Before her. I am a cursed prince, bound to a cursed throne. Hated, loved, feared, and desired in equal measure. The favored son of an ill-fated house, my name lingers in whispers meant for horrors too dreadful to speak aloud, the kind that haunt your dreams and leave you trembling in the dead of night. The shadows do not own me. I command them. Born of smoke and ash, betrayal and blood, I am the terror they dare not name. To face me on the battlefield is to meet your end, your final breath stolen before the void consumes you whole.

But today, there is something greater than my curse, greater than the weight of my name. An omen so terrible that the mighty Fae houses tremble at its coming. Whispers of its existence ripple through the Sundered Kingdoms, seeding panic where arrogance once reigned.

And so I am dispatched, my presence a reluctant admission that this threat could undo even us. I am to find it, this nameless dread, and drag it into the dark where it belongs.

A hard, echoing knock shatters the silence of my cabin. The door swings open, and Reaper Arax stands tall and broad in his black armor.

"Prince Daedalus," he says, pounding his gloved fist to his chest in salute. "We've arrived in Valorne."

I glance up from my table, where maps and scrolls are strewn amid an empty goblet and a drained jug of wine.

Fuck, he looks old. Is this what I have to look forward to when the years pass in their thousands? Hair long and fine as silk, streaked through with gray. Deep lines carved into my brow from too many years of scowling. I suppose it's a testament to his endurance. To the sheer stubbornness it takes to live this long after all the battles he's fought and won.

Insufferable as he may be, with his rigid sense of duty, he is a warrior of the highest caliber, and I trust him with my life.

His gaze narrows at my empty goblet, and I hear the disapproving grumble in his throat. But he says nothing. He knows better.

"Good," I say. "I will meet with Lord Eryndor alone."

My words earn another rumble of disagreement.

"I do not recommend such an action, my prince," Arax says. "The Sundered Kingdoms are vast, with many who wish you harm."

A laugh escapes me. A sharp, bitter thing that doesn't suit the gravity of his tone.

"I would welcome any fool who thinks my crown would look better atop their head. I hope its weight crushes their skulls." I rise from my chair, pressing my hands against the table, the runes tattooed on my knuckles pulsing faintly. "Or I'll separate that ambitious head from their shoulders. Either way, it won't end well for them."

Arax is still unconvinced. I can't see his lips beneath his thick, gray beard, but I'm certain they're twitching.

I exhale. "Fine. You may come. But only you."

Now I'm certain he's grinning.

"As you command, my prince." The thump of his fist on his chest signals his exit.

I stand for a moment, the room falling still around me. My thoughts press in too close, spilling into the space that wine should have dulled. Jugs of it emptied since leaving Baev'kalath.

This is no easy task. No simple squabble between Fae houses that bend to Mordorin's will, nor an uprising from humans who bend even lower. If Eryndor is right, if what he claims has risen in this forest of his, this... Grove, then it is a threat I must tear from the earth like a weed and burn to ash before it spreads. Father's patience is already running thin with me.

When I step out of the dark of my cabin, the sun strikes me, harsh and unforgiving. I raise a hand to shield my eyes from the glare, its intensity unbearable. And the heat... it's worse. It creeps under my skin, like it's trying to worm its way into my blood.

Baev'kalath is cold, dark, and hard, and centuries spent within the insidious walls of its fortress have shaped me into its image. This sunlight will not undo that, no matter how much its warmth tries to soften me. I am beyond saving.

The Reapers stand in formation along the deck. My lieutenants, my elite warriors, the finest killers in the Sundered Kingdoms. Clad in black armor and heavy cloaks, they are a stark defiance against the endless expanse of blue sky, where wisps of white cloud drift like specters. Their faces remain unseen, swallowed by the shadows of their shroud helms, faceless harbingers of death awaiting my command.

Arax tugs his own helm roughly over his head, then arches his back, and with a rippling sound, his wings burst forth, black feathers streaked with gray, a marker of age that gnaws at even him.

"My prince," he says, dipping his head.

I step to the railing, letting my gaze sweep over the land. Green. A sea of it, stretching on forever. Rolling hills, endless forest, and mountains in the distance, their peaks lost to the clouds and gleaming like a gem amongst the beauty of this land, is the seat of House Maledannan.

Their castle rises from the earth like something torn from another world. Spires reaching for the heavens, stained glass windows glinting in the sun. If storms raged around it, it might look like home. The Vornahl, or the First Fae as the humans call them, made their mark on this world with their love of towering, elaborate monstrosities. Structures meant to awe and unsettle. But this one is cloaked in green. Vines creep across the stone as if the forest is intent on swallowing it whole.

Arax watches me, his wings flexing as he waits for my word. I roll my shoulders, and with a satisfying snap, my own wings erupt, stretching wide and sending a sharp gust across the deck.

"I will fly ahead," Arax says. "If there are archers, I will draw their fire."

I roll my eyes at his noble theatrics, letting my wings shift and stretch, their splay loosening knots I hadn't even noticed.

"And let you have all the fun?" I scoff. "The only pain I've had lately is the endless nagging from the king and queen. An arrow through the flesh might be just what I need to make these dull days more interesting."

Arax frowns, his voice tight. "Prince Daedalus, I must..."

But before he can finish, I push off the deck, shooting into the air like a stormwyrm bursting from the sea. The wind slams into my wings, and they spread wide, casting a long shadow over the tiny specks of life below.

Old gods, it feels good to be in the air. To rise so high above the noise, where it can't sting my ears or flood my mind with things I don't want to hear. Sometimes, I think even the voice I can never escape, the voice of my master, the one that haunts me day and night, can't reach me up here.

But before I can savor my moment of peace, Arax makes sure to remind me he's never far behind. His wings beat the wind, a sound that somehow carries his disapproving grumble. I swoop away, pinning my wings back as I dart toward Castle Maledannan.

As I fly over villages, the scent of the humans rises, as pungent as any earthy broth or charred meat. The little people glance up at me, and I can see it in their eyes. The fear. Not just because I'm Fae, or their crown prince, but because I am something beyond what they can understand that fills them with dread. Like the snap of a twig in the dead of night, or the shadow that passes by your window when you're huddled beneath the covers.

How Arax thinks these fragile creatures could ever threaten the Fae, I'll never know. Then the weight of my purpose here sinks in, and the lump in my throat unsettles me. I swallow it down before it can spread.

With the castle close, the last thing to pass beneath me is a stretch of forest, its canopy so thick I can see nothing that lies beneath. But as I watch my shadow darken the leaves, I feel a piercing ache rip through me with such ferocity it steals my breath.

At first, I fear I was foolish not to listen to Arax. It has the sharp sear of an arrow tearing through skin. But there is no wound, no blood, and this pain comes from somewhere deeper than flesh. From a place I believed only darkness lingered.

But this sensation is anything but dark. It blinds me just as brightly as this damned sun.

I slow to a stop, my wings beating the air hard as I hover above the forest. I strain my eyes, but there are no gaps between the thick branches and densely packed leaves, no way for me to see what lies below. But I can feel it. Down there. The cause of this agony.

Arax halts beside me.

"My prince. What is it? Is there danger?"

My first instinct is yes. Why else would something like me, something that causes fear, be suddenly...nervous?

"It's nothing," I say, more to myself than Arax. I turn, my wings snapping, propelling me toward the castle at speed, and Arax follows.

We touch down in the courtyard with resounding thuds, and I feel the tremble of the moss-covered stone underfoot.

The Fae standing guard before the giant doors wear glinting silver armor, so pristine that I doubt it has ever known battle, and the pretty green silk draped over one shoulder doesn't help me think any better of them.

4

House Maledannan's banners fly from their spires, the deep green fabric emblazoned with a white lotus flower flanked by two sleek silver serpents, their tails entwined.

These sigils are meant to symbolize new life and infinite wisdom, yet they've always sparked suspicion in me, a hint of something darker lurking beneath the surface. After all, the Maledannan once sought to rule the Sundered Kingdoms, and it was the Mordorin who had to remind them, not so gently, who truly held power in these lands. Fortunately, that reminder didn't cost their house too many lives.

But the Mordorin have never forgotten. While the Maledannan may be Fae of nature and healing, that doesn't mean they don't secretly long for the glory of the crown. After all, why rule over humans alone when they could rule over Fae as well?

I stalk towards the doors, rolling my shoulders as my wings retract and vanish, my runes pulsing. The Maledannan guards immediately bow their heads and lower their polearms when they see me coming. The doors open with a long, low groan like old waking giants and then close behind Arax and I with the same laborious slowness.

Within the walls of House Maledannan, the gray stone is dappled by soft light, shaded by the vines that creep over the windows, some even managing to work their way through cracks and spaces between the old brick, crawling along the walls and curling from the rafters.

Arax and I walk the long green rug down the central corridor, guards with their heads bowed lining the way like statues. The silence here is eerie, with only our heavy boots and the clink of Arax's armor. No rain. Not like in Baev'kalath, but no voices either.

It's as if this whole place is trapped in silence.

Soon the corridor widens into a round room, framed with two winding staircases on either side of another set of gigantic doors. The Fae standing guard there pull these doors open as soon as they sight us, and when Arax and I step into the throne room, we're presented with the ruling family of one of the six great houses of the Sundered Kingdoms. Descendants of the Vornahl. The Fae of the old world.

Lord Eryndor and his wife Elyss, a male and female so vastly different in appearance, like night and day, yet so perfectly suited they can only be mates.

Eryndor startles with his alabaster skin and fine silver hair, braided into thin plaits that fall flat down his back. Elyss, in stark contrast, boasts a cascade of black curls and a complexion of the richest, warmest brown, her brightness held in striking sky-blue eyes that seem almost otherworldly.

Both wear crowns intricately woven from wood and leaf, their natural elegance elevated by diamonds and emeralds. Their signature green threads through everything. Flowing robes that sweep the floor, the cushioned thrones they sit upon, and the billowing silks that adorn the walls. Vines ensnare every surface, a living tapestry that weaves through the castle, making it as much a part of nature as the rulers themselves.

Eryndor lifts his head, and it takes him a moment before he acknowledges me with a smile that feels rehearsed. He rises slowly.

"Prince Daedalus," he says. "Welcome to Valorne."

He extends his hand to Elyss, and she rises also, dropping into a half curtsy and dipping her chin.

"Your Highness," she says, her voice so low and raspy I can't help but compare it to the serpents on their banners.

I barely have time to go through the formalities of my arrival before a pair of loud shrieks tear through the air, shattering the hollow silence, and I wince at the sting in my ears.

Two tawny-skinned Fae children, one male and one female, dart into the room, laughing and screaming as they chase each other without a care, oblivious to the fact their prince stands before them.

It is strange as I watch them to see no runes on their skin. They're far too young to be marked yet, but all it does is remind me how rare Fae children are, and the fact that Eryndor and Elyss have produced two of them not only says much for their fated match, or the amount of fucking they must have done over the centuries, but also for the longevity of their house. These are not just children, but two healthy heirs for House Maledannan, which is more than I have.

The children continue to chase each other while I watch them in silence, an impatient glower on my hard face, but they don't notice. They even weave between my legs in pursuit of each other. The male knocks my knee on his exit, and I buckle, stumbling forward, almost tripping over myself.

My eyes widen and I hear Arax clearing his throat, preparing for what I imagine will be the world's greatest admonishing, but I raise my hand to him, cutting off the words before he can let them fly.

Instead, the hint of a grin tugs at the corner of my mouth and I find the sound they make, the laughter full of pure, innocent joy, is not as offensive as I found it a moment ago.

"Lysander. Sylara," Elyss calls, with both her and Eryndor looking suitably nervous. "Come here. Now."

The children race off, still giggling as they leap into their parents' arms, the male to Elyss while the female latches onto Eryndor, tugging at her father's braids. It catches me off guard the way the little one looks at him with such affection and adoration and...love.

The tightness in my chest is foreign and I can't decide whether it is welcome amidst the cold inside me.

"Forgive them, Your Highness," Eryndor says quickly, anxiety in his tone. "I told them to stay in their rooms, but it seems they do not want to listen to what their father says."

Eryndor is speaking to his children, as much as he is speaking to me and I watch them pout.

"Sorry, Papa," Sylara squeaks.

Eryndor goes to speak again, but I speak first.

"No need for apologies, Lord." And the look of pure shock on their faces when I wink at Sylara is enough to undo the world. "They are just children being children."

Eryndor bows his head appreciatively before pinching his daughter's chin playfully between his fingers. "They can be a blessing and a curse."

"I'm sure there are others who can only hope to be as burdened as you are."

Eryndor and Elyss glance at me with confusion, and I don't realize my words have escaped my thoughts. I draw back my shoulders and exhale the sentiment before it gets too comfortable.

"But if you wouldn't mind?" I tip my head towards the door, and the lord and lady respond quickly, handing their children off to a maid who hurries them out of the room, snipping at their quiet protests.

"Now," I say, straightening the collar of my black shirt and running a hand through my hair as if to reset myself. "You sent word of a very serious manner and I am here to settle it swiftly." My eyes narrow. "So show me, Lord Eryndor. Show me this threat to the Fae that you have let thrive within your borders."

Eryndor gulps, exchanging fleeting glances with Elyss that they don't think I notice. But I notice everything. They're scared, which means this must indeed be dire.

7

Eryndor extends his long, willowy arm, his green robe falling in a silken sheet as he gestures toward a wall completely overtaken by vines. They're as thick as mooring ropes, their massive heart-shaped leaves marked with white mottled patterns that gleam faintly in the light.

"This way, Your Highness," he says.

Over my shoulder, I catch a glimpse of Arax, his expression a mirror of my own. Curiosity tinged with mounting impatience.

I follow, crossing the room to where Eryndor stands before the living wall. He waits, far longer than I care for, his silence grating. Just as I'm about to speak, his hand moves in a slow, deliberate wave. The vines react instantly, slithering back like serpents, untangling themselves with unsettling grace. They reveal a large mirror, its surface dull and tarnished, the glass so clouded I can barely discern the faintest outline of our reflections.

Then, almost imperceptibly, the foggy surface begins to change. Swirls of mist gather, twisting and churning with the intensity of a storm. Slowly, the chaos subsides, clearing like smoke drawn away by the wind. And there, in the heart of the glass, I see a vision: a lush forest, the grass thick and wild, encircled by ancient, towering trees. A deer darts through the undergrowth, its movement so vivid I half expect it to leap from the mirror.

"Where is this?" I ask, my voice tight.

"The Grove, Your Highness," Eryndor replies, his tone heavy. "A large forest not far from here. You would have flown over it when you arrived."

The memory hits like a blade. The sharp ache of it cuts through flesh and digs deeper, to a place I can never reach. I remember the moment too well, the pain that was more than physical, the sense of something lost before I even knew it existed.

"And this is where the threat lies?" I ask, my voice quieter now, though no less sharp.

Eryndor nods. His fingers move with an elegant, mystical flourish, and the mirror's image shifts. It feels as though I'm there, walking the forest's overgrown paths. The scene expands, bringing us to a sunlit clearing where lavender-colored flowers blanket the ground. The sunlight is dazzling, almost blinding as it spills over the blossoms. At the clearing's center, next to a large boulder, sits a human.

A woman, young, though with humans, age is deceptive, always slipping just beyond my grasp.

She's singing, her voice lilting and unfamiliar, the melody strange to my ears. The breeze tugs strands of her hair across her face, and she brushes them back with a delicate hand. I can't discern the color of her hair. It could be brown, yet the thudding in my chest resists such simplicity. The same confusion grips me as I try to name the glimmering shade of her eyes. Both the song and the sight of her unsettle something deep within me, something I don't yet have the words to name.

I stand here, Prince of the Mordorin, Commander of the Ebon Flight, a leader, a warrior, a being who has watched decades fold into centuries, unbent and unyielding. Yet before this girl, this human with her haunting song and unassuming grace, I feel undone.

"Your Highness," Eryndor says, his voice slicing through my reverie. Only then do I realize I have been staring. How long I do not know, so intent was I on studying the delicate curve of her neck, the way her hair brushed her shoulder like silk.

"What?" I snap, the edge of my voice cutting sharper than I intend. Eryndor lowers his head, his posture contrite.

"My apologies, Your Highness. But this is her...the girl I sent word of."

My stomach tightens. Impossible. It cannot be her.

"Who is she?" I demand, swallowing a lump that rises unbidden in my throat.

"She appears to be favored, not only by the village but by the elementals who dwell within the forest," Eryndor replies cautiously. "It seems they are teaching her our magic, and her response to it is...unprecedented. Stronger than any we've seen before."

I glare, my lips curling into a sneer. "The elementals? *Your* elementals? The ones you failed to control?"

Eryndor flinches but presses on, glancing at Elyss as if seeking silent reinforcement. "The villagers worship them as gods. The Maledannan deemed it wiser to let them remain untouched, undisturbed."

"And look where that wisdom has brought you." My voice drips with disdain. "The humans in this forest revere those lesser Fae more than they revere you. You should have crushed this nonsense centuries ago, Eryndor, but you were too busy clawing at power over the Sundered Kingdoms." My smirk sharpens, cutting deep. "You cannot even control the lands you were gifted."

Eryndor's lip twitches, a crack in his carefully constructed composure. The Lord of the Maledannan may shroud himself in civility, but there is darkness in him, vengeful, brooding. He needs only to slip, to let an ounce of that malice show, and I would gladly make a widow of his female.

"You are right," he admits slowly, his tone tight with restraint. It disappoints me. "But despite my house's failures, this matter must be addressed. If she is what we suspect..."

"Awakened," I cut in, the single word heavy enough to stir unease in the room. Even Arax shifts behind me, dipping his chin, disbelief shadowing his eyes.

I step closer to the mirror, drawn toward the image of the girl like a moth to a flame. My gaze fastens on her, every fiber of my being resisting the urge to reach out and feel her warmth through the cold glass.

Arax's grumbling voice rumbles at my back. "If she is Awakened, Your Highness, a human Awakened, she could be a greater danger that any Awakened before her."

"Or a great asset," I counter to him quietly over my shoulder, my eyes narrowing as I turn my accusing stare on Eryndor. "It surprises me the Maledannan even brought their suspicions to us."

"They know better than to test us after last time," Arax mutters darkly. "They'd be fools to repeat their mistakes."

I shake my head slowly. "No," I murmur. "I don't believe for a second that anyone wouldn't want to possess...her."

My voice trails off, the words faltering under the sudden weight of my breath as I exhale. My chest tightens, the telltale shudder impossible to mask. Arax notices. His brow furrows, his gaze sharpening on me with quiet scrutiny.

"What now, my prince?" he asks.

"Now, I do what I came here to do," I reply, rolling my neck as tension coils in my jaw. "I will determine if this human truly poses a threat to the Fae." My gaze returns to the mirror, to the girl sitting in the clearing, oblivious to the storm she has summoned. "What is her name?"

Eryndor hesitates, glancing at the mirror. The girl plucks a flower from the grass, tucking it behind her ear with such simple grace it feels like an affront to the chaos she has already wrought in me.

"The humans call her Amara Tyne," he says at last.

CHAPTER 2
AMARA

Empty. I had always known the meaning of the word. I knew empty when I saw it. But to feel it, truly and deeply, was not anything I had ever known. It is a hollowness that aches and hungers. It is all consuming, as if it could devour you in one bite from the inside. There is no sating the emptiness. No amount of food or drink will fill that hole. It is bottomless. Fathomless. I have no doubt that if you tried to walk the emptiness you would perish without ever knowing you were nowhere near its end. It is a beast. A monster. Emptiness is a demon that preys and it has been my only companion since the night I was torn from the arms of my prince.

The days melted into weeks, weeks bled into months, and now time is a shapeless thing I cannot hold. I no longer know how long it has been since I last felt his skin against mine. I fear I cannot recall its warmth, the exact place where the smooth hardness of him softened. Was it just beneath his ribs? The subtle dip of his waist before the rigid edge of his hip?

I close my eyes and try to summon it. Yes. That was the spot. There, he would stifle a grin when my fingers grazed him, this dark Fae warrior, whose laughter was as rare as the bright dawn in bleak winter. If only the warriors he commanded knew their fierce leader was ticklish...if you found the right place. It was a secret part of him, a joy only I knew.

But we had no time.

We were thrown together, two forces of nature colliding, leaving destruction in our wake. In the brief, turbulent span we shared, we lived lifetimes. Of heartache and betrayal, of desire and passion. I felt more pain and pleasure in those moments with him than many endure in the fullness of their years.

He is all things to me. All the things I crave and all the things I despise.

My husband. My betrayer. My enemy. My love.

But how long will I wait here? How long until he comes for me? How long until I forget the warmth of his skin beneath my fingers, or the timbre of his voice, or the sharp lines of his face?

My hands drift down, resting on the curve of my stomach, on the small swell beneath my flowing silk dress. A bittersweet tether to him, this growing life within me.

How long until this child is the only memory I have of Daedalus Phaedren?

The breeze brushes my face, cool and gentle, and I tilt my head toward the mists of cloud and the pallid blue of the sky.

The city outside my window is an astonishing patchwork of floating isles, each suspended in the endless expanse of sky like shards of a shattered world, held aloft by ancient magic. Some are small and rugged, little more than rocky crags with tufts of greenery. Others spill waterfalls from their edges, the torrents vanishing into the clouds below. And then there are the sprawling platforms of life, dotted with spired towers no different from my own.

Never before had I seen such a place. But even in my awe, I quickly noticed the absence of bridges or platforms linking the islands. The Ithranor, with their command over the wind, can travel wherever they please in this city in the sky, a stark reminder that I, a human, cannot.

We are so high I doubt the world below even knows we exist up here. Driftspire, the sanctuary the Ithranor carved out for themselves when they fled the Sundered Kingdoms during the Betrayer's Battle.

But this home is out of necessity. It is not the home they want.

What I've pieced together over these long, suffocating months is this: the Ithranor ache for the land where they truly belong. The birthplace of the First Fae, where they boarded their ships and set out for the Sundered Kingdoms centuries ago. A land long vanished from maps, its coordinates swallowed by time. A place spoken of only in myth and memory. This much they've shared freely.

What they haven't been so forthcoming with is why any of this involves me. Or my child.

I have not been treated terribly. Not by most standards. They feed me, clothe me. My room is clean and well-appointed, stocked with books, paper, ink for writing or drawing, and even a chess table to keep my mind occupied. But a gilded cage is still a cage.

When I step toward the balcony, I am reminded of that truth. The moment my foot crosses the threshold, something cinches around my neck, and I inhale sharply as the pressure builds. Light shimmers against my skin, and a silver collar materializes. Inch by inch, a chain emerges, extending to a thick steel ring embedded in the center of the room.

My lip curls as I glare at the restraints, but defiance costs me. The collar tightens with each passing second, biting into my skin until the rune etched into my flesh burns. Pain blooms, sharp and all-encompassing, and I clench my teeth against it.

But it's no use.

The ache creeps into my skull, a vise tightening until my vision falters and my body betrays me. With a growl of frustration, I retreat, the curse on my lips barely a whisper. The moment I step back, the collar slackens, the chain vanishing into thin air as though it was never there.

But I know better. It's always there. Invisible. Waiting.

It is how the Ithranor keep me prisoner in this luxurious cell. How they strip me of my power.

No amount of broken fingers will summon the pain I need to channel. Even the agony from the collar itself cannot stir my magic. This collar is laced with a spell so potent, it drains my abilities, rendering me helpless. And with each passing moment, the emptiness grows, creeping closer, threatening to consume me before I can escape.

Footsteps echo beyond the heavy door. I glance toward the cloud-shrouded sun, its pallid light barely reaching this forsaken height. Lunch. The Ithranor are nothing if not prompt.

I turn toward the door, waiting for the usual arrival of my meal, brought by a quiet maid, one who has clearly been ordered not to look at me, let alone speak. She always sets the food down in silence and leaves with her eyes fixed firmly on the floor. She might like me if given the chance. I have a way of turning stubborn maids into loyal friends.

The heavy blue door swings open, but instead of the familiar maid, I'm met with the towering presence of the Golden Son. His broad frame fills the doorway and I instinctively take a step back, my body colliding with the wooden post of my bed. My arm curls around it for support, steadying myself as his gaze holds mine.

"You're back. I thought…"

He shrugs, stepping inside with an ease that makes my blood simmer. The door clicks shut behind him. "It's best if you don't think, princess. You're far more pleasant that way."

He moves through the room with an air of nonchalance that only adds to the fury curling in my chest. He sheds his red coat, draping it casually over the back of one of the leather chairs near the chess table. He adjusts his collar, his gaze flicking to me over his shoulder.

It would be impossible not to recognize him. That shock of pale blond hair, those eyes like the clearest, bluest ocean. But I've had to adjust to the new mask he wears. Before I was taken, I knew only one face. The gilded mask of flames, a symbol of fury and destruction, worn like a beacon on the battlefield.

Now, he wears something different. A simpler mask, a bronze thing that covers only half his face, curving from his brow to shield his left eye, around his nose, down to his jaw. His mouth is exposed, a cruel reminder of who he is beneath. I assume the scars he hides are confined to that side of his face.

The side he leaves visible is flawless. Fair, smooth skin with just the faintest hint of color in his cheeks. Even after all these months, it's unsettling, as though he's trying to show me how perfect he once was. How human. I would rather he wore his full gold mask. At least then, he'd look every bit the monster I know him to be.

"You shouldn't be surprised to see me." His voice is smooth, almost mocking. "I visit you often, do I not?"

"Far too often, and always uninvited," I snap back, sharp and cold.

He chuckles, his tone dripping with amusement. "I thought princesses were supposed to have better manners."

"Maybe you need to do less thinking yourself," I shoot back.

He smirks, dragging the leather chair with a loud scrape before sinking into it, legs spread wide. He leans forward, elbows resting on his knees, eyes narrowing as they lock onto me.

"How have they been treating you?"

"Why do you care?" My words are low, growled with disdain.

"Because you are my prisoner," he answers, the coolness in his voice matching the coldness in his eyes. "The Ithranor are just providing the cage. I couldn't exactly take you back to the Sundered Kingdoms, could I? That'd be the first place they'd look for you." He leans back, his posture arrogant, eyes never leaving mine. "So?"

My jaw clenches, and I force a sarcastic smile. "Oh, it's beautiful. The view is stunning, and the fresh fruit and vegetables they serve are the most delicious I've ever tasted. But by far, my favorite part is the magical collar around my neck that strangles me if I get anywhere near the balcony."

He exhales sharply, nostrils flaring, but it's his eyes that betray him, flicking to the rune carved into the side of my neck.

"If only it covered that *thing* they branded you with," he says, voice low and bitter. "Wearing it, you spit on every human who ever bled under their rule."

My chin lifts, the weight of his words striking something hot in my chest. But I don't flinch.

Instead, I let my gaze drop deliberately to the edge of his sleeve, where a sliver of dark ink curls just beneath the fabric.

"You dare," I say, voice smooth as glass. "When you wear their mark just the same?"

A low growl vibrates in his chest and he yanks the sleeve down.

"I had no choice," he grits out. "How else would I travel through Driftspire? I need their winds."

"I don't give a damn how you come and go," I snap, the fire in my throat finally breaking free. "What matters is my freedom. Whether I'm a prisoner of the Ithranor or the Golden Son, I belong to neither of you. I demand you release me."

He leans forward, his gaze lowering to the marble floor, and then, with a voice like gravel, he says, "Ronin."

I don't respond, my silence louder than any words could be. But he knows I heard him, so he speaks again, his voice insistent, as if I haven't. "I told you to call me Ronin."

Still, I say nothing.

After the first month, when I was at my lowest and his visits became both more frequent and more unwelcome, he told me his name.

I don't know why.

The only names that matter are the ones he's stolen. The names of everyone I've lost to his blade.

Arax's name.

I don't care what his name is.

Yet he expects me to call him by it, like we're somehow...friends.

Souls. If I didn't think he was insane before, I certainly do now.

I will never call him by his name. He deserves nothing but the title of murderer.

When I don't respond, he turns in his chair to face the chessboard.

"It's your move," he says.

I glare at him.

"Don't keep me waiting, Jewel," he sighs, the wood of the chair groaning under his weight as he shifts. "The sooner you make your move, the sooner I'll leave you in peace."

"Peace," I scoff as I trudge to the chessboard. "I'm surprised you even know what that word means."

I pull out the chair and sit across from him. His eyes lift, meeting mine, but then they wander. They take me in, the brown hair cascading down my back, the red ribbon looped around my wrist, the blue silk dress, lighter than air, slipping off my shoulders with long, flimsy veils that cascade down my arms. It clings tight below my bust, flaring out, but even so, the bump of my belly is obvious.

His eyes linger there longer than I like, and I shift uncomfortably under his gaze. He notices, his focus snapping back to my eyes.

"How are you... feeling?"

"Fine," I answer curtly, my gaze drifting over the chess pieces as I think through my move.

Where his voice had once been hard and demanding, now it's softer, hesitant, as if he's struggling to find words. "Do you need anything?"

I glance up at him with a frown. "I said I'm fine."

His palm rubs roughly over his knee. "I don't know what happens in these situations."

"Well, maybe you should have thought twice before kidnapping a pregnant woman," I snap, tilting my head, letting my glare sharpen.

"I didn't know you were pregnant. Neither did Anethesis. It was an unexpected development."

"Well, you weren't the only one who was surprised," I reply, my chest tightening as my eyes lock on the black rook.

At first, I assumed that was why they took me. Because I carried the child of Prince Daedalus Phaedren. That they would demand some sort of twisted ransom. But I was wrong. I tried to keep it a secret when I realized they did not know, but in the last few weeks, when my bump refused to be hidden, it gave me away.

Now it feels like they do not know what to do with me, as if my child is not leverage but a burden to whatever plans they have. All I know is that they leave me alone more often now, and apart from the maid who brings my food and Anethesis and his endless questions, I barely see any Fae. It's almost as if they are frightened of me.

Good. Whatever keeps them away is welcome.

I pinch the rook between my fingers, my tongue peeking out the corner of my mouth involuntarily as I think. I hear a laugh under his breath.

"What?" I snap, irritation lacing my voice.

He squares his shoulders and coughs, clearing his throat. "Nothing. Can you hurry up? I'll die of old age at this rate."

I glare at him, my response sharp. "Then I'll take my time."

He growls low in his throat, his fist clenching. "Just hurry up."

I make my move, sliding the black rook across the board with a decisive flick.

The Golden Son leans back, a grin tugging at his lips as he watches me. "Interesting."

I watch him study the board, his eyes fixed on the pieces, his body tense as he thinks.

"What will you do with me?" I ask bluntly. "Do I die today?"

He looks up, almost annoyed with my distraction. "If I were here to kill you, I wouldn't have bothered taking off my coat."

"Perhaps you did not want to get blood on it?"

"Then I would have sent someone else to kill you," he sighs.

I shrug, not remotely frightened by his words. After living as the wife of the cursed prince, it takes more than petty threats to rattle me.

"I assumed you would want to pleasure of killing me yourself."

He spits a mocking laugh, his eyes flicking back to the chessboard. "There you go again, thinking too much of yourself."

"Then why?" I repeat, the question a razor edge. When he ignores me, I slam my fist onto the table, the pieces rattling on the board.

He sighs, dragging his gaze back to me, blue eyes brimming with irritation. "Because I'm convinced you can see reason. It was you who defeated my army that day in the Grove, not the Fae. You. Power like that, I cannot ignore. And when the Ithranor get what they need from you, you'll join the Legion."

My laugh dies on my tongue as I realize he's dead serious.

"You think after everything you've done to me, I'll fight for you?"

"You'd rather fight for him? A Fae who lied to you? Betrayed you? A prince who could not protect you?"

"You know nothing about Daed and me," I snap, the words sharp as a knife.

"You're right. All I know is what you scream in your sleep. The pain in your voice. No one who truly cares for you could cause that kind of agony."

Rage burns through me, so hot it blinds me, but, for some reason, the venom he's spitting locks my throat, and I can't find the words to shut him down.

"Don't be afraid, Jewel," he continues, his voice softening with mock sympathy. "You're not the only one he's failed. The fragile alliances he fought so hard to secure are unraveling. The Legion won't even have to lift a finger. The Mordorin will tear each other apart for us, and the Sundered Kingdoms will fall into my hands without a fight. He has abandoned all of you."

"And what of you?" I retort. "Instead of leading your armies, instead of fighting for the Sundered Kingdoms, you're here in this glittering city, wrapped in fine red coats, wearing Fae runes, playing chess with a pregnant woman who has considered more than once stabbing you through the eye." My fingers trace the sharp-tipped crown of the queen chess piece.

His scowl deepens. "Do not compare me to your bastard husband. You put your faith in the wrong monster, Jewel. You should have aligned yourself with your own kind. Imagine what we could have accomplished if you had fought with us instead of against us. Look where your foolish choices have gotten you." He pauses, then smirks. "So quiet," he taunts. "Nothing to say?"

The words are fire in my veins, but the fury they ignite only makes my hands tighten on the edge of the table.

"He hasn't abandoned me," I say, my voice steady.

The Golden Son looks up, a single eyebrow arching.

"Me or anyone else." The are words stronger now, a declaration. "He is searching for me. Across every ocean, over every mountain, through every shadowed corner of this land and beyond, my husband hunts for me. Because we... we are two halves of the same soul. Two flames that burn brighter together. Without me, he cannot rest. Without him, I cannot endure. We are the sun and the sky, the tide and the shore, the night and the day. Alone, we falter. But together...we are unstoppable. No force in this world...no monster, no army, no betrayal...will ever keep us apart and when we are together once more, we will rule the Sundered Kingdoms, and you will be no more than you are now."

The Golden Son's lip trembles with barely contained fury, his icy blue eyes like jagged shards of glass, cutting into me with a ferocity that sends a chill down my spine. His hand wraps around the white knight on the chessboard, his fingers tightening as though he were choking the life from it. "That's where you're wrong, Jewel," he growls, his voice low and dangerous. "I am a force of righteousness, and once I win this war, I will hunt him down and finish what I started with his pretty little wings."

He knocks my black rook off the board with ruthless precision, sending it clattering to the floor. His knight takes its place, his gaze never leaving me. "Your move."

Every shred of control I've been holding on to shatters. His smugness. His arrogance. I've suffered this for months, the weight of his crimes hanging over me. He murdered Arax. He brought bloodshed to the Grove. He stole me from the man I love and robbed me of not only my freedom, but the freedom of my child.

I can't stand it any longer. I grit my teeth, and in a flash, I lunge across the table, reaching for his throat with a guttural shriek. He catches my wrists effortlessly, squeezing until the burn of his grip sears my skin, but he doesn't speak, doesn't flinch. Not even when I spit in his face, the saliva glistening on the bronze of his mask. His expression remains unchanged, the same chilling calm that has haunted me for far too long.

The chess pieces fall to the floor with a sharp, hollow clatter as I lean further over the table, fury and frustration bubbling inside me like molten lava. "I hate you!" I scream, the words laced with all the pain I've kept hidden. The tremor in my voice betrays me, a near sob that claws at my chest. "Release me! Please! Let my child go!"

Still, he says nothing, his grip unyielding, his strength a cold wall I cannot break through. My body thrashes against his hold, but it's as if I'm struggling against stone, his hands tightening around my wrists. It's not until my eyes snap open, tears gathering in the corners, that I realize how close we are, how close his face is, his sharp breath mingling with mine. His gaze has shifted, focused now on my trembling lips.

I freeze, caught in the intensity of his stare. A hunger I don't want to acknowledge flickers in his eyes. A wave of disgust crashes over me. A moment ago, I wanted nothing more than to be over this table, strangling the life from him with my bare hands. Now I want to get as far away from him as possible.

The door suddenly swings open, the sound cutting through the charged air. A tall, lean Fae enters, gliding into the room with effortless grace, his midnight blue robes sweeping across the floor. His long fingers, tipped with curled nails, are steepled beneath his chin, his calm and indifferent demeanor giving way to shock and confusion the moment his eyes land on the scene before him.

"What is going on here?" Anethesis snaps, his tone jagged, fluctuating between high and low with agitation.

Neither of us answers.

"Ronin," Anethesis accuses and the Golden Son turns to face him.

"Would you mind releasing Princess Amara? I would hate for you to damage something of such great importance."

With that, Anethesis glides forward, his movements smooth. His fingers wrap around the Golden Son's wrists, prying his hands away from me. The scrape of his long, cold nails against my skin leaves an eerie, lingering sensation. He gently guides me back into my seat, the proximity of his presence unnervingly close.

"Great importance," I repeat, the weight of the words hanging between us. It's the first time he's said anything like that.

Anethesis smiles, but it's not a smile that reaches his lips. Instead, it radiates from his eyes, something colder, darker, that makes my stomach tighten. "Yes, Princess," he replies softly. "Our preparations are complete, and we are so very excited."

I catch the flicker of confusion that passes over the Golden Son's face, and for the first time, I see that he's just as much in the dark as I am. His brow furrows, and for a split second, doubt flits across his features.

"For what?" I demand, my voice sharper than I intend.

Anethesis takes a slow, deliberate breath, his shoulders rising and falling as though the weight of what he's about to say is almost too much to bear. "At long last, the Ithranor are going home," he announces, his voice thick with a quiet pride. "To our true home, to the lands of the Vornahl, and away from this wretched place that has caused us nothing but pain."

His eyes lock onto mine, a glimmer of something disconcerting in their depths. "It is time to get to work, our blessed Awakened."

CHAPTER 3
DAED

I lie sprawled across the table, the heat of the wood seeping into my skin, slick with the salt and sweat of endless days at sea. The ship rocks with the rhythm of the waves, their ceaseless lap against the hull a taunting melody. A reminder that I have been adrift far longer than my feet have known solid ground these last months.

Feet. Ground. Not wings. Not air.

Not since they were sliced from my back, leaving jagged, mocking scars.

The ache of their absence cuts deep, sharper than the blade that took them. I remember the wind rushing through my feathers, the cool caress of clouds on my skin. But even those memories, so sacred, so bittersweet, are nothing compared to the hollow agony of my true loss.

Amara.

My woman. My wife. My love. My salvation.

The gift my wretched soul never deserved.

I knew it was a matter of time before fate took her from me. But never did I imagine it would be like this. I failed her. These hands, this body, forged to protect and destroy, failed to shield the only light I've ever known. And not just Amara. My beautiful, good Amara. I failed the child I cursed her with. The child who carries my blood, my strength, and my ruin.

I was going to tell her in Pariseth. Tell her everything. The truth of what lay ahead, the weight of what we could never escape. That to build a life together would mean fighting tooth and claw for every fragile moment of peace. But I never got the chance.

Now she's out there, alone, with nothing but lies to cling to. Lies spun by Anethesis, that Fae snake. Yet even his venom pales beside the threat that haunts my every thought.

The Golden Son.

It was never his army that concerned me. Nor the alliance he forged with a Fae house. No, it was the look in his eyes when he gazed at Amara. The look of a man who covets something he cannot have. I've seen it before, in war, in life, in death. And I saw it again, clear as day, on the fields of the Grove and in Pariseth.

He dares to think he can have her.

But she is mine.

I will find her. I will bring her back. I will tear apart any who dared to touch her, who dared to think they could keep her from me. And when I stand before her again, I will say the words I should have said that night on the balcony.

The truth that could have saved us both from this curse.

From this agony.

From this endless, unyielding ache.

I wince as Solena jabs the needle into my skin again with a hiss of impatience. She shoves a half-empty bottle of rum toward me. "Take another drink," she snaps. "And stay still. These runes are melting off faster than I can ink them."

I grab the bottle, raising my head just enough to pour another burning swig down my throat. The fire of it barely registers anymore, dulled by overuse and the ache deep in my bones. "Then carve them deeper," I growl, my voice hoarse.

"Any deeper, and I'll be etching them into your damn bones," she retorts.

"Good. Maybe then they'll last."

Solena doesn't bother responding. She just sets her jaw and leans over me, needle in hand. The sharp sting of it punctuates her determination as she inks the sigils of the unseen into my flesh. Runes for those desperate to disappear.

I cannot afford to falter. If Gygarth finds me, he'll drag me under his thrall, and this cursed soul will become a weapon against the ones I swore to protect.

Theos, the Archdruid, claimed these sigils were my only chance of evading Gygarth. I dragged the truth from him, inch by bloody inch, until he broke and spilled it like wine on stone. But he warned me, warned that the magic would not last, that the runes would eventually burn away. He begged for mercy. Swore he was speaking the truth, and I believed him. I told him so before I threw him from the courtyard wall, his screams lost to the rocks below.

Now, I endure this endless torment, grateful and guilty for Solena's tireless hands. She spends more time carving into me than she does sleeping, her fingers raw and callused from hours of work. She never complains, though. She understands what's at stake. She wants Amara back as much as I do.

Still, the magic is fleeting. The runes blister and melt off my skin within days, dripping like black tar in the sun. The searing pain doesn't matter. The sight of the mess. Ink, blood, and burned flesh pooling at my feet only steels my resolve. I demand Solena start again, each time fiercer than the last.

So far, the sigils have held. Gygarth has not found me, his influence unable to seep from the void. But if I do not find Amara soon. If the sigils fail, the contingency remains. My sister, Zyphoro, will drive her blade through my heart and finally end the claim the Father Below has held on my soul since my birth.

I hope it never comes to that.

But hope is a fragile thing, easily shattered.

The cabin door crashes open, banging against the wall, and a whirlwind of copper hair and incoherent cursing announces Lord Reon of Eyr'Drogul. He stumbles inside, barely catching himself on the doorframe.

"Fuck this boat," he groans, bracing a hand against the wall. His hazel eyes flick to me, sharp despite the exhaustion painted across his face. "When you're done lying around, we've sighted land. Ballamar City's on the horizon."

I glance over my shoulder at Solena, who doesn't even look up from her work.

"Just a few more minutes," she murmurs, her hands deftly arranging her tools.

My brow furrows as I turn back to Reon. "This detour has thrown us miles off course. Are you certain this information is credible? That Ithranor Fae have been sighted in the city?"

He leans lazily against the wall in his loose linen shirt and tan leather vest and trousers, folding his arms over his chest. "My source was very convincing."

I take another swig of rum, feeling the slow burn settle in my chest. "When were you most convinced? While she was riding you, or in the seconds after you came?"

Reon's smirk curls. "Things get a bit hazy around that part."

"Done," Solena interrupts, stepping back from the table as she tidies up.

I sit up, the sting of fresh ink flaring across my skin as I swing my legs over the edge of the table. "We're here for a reason, Reon. To find Amara. Not to spread your seed through the lands beyond the Untold Sea."

He exhales dramatically, the faintest pout tugging at his lips. "You exaggerate."

I pin him with a flat stare. "I have no doubt that within a year's time there will be an abundance of ginger-haired babes with pointy ears crawling about."

"That's unfair," he counters, his smirk growing wider. "Not all will have pointy ears. Most will be only half-Fae, after all."

I narrow my eyes, biting back a laugh despite myself. Reon is a contradiction. A warrior whose fierce loyalty and honorable blade have fought for me without hesitation and a walking scandal who somehow still holds the respect of the Fae courts. He's a strategist and a fighter, and when we drink ourselves into oblivion, no one can make me laugh harder.

But this isn't the time for levity.

"Listen, Reon," I say, voice hardening. "While I would never deny you an excuse to drink and fuck yourself stupid, I need the warrior, the Fae I trust more than any other. Not the infamous rake of Eyr'Drogul. Amara's life depends on it, and so does the vengeance I plan to reap on the bastards who took her from me."

Reon's smirk fades, his hazel eyes darkening. "You'll have him when it matters," he says quietly.

I push off the table and my boots hit the floorboards with a hollow thud, the wood groaning beneath my steps as I cross the room. Reon and I lock eyes, a charged silence stretching between us.

After a moment, we clasp each other's forearms, an iron pact passing in the grip.

"I know I will," I say, my voice firm.

Reon nods, his expression grim but resolute. Without another word, I move past him, climbing the stairs to the deck.

Dawn greets me in a wash of amber light, spilling over the horizon and casting long, slanted shadows across the deck of *The Shattered Edge*. Smaller than most Mordorin vessels, it requires only a modest crew. But what it lacks in size, it makes up for in speed. We've cut across the sea swiftly, the wind at our backs and yet, we are still chasing shadows and whispers, always one step behind.

The cries of seabirds grow louder, mingling with the rhythmic slap of waves against the hull. Ahead, a dark mass looms on the edge of sight. The land of Moltas and the city of Ballamar inch closer.

The snap of the sails draws my eyes upward, where the silhouette of my sister stands perched in the crow's nest, high above me. Seeing her there is a bitter reminder: if I want her counsel, I'll have to climb.

I grunt, gripping the ladder and hauling myself upward. The wood bites into my palms as I ascend, the distance between us shrinking until I pull myself onto the narrow platform where she sits, her gaze fixed on the city ahead.

"How long do you think the sigils will last this time?" she asks without turning, her voice low and steady.

"As long as they can," I reply, settling beside her. "And when they fade, I'll have Solena ink them again."

"At this rate, the maid's fingers will fall off before we find Amara," she says dryly. "And then what?"

I exhale, my patience thinning. "What would you have me do? Without the sigils, we risk being found by Gygarth."

Her silence stretches like a taut string before she finally speaks. "You acknowledge the risk. You *are* the risk, brother. If the sigils fail, they could lead the demon straight to us. To her." She turns slightly, her profile sharp against the dawn. "Have you ever considered that if we can't find her, it means Gygarth can't either? And maybe it's better that way?"

I scoff, the sound bitter in my throat. "What are you saying? That it's better for Amara to remain lost?"

Her stony gaze flicks to me. "We both know what will happen if we fail. She'll die, and your child will be infused with the void's power, just as you were. But if she stays hidden, she and the child might be spared. Is that not worth giving up this quest?"

Her words strike deep, drawing anger from a place I've tried to bury.

"You forget," I say, my voice edged with ire. "Gygarth is not the only one who wishes Amara harm. The Golden Son is a part of this, and whatever the Ithranor are planning, it was worth crossing me to get to her. Do you think I can just leave her to that fate?"

Zyphoro shakes her head, a dry snicker slipping from her lips. "You could have stopped this."

"How could I have known the Golden Son had allied with the Ithranor?" I reply tersely.

"Not that," she snaps, spinning to face me. Her black curls whip in the wind, framing her storm-lit eyes as they burn into mine. "You knew what she was before she ever set foot in Baev'kalath, but you said nothing. Did nothing. You kept her as your little secret,

25

all the while knowing what she would become. You knew she would be more than just a prize to Gygarth and his wretched consort, Lanneth. She would be coveted and feared by every Fae in existence, because she's Awakened. You knew what that meant, and instead of doing what was necessary, what was expected of you, you let her live. You should have killed her in that forest."

The venom in her words ignites something primal in me. My teeth bare, smoke curling between my fingers like serpents in the air, but Zyphoro does not flinch. Nothing ever frightens Zyphoro.

"How dare you," I hiss, my voice low and venomous. "I told you everything in confidence, and now you use it against me?"

But her gaze is not laced with malice or hatred. It holds something heavier. Sadder. A truth I refuse to accept.

"If you had killed her then," she says, her voice quiet now, almost a whisper, "she wouldn't be suffering as she is now. She wouldn't have become the weapon everyone desires. The tool they will destroy each other to possess."

"You forget, sister," I snarl through clenched teeth, the smoke around me thickening into an ominous mist. "If not for Amara, you would still be rotting in that enchanted cage. Lanneth would still rule, and our father would still be her puppet."

A ghost of a grin tugs at her lips, one laced with resignation, not humor. She bows her head, a bitter chuckle escaping her. "That's the difference between us, brother. The difference that has always been." She lifts her gaze. "I would have stayed in that cage gladly if it meant preventing this cursed cycle. If it meant sparing you from being bound to Gygarth's shadow. But you...you weren't willing to sacrifice your happiness for hers. You wanted her too much to see reason. You convinced yourself you could save her."

"I tried to resist," I say, the admission barely a breath.

Her laugh pierces the air, mocking and bitter. "And yet you failed miserably."

I step closer, my anger barely contained. "Then why are you here? Why bother helping me when you think she's better off lost?"

Her gaze hardens, her expression unreadable as she raises a hand. Shadows twist and writhe around her fingers, coalescing into a dagger as dark as night.

"You know why," she says softly. The blade gleams menacingly as it catches the faintest light. "I'm here in case you fail again...or if you succeed. I am the bones that rattle beneath the rock, the reminder of a fate written in blood that cannot be unwritten, no matter how much you wish it so. And I will have my vengeance, Daedalus. Whether it be on Gygarth...or you."

I know exactly what she speaks of, and the thought of her trapped in that cage for all those years grips my chest with an iron fist, each breath crushed beneath the weight of regret. "You were lost to me," I murmur, my voice hoarse with unspoken sorrow. "Just as much as you were to everyone else. I couldn't help you, Zyphoro." A bitter sting pricks behind my eyes, and I swallow hard against it. "I couldn't even remember that I'd lost you."

A wry smile tugs at the corner of her mouth, sharp and knowing, as she waves her fingers. The shadowy blade in her hand dissipates into nothingness, a phantom of her fury. "I wish I could believe that, brother," she says, her tone laced with quiet cynicism. "I truly do. But as every creature who's had the misfortune of loving you learns sooner or later, you and deceit walk hand in hand."

Before I can muster another word, she ensures she has the last. Her wings burst from her back, the motion so forceful it tears through the air with a whip-crack sound. The updraft nearly stings my face, forcing me to turn away as feathers scatter like dark embers in the wind. She steps backward without hesitation, falling over the edge, her silhouette vanishing from sight before reappearing in a graceful arc. She swoops across the deck and climbs into the sky, weaving effortlessly among the seabirds as she heads for the shore, her figure cutting through the burnt orange glow of dawn.

"I would have saved you if I could," I murmur to her distant form, though I know my words will never reach her.

The descent down the ladder gives me far too much time to stew in my thoughts, her words lingering like echoes in my head. Zyphoro has never softened her truths, nor has she hidden the cold fact that she would kill me if it came to that. I do not doubt her. In some strange, twisted way, I appreciate her candor. She has made my failings unmistakably clear, and if I fall short again, knowing she would end me feels almost...reassuring.

When my boots finally hit the deck, I hear a rough cough behind me. Turning, I find Orios standing there, and as always, I'm struck by the sheer immensity of him. Even stripped of his Reaper's armor, he remains a towering monolith of muscle with his long, thick black hair tied back in a knot, though lately, he leaves much of it loose to fall over his broad shoulders, the dark strands framing his stony expression.

Orios never waits for orders. By the time I notice a task needs doing, he's already halfway through it, no matter how grueling or thankless the work. It's a quality I respect, perhaps the one I admire most. But above all, what sets him apart is his silence. Unlike the other Fae aboard this damned vessel, who seem to relish every opportunity to point out their prince's flaws, Orios keeps his opinions and his judgments to himself.

For that alone, he's earned my favor.

"Rook," Orios says, his tone steady. "Do you want us to go ashore armored and armed?"

I appreciate his vigilance. "Only lightly. It's best we move among the people quietly and avoid drawing attention. Wear layers. Hide your runes."

He nods, still so rigid and disciplined, as if he were back in line with the Reapers on the sparring grounds. "As you wish."

With a sharp turn, he heads below deck, his every step a stark reminder of Baev'kalath. Much like that cursed ladder is of losing my wings.

Word has reached me of the chaos consuming my kingdom. Lady Ilyra's spies have proven invaluable. Their messages carried on the wind, painting a grim portrait of what's unfolding. As one of my most trusted advisors, she governs in my absence, but even her influence falters. The noble thrall houses, already fractious, refuse to yield, their infighting so bitter that the Legion of Saints roams freely, unchecked and unchallenged. The Sundered Kingdoms are living up to their name in ways I never dared imagine.

While the Mordorin holds dominion over the Untold Sea, no Fae stands to oppose the human army on the mainland.

I tighten my jaw, a wave of guilt and dread crashing over me. Baev'kalath crumbles in my absence while I chase something I desire more. More than my kingdom. More than my duty.

And when I return, if I return, I may find nothing waiting for me but ash and ruin.

The world I knew may be gone, overtaken by the very enemies I once swore to hold at bay. Their banners might hang from the towers I was meant to protect. Their laws written over the bones of my people. I may come back to silence, to strangers, to a kingdom that no longer remembers my name.But I would make the same choice again.

Again and again.

Century after century.

For even the smallest chance that she might smile at me once more...and say her heart is still mine.

CHAPTER 4

AMARA

With a wave of Anethesis' hand, my invisible chain vanishes, but not my collar. My gaze follows the Golden Son as he departs, catching one last glimpse of his masked face when he pauses at the threshold and glances back. Then he is gone.

"Apologies, Princess," Anethesis says, his voice carrying a silkiness that mirrors his long, pale hair. It falls in perfect sheets, framing his sharp features. "Ronin is an unfortunate necessity. I hope his visits do not cause you distress, especially in your condition."

"I welcome his visits as much as I welcome yours," I say coldly. "With all the enthusiasm of a hot poker to the eye." I narrow my gaze. "Do you know he asks me the same thing? If the Ithranor are treating me well? Makes me question who I should be more wary of. Him or you."

Anethesis laughs, the sound tight and clipped, as though forced through his lips. "Don't be absurd. Driftspire is the safest place in all the realms, and no Fae will treat you more kindly than House Ithranor." He lifts a hand, and I flinch, but he stops just short of my face. "Have we not fed you? Clothed you? Given you every comfort?"

I glare at him. "You've chained me like an animal."

He nods, utterly unfazed. "If we hadn't, you'd likely harm us or worse, try to escape, and we can't allow that. We've waited far too long for you." He exhales, his smile broadening with unnerving ease. "You don't understand how precious you are to House Ithranor. You've given us the rarest gift of all. Hope."

"Hope for what?" I ask, unease crawling under my skin.

"For a return to the old ways. To the world we should never have left." His smile falters, replaced by a grim shadow of longing. "This new world has brought us nothing but death and suffering." Then a flicker of light dances in his eyes, like the first rays of dawn. "But you can take us back. Back to Meranor, the ancestral lands of the Vornahl."

I scoff, the sound sharp and mocking. "You have had your head in these clouds too long."

Anethesis' glare slices my words to shreds. He grabs my wrists, his nails scraping against my skin. "These are the hands of an Awakened," he growls, his calm slipping. "Hands capable of miracles. Portals, Princess. That's the miracle we need. You will open a portal to Meranor."

I yank against his grip, shaking my head fiercely. "I know nothing about portals."

"You will." Anethesis releases me abruptly, and I jerk my hands away, cradling them to my chest.

"An Awakened is a rarity," he says, voice laced with reverence. "Feared and worshiped in the same breath. They possess magic beyond imagining, but their light is usually snuffed out long before it can grow. Do you understand how extraordinary it is that you've survived this long? I imagine it's because you're human. No one would ever think to look for an Awakened among humans. Fae Awakened are easier to find...and easier to give up. Mothers turn in their own children without hesitation."

His eyes gleam with raw excitement, his very skin seeming to brighten, almost childlike in his awe. My shoulders stiffen. But then, as if catching himself, Anethesis exhales, forcing his thoughts back into order.

"Normally, it takes years for an Awakened to grow into their power, and though I would love to let you blossom at your own pace, we don't have that luxury. Mortals live brief lives as it is, and we've already waited too long."

"I know as much about being Awakened as I do about portals," I snap, gritting my teeth. "You have the wrong person."

Anethesis laughs, low and disbelieving, his smile twisting into something almost amused. "Please, Princess. Don't insult us both with such nonsense. You don't dream, do you? You see through magic...glamors...enchantments?"

I say nothing, but his smug grin only deepens.

"Those are the signs of an Awakened. And we *know* that's what you are."

My resolve crumbles under the weight of his certainty. "How?" I demand, my voice trembling despite my best efforts. "How could you possibly know when I barely know myself?"

Anethesis glides to the window, his movements fluid, almost serpentine. He stares out over the floating city, sunlight shimmering in his jade eyes. "Do you know what a scrying mirror is?" he asks, his back still to me.

"No," I admit.

"It is an artifact of immense power, crafted by the arcane scholars of House Taramethos. A scrying mirror acts as a window to the world. A prying eye into what lies beyond." His fingers lightly twirl in the wind as he speaks. "Long before the Betrayer's Battle, Lady Elyss of House Taramethos wed Lord Eryndor of House Maledannan. As a wedding gift, Taramethos presented them with a scrying mirror. It became a cornerstone of their power, as well as a tool of guidance for all the houses. But power like that...it breeds envy. The Mordorin coveted it, as they covet all things. When war consumed the land and House Maledannan fell, House Ithranor acted swiftly."

"You took the mirror?"

He turns slightly, a faint smile tugging at his lips. "We were neighbors of the Maledannan. We saw their castle burn, smoke rising like a funeral shroud. The mirror was too valuable to lose, too dangerous to leave behind."

"So you stole it and fled," I say, trying to keep my voice steady.

His expression sharpens, and his eyes narrow, chilling the air between us. "You understand so little," he says. "When the castles burned, it wasn't just humans setting the fires. Other Fae took advantage, driven by greed. The mirror was but one prize in a war of plunder and betrayal."

He clasps his hands behind his back, his tone softening slightly. "Yes, we claimed the mirror. We sailed across the Untold Sea, beyond the reach of war. We took to the skies and waited. For the fighting to end, for the ashes to settle, and we watched. We have always watched."

He smiles now, and the curve of his lips perturbs me. "The mirror reveals your deepest desire or your darkest dread. And it showed us both: a human girl who saw through ancient Fae magic and defied an army of golden warriors on a battlefield of green, wielding the power of the Maledannan...and something far greater."

I shake my head, disbelief coursing through me. The thought of being silently watched for so long sends a sickening twist through my stomach.

"When we returned to the Sundered Kingdoms to find you, we encountered Ronin instead and discovered we could prove valuable to one another."

"How could you possibly be allies after everything that's happened between man and Fae?" I ask curtly.

Anethesis gestures toward me, and his smile tightens. "It is astounding what compromises one will make for the right prize," he replies smoothly. "House Ithranor's numbers have dwindled, and we needed an army if we were to confront Daedalus, especially in his own domain, while the Legion requires a way across the Untold Sea to finish House Mordorin once and for all. But I wonder sometimes if Ronin's motives are fare more...intimate."

I scowl, but before I can voice my disdain, the stone trembles beneath us, and a deep, hollow roar reverberates through the sky. Its vibrations seem to part the clouds themselves, sending a dull ache through my chest. Anethesis gives an irritated sigh.

"That beast of yours continues to be a nuisance," he says.

"Then release him," I snap. "If I am what you need, free him."

"And let him alert your prince or tear Driftspire apart in search of you?" He shakes his head. "Enough Ithranor lives were lost securing him in the first place. No, the monster is best where he is. Be grateful we did not destroy him."

I suppress a grin. For all his boasting, Anethesis cannot hide the truth from me. They couldn't kill Ashen. How do you kill smoke? How do you kill shadow?

All they could do was try to contain him.

"May I see him, then?" I ask, forcing softness into my voice, though it makes my stomach churn. "It has been so long."

Anethesis takes his time considering my request. So long that my impatience nearly eclipses the burn of my collar, almost driving me to charge him. But at last, he nods.

"If it pleases our precious Awakened and makes her more agreeable," he muses, "I would be happy to take you to the beast."

His eyes narrow, his gaze searching. Less of an offer, more a question. A test of my compliance.

I nod resentfully and his shoulders ease. Anethesis moves his hands in those delicate, sweeping motions. The ones he uses to summon his power. I've nearly memorized the subtle twirls and curls of his fingers, the effortless hypnotic grace of it. He steps onto the balcony, but I am not fortunate enough to see him plummet to his death. Instead, a swirl of wind gathers beneath his feet, lifting him effortlessly. He extends his hand toward me, long bony fingers and sharp nails outstretched.

I hesitate, my scowl deepening. The thought of feeling his icy touch makes bile rise in my throat, but the chance to see Ashen is too much to resist. He is my only comfort in Driftspire, yet all I can do is listen to his mournful howls, which strike fear into the Fae, but to me, they carry only sadness.

With reluctance, I take Anethesis' hand, and he pulls me onto the swirling pillow of air. Together, we glide past the floating islands, the Ithranor Fae staring silently from their towers as we drift through the ethereal city. Our destination looms ahead: a massive hovering cavern, a waterfall tumbling from its mouth into the endless clouds below.

The sunlight's warmth vanishes as we enter. Inside, it is pitch black and so cold my breath turns to mist. I can barely see Anethesis, even though he floats right beside me. Then, a pulsing purple glow blooms within the darkness, faint at first but growing stronger, illuminating the jagged crystal lining the cavern walls.

The tunnel opens into a vast chamber with a shimmering lake at its center, and suspended above the water in a gigantic cage is my beautiful Ashen.

At first, he looks so small, pacing in tight circles, little more than a black smudge against the enormous barred frame. But the moment I arrive in the chamber, his nose lifts, and the bright white of his eyes locks onto me.

He hisses, a sharp, high-pitched sound, but it quickly morphs into a deep, thunderous roar that shakes the stone around us. He lunges at the bars, his body transforming in an instant into the fierce, massive protector I know him to be. Smoky tentacles lash out from his back, striking at the cage with fury.

Then he cries out in pain.

A collar materializes around his neck, pulsing with cruel, binding magic. Chains follow, first around his front legs, then his back, each one tightening with every struggle. The harder he fights, the more mercilessly they constrict, dragging him down to the cage floor. He thrashes, desperate, but the restraints only force him lower and lower until, at last, he is pinned, face pressed against the cold steel.

"No! Stop it! You're hurting him!" I snap, my voice cutting through Ashen's agonized roars.

"Hurting him? Impossible," Anethesis replies, his tone cool and dismissive. "He is a demon of the void. They do not feel pain."

"Yes, he does!" I scream, my hands curling into fists. "Let him up!"

34

Anethesis sighs as if I am the one being unreasonable. "He is doing this to himself. All he needs to do is stop resisting the collar."

My jaw tightens, and anger burns hot in my chest, sending tears stinging at the corners of my eyes. "Ashen!" I call, my voice trembling despite my best efforts to hold it steady. "It's alright. Please calm yourself."

Ashen thrashes harder, his claws scraping against the floor of the cage as he tries to rise. The chains respond viciously, dragging him down again with ruthless force.

"Please, my darling!" I call again, swallowing the sob rising in my throat. "Calm yourself. For me."

His roar tears through the cavern once more, but this time, it falters towards the end. Slowly, reluctantly, the fight drains from his body. He collapses with a defeated groan, his glowing white eyes dimming to a muted gray. As his strength fades, the collar and chains shimmer and vanish, but Ashen doesn't move. He lies still on the cage floor, utterly spent, as if the struggle has left him hollow.

"See?" Anethesis murmurs, his voice almost mocking. "That wasn't so hard, was it?"

I whirl on him, fury surging through me like fire. "Take me to him," I snarl. "He needs me."

Anethesis tilts his head. "I was hoping he would relax you," he says with an air of disappointment. "But it seems he has done quite the opposite. We cannot predict the effect the first trial will have on you in your...condition."

His gaze flicks to my belly, and his thin nose wrinkles as though he's caught the scent of something foul.

"What are you talking about? What trial?"

Anethesis dips his head, his nod so steeped in false sympathy that, for a fleeting moment, I almost believe it's genuine. I'm too tired, too confused, too angry, and that glimmer of doubt flickers dangerously close to hope.

"Let me make this plain," he says slowly. "Perform these tests without resistance, and we will release you and your pet."

My head snaps up, my tired eyes narrowing as I scrutinize him for any shred of truth. "You will?"

"All the Ithranor want is to go home, Princess. To leave this suffering behind." His voice drips with sincerity, but it's his next words that truly sink their claws into me. "You offer us that opportunity. We can both get what we want. It's no different from the collar.

Stop fighting, and this could be so easy for you." His gaze dips to my belly, his lip curling slightly. "For you and your little one."

My thoughts race, a torrent of fears and desires crashing into one another faster than I can catch them. Ashen, confined in his cage, his brilliant presence dimming with every passing moment until I can almost see through him. My child growing inside me, larger and stronger than it should be. The Grove, left defenseless without me. And then there's him. My husband. The man I have no right to love, yet whose absence gnaws at my soul every waking moment.

This could be my way out. My chance to protect them all without risking everything I hold dear.

My eyes flick to Anethesis. His gaze hasn't wavered, and I swear I see the faintest trace of satisfaction in his expression.

"What is the first test?" I ask, my voice steady despite the desperation raging inside me.

He exhales, long and measured, as if savoring my surrender. "Thank you for seeing reason, Princess."

The cavern fills with sound as the lake churns below, the water twisting and frothing violently, the purple glow pulsing like a heartbeat. I glance down, the flickering light slicing through the darkness. Ashen rises shakily to his feet, his white eyes locking onto mine, reflecting the same mix of worry and confusion I feel.

"The Test of Veils," Anethesis intones, his voice reverberating with unnatural power. The purple light flashes across his face, casting shifting shadows that make him look even more sinister. "Here, you must discern what is real and what is illusion. If you succeed, your ability to see through the false will grow stronger."

"Wait," I say, my voice cracking as the light grows brighter, stinging my eyes. "What do I do?"

"You are Awakened." His gaze pierces through me. "You will know."

I open my mouth to protest, but before I can utter another word, Anethesis raises two fingers and taps my forehead. It's a gentle touch, but it feels like the weight of a mountain crashing into me.

My vision explodes into darkness, and I feel myself falling backward, weightless and untethered, plummeting into nothingness. Forever.

The air shifts and my eyes flash open, and suddenly I'm no longer in the dark cavern with Anethesis. My breath fogs as I stand in an open courtyard bathed in pale moonlight.

Surrounding me are towering walls of glass, each panel polished to a gleaming perfection that reflects my image back at me, dozens of me, each one distorted, stretched, or twisted in ways that make my stomach lurch. The maze stretches endlessly in every direction, the mirrored walls shimmering like liquid silver.

Anethesis' voice echoes in my mind, cold and distant. "Find the truth, Amara. Or let the maze claim you."

I step forward, and the glass seems to ripple under my gaze. I reach out a hand, my fingertips brushing a surface colder than ice. The moment I touch it, the world around me shifts. The moonlight dims, the mirrors flicker, and suddenly I'm not alone.

"Amara?"

I whip around. The voice is achingly familiar, a sound I thought I had forgotten. My mother stands a few feet away, her gentle smile tugging at my heart. She looks like the phantom of someone I once knew, her memory so lost and clouded in the forgotten edges of my mind. Still, some things I can never forget. Soft brown waves of hair framing her face, the warmth in her eyes, the same rich brown as mine, a balm I didn't know I still craved.

"Mother?" My voice cracks, and I take a step toward her.

She opens her arms. "Daughter. You've been so strong, but you don't have to fight anymore. Just come home."

I falter, something twisting in my chest. It's her voice, her face, everything about her flawless, but it's too perfect. Too clean, too untouched by the years that should have changed her. My gut twists.

"You're not real."

Her smile withers, and her eyes glisten with tears. "Amara, it's me. Don't you recognize your own mother?"

I step toward the mirror, my hand reaching out instinctively, even as a voice deep inside me screams that this isn't real. But I want to believe it is her. Desperately. Every part of me aches for the chance that this could be true. To feel her warmth again, to be with her under the dappled sunlight, her fingers brushing gently through my hair as birdsong fills the air. The longing is so strong it burns through me, a cruel, aching need. I would give up everything for it.

But it's not real. It's a glamor.

A sudden flash of bright orange light sears my vision, and I stagger back, wincing. When I look again, the mirror is engulfed in flames. Blistering, suffocating, all-consuming. The heat presses against my skin, and my mother's form flickers within the inferno. She shifts, flashing between the woman I remember and the unrecognizable, charred figure left after the fire stole her from me.

Tears sting my eyes, but I clench my jaw against the tremor threatening to break my voice. "I'm sorry," I whisper, my words trembling despite my resolve. "But you are not real." My voice hardens, cutting through the illusion like a blade. "You died, and you're not coming back."

The flames flicker and die, vanishing as if extinguished by my words. She stands before me again, whole and untouched, her smile soft and bittersweet. For a moment, I think she'll speak. But she doesn't.

The mirror shatters, splintering into a thousand glittering shards, and with it, she disappears.

I barely have time to draw a breath through my grief before the maze shifts again. The mirrors ripple and twist, reforming into new, cruel visions.

Ashen dissolves into tendrils of smoke, fading until there's nothing left. Keeper Erania appears next, her screams piercing the air, her face obscured by streaks of blood. A cradle rocks in eerie silence, its emptiness louder than any cry.

I spin on my heels, turn away from the scenes, but the torment doesn't stop. Rain pours as Daed kneels in the courtyard of Baev'Kalath, his shoulders slumped in despair. A blade arcs downward toward him, and his eyes meet mine as he whispers, "It was all a lie."

"No!" I cry, spinning wildly, desperate for an exit, but every path only leads to more torment.

My Sisters of the Vine call out to me, their voices heavy with accusation, their faces twisted in anguish. "You failed us!" they scream, and I stumble backward into another vision. Solena stands by a bathtub, serene for a heartbeat, before the image shifts, her lifeless body now submerged beneath the water.

I whirl again, only to face Arax. Lightning splits the sky behind him, illuminating the grotesque truth: half his face stripped to bone, the skeletal grin a cruel mockery.

But the worst is still to come. I see myself reflected in endless mirrors, splintering into countless versions. Each one smaller, weaker, more fragile. Each version breaking under the crushing weight of my fears, shattered and defeated and alone.

I force myself to breathe. This isn't real. None of it is real.

I close my eyes, blocking out the images, the sounds, the whispers clawing at my mind. I focus instead on the faintest sensation, the tug of something deeper, something true, pulling me forward. It's barely there, like the faintest thread brushing against my soul, but I follow it.

When I open my eyes, the illusions have grown more desperate. The mirrors crack and shift, now throwing images of everything I've ever wanted: Ashen, free and unchained. My home, my friends, my love, my child. Safe and happy. Those I've lost, watching over me, at peace. They all call to me, urging me to join them. To rest at last.

But there is no rest. Not until my task is done. I must be close.

Tears blur my vision, but I grit my teeth and push forward. Each step is harder than the last, the images growing sharper, more tempting, more cruel. But I don't stop. The pull grows stronger, guiding me toward the heart of the maze.

Finally, I step into a clearing. The air feels different here, fresher, as though the weight of the illusions has finally lifted. The mirrors fall away, their haunting reflections vanishing into the ether. I'm left standing before a single, unbroken surface. It doesn't reflect me, not even a hint of my image. It reflects nothing at all. Pure. Untouched by illusion. A blank canvas, waiting to be filled with truth.

"This is it," I whisper, the words barely leaving my lips before I realize how final they sound. How final *it* feels. There is no more trickery, no more deception. This is the truth.

I reach out, my hand trembling slightly. The mirror surface is cool against my fingertips, but it's not hard like glass. There's an odd sense of yielding, like the very fabric of reality is ready to bend beneath my touch. My heart beats louder, echoing in my chest as I press forward. The moment my fingers make contact, the mirror doesn't crack or shatter with violence, it dissolves, as if it's been waiting for me to unlock it. The surface breaks apart gently, each piece turning into light that swirls upward, vanishing into the air like stardust.

Suddenly, I gasp for air, my chest heaving, eyes snapping open, but before I can scream, before the fear and anguish can claw their way out of me, I feel it, soft, familiar, the warm nuzzle of a nose against my face. I blink, my mind struggling to catch up, and as I focus, reality slowly settles into place. I'm inside Ashen's cage, his body curled around me like a shield, his purrs rumbling in my ear.

I don't think. I just move, pressing myself into him, burying my face in his thick mane, wrapping my arms around his neck as tightly as I can.

"Congratulations, Princess," Anethesis says from outside the cage, his voice floating in like ice water. "You passed with ease. You've earned this reward." His words are as empty as they are cold. "I'll give you some time alone. Someone will attend to you when dinner is served. I believe you're having seasoned squash with a selection of tubers," he says, nose twitching ever so slightly as his expression curdles. "Delicious."

I glare at him through the mist of Ashen's mane, my heart still pounding in my chest as I snap, "Anethesis."

He pauses, glancing over his shoulder. "Yes, Princess?"

"When I've completed these tests, when I've opened this portal..." I force the words out. "Give me your word that you'll release us."

He dips his chin. "You have my word."

And then, just like that, he's gone. The cavern falls into a strange, aching silence. A hollowness gnaws at me, deeper than anything I've ever felt. I've passed the test, but I don't feel victorious. I feel...broken. The toll of it all, the illusions, the false hopes, the fears I had to face, still echoes inside me, like a distant, unwelcome voice.

I glance around, half-expecting the darkness to swirl back to life, for the maze to rise again. But it doesn't.

I burrow further into Ashen's mane, the comfort of his warmth sinking deep into my bones. I remind myself over and over that none of it was real. That it was all just an illusion. But the images that flash behind my eyes, the voices that scream in my head, those feel anything but.

Chapter 5
Daed

*B**efore her.* What a curious thing this human is. This Amara Tyne.

I have been watching her for some time now, studying the way she works the soil, her hands caked in mud, dirt wedged beneath her nails. She brushes a stray strand of hair from her face without care, smearing dirt across her cheek, so unlike the pristine, delicate females of the Fae courts.

I can smell the sweat on her skin, mingling with the natural sweetness that lingers there. But beneath that, another scent emerges, something deeper, sharper. It fills my head, burns through my veins like molten fire. It is intoxicating.

She is unlike any human female I have encountered. Every small, insignificant movement she makes strikes me with such force that she might as well be a titan. I am captivated by her, by her mannerisms, her subtleties, her presence.

It seems almost a pity that something so fascinating must die.

But on the absurd chance she is Awakened—a human Awakened—then she is far too dangerous to be allowed to live.

Amara rocks back onto her knees, gently patting the soil around a leafy green plant. She wipes her hands on her simple green dress and exhales a satisfied sigh. Lifting her face, she shields her eyes from the sun cutting through the canopy. The light catches her warm brown skin, illuminating her like some divine artifact. At that moment, I have never envied sunlight more.

I could kill her now if I wished. Step out of the shadows of this tree, appear behind her in an instant, and drive my blade between her ribs before she even senses me. It would be quick. She intrigues me enough that I wouldn't let her suffer.

Smoke curls between my fingers, dark and restless, as I weigh my next move. Why am I still sitting here, lingering? Perhaps because killing her without cause would be...unprincely. I am the human's sovereign, after all. I am no tyrant, no matter how much they whisper otherwise.

Still, she cannot be Awakened. There are no signs, no mystical aura surrounding her. Nothing ethereal to suggest she wields magic older than the stars themselves. She's just a human playing in the dirt.

She is nothing.

The silver edge of a blade shimmers as it forms in my hand, the runes inked into my skin pulsing faintly. I tighten my grip on the hilt. Perhaps I should get closer just to be sure.

Suddenly, the branches around me groan and creak, wood twisting like waking limbs. I narrow my eyes as the branch beneath me sprouts new growth, tendrils wrapping around my legs, locking me in place.

I jerk against the restraints, snarling, as another branch coils around my chest, squeezing tight.

"Do you know who I am, elemental?" My voice is sharp, my canines elongating in warning.

The forest spirit does not respond. It only tightens its grip, wood groaning as it constricts me further.

Ah, this girl. The Jewel of the Tenders, Eryndor called her. So, she is guarded by these lesser fae.

How precious.

"This will not end well for you," I growl, my voice strained. "The Maledannan may allow you your freedom, but I will not. You know the darkness that runs through me. You dare seek it out?"

My curse wells up inside me, the void that is both my prison and my power. It rises like a tide, swallowing everything within me. The memories, the scraps of joy, the faintest hints of hope, until there is nothing left but hollow hunger.

My eyes roll back, and when they open again, I know they are black pits. Smoke spills from my skin, curling in tendrils as the branches gripping me recoil, their instinct for survival stronger than their loyalty to the girl.

The wood creaks and groans, turning brittle in an instant, bark splitting and cracking as rot races along the vines like poison through veins. With a sharp snap, they splinter and crumble, and I fall free.

I drop from the tree in a crouch, landing hard enough to snap twigs and send the forest into chaos. Birds explode from the branches above, shrieking as they flee. My ears catch the sound of footsteps behind me, and the darkness inside me coils tighter, demanding blood, demanding flesh to sate its endless hunger.

The dagger in my hand feels heavier, pulsing in time with the void that threatens to consume me. My grip tightens until my knuckles ache, and I feel it happening. The moment I lose myself.

The moment *he* takes over.

The ancient force within me, older than this forest, older than the first dawn, tears through my control like a blade through silk. I am shoved aside, a passenger in my own body, watching as the beast claims me.

"Who are you?"

Her voice cuts through the shadows. Steady, curious, lacking the fear I am so used to hearing, and it carries a warmth that stops the tide just before it drowns me.

The dagger vanishes as my form shifts. Fangs retract and pointed ears soften as I glamor myself, and my features bend into something more familiar to her. Something human.

I step out of the shadows, and her gaze narrows, assessing me as the sunlight filters through the canopy, catching her dark eyes, the line of her jaw, the curve of her lips.

"Who are you?" she demands again, her voice steady. "You are not of the Grove."

"No," I reply, stepping closer, so near now that I could snap her neck with a flick of my wrist if I wished.

Her expression hardens, the softness of her face giving way to steel. "You're a poacher, then. Here to murder the creatures of this forest. You are not welcome here."

My lip twitches in amusement, her defiance sparking something unexpectedly warm in my chest. "And what will you do about it? You're alone, with no one around for miles."

I take another step forward, testing her resolve, but she doesn't flinch.

"You have no weapons. No magic. Nothing to protect you."

She raises her chin, eyes blazing. "I need neither to defend myself from a coward like you. Someone who preys on the innocent, skulking in shadows and threatening a young girl to feel powerful." She flexes her fingers, her nails filthy. "These will do just fine to scratch your eyes out if you come any closer. Now leave, while you still have your dignity and your sight."

Laughter erupts from my throat, unbidden and genuine, but not cruel. It's a foreign sound to my ears, more of a surprise than an insult. Warmth spreads through me, uncoiling the darkness that clawed at the edges of my mind. It retreats, slinking back into the void it came from.

There is no fear in her. Only fire. A fierce passion that stirs something unfamiliar.

But she doesn't find my amusement endearing. Her expression sharpens.

"I've warned you," she says firmly, her voice calm but unrelenting. "I have a power within me. Don't make me summon it to my side."

The laughter dies in my throat. My eyes narrow on her, and I take a half step closer.

"Power?" I ask, the word tasting like bait. "What power?"

Her hand lifts to the rune hanging from a leather string around her neck. She clasps it tightly, her knuckles whitening as she holds her ground. "I am the forest," she says, her voice low but fierce, each word crackling with conviction. "I am the Jewel of the Tenders."

The anticipation inside me vanishes. My eyes flick to the rune. It's Maledannan. A relic for healing. Nothing more.

The realization washes over me like cold water, extinguishing whatever simmering tension remained. This girl isn't Awakened. She's no threat to me.

There is nothing more to be gained here.

"Very well," I say, taking a deliberate step back. "I will leave."

Her head jerks slightly, startled by my sudden compliance. "You will?"

I smirk. "Isn't that what you wanted?"

"Yes," she says quickly, straightening her shoulders as if to regain the upper hand. "Leave and be quick about it."

The Prince of the Sundered Kingdoms isn't accustomed to being ordered about, especially by a human, but there's something oddly charming about her obliviousness to who I truly am. An Awakened would see through my glamor in an instant, pierce the enchantments masking my true form. Amara Tyne is just another human.

I dip my chin, striding past her, the scintillating scent of her filling my head once more. It's maddening, almost intoxicating, and an involuntary groan escapes my lips before I can stop it. I grit my teeth, trying to will the reaction away.

I've barely taken a few steps when I hear the rustle of grass behind me.

"Wait," she calls.

The word hooks me, curiosity forcing my steps to still. I glance over my shoulder.

"What is that?" she asks, her brow furrowing as she stares at me, her voice trailing off.

My eyes narrow. "What's what?"

"That light around you," she says, her gaze distant, her lids half-closed as though seeing something beyond what I can. "That...shimmer."

My heart stumbles in its rhythm, the beat thundering in my ears. I turn slowly to face her, every muscle taut. "What did you say?"

Amara steps toward me, her movements fluid, almost dreamlike. The wind catches her hair, sending it tumbling over her shoulders, and the long grass sways in harmony with the fabric of her dress. For a moment, she's otherworldly, a vision so radiant it steals the breath from my lungs.

Her hand rises toward my face. I flinch before her fingers can make contact.

"It's beautiful," she murmurs, her voice barely above a whisper. "I've... I've seen it before."

The words send a jolt through me, and without thinking, I step back. *I* never step back.

"I'm leaving," I say quickly, the urgency in my voice betraying me.

"No, wait!" she calls again, closing the distance faster than I expect.

Her hand reaches up, dirt and all, cupping the side of my face with a gentleness that makes me freeze.

The moment her hand touches my skin, something fierce awakens within me, a surge of heat that rushes through my veins, burning away the cold, hollow darkness that has lived in me for so long.

I see it then, the golden threads, delicate yet unbreakable, curling from her fingertips like living tendrils of sunlight. They wind their way across her hand, flowing to where her skin touches mine. The light is blinding yet soft, a warmth that seeps into the marrow of my bones, illuminating every darkened place inside me. It chases the shadows from my vision, filling the void with something pure, something I feel with every fragment of my fractured soul. It is as if it knows me, as if it has *always* known me.

She is not just a human. She is mine.

Amara Tyne is my salvation. My ruin. My *mate*.

The realization strikes me with the force of a storm, wild and uncontrollable, and I fight the instinct to claim her then and there. My fingers ache with the need to touch her, to pull her closer, to feel every inch of her against me. The beast inside me howls, clawing at the walls of my control, demanding that I give in, that I take what is mine by right, by fate, by the threads that tie our souls together.

I swallow hard, my gaze fixed on hers as she meets it without hesitation. Yet, in the reflection of her eyes, there's no trace of the golden threads. Am I the only one who can see them? Still, I'm almost certain she *feels* them. Her lips part slightly, her brow knitting in quiet confusion, as though she's trying to piece together what's unfolding between us.

It's too much. It's not enough. The need to savor this moment wars with the instinct to escape it. I grip her wrist gently, holding her hand in place, and the threads pulse brighter, as if recognizing the act.

"What are you?" I whisper, my voice rough, trembling under the weight of the question, but the threads don't answer. They simply shimmer, binding us tighter, burning with the truth I'm too afraid to speak aloud.

"I could ask you the same question," she replies.

My mind whirls, a storm of disbelief and dread. This cannot be. I have waited centuries, endless, hollow centuries, for a mate, for the one who would complete me, who might pull me from the abyss of my loneliness. But I have feared this moment just as much as I have longed for it.

I am cursed. Anyone I love is destined to die. This is my birthright, my inescapable fate, and, as if the gods weren't cruel enough, she is human. Yet now I see clearly that she is more than that. She is what Eryndor feared, what he warned me against. Awakened, and a human Awakened cannot be allowed to live.

My other hand drifts behind my back, smoke curling in the air like an unholy whisper, pooling into solid form around my fingers. The dagger materializes, cold and familiar, the hilt fitting perfectly into my grip. One strike, swift, precise, between her ribs and into her heart. It would be over before her next breath. One act of mercy to spare her from a lifetime of suffering, from the curse that would destroy her if I made her mine.

I gaze numbly at her, the world narrowing to the touch of her hand and the weight of her presence. My eyes fall to the cascade of her hair, and I see it now. Brown, but not simply brown. It's the deep, earthy hue of forest soil after a rain, rich and alive, catching the light in glimmers of gold and auburn as it tumbles over her shoulders and her eyes—*gods above and below, her eyes*—are endless. Dark as night but flickering with flecks of copper that shimmer like sunlight streaming through autumn leaves. There's a depth to them, as if they hold secrets older than the trees around us, as if they've seen me—*truly seen me*—in a way no one else ever has.

Make it quick.

Suddenly, movement stirs in the trees behind us, drawing her attention. Her hand slips from my skin as she turns, breaking the fragile connection that had tethered me to this moment. Her scent lingers in the air, wildflowers and earth, a breath of life that fills my lungs one final time.

When she turns back to look for me, I am already gone.

Arax waits for me on the ship, his eyes scanning the skies as I descend and land deftly beside him.

"My prince. Did you find her?"

I stride past him without so much as a glance. "Yes, and Eryndor has accomplished nothing but wasting my time."

Arax falls into step behind me. "So she is not Awakened?"

I move past the Reapers standing at attention along the deck, each of their heads bowed in deference.

"No," I say curtly, gripping the wooden frame of my cabin door as I stop, still refusing to meet his questioning gaze. "She is human. Nothing more."

He exhales slowly, relief evident in the sound. "This is good news. The king and queen will be pleased to avoid the complications of dealing with another Awakened."

I nod, swallowing the ache rising in my throat. "Send a Blade to House Maledannan. Have them inform Eryndor that the girl is nothing to be concerned with." My voice drops lower. "In fact, tell him to forget about her completely. Let her live in peace."

Out of the corner of my eye, I see Arax's brow furrow in curiosity, but he doesn't press. "Very well, my prince."

The stomp of his boots echoes across the deck as he gives my orders. Moments later, the sharp sound of wings slicing through the air signals the messenger's departure. Without another word, I step into my cabin, slamming the door behind me.

A full bottle of rum sits on the table, and I waste no time grabbing it, wrenching the cork free, and throwing back a long gulp. The burn scorches my throat, but it dulls the edge of the emotions clawing at me. Emotions that linger far too long to be dismissed as fleeting.

No matter how I try to convince myself otherwise, I cannot ignore the truth. It thrums in my veins, as undeniable as the runes etched into my skin. After centuries of searching, I have found her. And she is more radiant and pure than I ever imagined. Too perfect, too untainted for me to darken her life with the shadows that haunt me. To curse her. To see her consumed by a fate I am powerless to prevent.

For though I may be a prince, a warrior, a Fae who commands smoke and shadows, though I may make my enemies kneel and feast on their fear, I am utterly helpless against the force that shares my body. The vile essence that taints my blood.

I would rather endure an eternity of solitude, clinging to the memory of what could have been, then see something so splendid as her torn from this world because of me.

And so I will lie. To Arax. To Eryndor. To the king and queen. I will lie to protect her.

A knock at the door breaks through my thoughts, and I take another long swig before calling out. "What is it?"

The door creaks open, and a Blade steps forward. "Your Highness. We are ready to depart for Baev'kalath."

I nod, dismissing him with a wave, eager to be alone again.

Sinking into the chair, the rum sloshes in the bottle as I tip it to my lips. The groan of the anchor being raised and the bustle of Blades readying the ship filters through the thick wooden walls, but it isn't fast enough.

I wish to leave Valorne, never to set foot on its soil again, praying another five centuries pass me by without ever seeing Amara Tyne again. For both our sakes.

CHAPTER 6
DAED

*A*fter her. The scar on my palm stares back at me, a jagged, pale line carved into my flesh. A cruel reminder of the night Amara became my wife. I trace it with my thumb, feeling the ridges of old pain, and wonder how I ever thought I could defy fate. Our marriage was never a bargain struck in desperation; it was destiny, written in the stars long before I first laid eyes on her. But destiny is no kind force. It cares nothing for the lives it shatters, only that its plans unfold as ordained. Even Amara being stolen from me was likely etched into some distant constellation, and for that, I damn the stars to the void.

Her scar is gone now. Her power to heal ensures no mark remains to mirror mine. Yet I've left enough scars on her heart to more than make up for it.

The ship rocks gently as it docks in the harbor of Ballamar City, the humid air clinging to my skin like a second layer. The docks are chaos, a cacophony of creaking wood, shouting merchants, and the slap of waves against ship hulls. The sharp tang of salt saturates the air, mingling with the earthy scent of dust kicked up by hurried feet. Ahead, the streets simmer beneath a cloudless sky, the sun blazing mercilessly above. Tall sandstone buildings rise, their timeworn walls smooth and bleached by heat. Narrow alleys snake between them, shadows pooling in fleeting reprieve from the inferno.

I take a slow breath, letting the scene settle over me, wincing as vendors bellow their wares, their voices rising above the city's relentless hum. There is nothing like this in the Sundered Kingdoms. Every land across the sea is stranger than the last, but none have brought me closer to her. Even now, with Reon's flimsy leads, I fear this will only be another dead end, more precious time wasted. Impatience and dread gnaw at me as I watch barefoot children dart through the crowds, painfully reminded that more than Amara is at stake.

I've been merciful so far, using tact and diplomacy to gather whispers of House Ithranor's plans. But I feel that mercy slipping away. How much longer until I tear what I need from anyone I suspect of withholding it, until I leave broken bodies in my wake and drown my enemies' cries in blood?

"Daed," Reon's voice interrupts, his firm slap on my back dragging me from the edge of my violent imaginings. "We're looking for the Red Room. The Ithranor we seek are said to frequent it."

I grunt. "The Red Room? Sounds like a brothel."

When Reon doesn't answer immediately, I pinch the bridge of my nose. "I swear, if this is an excursion for your fucking cock…"

He shakes his head quickly, but the poorly hidden smirk twitching at his lips betrays him. "Of course not. It's just… a happy coincidence." He glances around the ship, his brow furrowed. "Where is your sister?"

I lift my chin toward the city sprawling before us. "Somewhere out there. Hopefully not getting into more trouble. I'm in no mood to clean up another of her messes."

"Yes, it is strange that you are not the reckless one," Reon remarks with a smirk.

"I cannot afford to be," I reply, my tone firm. "Not when the world is mine to lose."

His fingers curl on my shoulder, his grip steady and reassuring. "We will find her, Daedalus. If we have to search every land beyond the sea, we'll bring her back to you."

A faint grin tugs at the corner of my mouth. Reon's loyalty has never been in doubt. We've faced too much together, endured too many battles, for me to question his word. He didn't need convincing to leave Eyr'Drogul; he volunteered before he even knew the dangers we would face. That kind of unwavering devotion earns a great deal of forgiveness, including his penchant for spending every quiet moment in the arms of some beauty. Human, Fae, or otherwise. If those nights leave him sharper and stronger when he rises, who am I to begrudge him his indulgences?

The ramp slams onto the dock with a jarring thud, and we disembark with our heads bowed, cloaks and hoods draped over us in an attempt to blend in. In this stifling heat, however, the layers do little but draw unwanted attention. Sweat clings to my skin, and the air is thick, almost suffocating, as we step into the chaos of Ballamar.

At the rear, Orios and Solena walk in step, their fingers brushing in a fleeting, intimate gesture. When I glance back, Solena's eyes meet mine, and we exchange polite, strained smiles before quickly looking away.

She didn't hesitate to join me, much like Reon. At first, I questioned what use a maid could be on a voyage across the seas, but after the Archdruid's confession, I found her purpose and it has proven invaluable. Solena is no longer just a maid; she's the most critical member of my crew. The long hours we've spent together have unveiled parts of her I never would have known otherwise, bound as we are by one undeniable truth: a shared love for Amara.

Orios, naturally, follows wherever Solena goes. His love for her is endless, and in exchange for his service, I have released him from his Reaper's vow. If he wishes to claim her as his mate, he has my blessing. It is a small price to pay for the loyalty of such a formidable warrior.

Reon sidles up to me as we weave through the bustling streets. "That one still hasn't warmed to me," he says, nodding toward Solena. "There must be something wrong with her."

"She has standards, Reon," I reply dryly, earning myself an elbow in the ribs. "Besides, she's with Orios. Why would she show you even a hint of interest?"

Reon shrugs, an easy grin tugging at his lips. "He hasn't marked her yet. No bite, no claim. Until then, she's an unclaimed female, is she not?"

I glance at him, unamused. "You might want to keep that sentiment to yourself if you're fond of your balls being attached to your body."

Reon throws a look over his shoulder at Solena, whose hooded face still manages to convey a sharp glare. He smirks. "I'd bite her in an instant. Feisty little thing. Seal the bond with teeth and flesh and blood."

I can feel his gaze shift back to me, that telltale glint in his eyes, and I know exactly where this conversation is headed.

"Don't start," I groan, sidestepping a woman berating her children as they shuffle down the street. "I thought I'd have more time. I wanted to explain everything to her first."

Reon frowns, his playful edge dimming. "You should've bitten her at the wedding. Got it over and done with. I'd have reminded you, but your *best friend* didn't even make the guest list."

I sigh, bored and weary. "We've been over this."

"We have," he says with a shrug, the grin returning. "But giving you shit is an excellent way to pass the time."

"Sometimes I wonder if you're worth the trouble."

"You know I am." His tone turns pointed. "Just like you know you should've marked her when you had the chance. Would've made finding her a hell of a lot easier."

I shake my head, my jaw tightening. "I couldn't. I'd already put her through so much."

For once, Reon's voice softens, a rare seriousness creeping into his words. "When we find her, Daedalus, will you tell her then? Or will there always be a reason to wait?"

I lift my chin, my voice firm with conviction. "I won't waste another moment. I'll tell her she's my mate and I'll bite her and never let go."

Reon waggles a finger, his smirk sliding back into place. "Not too deep. Humans can be delicate, you know. Don't want to tear out her jugular after all this effort."

I grin despite myself. "She's no ordinary human."

His smirk falters, replaced by a contemplative look. "I'm beginning to see that."

I barely take a step before a small body slams into me, a child, barely taller than my knees, clutching a sticky sweet on a stick. He looks up, tongue still dragging across the candy, but the moment his eyes meet mine, he gasps. It's as if he sees past the hood and cloak, straight through to the monster beneath.

He stumbles back, his foot catching on a rock. The candy flies from his hand. But before either boy or sweet can hit the ground, they freeze mid-motion, suspended in the air like marionettes caught in time.

I glance at Reon beside me. He's pointing a finger at the child, an amber light crackling at its tip.

With a groan, I step forward, grab the boy rigid as stone and set him upright. Then I snatch the candy from the air and place it carefully back in his hand, mindful I could snap his little digits straight off in this state.

When the moment is as it was, Reon clicks his fingers, and the sparks vanish. The boy blinks, his head whipping around, dazed and disoriented.

"Go," I say sharply. "Away with you."

He doesn't need to be told twice. One last lick of his candy, and he darts off into the crowd.

I scan the street, searching for any eyes that might've caught Reon's display, but the people seem blissfully unaware.

"We're trying to keep a low profile," I mutter under my breath.

Reon shrugs. "What? My power's like a muscle. I've got to stretch it. Besides, all I did was stop a kid from falling on his ass."

I shoot him a dark glare, brow furrowing. He lifts both hands in mock surrender.

"Okay, okay. I get it. No time warps."

We push deeper into the city, the salty tang of the sea fading into the stench of unwashed bodies, rancid gutters, and sour ale. The streets pulse with noise and movement, a chaotic tangle of vendors shouting over each other and the occasional yelp of a stray dog dodging a cart wheel.

In a shadowed corner, I spot a group of men clustered like flies over rot. Even from here, the rank mix of ale, sweat, and piss bites at my senses. If anyone knows where the Red Room is, it's them.

I approach with measured steps, the others trailing close behind. When the men look up, their faces harden with hostility, their conversation silenced.

"Piss off," one of them spits without hesitation.

I remind myself I'm here for information, not a fight, though their arrogance scrapes my patience thin.

"The Red Room," I say, keeping my voice low and firm. "Where is it?"

The man who spoke first leans off the wall, the others following his lead, closing ranks.

"I said, piss off. You deaf? Or do I need to show you with my fists?"

Reon shifts forward, but I press a firm hand against his chest, holding him back.

"I don't want trouble," I say, though the growl in my throat betrays the truth. "Just give me what I need, and no one gets hurt."

The men laugh. Loud, grating, and obnoxious.

"Or maybe we'll beat the shit out of you and your boyfriend for the fun of it," the leader sneers.

Reon snorts. "Boyfriend? He fucking wishes."

I grit my teeth. "Last chance," I warn, my voice a low rumble. "This doesn't need to get..."

The leader's fist flies at my face, but I catch it midair, my grip locking like steel. He freezes, his bravado cracking as I tighten my hold. Smoke begins to curl from between my fingers, slithering up his arm like a living thing.

He thrashes, trying to pull free, but my grip doesn't falter. His fear is a tangible thing now, a bitter taste in the air.

I shake my head, disappointed. "...ugly."

The smoke coils tighter, and a sickening snap echoes as his arm gives way. He drops to his knees with a howl, his body trembling as the smoke climbs to his throat, winding around it like a serpent preparing to strike.

"The arm will heal," I say coldly, watching his face contort with pain. "But a broken neck? That's more permanent."

He gasps, choking on incoherent words as the smoke squeezes.

"What was that?" I lean closer, twisting his mangled hand until the bones in his fingers crack like dry twigs.

The sound of his suffering is music, but one of his companions breaks the symphony, shouting, "That way! Down the street, an alley on the left. There's a door at the bottom of the stairs. That's the Red Room!"

I hear him, but I'm in no rush to release the bastard in my grasp.

Reon leans in, his tone dry. "Unless you're aiming to leave a puddle of human goo behind, maybe ease up? Not exactly low profile."

He's right. A crowd is beginning to gather. The last thing I need is the city guard sticking their noses into my business. With a flick of my wrist, I release the man.

The smoke retreats, leaving his arm limp and mangled, fingers little more than splintered bone and shredded flesh. His companions rush to his side, hauling him to his feet and dragging him away as he howls in pain.

The murmurs grow louder, the word *Fae* spreading like wildfire.

Solena steps closer, her hood casting deep shadows over her face. "We should move. Quickly."

Reon tilts his head. "What about Zyphoro?"

Before I can answer, a shadow sweeps across the dusty street, and we look up to see Zyphoro gliding above, her black wings blocking out the sun.

Reon clicks his tongue. "You and your sister are absolutely shit at blending in, you know that?"

I glance at the growing crowd and sigh. "Let's go."

We follow the man's directions down the narrow street, then turn left into a cramped alleyway. The space is so tight we're forced into single file. A creeping suspicion gnaws at me that we've walked straight into a trap. But then, my foot catches on something, and I almost stumble.

I glance down to find a small gap in the wall. The stairs that descend into pitch-blackness are barely visible. It's even less inviting than the claustrophobic alleyway.

A sharp gust of wind blows my hair out of my eyes as Zyphoro lands beside me.

"Decided to join us, then?" I say, my tone laced with sarcasm.

Zyphoro arches an eyebrow, the faintest trace of a smirk on her lips. "Apologies, brother. I sometimes forget your wing situation is... less than desirable."

Reon snorts, and when I catch Solena and Orios laughing softly, I can't help but feel the sting of their amusement. I am their prince, yes, but also the only one who can't fly.

We move down the stairs one after the other, the stone walls scraping against my shoulders, the low ceiling forcing me to duck. The only light comes from the flickering glow of candlelight, which reveals a steel door at the bottom.

I raise my fist and pound against it. The sound echoes in the silence, and almost immediately, a slot slides open with a metallic scrape, revealing only a pair of drooping blue eyes.

"Password," a gruff male voice demands.

I furrow my brow and turn to Reon. His eyes flicker, but he's chewing on his lip, clearly uncertain.

"Password?" I repeat to him, my voice edged with frustration. "She gave you one, didn't she? What did she say?"

Reon looks sheepish. "Apart from my name over and over, not much," he mutters.

The voice behind the slot grunts. "No password. No entry," before slamming the slot shut with finality.

"Fuck," I mutter, clenching my fist, smoke beginning to curl from my fingers. The temptation to break through the door is overwhelming, but before I can act, Zyphoro steps forward, placing a hand on my fist to steady me.

"I love bloodshed as much as the next, brother," she says softly, "but we are here for information, and people talk easier when they're still breathing."

She pushes me aside and bangs on the door. Once again, the slot opens with a harsh clang.

"Password," the voice demands.

Zyphoro pauses for a moment, and I expect the slot to slam shut once more. But instead, the hardness in the doorman's eyes softens, pupils dilating as they fixate on her. His gaze goes distant, as if he's caught in a trance.

Zyphoro's voice drops sweetly, and I can hear the honeyed edge in her words. "Be a dear and open the door, would you?"

"Yes. Of course," the voice replies, now dripping with eager submission. "Anything you want."

Several locks click, bolts unlatch, and with a loud groan, the door swings open. Zyphoro steps back, giving me a mock bow as she gestures for me to go ahead.

I frown but step forward, pushing past the door into the dim light. Behind it stands a dwarf, short, stout and shaggy-haired, standing on a box. He looks up as I enter, his breath catching when his eyes meet Zyphoro's.

"Go straight through," he mutters, gesturing to a heavy red curtain a few steps away.

Zyphoro, ever playful, reaches over and pinches the hanging skin of his cheek. "Thank you, darling," she coos with an exaggerated sweetness.

She turns to us, her lips curling into a sly grin. "Glamor. Ever heard of it? You'd think you were the ones trapped in an enchanted prison for centuries."

With that, she boldly parts the curtains as the dwarf shuts the door behind us, and we're hit by the seductive murmur of string music, the low hum of laughter, and the occasional sensuous moan that hangs in the air, thick with the sweet scent of smoke.

A dim, sultry light bathes the crimson room, casting its warm glow over the sea of plush, tasseled cushions that carpet the floor in rich shades of scarlet and deep violet. The space feels alive with movement, every surface seemingly writhed upon by bodies, every hand clutching a goblet, wine spilling carelessly over bare skin as fingers dance along smooth, exposed flesh and feed grapes to gaping mouths.

Sheer silk veils flutter between rooms, their delicate fabric swaying in a breathless, unseen breeze. But these veils do nothing to conceal the hedonistic scenes unfolding beyond them. Through the translucent curtains, the silhouettes of entwined bodies twist together in various positions, some that even take me a moment to figure out.

The allure of the room is undeniable, the sounds stirring something deep within me, tugging at my senses. The sight of bare skin makes me think of Amara. Her smoothness, the softness of her beneath my fingers, the way she tasted on my tongue. I clench my fists, fighting the heat rising in me, willing it to stay contained.

A terse voice slices through the air. "What are you doing here? How did you get in?"

I turn to face the human woman, her silk robe barely drawn around her, blonde hair piled high on her head, jewels dripping from her ears and clinging to the delicate curve of her neck.

"We mean you no harm," I say, my tone steady. "We're looking for someone."

She narrows her gaze, sizing us up. "As is everyone who visits the Red Room. But we are strictly members only, and I've never seen any of you before." Her eyes sweep over me, and for a moment, her expression softens. "I would remember."

I grin in response, and she seems to take it as an invitation. Her hands loosen their grip on the robe, the silk parting over her thigh, revealing just enough, but I am not interested.

"Do you have any Ithranor Fae as members?" I ask, staying on task.

"Ithranor... Fae?" she gasps, eyes widening in surprise.

I lower my hood, revealing the pointed tips of my ears, and the others follow suit. The woman's gaze flickers between us, a moment of hesitation before she nods, gesturing toward one of the curtained rooms.

I offer a silent smile, dipping my chin in gratitude as I move toward the curtain. When I slip inside, the Fae male splayed on the edge of the bed doesn't even notice, far too absorbed in the woman kneeling between his legs, her head bobbing enthusiastically. Only when I clear my throat do his eyes snap open, and his expression morphs into one of panic as he sees us.

"Fuck," he curses, shoving the woman away and grabbing for a sheet to cover his lower half.

The woman gasps, scrambling to gather her clothes as she hurries out of the room.

"Who the fuck are you?!" he bellows, his voice filled with indignation.

I step forward, rolling my shoulders. "Oh, I think you know."

His eyes widen as he leans forward from the soft embrace of the round bed. When he finally recognizes me, it's as if the weight of his world shifts.

"Prince Daedalus... but how... why... what are you doing in Ballamar City?" His voice cracks with disbelief.

I don't hesitate. "I think you know that as well, so let's stop wasting time. Shall we?" My jaw tightens as my voice lowers, rough like gravel. "Where is my wife?"

"Please," the male stammers, one hand outstretched while the other clutches the sheet at his waist. "I have no ties to my house anymore. I've broken from them."

"That's not what my brother asked," Zyphoro cuts in, her fingers idly tracing the intricate gold threads that edge the silk curtains. "Amara Phaedren. Princess of the Sundered Kingdoms. You know of whom we speak?"

The male nods.

"And you know she was stolen?"

Another nod, slower this time, his throat bobbing.

"So you know where she is?"

He shakes his head vehemently. "That, I do not know. I swear it."

Zyphoro and I exchange a weary glance.

"Glamor him?" I suggest.

She smirks, tilting her head like a predator deciding how much to toy with its prey. "There are far more entertaining ways to make him talk."

Smoke weaves between my fingers as I consider. "Strangulation? Decapitation? Evisceration?"

She taps her chin, feigning thoughtfulness as the male squirms, sweat beading on his brow. "Tempting options, but no. Maybe something a little more visceral." Her eyes flick to Orios, standing like a stoic giant in the corner, towering over Solena at his side. "Reaper, how long has it been since you crushed a skull with your bare hands?" Zyphoro asks, her tone almost conversational.

A slow grin pulls at the corner of his mouth. "Too long," Orios rumbles.

"Then, by all means, when you're ready," Zyphoro says, nodding her approval.

Orios steps forward, his massive hands flexing, and the male pales as if all the blood has drained from his face.

"Wait!" he shouts, panic cracking his voice. "I'm telling the truth! I don't know where she is. Not now."

Orios looms over the bed, his hands closing around the male's head like he's holding an overripe melon, ready to crush.

"What do you mean, *not now*?" I ask, stepping closer.

"Because it moves," the male whimpers, Orios' grip tightening, his thumbs pressing against his jaw. "Driftspire moves!"

I raise a hand, and Orios halts. "Driftspire. What is that?"

The male peeks out from between Orios' fingers, his voice trembling. "When House Ithranor fled the Sundered Kingdoms, we built a new home in the sky. It's where we've lived all these years. But it doesn't stay in one place. It moves with the wind. Almost impossible to find."

"Then where was it last?" I demand.

The male hesitates, his eyes darting nervously. I nod at Orios, who resumes his squeezing.

"Here!" the male shrieks. "Not far from Ballamar City. I broke from my house here and chose to stay."

"How long ago?" Zyphoro presses.

He shrugs helplessly as Orios tightens his grip again. "Weeks! I've lost track!"

I glance at Zyphoro and find her already looking at me. Her expression is grim, the truth settling between us like an uninvited guest. "If this city moves, they could be anywhere by now," she says quietly.

She's right, and the reality of it ignites something dark and restless in me. My anger surges, curling my fingers into fists. I barely register Orios still poised to crush the male's skull.

"Enough, Orios," I command.

He obeys immediately, and the male collapses onto the bed, trembling, his hands roaming over his head as if to reassure himself it's still intact.

My jaw tightens, and I force the anger clawing at my throat into words. "But she is alive?" The question leaves me in a hoarse voice I hardly recognize.

"Yes," the male whispers. "She is alive. They keep her well. And not only Anethesis... she is protected too... by the Golden Son."

The fire in my veins ignites into an inferno, my canines lengthening as the shadows gather thick and hungry around me.

"He is with her?" I snarl, my voice a low growl as rage twists inside me and the shadows coil tighter.

The male's heartbeat pounds in my ears, frantic and shallow, the scent of his fear thick and intoxicating. I'm one step from the edge, ready to let the darkness devour me, when Zyphoro's hand clamps down on my shoulder.

"You knew he would be," she says firmly, her voice cutting through the haze of rage. "Calm yourself, brother."

"We could take to the air," Reon suggests.

"But where would we even begin?" I snap, bitterness edging every word. "If the city moves, it could be anywhere. It might've passed right over us, and we'd never have known."

"There might be a way," the male mutters, barely audible.

All eyes snap to him, and he shrinks back, hands raised defensively. "I'm not the only Fae who found refuge in Ballamar City. There are others, and they have something you might find useful."

I narrow my eyes, scrutinizing him. "What other Fae? More Ithranor?"

"No." He gulps, his gaze darting around the room as if afraid of being overheard. "House Taramethos."

I scoff, disbelief flooding my tone. "House Taramethos? Here?"

He nods quickly, desperation in his movements. "They practically rule this city from the shadows."

Reon's gaze drills into me. "If House Taramethos is here... they might have a..."

"Scrying mirror," the male interrupts. "Yes. I've seen it with my own eyes."

"A scrying mirror could show us exactly where the city is," Solena says, her voice trembling with barely contained hope. "And Amara."

I step closer to the male, my face set, my tone leaving no room for compromise. "Where is this mirror?"

"They host a masquerade ball once a month at midnight and show it off like a party favor. The next ball is in a couple of days. The location is secret until the night before. I will tell you as soon as I know. Please just... leave me in peace. I didn't sever my ties with my house just to die in a brothel."

I nod curtly. "Very well. Your life is spared... for now. But I'm not letting you out of my sight, and I swear, if what you've told us leads nowhere, there are far worse things in this world than death."

He bows his head, clasping his hands as though in prayer. "You are a merciful prince."

Such words offend me.

"Get dressed," I order coldly. "We're leaving."

I nod to the others, and they slip past the curtain.

Reon leans close, his voice low. "So, we're heading out straight away, then?"

I glare at him. "Move your fucking ass."

He smirks faintly. "Got it."

As I follow the others, I pause at the threshold, turning back to the male as he frantically searches for his pants beneath the mound of cushions.

"Tell me," I say, and he freezes, looking up nervously. "Why did you break from House Ithranor?"

His shoulders sag, and he sweeps his long, golden hair out of his face. "They're planning to return to Meranor," he admits, his voice hollow. "But I'm quite content here. I like the humans... more than my own kind, if I'm being honest."

"That's impossible," I mutter bitterly. "There's no way back to Meranor."

His silence speaks louder than words, and he avoids my gaze.

"Amara," I mutter, realization striking like a blow.

He nods slowly. "Anethesis plans for her to open a portal."

My jaw clenches, fury surging through me. "Hurry up."

I storm out of the room, where the others are waiting.

"What is it?" Zyphoro asks, immediately noticing the tension radiating off me.

My heart pounds violently in my chest as I glance down at the scar on my palm. "We have less time than I thought."

CHAPTER 7

AMARA

I feel strange tonight. The moonlight spills through the balcony, draping my room in a somber blue hue that casts everything in an eerie, spectral glow. But it's not just the melancholy light. Something is different. As though my eyes are open for the first time, and that I can see this pretty cage, this tortuous world, for what it truly is.

It's not the shimmer I've learned to spot when the Fae weave their illusions. That I can see plainly now, their tricks laid bare. No, this is deeper. As if I'm seeing the very essence of everything around me. Not just the paint, the wood, or the stone, but the imprint they leave on the world, the threads that tie it all together.

I lie on my bed, staring at the ceiling, my hands raised above me. Slowly, I move them through the air, and as they drift, they leave behind a trail of silvery glitter, like faint stardust. If I look closer, closer still, I can see the blood coursing through my veins beneath the skin, beneath the muscle.

My hands drop to my sides, and a shiver crawls over me.

I see all this with my collar on, so it cannot be magic.

What are they doing to me?

A twist churns in my stomach, and I glance down, catching a movement so strong it's visible even through my dress. This may be my first pregnancy, but I know enough to recognize that I'm larger than I should be for how far along I am. I devour every meal, leaving not a scrap behind while always hungering for more, and I'm endlessly thirsty. Is this because my child is half-Fae?

A sharp kick suddenly jolts me, as if the child is answering my question with an emphatic *yes*. It already has a temper, that much is certain. But with parents like me and Daedalus, it was never destined to be a calm, placid thing. I smooth my hands over my belly, trying to soothe it, and begin to hum softly. Slowly, the flutters and flips quiet.

The melody has no words, just a tune born of the sounds I've heard in moments of stillness: birdsong, rustling leaves, the whisper of the wind. I hum it often to my child, not just to comfort them, but to calm myself as well.

Soon, I'm certain my child has drifted to sleep, but sleep evades me. My gifts can't save me here. Even if the collar around my neck didn't suppress my power, I have no earth to draw from, no Souls to channel. If I could free Ashen, we would escape with ease, but that would mean flying to the cave where he is imprisoned and somehow breaking the enchantments that bind him, dulling his power as effectively as the collar dulls mine.

I hold on to hope, but I can feel Ashen's slipping away. I fear the next time I'm allowed a visit with him, I'll find his cage empty, nothing left but a faint wisp of smoke.

Suddenly, my thoughts are interrupted by the familiar groan of shifting rock. I turn toward the balcony, watching as clouds drift past, but it isn't the clouds moving. It's Driftspire. Has it already been that long?

Every few days, the Ithranor gather and channel their magic to move the city to a new location. But where they take us, I never know. That information is not shared with me, nor am I meant to be privy to it.

The thought gnaws at me. If I have no clue where I am, what chance does Daedalus have of finding me? Am I to wait for him? For how much longer? Weeks? Months? Years?

No, I cannot wait for him.

I cannot wait for Ashen to fade into nothingness or for my child to be born a prisoner.

If I want freedom, I must take the bargain Anethesis offers.

Endure the trials, and I will be released.

I drift in and out of tormenting awareness, blinking through fragments of sleep, until the sun finally rises. Stumbling out of bed, I wander dazed to the balcony, squinting into the sharp morning light. The sky is flawless, a stunning blue. The rocky islands of Driftspire hover around me, and when I glance down, I see nothing but an endless sea of white, misty clouds. No landmarks. No clues. Just emptiness. Once again, I'm granted no insight into where we might be, but deep in my gut, I feel it. I'm even further from Daed than I was before.

A knock sounds at the door, but I don't bother answering. After a pause, it creaks open, and the maid peeks in, carrying a silver tray.

She doesn't say a word, just hurries inside with her head bowed, as though even looking at me might curse her. She lifts the dome lid from the tray, revealing a vibrant sprawl of freshly cut fruit. Then scurries out, closing the door softly behind her.

I glance over my shoulder at the platter. Some of the fruit is familiar, but other pieces, bright pink with large black seeds or brilliant yellow with an almost glowing flesh, I've never seen before. Could this be a clue to where we are? These fruits aren't common in the Sundered Kingdoms.

But the thought doesn't linger. Hunger wins. I dive upon the platter, scooping up pieces of fruit and biting into the firm, sweet flesh with urgency, half-afraid it might vanish if I don't eat it fast enough. The juices drip down my chin, sticky and sweet, and anyone watching would think I was being starved.

If nothing else, I can say my captors feed me well. They even respect the fact I do not eat meat, unlike my Mordorin hosts.

When I'm finished, the tray is littered with mangled skins and scattered seeds, yet the hollowness in my stomach remains. I could devour three more platters like this, and it might not make a difference. This baby is insatiable.

I glance at the water jug, debating whether to drink straight from it, but I decide to maintain a semblance of decorum and pour myself a cup instead.

Taking a seat at the chess table, I notice the board has been reset. Clearly tidied while I was trapped in the maze of mirrors. The game I've been playing with the Golden Son is wiped clean. I have no desire to see him, yet I have my first move planned out.

I sip my water, avoiding the chess pieces, trying to keep my hands from reaching for them. But eventually, I give in. Setting the cup down, I pick up a black pawn and move it forward on the board.

There's another knock on the door, but before I have time to respond, Anethesis glides in, his eyes flickering toward the tray with a hint of surprise.

"I'm glad to see your appetite is strong," he says smoothly. "I'll inform the kitchen to double your servings."

I don't acknowledge him, but I don't argue either. At this point, extra portions feel less like a luxury and more like a necessity.

An awkward silence stretches between us, and I lack the patience to draw this interaction out any longer.

"Is there something you want, Anethesis?"

"Yes," he replies promptly, as if he's been waiting for permission. I still find his placating demeanor strange, especially coming from my jailer. "It's time for your next test."

"Already?" I ask, unable to hide my annoyance.

He steeples his fingers beneath his chin, calm as ever. "I'm afraid so. The sooner we complete these tests, the sooner you'll be free, Princess."

I can't deny the logic, infuriating though it may be. If freedom lies at the end of this, I should be grateful for his eagerness to move things along, especially after weeks of confinement, reduced to playing chess with my enemy.

"Very well," I reply tersely. "What must I do next?"

"The Test of Threads," Anethesis says, his voice smooth and measured. "To measure your control over the threads of magic."

"Magic?" I echo, incredulous. "I don't have any magic. And whatever I *might* possess is severed by this." I gesture to the invisible collar wrapped around my neck.

Without a word, Anethesis waves his hand, and the collar vanishes. I rub at my neck where it had pressed against my skin, glaring at him with narrowed eyes.

"This is bold of you," I warn.

He remains unfazed, his indifference grating. "I think you are wiser than that, Princess. You know the limitations of your power, as do we. We've been studying you since the moment you arrived." He pauses, his jade eyes boring into mine. "Your strengths. Your weaknesses. And the truth is, even without the collar, you cannot escape Driftspire. Even if you managed to dispatch me and my brethren waiting just beyond that door, where would you go? There's nothing but sky and mist. A single misstep, and you'd plummet to your death." He tilts his head, staring at me intently. "I don't think that's the outcome you desire."

I grind my teeth, a wave of fury surging through me. I am so tired of being manipulated by Fae. They've haunted my life from the beginning, different shades, different magic, different allures, but always the same in one respect. None of them can be trusted.

"Let's get this over with," I snarl, pushing to my feet.

Anethesis shakes his head, clicking his tongue as if scolding a child.

"This test can be completed right here, Princess," he says smoothly. "Let us begin."

Anethesis stretches his arms wide, and the walls around us dissolve into an endless stretch of rippling midnight blue. The furniture vanishes in an instant, leaving us alone in this strange, boundless place. It feels as though the ground beneath me is shifting, but I'm not moving. My feet remain rooted, yet I struggle to maintain my balance as this surreal realm swirls and undulates.

A wave of nausea rises, and I clutch my stomach, dry-heaving as the world pitches and rolls like a stormy sea.

"Breathe," Anethesis says, his tone maddeningly calm. "It will pass soon enough."

He lifts his hand, and the air ripples.

Before me, a shattered mirror materializes, its jagged shards suspended in midair, each fragment catching the light and splintering it into fractured reflections of my face. Beside it hovers an hourglass, its golden frame carved with intricate, swirling runes that seem to shift as I watch, while inside silver sand falls in a slow, shimmering stream, each grain marking the start of a countdown I can feel in my bones.

"The Test of Threads," Anethesis says, his voice echoing around me. "Weave it whole again. Use the threads of magic that bind all things. Your time is limited, Princess."

Without another word, he vanishes, abandoning me to my task.

I stare at the broken mirror, my reflection scattered and distorted across its many pieces. My heart pounds. Magic? How am I supposed to do this when my power has always been stifled or stolen? The collar may be gone, but I've never wielded the sort of magic required for this task freely. This is impossible.

Still, I stand before the shattered mirror, extending my hands hesitantly. I try to focus, reaching deep within myself, searching for some spark of energy, some hidden well of power. My fingers tremble, and I press harder, willing the shards to move, to respond.

Nothing happens.

The silver sand slips through the hourglass, each grain a cruel reminder of time slipping away. A knot tightens in my chest. I don't know what I'm doing. I've failed.

But then, pain.

A sharp sting on my arm makes me gasp. I look down to find a thin, fresh cut stretching across my skin, beads of blood welling up along its line. Confused, I clutch my arm, staring at the wound as my mind races. What caused this?

Before I can gather my thoughts, another cut slashes across my opposite arm, the sting sharper this time. My breath quickens as the realization dawns. This is part of the test. The longer I fail, the more the magic will punish me. And I don't want to know what will happen when the last grain of sand falls.

Panic claws at me, but I force myself to focus. I stare at the shattered mirror, closing my eyes and trying to feel it, to sense the threads of magic that Anethesis spoke of. I reach deeper inside myself than I ever have before, past the fear, past the doubt, searching for that elusive spark.

It's faint at first. A shimmer in my mind's eye, like spider silk glinting in sunlight. I reach for it, and suddenly, I see the mirror differently. The shards glow faintly, connected by invisible threads, their broken edges aching to be whole again.

I stretch my hands over the pieces, willing the threads to bind them together. Slowly, haltingly, they begin to respond. The shards quiver, then lift, their edges aligning as if pulled by unseen strings. A glimmer of hope sparks within me, but my concentration wavers as pain flares again. A fresh cut across my cheek.

I grit my teeth and push forward, ignoring the stinging lines that now mark my arms and face. The fabric of the mirror becomes clearer, its imprint on the world unraveling and reforming under my will. The shards piece together, one by one, like a puzzle slotting into place.

The sand continues to fall, and so do the cuts. A line across my collarbone. Another down my leg. My body screams in protest, but I refuse to stop. I pour everything I have into the mirror, weaving its threads with my mind, pulling it back from its fractured state.

My mind reels with everything I'm not ready to lose. The life I've barely begun to live. It cannot end here, not in this place, far from the people and places that I love. Not before my child has a chance to feel the soft earth of the Grove beneath their feet or the icy rain of Baev'kalath on their skin.

A fierce rage rises, feeding on my fear, burning away the edges of my panic. Anethesis did not warn me that these tests weren't just trials of skill but trials of survival, paid for with my blood, maybe even my life.

Damn the Fae and their twisted games. Damn their lies wrapped in pretty words.

I am not a pawn to be played with.

I clench my fists, feeling the slick warmth of my blood on my skin, and let the fire within me roar to life. If this is the cost of their test, then I will pay it, but on my terms, not theirs. They will not break me.

As the final grains of sand slip through the hourglass, the mirror snaps into place, whole and gleaming, its surface flawless once more. Relief washes over me, but only for a moment.

A searing pain slashes across my throat, and the world tilts. My hands fly to my neck. Darkness creeps in at the edges of my vision, and the last thing I see before everything fades is my reflection in the mirror, my face going pale beneath a crimson mask, blood seeping between my fingers as they clutch my throat.

Then, nothing.

CHAPTER 8

DAED

*B*efore her. The rain and lightning welcome me back to Baev'kalath as the ocean hurls itself relentlessly against the ship's hull. The moment we dock, I launch myself off the deck, soaring through the storm-laden air toward the fortress. My boots strike the stone hard just as a crack of thunder tears through the sky, the force reverberating in my chest.

The Blades lining the walls bow their heads, their faces hidden beneath dripping hoods, as I march past. My focus is fixed on the throne room doors, looming ahead like the maw of some great beast.

When I throw them open, the grand hall is bathed in flashes of blue and violet from the lightning illuminating the stained glass window behind the thrones. King Kaelus and Queen Lanneth sit side by side on their cold, carved thrones. The king's gaze is, as always, fixated on his queen, as though her very presence bends his will.

Even the echo of my boots on the stone doesn't stir him. It isn't until I reach the foot of the dais, soaked and breathless, that his bright gray eyes flicker toward me.

"Father," I say, urgency sharpening my voice, as I push my rain-soaked hair from my eyes.

My father is ageless. He carries the kind of stillness that only comes after watching centuries crawl by. There's a distinction to him, etched deep. Every feature of his is sharp, noble. Not rough like stone, but fine marble, all smooth edges and elegance that only seems to grow harder with time. And just like marble, there's no warmth to him. Only cold. Heavy and perfect beneath flawless skin.

I see pieces of myself in him. The way our ebony hair curls at the ends when it's wet. The exact line of our ears, pointed, proud, Fae-blooded. But that's where the likeness ends.

I'm not as splendid as he is. Not as clean-cut or untouchable. My edges are rougher. My shine dulled by ghosts I can't shake.

Whatever fineness I had, if I ever had it, has been chipped away by grief, by rage, by everything I've had to survive.

And neither of us has warmth.

Only she ever had warmth.

My mother. Queen Veloria.

Her portraits are all I have to remember her now, but they too are starting to fade.

This place can't stand anything pure. It sniffs it out like a sick dog and drags it into the dark.

Even memories rot here. Even love fades.

Sometimes I see her. My mother.

In that thin moment between sleep and waking, when I float just outside myself. Numb, weightless, and my demon's claws haven't quite sunk in. She's beautiful. Even in childbirth, body shaking with pain, she glows with a light the world doesn't deserve. She's screaming, and under her cries, I hear mine, sharp and new. A Fae prince born into a world that will break him.

But I hear something else too.

Another cry. Almost the same as mine.

A second baby born into the same twisted legacy.

For a heartbeat, we're together.

Tiny hands touching before we're pulled apart.

Then it's gone.

Pain sears through my head, sharp enough to blind me. My skull feels like it's caving in. The dream rips away, torn to pieces until there's nothing left. It always ends like this. When I remember her.

I pinch the bridge of my nose and hiss through my teeth.

Where the fuck did this headache come from? What was I...

Queen Lanneth shifts in her seat. "Daedalus. Are you alright?"

I manage a glance through half-lidded eyes as the pain recedes. "I'm fine," I say.

The words are barely out before the ache is gone, like it was never there at all.

King Kaelus drags his gaze away from his queen and studies me for a moment before finally speaking. "Welcome home, son. What news do you bring from Valorne?"

Queen Lanneth's icy gaze slides over me, piercing and clinical. A pearl choker encircles her neck, and her ivory satin gown clings to her pale skin, damp in the humid storm air. She is his shadow, always at his side, granting him no respite from her presence, and I fear she taints even his thoughts.

I keep my gaze fixed on my father, the response I've practiced resting at the edge of my tongue, but the words refuse to come. I rarely feel the cold, yet tonight the water soaking through my leathers seeps deep into my bones. Somehow, I know it isn't the chill of the night that freezes me. It's the weight of what's coming, because I'm about to lie to my father.

"Well?" Kaelus repeats, his gaze narrowed and curious, with a deep crease through his brow. "Speak. Is it as the Maledannan feared? Did you find an Awakened?"

I clear my throat, shoving my hesitation into some dark corner of my mind. "No," I reply, my voice even. "She is nothing."

"She?" the queen interjects, her voice a dagger, her gaze boring into me.

"Yes," I answer, glancing at her briefly before returning my focus to my father. "A young girl of the forest."

"And you're sure?" Kaelus presses, his voice heavy with expectation. "There can be no doubt about this, Daedalus. These things must be dealt with swiftly."

Deception is no stranger to me. I have worn lies like a second skin, wielded them as tools to serve my purpose time and time again. But never have I borne a falsehood so heavy, one that carries the weight of my people's fate. And yet, despite the risk, despite the shadow of treason that now looms over me, I cannot force the truth past my lips. Not when I know it would condemn her to death.

"I am certain," I lie, the finality of the words feeling like a noose around my neck.

My father leans back in his chair, a slow smile curling at the corners of his lips. In that moment, I feel it. His unwavering belief in my words. The sting of my deception cuts deep, carving its way down to the bone.

"Very well," he says. "This spares us bloodshed. An execution would only stoke the flames of their defiance, and these humans already test the boundaries of their leash. If they do not quiet themselves, the House Lords may be forced to pull them back into line."

The queen sighs theatrically, her voice dripping disdain. "A few burned fields or poisoned wells should be sufficient to curb their insolence. We have been far too lenient with the humans for far too long. I've said this for years."

My father turns to her, taking her skeletal hand in his, a gesture that sets my teeth on edge. "I know, my love. I should always heed your wise counsel," he murmurs, pressing a kiss to her knuckles. Her pale lips curve into a satisfied smile, and the sight makes my gut twist.

"Now, onto other matters," my father says, his voice cooling like steel left to temper. His gaze returns to me. "Did you meet Eryndor's children during your visit?"

I nod once.

He lifts his chin, his stern expression set. "Two heirs," he says. "A legacy secured. A future for his line. And yet House Mordorin stands on a precipice, threatened not by war, but by your continued inaction. You need an heir, Daedalus. It is past time you took a wife."

At the king's words, the queen's glacial eyes flash with interest, her posture shifting forward like a predator scenting prey.

I force myself to look past her. "I have told you. When the time is right."

"The time has been right for centuries," my father growls. "These humans are a nuisance, but the Lords are a threat. They breed heirs while the King's line remains vulnerable. It's not only embarrassing, it's dangerous. You know how they covet the throne, Daedalus. Without an heir, our position grows weaker by the day."

"They would have to kill us both for that to happen," I snap, my voice laced with mockery, "and I welcome any who think they have the courage. I've swatted flies more menacing than these cowardly lords."

My father exhales, long and heavy, his breath thick with the weight of his endless frustration over my refusal to wed. "House Merrin of Mor'Thravar has bred strong warriors, especially for a thrall house. Modok's sister, Nyraxes, has her... charms."

I arch a brow, searching his face for any trace of humor. "She is insane."

He smirks. "I thought you might enjoy the challenge."

I don't dignify that with a response, but I don't have to. The queen is even more repulsed by the idea than I am.

"They may produce capable warriors, but the Merrins themselves are *vile*," she spits, as if merely speaking their name taints her tongue. "And have you forgotten, Kaelus, the trouble their youngest sibling has caused?"

My head snaps toward her, the sharpness of my gaze enough to wound. But she does not relent.

"It is fortunate this human was not Awakened," she continues. "Has there ever been a time in history when two have existed? Though I would welcome a *Fae* witch over a *human* one." She shudders. "Abomination."

"Zema is *not* a witch," I say, my tone cutting. "And she has nothing to do with this. Leave her be."

My father and the queen exchange knowing glances. The unspoken weight of their meaning settles in my chest like a stone.

"You cannot still be sentimental, Daedalus," my father muses, leaning forward, resting his elbows on his knees. "Regardless of the friendship you once shared, Zema is Awakened. That seals her fate."

I glare. "You give my heart too much credit. The fate of Zema Merrin does not trouble my sleep." My teeth grind behind my scowl. "If that is all, I can think of an infinite number of places I would rather be."

My father opens his mouth, likely to rebuke my insolence, but before he can speak, the air in the throne room shifts.

Darkness slithers from the corners, stretching and coiling like the creeping fingers of dusk swallowing the last light of day. With it comes a cold so sharp and biting it turns my breath to mist, yet the air is too still, the tendrils of white fog barely curl before hanging motionless.

Then, the world holds its breath.

A glimmer of silvery black flickers at the center of the room, no larger than a pinprick. It twitches, pulses, then stretches, widening into a yawning maw.

A portal.

Within is the void. Black and fathomless. So endlessly, impossibly dark that just looking at it feels like falling. Forever.

But the void is only the veil between the realms. It is not where the demons dwell.

Like a tear ripped through the skin of shadow, a city forms in the darkness, its skyline jagged with spires of rock that claw into a sky of endless gray. Winged terrors scream as they circle above, their cries shrill and blood-curdling, sharp enough to rattle bone.

The landscape below is ash and ruin. Barren. Cracked. No place for life to take root.

And at its center stands a fortress, high and grim. A temple fit for a god of death. Pillars rise into the gloom, endless steps crawling up toward blackened gates, each one flanked by pyres that burn with ceaseless flame. The stone is etched with the faces of fiends, snarling, shrieking, immortalized in agony.

This is the temple of Gygarth. The city of An'kel.

Here, the demons of the void gather. Here, they kneel. They serve. They worship.

And I stand frozen, powerless to move, breath caught in my throat, forced to watch as Gygarth's most lethal harbinger steps forth from the abyss.

A heavy, tattered black robe drapes over him, the hood drawn low, concealing most of his face. The sleeves hang long enough to shroud his hands, the fabric pooling and shifting as if darkness itself clings to him. He does not *walk*, nor *step*, he *glides*, soundless and unburdened by weight, an eerie movement that sends unease crawling down my spine.

Then, his head lifts.

Two stark-white eyes glow beneath the hood, casting sickly illumination across his face. His skin is blackened and dry, stretched taut over the bones like ancient, desiccated leather. Torn flesh mars his cheeks and brow, revealing glimpses of the skull beneath and below his mouth, writhing and twisting with a mind of their own, dangle several grayish tentacles, curling and shifting around his throat like sentient, grasping limbs.

The air thickens, pressing down on my lungs, filling me with dread.

A name forms at the edge of my mind, crawling through my skull like a whisper from the void.

Emranth. Lord of the Void. Envoy of Gygarth. Harbinger of the unseen abyss.

He moves among us, untouched by the sluggish pull of time, for time itself bends to his will. As he passes me, his presence thickens the air like tar, cloying, suffocating.

"Favored one," he whispers, his voice layered with a thousand echoes, as if countless souls speak through him. He inhales slowly, as if tasting the air between us. "You look well. Strong. If only the same could be said for your master."

The tentacles beneath his chin writhe with a slick, wet sound, twisting restlessly.

"You rule this land by his generosity, and yet you ignore the bargain that placed the crown upon your head. The pact that holds your kingdom in place. If you wish to keep your power, your master demands his taste." He leans forward, his voice dropping. "He hungers. He starves. He must be fed."

I try to speak, but even the smallest movement feels impossible, as though my body has been bound in invisible chains. Emranth does not require my response.

"If his hunger is not sated, then you and all who know you will fill his belly instead. Do you understand, little prince?"

Even if I wished to resist, I know there is no answer he would accept but obedience.

"Good." His satisfaction slithers through the air. "But be mindful. Time is not on your side."

With that, Emranth drifts backward, smooth and spectral, retreating into the void. The portal contracts around him, shrinking to a single silver speck before vanishing entirely. The moment he is gone, time snaps back into motion, and I stumble forward, gasping for breath.

I hear the ragged inhalations of my father and the queen. They slump weakly against their thrones, drained, their power meaningless against a force like Emranth. My father clenches his fists so tightly his knuckles are bone white, his gaze fixed on the floor.

"What have we done?" His voice is barely a breath.

"I've had enough of this," I snarl through gritted teeth. "What use is this power, this sacrifice, if I'm to live my life as some puppet to Gygarth and his dog?"

"Watch your tongue, Daedalus," the queen snaps. Her gaze flicks toward the darkened corners of the throne room. "You do not want to anger the Father Below."

"Why? Because he'll kill me? Take control of me? Tear away what's left of my will, twist my mind until I wake with blood on my hands and no memory of how it got there?"

"Consider that a blessing, son," my father says, voice grim and hollow.

I bark a laugh, sharp and bitter. "A blessing? Then *you* take it. You offer yourself to the void. You become something worse than the monsters."

A flash of thought rips through me, and my jaw clenches tight.

"We could end this," I mutter, half to myself, half to them. "Take the Blades. Rally the armies of Mordorin. Unite the Fae houses. March on An'kel and bring the war to *them*. To the gates of the abyss."

The queen's hands clutch the arms of her throne, nails scraping hard stone. "Silence, Daedalus."

But I don't stop. I *can't*.

"We could be free. All of us. We don't have to live like this."

And then, just for a breath, I see something stir in my father. A flicker of light in those frostbitten eyes. A spark of the warrior he once was, before time and terror turned him to stone.

"Walking the void is one thing, Daedalus," he says quietly. "But opening a portal to An'kel... that is something else entirely. It is beyond even your power."

"There is no time for regrets, Kaelus," the queen snaps, her chest rising and falling in rapid, furious bursts. Then she turns to me. "If the word of your father and I is not enough to move you, Daedalus, then heed the warning of the void's warden. If you do not wed, if you do not produce an heir, if you do not give Gygarth what was promised, then you risk the lives of all Mordorin."

I turn away, but her voice cuts through the air like a lash.

"Do you hear me? You will bring ruin to your house! You must choose Daedalus, or we will choose for you. Do you understand?"

I inhale, steadying my breath, then roll my shoulders back, straightening beneath the weight of their demands. My gaze locks onto the queen, my stepmother, the thing I despise most in this world, second only to myself.

"I understand," I say, voice low and seething, before turning my back on them and leaving the throne room.

After her. We find a local inn. Small, filthy, cheap. The kind of place where, if we're lucky, the patrons are too drunk or too stupid to recognize what we are, let alone care enough to tell someone.

The Ithranor male comes with us. Or rather, Zyphoro keeps him with us. She toys with him like a cat batting around a stunned mouse, and I honestly can't tell if the poor bastard is in love or scared shitless.

Tonight, we've got the dining hall to ourselves. Low ceilings, smoky air, the faint stink of mildew in the walls. It's as tight and claustrophobic as the ship's cabin. We're gathered around a table as filthy as my boots, its surface sticky with gods-know-what. The hunched innkeeper shuffles out from the kitchen, arms full of plates. Bread and cheese, a chunk of charred meat still speckled with burnt hair. I don't ask what animal it came from. I don't care. My eyes are on the jugs of wine he drops on the table with a heavy thud, dark liquid sloshing over the edge and dripping through the cracks into the floorboards below.

I pour myself a cup before he's barely let go of the handle.

"Will there be anything else?" he croaks, coughing into his hand, barely catching the spittle.

I don't look at him. "That's all. Leave us."

He grumbles something under his breath, but Reon is already pulling a gold coin from his vest. He flicks it into the air.

"For your trouble."

The old human may be stooped and shriveled, but he's fast enough to snatch that coin midair and bite it with the few teeth he has left. He nods, grunts, and hobbles away.

I bring the cup of wine to my lips and drink deep. Over the rim, I watch Zyphoro across from me, curled around the Ithranor male. Tamis, I think his name is, from what I could make out between the stammering and stuttering. She's wrapped around him like smoke, fingers trailing through his long hair, dragging slow and lazy. His throat bobs with a nervous swallow. His hands tremble. He looks absolutely fucking terrified, but I'd wager a small fortune that he's hard beneath this table.

"What was your name again?" I ask for clarity, lowering my cup.

"Tamis," he confirms.

"Such a pretty name," Zyphoro purrs, draping a leg over his lap. "Did your mother give you that name?"

He nods, hesitant. "Yes."

"How fortunate," she sighs, casting a glance at me. "Our mother didn't get the chance to name us, did she, Daedalus?"

I roll my tongue across my teeth. "No, she did not, Zyphoro."

She snaps her attention back to Tamis, voice all poison and silk. "I'd like to meet your mother. Maybe she'll braid my hair. Read me bedtime stories. Tell me what a good little girl I am."

A low, mocking laugh cuts through the room.

Zyphoro's gaze sharpens, snapping to Solena sitting in the shadows beside Orios, who's the only one brave or dumb enough to be chewing the fuzzy meat.

"Something funny, maid?" Zyphoro spits.

Solena doesn't flinch. She just smirks, sliding one hand across Orios' broad shoulder, while the fingers on her other idly trace circles on his forearm.

"A mother might also tell you not to play with your food," she says sweetly. "So fuck him already or leave him be. Either way, you're boring me."

A bark of laughter escapes me before I can stop it, and Reon, seated to my right, chokes down his own with a cough. Zyphoro's glare cuts through both of us, silencing the table.

Only Orios seems unfazed, gnawing contentedly at the charred remains of whatever creature died for our supper.

Zyphoro's attention shifts. She leans across the table and pushes Tamis aside with the casual cruelty of someone bored with a toy.

"You dare speak to me like that?" she hisses.

Solena doesn't flinch. She sighs, long and tired, like she's had this argument before in another lifetime. "I'd rather not speak to you at all. So why don't you take your pet and leave the rest of us in peace?"

I watch them in silence, one corner of my mouth curling. You'd think after months trapped together on that damned ship, they'd have grown tired of sparring. But no. If anything, they've turned it into a sport. Neither willing to yield. Neither knowing how.

At least it makes for good entertainment.

Where I expect my sister to snap, to bare her fangs and rip into Solena with the fury she's known for, Zyphoro does something far more dangerous. She smiles. The kind of smile that never ends well for anyone.

I know it too. It's the same one I wear when I've found a game worth playing. The kind that Amara drew from my lips when she would do her best to resist me, even though I could smell her need clinging to her skin like perfume.

"Jealous, maid?" Zyphoro purrs. Her eyes flick to Orios. "Is someone not scratching your itch?"

Orios looks up from the slab of meat in his hands, brows raised.

Solena stiffens. "That's none of your business."

"Oh dear. Just as I thought," Zyphoro sighs. "The only thing worse than not getting enough... is getting none at all."

Reon lifts an eyebrow. "Surely you two have fucked."

I lift my cup. "I'd wager they have."

Zyphoro shrugs one delicate shoulder. "It's a small ship and I haven't heard so much as a swallow from your cabin." She leans forward. "And trust me, I've been listening."

Solena shoots her a look like she's about to throw a knife, or a plate, or both. "You're vile."

Zyphoro feigns offense. "Where else would I look for fun? The Mordorin don't dabble in incest like some other Fae houses and I'd rather carve out my own heart than let the ginger lay a single finger on me."

Reon snorts. "What the fuck?"

Zyphoro laces her fingers under her chin innocently. "Which leaves you and the boulder as my only options for... release."

The meat slips from Orios' fingers and hits the table with a wet thud, his mouth agape.

Solena's hand flies to his back, smacking him once before shoving him so hard he jolts in his seat and wipes his mouth on his sleeve.

Zyphoro giggles. "Maybe I'm not the only one who's considered it."

Solena's voice drops an octave. "You think too much of yourself."

"Perhaps." Zyphoro's smile never wavers. "But when you decide to prove me wrong, I'll be right outside your door."

Solena bolts to her feet. Her hand closes around Orios' forearm, and that alone is enough to haul the brute to standing. Zyphoro rolls her eyes.

"So dramatic."

"We're going to bed," Solena says flatly. "As should you all. We are here for a purpose? Remember?"

I nod at her scolding. How could I forget? But there's a strange comfort in knowing I'm not the only one, like we're both limping from the same wound.

"Sweet dreams," Zyphoro sings after them, though neither looks back as they disappear up the stairs.

I lean back in my chair, swirling the wine in my cup. "I thought you two would've found common ground by now."

Zyphoro grins, unapologetic. "Where's the fun in that?"

She rises suddenly, stretching her arms like a cat waking from a nap. She casts a glance at Tamis, who's still seated, paralyzed with uncertainty.

"But the maid does have a point," she murmurs. "I'm done playing with my food."

She strides toward the stairs, hips swaying with purpose. Halfway up, she pauses, glancing behind her with a theatrical sigh.

"Well? Move your ass."

Tamis scrambles after her, his face pale and lips bitten red.

"Poor bastard," Reon mutters, reaching for the wine and refilling his cup. "Let's pray the gods fancy him enough not to get fucked to death. We still need him."

I laugh under my breath. "Just the two of us, then."

Reon lifts his cup toward mine. "And you made it very clear today that I'm not your type. Seems you and your sister have that in common."

I nod, and whether it's the wine or the company, the tight coil in my chest loosens for the first time in weeks.

"Don't take it personally, Reon," I murmur. "My miserable heart only beats for one."

Quiet settles between us as we sip our drinks. Then *thump...thump...thump.* A slow, rhythmic pounding echoes from the ceiling above, followed by a soft drift of dust sifting down from the rafters. We glance up together, then back at each other with matching frowns.

Reon adjusts the front of his leathers with a grimace. "Might have to pay a visit to the Red Room before the night's through."

I chuckle into my cup, the sound low and tired. But even that small warmth can't quiet the ache that lingers beneath my skin. The longing for the only touch I've ever truly craved... and the quiet fear that I may never feel it again.

CHAPTER 9
DAED

The next few days drag like a lame mule, and the inn's no better than the ship, just a different kind of dank hole to dwell in. We don't go out. Can't risk drawing eyes, not when we're this close. Close to what, exactly? I couldn't say. The answers might come tonight, or this could be another waste of time, another false thread unraveling in my hands while Amara slips further from my reach. And then there's the other rot blooming under my skin. The sigils of the unseen grow weaker each time Solena carves them. I can feel the void creeping in, smoke curling at the corners of my sight, whispering through the cracks of my mind. It wants me. Wants to take me, twist me, use me. If Gygarth wins, if he gets his claws in deep enough, then I'll no longer be the Fae who aches for Amara with every cursed beat of his heart. I'll be his hound. His butcher. My only purpose, a blind, brutal hunger to hunt meat for the beast.

I must find answers tonight. Before I lose everything.

The evening breeze rushes through the open window, cool against my skin, but all I feel is her. Amara. The whisper of wind becomes the ghost of her fingers, tracing along my flesh. My eyes slip shut, surrendering to the memory. The way she touched me, how her hands mapped my body with a knowledge that should have taken a lifetime to learn.

But that was the secret, wasn't it?

She wasn't just any human. Nor any other Awakened.

She was mine. My mate. My destiny.

And she carried the map of me within her, etched into her soul as surely as I carried hers. I knew her. Every lush, tempting curve, every dip that beckoned my touch, every mouthwatering crevice that even now has my cock stiff and aching beneath my leathers.

The way her body hummed for me. The way her breathy moans tangled with mine. The feel of her soft breasts crushed against my chest as I stole the air from her lungs, claiming her so fully, so completely, that there could be no doubt she was mine to possess, to love, to fuck.

A sharp growl rumbles in my throat as I grip myself roughly, the throbbing demand between my legs a cruel reminder of what was stolen from me. Of what I will kill to get back.

Then the wind shifts.

The warmth of memory is replaced by something colder, more formal, laced with power, and then a voice follows.

"My prince. I bring news from Baev'kalath."

The breeze coils into the shape of a female, her features indistinct, a mere echo of something Fae, a whisper on the wind.

Lady Ilyra's spies are everywhere and nowhere, unseen but ever-present. Without them, I would be blind to what has become of my kingdom in my absence. Ilyra is as loyal as she is ruthless, and through her, I remain informed.

I force my need aside, moving from the window to the edge of the bed.

"What news do you bring?"

"All goes well, Your Highness. Lady Ilyra holds Baev'kalath with the aid of the warriors of Eyr'Drogul, despite Lord Modok's persistence."

My jaw tightens. "Has he crossed the sea? Does he bring more than threats?"

The wind-wrought figure shudders. "Not yet, Your Highness. But with the Lady twins and Lord Horax unwilling to continue negotiations, a challenge is not implausible."

My teeth clench. "And what of Sarberos?"

"Nothing yet," the voice murmurs. "He fortifies himself and his people within Thal'Morven, refusing communication with anyone."

"And the Sundered Kingdoms? The Legion?"

"They hold the mainland strong. Without contestation. It seems they are now led by a coven of generals."

I barely contain my snarl, my teeth grinding against the words I know I must ask.

"And the Golden Son?"

A pause.

"No, Your Highness. There is still no sign."

The confirmation is a knife in my gut.

His absence can mean only one thing.

He is with her.

And the thought of it, of him anywhere near Amara, festers inside me like a sickness, like a rot devouring me from within.

The edges of the figure waver, its form unraveling inch by inch, carried away on the breeze slipping through the open window.

"Is that all, Your Highness?" The voice cracks, strained with the effort of holding itself together.

"Yes, go now to your mistress."

The faceless shadow bows its head in silent regard before sweeping out into the night, dissolving in a slant of moonlight.

The door swings open, slamming against the wall, and Zyphoro steps inside. Her sharp gaze flickers around the room before settling on me.

"Talking to yourself again, brother?"

I exhale sharply, rubbing my brow. "A visit from Ilyra's spies. She holds strong, but I fear there will be little left of our kingdom by the time we return home."

Zyphoro folds her arms, leaning against the doorframe. "I should have stayed."

"No." My voice is sharper than I intend, my head snapping toward her. She stiffens, surprised. "You were trapped there long enough. I will not leave you in the dark again."

Her shoulders ease, though she does not dare smile.

"Besides," I add, a smirk tugging at my lips. "If I need to raze House Ithranor to the ground, I'll require the finest Fae warrior to ever live."

To that, she grins. "You flatter me, Daedalus. But you aren't wrong."

Her expression stirs something bittersweet in my chest. I wish it could always be like this between us. Light, easy, unburdened. But the past is a scar that will never fade, tainting what should be an unbreakable bond. The sharing of a womb. A brother and sister forged from the same blood, the same great lineage, bound by the same cursed power.

And yet, every time I look upon Zyphoro, I am lashed with the guilt of knowing I could not save her. That no matter what I do, I will never reclaim the time she lost, nor ease the solitude that had been as much her prison as the enchanted cage that bound her.

Even now, her presence on this mission, to restore my wife, to restore my happiness, feels like a cruel joke at her expense.

"Are you ready?" she asks. "The hour grows close."

I turn to the window. The full moon looms in the ink-dark sky, and I breathe deep, slow, steadying myself. Bowing my head, I rest my elbows on my knees, clasping my hands.

Smoke coils from my skin, thick and curling, sliding over my worn leathers, swallowing my muddied boots. It moves with purpose, threading through every seam, devouring every frayed edge, until the tattered remnants of travel and violence are erased. When it recedes, it leaves behind a suit of deep violet, woven with an almost imperceptible shimmer, as if stardust itself has been spun into the fabric.

The silver-threaded cuffs catch the light, their delicate curls forming ancient, arcane patterns. The jacket molds perfectly to my frame, the cut precise enough to trace the shape of my shoulders and the breadth of my chest, as though it had been stitched by someone who knew every inch of me. Its sharp lapels draw the eye to the crisp, high collar of the shirt beneath, black as midnight, and the sleek fabric moves with me, tapering into fitted trousers and black leather boots polished to a mirror sheen.

The smoke continues up my throat, curling over my jaw, teasing at my cheekbones before washing over my face. When it vanishes, a silver mask remains, wicked, baroque, twisted and gleaming beneath the moonlight. The metal is molded into intricate swirls, sharp at the edges, curling like the horns of a forgotten god. It obscures my eyes, save for the slits that cut through, allowing me to see the world while revealing nothing in return.

And around my neck, on a simple leather cord, hangs the only piece of me that remains untouched: a hewn moonstone, swirling and restless with its quiet glow. It once belonged to my mother. Its other half dangles from Zyphoro's throat.

I flex my fingers, feeling the shift of fabric, the hidden strength beneath the decadence. A suit fit for a prince. A mask fit for a monster.

Zyphoro rolls her eyes, unimpressed. Smoke pools at her heels, thick as storm clouds, swirling in restless tendrils around her legs. It rises, licking at her skin, and when it fades, she stands transformed.

A gown of the deepest obsidian clings to her frame, but unlike the sharp lines of my suit, there's nothing modest or subtle about my sister's choice tonight. The dress is cut high in the front, revealing far more leg than I'm comfortable seeing, her thigh-high stockings disappearing beneath a tangle of black tulle that spills into a dramatic train behind her.

Her heels are sharp enough to wound, meant to be heard before she enters the room, and her long black gloves cling to her arms like a second skin. But it's the bodice... strapless, tight, and straining against the full rise of her chest, that has my gaze darting away.

Smoke curls around her face, thick and inky, sliding over her sharp cheekbones and smirking lips. When it recedes, it leaves behind a mask of ebony filigree, its edges tapering into delicate thorns that frame her temples.

She flicks a hand, and in her palm, the silver pommel of a dagger gleams, conjured from nothing, a casual reminder that beauty and death are often the same thing. Beneath the veil of shadow and lace, her silver eyes gleam. "Shall we?"

I rise from the edge of the bed and step toward her, drawn by the bond that hums in the space between us. Our eyes lock in a hollow silence, the only sound being the restless whisper of the breeze slipping through the open window. I extend my arm.

"Sister."

She tilts her head, studying me with that rare, quiet softness. Then, with a ghost of a smile, she slips her arm through mine.

"Brother."

A grin tugs at my lips as I push open the door, and side by side, we step into the candlelit corridor of the inn, where the others wait.

Golden light flickers over their masked faces, casting shifting shadows against the worn wooden walls. Reon stands in a blaze of crimson, his coat embroidered with curling patterns of gold, while Orios is clad in midnight blue, the fabric stretched so taut across his broad frame I wonder if he simply refused to conjure a size larger.

I let the door click shut behind me. "Let us go." Then, frowning, I scan the hall. "Where is Solena?"

A door creaks open further down the hall, and soft footsteps sound against the wooden floor. Solena steps forward, the candlelight catching on the pale silver of her gown, its fabric fluid as moonlight, draping elegantly over her frame. The bodice is fitted, its delicate embroidery glimmering with frost-kissed threads, the neckline a graceful sweep that bares the smooth expanse of her collarbones. Her long black hair spills in perfect sheets down her back, a river of night against the cool shimmer of her dress.

For a heartbeat, I forget to breathe.

It is not Solena I see standing before me, but *her*. Amara. The shape of her lips, the way the candlelight pools in her dark eyes, the soft cascade of her hair. It's all so painfully, impossibly familiar. My pulse stutters, my throat tightens, and for a single, wretched moment, I am caught in the cruel jaws of memory.

I do not know how long I stand there, lost in the trick of candlelight, before awareness drags me back. Too late.

Solena shifts, uneasy, adjusting her silver mask, her fingers twitching. The air in the hall thickens, tension creeping in like an unwelcome guest. One by one, the others notice. Reon's smile fades, Orios stiffens at her side, and Zyphoro's sharp gaze flicks between us.

I blink, shattering the illusion, and exhale through my nose, forcing the weight from my chest.

A muscle in Orios' jaw ticks as he steps closer to Solena, glaring at me from beneath his heavy brow, his broad form shifting between us. His hand finds the small of her back, his fingers pressing just firmly enough to remind her, and me, of where she belongs.

I'm not about to waste time in a pissing contest with him, and I have far more pressing matters than justifying myself to anyone.

"Let's move," I grind out, my voice a low rasp against the uneasy silence. My eyes flit to Zyphoro. "Is your plaything ready?"

She nods. "He is downstairs. Exhausted but able-bodied enough to serve his purpose."

I do not care for the sordid details, though I'm glad Tamis has survived the last few nights as Zyphoro's bedmate. I press forward, Zyphoro at my side. Behind me, I hear Solena's quiet breath as she clings to Orios' arm, her fingers tightening just slightly. His frown deepens, but he says nothing.

No one does.

We descend the narrow stairs and move through the tavern, no longer a quiet hovel cloaked in midnight hush. Now it thrums with life. Music curls through the air, tangled with raucous laughter, the thrum of voices, and the sharp clatter of mugs colliding in drunken celebration. The patrons, soaked in ale and blissful ignorance, barely glance up as the finely dressed Fae, masked and glittering, slip like shadows through their midst.

When we step outside, the warm breeze clings, offering no reprieve from the choke of the humid night. Tamis leads the way, but he falters, his eyes flicking toward the dark alleyways that split off from the street like veins. I catch his elbow before he can get clever.

"Not thinking of making a run for it, are you?" My voice grates rough as gravel. "I'd hate to snap your neck after my sister's taken such a liking to you."

Zyphoro laughs, soft and dangerous, as Tamis swallows hard.

"Of course not, Your Highness. I'm only... orienting myself." He stiffens his spine, gaze sweeping over the crowd-packed street, thick with bodies drifting between taverns and brothels like moths to a flame. Then his eyes catch something and widen beneath the edge of his mask.

"There," he says, voice steadier now.

My gaze drifts down the street to the large domed building looming at the edge of the city's chaos. A place that seems to exist apart from the noise. Even the staggering drunks and scavenging dogs give it a wide berth, as though something unseen warns them away.

If Tamis speaks the truth, then hidden within those shadowed halls lies another Fae House long thought to be lost, and within it, a mirror of whispered legend. A thing of impossible magic, said to reveal either your greatest desire or your most harrowing fear.

The others walk ahead, their footfalls swallowed by the thrum of the city. But Zyphoro lingers at my side, her steps as light as breath. She tips her chin toward Solena's back, where Orios' thick arm is wrapped around her waist, keeping her close.

"And what was that?" she murmurs at my ear.

"It was nothing," I grumble.

Zyphoro exhales. "The fact that you understand my meaning says it was something."

My jaw tightens. Canines lengthen. My body reacts to her insinuation with an insulted sort of rage, lip curling, fingers flexing at my sides.

"For a fleeting moment..." I begin, the words like ash in my mouth. "She looked like Amara. That is all."

Zyphoro sighs, and the weight of it is somehow worse than any blade. "That is much."

I halt abruptly, seizing her elbow in my grip. "I dislike what you imply."

The others continue on, their shadows shifting against the buildings like ghosts.

Zyphoro tilts her head, her gaze sharp, assessing. That familiar, predatory curiosity slides over her face, and a chill licks up my spine. It is the look that always makes me feel as if I have been flayed open, as if she is sifting through my ribs, through the sinew and marrow, searching for my deepest truths.

"You spend much time with the maid," she muses. "Her hands are on your skin almost daily."

I roll my eyes. "To ink the sigils, Zyphoro."

"A convenient excuse," she murmurs. "Perhaps even a pleasant side effect."

My fists clench.

87

"I know this journey has worn you thin," she continues, softer now, almost gentle. Almost. "Your mind, your body, your will, all stretched to the breaking point. A spider's web trembling on the edge of snapping."

I turn my head away, but she catches my chin between two fingers, forcing me to meet her gaze.

"I know your grief consumes you," she whispers. "Be careful where you seek solace."

A growl rumbles through me. I slap her hand away, hard enough that she stumbles back a step.

"Watch your tongue, sister," I snarl. "Before you lose it."

She laughs. *Laughs.*

"Just an observation, brother."

Shadows curl at my fingertips.

"Then do not make me take your eyes as well," I hiss.

But she merely spins in the middle of the street, arms outstretched, before striding ahead, leaving me alone with the gnawing weight of her words.

Zyphoro fears nothing.

And I am beginning to think she feels nothing just as strongly.

Her words, her jests, her cutting little observations. Are they just weapons she wields for her own amusement? A way to stave off the boredom?

Or is she testing me, watching, waiting? Hoping to unearth something raw, something visceral?

Perhaps she only wishes to see me feel so that, for just one fleeting moment, she might feel something, too.

I carry on, my steps steady, my gaze fixed ahead as Zyphoro melds into the others without so much as a backward glance.

She has sworn to take my life if the darkness within me rises.

If my curse fights its way to the surface.

And I am beginning to think I must be ready to return the favor.

CHAPTER 10
DAED

As we near the domed building, the low thrum of music pulses through the air, muffled yet insistent, like a heartbeat beneath stone.

We ascend the stairs, and from the city's darkened corners, figures slip from the shadows. Their faces remain obscured behind masks that catch and refract the moonlight, their eerie smiles dipped in a courtesy that feels strangely familiar, though we have not earned it.

Good. That means we look as though we belong.

At the top of the landing, two tall, lithe males stand in silence. Even before I see the sharp angles of their faces or catch the faint glint of eyes beneath their hoods, I know what they are. Fae. Their scent confirms it.

Tamis takes a step forward, and Zyphoro slinks her arm through his, the perfect illusion of a doting consort rather than his beautiful tormentor. Orios moves in close to Solena, silent and imposing, a wall of stone at her back. I catch the flick of his glare, the bitter twist of his mouth. He says nothing. Of course he doesn't. He's a Reaper of the Ebon Flight, centuries under my command, forged in loyalty and discipline. That loyalty is carved into him, and it runs deeper than blood.

But I know the lengths a male will go to for what he loves. What violence he will endure and what violence he will inflict just to keep her close.

We Fae pretend we are refined, detached. Above petty emotions. Weakness is for humans, we say. But the truth is, time doesn't dull us. Not always. Sometimes it sharpens the edge, deepens the hunger. And I would not be surprised if one day it overtakes Orios entirely. If his restraint snaps, and I feel his blade between my ribs.

I hope it never comes to that.

It would be a shame to cut him open—throat, belly, and balls—and let him bleed out into the dirt.

What a waste of a fine warrior.

At the entrance, the guards square their shoulders as Tamis approaches. But their posture falters the moment Zyphoro steps into view, impossible to ignore, like an eclipse slipping across the sun.

"Tamis Efrain," he says with cool confidence, gesturing to us. "And these are my guests."

The guards make a show of inspecting us, but their eyes keep dragging back to my sister. They hesitate too long, caught somewhere between suspicion and awe.

Then the doors swing open, spilling golden light across the worn stone steps.

We step through the threshold with the feigned ease of those who have walked these halls before. Our eyes, however, betray our caution, scanning every alcove and shadowed corner, sweeping the balcony above. Our heads snap toward each burst of laughter, each ripple of conversation.

Because though we may be Fae, we were not invited.

And if House Taramethos holds the same contempt for me as Ithranor does, then my title will be worth nothing here.

On this side of the Untold Sea, I rule no one.

The doors slam shut behind us with a thunderous boom, sealing us inside the opulence of the masquerade.

The ballroom is vast, its domed ceiling a decadent masterpiece—a mural of Fae desire and ruin. Celestials and demons entwine in an eternal embrace, hands reaching through a shimmer of stars, faces caught between rapture and despair, ecstasy and agony made one. Golden constellations glimmer faintly in the lacquered paint, the illusion of motion making it seem as though the figures still writhe, still yearn.

Soft light spills from crystal sconces, gliding across walls of black marble veined with smoke-grey. It fractures through curtains of silver beads that drape the obsidian floor like falling starlight, swaying with every pulse of sound and movement.

Within those shifting veils, masked figures move as one, swirling beneath the mournful wail of violins. Every step deliberate. Every turn flawless. Not a single misstep, only the seamless rhythm of dancers who've known this waltz for lifetimes.

I part the beaded curtain and step through as the melody coils through the air, slow and hypnotic. The cool strands brush against my fingers as they sway closed behind me. The air is thick with heady perfume, spiced wine, bodies pressed dangerously close. I do not need to look at the others to know they feel it, too. The unseen undercurrent beneath all this beauty. The tension wound tight enough to snap.

It hums in my blood. It feels like home.

I let my gaze sweep the room, cataloging the players in this game before they can do the same to me.

And then I see her.

Seated upon a gilded chair that is no throne but might as well be, her posture languid. As if all of this, this performance, this illusion, exists purely for her amusement.

Her pitch-black hair falls in sleek ringlets, a thin golden circlet resting against her brow. It glints softly in the light, forged from the same delicate metal as the mask that conceals most of her face. But her eyes, an eerie, liquid blue, are unmistakable.

Lady Marlayna of House Taramethos.

Of course, she is still here. Of course, she still rules them.

I do not know why I am surprised.

But if I recognize Marlayna, then without a doubt, she will recognize me.

I cannot risk that.

My gaze lifts to the balconies above, shadowed alcoves hanging watchfully over the masquerade.

"Where is the mirror?" I whisper to Tamis.

"I'm not sure," he says.

It takes every ounce of restraint not to gut him where he stands for such a worthless answer.

"Sometimes it's beside her," he adds, voice low. "Other times... upstairs. In the parlor."

I scan the chamber again, my eyes dragging over every surface. Nothing. No glint of silver, no sign of it at all.

"It must be upstairs," I mutter, the frustration coiling tight beneath my ribs.

"Possibly," Reon murmurs, following my line of sight. He tips his head toward the Fae guards at the base of the stairs, their expressions blank, their presence anything but idle. "They are clearly guarding something."

I nod. "Then upstairs is where I must go."

Zyphoro smirks, eyes gleaming with that signature reckless amusement. "You'll need a distraction, I assume?"

She turns to Reon, head tilting just so, eyes of the storm flashing beneath her mask. "May I have this dance, Lord of Eyr'Drogul?"

His tongue rolls against the inside of his cheek as he casts his gaze over her in a slow, appreciative sweep. His smile is crooked, shameless and enough to make my stomach churn.

"I thought this ginger wasn't allowed to touch that flawless skin of yours?"

In a flash, Zyphoro grabs him by the collar and yanks him close, their faces nearly touching, a breath of a whisper separating their indulgent smirks.

"It must be your lucky night, then," she purrs. "Be sure to savor it."

Reon grins, biting back a groan as he seizes her wrists and drapes them over his shoulders, hands sliding down to clutch her waist. He takes control, rough and eager, and Zyphoro laughs, surrendering to his lead with a glint in her eyes that dares him to try harder.

In an instant, he spins her into the swell of masked bodies, their steps sliding into rhythm as the violinists quicken their tempo. The eerie melody winds tighter, a noose of sound pulling the dancers deeper into its thrall, each movement more fevered, like they've all forgotten where the music ends and the spell begins.

I catch the way Tamis' chin drops to his chest, shoulders caving in. Poor, pathetic, fucking soul.

"I'm getting a drink," he mutters, sulking off.

"Don't even think about breathing a word of us to anyone," I call after him, voice low and lethal.

But he doesn't bother to answer, too busy dragging his sorry carcass to the bar.

And now I am left standing with Orios and Solena.

The Reaper still glowers at me, his silence deadlier than any sharpened steel, his gaze an unspoken accusation.

But Solena, ever soft where he is hard, runs a delicate hand over his forearm, leaning into him as if she alone has the power to thaw the ice beneath his ribs.

"Come, my love," she whispers, and the words coil around him like a spell, drawing the anger from his blood, smoothing the edges of his rigid stance.

Orios exhales slow. "Yes, my love."

It is spoken to Solena, and yet, somehow, it is meant for me to hear too.

A warning. A reminder. A parting word.

Then he takes her in his arms, their bodies molding together as they step onto the floor, slipping into the dance. They twirl and glide in perfect synchrony, arms taut, hands clasped, leaning back as they spin.

I shouldn't watch.

But as Solena moves, the candlelight catches her face just enough, and the world warps.

For the briefest moment, I see Amara once more.

Smiling at me, beckoning, her eyes bright with something she never got to say.

My breath stumbles. My fingers twitch. Before I can stop myself, my hand lifts, reaching but just as swiftly, the illusion splinters. I grit my teeth, curling my hand into a fist, wrenching myself back from the brink.

Zyphoro was right.

This journey, this grief, is unraveling me thread by thread, leaving nothing but frayed edges and shadows where certainty used to be.

I know she is not Amara.

And yet, my twisted heart still wants so desperately that it is willing to deceive me.

This is madness.

And I cannot afford to lose focus. Not when, for the first time in weeks, I am close.

I turn away from the dancers, pushing through the beaded curtain and slipping toward the stairs.

I move like a whisper, curving around the guests who flock to the dance floor, careful not to brush too close, careful not to let the guards catch the shift in the air as I slip past. They stand vigilant, but I've long mastered the art of being unseen.

Then, as if on cue, a heavy thud shakes the floor, followed by a sharp shriek.

The music screeches to a halt.

"My apologies," a voice calls from the dance floor, dripping with false remorse. Even through its disguised lilt, I recognize the mischief woven through Zyphoro's words. "How clumsy of me."

A ripple of irritation spreads through the ballroom, the warmth of idle conversation turning to annoyed whispers. Raised voices grumble, and that is all it takes.

The guards at the base of the stairs abandon their posts, moving toward the commotion.

Perfect.

I slip into the shadows along the wall, silent as smoke, and ascend the staircase.

As I go, I glance back, catching the chaos Zyphoro has left in her wake. A mess of tumbled dancers, overturned goblets, Fae nobles brushing their embroidered sleeves with wounded pride. My lips curl into a grin.

I don't get to enjoy it for long.

I barely reach the landing before I find myself staring into a pair of azure eyes.

Fuck.

"Your Highness." Marlayna's voice is smooth as silk. She stands flanked by guards, the hilts of their swords gleaming. "How honored I am to have Sundered Kingdoms royalty in my humble home."

Despite my mask, she must have recognized me just as swiftly as I did her. I hadn't even noticed her rise from the throne, so focused on the mirror, blind to the one who guarded it. I curse myself, frustration curling deep in my chest. In my hunger for answers, I'm growing careless. Still, I manage to summon a smile. Effortless, charming, the kind I've worn too many times to count, the kind that's kept me alive far longer than I deserve.

"Lady Marlayna," I say, inclining my head just enough to be polite. "You look well."

Her gaze drags over me, unhurried.

"As do you, my prince. It has been some time."

She tilts her head toward the wreckage below.

"Friends of yours?"

I follow her gaze, watching as Zyphoro, the cause of the disaster, twirls innocently away from the sputtering nobles.

"I've never seen them before in my life."

Marlayna hums unconvinced, the corner of her glossy red mouth curling upward.

"You know, Your Highness, etiquette states that a visiting prince owes the lady of the house a dance."

I lift an eyebrow. "Does it now?"

She extends her arm, fingers curling in silent command.

A test I can't refuse.

I inhale deeply, and the scent of her is immediate. The charged pulse of her blood just beneath her skin, the sheen of sweat gathering at her collarbone, the way her breath catches ever so slightly.

If I deny her, I lose any chance of getting close to that mirror. But if I summon the shadows and reduce this place to rubble to get what I want, I risk drawing the attention of the void.

Which leaves only one option.

I take her hand.

"I would be honored," I lie.

I guide Marlayna down the stairs, grinding my impatience into something passable for calm. I'd hoped this would be quick and simple. How arrogant of me to believe it ever could be.

As we approach the dance floor, her guards part the beaded curtain, and the din of the ballroom hushes just enough for the shift in focus to land on us.

This mask does little to shield me from their scrutiny, though I don't think they recognize me as easily as Marlayna did. Their curiosity, no doubt, is aimed at the stranger who's earned their lady's favor.

The crowd parts, and we step onto the center of the dance floor. I take Marlayna into my arms with the kind of boldness I know she expects. Anything less, and she'd be suspicious. She knows my reputation far too well.

I pull her close. Her heartbeat pounds against my chest, a frantic, fluttering thing. She drags her nails slowly up my arm, tracing every flexed muscle, humming in approval before sliding her hand across my shoulder and curling her fingers around the back of my neck.

I fight the urge to flinch. To recoil from the sour churn of disgust rising in my throat. Focus.

This isn't the first dalliance you've had to pretend was different. Special.

Just do what you came here to do. Get what you need.

The violins resume, long and aching. We glide into motion, letting the rhythm pull us forward. The dance is seamless, our bodies moving as one. Graceful, elegant, calculated. The other couples blur around us, reduced to shadows at the edge of my vision.

As we spin, I catch glimpses of my companions. Zyphoro's sharp gaze. Reon's jaw tight with tension. Solena, trying and failing to conceal her worry. And Orios, all pensive stares and misplaced jealousy.

They are waiting. Watching. But none of them can help me now.

Only Marlayna can.

The mirror is within these walls. She is my key, my obstacle, my prey.

And judging by the way her eyes drink me in, her hunger barely veiled, I am hers.

Her fingers glide over my neck, long red nails tracing the runes etched into my skin. She licks her lips.

"You wear power well, my prince," she murmurs, her voice a velvet purr beneath the music. "It fits you as beautifully as this suit. Tell me... do you ever let anyone beneath it?"

I smirk, tilting my head just enough to let her touch trail down the column of my throat. I let her think she's in control. Let her believe she's unraveling me.

"So forward," I murmur. "Do you flirt like this with all your guests?"

Marlayna drags her teeth over her lower lip, eyes caught in mine like she's falling into a trance.

"Forgive me," she breathes. "I've never hosted a guest quite like you. It's not every day the prince of the Sundered Kingdoms stands at my disposal."

"Is that what you think?" I ask, voice low and edged. "That a few guards make me yours to command? That I'll obey?" I lean closer, close enough to feel the hitch in her breath, the subtle stiffness of her spine. "Is that part of the fantasy, Marlayna? The prince on his knees before you?"

She doesn't falter. She shakes her head once, slow and sure.

"No," she says. "In my fantasy, I'm the one on my knees."

I let that hang between us a beat too long, watching the desire spark in her eyes.

"You must earn that right," I say.

Her grin sharpens.

"And how," she whispers, "does one earn such a right?"

"How do we Fae work?" I whisper, a teasing edge to my voice. "With bargains and favors."

Her laugh is soft and indulgent, like she's savoring something far more delicious than the dance itself. She leans in, her nose grazing my chin, breath warm against my throat.

"I have a feeling you've come with one such bargain in mind," she murmurs. "Why else arrive in disguise? You need something."

At least she sees that much. It means I won't have to play quite as long.

"You have a scrying mirror," I say, voice low, barely audible over the music. "I want to see it."

The music swells, the tempo quickening, pulling us into a faster, more intimate rhythm.

Marlayna giggles, almost cruelly, and I'm starting to wonder if she holds more control than I'd like to admit.

"And what do I get in return?" she purrs.

My patience thins. I halt in the center of the dance floor, one hand curling around her jaw, angling her face toward mine. The crowd fades. My gaze snags hers, and her breath falters, knees softening as she sinks deeper beneath the spell I cast.

"A warm and willing body in your bed tonight," I say, voice calm, steady, dark with promise.

Let her believe she's won.

Let her believe it's real.

Marlayna bites her bottom lip, something fierce, something hungry flickering within her eyes. She craves me. That has never been in question. Long before this night, before the humans took up arms and burned her castle to ash, Marlayna wanted me with the same inevitability that winter longs for the first breath of spring. Had things been different, had fate bent to her will, I have no doubt she would have pursued me as a husband.

If not for two things.

Her Lord husband, Rourke, and the simple, unshakable truth that when I look upon her, I see nothing but a hollow, vapid shell of a female who, for all her vanity, I doubt even casts a reflection in a mirror.

Many believe our long lives to be a gift, but among their cruelties is this: for some of us, with every passing year, we become a little less. A little emptier. I have watched the light drain from the eyes of the immortal, turning them into these exquisite, soulless monsters. That is what I see when I look at Marlayna. A creature of devastating beauty, yes, enough to bring even the strongest of beings to their knees, to make them beg for the privilege of feeling her warmth beneath them.

But for all her flawlessness, all her charm, all her power, she could only ever dream, in a thousand lifetimes, of being even a glimmer of the companion Amara has become in just one.

Marlayna's lips curl into a wicked smile. "Very well," she says. "Follow me." Her eyes flick to my company, her expression flattening with irritation. "And bring your friends before they cause another scene."

She slips from my arms and turns, hips swaying with deliberate grace as she strides ahead. Her guards part the beaded curtain, heads bowed.

We pass through one by one, but when it's Tamis' turn, Marlayna's guards block his path with a hard shove to the chest.

She glances over her shoulder, her eyes narrowing with disdain as they settle on him.

"This is the Fae who brought you here."

It is not a question, but an accusation.

I exchange a glance with the others, then meet Tamis' eyes. Wide, glassy, full of silent pleading.

I shake my head. "I've never seen him before in my life."

Marlayna arches a brow. "That answer won't work a second time. If I didn't know better, Prince, I'd think you were trying to protect him."

"Why would I?" I sigh, bored. "I don't care what happens to him."

"Good."

She lifts her chin, and the beaded curtain stirs as if it's alive. It weaves and twists, the strands writhing like serpents, then strikes, coiling around Tamis' throat. He chokes, clutching at the beads, fighting to tear them free, but he's powerless. The curtain lifts him into the air, feet kicking, eyes bulging, skin turning a bruised, awful shade of purple.

I move to step forward but I'm met by a wall of muscle, Taramethos guards barring my way.

"Now, now," Marlayna purrs. "I thought you didn't care."

I force myself to look away, to shut out the ugly sounds clawing their way out of Tamis' throat. It should be easy, once, it would have been. But now... now I feel something dangerously close to regret.

Even through her cruelty, I catch the slight arch of Zyphoro's back, her eyes flicking between me and Tamis. She knows the cost. Just as well as I do. We're here for the mirror. Everything else, especially Tamis's life, is irrelevant.

I shrug and let out a long, exaggerated sigh.

"Do what you want," I say, voice flat. "But can we speed it up? I'd rather not listen to him gurgle all night."

Marlayna frowns. With a flick of her fingers, the beads snap back into their decorative form, dropping Tamis to the floor in a heap. He lands hard, coughing and gasping, but alive.

"Well, it's no fun if I'm the only one enjoying it," she says.

I force a grin to appease her and give her a slight nod.

She turns and climbs the stairs. But when she notices I haven't followed, she glances back, her narrowed gaze a silent command.

And of course, I follow.

What else is there to do but obey and surrender to whatever bargain she's ready to make?

CHAPTER 11
DAED

I see the echoes of House Taramethos woven into the bones of this place, the remnants of a world before war, before destruction. Before the rebellion that burned their legacy to the ground. Marlayna has done what she can to salvage that lost grandeur. The walls bearing the mark of artisans, etched with intricate filigree, pulsing with old enchantments that no longer have purpose. Gilded archways curve like the delicate strokes of a painter's brush, their edges adorned with faded sigils of prosperity and power, now little more than relics of a dynasty that chose exile over honor.

Once, House Taramethos ruled over Thyros, a stronghold nestled within the embrace of the Thraelis Mountains. Their castle had been more than a seat of power. It was a temple of creation, a sanctum where magic was not merely wielded but shaped. They crafted artifacts that could shake empires: crowns that made kings kneel, blades that turned the tide of war, mirrors that could unravel the very fabric of fate. But time tarnishes even the finest craft.

Here in Ballamar City, what remains of that splendor is a poor imitation of its former self. The artistry, the tapestries, the hoarded relics of a lost age. They do not inspire awe. They clutter, they crowd, as though Marlayna is desperately trying to press the past into the narrow walls of a place unworthy of its history. I almost feel sorry for her. Almost.

Because I have not forgotten. When the war came, when the firestorm of the Legion rose against us, House Taramethos turned their backs. They fled, taking their weapons, their magic, their carefully hoarded power with them. They abandoned the Mordorin warriors at Greenmist Gorge, left them to be slaughtered while their promised reinforcements never came.

As if sensing the bitterness in my gaze, Marlayna glances over her shoulder, her lips curling into a sly smile. I return it, forced and placating, though my mind is still with the bodies that once littered the gorge.

100

Like its mistress, this house wears its splendor like a mask. Dazzling, breathtaking, but hollow beneath the surface.

Marlayna guides us into a large room, and the moment I lift my head, I realize we are not alone.

The parlor is steeped in darkness, shadows flickering over silk and skin. Candlelight trembles across the walls, painting the silhouettes of writhing bodies, limbs entwined, sweat-slicked and glistening beneath the spill of moonlight slanting through the open windows.Scents of musk and wine linger in the air, threaded with sighs and whispered names. Those not lost to pleasure lounge on velvet divans, sipping wine dark as spilled blood, indulging in silver platters piled high with cream-filled confections and sun-ripe fruit, their sweet juice running down eager chins.

Ballamar City is far more of a hedonistic pleasure nest than I ever imagined.

I turn to Marlayna, ready to demand why she has brought us here, but then I see it, past the haze of desire and debauchery, a small cluster of Fae huddled in the farthest corner. Unlike the others, they are not indulging. They murmur in hushed tones, their gazes fixed on something between them.

I strain to see, stepping closer, and when the figures shift, my breath stills.

A gleam of tarnished silver. A surface I would recognize anywhere.

The scrying mirror.

I move toward it, but before I can take another step, Marlayna's hand presses against my chest, fingers curling, kneading as if she can make my body yield with touch alone.

"There will be time for that," she murmurs, her voice silk-soft. "I have many, many questions. Please, you and your companions must eat. Drink."

I shake my head. "The mirror..."

"Eat and drink," she interrupts sharply, the command hidden beneath honeyed words as her guards close around me.

My eyes narrow, but she shows no regard for my irritation. Instead she laughs, light and musical, her lashes lowering as if in feigned modesty. But there is nothing coy about her.

"You are in my kingdom now," she says. "And we will play by my rules."

I lean in, my voice low, edged with warning. "You are brave to think you hold any true power over me. Especially when you know exactly what I am capable of."

Her brows lift, amusement curling at the corner of her lips. "Oh, I know," she says, stepping even closer, so close I can feel the warmth of her breath. "But the fact that you have not murdered me and my guests already tells me you will not use that power. And that makes me curious."

She tilts her head. "So, please," she breathes. "Eat. Drink."

I turn my back on Marlayna for only a moment, my allies pressing in close. We take in the scene with guarded detachment. The moans, the clinking goblets, the scent of sweat and spice. These indulgences do not rattle us. Such things are common in our world.

But we are not in our world.

And the Fae cannot be trusted.

"What does she want?" Zyphoro murmurs, arms folding across her waist, long, dark nails tapping a slow, deliberate rhythm against her ribs.

Reon sighs, exasperated. "Surely you are not that oblivious?" He flicks a glance toward Marlayna. "I believe she wants your brother."

Zyphoro scrunches her face in distaste. "What for?"

Reon smirks. "I imagine she'd like to sample the royal cock."

Zyphoro gags, sticking out her tongue, throat bobbing with visible disgust. I frown at her overreaction.

"You cannot bed her," Solena interjects, her voice firm, her brow furrowed.

I turn to her, exhaling slowly. "We need access to that mirror."

"Then kill them," she says simply. "Kill them all. Any who stands in our way."

Orios nods his agreement.

I shake my head. "I must tread carefully with the void. If I summon too much, if I step through it, I will make myself known to him."

Orios shrugs. "Then I will kill them."

Zyphoro raises a hand. "I'll help."

"No." The word is a snarl, my canines pressing against my lip. "We do this my way. Without bloodshed."

Their gazes weigh heavy on me, unspoken questions thick between us. The prince who carved a reputation in blood and battle now speaks of restraint?

I answer before they can voice their doubts.

"This conflict cannot be solved with smoke and steel. Carving my way through land and sea will not bring me closer to my love. No amount of blood on my hands will make my heart whole. Only Amara can do that and so I must play their game."

Zyphoro studies me through half-lidded eyes, skepticism laced in her smirk.

"How admirable of you, brother." She exhales, rolling her neck. "Boring as fuck. But admirable nonetheless."

The others nod, but there is something different in their eyes, something searching, as if they are seeing me for the first time, as if this shift within me unsettles even them.

I do not like it.

I have never needed their approval, only their obedience. I want them to see me as they always have. The wicked prince of the Mordorin, the creature they fear, the warlord who does not bend. But now, beneath their scrutiny, I feel something I have never allowed myself to feel. Exposed.

And I know the reason.

Amara has stripped me bare. She has unraveled me, unmade me, and I let her. My need for her outweighs the mask I once wore so effortlessly. She has changed me, and now I fear I cannot be both.

The prince I was feared nothing.

But the husband I am now is *nothing* without her.

Without my mate.

"Prince Daedalus," Marlayna says, her voice laced with formality, though we both know my title holds no weight here. "Would you care to join me?"

She gestures to a deep blue chaise, its gilded baroque edges gleaming in the dim light.

I nod stiffly, though the irritation gnawing at me feels sharp enough to draw blood. She smiles, a knowing curve of her lips, and sways toward the chaise. I take a moment to glance at the others.

"Leave this to me. Blend in. Try to enjoy yourselves," I murmur. Before they can scatter, I glance back at them, eyes narrowing. "And don't kill anyone."

Zyphoro and Orios exchange disappointed looks, but they fade into the crowd. Reon, however, takes to the scene like a fish to water, slipping into the company of two masked females whose pale, naked forms entwine slowly, almost languorously. Zyphoro sprawls in a large chair, legs draped over the arm as she casually plucks a string of grapes from the table while Solena and Orios help themselves to goblets of wine.

I stride toward Marlayna, and she pats the velvet cushion beside her in invitation. Unbuttoning my coat, I shrug it back, letting the fabric settle as I sink onto the chaise. My legs sprawl apart, a deliberate display of ease I don't quite feel, my chin resting between my fingers as I stare into the space before me, lost in thought.

A slender male approaches, his face hidden behind a silver mask, and offers us each a goblet. When I lift it to my lips, the dry ache in my throat nags at me, but I pause, my gaze flicking to Marlayna. She watches me with a curious gleam in her eyes.

I pull the goblet back, inspecting the blood-red liquid, inhaling its scent, looking for any trace of poison.

She laughs softly, a melodic sound that only adds to my suspicion. "Do not fear, Prince Daedalus," she says with a teasing smile. "Your bargain has me far too intrigued to kill you."

"Why do you call me that?" I ask sharply, the word bitter on my tongue as I hold the goblet aloft, still wary. "I am no prince here in Ballamar, and no law forces you to bow."

She shrugs nonchalantly, then takes a slow sip of her wine, letting the gesture speak for itself. When she lowers the goblet, a single drop clings to her lips, which she licks off with a subtle, deliberate motion. "It's nice to pretend sometimes, that the world is as it once was," she admits. Her gaze drifts around the room, lingering on the paintings hanging on the walls. Landscapes of Thyros, the Thraelis Mountains, and the distant silhouette of Castle Taramethos.

"You miss it," I say, a faint bitterness curling in my chest.

Her eyes drop, a flicker of vulnerability passing over her face. "I do," she confesses quietly.

"You could have helped to save it," I say, unable to stop the words from spilling out.

Marlayna lifts her gaze, meeting my eyes. "Does it make me pathetic that, after a thousand years of life, the reality of death terrified me?"

I consider this for a moment. "No," I finally reply, my voice steady. "Death should frighten us more than any other creature. It's a finality in a life that otherwise stretches on forever. I do not judge your reluctance to die. But your eagerness to flee your oaths..." My words turn sharper, a biting edge slipping through. "That is something I cannot abide."

I watch her throat bob, the faintest sign of hesitation in her movement.

"I am not proud of the actions of my house, but as I heard not long after, the forces of the Mordorin stood victorious in the end."

A dark chuckle escapes me, one I can't quite suppress, my disdain curling at the edges of my words. "Oh, we may have been left standing," I reply, my tone dripping with irony, "but the Sundered Kingdoms are hardly ours to claim."

Marlayna lifts her chin. "Perhaps it is time House Taramethos returned to the Sundered Kingdoms." Her fingers drift across the velvet, skimming over my leg in a caress meant to entice, but her touch is no more alluring than a buzzing fly. "We could claim it together. Join our houses."

My gaze flicks to the mirror, still surrounded by entranced guests, some laughing, others weeping at whatever visions torment them. I let her hand remain but weigh my words with care.

"I have no need for a wife, Lady Marlayna, and last I heard, you already had a husband."

A flush rises over her skin, smooth and dark like midnight silk. She shifts, fingers tightening around the stem of her goblet. "My beloved Rourke did not survive the journey."

She does not meet my eyes as she takes a measured sip of wine.

"My condolences," I offer, though I suspect she has no use for them. "I hope he did not suffer."

"No," she murmurs, gaze still evading mine. "It was swift."

But when her eyes flicker back to me, they carry something else, a guarded truth, a quiver beneath her practiced grace. I hear the phantom pulse of blood beneath her skin, taste the unspoken in the air between us. I arch a brow.

"And how did you say he died again?"

Marlayna straightens, her reply curt. "I didn't."

I nod, and with that, I place my untouched wine on the round table beside me. "I did wonder how Lord Rourke would take to such... titillating surroundings. He was always rather pious."

"I miss him every day, of course. But the freedom I've had since settling in Ballamar has been quite liberating."

"I can see that," I murmur.

She lifts her empty goblet and gives a lazy flick of her wrist that sends a servant scurrying to refill it. As the servant vanishes, Marlayna turns back to me, curiosity darkening her gaze.

"Now it is my turn," she says. "Why do you seek the mirror? What is it you hope to find?"

"Something I lost," I reply. "And a city that moves with the clouds."

"Driftspire," she says casually, and my head snaps toward her.

"You know Driftspire?"

"The floating city of House Ithranor. Yes, I have heard of it. But if you're about to ask where it is, I'm afraid I can't help you."

"The mirror will tell me," I say.

She tilts her head. "You desire the city that much?"

"I desire only what the city has stolen from me."

My gaze flicks again to the scrying mirror, restless, impatient to rid myself of this conversation and claim my moment with the tarnished window to the unseen.

"It may show you what you seek," Marlayna murmurs, reclining against the chaise with the sinuous grace of a cat in sunlight. She crosses her legs, revealing a flash of smooth thigh. I make a point of not noticing. "But you know scrying mirrors are fickle things. They unveil not only what you desire... they expose what you fear."

"It is a risk I am willing to take," I say.

"It must be a great treasure indeed you've been robbed of."

I offer no further details. It's blessing enough that she seems unaware of all that has transpired.

"Very well." She exhales as if she's already won the game. "Keep to your bargain, and the scrying mirror is yours to use as you will."

I tip my head toward the six or seven Fae still gathered around the mirror, their expressions rapt with awe or horror.

"Did they bargain with you as well?"

Marlayna hums, thoughtful. "No. They use it freely. But they have nothing I want."

I draw a slow, measured breath, reminding myself, forcing myself, to remember that while Marlayna's slender neck would be so very easy to snap, that is not the path I have chosen. Not tonight. Instead, I pick up the goblet and throw back the wine, letting it sear its way down my throat before handing the empty goblet to a hovering servant.

"Then why waste time with this meaningless chatter?" I say, rough as gravel. "Where is your bedchamber, my lady?"

I can practically feel her blood run hot through her veins, her breath hitching as much from surprise as anticipation. She hastily drains the last of her wine, though in her eagerness, most of it dribbles down her chin. She wipes it away with the back of her hand, ignoring the stain it leaves against her skin, and shoves her goblet into the waiting hands of another servant.

106

"Follow me," she says, her voice slurred from the wine or her nerves, or a little of both.

She waves off her guards with a flick of her wrist and strides toward the exit. I fall into step behind her, feeling the weight of a dozen curious eyes on me. Reon and Zyphoro are among them, their brows arched in pointed intrigue. But I do not stop.

Marlayna extends a hand behind her, fingers curling, searching for mine.

I have held back armies. Fought through waves of enemies with nothing but my fists until my knuckles split and my arms went numb. I have walked through fire, through ruin, through the jaws of beasts that would tear lesser creatures apart.

And yet none of it, not a single battle, has ever required the strength it takes to lace my fingers through hers and make her believe it is what I want.

Marlayna leads me down the corridor in silence, her footsteps a steady staccato against the wood, echoing the hollow thud of my own heartbeat. We pass so many doors I lose count, the hush between us stretching taut. At last, she halts and at her unspoken command, the double doors glide open, revealing a chamber draped in quiet opulence.

Midnight-blue marble glistens beneath the flickering sconces, their golden light catching in the gossamer drapes that whisper with the night breeze. A grand hearth of black stone commands one wall, its fire casting long, shifting shadows over low tables scattered with scrolls and half-filled inkwells, plans and sketches sprawled in careful disorder.

House Taramethos has always been a house of builders, of visionaries who shape the world with steady hands and restless minds. Even here in Ballamar, far from their ancestral seat, that legacy endures.

But for all the intrigue scattered across those tables, my attention is pulled inexorably to the massive bed that looms at the center of it all, its dark silks rippling in the breeze like the surface of some deep, unknowable sea. It is a stark reminder of why I am here, of the role I must play.

I do not have the luxury of distraction.

Marlayna moves with the confidence of a female who has never once doubted her own allure. She turns her back to me, not so subtly nudging my groin with the curve of her ass. Then, with a sweep of her hand, she drapes her hair over one shoulder, revealing the neat row of buttons running down the back of her gown.

"Would you?" she asks, glancing at me over her shoulder, her bottom lip clenched between her teeth.

I do not answer. Words are unnecessary.

Instead, my fingers find the first button. I work them loose with swift, practiced efficiency, the fine fabric parting beneath my touch. Her skin is warm and unblemished, a study in perfection.

And yet I feel nothing.

No hunger. No heat. Not even the ghost of a stirring in my blood.

Marlayna tilts her head, as if waiting for something more, but I give her nothing. This is not seduction. This is strategy. A game played in whispers and shadows, in silk sheets and half-truths.

The last button slips free. Her gown slackens around her shoulders, the fine fabric whispering against her skin, threatening to slide away completely. But just before it can pool at her feet, she catches it in her fists, holding it tight as she glides toward the bed.

She moves like she expects to be worshipped. Like the sight of her reclining across the silken sheets, her gown slipping just enough to bare the soft swell of her breasts, should send me into a frenzy.

But the only thing that burns in me is the consuming ache of absence.

Not for her.

For Amara.

If it were Amara stretched out before me, there'd be no hesitation. No strategy. Just raw, ruinous need to have her, claim her, hear her cry my name as she clawed at my skin. I'd take my time unraveling her, tasting every inch, coaxing the sweetest sounds from her lips until she was trembling beneath my tongue. I would worship her, over and over, until she came undone in my mouth, her pleasure washing over me like a blessing, long before I ever sank into the unbearable heat of her. The only warmth that could ever truly sate me.

The thought alone sends a sharp rush of hunger through me, but it is not for the female sprawled before me. Even in the haze of my own longing, Marlayna remains nothing more than a pale imitation of desire.

"Come, my prince," she murmurs, her voice threaded with anticipation as her hair lifts in the breeze. "Time to honor our bargain."

"Yes," I say, my voice low, carried on the same wind that catches her hair. "A warm and willing body between your sheets."

She nods, lips parting, teeth grazing the curve of her bottom lip in anxious excitement.

But then the door groans open behind me.

Marlayna stiffens, her eager expression vanishing in an instant, swallowed by something colder.

Boot steps sound against the floor, measured and unhurried, and then the door clicks shut once more.

Reon steps forward from the dark, coming to stand at my side.

And in the quiet that follows, I can almost hear the pulse hammering in Marlayna's throat.

"What is this?" she snarls, eyes flashing with fury.

"This," I say smoothly, barely restraining my grin, "is Lord Reon of Eyr'Drogul." I tilt my head toward him. "And he is more than happy to honor our bargain on my behalf."

With the ease of someone born to charm, Reon sweeps back his copper hair and offers a lazy half-bow, the moonlight catching on the sharp gleam of his canines as he straightens.

"Lady Marlayna," his voice a low rumble beneath his grin. "It will be my pleasure."

Her face twists in disbelief. "This is not what was bargained."

My brows lift in mock confusion. "A warm, willing body. Was that not your request?" I clap Reon's shoulder. "You'll find he meets those requirements very well."

"Deceiver," she spits, her hands curling into fists. "I could have you killed for this."

I step closer, letting the weight of my gaze settle over her. "Bargains are dangerous things, my lady. Especially when made by Fae." I let the words hang between us, then smirk. "For one who so longs for the old ways, perhaps instead of outrage, you should embrace this moment."

The silence draws taut between us, each waiting to see who will make the first move. In the end, it is Marlayna who yields, though not without a flash of irritation in her eyes.

"Fine," she concedes, voice clipped. "I've had too much wine to be particular. Lord Reon may not be your equal, but he will do."

Reon exhales a laugh, rolling his shoulders. "I've had worse foreplay, my lady."

Marlayna's gaze cuts to me like a dagger. "The mirror is yours to use," she snaps. "Now get out." Then her eyes slide back to Reon, considering him like a merchant inspecting wares. "You can have your friend in the morning. No sooner."

Before I can turn on my heel, Reon reaches behind his back, fisting his shirt and dragging it over his head in one smooth motion, the hard muscle of his chest freckled like sun-kissed stone.

"I'll accept that challenge," he says, voice laced with amusement.

I waste no time in leaving, turning my back just as Marlayna's delighted giggle fills the chamber. The last thing I hear before the door shuts behind me is the sharp snap of Reon's belt.

I step into the dimly lit corridor and try to ignore the churning in my stomach at whatever is about to unfold in that room.

The mirror. That is all that matters.

CHAPTER 12

AMARA

When I feel the heat of the morning sun cross my face, I gasp and bolt upright, my breath tearing from my lungs in a frantic rush. It takes a moment, just a beat, to find my bearings, to realize I'm in the bed of my prison. The weight of the invisible collar around my neck presses down on me, its cold grip suffocating. My eyes widen in sudden horror. My neck. The blood. I remember the blood seeping through my fingers, the warmth, the sickening thickness.

I reach for my skin, panic flooding through me, my fingers trembling with the dread of what I might find. But there's nothing. No wound, no blood, no scar to mark the nightmare that clung to me. But it wasn't a nightmare. I know it wasn't. I saw it. I *felt* it.

Desperation claws at me as I check my arms, my breath shallow, praying that my trembling fingers won't be met with the evidence of my madness. But once again, there is nothing. Nothing but a faint memory of the pain.

No. Please. *No.* I can't be going mad. Not again.

"You didn't imagine it," a deep voice murmurs from the shadows, its tone a rich baritone that seems to reverberate through the silence of the room. My body jerks upright, heart racing as I scramble against the headboard, drawing my knees tightly to my chest.

The Golden Son is sitting with casual indifference at the chess table, his fingers toying with the white queen, rolling it in slow circles across the polished surface. His eyes are locked on the board, distant, detached, as though nothing in this room could truly demand his attention, least of all me.

"You've been asleep for days," he continues.

"My throat..." I rasp, the words barely escaping, my voice a rough, jagged whisper. The dry pain of it makes me flinch.

Finally, his gaze lifts, locking onto mine. Those ice-blue eyes gleam beneath his mask, cold and sharp as a blade forged from glass. "They healed you, but even so..." The words are measured, reluctant, as though forcing them out costs him something. He exhales slowly. "I didn't know if you'd wake up."

Then his voice shifts, cutting through the dim light like steel. "What are these tests Anethesis has you performing?"

I find enough strength to scowl. "As if you do not know."

His fingers tighten around the chess piece, knuckles whitening. "I did not know they were tearing you to shreds." His voice is steady, but there's an edge to it, something close to anger.

"Well, now you do." My tone is sharp, but there's no satisfaction in it. "What difference does it make?"

His grip on the white queen turns crushing. "It makes all the difference," he snarls. "That was not our bargain."

That word. Bargain. Spoken from his mouth, laced with fury, with meaning and, Souls help me, it sparks something absurd in me. A laugh, hoarse and broken, bubbles up before I can stop it. At first, I slap a hand over my mouth, but it forces its way out, rolling from my throat, ragged and uncontrollable. I tip my head back and laugh.

The Golden Son watches in baffled silence.

"Bargain?" I spit the word, amusement turning to something bitter. "Do you know nothing of the Fae and their bargains?" I lean forward, eyes narrowing. "You cannot trust the Fae."

His jaw tightens. "Yet you married one."

"What does that matter?" I mutter, my voice dull with exhaustion.

"You lay with him," he presses, voice sharpening, "You carry his child."

"None of that means I trust him."

The Golden Son shakes his head, vehement, nearly disgusted. "Then that is not love. There cannot be one without the other."

I hold his gaze, letting the weight of his words settle.

A slow exhale slips from my lips.

"Love and trust are not the same," I say, my voice quieter now. "They should be. In a perfect world, maybe they are. But not for me and not for Daed."

"Then that is not love. That is surrender," he snaps.

I shake my head. "No. It's survival."

He says nothing, but I see it in the rigid line of his shoulders. His refusal to accept it.

"Daed is Fae," I continue. "And I knew what that meant before I ever let him touch me. He lies when it suits him. He withholds when it's to his advantage. His nature is not kindness, nor is it cruelty, because that is what Fae truly are. The gray between the black and white world we humans live in. And yet, I know with absolute certainty, if I asked him to fall on a blade, he would. If my life meant his death, he would not hesitate."

The Golden Son scoffs, sharp and disbelieving. "That is your standard for love?"

"No," I say simply. "That is my standard for him."

His head tilts slightly, but he says nothing, waiting.

"What Daed and I have, it isn't built on trust the way you understand it. It's built on something else. On knowing exactly what the other is capable of. On knowing how far the other will go, and where the line is drawn. You think trust is blind faith." I shake my head again. "But love can exist in spite of mistrust. In spite of doubt. It can still be real, even when it's complicated, even when it's dangerous."

He studies me, his mouth pressing into a thin line.

"If you do not trust him," he says at last, "then what keeps you by his side?"

"Because he never pretends to be anything other than what he is and in return, I never have to pretend either. There is no illusion between us, no lies to fall into and be broken by. What we have is something deeper than trust."

A muscle feathers in his jaw. "And what is that?"

I lift my chin. "Certainty. The certainty that no matter how this world tries to tear us apart, we will never be separated."

Still, the Golden Son remains unmoved, his expression carved from stone.

"Love does not need to be so complicated."

I glare at him, frustration curling in my chest, perhaps because in my heart I know he is right, though I would rather die than admit such a thing.

"What would you know?" I spit bitterly.

I move to turn away, to put my back to him, but the scrape of his chair against the stone floor stops me cold.

"Of what?" he snaps. "Of love? Of trust? Of certainty? Is that what you're asking?"

He pounds a fist against his chest, the sound reverberating through the room. "Do you think this lump of blood and muscle behind my ribs does not beat? That it does not feel? Do you think you and that fucking Fae are the only two creatures in this world who have ever cared so fiercely for another?"

His jaw clenches, his throat bobs with a hard swallow. "Well? Do you?"

I've seen this man's rage before. Cold, ruthless, soaked in blood. I've seen the hatred in his eyes just before his boot slammed into my face at the Battle of the Grove. But this... this is something else entirely. This fury is raw, primal, clawing its way out from somewhere deeper. From that lump of muscle behind his ribs that he grips through his shirt like he's ready to rip it out with his bare hands.

I don't know what to say, don't know what he expects me to say. But when I don't answer, he moves.

I barely have time to gasp before he crosses the space between us, climbing onto the bed, dragging himself toward me where I sit pressed against the headboard.

"I feel," he snaps, his breath ragged. "More than you know. More than you could imagine."

His hands go to his collar, gripping the fabric of his shirt. With a harsh grunt, he rips it open, the material giving way to reveal the smooth planes of his chest, the powerful lines of muscle beneath, and the raw, unforgiving ripples of seared skin that scar his left side.

"Feel it," he snarls, but there is something hollow beneath his rage, something aching, something desperate.

He lunges, grabbing my wrist. I wrench away, kicking at him, but he's stronger, fueled by something I do not understand. He catches my hand again, rough fingers closing tight, and before I can fight him off, he drags me forward, pressing my palm flat against his chest.

"Feel it!" he demands, his voice a ragged growl.

My heart is pounding so fiercely, so loudly in my ears, that at first, I cannot tell his heartbeat from my own. I squeeze my eyes shut, as if willing him away, but there is no escaping the press of our heavy breaths, the way the silence between us stretches tight as a drawn bowstring.

But then, as my own chest settles, I feel it. The thud beneath my palm. Rapid, unrelenting, as though it might tear free from his ribs at any moment.

Slowly, hesitantly, I open my eyes and when our gazes lock, I nearly flinch. His ice-blue eyes are glassed over, shimmering like water held at bay.

"I am not a monster, Amara Tyne," he murmurs. Not Phaedren. Not Daed's wife. My name, stripped bare, raw on his tongue. "I am but a man burdened with the fates of my people. I am their champion, but in the dark of night, when I am alone, I feel like their failure. For all I have done is bring them death and despair."

His grip on my wrist slackens, and I pull my hand back to my chest. He kneels near me, shoulders caving inward, his head hanging low. For the first time, he looks defeated.

"Why are you telling me this?" My voice is barely a whisper.

"Because you and I are more alike than you think," he says. "We have both lost much to the flames that ravaged the Sundered Kingdoms. We are both orphans of the ashes."

His fingers drift to his mask, tracing the swirling engravings molded into the bronze. "My parents burned in the fires of Rethmar. I was asleep in my bed, unaware, until my brother shook me awake and dragged me through our bedroom window." He takes a steadying breath. "There was this smell. A stench that clung to us, no matter how fast we ran. Even when we reached the mountains, it lingered. We stood there, watching the flames of Rethmar lick the sky, turning night to day. Only then, in the eerie stillness, did I realize the smell was me. My skin, burnt. My bedclothes, fused to my little body. But I did not scream. Even when the pain had me wishing for death, I would not give the Fae the satisfaction of knowing they had broken me."

His voice never wavers, steady and measured. But his eyes betray him, heavy with the weight of memory.

"How does a little boy become the leader of an army?" I ask.

He scoffs. "He doesn't. His brother does. Starving to death was never an option, so we joined the Legion. Little more than a scattered rebellion back then. But my brother was ambitious, and that ambition earned him a name among the people. The Golden Son. The light that would save humans from the Fae. And when he died, the mask fell to me."

His hand stills over the bronze surface, his breath turning ragged. "But where he wore his as a symbol of honor, mine is a shroud to hide what the flames took from me that day. Not just my flesh, melted from my bones, but the boy I had been. That was the day the world changed forever. The day I became a man with a divine purpose... and a terrible vengeance."

Of course. For years, the Fae have asked the same question: *Who is the Golden Son?* His face has never been seen. Time itself seems to pass him by, untouched, an immortal force of reckoning.

But now, the answer is clear.

He is not the first Golden Son. Only the mask's newest heir.

He is Ronin. An orphaned boy from Rethmar, stripped of his past, burdened with a future too heavy to bear and now, before me, he is breaking.

"Your brother sounds like a good man," I say.

"Yes. He was," he murmurs, his voice hollow. "Far greater than his successor."

"Did he die fighting the Fae?" I ask.

The Golden Son lifts his gaze. "Ambushed near Lake Vysere," he says. "One of his men managed to tear the mask from his face before the Fae could search the bodies. Slipped away, bloodied and half-dead, and brought it back to me." He pauses. "The Fae didn't realize they had killed The Golden Son that day."

"And your parents?" I hesitate, gnawing my bottom lip. "Do you... do you remember their faces?"

Something flickers in his gaze, something knowing, something strangely familiar that sets me at ease.

He exhales. "I fear I have forgotten them."

A small, honest smile tugs at my lips. "As have I."

Without thought, without reason, my hand drifts from my chest, reaching for him.

He catches the movement from the corner of his eye and flinches. I freeze.

For a moment, neither of us breathes.

Then, slowly, he gives the smallest nod, a hesitant, fragile thing.

Only then do I continue, my fingertips brushing the cold of his mask.

I do not know what drives me. Curiosity, or the aching need to ease his suffering, as I do for all who bear pain. Despite *who* they are. Despite *what* they are.

Because pain is the great equalizer. It does not favor, does not discriminate. It takes, it breaks, it brands, and so I must tend to it with the same indifference, the same unwavering touch.

My fingers inch beneath the edges of his mask, curling into the grooves. He shivers. His throat bobs with a hard, audible swallow, but he does not stop me. He does not move at all, save for the tightening of his fists against his thighs.

So I pull.

The mask resists, a final act of defiance, but then it loosens. And with one firm tug, it comes free.

What lies beneath is a battlefield of scars. Scorched flesh stretched taut, ridges of deep purple and ashen white carved into the left side of his face. The burns claim his brow, twist into his hairline, consume half his nose and the corner of his mouth, curve cruelly down his jaw before trailing down his neck.

I do not flinch.

I do not recoil.

Because I know what it is to be marked by fire. To be remade by ruin.

The Golden Son does not look at me. His breath is shallow, uneven, his hands curled so tightly his knuckles go white. He is waiting. Bracing. As if he has been here before. As if he has seen the horror, the pity, the revulsion written on another's face and is readying himself for it once more.

I do none of those things.

Instead, I reach out, my touch featherlight as I trace the edges of his scars, the ridges and valleys of melted flesh. He inhales sharply, but does not pull away.

And softly, barely above a whisper, I say, "I see you."

I feel the relief well behind his eyes, a dam ready to break, but he does not let it. Instead, he leans into my touch, his breath shallow, as if afraid to disturb this fragile moment.

I must heal him. I must take this pain away.

I close my eyes, reaching inward, summoning the gift that is both my burden and my blessing. Warmth stirs within me, a familiar golden light unfurling like the first rays of dawn. It fills me, bright and boundless, spilling through my veins like a river of molten sun. I have missed this. This sacred power, this connection to something greater. It is the whisper of the Souls, the caress of my lost sisters, the memory of soft grass beneath my feet. It is *home*.

For one perfect moment, I lose myself in it.

And then...

Agony.

A burning, searing pain explodes around my throat, raw and all-consuming, as if fire itself has come alive and sunk its fangs into my flesh. My body jerks, the light within me twisting, turning, *rebelling*. I grit my teeth, willing myself to endure it, but the pain only deepens, sharper, crueler, until it rips a scream from my lips.

"Amara!"

His voice booms through the haze of agony, frantic, desperate. "No! I didn't ask you for this. Stop!"

I try, Souls, I try, but the pain holds me captive, an unrelenting inferno consuming me from the inside out. My vision blurs, stars bursting behind my eyelids, and somewhere through the haze, he grips my shoulders.

"Amara, stop!" The Golden Son shakes me, his voice raw with panic. "Please!"

I gasp, my eyes flying open, the world lurching back into focus. The collar around my neck glows red-hot, no longer just a shackle but a branding mark, searing, punishing.

He pushes my hand away from his face, his own trembling as they clutch at me, as if willing me back to myself.

"Please," he whispers again, and there is something in his voice I do not expect.

Fear.

Suddenly, the door bursts open, crashing against the wall as a flood of Ithranor Fae swarm the room.

"Ronin! What have you done?"

Even through the haze of pain, I recognize the voice. Anethesis. My vision swims, but I see them seize the Golden Son, ripping him from my bed, dragging him toward the door.

"Get the fuck off me!" he roars, thrashing against their grip. "What are you doing to her, Anethesis? You lying bastard!"

"Take him away!" Anethesis commands.

Even with Ronin torn from me, the agony doesn't fade. It burns, relentless, consuming. Anethesis is beside me now, his bony fingers pressing into my skin.

"Princess, you must calm yourself," he urges. "You're only making it worse."

But I can't stop. My fingers claw at the collar, nails scraping, snapping against the metal.

"I can't..." My breath shudders. My throat constricts. "I can't breathe."

"We must release her," a Fae voice insists.

"No!" Anethesis bellows, his voice cracking.

"Then she will choke to death, and all will be lost!" another voice pleads.

The room tilts, my vision narrowing. Anethesis is no more than a pale blur now, a wraith shifting in and out of focus. His hands close around my neck, and for a moment, I wonder if this is it. If he will grant me the mercy of ending it.

But then, I hear a click.

The collar falls away.

Agony unfurls from my body like a snapped chain, releasing its grip. My mouth opens, a scream tearing free, and the room explodes in a brilliant burst of blinding green light before everything turns black.

CHAPTER 13
DAED

Before her. The image of Emranth lingers, a specter in the shadows of my mind. Even here, beneath the endless night sky, far from the cursed halls of Baev'kalath, I feel him. Him and the demon god he serves.

Emranth is only a messenger, a wretched errand boy for something far older, far worse, and that I feel more than anything. For I am never alone. No matter how far I flee, no matter how many miles stretch between us, the void is within me. Bound to me. Cursed to me. And as long as I draw breath, I know I will never escape it.

Beneath me, the waves churn, a restless, raging thing. The sea is wild, untamed, as beautiful as it is deadly. My wings slice through the frigid night air, rain needling against my face, beading on my black feathers before sliding off in rivulets. I drag a hand across my eyes, blinking through the downpour, my gaze narrowing on the island ahead.

It is unremarkable. Barely more than a jagged rock jutting from the sea. It is not large enough to mark on a map, and even if it were, the Fae of the Untold Sea would scratch it from existence. Not because of the island itself. No, that is nothing but stone and dirt. It is what *lives* there that unsettles them so.

But not me.

Never me.

I tip my wings, streaking down in a swift, controlled descent, pulling up at the last second to hover before touching the ground. The island is as barren as I remember. Nothing grows here, nothing ever will. But ahead, nestled into the craggy rock, a cave glows with the flicker of orange light.

I move toward it slow and cautious. The roar of the ocean dulls, swallowed by the nearer crackle of burning wood. My wings fold against my back as I brace a hand on the cave's entrance, warmth brushing against my damp skin.

Inside, a wooden dish rests near the fire, littered with fish bones, a meager meal, long since cold. A bedroll lies crumpled in the corner, beside a haphazard stack of books, their pages curled with age and use.

But the one who calls this place home is nowhere to be seen.

My brow furrows. I duck my head, stepping forward but freeze when cold steel kisses my throat.

"You dare show your face here?" The voice is a low rasp, sharp as the blade pressing against my skin.

The slightest movement, even a breath, and it will cut.

Then my attacker inhales. "Wait. Is that..."

The blade eases.

I grin. "Yes, it is."

Reaching into the satchel strapped across my chest, I pull free a shiny red apple.

Before the apple has even tasted the night air, a grubby hand snatches it from my grasp. A figure, cloaked in tattered gray, sweeps past me into the cave, settling before the fire in a swirl of threadbare fabric.

A loud crunch fills the space.

"Dear Pale Mother," she sighs, her voice thick with satisfaction. "This tastes *wonderful*."

I duck inside, tossing my satchel at her feet. It lands with a heavy thud, apples spilling across the ground. "Well, lucky for you, I brought the whole tree, Zema."

The figure pulls back her hood, and the firelight reveals what the shadows tried to conceal.

Even beneath the layer of dirt that smudges her pale skin, she is stunning, breathtaking in the way only a Mordorin Fae can be. Her large brown eyes gleam with knowing mischief, her lips parted just enough to reveal the crisp white bite of apple between them. A thick braid of dark hair spills over her shoulder, so long it coils on the ground beside her like a waiting serpent.

She is cut from the same jagged stone as her kind. Mordorin females, whose beauty is only matched by their strength. There is no softness to them, no delicate refinement like the females of the other houses and as Zema tears into another bite of apple, her satisfaction written plainly across her face despite the desolation around her, I wonder if there is a single female in all the worlds who could have survived as she has.

She looks up, catching me staring.

"Well? Sit down," she says curtly, "unless you're just passing through."

I shake my head and lower myself onto the hard ground, the fire's warmth chasing away the rain clinging to my skin, seeping into my leathers.

"You look good," I say.

She snorts, leveling me with a glare. "I look like shit, Daedalus." Another crisp bite. "But I've been exiled here for half my life." She gives me a once-over. "What's your excuse?"

I chuckle. "It's like that, is it?"

She shrugs, the ghost of a grin playing at her lips. "Serves you right for taking your time between visits. Is the Prince of the Mordorin's schedule so full he has no time for an old friend?"

The playfulness fades from my face, replaced by something heavier. Something sadder.

"I *always* have time for you, Zema. You're right... I've been too distracted."

She waves me off with a chuckle. "I was joking, Daed."

"I wasn't," I say, and it startles her. "I have to do better by you." My gaze sweeps over the cramped cave, the worn books, the scraps that were her last meal. "I don't know how you suffer this."

She exhales through her nose, shaking her head. "What choice do I have?" Her voice is steady, but the certainty in it stuns me. "It's this or death, and I'm not ready to die just yet."

I drop my head as if her acceptance is too bright to look at. "How can you be so resigned to your fate?"

Zema shrugs. "I've had a lifetime to come to terms with it. I am Awakened. I saw this fate long ago."

My throat bobs, and she notices.

Her expression shifts, curiosity sharpening her features. "What is this?" she asks, a slow, knowing smile peeling back the tension. "Something's happened. You feel... different."

I frown. "You've been in this cave too long. Nothing is different."

But she only watches me, studying me like she can see straight through my skin, through my ribs, into the secrets curled tight within me. Then, suddenly, she tosses aside her apple core, picked clean as the fish bones by the fire, and shifts onto her knees, inching closer.

"No," she murmurs, eyes gleaming. "Something is different. I'm sure of it."

Before I can stop her, she scrambles around the fire, settling beside me. Her hands shoot out, grasping either side of my face.

"Zema," I groan, turning away, but as always, she ignores my protests.

She pulls me back, squeezing my cheeks like I'm some petulant child. Then she stills. A slow, wicked grin spreads across her face.

"Oh my," she laughs, dark and delighted. "Maybe you should have brought wine instead of apples. It seems we have reason to celebrate."

I sigh. "What nonsense are you spouting now?"

Her grin widens.

"You found her, didn't you?" she breathes.

My stomach knots.

"You found your mate."

My throat tightens, words stumbling over themselves before I manage, "How... how did you..."

Zema gives me a pointed look, as if the question itself is absurd, but then the excitement on her face wilts. Her grip on my face slackens.

"Oh, my. The fates didn't tell me she was..." Her voice is quieter now. Softer. "I'm sorry, Daedalus."

I place my hands over hers, gently peeling them away. "We are not here to talk about me, Zema."

But she doesn't let me go so easily. Even as I avoid her eyes, I can feel her watching me.

"Will they make you kill her?" she asks. The words are sharp, cutting through the space between us. She lets out a forced laugh, brittle and hollow. "Like they wanted you to kill me?"

My jaw clenches. "But I didn't kill you, did I? I *would never* have killed you."

She nods, her expression unreadable as she gestures around. "Yes, the perks of being the sister of a lord and the companion of a prince. A lovely little cave in the middle of nowhere, but I get to keep my head." A humorless smile tugs at her lips, but her eyes are dark. "I fear your human mate does not have the same privileges."

I lurch to my feet, desperate to put distance between us, to end this conversation before it burrows any deeper into me. But in my haste, I slam my head against the low ceiling with a dull thud.

122

"What is a human Awakened like?" she muses as I rub my head, her curiosity unde-terred. "Does she look any different? She must smell different."

"I don't want to talk about it, Zema," I groan, staggering away from the humble fire, which suddenly feels like a raging inferno.

"You knew, didn't you?" Zema presses, her voice a soft but persistent challenge. "That she was your mate. Just like I told you."

I don't answer immediately, my hand still rubbing the dull ache on my head as I turn to look down at her, surrendering to the weight of her gaze. It's the least I can do. Admit the truth, at least in this moment.

"Yes," I say quietly. "It was like lightning struck me."

Her shoulders relax, and the tension that clung to her melts away, replaced by some-thing lighter. A smile stretches across her face, as if my simple admission was a gift greater than my visit, greater than the apples I brought.

"Is she beautiful?"

The question feels heavier than it should. My chest tightens as I exhale, the breath burning in my lungs. "She is. Just as beautiful as you said she would be and just as fiery. Just as fierce." The memory of her stirs in me. Amara Tyne, with her wild eyes and unbroken spirit. "Just as tormented."

Zema's lips tighten as she nods in understanding. "Good. What will you do now?"

"Nothing," I say, my voice flat, resolute. "I'll forget I ever met her and never think of her again."

Zema frowns. "And then what, Daedalus? Will you stop the sun from rising? The moon from shining?"

"What would you have me do, then?" I mumble, frustration creeping into my voice. "The truth will only bring her death."

She shakes her head, unphased by my words. "You will not let her die."

I growl, clenching my fists. "Then what? What the fuck do I do?"

Zema still isn't moved by the sharp edge in my voice.

"That, I haven't seen yet. But I'm sure you'll figure it out. You're the favored son, after all."

"Favored?" I scoff, bitterness rising like bile in my throat. "To be alone? For my dearest friend to be exiled to some rock? For my mate to be a human? For me to be a slave to the void? How does any of this make me fortunate?"

The words burn through me, and I clench my jaw, my fingers gripping my hair at the roots as I tug at it, trying to expel the anger that twists in my gut, the frustration clawing at me.

Zema doesn't flinch at my outburst. Instead, she reaches for me, her fingers curling in invitation. "Come, Daedalus."

I hesitate, resisting the pull at first, my anger flaring hotter, but her soft smile, her gentle motion, draws me in. Slowly, I sink to my knees beside her, surrendering once again to the quiet strength she offers.

She taps her lap, and I lay my head down there, the fire's crackle now seeming distant, almost forgotten, as her steady hand moves over my head. The warmth of her touch spreads through me, and something in the air shifts. Calming, soothing.

The sound of my heartbeat fades into the background. It's as if her hands are not just brushing over my skin, but weaving something deeper, threads of something far more profound sinking into my bones, reaching into the depths of my mind.

As Zema's fingers gently trace the line of my scalp, a memory flickers, fragile as the light from the fire.

I'm a child again, standing in a garden. The sun is warm, but there's a cool breeze that smells like the earth after rain. Zema is there, her small hands holding a bundle of wildflowers, a smile stretching wide across her face. Her hair is unbound, flowing like the wind itself, and for a moment, she looks like a spirit, something untouchable and free.

She hands me a flower, violet petals, soft as the clouds overhead, and tells me that one day, when we're older, we'll return here together, and the flowers will still be blooming. That everything will be as it was.

I laugh, and she giggles too, her eyes sparkling as we spin around the garden, pretending we could dance forever.

"Do you see it, Daed?" she asks. "Do you remember?"

"Yes," I murmur. "I remember."

But the memory fades as quickly as it came. I blink, and I'm back in the cave.

I close my eyes, my arms instinctively wrapping around Zema's knees, pulling her closer without a second thought. Her hand continues its steady, gentle caress through my hair, and I let myself fall into the sensation, seeking refuge in the comfort of her touch. The warmth of the memory washes over me, a fleeting glimpse of a time when the world was simpler, before it all fractured.

As much as the peace she offers soothes the ache, it also sharpens the pain. A cruel contrast, carving deep the truth of all we've lost. The innocence, the laughter, the golden days before the weight of destiny crushed the lightness of youth.

Before the world turned against her. Before they discovered what she was.

Before her own blood, her brother Modok, her sister Nyraxes, cast her out, shamed her, stripped her of her name until it was nothing but a whispered curse among the Mordorin Fae.

And yet, here in this hollowed-out refuge, with the fire flickering low and her fingers threading through my hair, I let myself feel it all. The warmth, the sorrow, the longing for a time that will never return.

After her. The hour is late, well past midnight, and the revelry is finally unraveling. One by one, they drift away. Some with the ones they came with, others in newfound entanglements, and the rest stumbling drunkenly into the night. I remain. Silent. Watchful. Seated in the shadowed corner, legs spread, hands braced on the arms of the chair as I stare at it.

The scrying mirror.

I've watched it for hours, long after I left Reon to fulfill my bargain. Long after Solena and Orios departed, and my sister not long after that. Still, the mirror remains the room's gravitational center, its shimmering surface drawing the last few stragglers, each seeing something different in its depths.

Eventually the crowd thins, leaving only one.

I have waited long enough.

I rise, moving through the staggering remnants of the night, indifferent to the drunken bodies that lurch into my path. They are nothing. Only the mirror matters.

I stop before it, the lone viewer oblivious to my presence. Oblivious to the prince of the Mordorin. The commander of the Ebon Flight. The wielder of Death Singer. The favored one.

But of course, none of that matters to a man lost in his own desires. Just as the revelers meant nothing to me, my titles mean nothing to him. He is ensnared, his gaze swallowed whole by the mirror's promise.

From behind the male, I see nothing. Not what he sees. Not what I need. Only the tarnished surface of the mirror.

I must get closer.

I must move him.

I set a firm hand on his shoulder, but he doesn't flinch. Doesn't so much as breathe in acknowledgment.

My fingers tighten. I step forward.

"You must move," I say, my voice edged with command. No patience. No politeness.

Still, he stays.

For a moment, I wonder... is he truly lost? Or does he dare to ignore me? Either choice will end poorly for him.

I lean in, my lips near his ear. "Move. Now. Or I will move you myself. You do not want that."

A breath of silence.

Then, in a snap of motion, he turns his head and what I see is not Fae.

The face before me is gray, hollow-cheeked, its skin stretched too thin over bone. Bulging, glassy eyes roll in their sockets, unfocused and wild. A mouth, dry and cracked, splits open to reveal rows of razored teeth. It hisses, then screeches, a jagged, unnatural sound, and lunges at me with gnarled claws.

Smoke curls instinctively at my fingertips. The void stirs, waiting, whispering the promise of Death Singer. But I do not draw it. Not yet. Not unless her life depends on it.

Instead, I strike.

My hand snaps to its throat, closing around the sinewy column. The creature writhes, clawing at my wrist, but I do not loosen my hold. I squeeze.

And then... it changes.

The monstrous features ripple, distorting. The bulging eyes recede. The jagged teeth dull and shrink. The sallow, corpse-like skin flushes, softening back into something familiar. Something Fae.

By the time I release him, he is gasping, staggering backward, his chest rising and falling in ragged desperation.

I watch him, my gaze cutting over his form, then flicking back to the mirror. I have always known its power, the way it can ensnare, consume, devour. But this? *This* I have never seen.

A soul so lost that it forgets itself entirely.

The male collapses at my feet.

"Leave," I command.

He nods weakly, his body shaking as he staggers from the room. He does not look back at the mirror, though I can see the battle warring in his eyes, the desperate pull of whatever he saw. He folds into himself as he stumbles through the doorway, a broken thing, sobbing.

I turn to the mirror, and doubt flickers like a cold ember behind my eyes. What if I become lost as he did? I like to think myself stronger, immune to such enchantments. But the House of Taramethos is wise and wicked, their power of creation unrivaled, their methods unknown. That secrecy is what makes their artifacts so coveted and so feared.

I step closer, my eyes half-lidded, as if only offering a sliver of myself to its call. The mirror's tarnished surface remains still, unremarkable, reflecting nothing more than my own face at first. But then, subtle as a breath, the image shifts.

The room behind me is not the one I stand in. Gone are the velvet-draped settees with their gilded edges, the sweeping tapestries, the grandeur of this forgotten house. In its place, something I know well. A massive hearth, its mantle carved with writhing serpents and grim-faced gargoyles. And above it... a painting.

A Fae female, her flowing gown gathered over the gentle swell of her belly.

I swallow hard. My pulse trips over itself.

"Mother?"

I step closer. A single step. And it is like plummeting from a great height.

The world shatters.

Shapes blur, colors bleed into a violent swirl. The sounds of the chamber turn hollow, distant, until even my own breath feels impossibly far away.

Then silence.

Darkness, vast and suffocating. The kind that presses in on all sides, black as the void itself.

For one brief, breathless moment, I fear that is exactly where I am.

But he is not here.

Gygarth.

I do not feel his presence. His poison.

I inhale slowly, steadying.

In this silence, it is only me and the mirror, and when its surface ripples like disturbed water, I brace myself for what awaits on the other side.

Suddenly I am falling.

Not through space, not through time, but through something deeper. My body remains rooted before the glass, yet my soul is wrenched forward, dragged into the vision with a force that steals my breath.

A sea stretches beneath me, endless and glistening like liquid sapphire. The mirror pulls me across its rolling expanse, faster than the wind, until the waters blur into nothing but streaks of light. Then, without warning, I ascend.

Higher.

Higher.

The air turns thin, crisp, charged with raw magic.

Driftspire.

Its floating isles materialize before me, wreathed in mist and clouds. The vision surges forward, spiraling upward, until at last, it fixes upon a lone tower.

A window.

And within it... Amara.

My heart clenches as I see her standing there, framed by sunlight, her hands cradling her belly.

Our child.

She is radiant, with her waves of hair cascading over her shoulders, her brown skin glistening, almost golden. But her face is solemn, her gaze lost to the horizon, as if she is searching. Yearning.

For me.

Emotion crashes through me. Love, longing, loss, each one sharp as a dagger to the ribs.

I reach out, my fingers trembling as they press to the mirror's surface. It is cold and hard, but still, I touch her. I trace the curve of her cheek, caress the lips I have kissed a thousand times.

She closes her eyes.

I freeze, my breath catching.

Can she *feel* me?

For a moment, a single, aching moment, I allow myself to believe. To hope. To bask in the solace of this stolen closeness.

Then a hand.

Not mine.

It rests gently atop her belly.

My blood turns to ice.

The figure behind her shifts into view.

A shock of pale blond hair. Piercing blue eyes behind a bronze mask.

The Golden Son.

He leans in, his lips hovering near my wife's ear.

No.

He presses a slow, reverent kiss to her temple.

No.

I roar.

The sound rips from my chest, a violent, shattering thing, shaking the very walls of the chamber. The mirror fractures, the image vanishing in an explosion of light and darkness.

I stagger back, my breath ragged, my fists clenched so tightly my nails cut into my palms.

I do not dare look back.

Even the memory of what I saw is agony, raw and festering, a wound torn open too wide to close. The rage coiling inside me is enough to burn this house to the ground, to reduce every stone and artifact to nothing but cinders if it means destroying that fucking mirror forever.

But I am no better than the male before me. I am not immune.

The pull of the mirror is insidious, a force that sinks its hooks deep. Even as fury surges through me, I feel it dragging at my gaze, whispering, calling.

And before I can stop myself, I am standing before it once more.

My hands brace against its cold, molded edges, my breath uneven, my body taut as if awaiting a blow.

But it does not show me Amara or the Golden Son.

Instead, the mirror delivers me elsewhere.

To the cold, darkened halls of Baev'kalath.

Lightning tears open the blackened sky. Thunder roars, rolling like war drums, a relentless beat that matches the crashing of waves against jagged stone.

It is so real. So vivid, I can almost feel the icy rain pelting my skin, seeping into my bones.

Then I find myself in a room, a pulsing blue circle etched into the stone beneath my feet, glowing with a slow, rhythmic throb, as if the very rock is alive.

Voices chant, low and rasping.

Then a scream.

A sound so raw, so desperate, it carves through the solemn thrum like a blade through flesh.

"Calm yourself, Queen Veloria," a voice soothes. "Breathe."

A long, shuddering sob. Another scream, more ragged, more broken.

I lift my gaze, and my breath leaves me in a sharp, brutal exhale.

There she is.

My mother.

Lying upon a stone altar, her body wracked with pain, the same gown I remember from her portrait now soaked in blood.

Cloaked figures surround her. They do not move to help her.

They only watch.

I step forward with urgency, only to slam into an invisible wall. The force of it knocks me back, a blinding snap of magic striking my forehead. I stagger, cursing, my vision swimming. My fingers press against my skin where the unseen barrier struck me.

But the discomfort vanishes when my mother screams again and a blade arcs through the air.

I slam my fists against the barrier as it comes down upon her.

I have seen war. I have seen the ruin left in its wake, human and Fae alike, bleeding out upon the battlefield, their bodies torn, their souls unmade.

But *this... this* I cannot watch.

I do not want this memory.

I wrench my gaze away, my breath ragged, my throat tight with something dangerously close to a sob. The chanting stops, and so does the screaming. For a long, terrible moment, there is only silence.

Then, a sound cuts through it.

Not my mother's voice.

Not a cry of pain.

But the sharp, trembling wail of a newborn.

My heart slams against my ribs. My hands tremble as I force myself to look.

My mother's arms dangle limply over the edge of the altar, fingers pale, lifeless. Her chest does not rise. Does not fall. And in the arms of the cloaked figures, not one child, but *two*.

I do not have time to comprehend it.

Because above them, a darkness swirls. Slow at first, then faster, hungrier.

The void.

The figures retreat, their reverence turning to fear, and within the churning abyss, a pair of burning white eyes lock onto mine.

It is no longer a vision. It is *real*. As real as the rain. As real as the pain.

No.

What have I done?

He *sees* me.

And if he sees me... he can *find* me.

A whisper slithers through the void, low and ancient, curling through my bones, wrapping tight around my lungs like chains. *Daedalus.*

My name, spoken from lips that do not exist.

A cold touch skims my cheek.

I shudder, every muscle in my body locking up as if unseen hands are winding around my throat, my wrists, dragging me closer.

I thrash against it, against the pull of the mirror, against the force sinking its claws into my mind, trying to root me in place.

It takes every ounce of my will, every scrap of strength I possess, to wrench myself free.

The world lurches, and suddenly the vision shatters.

I stagger back, gasping, my chest heaving. The weight of the magic clings to me, whispering my name in the hollows of my mind. My vision swims, my knees nearly buckling, but I force myself to focus, on the room, on the mirror, on the crack now spiderwebbing across its surface.

The magic hums, furious at my escape.

I do not wait to see what happens next.

I turn, storming from the parlor before the mirror can show me anything else.

CHAPTER 14
DAED

That night, sleep eludes me. I wander the moonlit streets of Ballamar, haunted by the visions the scrying mirror forced upon me. Ghosts of desire twisted into nightmares. I should have known better. I had hoped it would show me only what my heart longs for most. All I needed was to think of Amara, to let the warmth she ignites within me guide the way, like a beacon through the dark. Instead, the rot inside me poisoned that beauty, warping it into something else. Because the mirror does not show only dreams. It reveals your deepest fear.

Amara and the Golden Son. His hands on her. On my wife. As if he dares to believe himself worthy of breathing the same air as my queen, let alone touching her skin. My fists tighten, the rage coiling through me like a viper ready to strike. But I cannot lose myself to this fury. The mirror, for all its power, cannot be trusted. Its magic is ancient, wild. Though crafted by the Fae, it bows to no master, answers to no soul. It does not soothe. It does not guide. It only hungers for chaos.

As the sun crests the horizon, bleeding burnt orange across the sky, it strikes me full in the face, dragging me back to the present. I have lost time. Again. Another fruitless errand, another night wasted, and I am no closer to Amara. The mirror may have revealed Driftspire, but not where to find it. The city in the sky remains a phantom, offering no hint of where it hovers and I do not dare test the mirror again.

Because the Golden Son coveting my wife is not the only nightmare it showed me.

Baev'kalath. The chamber buried deep within the stone. The place where my mother was murdered. Where my sister and I were brought into this cursed world. Where Gygarth took his offering of flesh.

I feel his eyes still on me, searing through my skin, through the wretched soul he has claimed as his own. Again, I try to convince myself it was not real. That Gygarth did not see me in that moment. That the sigils held, and I am still beyond his reach. But his power is infinite. His hunger is boundless. Even a glimpse of the void could be enough.

The sigils. I feel them burned into my back, raw and aching where the fabric of my shirt rubs against the wounds. I must find Solena. She must carve fresh runes.

The inn looms before me, its doors yawning open to the reek of stale ale and unwashed bodies. I push through, stepping over drunks crumpled on the floor, while others slump across the tavern's tables, their snores rattling through the dim room. Up the stairs, down the narrow hall lined with doors, I pass Zyphoro's room and rap my knuckles sharply against the door of Solena and Orios.

No reply. I barely wait for one. Desperation claws at me. I have traveled too far, suffered too much, to let Gygarth take hold of me now.

"Solena. Orios. Are you awake?"

I don't allow time for an answer. I shove the door open, heedless of the consequences.

The bed jerks on its legs, the covers rustling, shifting. Someone, or rather, *someones*, are beneath them, writhing in a tangled mess. The only thing in plain sight is Orios' enormous feet dangling off the end of the mattress.

"I'm sorry to intrude," I say, though my tone lacks any true remorse. "I need Solena to check my sigils."

A hushed flurry of whispers. No response.

My brow furrows. "Did you hear me? This is urgent."

After a long pause, Solena's breathless voice finally emerges from beneath the covers.

"Yes, Rook. I will be out in a moment."

More rustling follows, then a furious whispered hiss. "*Stop that!*"

I stiffen. "Excuse me?"

"Not you. I mean... nothing... just...please, I'll be right out."

My eyes narrow at the strange, shifting bulge beneath the blankets, writhing like a sack of trapped serpents.

I grip the edge of the blanket and give it a sharp tug, just enough to expose Orios on the left. His hair tumbles free in a wild, disheveled mane, the dark strands curling over his bare chest. He gulps, knuckles white as he fists the covers, holding them in place with a silent plea for mercy.

"Rook," he stammers, his voice hoarse. "Please, if you... give us a moment."

Before I can respond, Solena pops out on the right, her hair a tangled mess, bare shoulders stark against the sheets. There is no mistaking what I've walked in on. If I weren't so anxious, I might even be amused.

"I'm sorry to have disturbed you," I say at last, genuinely, realizing I've made this far more uncomfortable than necessary. "I'll wait downstairs."

I turn, gripping the door handle to grant them their privacy, but something tugs at my instincts. My spine stiffens. I glance back, eyes narrowing at the bed where Solena and Orios lie, covers clutched to their chests. They are sprawled apart, yet the space between them is not empty.

I pause. Then tilt my head.

"Who is your friend, Solena?" I ask.

Color drains from her face. "My... friend?"

I shift my gaze to Orios. If she is a bad liar, he will be worse.

"Reaper," I say, watching him flinch at the command. "Will you answer me?"

"Yes, Rook," he blurts, then blanches. "I mean...no. I mean..." His eyes dart helplessly to Solena, begging for rescue.

I roll my eyes, already bored. "Fine. I'll find out myself."

I plant a knee on the edge of the bed and grip the covers, but before I can yank them away, a third head bobs up between them.

Zyphoro.

She sweeps a hand through her raven curls, shaking them back from her face, her bare shoulders inked with runes. I thank every god in existence that I stopped myself before pulling the blanket further. There are some things I never need to see.

"Really?" I ask dryly, arching a brow.

Zyphoro shrugs. "They seduced me and I've never been so happy to be proved wrong."

I stare at her. Then at them. Then back again. I have heard nothing more preposterous in my life.

Slowly, I turn to Orios, smirking. "Have a good night, Reaper?"

He doesn't answer. But his burning red cheeks and the reluctant curve of his mouth tell me everything I need to know.

"Well," I sigh, shaking my head. "When the three of you manage to untangle yourselves from whatever *that* is, can we get the fuck out of here? Ballamar has given nothing." My gaze sweeps over them, unimpressed. "To me, anyway."

135

I leave them at last, and the moment the door clicks shut behind me, I swear I hear their collective sigh of relief.

Downstairs, I push aside a slumbering drunk slumped over the bar, claiming his spot without remorse. No bartender in sight. Fine. I help myself to a shot of rum, pouring generously before knocking it back in one sharp motion. The burn scalds its way down my throat, a brief distraction from the rot in my mind.

The tension coiled in my muscles refuses to unwind. My crew had their fun last night, but I find no envy in their indulgences. The fire in my blood is not so easily quenched.

I am a Fae of flesh, of heat and hunger, and I do not deny my nature. I know the sweet relief of a warm body, the way pleasure can be both an escape and a reckoning. I know how it feels to sink into heat, to lose myself in the rhythm of lust until there is nothing left but breath and skin and the fleeting illusion of peace.

But no nameless body can sate me now. No indulgence would be enough. The hunger twisting in my gut is for Amara alone. Only her hands, her mouth, her body, can ease this ache. Only she can unravel me, soothe the rage and the want that has me wound so tight I might snap.

I brace my hands on the bar, breathing deep, willing myself to be still. But stillness is impossible. Not when I burn for her.

I pour another rum, polishing it off quicker than the first, when at last I hear the steady rhythm of boots descending the stairs. I don't need to look up to know it's Zyphoro. She slides onto the stool beside me, one hand tightening the straps of her leather harness while the other helps itself to the bottle of rum.

"Not for a moment do I believe that was their idea," I say, my fingers tightening around the empty glass.

"They seemed eager to prove a point, and I was not about to refuse them," she replies, her tone light. "What's the matter, brother? Jealous I got there first?"

"Watch your tongue, sister," I warn, low and sharp.

She grins, unrepentant. "My tongue has been doing far more than watching. In fact, it's exhausted."

"Then by all means, be silent. It clearly needs the rest."

Her laughter is quiet, a purr of amusement as she swirls the rum in her glass. "I don't doubt the love you have for Amara. It's one of the few things I find admirable about you."

I exhale through my nose, pushing past her jibes. "You are too kind."

"But you'd be a fool to think you are not desired by others," she continues, tossing back her drink in one smooth motion.

I finally glance at her, my gaze narrowing as she slams the glass onto the bar. "What are you talking about?"

"You're not so clueless as to miss the way Solena looks at you."

The scrape of my chair against the wooden floor is sharp as I push back from the bar. "I've heard and *seen* enough from you for one morning, Zyphoro."

"Fine, fine." She raises her hands in mock surrender, though mischief lingers in her smirk. "Forget I mentioned it. Perhaps I'm mistaken."

"You are," I snap, leaving no room for argument. "The bond between Solena and Orios is a strong one. I can attest to that and her runeweaving has been invaluable."

Zyphoro hums, watching me with a knowing glint in her eye. "Indeed, brother. And I'm sure the long hours with your bare, muscled flesh beneath her hands have had no effect on her at all."

I don't reply. I don't indulge her. Zyphoro wants a reaction, craves the sport of getting under my skin. But I won't fill her boredom with easy bait. Not when Driftspire sails the skies above us.

The arrival of Solena and Orios is timely, though neither of them meets my eyes. The air between us turns thick, awkward. I cut through it.

"Let's collect Reon and get back to the ship. This has been a complete waste of time."

"Where is Reon?" Solena asks, her voice quiet, her gaze darting to her boots the second I meet it.

"Hopefully, just where I left him. In Lady Marlayna's bed. I'm in no mood to go searching for him."

By the time we leave the inn, the streets are already alive. Awnings unfurl, shading stalls nestled between the towering sandstone buildings, while a cloudless sky and a blazing sun promise a blistering day ahead.

We weave through the chaos, dodging wagons brimming with fruit and vegetables, sidestepping vendors who bark at us to clear the way as they push wheelbarrows stacked with fresh-caught fish, some still gasping for breath. The desperation in their round, glassy eyes lingers with me long after they vanish into the crowd.

Only the enormous domed estate of House Taramethos and Lady Marlayna stands untouched by the morning frenzy, as if it exists solely in the realm of night, thriving in darkness and abandoned by daylight.

When we climb the steps, we find the door ajar, the menacing guards of the previous night nowhere in sight. A long creak echoes as I push it open, my eyes adjusting from the blinding sun to the ballroom shrouded in shadow. Heavy curtains are drawn, though thin slivers of light break through in places, illuminating the aftermath of excess. The once-vibrant obsidian dance floor lies empty, goblets strewn across the floor, platters abandoned with only a few stray grapes and scraps of last night's indulgence.

But the silence. Gods, the silence.

It is as if we have stepped into a tomb rather than a place where hundreds of Fae had danced, drunk, laughed, and fucked in a decadent display of indulgence.

I glance up the grand staircase, then back at my companions. I signal to Orios, a silent understanding that I will go first, and he will follow. He straightens his shoulders, offering a nod in return. Solena and Zyphoro linger near the entrance as Orios and I ascend.

Still, not a soul in sight. No guards, no lingering revelers slinking away in the harsh light of morning. Only silence. We move deftly, our steps ghosts upon the wooden floor.

We pass the slightly open door of the parlor, and in the sliver of space, I catch the glint of the mirror.

My head snaps away before I can see more. The movement is sharp enough that Orios shoots me a questioning look. I do not offer him an answer. I keep moving, approaching the door where I left Reon to do his work on my behalf.

Again, no guards.

A slow, creeping dread curls through my gut, tingling at my fingertips.

Then a creak. Floorboards shifting beneath a weight that isn't mine or Orios'.

A muffled groan follows.

I press a hand to Orios' chest, halting him.

He turns to me, but I shake my head. A silent command.

Not another step.

But my instincts flare embarrassingly late.

The doors to Marlayna's chambers swing open, revealing Reon on his knees, a gag tied tightly around his mouth. His captors flank him, one with a fistful of his hair, yanking his head back, the other pressing the sharp edge of a sword to his throat.

"Good morning," Lady Marlayna greets, lounging on a chaise, draped in a silk robe, swirling wine in the bottom of her goblet. "For a moment, I thought you wouldn't come to reclaim your friend."

A rush of wind stirs at my back, my instincts screaming just as I glance over my shoulder. More of them. A dozen Taramethos Fae filing in, Zyphoro and Solena in their grasp, each held still by a blade at their throats.

Marlayna sighs, tipping her head back against the chaise. "This feels *too* easy," she muses. "Not that I'm complaining, but I was hoping for more of a challenge. A little struggle. Maybe even a bit of bloodshed." Her gaze flicks lazily toward me.

"Here, in this human world, we Fae can do as we please. No punishment. No consequences and I must admit..." She smiles, slow and sweet, the kind of smile that curdles the air between us. "I have done truly *horrible* things to the people of Ballamar in the name of boredom."

My fingers twitch at my sides.

"In the Sundered Kingdoms, under House Mordorin, we wouldn't have dared step a toe out of line. We all knew the punishment the Mordorin prince would exact on those who displeased him." She exhales wistfully. "Another thing I miss, I suppose." Then, a sigh. A shrug. "What a disappointment."

I grind my teeth, the rage barely caged behind them. *Careful.* One wrong move, and Reon, Solena, Orios Zyphoro are all dead.

"This is unnecessary," I growl, forcing steel into my voice. "We mean you no harm. I did not come to exact *any* punishment. I only wanted the mirror, and I met the terms of our bargain."

Marlayna's languid gaze drifts over Reon's bare torso, and my stomach twists. Bruises bloom across his fair, freckled skin, scratches raking down his ribs. One eye is swollen and darkening, his lower lip split, a smear of dried blood crusting at the corner of his mouth.

"I had rather hoped to know what a Mordorin prince felt like between my thighs," Marlayna muses, dragging a finger along the rim of her goblet, "but your substitute proved to be an... *enthusiastic* bedmate."

Reon's jaw clenches, his nostrils flaring, but he says nothing. Marlayna takes a sip of her wine, savoring the taste with a smack of her lips before lifting her gaze back to me.

"But I've decided I desire more from our arrangement. A husband."

My brow furrows. "You wish to marry *Reon*?"

139

Marlayna laughs, rich and honeyed, and even in his perilous predicament, Reon frowns at her amusement.

"You, Daedalus," she purrs, her smile curling like a cat's tail. "I want *you*. We will return to the Sundered Kingdoms as king and queen."

Now it's *my* turn to laugh, sharp and cold, and for the first time, Marlayna looks foolish.

"And what kingdom do you think we'll return to?" I ask, voice laced with quiet mockery. "The Sundered Kingdoms is in chaos. The human rebellion holds the mainland. The thrall houses of Mordorin squabble amongst themselves. Half of them remain loyal to me. The rest would rather see me dead than welcome me home." I tilt my head. "You think returning with a Taramethos traitor who fled the war on my arm will change anything?"

Marlayna's confidence falters, just a flicker, a single heartbeat of hesitation, but I see it.

"I have enough warriors of Taramethos to *force* them to kneel," she snaps, though the bite in her voice is dull, worn down to little more than a chew.

I let my gaze sweep across the room, across her so-called warriors.

"Fae they may be, but if all they have done these long years is torment the fruit vendors and fishermen of this shithole, I doubt they will be much of a match for what awaits them across the Untold Sea."

Marlayna's lips press into a thin line, but I see the crack in her poise, the way her nails dig into the silk of her robe.

"Do *not* underestimate me, Daedalus," she hisses. "Rourke underestimated me to his peril. You will do as I command."

And that is her fatal mistake.

"You *dare* spit orders at *me*?" The words leave me in a low, rumbling growl, curling through the stale air like a storm on the verge of breaking.

"You *dare* think yourself worthy to stand at my side?" I step forward, and the shadows at my feet slither in response.

"You *dare* believe you are beautiful enough to capture my eye?" My voice darkens, and so does the room.

"You *dare* think yourself *strong enough* to tame my heart?"

The last sliver of light is swallowed as the darkness rushes in.

I can taste their fear, sharp, metallic, intoxicating. The air hums with it, thick and suffocating, pressing in from all sides. I hear the hard swallows, see the way their skin prickles beneath the weight of what dwells inside me. It surges hot and feral through my veins, something I have fought to keep buried for so long. Too long. The darkness of the void, the immeasurable power, the sheer exhilaration of walking hand in hand with death. Of being its master.

Smoke unfurls from my fingertips, shadows curling, waiting, pleading for release.

"You are not her," I breathe, my vision laced with darkness. "You will never be her."

"Daedalus." Solena's voice reaches me as if from a great distance, though she stands just behind me. A beat. A sharp inhale. Then firmer, more urgent. "Rook." A snap of my name, meant to pull me back. "Don't. He will find you."

I know what she means. I know what she fears. But the hunger, the need, is too strong. The power sings to me, calls me home. For the briefest of moments, I consider giving in. Consider letting it consume me. The freedom of it. The raw, unrelenting force of what I am.

Across the room, Marlayna rises from her chaise, every movement controlled, every inch of her fighting to maintain composure. But I see the flicker in her eyes, the swallow that betrays her fear.

"Very well then," she murmurs, voice carefully measured even as her throat bobs. "If you will not see reason, then I will take your head back to the Sundered Kingdoms instead and claim your throne for myself."

My chin dips, and a low, mocking chuckle spills from my lips.

"No, Lady Marlayna," I murmur. "The only thing claimed today will be your soul."

Marlayna's cry rings out like a bell of war. "Kill them!"

Steel glints in the dim light as Reon's captors move to sever his throat, but they are far too slow.

Darkness uncoils from my fingers like serpents, striking with ruthless precision. One Fae is ripped from his feet, sent crashing into the wall with a sickening crack, his body crumpling like discarded parchment. The other barely has time to blink before the tendrils latch onto his wrist. A sharp pull, a wet, tearing sound. His sword arm is severed at the elbow, the blade clattering uselessly to the floor as a spray of crimson arcs through the air.

The blood splashes across Marlayna's face, staining her silk robe in violent reds. She gasps, stumbling back, her perfect features twisted in a grotesque mask of horror. But she doesn't remain still for long.

I watch, frozen, as the blood splattered across Marlayna's chest writhes unnaturally, like it has a life of its own. It hardens into jagged crimson needles, and with a deafening scream, they rip through the air toward me, faster than I can conjure a shield of smoke to protect myself. The deadly projectiles are mere inches away when time suddenly shudders to a halt.

My gaze locks onto Reon, still kneeling on the floor, his captor's blood staining his freckled face. His hands tremble as he molds a golden orb of glittering light, and as his power warps time, everything around us slows, becomes a blur, while we remain untouched by the suspension of reality.

Zyphoro and Solena slip from their captors' reach. The soldiers stand paralyzed, reduced to trembling, sluggish statues. Blades droop uselessly from their hands as Reon's power drags them down, turning flesh and bone to stone.

"Disarm them, Orios," I command, my eyes still fixed on Marlayna, frozen in the moments before the needle-thin blood can pierce me.

This is what it feels like to be at the mercy of time itself. To know what is coming, to feel its inevitability, but to be powerless to change it. I imagine this is what it is like for Emranth, how he can play with me, slow me, make me feel like a toy in his hands. But Reon's is not as powerful. His power is specific, localized, and fleeting. It won't last long. I can already see the strain in his jaw, his muscles taut as he holds the orb, exerting every ounce of his strength.

I step closer to Marlayna, watching as her eyes water, her breath ragged, each inhale a struggle against the invisible force pressing against her chest. The hunger within me stirs, dark and insatiable. The beast of the void whispers, urging me to take control, to feed.

Orios moves swiftly, peeling back the numb fingers of the Taramethos guards and disarming them.

I tower over Marlayna, watching as her mouth twists with words she cannot speak.

"Pathetic Fae," I growl, my voice guttural. "Your House should have stayed lost. At least then, you would have lived on. But for your vanity... for your disrespect... I will end your line. The name Taramethos will be forgotten by time, and you, Lady Marlayna, will be remembered by no one."

I lean in close, my breath hot against her ear, my voice dripping with venom. "His teeth will be the last thing you see before they devour you."

"Rook," Orios calls from behind me. "What should I do with them?"

"Kill them. Kill them all," I command, my voice morphing into a deep, otherworldly resonance. A chorus of a thousand voices that is no longer entirely mine.

Orios hesitates. "Like this? But they cannot fight back."

"Then it will be easy," I snap, my eyes dark with fury.

I close my hand around Marlayna's throat, smoke weaving through my fingers, as Death Singer calls to me. It has been too long since I've felt its weight, since I've heard the dark hum of its power vibrating through my veins. But this time, the darkness that fills the room is not just the shadows I summon.

My eyes roll over black as I feel the steel solidify in my hand, the familiar coldness of the blade taking shape, the power thrumming through my fingertips.

House Taramethos stands frozen, their helpless eyes pleading, but their fate is already sealed.

CHAPTER 15
DAED

I've spent too long fighting it. Too long holding back the darkness that rages inside me. My body is a shell, worn and battered, every muscle aching with exhaustion, every bone heavy with the weight of restraint. My mind is unraveling, hanging by a thread so thin, I can barely keep my grip. But I've done it for her.

For Amara.

Everything is for Amara.

I've lived in the shadows of this torment because I promised I would. Because I swore I would hold onto what little control I have left, even if it means suffocating the part of me that craves the release, the freedom. I've searched for her in every corner of this broken world, but she is always just out of reach, slipping through my fingers like sand. Maybe... maybe she doesn't want to be found. Maybe she has moved on, leaving me to wallow in the darkness of my own making.

And it's maddening.

The ache in my chest grows, the emptiness gnawing at my insides. I can feel the darkness creeping in, filling the cracks in my fractured mind. It calls to me, tempting me with the release I crave. And for just a moment, I wonder, what if I had given in that day when I had the chance to end her life in the forest?

Would it have been better? Would I be free of this endless longing?

The thought haunts me, but before I can linger on it, the anger boils over, sharp and bitter, and I curse her in my mind.

This love... this twisted, suffocating love.

It torments me more than anything else in this world, dragging me deeper into madness with every passing day. If only I had never known her, never felt her warmth, never let myself believe that something beautiful could exist in the midst of the ruin I've made of my life.

But I am weak. I always have been. And I let the need for her consume me.

As the darkness wraps its cold fingers around my heart, the world tilts, spinning out of control. I feel it. My sword is heavy, but I've lost all sense of where it should go and in that moment, as the darkness pulls me under, I feel a sharp, searing pain shoot through me.

I blink, eyes blurry, and the world comes back into focus.

The sword is not where it should be. It's not buried in Marlayna's chest as I intended, not sending her to the void as I had planned. No... the blade is embedded in my own side, the crimson flow staining my hands as the pain flares and my breath catches in my throat.

I've done it again. I've failed.

I've fallen to the darkness within me, and now it's too late.

"Daedalus!" Zyphoro's voice is numb to my ears like a scream underwater.

My hand slips from around Marlayna's throat as I stumble backwards, as Death Singer dissolves into smoke in my grasp, but I fall into my sister's arms before I can hit the floor.

"You stupid fool," she hisses at me as my hands press down on my wound, blood gushing between my fingers.

The world around me is a blur of shadows and pain, the darkness clawing at my vision as the stab in my side sends waves of agony through my body. The golden orb of Reon's power flickers dimly, sputters like a dying flame, its grip on time beginning to slip as my consciousness wavers.

Suddenly the armless guard's scream, long trapped in frozen silence, erupts with bone-chilling volume. It shatters the quiet tension that hangs over the room, ripping through the air like a whip. His mouth opens wide, but his voice is like the tearing of fabric, raw and violent. The sound itself seems to crack the spell, and in an instant, everything comes rushing back.

Solena, caught off guard, is tackled to the ground by one of the reanimated guards, her shocked cry barely leaving her lips as his body slams into hers. Her hands go instinctively to defend herself, but she's overwhelmed, pinned beneath the weight of the male's armor-clad form. Her breath is crushed out of her, and she fights, desperate to regain her footing.

The other Fae guards, once frozen in Reon's time-bind, spring into motion. They are swarming, their movements swift. Without their weapons in their hands, the Taramethos art of transmutation does not leave them defenseless for long. They bend, reshape, and forge new weapons from the very essence of their surroundings.

One of the guards raises his hand, palm outstretched, and in a flash of fiery magic, the floor beneath him splinters, fragments of stone shooting upward. With a snap of his fingers, the jagged shards twist and meld into a spear as he swings it at Orios.

Without as much as a glance, Orios' thick arm raises to defend himself, catching the spear in its swing, his teeth grit as it impacts but he does not move an inch. Another guard, a lithe figure with silver hair, flicks his wrist, and the leather straps of his armor ripple and shift. Within seconds, the straps have morphed into a long whip. It lashes out, seeking Orios' neck, but instead he fists its end then winds it around his wrist over and over, dragging the guard closer while still grasping the spear in his other hand.

Both Taramethos Fae go pale with panic as Orios steps forward, his massive frame holding them at bay. Muscles straining, he lets out a low, guttural growl.

Then he moves. Fast.

He grabs the whip-wielding guard and yanks him across the room, pulling him close enough to drive his forehead into the male's nose with a sickening crunch. Blood sprays across both their faces.

Before the guard can recover, Orios tears the whip from his limp hand, spins, and loops it around the neck of the second Fae.

He pulls.

Hard.

The guard claws at the tightening coil, his face shifting from panic to purple, eyes spiderwebbing with red. His spear clatters to the floor a second before his body goes limp.

Orios lets him fall with a heavy thud.

Reon's breath comes in ragged bursts, the golden orb in his palm flickering weakly as the massive Fae guard barrels toward him, weapon raised with a roar.

With a flick of his wrist, the world stutters, then slows.

A single heartbeat stretches impossibly thin. Time bends. The guard's swing freezes midair, his face twisted in a snarl.

Reon pivots. His sword flashes like lightning, slicing through the guard's side with a crunch as the blade bites into armor and flesh.

Time snaps back.

The guard howls in pain, stumbling, but Reon is already moving.

He slows time again, just long enough to duck beneath the guard's wild counterstrike, the blade singing past his head by inches.

In that fleeting breath between heartbeats, Reon drives his sword deep into the guard's abdomen, each motion clean and precise, guided by time itself.

Then, with a gasp, he lets go of the magic. The air crackles as the world resumes its natural pace and the guard collapses. But Reon's strength begins to fail him. His knees buckle. He catches himself, teeth clenched, the last dregs of power slipping through his fingers.

The guard looming over Solena fumbles at his belt, hands trembling until they finally close around a dagger.

Reon's eyes narrow.

He summons the last of his strength, golden sparks barely flickering between his fingers, until one catches, flaring to life.

Time stretches.

The dagger hovers in the air, suspended above Solena's vulnerable form, the guard's face twisted into a vicious sneer, frozen in that final moment.

In the unnatural stillness, Orios moves.

Like a shadow with teeth.

He snatches a fallen sword from the blood-slick ground, then, with a roar that shakes the room, he charges.

The guard doesn't stand a chance.

Orios's blade whistles through the air, cleaving clean through flesh and bone. The head separates from the body, which stumbles once, twice, then collapses. The severed head rolls across the floor, eyes still wide in disbelief.

There's no time to breathe, no time to revel in the kill.

With a growl, Orios and Reon turn on the remaining guards. Steel clashes. Flesh yields.

The bedchamber rings with the sounds of violence, and blood stains the floor beneath them, deep and dark and final.

And then, the sound of heavy footsteps reverberates through the hall, voices echoing in the distance. Reinforcements. More warriors. Marlayna's forces are far from depleted.

"We can't fight them all," Reon mutters, eyes flashing toward Orios.

With a shared look, the two of them lunge for the doors, slamming them shut just as the reinforcements reach the threshold. They shove everything they can find against the doors—a dresser, a side table, a stack of velvet chairs—anything to delay the oncoming storm. The wood groans in protest, but the barricade holds... for now.

In the chaos, I lie in Zyphoro's arms, my gaze fixed on the ceiling above, struggling to stay conscious. Her breath hisses through clenched teeth, the tension in her body palpable. She mutters curses under her breath, her fingers tightly laced over mine, pressing harder against the wound in my side, sending waves of pain through me. Meanwhile, Marlayna trembles in the corner, her eyes wide with fear, unable to summon the strength to move.

"We need to get out of here," Reon says, his voice tense as the doors begin to bow under the pressure. "This won't hold long."

Orios lifts Solena onto her feet, his hands cradling her face with surprising tenderness before he presses soft kisses to her brow and chin, a stark contrast to the brutal scene unfolding around us.

"I'm fine, my love," she murmurs, her small hands wrapped around his thick, vein-corded forearms as he looms above her.

"Get up, brother," Zyphoro orders tersely. "We've overstayed our welcome."

With Reon's help, they haul me to my feet, but my legs feel like lead beneath me. I stumble, and they catch me again, Reon throwing my arm over his shoulder.

"Get your shit together," he scowls. "I didn't cross an ocean and get syphilis twice, just to have you die before we've even found your sweetie."

Orios strides past us, heading to the window, his massive hands gripping the curtains and tearing them down. The sunlight floods the room, blinding and stinging like fire on my skin. Zyphoro steps back, and even through the pain, even in my weakness, I flinch when Reon goes to sweep me into his arms.

He frowns, sensing my hesitation at being scooped up like some helpless damsel.

"I get no pleasure from this either," he drawls.

"What do we do with her?" Zyphoro asks, her gaze fixed bitterly on Marlayna.

I'm too weak to form the words, but Solena speaks up instead, her voice venomous and unforgiving. "Leave her. She is nothing. Her house is nothing."

But Solena's words fall on deaf ears.

In a blink, Zyphoro moves, a flash of smoke and steel, and her dagger finds its mark, plunging deep into Marlayna's heart.

The Lady of Taramethos gasps, her lips parting soundlessly as disbelief freezes her features. For a heartbeat she stands trembling, eyes wide and glassy, before Zyphoro twists the blade. A sharp, shuddering breath escapes Marlayna's throat. Then she slips from the steel's edge and crumples to the floor.

Zyphoro wipes the blade on the leather of her trousers with casual indifference, as if the act were little more than an afterthought. "You feared punishment from a Mordorin prince. Perhaps it is the princess you should have concerned yourself with." Her eyes meet mine, and I glimpse something dark behind them. "Vengeance served, brother."

Despite my protests, Reon lifts me up with less effort than I'd hoped, and Orios, without a word, raises his boot and kicks the glass from the windowpane. The shattering sound echoes in the room as Reon steps onto the ledge, staring out across the sandstone rooftops of Ballamar. For a moment, he simply breathes in the air.

Then, with a single step, we plummet. The wind roars around us as we fall toward the bustling streets stories below. Gravity drags us down until, with a powerful beat of his copper wings, Reon catches the air. We soar upward, climbing higher into the sky, the wind rushing past us, sending dust and dirt swirling through the streets.

Zyphoro, Solena, and Orios follow close behind, the wind carrying us swiftly toward *The Shattered Edge*, its dark sails billowing where it lies anchored. Reon's landing is anything but graceful, his footing falters under my weight, a grunt slipping from his lips, but he manages to stay upright.

"Bring him below deck," Solena commands as she touches down in a seamless, fluid motion, wasting no time before storming toward the cabin door. She throws it open, and Reon obeys without question, hauling me down the narrow steps before laying me across the familiar smoothness of the table.

Zyphoro and Orios linger in the doorway, their forms blocking the light, but Solena turns on them before they can step inside.

"All of you. Out," she barks, her glare daring them to defy her. "If I need help, I will ask for it."

My vision swims, but I catch the smirk playing at Zyphoro's lips and the heavy sag of Orios' shoulders before Reon shuts the door behind them.

Solena moves fast, her fingers ripping open my shirt without hesitation, exposing the wound beneath. She doesn't flinch. Doesn't hesitate.

"What were you thinking?" she hisses, grabbing a nearby rag. "As if you do not already have enough enemies eager to see you dead, you decide to take matters into your own hands?"

"I do not deserve to live," I mutter, my voice hoarse. "Not after what I've done to Amara. Not after the pain I've caused her."

The sharp clang of glass and metal fills the space as Solena roughly rummages through a shelf, ensuring I hear every scrape and clatter.

"So this is your penance?" she scoffs, her voice laced with biting disapproval.

I turn my head away, unwilling to meet her eyes, unwilling to answer. Then, the sound I do recognize. A slosh of liquid in a bottle. A second later, warmth splashes against my torn flesh.

A fresh pain tears through me, and I suck in a hard gulp of air, gritting my teeth as the burn spreads deep into the wound.

"If you were truly so wracked with guilt, you would have skewered something vital," Solena remarks, far too unimpressed for my liking. She tips the bottle again, letting another generous pour of rum wash over me. "You didn't even hit an organ. This is little more than a flesh wound."

I squeeze my eyes shut as she presses a cloth against my side, not bothering with delicacy as she binds it tightly with whatever rags she can find, cleanliness be damned.

"What would Amara think if she knew you had done something so incredibly stupid?" she demands.

"I don't know what came over me," I admit, exhaling shakily. "For a moment, I thought I was doing her a kindness."

Solena doesn't soften. If anything, her expression darkens. "Not just throwing yourself on your sword like an idiot," she snaps, her hands pausing for only a second. "You summoned Death Singer from the void." Her gaze drills into me, searching. "Did he see you?"

Regret rises thick and acidic in my throat. I stare at the ceiling, my chest tight. "I do not know."

Solena shakes her head, disappointment cutting almost as deep as the wound. "On your stomach," she orders. "I'll draw more sigils. Just in case."

I shift, but pain lances through my ribs, sending stars bursting behind my eyes. A groan slips out before I can stop it.

Solena, unsurprisingly, offers no sympathy.

"That's what happens when you stab yourself," she snaps. "I'll mix the ink. Be on your stomach by the time I'm ready."

I bite down on my lip, my canines nearly piercing the skin as I force my battered body onto my stomach with one final, agonizing roll. A sharp breath hisses through my teeth, but I make no sound beyond that. I lie still, my body pressed against the cool surface of the table, waiting for Solena's return as she continues her scolding, relentless words that blur in my ears, fading beneath the rush of blood pounding through my skull.

Then, another voice cuts through.

"Favored son," it whispers. *"So long have you been unseen by his eye. But not now. We see you."*

A slow, slithering dread knots in my gut. My eyes burn, red and sore, and at first, I tell myself it's nothing, just exhaustion, a trick of my blurred vision. But then I see it. A black speck, flickering in the periphery, shimmering like heat off distant dunes. I squeeze my eyes shut, willing it away, but when I open them, the darkness is still there.

Larger. Expanding.

The blackness unfurls, stretching wide until it is no longer a speck but a fathomless abyss so absent of light, so empty of hope, it can only be one thing.

The void.

And within its pitch-dark depths, something stirs.

A glint of pale white cuts through the darkness. An eye, enormous and all-seeing, unblinking in its endless hunger. And below it, a clawed hand, its fingers impossibly long, reaching.

"Come home, favored son," the voice beckons, dark and sweet as a hymn. A call that slides into my bones, curling around my ribs. *"It is time to feed the beast."*

A sharp clatter rips through the air. A bowl of ink spilling onto the floor, the thick black liquid pooling at the table leg.

Before my vision is swallowed whole, before my eyes roll over black, I hear Solena scream.

"Zyphoro! Gygarth has found him!"

The door explodes open, wood splintering beneath the force of Zyphoro's arrival. My vision swims, edges blurring, but she moves with lethal grace. Her daggers cut through the air, silver flashing like shards of a dying star. I don't even have time to brace. The air hums, sharp with the promise of steel, and before I can take another breath, before I can blink, my eyes roll over black.

CHAPTER 16

AMARA

There are no dreams.

Only falling.

A slow descent into darkness, weightless yet drowning in silence. Cold presses against my skin until something warm and rough drags across my cheek.

My lashes flutter, awareness drifting back to me in pieces. The damp chill in the air. The faint lap of water against stone. And something beside me.

A shadowed form shifts, smoke given flesh.

Ashen.

He hovers just above me in his kitten shape, his body unfurling and curling like mist caught in a breeze. His ivory-bright eyes watch me before he gives another slow swipe of his tongue across my cheek.

I manage a smile. My fingers lift weakly, threading through the drifting strands of his fur, warm despite its insubstantial, smoky form. He leans into the touch, his ever-shifting body curving around my hand, as though relieved to find me whole.

Slowly, the world stitches itself back together. Sound, breath, thought. My mind sharpens, pulling itself from the fog. And then I realize. If Ashen is here... where am I?

My gaze drifts to the bars encasing us, to the dim, flickering gloom of the cave beyond.

I bolt upright, the last remnants of sleep vanishing in an instant. My hands fly to the bars, gripping them, shoving against them. But the moment I do, I feel the snap of my chain, dragging me to the center of the cage with such force I nearly fall.

Ashen growls at my side, the sound low and rumbling. His body expands, shadows rippling over muscle and sinew as he grows. He presses against my legs, anchoring me as the truth crashes in.

We're in his cage suspended above the lake. The cavern swallows the sound of my breath as confusion claws up my throat.

Then I hear something, see something in the shadows, and my gaze darts beyond the bars, straining to see past the thick shroud of darkness.

"Who's there!" I demand.

A figure steps forward, emerging from the gloom.

"Calm yourself, Princess."

I know that voice.

But there's a rasp to it now, twisted and raw, so unfamiliar it makes me doubt myself.

Then he lifts his head toward the dim light, and the air rushes from my lungs.

For a moment, I'm certain it's a trick of the dark. A mirage conjured by exhaustion and shadows. But then I see his eyes... one of them. The same eye I've stared into day after day, the eye of my warden.

There's no mistaking him.

"Anethesis," I breathe, the name scraping from my throat like gravel, half disbelief, half fury.

His once-flawless face is unrecognizable now. A grotesque canvas of scorched flesh and twisted sinew, like wax left too close to flame. One eye is fused shut, a warped ridge of scar where it used to be. The other, untouched, unchanged, glints in the dark like a shard of jade. His golden hair, once long and regal, is gone. Only uneven stubble remains, clinging to the wreckage of what he was.

I choke on a gasp, horror rising in my throat. My stomach lurches, a sick twist of revulsion and shock.

"What..." My voice falters. "What *happened* to you?"

"You did, Princess." His voice is quiet. "This is your work."

I shake my head, my breath coming hard and fast. "No. That's not true. I would *never*."

"Oh, but you did, and if not for my misfortune..." he gestures vaguely to the melted ruin of his skin, the drooping curve of his mouth, the eye sealed shut by scar tissue. "I must admit, it was... wondrous."

I refuse to believe it. Refuse to let his words take root. That I could have done this.

"How?" My voice is sharp. "I'm shackled. You made sure of that."

He exhales heavily, the sound wet, tinged with a drool he can no longer control. "Ah, well. I am too kindhearted for my own good." His lips pull into something resembling a smile, but it only makes him look more hideous. "I feared for your safety, princess. So I removed your collar."

A cold rush of dread slices through me.

His voice dips lower. "That mistake cost a dozen Ithranor Fae their lives. Burnt to a crisp in a blaze of green fire." His good eye gleams. "Fire you conjured."

"You're lying." The words scrape from my throat, barely more than a whisper. "Another trick."

He laughs, but the sound is wrong. Strangled. Almost painful. "Then it is a trick I've played on both of us. Believe what you will, princess, but know this. I hold you no ill will." His gaze drifts over the bars. "All you have done is prove exactly what we hoped. You are the power we need."

I wrap my arms around myself, resisting the icy fingers of his words.

"But such power must be contained," he continues, tone almost... regretful. "So we've had to increase our precautions. I'm sure you understand."

The question on my tongue is desperate for escape.

"Where is the Golden Son?"

Anethesis studies me curiously. "Do not worry yourself about Ronin. We will not allow him to hurt you again."

"Hurt me?" I let out a short, incredulous laugh. "You and your tests are what slashed me to pieces. What nearly killed me. Not Ro..." I catch myself, my pulse hammering. "The Golden Son."

He inclines his head as if acknowledging his own guilt. "You are right. The last test was... intense."

I let out a bitter breath. "And what if I *hadn't* survived?"

He smiles, and the sight of it curdles my stomach.

"Then we wouldn't be having this conversation," he says lightly, "and we wouldn't be one step closer to returning home." He clears his throat and slurps. "Just one test left."

I jerk at another surge of disbelief. "No." My voice cracks with defiance. "What makes you think I will do anything more to help you after what happened last time?"

Anethesis doesn't flinch. His expression is as cold and calculated as ever. "Because I still possess what you desire most." His words are dripping with cruel confidence. "Your freedom. Even with your power. Even after you incinerated my dear brothers and sisters of House Ithranor. You are still trapped in Driftspire, locked in a cage with a collar around your neck. And that is where your child will be born if you do not finish what we have started."

A torrent of rage builds within me, a chorus of curses and venomous hate burning on the tip of my tongue, desperate to be unleashed. I loathe him. I loathe everything about him. But more than that, I hate that he's right. He has power over me. He wields my child like a weapon, using my very flesh against me. The truth is merciless, and it digs deep into the wound of my pride.

I don't doubt his threat. I don't doubt the lengths he will go to for the one thing he desires most. Who wouldn't? Who wouldn't do whatever it took for what they love?

One last test. One more, and then we will be free. Ashen. Me. My hand brushes over my stomach, where my child stirs. Our child.

My chin dips in silent submission, and the soft, almost satisfied sigh from Anethesis grates on my nerves. At least, I think bitterly, I'm wearing him thin.

"The trial of portals," he says, his voice cold as ice.

He crosses his arms, his hands beginning a mystic dance in the air. A surge of magic rips through the air around me, and suddenly the breath is torn from my lungs as the cage that held me vanishes, dismantling into thin air. I'm left suspended over the lake, floating in nothing.

I twist, searching for Ashen, but he's gone.

I know what this is. Another illusion. Another one of his cruel tricks. Like all the tests before.

The world shifts beneath me without warning. One moment, I am suspended in the air, and the next, the surface of the lake rushes toward me. But when I land, there is no splash, no soft embrace of water. Only the unforgiving impact of solid earth.

I glance around, my heart pounding, then, without warning, several closed doors appear out of the blackness like apparitions.

The stillness of this place is unnerving, and a sense of urgency pulses through me. If this is anything like the previous test, I know that I cannot stand still for long. Not without deadly consequences.

I move toward the first door cautiously, every step a whisper against the hard ground. My hand hovers above the handle. The moment my fingers close around it, pain lances through my body. It's not physical, not exactly, but it feels as though my very soul is being pulled from my body. I gasp, releasing the handle instantly, but the sensation lingers, scorching through my chest, crawling up my spine.

I bite back the scream rising in my throat.

My hands have never been the instruments in these trials. It has always been my mind, the sharp edge of thought, not the blunt force of touch. The realization strikes, swift and brutal. These doors were never meant to be opened with hands.

My eyes snap back to the door in front of me. I concentrate, forcing my mind to focus, to hone in on the task that stands between me and freedom. The words are unspoken, but my thoughts are clear. *Open.* I picture the door swinging wide, my will the force that moves it.

The moment I do, the air changes, power surges through me and the door flies open with a deafening crack, the sound of splintering wood echoing in the hollow dark. The darkness that had been closing in on me halts, frozen for a heartbeat, and then, with a violent burst, the other doors explode into silver dust, swirling away into nothing.

I stand motionless at the threshold, the open doorway yawning like a wound in the world. Something inside calls to me, whispering dark promises with every breath of stale air. My chest tightens as I take a cautious step forward, gaze locked on the abyss beyond. The air ripples with malevolence, pressing against my skin. Then, without warning, a hand of pure shadow lunges from the darkness, its fingers slick and inky, curling around my throat. I choke, scratching at the thing as it tightens, twisting until my breath is no longer mine to take.

Suddenly, a wave of winged creatures bursts from the doorway, their screeching cries splitting the air. Their wings flutter in a frenzy, and their black eyes gleam with hunger. The swarm grows, multiplying as they rush toward me, closing in from every side.

I scream, but no sound comes out. The hand around my throat tightens again, dragging me toward the void. My body thrashes in its grasp, but the darkness is too strong.

And then, suddenly, everything stops.

The hand vanishes, and the creatures, all of them, disappear into the shadows, swallowed by the swirling blackness. A gasp escapes my lips, and I fall to my knees, the sudden absence of pressure in my chest like the first breath after being underwater for too long.

The void is gone. The creatures are gone. The sensation of being dragged toward the darkness fades as quickly as it had come.

I blink rapidly, trying to clear my vision, the taste of fear still sharp in my mouth. My hands tremble as I reach up to touch my throat, feeling the bruises left behind by the shadow's grip. But when I look around, it's not the endless dark I see. Instead, I'm back in the cage.

The illusion. It's over.

Still, I feel the phantom touch of the shadow's hand on my throat, the screeching creatures in my ears, and the overwhelming dread that follows me now, clinging to me like a second skin.

Ashen curls against me, his warmth a silent comfort, grounding me in the midst of this chaos. I hold him close, drawing strength from his steady breathing, but in the stillness of the cave, a sound breaks through. Soft, hesitant, barely audible at first. A sob.

Anethesis.

I freeze, my heart lurching as I hear him. His voice trembles, raw with emotion.

"Princess," he struggles to find the words. "You cannot possibly know the magnitude of the gift you grant us. We are so very thankful."

I exhale slowly, the breath leaving me in a quiet, bitter sigh. My gaze drags up from the cold floor of the cage to meet his. His one good eye is wide, glazed with what might be gratitude, but it isn't enough to move me.

"We are done then," I say, my voice hoarse but steady. "I am free now?"

"There is a last task," Anethesis responds. "The final portal home, and then your work is done. You will be set free."

"When?" I demand, my throat tight with a desperate need for answers.

"Soon," he answers, his tone distant, almost reluctant. "We must ready ourselves for what comes."

The words are like a slap, sending a chill through me that has nothing to do with the cold of the cage. What comes? I stagger to my feet, my legs unsteady beneath me, and I lurch toward the bars of the cage, gripping them so tightly my knuckles whiten.

"What do you mean? What is to come?" I grit out, my voice breaking.

But Anethesis doesn't respond. Instead, his fingers move in their familiar, graceful dance, the air around him stirring. With a fluid motion, he rises from the ground, weightless, the very air bending to his will. I watch, powerless, as he ascends, his figure fading into the black abyss of the cave

"Anethesis!" I scream, my voice a ragged echo in the silence, but he doesn't answer. He doesn't even glance back. "You promised!" I shout, but the words are swallowed by the emptiness.

Slowly, the heat drains from my limbs, and I collapse, sliding down the bars to crumple upon the floor. My body trembles with the weight of exhaustion, the anger, the confusion. My hands still grip the bars, my knuckles aching with the pressure, as if holding on to something, anything, will keep me from losing myself entirely.

Have I truly been such a fool?

Falling for another Fae bargain.

I press my forehead to the bars, closing my eyes as I try to stifle the bitter laugh that rises in my throat. This will never be over. It can't be. Not with him. Not with any of them. They take what they want, they break you, and then they disappear into the shadows until they're ready to take more.

I feel it deep in my bones, knowing that Anethesis will take far more than I ever imagined. My freedom, my soul, maybe even my child. And I... I will have no choice but to give it to him.

I don't know how many days pass in the cage. The world outside is a blur of darkness, no sunlight to mark the passage of time, no moonlight to guide me. The only certainty is the stillness, and the occasional drip of water, echoing through the vast emptiness. It is haunting, relentless, as if the very air is too heavy to breathe.

The food they give me is delivered with the same cold detachment. I never see their faces, not that I care to. The wind carries it to me, like scraps tossed to a wild animal, meant to keep me alive but never treated as anything more and yet, I devour it with a hunger that feels beyond me, a gnawing need that has nothing to do with my own body. The baby inside me demands it.

When I ask for more, they never refuse me. They may view me as nothing more than a means to an end, but they need me alive, need me well. I know this. I feel it in the weight of their eyes, watching from the shadows.

But food doesn't satisfy Ashen.

I feel him weakening. Each passing day carves something out of him, and my heart aches with every breath he struggles to draw. Sometimes, when he's too tired to hold himself together, my hand slips right through him. There's a cruel comfort in the certainty that, if nothing else, we'll go together. All of us.

A soft kick presses against the inside of my belly and despite the weight of dread anchoring me, a smile tugs at my lips.

On another day or another night, I'm not sure which, I sit in my cage, the hours stretching on in a dull, endless haze, when I hear a sudden crack from below. I jerk upright, and my gaze drops to the darkness beneath me. There's nothing there at first, just the glimmer of the water's surface, reflecting the faintest hint of light.

Then, a hand grips the bar, sending a jolt through my chest.

Another hand appears, followed by a shimmer of bronze.

"You," I snap as I meet the blue eyes of the Golden Son. "What are you doing here?"

I glance down through the bars and see the air pooling at his feet as he levitates next to the cage, the ink of his Ithranor rune peeking from beneath his sleeve.

"I'm getting you out of here," he says.

I let out a dry laugh. "Are you now?"

He nods slowly, seeming equal parts confused and offended by my response.

I shake my head, crossing my arms over my chest. "I do not need your help."

"I know, but you will receive it, anyway."

I scoff. "For someone so eager to help, you have taken your time. Where was this help when they threw me in this cage?"

"I couldn't stop them. If they hadn't dragged me away from you when they did, I'd be ash like the rest of them."

I glare at him. "What a shame."

He exhales harder this time, shoulders rising and falling. "I'm trying to make this easier."

"Why?" I snap.

"Because we shared a past. A torment. A memory, you and I," he says, low. "And I thought..."

"Don't think," I cut him off. "Not for a second. You and I are *not* the same. You're a murderer."

My gaze drops to the red ribbon around my wrist. The memory bites.

But instead of silence or shame, he laughs. A mirror of my own cruelty.

"Oh, but we *are* the same, Amara," he says. "Yes, I have killed. But so have you. When you summoned your beasts. When your husband cut through my men like animals. You weren't innocent that day. There's blood on both our hands."

He grips the bars tighter, his face pressed against the cage, his mask scraping the steel.

"Those were my brothers. My sisters. My Legion. Some I'd known since we were children. Some ran barefoot from the fire in Rethmar, like I did. Don't think for a second you were the only one who lost someone that day. We were just fighting on different sides."

"And nothing has changed," I say, curt and cold.

"Really?" he replies, tilting his head as though trying to see through me. "Did you not try to heal me? Is that something you do for your enemies?"

I snort. "Unfortunately, yes. From time to time. It is my weakness."

"No," he says gently now, his head shaking. "It is your goodness. That has become... clearer to me these past weeks."

I don't like the way he looks at me. Eyes too soft. Voice too warm. I prefer him cruel. Condescending. The version I can hate without guilt. The version I can imagine strangling across a table without hesitation.

"I know what the Ithranor have planned," he continues, his voice steadying, the exhaustion momentarily forgotten. "I know exactly what they need from you."

"The portal," I say, my tone sharp, unwilling to be fooled. "It is the price for everything. Perhaps even what you bargained with them for."

He nods, and his eyes dim like the sun slipping behind a cloud. "The Sundered Kingdoms. The throne. House Ithranor will turn the tide of this war. We'll defeat the Mordorin. Once and for all."

"That's what you desire?"

He doesn't answer at first. Just stares. Lips parted. Words caught on the edge of his breath. His gaze pins me, sharp enough to make me blink first. I look away.

"Yes," he murmurs. "That's what I desire. It is what my brother died for."

"Then enjoy it while it lasts," I say, voice tightening. "Because when I'm reunited with Daed, we will..."

"There will be no reuniting, Amara," he cuts in, the words spilling from him like a cracked goblet pouring water.

I frown. "We cannot be apart. Daedalus and I..."

"Yes, you can." His voice sharpens. "And you will. If you open that portal."

His eyes drift upward, his jaw clenched. When he finally forces the next words out, they scrape.

"You're not meant to survive it, Amara."

A short, stunned laugh escapes me. Disbelief. Another lie, surely. But when I search his face, I find no deception.

Only regret.

And when he realizes I see the truth written there, he nods.

"You've been tested," he says. "To see how long you can last. How much pain your body can take. They need you to stay alive, just long enough to keep the portal open. Long enough to bleed you dry."

I shake my head fiercely. "If I open the portal, he promised we'd be released."

The Golden Son's shoulders draw tight. He inhales like it hurts. "He didn't mean your freedom."

My chin falls. Water wells behind my eyes, the weight of it makes everything blur. My hand drifts to my swollen belly.

A kick. Small, but there.

"But my baby..."

"They want to return to Meranor, Amara," he says. "They don't care who dies to make that possible."

These bastard Fae. All of them would see me dead for their own power. Their greed.

I may be able to see through their glamors, but I am still so blind.

Blind to their finely tuned deceptions. Their silk-spun lies. Their perfectly measured truths. They plot and kill as easily as they breathe, all smiling mouths and silver tongues, hands slick with blood they pretend is wine.

They call it sacrifice. But it is murder.

I glance at the Golden Son, at the shadow crossing his face. At the sorrow in his gaze. It is genuine. Perhaps. But it changes nothing.

"You knew," I whisper, and my voice no longer trembles. "You knew, and you still let me believe..."

"I wanted to tell you."

"But you didn't."

His mouth presses into a hard line. He does not deny it.

I turn my back to him, my fingers curling over my stomach as my child kicks again, stronger this time, as if sensing the storm inside me.

If Daed cannot find me, then I will free myself, for there is one thing the Ithranor cannot bind: my will.

My power was never theirs to use, and I will burn this realm to cinders before I let them harm my child.

Let them lie. Let them plot. Let them come.

Because I'm done being their sacrifice.

It's time I became their reckoning.

I spin on my heel, ready to tear another shred from the Golden Son, but a gust of wind slams through the cavern before I can.

It knocks the breath from my lungs as I'm thrown to the ground. The current barrels past me, shrieking before hurling the Golden Son against the cavern wall.

His body hits with a crack that echoes through the darkness, and he slumps, pinned by nothing but the crushing force of the wind. He groans, straining against it, muscles trembling.

Ashen brushes against me as I sit on the floor of the cage, a low, worried purr vibrating from his chest. I reach for him, stroking his spine to soothe his worry, then I lift my gaze to the mouth of the cavern.

Anethesis drifts toward us, his jaw tight, face twisted in rage.

"Ronin," he says. "I am so very disappointed in you."

He clenches his fist.

The wind crushes harder against the Golden Son, pinning him deeper into the rock. Stone splinters. Rubble rains down into the lake below with heavy splashes. The Golden Son can only groan, helpless beneath the unseen force.

Anethesis sighs. His voice softens, but there's no kindness in it.

"I'm sorry, Princess. I did promise to keep you safe from him."

He clicks his tongue, almost thoughtfully.

"We will have to discipline him. Harshly." A pause. "Such a shame when friendships take an ugly turn."

Before I can demand what that means, Anethesis slices a hand through the air. The wind obeys.

Ronin is ripped from the wall and flung into the distance, vanishing like a discarded thought.

Anethesis bows his head in mock civility. "Rest now, Princess. There is so much to do."

CHAPTER 17

AMARA

I f the Golden Son is right, if the Ithranor truly intend to spill my blood, every last drop, to tear open the portal to their home, then this cage, this cavern, will be the last thing I ever see.

I have proven myself, done as they asked, played the obedient fool. And now I wait. A lamb fattened for slaughter. Even my meals have doubled. Perhaps the only mercy they will grant me. A feast for my final days.

I sink into the cushions of my cage, Ashen curled against me, his smoke-thin body rising and falling with each shallow breath.

The tests may have ended, but Anethesis still comes, as he always does, at the same hour each evening. When the trays are cleared, when the silence is thick enough to suffocate. He makes me recite words whose meanings are lost to me, spoken in a tongue far older than the little Fae I know.

Véthari lios an'thera. Véthari lios an'thera. Véthari lios an'thera.

Over and over, I recite the words. Anethesis insists I must know them as intimately as my own name, that they are not merely spoken but felt, carved into the marrow of my bones.

I submit. Committing to memory the last words I will ever speak. It twists my stomach to see how pleased he is by my obedience. Every time he tells me what a good job I'm doing, I imagine tearing apart what's left of his face.

But I can't let him see the truth. He must believe I'm just another pawn. An unwitting slave to his ambition. It's the only way out. The only way to save my family.

When I am not practicing the words, when it's just me and Ashen, alone in the hush of the cave, I hear him. The Golden Son.

His screams echo from somewhere deep within Driftspire. His torment too constant, too cruel, to be anything but entertainment for whoever holds the reins.

And yet, I cannot bring myself to feel only rage towards him. Not anymore.

I tell myself we are nothing alike, no matter how often he insists otherwise. But it clings to me, that truth hidden in his words. Buried like a splinter I can't quite dig out.

There's been a shift.

Not a softening. Not exactly. But the jagged edges of my hate have dulled, worn down by proximity, by shared pain, by something I don't want to name.

Hatred is clean. Simple. It lives in black and white.

But this, this strange, uneasy tether between us, is a space streaked with gray.

The Fae who set fire to my world burned his too. I've seen the flicker in his eyes, in the way he speaks of what he's lost. And whether I like it or not, he has shown me slivers of kindness, shards of something like respect. As much as someone like him can give, and every time his broken cries find me in the dark, I remember I am the reason he screams.

He found me here. Broke the rules of his allies. He gave me truths when no one else would.

So when I finally figure out how to escape this wretched prison of rock and wind and silence, I wonder if I'll owe him his freedom too.

In our cage, I run my fingers through Ashen's fading form. His drifting smoke reminds me of another who exists in that gray space. Daedalus.

I should only think of holding him again, but part of me aches with the question: Why hasn't Daedalus come for me?

I try not to dwell. The world beyond the Sundered Kingdoms is vast, and I am not easily found. My prison lies high in the clouds. Even so, doubt creeps in.

Then, suddenly, a sharp kick lurches me forward. Another follows, stronger.

Even Ashen flinches as my belly twists, the life inside me not just stirring, but commanding. I feel it in my bones, in my soul. A demand, not a plea.

Do not give in to despair.

I press a hand to my stomach, fingers splayed over taut skin, a living reminder of all I've fought for.

All I've survived.

No, Amara. Guardian of the Grove. Jewel of the Tenders.

You did not endure all of this just to be broken by doubt now.

Not when there is still so much to live for.

Far too much to lose.

A flicker of movement at the cavern's entrance snaps me from my thoughts. My gaze locks on the approaching figure, the shadows barely stirring as Anethesis glides forward.

It must be time.

Time to recite those damned words, again and again, until my throat burns dry and my spirit splinters beneath the weight of them.

As always, he keeps his distance. Never straying too close to the cage.

Does he still fear my fire? The green flames that marked him seared into his memory as much as his skin?

He does not need to worry. I remember nothing. I don't know how I did it, don't know if I could do it again, even if I tried.

And yet, for the first time, he dares to step onto the narrow rock ledge circling the lake beneath me.

"Good evening, princess," he says, dipping his chin in that way of his, always just a sliver of respect, never more. "How was your dinner?"

"Fine," I bite out.

"That is good to hear. I have instructed the cooks to..."

"Véthari lios an'thera." I cut him off.

He steeples his fingers, nodding once. "Véthari lios an'thera."

And so it begins. The same rehearsed ritual. The same exchange, repeated until the words feel like nothing. Until I feel like nothing.

Then, Ashen hisses, his back arching, smoke flickering like firelight along his spine. Anethesis halts mid-step, watching him with thinly veiled disdain.

"What is wrong with... it?"

"With Ashen?" I reply coolly, running a hand down his twitching back. "I imagine he's had enough. Of bargains. Of lies. Of this cage."

Anethesis's lip curls. "Has he now?"

I nod, letting silence bloom between us before I finally speak. "He yearns to be free. To fly. To feed on flesh, down to the bone."

Anethesis' throat bobs with a swallow. "How colorful. Unfortunately for your pet, the collar around his neck makes such appetites... impossible."

I lift my chin. "Yes. The collars. They are a problem. Only you can remove them, I assume?"

165

His gaze narrows. "I crafted the enchantment. Naturally, only I can undo it." A beat. "Your questions concern me, Princess. I hope you're not planning anything foolish. Not after we've come to... trust each other."

A laugh nearly escapes me, but I swallow it whole.

"I wouldn't dream of it," I say with a smile too soft to be sincere. "But what if there were another accident? What if I summoned the green fire again?"

His hand twitches toward his face, fingers hovering near the jagged ridges of his scars.

"You'd have to remove the collar, wouldn't you?" I press. "Or risk me turning this place to ash. Including myself."

Anethesis frowns, suspicion clouding his expression. "It's true. I cannot allow you to come to harm. However, we've learned, haven't we? You have no catalyst. No one to heal. No one to channel your gifts through. Even your beast is more smoke than flesh now."

"That may be," I murmur, watching Ashen's dark form ripple, his body slowly expanding. Tendrils of living shadow coil around my fingers. "There's not enough left of him to heal, but there is far more to me than you understand."

Ashen bares his teeth, the air crackling as he grows. His bellowing snarl cuts through the cavern. I trail a finger along his jaw, then press my wrist to his fang.

A slice of agony. A bloom of blood.

Anethesis takes a startled step forward as crimson drips to the floor.

I breathe through the sting, head lifted.

"Pain," I whisper, feeling it surge inside me, hot, untamed. "Pain is my true gift."

Green light crackles through me, threading like vines beneath the surface, glowing through my veins. My body shudders, spine bowing, as the cut on my wrist seals with a hiss. My magic has always been tied to healing, to life, but now, it's different. Wilder. Hungrier.

And the collar feels it.

The metal tightens like a noose, a searing ring of fire at my throat. I gasp, clutching at it as it burns, branding me from the inside out. Magic clashes with restraint, power with prison and I am the battlefield.

But I do not stop.

I will not be broken.

Anethesis stumbles back, eyes wide with horror as the green glow bleeds from my pores. I hear the fear in his voice now. I see it plain.

"Stop!" he shouts, voice cracking. "You'll kill yourself. You'll destroy everything!"

Good.

Let it burn. Let it all turn to ash.

"Please!" he pleads, stepping forward, hands raised. "You don't understand... if the collar stays on and your power keeps rising..."

"I know exactly what happens," I snarl, power surging again, but I can't ignore how different it feels.

I glance down and my skin is no longer just aglow with emerald. It pulses with shadow too. A marriage of verdant light and oily black, not smoke, not vines, but something new. Something more.

The collar lashes back violently, its enchantment tightening with a cruel, serpentine strength. My vision blurs. My knees buckle. Ashen snarls. The pain is blinding now, stars bursting behind my eyes.

Still, I do not yield.

Because I know Anethesis' fatal flaw. He cannot watch me die. I am the linchpin of his plan. The key to power. His precious trophy. He cannot bear losing me.

So I scream, daring him to look away. Daring him to let me burn.

And just when I think he will, just when I think he'll let me perish, a husk of power and blood and flame, the door swings open.

The heat blasts outward as Anethesis stumbles through, shielding his face, his long robes catching the shimmer of magic in the air and with a trembling hand, he grabs the collar, fingers curling around it, mouth twisted in disgust, and yanks it free.

The moment it's gone, the world shatters.

My magic explodes outward. Green and black fire licking the walls, wrapping around my limbs, spilling from my chest like a storm. My scream rips through the cavern, fury and freedom and grief all in one violent crescendo.

And I rise.

No longer just a princess. No longer just a prisoner.

But something *else*.

Something born of pain and shadow. Of healing and destruction. Of fire and bloom.

Anethesis stumbles back, teeth bared in a grimace.

"Amara!" he roars, and for the first time, his voice breaks with an unfamiliar rage. "Enough!"

He flings his hands forward, and the air erupts with force. A violent gust slams into me, throwing me against the side of the cage, the bars biting into my spine. My flames gutter, but they do not die.

I snarl, pushing against the wind, muscles trembling with effort as I stalk forward. The flames rise with me, green and black twisting in frenzied spirals around my arms, devouring the air between us.

Panic sparks in Anethesis's eyes. He grits his teeth and thrusts both hands out, wind lashing harder, his body trembling from the exertion.

"Princess!" he cries. "Please! Don't do this! I don't want to hurt you!"

"Lies!" I scream, voice booming like thunder. "That's all you Fae ever do. All you know how to do!"

Step by step, I force myself closer. The gusts howl, ripping at my hair, my clothes, but I don't stop. I won't stop. My hand rises, wrapped in fire and smoke, the red ribbon at my wrist snapping in the wind like a battle flag.

My open palm nears his face.

Anethesis flinches, turning his head with a cry as the flames lick across his cheek.

"Stop!" he bellows. "I beg of you!"

I smile, slow and merciless, and lower my hand.

"Good," I murmur, voice cold as ice, hard as stone. "That's a start. Now, release Ashen."

He shudders, backing away, his breath coming shallow.

"But... how do I know you won't kill me?"

"You don't," I snap. "Now. Do it."

He skirts around me, keeping to the edges. His back scrapes the bars as he nears Ashen, still no larger than a hunting cat, crouched low, his ivory eyes ever watchful.

Anethesis's hands shake as he reaches for the collar. I can smell his fear now, thick and metallic on his skin, and it stirs something within me I'm not ready to embrace.

The clasp clicks and the collar falls.

Ashen unleashes a roar that shakes the cavern to its bones. The stone groans. The cage sways. Far below, the lake ripples.

Smoke pours from Ashen's body, swallowing him whole. Tentacles explode from his back with a wet, snarling sound, thrashing like serpents. His limbs stretch, his torso bulging with muscle and mist, until he towers, massive and monstrous, his true form no longer constrained.

The cage groans under his bulk, metal creaking in protest.

Anethesis presses himself against the bars, clutching them like a lifeline, his eyes screwed shut, desperate, praying. Pretending this is a dream.

But it isn't.

This is real.

This is the nightmare he made with his own hands.

I step forward and place my hands on Ashen's neck, burying my face against the thick, solid heat of him as he growls low in his throat

"Welcome back," I murmur.

"Now is a time for calm, Princess," Anethesis says, only turning half his face toward me, his hands still clinging to the bars. "I was promised mercy!"

"You were promised nothing and took everything!" The words tear from me, raw with everything he's done, every agony I've endured at his hands. "You stole me from my love. Threatened the safety of my child. Forced me to endure your trials. But you never intended for me to survive, did you, Lord of Ithranor?"

Ashen snarls, his lips peeling back, canines glinting.

Anethesis swallows.

"This world has given us nothing but pain," he says hoarsely. "We just wanted to go home, Amara."

I stare at him, at the broken man before me.

"That's all I wanted, too. But we cannot both get what we want and live."

Anethesis's lip twitches, his expression curdling with fury. "Awakened whore!" he spits, voice cracking like a whip. He whirls from the bars, thrusting his hands forward as violent gusts tear through the air, wind shrieking at his command. But it's no use.

Ashen lunges.

A single snap of teeth, swift, brutal, and Anethesis' hands are gone. Blood spatters across the cage, deep crimson dripping between the grates. He stares at the severed stumps in mute horror before realization slams into him.

Then he screams.

Ashen doesn't stop.

He lunges again, massive jaws clamping down around Anethesis's leg before hurling him across the cage like a ragdoll. His body slams into the bars with a sickening crack before crumpling to the floor, motionless but groaning.

Ashen lowers himself, and I climb onto his back, fingers sinking into the thick smoke of his mane. His paws pad toward the door, each step thunderous in the silence, but I glance back one last time.

Anethesis lies curled on his side, sobbing, blood pouring from him in heavy sheets, a waterfall of crimson spilling into the black water below, swirling like ink.

"You will never truly escape," he rasps, voice warped by pain. "You are Awakened. Death will find you. One way or another."

I meet his gaze without flinching. "Then let it try."

Wings of smoke burst from Ashen's shoulders. He rears back, then leaps into the open air. Wind surges beneath us. The cage door swings shut behind with a final, echoing clang.

He flies us from the cage, from the cavern, from the doom that awaited us and, as the sunlight spills through the mouth of the cave, I lift my face to it, my smile stretching wide.

My first instinct is to tuck myself against Ashen, to press low against his neck and urge him to fly, ears pinned, wings beating fast and true, as far from Driftspire as he can. Especially when his shadow cuts across the floating isles and draws the gaze of the Fae below.

We do not have the advantage here. Not in their sky. Not against creatures who command the wind, who fly just as high and just as fast as Ashen can.

We must run. Now, or not at all.

And we almost do.

Until I hear his scream.

The Golden Son.

I tell myself not to look. Not to feel.

But I do.

I always do.

I tug on Ashen's mane, hard.

"Down there," I whisper.

He growls beneath me, a low, warning rumble in his chest. He knows what this means. What it risks.

Still, I pull again, more forceful this time.

Ashen resists. Then snarls. Then folds his wings and drops.

He hits the stone balcony of the tower with a bone-shaking thud, his massive body slamming through the ledge. Stone splits and crumbles, dust blooming in a thick cloud around us.

I slide off his back, and when the dust clears, I see him.

The Golden Son.

Maskless.

Chained against a wall, dangling from shackles at his wrists.

I've never seen him so pale, his blond hair stuck to his face with sweat, his chest barely lifting with breath. But he stirs when he hears me. Eyes slitting open, dazed and unfocused.

"Amara? What are you..."

"Be quiet," I snap. "Or I'll change my mind."

I lift my hands, the last of my power flickering to life, green fire curling over my skin. I grip the shackles around his wrists, feel the metal sizzle beneath my touch, until it melts and drips down the wall in black streaks.

That's when I see it.

The raw, flayed flesh of his wrist.

The rune that once marked him carved away.

Cut straight from his skin.

He falls forward, and I catch him.

His weight knocks the breath from me. Sweat and grime coat his skin. His head drops against my shoulder, limp as a broken doll.

"Thank you," he whispers.

"Say another word," I growl, "and I'll leave you here, I swear."

But there is no time to breathe.

The wind shrieks around the tower, and the raised voices of the Ithranor rise like a storm in the sky. With the Golden Son's arm slung over my shoulder, I drag him toward Ashen, who waits on the shattered ledge, and too late, I realize he was far wiser than I.

The tower is surrounded.

The sky churns with Fae riding the currents, their eyes locked on us, their blades drawn. If they do not already know what has become of Anethesis, they soon will, and I do not expect mercy.

Suddenly, the Golden Son's legs give out beneath him, and he crashes to one knee, dragging me with him.

"Get up!" I bark.

"Leave me," he breathes. "I'll slow you down. Hold you back. Save yourself, Amara."

I roll my eyes. "Be quiet. You're coming with me. That is not up for discussion."

He doesn't argue again. He can't and even if I left him, the odds of escape would still be razor-thin. But I didn't come this far to fail.

I'll carve a path in green flame.

I'll let Ashen gorge himself on as many Ithranor as he can stomach.

I will be free.

I drag the Golden Son to Ashen, shove him toward the demon's side.

"You're going to have to lift yourself up," I snap. "I'm not strong enough."

He mumbles something too soft, too slurred, and his eyes begin to fall shut.

"Ronin!" I shout.

That awakens him. His eyes snap open, vivid blue slicing into mine.

"Pull yourself up. Now."

He nods barely, but somewhere inside that wrecked body, he finds the strength to grasp Ashen's fur and haul himself onto his back.

I climb up after him, patting Ashen's neck, trying to soothe the beast as he snarls at the Ithranor circling like vultures.

My power is already slipping, the pain ebbing into nothing. I can only hope there's enough left in me to put up a fight.

My hand drifts to my belly, to the faint flutter beneath my palm. A breath, a life. Fragile and fierce. I close my eyes for the span of a heartbeat, square my shoulders, and exhale.

"Home, Ashen," I whisper.

Ashen's stark white eyes flare with eerie light, and I brace for the rush of wind, for the sky to tilt as he leaps from the ledge, slicing through the storm of Fae, carrying us away from Driftspire toward the distant arms of my husband.

But he does not rise.

The stone beneath us trembles as his massive paws strike the tower with purpose, a deep growl rumbling in his chest. Then the air before us bends. It flickers, warps and a sliver of darkness tears through the space ahead. A speck at first. Then a widening ripple. Something darker. Vast. Infinite.

The void.

My breath catches. I grip Ashen's mane tighter.

The cold unfurls inside me like smoke, familiar and terrible. That emptiness. That hunger. The thing I had nearly forgotten, but which never truly leaves.

Before I can stop him, before I can speak or even think, Ashen hurls himself forward. Into the dark.

The void swallows us whole, the world vanishing in a rush of shadow and cold. Behind us, the rift seals with a sound like cracking bone, just as the Ithranor crash upon the tower.

CHAPTER 18
DAED

Before her. Zema's island looms larger as I approach, its silhouette dark against the storm-lit sky. The wind is vicious tonight, howling like a beast, driving the rain in stinging needles against my skin. Thunder cracks, rolling with the fury of a wrathful god, and a sense of unease rises in my gut, tightening with each beat of my wings. I push forward, muscles straining against the storm's weight, and feel relief when my feet finally touch solid ground.

The island itself is eerily silent, untouched by the tempest raging around it. I adjust the satchel at my side, fingers brushing against the apples I brought, redder, juicier than the last, a small offering to bring Zema a glimmer of joy. But something about the quiet tonight prickles at the back of my neck.

I step forward, the cave just ahead, barely visible through the sheets of rain. I narrow my eyes, scanning for movement, the familiar flicker of firelight. But there is nothing. Only stillness. Only dark.

"Zema?" I call.

Silence.

I move closer, arriving at the mouth of the cave and ducking my head inside. My gaze sweeps over the empty bed, the abandoned plate, the firepit long gone cold. The embers are stone-hard, scattered ash curling in the draft. There has always been fire here. Even on the worst nights.

I straighten, pulse quickening. "Zema!"

No answer.

The storm rages on, the thunder a constant growl in the sky, but I do not know how many times I call her name. Each time, my hope both swells and withers. Then, somehow, even through the fury of the storm, I hear something softer. A slap. Low, dull. Wet.

I follow the sound to the island's edge, where the wind howls louder. There, snagged on the jagged lip of a rock, a strip of fabric thrashes like a shredded flag.

My stomach knots.

I step closer, heart thundering, and reach for it. The wind fights me, pulling it back like it wants to keep the truth hidden. But I seize it anyway, fingers closing tight around the tattered cloth.

The moment I touch it, I know.

Zema's cloak.

It is soaked through, but not only with rain.

Blood.

I lift my gaze to the ocean, to the waves that crash and churn.

"Looking for someone, Your Highness?" a voice says behind me.

Smoke curls between my fingers, and I feel the leather-wrapped grip of Death Singer solidify in my hand. I spin, blade flashing in the moonlight, the tip a breath from the throat of the male before me.

Modok, Lord of Mor'Thravar.

His leathers are rain-darkened, his face cast in shadow. The sides of his head are shaved close, but a long, frayed braid whips in the wind. His presence stinks of rot, of the thing festering inside him, leeching through his skin.

"What are you doing here?" I demand.

Modok clasps his hands at his waist, his thumbs brushing together in thought. The blade at his throat does not make him flinch.

"I could ask you the same question," he says. "This island is within my territory."

I do not waste breath on his claim.

"Where is she?" My grip tightens on Death Singer. "Where is Zema?"

"My Prince," he says, shaking his head slowly, his voice thick with mock regret. "You knew this was inevitable."

"No." The word is barely more than a breath, but my grip on the blade does not waver, though beneath my skin, my muscles tremble, and my blood turns sluggish with dread. "You had no right."

Modok's lips curl. "I had every right, Your Highness." The title drips from his tongue like something bitter. "She was my kin. My house. My sister. And I am bound by duty to obey my king's command."

"King," I bite out. "My father."

Modok nods once. "He wished to free you from distractions."

The words strike like a blade to the ribs. I swallow against the bile rising in my throat. "You speak as if she meant nothing. She was your sister."

His jaw tightens, the muscles ticking beneath his bristled skin. "She was Awakened," he grits out. "An abomination. A curse upon my house." His eyes gleam like embers in the dark. "But I have taken care of it."

Death Singer dissolves into smoke, curling away from my grip like mist in the wind. My wings flare wide, the sudden gust kicking up dirt and rain as I lunge. The force of my leap sends us both crashing to the ground, my knees pinning his ribs, my fists slamming into his face. Once. Twice. Over and over.

Bone cracks beneath my knuckles. His head snaps back against the wet earth, his lip splits, blood staining his teeth. But still, he smiles. That same smug, infuriating smirk. He does not fight back.

"Retaliate, Modok," I growl, slamming my fist into his jaw. "Fight me." Another strike. Another. "Give me a reason."

He only laughs, the sound wet, gurgling, but full of knowing. He understands. He sees through me. He knows I want this, need this, need to rip him apart, to make him feel even a fraction of what I feel.

And so he does nothing.

I freeze, my breath ragged, my chest heaving. The storm rages around us, rain pouring, thunder rolling, but I feel nothing but the sick, empty pit of grief yawning inside me. My hands tremble as I slowly climb off him, staggering back.

Modok does not rise. He does not gloat. He only watches.

I can't bear it.

With a sharp beat of my wings, I take to the sky, leaving the island, the storm, and my grief behind.

***

After Her. The ship sways, and the creak of the wood burrows deep into my bones. Each sharp prick on my back drags me between dreaming and waking, my body caught in a haze of pain and exhaustion. My arms ache, my muscles taut, my wrists burning.

"Almost done," Solena hisses from the darkness. "Hold him still."

176

My eyes flicker open. My cheek is pressed against the smooth wood of the table, and the first thing I see is Orios, jaw clenched, teeth bared as he pulls against a leather strap with all his strength. I grunt and shift, turning my head just enough to glimpse Reon on my other side, his hands red and raw, gripping another strap as if his life depends on it. My vision clears, and the realization sets in. The straps they're hauling on so fiercely are bound to my wrists. They're holding me down.

A fresh sting flares along my spine, and I suck in a breath. But there's more than just the pain. A weight presses against me, a knee digging into my back. Solena must be astride me, inking the sigils.

"Morning, brother," Zyphoro murmurs.

I lift my head against the restraints, just enough to meet her gaze. She clicks her tongue. "You just can't behave yourself, can you?"

My throat is dry, and the words scrape as I force them out. "I'm alive. You didn't kill me."

Zyphoro tips her head toward Solena. "The maid assured me she could buy us time, and I've recently discovered she is a female of many talents."

"Enough, Zyph," Solena snaps. "Just a few more."

The glint of Zyphoro's dagger tapping against her palm catches my eye. Her expression darkens when she asks me. "Do you feel him?"

I want to lie. Maybe to save my own skin. Maybe because I need to believe I have more time. But neither is true.

"Yes," I mutter. "The sigils are failing."

I brace for the cold press of her blade at my throat, but it doesn't come. Only the judgment in her eyes.

"Then we have little time to find Amara before you lose control."

"I can fight it," I snarl through clenched teeth.

"I have no doubt you'll fight to the end, Daedalus." Her voice is calm. "But you will not win. Not until one of you is dead."

"There," Solena exclaims, almost to silence Zyphoro's warning, punctuating her last stroke with a searing jab of the needle.

A hush settles over the cabin. They watch me, waiting.

Waiting to see if I am still myself.

The darkness recedes. The thousands of voices shrivel into silence. The master's hand on my shoulder loosens its grip. But something is different.

Despite the sigils seared into my skin, I am not alone in my body.

There's a presence inside me, distant, weak, but there all the same. A passenger, lingering in the shadows.

"Can we let go now?" Reon grumbles. "My arms are fucking killing me."

Zyphoro doesn't answer right away. She watches me, still waiting for the void to rupture, for the darkness to seize control.

Then, at last, she exhales. Her shoulders ease.

"Let him go."

Reon and Orios release me in unison, both collapsing onto their backsides with ragged breaths. The leather around my wrists loosens, and I flex my fingers, the sting immediate. My skin is raw, torn, blood seeping into the worn straps. I shake them off and shift, casting a glance over my shoulder.

Solena is still there, still straddling my back.

"If you're done," I say.

"Right," she mutters, blinking as if just remembering herself. Then, with a quick movement, she swings her leg over and slides off the table, her boots landing softly on the floor.

Slowly, I push myself upright, hauling my legs over the edge of the table. Every motion awakens the ache of bruises, the sting of fresh wounds. My shoulders roll, stiff and sore, but the real reminder of my condition comes when I straighten. My canines lengthen, pain flaring sharp and deep from the stab wound in my side.

"You're a mess," Reon remarks.

I lift my gaze, studying the black eye and split lip he earned in Ballamar City.

"You're one to talk," I mutter. "House Taramethos did a fine job ruining that pretty face of yours."

"Hah." He scoffs, fingers grazing the raw cut on his cheek. "Lady Marlayna did this herself, long before I figured out she planned to turn on us." He gestures vaguely to his battered face. "This was foreplay."

My brow furrows, just enough to send another pulse of pain through my skull. "She did that to you?"

Reon nods. "You owe me one."

I manage half a grin. "I'm sure you hated every second of it."

Reon stifles a smirk of his own. "Without a doubt. Getting hard just thinking about it is an unfortunate reflex."

Solena sighs, frustrated. "Really? After everything? After almost losing our prince to the void, this is what you're joking about?"

Her scorn is enough to strip the amusement from both of our faces.

"You need to clean yourself up," she says, tone firm. "Then come above deck. We need to decide what happens next."

No one argues. We only nod, as if this once-maid is the wisest among us.

Zyphoro and Reon leave as Solena turns to Orios, reaching for his hand. "Come," she beckons.

"I'm right behind you," Orios murmurs, leaning down to press a kiss to her forehead.

Their hands drift apart as she steps past me, sparing the briefest glance before she disappears through the door.

Orios lingers there in the corner, and I think nothing of it at first until I feel his eyes burning through me like flaming arrows.

I lift an eyebrow. "Is something wrong, Reaper?"

His fingers curl, knuckles cracking as he closes the space between us in a single stride.

"I am not a Reaper here," he says, voice lower, rougher. "Here I am Orios. Fae. Male. No different from you."

"Is that right?" I drawl, letting my legs spread a little wider on the edge of the table, watching him. "And why do you feel the need to remind me of this... Orios?"

He squares his shoulders. "Because I don't want titles getting in the way of what I'm about to say."

My canines lengthen again. I run my tongue over one, slow, letting my gaze narrow. "Then, by all means. Speak your mind."

Orios bares his own teeth, his lip curling just enough to reveal the sharp tips of his fangs. Arms folding, he leans forward, voice quiet but unmistakably clear.

"Solena is mine. Bitten or not and I will not hesitate to cut through anyone who comes between us."

"I have appreciated your service," I say. "So I will forgive your puny threats and insolent fucking tone. But if this is you telling me to stay away from *your* female, you are wasting your breath. I have no interest in Solena."

He straightens, shoulders broadening.

"We may be far from Baev'kalath, but never forget who you are talking to. Understand me?"

Orios' jaw tightens, his breath heaving in his chest. "Yes, *Your Highness*," he says, voice smooth but taut. "I understand."

Then he leans in, his words a low rasp against my ear.

"But if you dare stare at her too long, if your hands wander too close, I *will* kill you."

He straightens, brushes past me, shoving my shoulder in a way that's nothing short of deliberate.

I grin as he reaches the door, a quiet chuckle slipping free. "For someone so concerned about who touches Solena, maybe you should've thought twice before taking *my sister* as a bedmate."

His hand stills on the door, fingers curling against the wood. Then, slowly, he glances back over his shoulder. "Worry less about who shares my bed and more about finding your own female."

The words hit their mark like a hammer. He doesn't wait for a reply. The door slams behind him, rattling on its hinges, the final punctuation to his parting shot.

I exhale through clenched teeth, fury tight in my chest. Sliding off the table, I curl my fingers into a fist and drive it down. Once, twice, again and again until the wood gives, splintering beneath my knuckles. Pain blooms through my hand, grounding me, but it is nothing compared to the war raging inside me.

Because he's right.

I have been lost, adrift in the chaos, tangled in distractions, drowning in the ghosts of my past and the weight of what hunts me. I have strayed too far from my path, too consumed by my own torment to see the truth. I must find my way back. Back to her.

I brace myself against the table, fingers pressed into the blood-slick wood, scattered with splinters and spilled ink. My head bows beneath the weight of it all as I struggle to steady my breath, to find calm.

In the hush that follows, I swear I hear her voice.

Good. I need to remember why I'm doing this. What I've lost.

At first, I tell myself it's a dream. A longing twisted into sound. But then I hear her again, closer this time. So close, it's as if she's at my ear, calling my name.

My shoulders go rigid. My head whips around, searching the shadows.

What is this? Why does she should so close? Why does she sound afraid?

My breath snags, the truth clawing up my throat.

This isn't memory. This isn't madness.

It's her.

"Amara!" I cry, my voice breaking as it rips free. "I hear you!"

She calls again. But from where?

I shove aside the table and lunge for the door, throwing it open as I bolt above deck. Sunlight slams into my eyes, and I lift a hand against the glare.

"Amara!" I shout, scanning the horizon, my heart a frantic drum in my ribs.

Zyphoro straightens from where she leans against the railing, her gaze tracking me. "Daedalus. What is it?"

"I can hear her!" The words claw out of me, desperate. I pace across the deck, searching. "She's here!"

Reon and Solena exchange wary glances.

"What do you mean?" Reon asks, his voice cautious. "Who is here?"

"Amara!" I snap, my pulse roaring in my ears. I drag my fingers through my hair, gripping at the roots. "Can you not hear her? She's calling my name."

Zyphoro moves to follow, but when I turn back on my own path, searching the same stretch of deck again, she snatches my elbow.

"Brother, stop," she says, voice firm, but I rip free.

"I can hear her!" I clutch at my skull, my fingers digging in. "She's in here!" I slap the side of my head so hard that Zyphoro flinches.

The impact rings through me, and as the words leave my lips, their meaning takes hold.

In here.

Inside me.

Not on this ship. Not in the ocean.

She's in the part of me that lingers just out of reach. The part that refuses to die despite the sigils burned into my back.

"Brother." Zyphoro's voice softens, wary now. "What is happening?"

My breath shudders. My heart races and yet feels still, suspended in time.

I lift my gaze to hers, twin mirrors of my own, filled with the same terrible realization.

"I've found her," I whisper, dread like ice in my veins. "Amara is in the void."

"You are exhausted and wounded," Zyphoro says, gripping my shoulder. "She cannot be in the void. Why would she be in the void?"

"I know her voice." My heart slams against my ribs, a drumbeat of certainty. "When she calls, I answer. Always." I lift my hand, and smoke curls between my fingers, twisting with purpose. "I must go to her."

Zyphoro tightens her hold, her nails digging into my skin. "Do you hear yourself? After everything we've been through, after we nearly lost you, do you truly mean to step into the void willingly?"

The alternatives claw at my mind, dark and unbearable. "This could be my only chance to bring her back before..." My throat tightens. "Before Gygarth finds her first."

Reon, Solena, and Orios close in, their heads shaking in unison.

"This is madness," Reon snaps. "We have spent all this time keeping you away from the void. Away from Gygarth."

"And now fate drags me back into his shadow," I say bitterly. "By dangling before me the one thing I cannot ignore."

Solena's hand presses gently against my back, just as Orios' gaze hardens.

"You cannot do this," she pleads.

I step away, shaking her off with careful resolve. "If the void is what stands between me and my love, then there is only one choice, and we have already wasted too much time."

CHAPTER 19

AMARA

The void is endless. A world without time, without breath, without light. Smoke coils and drifts like specters in the dark. Ashen paces, though I do not know if we move. There is no way to tell. No point of reference, no sound except the distant echo of my own thoughts. How long has it been? Hours? Days? I cannot tell if time still applies to me. If I still exist the way I once did.

Tears burn, but they do not fall. My chest tightens, an ache so raw it threatens to break me. And then, for the first time since the darkness swallowed me, I part my lips and let my voice reach into the abyss.

"Daedalus."

The silence swallows his name whole.

But I call again. Louder. Desperate.

"Daedalus!"

A hand clamps over my mouth as the Golden Son pulls me close. His blue eyes, so piercing, so starkly bright, seem almost too pure for the suffocating dark that swallows us whole.

"Quiet," he warns, his strained voice still threaded with pain. His gaze sweeps the shifting shadows, muscles taut, every line of him sharpened with tension. "We are not alone, and we do not want to draw attention."

His hand drags away from my mouth, lingering for just a breath too long, fingers grazing my skin as he withdraws his touch. He tips his chin towards Ashen.

"Can you command this beast to get us out of here?"

Suddenly a fresh wave of nausea twists through me, a deep, curling discomfort that is not just mine. My hand finds my stomach instinctively, fingers pressing against the source of that strange stirring.

The Golden Son notices. "What's wrong?"

"Nothing," I say, too quick, too clipped. I grip Ashen's mane. "You must take us home. Now."

But Ashen does not obey. He drifts forward, unhurried, his paws pressing weightless against the swirling black, carrying us deeper into the abyss.

The Golden Son's jaw tightens. "He's brought us here on purpose. This is a trap."

"No," I snap back, defensive. "This is my fault. I asked him to take us home. He is a creature of the void. He only misunderstood."

"Then make him understand," the Golden Son growls. "We cannot stay here."

His words fracture into a brutal, hacking cough. He lurches forward, clutching his throat. A thin, writhing thread of smoke spills from his lips, alive, curling, vanishing into the abyss.

"What the fuck!" he gasps between coughs, voice raw. "What was that?"

My throat bobs, my pulse a wild thing. I shake my head, though my confusion isn't entirely feigned.

The void is not meant for humans. It never has been.

The Fae can walk its endless dark and survive. I can breathe this air, perhaps because something within me is neither wholly human nor Fae, but something in between. A child of smoke and vine. And yet, even with that possibility, the pain twisting through my stomach is something else entirely.

The Golden Son is right.

We must get out.

Before my body betrays me. Before the void seeps into his lungs and suffocates him. Before the master of this place wakes and finds us trespassing.

I tighten my grip on Ashen's mane, my voice steady despite the unease curling in my gut. "Ashen. Can you hear me? You must void walk. We must leave."

But he doesn't respond. Not to my voice, not to the silent plea I send through our bond. The smoke and shadows have claimed him, twisting around his form, sinking their claws into something deeper than obedience. He is not mine to command. Not here.

"He cannot help us," I murmur, biting down against the sharp twist in my stomach. My gaze drifts to his paws, gliding effortlessly over a sea of darkness and mist.

If I climbed down, would I find solid ground beneath my feet? Or would I plummet into the dark? I'm not willing to take that risk.

The next wave of pain is sharper, tearing through me like a blade, and I lurch forward, collapsing against Ashen's neck. He doesn't react. Doesn't so much as flinch.

"Don't tell me it's nothing again," the Golden Son growls.

Smoke spills from his mouth, his fingers digging into his chest.

I press a hand to my belly, my breath catching. My brow furrows. It's impossible, but Souls, I swear it's larger. Rounder. Firmer. The silk of my gown, once flowing, clings too tightly now, stretched taut over my skin.

No, this is wrong.

We have to get out of here. Now.

I inhale deeply, forcing the pain aside, pushing through the fog clouding my thoughts. If Ashen will not get us out of here. If the void has ensnared him in its grasp, then there is only one other who can wield that power.

Me.

I close my eyes, steadying myself against the inevitable.

"I will open a portal."

The Golden Son reaches around, pinching my chin between his fingers and forcing me to face him. I snarl, shoving him away, but he doesn't miss a beat, grabs me again, his grip more forceful this time. Like he wants me to feel it. Like he's daring me to fight him for control.

"You know what will happen," he growls. "What it costs."

I shake my head, defiant. "And what choice do we have? Linger here until the dark takes us? Wait for something worse to crawl out and devour us? If we're lucky?"

"No." His voice hardens. He shakes his head once, with finality. "I won't allow it."

My jaw tightens. "Luckily, I am not asking for your permission."

Before he can stop me, before he can rip the words from my lips, I speak them.

"Véthari lios an'thera."

The void devours them.

So I say them again. Louder. Then again, until my voice is all there is.

"Véthari lios an'thera. Véthari lios an'thera. Véthari lios an'thera."

But there is nothing but darkness.

Then I understand. Blood.

It must always be blood.

But how?

I have no weapons. And with Ashen under the sway of the void, I'm not eager to force his mouth open and shove an arm inside.Panic coils in my chest as I whirl, eyes scanning the Golden Son. His bare torso is a map of bruises and shallow cuts, smeared with dried blood, but no blade. Nothing sharp. Nothing useful.

I could claw at myself. Bite down hard and pray a drop is enough.

There's no time to hesitate. No time to hope for a cleaner way.

I seize my arm, teeth bared, ready to tear into my own flesh. But before I can, a curl of smoke unfurls across my lap.

I freeze. Watching, breathless, as the darkness writhes like smoke, then stills. Solidifies. The shadow evaporates, leaving behind a dagger, its blade glimmering like starlight, its leather-wrapped hilt fitted to my hand, its pommel a clear, flawless jewel.

I stare.

The only one more stunned than me is the Golden Son.

"That's Fae magic," he breathes. "But how..."

His voice fades as his gaze drops to my belly just before it jolts, a massive ripple rolling beneath my skin like the swell of a restless sea.

He shrieks, a high-pitched sound even louder than the one he scolded me for, his face contorting into something between horror and revulsion.

"Was that the baby? What's happening to it?" he chokes out.

"There's no time to figure that out," I snap, already slicing the dagger across my arm.

A crimson curtain spills down my skin, warm and fast.

The Golden Son snarls, lunging for the dagger, wrenching it from my grip. But it's too late.

The blood is already spilled.

"Véthari lios an'thera."

I close my eyes and think of the Grove. Of home. Of the ancient trees and the Souls that whisper through them. Of the ones I swore to protect.

But this place. This place does not let go so easily.

It seeps into me, thick as ink, curling through my ribs, my veins, my mind. It *stains* me. Poisons my thoughts until even my beloved Grove turns to rot and cinder in my memory.

My blood drips. My vision flickers.

The void before me rips.

A gash splits through the darkness, stretching wider, inch by inch. A portal. And despite the cost it demands, despite the truth that my life has been torn apart in the name of this magic, I can't help the swell of pride that rises in my chest. I've done this. It's enough to steady me, enough to chase back the fear of what I've become.

Within the portal, there is light, faint, dim, but blinding compared to what surrounds us.

The Grove?

I don't know. But Ashen moves toward it, drawn like a blade to its sheath.

The tear unravels, threads of shadow snapping apart like stretched sinew. At first, the view is muddled, unclear, but as Ashen carries us closer and the portal swells, clarity sharpens.

This is not my beloved Grove.

The land beyond is barren and cruel. A jagged expanse of dark stone, cracked and unforgiving, and there, carved into the spine of a mountain, looms a fortress. Crooked and rotting, like the corpse of a kingdom long dead. Fire pits flicker at its base, spitting embers into the sooty sky, casting shifting shadows that dance across shattered ramparts and broken spires.

Then, a screech cleaves the air, razor-sharp and unnatural.

A sky of wings. Black. Endless.

Not Mordorin Fae.

Not the Blades of Baev'kalath.

Worse.

Monsters.

But it isn't the only sound.

The first growls roll across the land like thunder. Deep tremors that rattle the bones of the world. Then come the screams. Shrieking. Unrelenting. Growing louder with each ragged breath.

And then I see them.

A flood of creatures bursts from the fortress, a living tide of shadow and snarling teeth, crashing down the mountain in a relentless swarm. They pour over the landscape like spilled ink, unstoppable, ravenous, fast as death.

"Amara," the Golden Son murmurs at my ear, calm despite the chaos, despite the death hurtling toward us. "Close the portal, please."

A cold weight drops into my stomach. My throat tightens.

"I... I don't know how," I admit, heat rising to my cheeks, burning down my neck. "I was never taught that part."

The Golden Son exhales sharply, muttering, "Because they expected you to be dead by this point, I imagine."

A bitter truth.

Then, a flicker of luck. The portal stops widening.

I glance down at my arm, where my blood, once a river, is now only a trickle.

"It needs more blood to open fully," I realize aloud. "They won't fit through."

The Golden Son's jaw tightens. "Do you want to test that theory?"

I don't answer. I don't have to.

I seize Ashen's mane, fingers knotting through the strands. I yank hard.

"Hear me, Ashen! Turn around! Please!"

But the beast does not stop. If anything, he moves faster, drawn to the world within the portal, an unholy pull dragging him forward.

The cries sharpen, rising to a fever pitch, matching the frantic hammering of my heart, the pulse in my throat, the blood pounding through my veins.

Then a white-hot pain rips through my stomach. A scream tears from my throat, raw and jagged, louder than the horrors swarming towards us.

I double over, clutching at my middle as my baby shifts inside me. My skin stretches so tight I think it might tear, veins pulsing beneath the surface.

I grit my teeth, my breath shuddering as I force my eyes open. The portal is closing.

Slowly, like a stitch drawn through fabric, the darkness begins to weave itself shut.

A small mercy.

But then, there's a hand. Skeletal, wrapped in blackened, withered flesh, the bones straining against their decaying sheath. It thrusts through the narrowing rift, fingers curling and clawing, desperate to rip the wound in the world even wider. And behind it, something follows. A figure cloaked in tattered black robes, the fabric snapping in a wind I cannot feel. Its eyes blaze, twin moons of searing white that cut through the dark, and from its chin, a writhing nest of tentacles, each one twitching in a slow, grotesque rhythm.

Those eyes. They don't just see me. They see through me. They burrow into my very soul.

Frozen. I can't move, can't breathe.

"You," the thing hisses, its voice a slithering whisper like serpents tangled in the depths of a black pit. It holds the portal open, its other hand stretching impossibly toward me, its fingers curling like the promise of doom.

No. Not toward *me*. Toward my stomach. My baby.

Fear churns in my veins, and the pressure in my belly intensifies, sharper than ever before. The tiny hands inside me claw, the little feet kicking with such force I fear they'll tear me apart from the inside. My breath comes in ragged gasps, the pain nearly overwhelming.

The thing's lips curl into something like a smile, its voice a hiss of hunger as it speaks. "You bring a feast for my master. Meat for the beast."

"No!" I scream, my voice a desperate cry that cracks through the air. "Daedalus!"

Then, somewhere in the distance, past the roar of my blood pounding in my ears, beyond the monstrous army crashing toward me, beyond the creature still reaching for my baby with its clawed, twisted hands, I hear it.

His voice.

"Amara!"

It cuts through the chaos, a lifeline, a tether in the storm, and for a moment, everything else fades.

My body jerks toward the voice, as if the very threads of my soul, our souls, are being pulled taut, stretching across the darkness to find him. Thin, golden strands shimmer like dust caught in moonlight, weaving through the abyss, parting the shadows as they reach for me.

Tears burn behind my eyes, hot with exhaustion, frustration, and anguish. Please, Souls, do not let this be a trick. Do not let this be another cruel illusion. I could not bear for this to be anything but real.

"Daedalus!"

I lean toward the glowing threads, desperate to meet them, desperate to feel him again. The darkness yawns beneath me, the void-demon still clawing at the portal's edges, but I don't care. Not anymore. All I care about is *him*—his hands on my skin, his arms crushing me against his chest, his lips against mine, erasing the nightmare with a single breath. I don't even realize I'm falling until the Golden Son's arms catch me, keeping me from tumbling off Ashen and into the dark.

"What are you doing!" he snaps with disbelief.

"Can you hear it?" I whisper, trembling. "Can you hear him calling my name?"

His silence stretches. He shakes his head at first, resolute, but then, Daedalus' voice carries through the air again, cutting through the storm of screams and screeches like a blade of pure light.

And the Golden Son flinches.

My breath hitches. My fingers dig into his arm, gripping tight, shaking him. "You hear him! Don't lie to me! You hear him!"

He swallows, throat bobbing. "Yes, Amara," he says at last. "I hear him."

The confirmation almost breaks me.

But before the relief can take hold, agony lances through me, wrenching the breath from my lungs. My stomach tightens, pain so deep and brutal that my vision swims. A cry rips from my throat as I double over, clutching myself, and through the haze, I see my gown, once soft teal silk, now blooming red.

Blood, seeping down my thighs in thick, trailing rivers.

My hands tremble as I press them to my belly. Souls, no. No. Not my child.

Tears spill freely now, raw and frantic, as I scream his name into the void, pleading, praying.

"Daedalus! Help me! Our baby!"

The world tilts, and I am weightless.

Pain pulses like a second heartbeat, tearing me apart from the inside, but I barely feel it now. My body is slipping, my strength unraveling, yet something—someone—holds me together. A warmth cradles me, steady and firm.

"Amara," The Golden Son breathes. "Hold on." His hand comes to my face, his fingers brushing my cheek with a tenderness that eases the pain.

But I can barely think beyond the steady drip of my blood, cooling as it slips from my toes into the dark below.

The air shudders with a scream, a thousand voices tangled into one, and I hear it again. My name. Louder. Closer.

The Golden Son stiffens, his grip on me tightening, desperate to protect me. But I know that voice. I know it in my bones, in my breath, in the places of me that have only ever belonged to him.

Another hand finds me, burning hot, familiar. My body knows before my mind does, my skin waking beneath his touch as though drawn to him even now. My fingers twitch, my heart stutters, and I open my eyes to a storm.

Not the howling dark around us. Not the raging void that waits to devour me whole. *His storm.*

Gray and violent and endless.

"Wife," Daedalus whispers, his lips parting, his fury and his relief braided into one.

A small, weak breath escapes me, something close to a laugh, something close to joy. My lips curve, even as the edges of the world blur.

"Husband," I whisper back.

CHAPTER 20
DAED

The void shifts around me, a swirling abyss of black and deeper black, shifting and writhing. The air is thick here, heavy with something unseen, something that clings to my skin like tar. But I do not stop. I do not hesitate.

The golden threads gleam in the darkness, thin as silk, delicate as whispers, yet stronger than any chain. They stretch before me, weaving through the nothingness, pulsing in time with the frantic beat of my heart. *Binds of Fate.* Threads of magic that only mates can see, spun from the fabric of destiny itself, a tether between two souls meant to find each other in life, in death, and beyond.

I saw them that day, when I first set eyes on Amara in the Grove. Now, they lead me to her.

My breath is ragged as I move forward, my steps soundless against the nothingness beneath me. The threads shimmer like stardust, guiding me, pulling me through the void. But in the corner of my eye, I see them.

Demons of smoke and shadow.

They hover in the darkness, stalking, watching. Their jagged-toothed mouths hang open, drool thick and shining, their hollow eyes fixed on me. Their hunger is palpable, a gnawing presence in the air, their talons twitching in anticipation. But they do not lunge. They do not attack.

And more troubling still, they have not summoned him.

Our master.

A chill slithers down my spine, colder than the void itself. Why do they hesitate? Why do they wait?

I do not waste time questioning. If I remain undiscovered, it is a mercy I will not squander. Every moment here is a risk, and I will not give them time to reconsider their inaction.

Amara needs me.

I grip the golden threads tighter and push forward, faster now, chasing the echo of her voice. I feel her pain through the tether, a cry in the dark that sets my soul ablaze.

The closer I get, the more desperate her cries become. Every muscle in my body is wound tight, stretched past its limits, but it's still not fast enough, not when her next words hit me like a blade to the gut.

"Daedalus! Help me! Our baby!"

The world narrows to that single, fractured plea. Nothing has ever sliced through me so deep, so violently. My blood turns molten, my veins searing with the force of my desperation. My legs burn as I push harder, faster, void-walking in reckless bursts. The threads between us pulse like a heartbeat, dragging me forward. My hands claw at the air. I will rip through the very fabric of this realm if I have to.

My body is nothing. My pain is nothing. If it means getting to her, I would run until my bones shattered, until my lungs bled, until my very soul burned itself out. I will tear through every demon that dares to stand between us.

I *will* reach her.

And I will *destroy* anything that threatens what's mine.

The golden threads coil through the darkness, weaving around a figure bathed in their glow, and my heart both shatters and mends in the same breath. She is here. Every step forward is agony, every heartbeat a war between relief and terror.

I void-walk again, stepping through the abyss to emerge at her side. The moment I do, her scent engulfs me. *Hers.* No soaps, no oils, no perfumes. Just *her.* The scent I feared I'd never breathe again, the one that lingered on my sheets long after she had gone, that clung to my skin the first time our bodies tangled in Pariseth, slick and burning, mouths desperate, limbs shaking. But beneath that, something sharp, something wrong.

Blood.

Fresh. Hot. Spilling too fast.

Ashen drifts forward, eyes hollow, paws dragging, bewitched by the dark force that still calls to him. I seize a fistful of his smoky mane, wrenching him to a stop, and he lets out a startled grunt. But my attention is already locked elsewhere.

A scent. A presence. *A man.*

I drag my gaze upward and see him. The one holding her.

The Golden Son.

Our eyes collide, and for a moment, time bends, thick with a silence that could shatter mountains, turn tides, split the sky in two.

Rage surges through me, the taste of blood sharp on my tongue. My canines lengthen, my breath shortens, my fists clench so tight I might break my own bones. This glare is one of war, of unfinished battles, of violence yet to come.

But even my fury must wait.

Because Amara is in pain. *My Amara.* And that matters more than anything.

I reach out, brushing my fingers against her skin. She is warm, tingling against my touch.

"Wife," I whisper.

Her eyes flicker open, and her lips tremble, curving into a soft, fragile smile, her tears pooling on the curve of her mouth.

"Husband," she breathes.

But nothing is ever simple for Amara and me.

I tear my eyes from her long enough to see the wound in the fabric of this realm. A portal barely holding itself open, and through that shrinking gap, I see him.

Emranth.

The servant of the Father Below grins at me, his mouth a wicked curve, his eyes brimming with malice.

"Prince Daedalus," he croons, voice slick as oil. "What a wondrous day this is! Delivering us both a feast and an heir at once."

My grip on Amara tightens. Over my dead body.

But Emranth's smirk doesn't have time to settle before his face twists with hunger. He lunges, teeth bared, claws swiping through the portal's shrinking space, his nails raking against the edges, sending sparks of dark energy scattering. When he realizes he cannot reach us, his mouth splits, a cavernous, yawning maw that stretches too wide, too deep, endless.

And from its depths, I hear them.

Screeches like shattered glass, a chorus of shrill, keening hunger. Then they come. A legion of winged horrors, bursting from his throat like he is regurgitating the void itself, their bodies sleek, their eyes burning with void-light. They dive toward us, talons outstretched, their cries slicing through my skull like daggers.

No time.

I seize Ashen's mane in one hand, cup Amara's jaw in the other, and with a single thought—*go*—the void rips open around us.

The world implodes in sound, Emranth's screech of rage swallowed in the rupture, the beasts howling as the darkness folds over them, sealing them away.

And then we are gone.

***

It is the squawks of the seabirds that pull me from unconsciousness. My eyes flicker open, and for a brief, weightless moment, my mind is blank. A slate wiped clean by salt air and sun. The world is nothing but the rhythmic crash of waves, the burn of heat on my skin.

Then Amara screams.

The sound cracks through me, and everything comes rushing back.

I bolt upright, twisting toward her voice, my body moving before thought can catch up. I scramble across the wooden deck, hands slipping on the damp boards, heart hammering as she screams again.

She is on her back, legs splayed wide, her full, heavy belly rising and falling with shuddered breaths. The silk of her dress fans around her like the petals of a wilting flower, once a delicate shade of teal, now soaked in deep crimson.

Blood. So much blood.

Solena kneels between Amara's legs, her hands slick with it, working quickly, her face a mask of grim concentration.

"Breathe, Amara," Solena instructs, her voice steady, but I hear the tight edge of concern beneath it. "You *must* breathe."

Ashen paces at her side, restless and low to the ground. A soft whimper escapes him as he leans down, nudging Amara's shoulder with his nose, smoke curling faintly from his mane. The worry in his eyes is almost human. Aching, helpless. But now is not the time for sentiment. I will spare him the sight of her suffering. With a flick of my wrist, he growls, a sound of protest more than defiance, before dissolving into a plume of smoke, leaving only the echo of his sorrow behind.

Orios and Reon hover nearby, their gazes dark with worry, while Zyphoro kneels at Amara's side, clutching her trembling hand. My sister looks up at me, and I see it in her eyes before she even speaks.

This is *wrong*.

Not how it should be.

I can feel it too, the unnatural energy thrumming in the air, thick as storm clouds. Amara's belly is *too full*, her body straining under the weight of a pregnancy that should not be this far along. The days apart have felt endless, but this... *this is not right*.

"The void," I mutter, realization striking like lightning. "Time moves differently there."

Zyphoro nods grimly in agreement, but my focus is only on Amara now. I grasp her hand, pressing it to my lips, kissing her knuckles as if I can will warmth back into her skin. But she is so cold. Clammy with sweat, her complexion leached of color.

Her fingers tighten weakly around mine. "Daedalus..." Her voice is barely a breath, pain twisting her features. Her eyes, hazy with suffering, flicker to mine. "Is it really you?"

"Yes, my love," I whisper fiercely, cradling her hand against my face. "I am here. We are together at last."

She sobs, the sound fractured, caught between agony and relief. "This isn't right. I'm not ready. I haven't carried long enough." Her breath hitches, and then, in a voice laced with raw terror, she chokes out, "There's too much blood."

I press her palm to my skin, closing my eyes, letting the familiarity of her touch anchor me. "You are strong. Our baby is strong. You do not know fear."

Her body convulses violently. A strangled cry rips from her lips as she lurches forward. Solena's eyes flare with panic.

"We must deliver this baby," she says, voice edged with urgency. "Or we will lose them both."

The pain tears through Amara, a violent storm that shakes her to the core, and I feel it as if it's my own. Her body trembles, her cries slipping through clenched teeth and every ragged gasp she takes, every plea she breathes, shreds me further. The ship rocks violently with each wave, rising higher, crashing louder, like the world itself is mirroring Amara's pain. A sharp gust of wind whips through, snapping the sails with loud cracks while the sky, once a pale canvas of daylight, darkens with an unnatural speed, clouds twisting above, birds scattering, fleeing the encroaching darkness that swallows the sun.

"Hold on, Amara. Please," I whisper, but she doesn't hear me.

She's too lost in the agony of labor to hear me, her grip like a vice around my hand as her body twists and convulses with something far too monstrous to name.

And her eyes... they're no longer hers.

Where there was once warmth, those beautiful, rich brown eyes that cast their spell on me long before she came into her magic, now there is only black. Slow and creeping, it overtakes them, like ink spilling through water.

Smoke, dark as tar, trickles from her mouth, her ears, her very pores. It spills over her skin, staining the wood beneath her, a spreading darkness that I can't stop.

I reach for her stomach, my fingers trembling, desperate to calm her, desperate to reach our child. My hand hovers just above her, barely grazing her writhing belly, but my hand snaps back to me when a flash of darkness strikes my vision, and within the shadows, I see him. Gygarth, his shadow looming over me, over her, over everything.

I jerk back, the air around me freezing, suffocating. My skin burns with the imprint of his darkness, his power, the same haunting force that has been chasing us, threatening to tear us apart since this nightmare began. His power is not just in the smoke, not just in her eyes, it is in the very soul of this moment, in the very fabric of this place.

I reach for Amara again, but I won't pull away this time. I can't. I won't let her slip into whatever dark void is calling to her, pulling her under with every breath she takes. The ship rocks violently again, the waves now towering over us, crashing like the world is falling in on us.

"Amara," I whisper fiercely, squeezing her hand. "Fight this. *Fight for us.*"

Her breath stutters and her body arches once more, wracked with forces I cannot soothe. And then, for the span of a single heartbeat, I see it. A flicker. Her eyes. The barest glimmer of brown, warm and aching, like a dying ember fighting to burn beneath an ocean of flame.

I do not know how much longer we can defy this. How much longer can I hold her in the light before the dark I summoned claims her completely?

This curse, this shadow, it wears my name. No god nor demon bears the blame for her agony. Only I do. My love wrought this. My yearning. My reckless, ruinous need.

But my wife...

She is forged from iron roots buried deep in the bones of the earth, tempered by the wild, unyielding fury of the untamed world. She is strength incarnate, older than fear, fiercer than fate. Stronger than me. Stronger than any darkness that dares to claim her.

"Amara," I whisper, my voice raw, desperate. "My queen. Do not leave me."

Kneeling at Amara's feet, Solena looks up and though her face maintains a stillness despite the chaos, the tautness of her shoulders and the slight trembling of her hands give away the fear that rattles her too. The smoke continues to ooze, slithering along the wood, mingling with Amara's blood.

"It's time," Solena says.

I nod, clutching Amara's hand, even though I'm not sure she knows I am even here. Her body tenses, her breath shallow as another wave of pain crashes over her. I grip her hand tighter, the sweat on her skin making it difficult to hold on, but I don't let go. I can't.

"Push, Amara," Solena commands, her voice rising over the thunder booming through the sky. "You have to push now."

She doesn't respond, but her body shifts, her hands clenching, and I can see the effort it takes her to fight against the overwhelming wave of pain.

The air feels colder now, so cold it seeps into my bones. The smoke intensifies, dark tendrils curling around Amara's form, suffocating the air, and the ink beneath her pools deeper.

And yet, still, Amara fights. She must.

"One more push, Amara," Solena says, her voice low but firm. "You're almost there. I can see the head."

Amara's body jerks violently, and I can feel her pulse quicken beneath my hand. My heart races in response, and I hold my breath, waiting for the moment I know is coming, the moment when the dark, energy around us finally breaks.

Another scream tears from her throat. Amara gives a final push. Her body convulses, and for a moment, everything stops. The waves, the thunder, the smoke. The world holds its breath.

And then, with the sound of a small, fragile cry, I hear it. The baby.

Tears fill my eyes before I even realize it, but I can't stop them. Not as Solena lifts the baby from Amara's trembling body.

"Amara," I whisper, my voice hoarse. "Look. Look at our baby."

But when I look down at her, she is silent. Still. Her eyes closed.

"Amara..."

A hush falls over the ship. Reon and Orios bow their heads, stepping back, turning away while Zyphoro moves closer, still holding Amara's other hand. Her eyes are fixed on me, a sheen of sadness glistening in them. But I refuse to acknowledge their pity.

"Amara," I say again, my voice trembling as I stroke her hand, unwilling to accept the way her skin has cooled, how her fingers hang limp in mine.

"Brother," Zyphoro says softly. "You must tend to your child. Let us take care of this."

"Take care of what?" I snap, my canines lengthening, fury surging through me like the storm itself. "There's nothing to take care of," I growl.

Zyphoro dips her chin in submission. "As you wish, Daedalus."

"No," Solena interjects with urgency, her voice tight, the child still squirming in her arms. "Look. She breathes."

I turn back to Amara's body. I see it. Just the faintest rise and fall of her chest. Barely there, but it's enough.

"Amara," I plead, my voice cracking, my chest tight with desperation. "Wife. Hold on. Please."

Time stretches around us. Seconds feel like hours, each one heavier than the last, the silence unbearable as we wait for her to return to us. To me. To our child. My chin dips toward my chest, my shoulders shaking with the weight of my pain. I grip her hand tighter, feeling the warmth slip away, feeling her fade.

This is the doom of Amara Tyne. A fate I could have saved her from. A bargain she could not escape.

But then, her finger moves.

At first, I think I imagined it. Perhaps I wanted it so badly that I thought I saw something. But then it happens again. Her index finger twitches, then her thumb. I feel warmth rushing back, her blood pumping, her pulse strengthening. A smile breaks through the despair, relief flooding me like a rushing tide.

"Wait," Zyphoro whispers, her voice a mix of awe and confusion. "She's getting so hot." She pulls her hand away from Amara's, her eyes wide in wonder. "Is that... fire?"

I blink away the haze of joy, still too overwhelmed by her return to notice the green flames rolling across Amara's skin.

"Yes, it's fire," a voice says from behind us.

I spin, my eyes narrowing, and catch sight of the Golden Son sitting casually on the deck. His legs are bent, hands resting on his knees, his bare chest bruised and battered. He may not wear his mask, but I would know his scent anywhere, and its stench makes my blood boil.

Rage surges through me, threatening to consume every last ounce of control I have. I want to tear him apart. But then, he nods toward Amara's still form as the green fire grows taller, hotter, until it consumes her entirely.

"I would move if I were you," he says, his tone almost bored. Without waiting for a response, he scrambles across the deck and leaps overboard.

A splash echoes, the sound of his body hitting the water, and we exchange looks of confusion. But as the fire intensifies, Reon and Orios inch closer to the railing, and Zyphoro clambers to her feet. They share a final glance before their wings burst forth. Reon, Orios, and Zyphoro soar upward, vanishing into the sky.

I glance at Solena just as the snap of her wings pierces the air. She holds my child tight against her chest before she too, takes flight. I'm reminded bitterly that I cannot follow them.

The emerald flames swallow Amara whole, and I turn my face away from the blistering heat. A low growl rumbles in my chest as I spring to my feet, my muscles burning with urgency. I dash across the deck, hurling myself overboard just as the fire erupts in a violent burst, sending a scorching wave across the ship before the flames recoil into themselves.

I crash into the water with a brutal splash, the heat of the flames searing my back just before I'm submerged. When I break the surface, I gasp for air, floating there for a moment, stunned and disoriented, trying to make sense of what just happened. Then I see him bobbing beside me, the Golden Son, water dripping from his blond hair, coursing down the ridges of his scarred face.

"How did you know that would happen?" I snarl.

He meets my glare with unsettling calm. "I've seen it before," he replies. "She killed a room full of Fae with that fire. It cleanses her, heals her, but..." He shrugs, as if indifferent to the lives burned in its wake. "Unfortunately, anyone nearby gets reduced to ash."

We float in tense silence, neither of us yielding an inch. Then, I hear a soft murmur carried on the wind. Amara's voice, fragile yet unmistakable.

Without hesitation, I swim back to the ship, grabbing hold of the mooring rope and hauling myself up. As I reach the railing, a hand suddenly clasps over mine. I look up to find Reon waiting.

He grips my forearm and pulls me aboard effortlessly. "Sorry about that, old friend. I forgot your wing situation."

I glare at him but don't waste time on words. There's no room for anything but action now. I rush to Amara's side, dropping to my knees and sliding across the floorboards to her.

"Wife," I say, the word barely escaping my lips. "Are you alright?"

My gaze scans over her, dreading the sight of a body shattered by childbirth, scarred by the fire. But my Amara... she is untouched. Perfect. The green flames have left no trace upon her. No burn, no mark, not even a singed hair. Even the ship has borne the brunt of her fire with only a few smoldering remnants, quickly extinguished by Reon and Orios.

She manages a smile, a soft curve of her lips, as I take her hand in mine, pressing a gentle kiss to her knuckles.

"I will survive," she whispers, her voice soft, her eyes half-closed in exhaustion. "Is it truly you?"

I nod, pressing her hand to my cheek, letting her feel the steady beat of my pulse beneath her fingers. "It is, wife. It is."

Her smile deepens, her flawless, warm brown eyes shimmering with the first true spark of life I've seen in what feels like forever. But then, suddenly, they widen with alarm.

"Our baby," she gasps.

Before I can respond, Solena's boots touch down softly on the deck, her wings folding neatly behind her. She approaches slowly, reverence in her every step, and kneels beside Amara. With a careful motion, she unfurls her arms to reveal our child.

Our perfect, tiny girl.

Her face is flushed with the heat of birth, her tiny hands clenched as if already grasping for the world, her cries soft but determined. The only sound that exists in the vastness of this moment.

Solena gently places the baby in Amara's arms, and I watch as my wife, still trembling with weakness, looks down at our daughter. Her gaze softens, and for the first time, I see a peace I thought lost forever.

A part of me wants to believe that this is it. That we've conquered the darkness. I want to believe that this child, this precious little girl, will be the light in a world fractured by shadows. But I know better. The void is still out there, watching, waiting. Emranth has caught our scent, and the Father Below demands his due. This child, so pure, so innocent, has entered a world twisted by smoke and vine. She is not human, not Fae, but something else entirely.

Still, I can't stop the smile that tugs at my lips, a surge of love and relief washing over me in a flood too overwhelming to resist. The world is broken, but in this moment, with my wife and daughter by my side, I find hope where I thought none could exist.

CHAPTER 21
DAED

*B*efore *her*. I watch from the ruined heights of House Maledannan as the Sundered Kingdoms burn. Villages smolder in the distance. Forests, once sacred, crackle with flame. This Legion of Saints, these rebels, these ungrateful humans, have summoned their own doom. Did they truly believe the Mordorin would show mercy? That we would share our power like beggars at a feast?

Fools. This blood is on their hands, not mine. And we will fight until only the Mordorin stand.

I walk the cold, silent halls of this once-proud house, and even here, high above the chaos, I hear the wails of the dying and the wind-fed roar of fire. House Maledannan's green banners lie torn and filthy, trampled under boot and soaked in blood. Shattered windows gape like wounds. The tapestries have been ripped from the walls. The Fae who guarded this place lie slumped in corners, blades still lodged in their bodies, their blood now dark and tacky on the stones.

The doors to the throne room, battered and barely on their hinges, groan as I push them open, the sound low and feral like a beast disturbed from sleep. A painting topples from the wall as I enter, ancient and priceless, and crashes to the floor in pieces. The twin thrones of Lord Eryndor and Lady Elyss lie overturned, discarded like the corpses of their house. The banners of the white lotus have been torn from their moorings, and near one toppled throne, a child's toy, a small doll, lies smeared with blood.

I move to the wall veiled in heavy vines. I cannot command them as Lord Eryndor once did. So I summon Death Singer. Smoke curls from my fingers as the blade takes shape in my palm, silver glinting as it settles into being. I strike the vines with a single cut. They fall away, revealing... nothing.

The scrying mirror is gone, stripped away like everything else in this place. Death Singer vanishes from my grasp, and for a moment, I sag beneath the weight of what isn't here.

I would be lying if I said I hadn't come to this devastated castle hoping to see her again in the mirror's glass. Even with war tearing the world apart, she haunts my every thought.

The missing mirror is for the best.

If I knew Amara Tyne lived, if I saw her again... I would only want her more.

A scent rides the air. Smoke. Blood. Steel. It slinks in before him, curling through the empty halls just ahead of the heavy clomp of Arax's boots on stone.

"My Prince," he says, entering with a fist to his chest. "I bring word from the front. The Legion has been driven back in the east, but we've lost Greenmist Gorge."

I turn, just slightly to glance at him over my shoulder. "How?"

"The reinforcements from House Taramethos never came," he answers. "An entire order of Ebon Flight... gone."

My breath hisses through my nose. My jaw clenches. Fingers curl into fists, gauntlets straining around them.

"I will go myself," I say.

"You cannot, Rook," Arax replies quickly. "It's too dangerous. The gorge is narrow, and they hold the high ground. Their numbers..."

"I will flood that gorge with their blood," I snap. "I did not ask for your counsel, Arax."

He nods. "Yes, my Prince." A beat passes, and I hear the thick bob in his throat.

"They've found the bodies of the Lord and Lady of House Maledannan," he says at last. "On a bonfire in the plains near the forest."

His eyes flick to the overturned thrones, to the smear of blood trailing toward the shattered door.

"Lady Ilyra's spies report the Legion passed through here several days ago."

Another pause and for a warrior as blooded as Arax, who has watched fields rot under corpses, this next truth cleaves clean through his composure.

"It seems the young ones were burned with them."

I don't answer. I don't need to. The sharp crack across my chest is answer enough.

"There was a mirror," I say, voice low. "Do you remember it?"

He nods. "Yes, Your Highness. The Legion must have taken it when they raided the castle."

"Perhaps."

"I'll assemble the Reapers and await your command," Arax says, already turning, his armor clanging with the shift.

But I stop him.

"I heard about Estra."

He halts.

"My condolences, Arax."

"Thank you, Your Highness," he says. The words don't tremble. They land like stone.He hides his grief the way I do. Deep and silent.

I listen to his footsteps retreat down the hall as I remain fixed on the wall where the mirror once hung. Whoever took it now holds a key to great power. Too great. I don't believe for a breath it fell into mortal hands. The Sundered Kingdoms are burning, yes, but both sides are lighting fires. And in war, I trust my own kind even less than I trust the human traitors.

Then, footsteps again. Arax, doubling back.

"Your Highness," he calls. "We've found something. A deserter."

I turn, my brow lowering, curiosity tightening into suspicion. We stride together through the corridor, pushing through the cracked doors onto the stone terrace where vines creep through every fracture.

The sky above us is choked with smoke, glowing orange, the air hangs heavy with ash and the stink of burning men.

An order of Blades stands ready outside, the line of Reapers behind them rigid as stone and at their feet, on his knees, trembles a lone male.

His dark hair is thick with blood and soot, his body shuddering with each sob as he stares at the ground. His armor is scorched, his blade discarded.

But it's unmistakable.

House Taramethos.

Crafters of relics. Masters of transmutation. The forge-born. His dusksteel breastplate, though battered and burned, still bears their mark. A single anvil wreathed in flame.

The Eternal Forge.

And now, its loyal son kneels in the mud.

"They caught him trying to flee into the mountains," Arax says.

I step forward, casting a long shadow over the trembling figure. He shivers, shoulders hunched, spine bent beneath shame.

"You desert not only your prince," I snarl, "but your house?"

"Mercy, Your Highness," he gasps, daring to lift his gaze, but not quite meeting mine, as if he knows what lives behind them will be his undoing. "My family. My wife and children. I was only trying to protect them."

Arax leans in, his voice low at my ear. "We found them with him. A female and three young ones. They're in the camp, down in the valley."

"Please," the deserter whispers, his voice cracked and raw. "Do what you must with me. Just let them live."

I raise my hand. Smoke coils between my fingers and in the next breath, the hilt of Death Singer nestles into my palm, its silver edge humming with hunger.

"You are a coward," I growl, dragging the blade's tip across the stone until it screams, "and a traitor. For such things, you forfeit your life."

He nods. Not in defiance, but acceptance.

The sobs still, hollowed out. He looks up, finally, and though his eyes are slick with tears, there's a brittle calm in them.

"As you wish, Your Highness. But my family... please."

But the void stirs in me.

Tendrils of shadow crawl up my spine. My vision darkens. My eyes roll black.

Death Singer arcs.

One clean strike.

His head topples from his shoulders with a wet thud, rolling across the stone. His body slumps after it, like a puppet whose strings were cut mid-beg.

I stand over what remains, breathing hard.

Then I lift my hand, and with a flick of my wrist, a veil of smoke rolls over the corpse, swallowing it whole.

Meat for the beast.

The Father Below, Gygarth, stirs inside me. That ancient, hungering dark that no offering can ever satisfy. Even now, after the kill, he leans close to my soul with clawed talons and a low, insatiable whisper:

Feed me, Favored One. Feed your master.

My jaw locks. Eyes squeeze shut. I fight to surface, to tear myself free from the abyss that claws at my ribs and would gladly drown me.

Then I hear Arax's voice at my ear. "Your Highness. The family. What do you want done with them?"

Death Singer fades from my grasp, vanishing into ash.

My silver eyes snap open.

"Give them food and water," I say at last. "Keep them safe."

Arax slams his fist to his chest, his head bowed in submission, but my reply startles him as much as it does me. Still, he does as he is commanded.

"Yes, Your Highness."

***

After her. I never believed I was worthy of love. Not once.

A wicked, cursed thing, born of death, wrapped in shadow and regret. I thought that was all I was. What I would always be. No light could touch me, no warmth could thaw the ice that had wrapped itself around my soul. I didn't deserve the simple joys that others had. The quiet moments, the laughter, the softness of a kiss, the feel of a child's hand curling around your finger. Not with the things I had done, the mistakes that haunted me, the blood that stained me, the deaths I had caused.

And yet, somehow fate has thrown my curses aside and given me blessings I could never have imagined.

A wife. A daughter.

For the first time in my life, I am a part of something good and pure.

I had never imagined this. Never thought I could have this. The feeling of Amara beside me, her soft breath, the warmth of her skin against mine. The tender gaze she gave me, the way her smile lit up the dark. And then our daughter. Our perfect daughter, so tiny, so fragile, her small hand curled in mine. Her soft, dark hair, her little eyes, gray like mine, her skin the perfect shade of tawny like her mother. She is our love made flesh, a promise between us, a child of two worlds, a princess of both.

I can't even wrap my mind around it. The three of us, together.

I gaze at them both now. Amara's peaceful form, our daughter resting in her arms and for the first time, I feel something more than guilt, more than despair. I feel *whole*.

My hand reaches out to touch Amara's cheek, the warmth of her skin grounding me, reminding me that I am not the monster I believed I was. I am her husband. I am the father of our child. I am worthy, *because of them.*

And I will never take this gift for granted.

I carry my wife to a small cabin below deck and tend to her while our daughter sleeps, swaddled and warm, in a makeshift crib Reon and Orios fashioned from a hewn barrel.

Time passes, though I cannot say how much. Hours, perhaps. I have not left Amara's side. I refuse to.

Slowly, the color begins to return to her cheeks. The ashen cast lifts. Her breathing grows deeper. The warmth of life creeps back into her skin, chasing out the cold that nearly stole her from me.

I cleanse her carefully, cloth and water in hand, wiping away the blood and sweat still clinging to her. Her body shivers beneath my touch, the tremors of agony still echoing through her limbs. I long to kiss away the hurt, to draw it from her bones and bury it in my own flesh. But I can't. I press my lips to her forehead instead, brushing aside the damp strands of hair that cling to her skin.

Her gown, which I imagine was splendid once, is ruined, soaked through in blood. I remove it with care, reverent in the way I slide the fabric from her limbs. My fingers graze her skin as I dress her in a soft linen nightgown.

She stirs faintly, her eyes barely opening. No words, only weak murmurs that seem to leave her more spent. She has endured enough. Let the world wait. She deserves peace.

A knock at the door draws a scowl to my face. When it creaks open and our daughter stirs in her crib, it takes everything in me not to rise in fury.

"What is it?" I snarl under my breath.

Reon clears his throat. His voice is quiet. "Daedalus. There is a matter above deck that requires your attention."

I exhale, the sound rough and reluctant. I already know what he means. Still, leaving this room feels impossible. I have waited so long for this. To have them. To hold them. And now that I do, I would trade every throne, every crown, just to remain here.

Reon speaks again when I don't answer. "We could kill him if that's what you want."

I believe he would, without hesitation. It would save me the trouble. The Golden Son does not deserve a trial. He does not deserve mercy. We could hang him from the mast for his crimes against the Fae and be fully justified.

But one question burns on my tongue, and I cannot let it go. If I let Reon take his life now, I will never have the answer.

I need to know what happened in Driftspire.

"No," I say, my voice low but steady. "I'll handle it."

Reon leaves the door open, and I follow. I look back once, unable to help myself. I seal them in with a soft click of the door, as if the whole world might shatter if I close it too loudly.

Above deck, the storm has passed. The same storm my daughter's birth summoned, scattered to the edges of the horizon. Dusk is near. The wind carries a sharper chill, and the sky burns gold and crimson as the sun sinks into the sea.

Reon and Orios stand on either side of the Golden Son, holding him fast. His arms are locked between their grips, but he does not resist. He stares at me with a slight tilt of the head, one brow raised, the one unmarred by scars, as if baffled to find himself still breathing.

He should be. I never meant for him to escape the void. I wanted to leave him there, suspended in nothingness, tossed around by the demons that feast on lost souls, his spirit torn from his body, dragged into the dark where it would be ripped apart again and again for all eternity.

But no. He had to have been touching Amara when I pulled her free. A stowaway when I void walked. My anger stirs again. The thought of his filthy hands on her, even in the smallest way, is enough to send me spiraling. Then I remember the scrying mirror, and the image it showed me. Amara in his arms.

My hand moves before I can even understand the urge. A punch. A brutal, vicious strike to his jaw. The sound of flesh meeting bone, followed by the sickening spray of blood that bursts from his mouth and splatters across Reon's boot.

"Brilliant," Reon sighs irritably, shaking off what he can.

But the Golden Son doesn't flinch. Doesn't crumple. Instead, his eyes lock with mine, and that, more than anything, sets my blood alight. There's something in his gaze, something defiant, something that dares me to do worse.

I take a step forward, my heart thundering in my chest as if it too wants to crush him. But not yet.

"Tell me everything," I demand.

He doesn't answer. Not at first. He just watches me, blood dripping from his swollen lip, eyes burning with something darker than hatred. It claws at me, gnawing at the edges of my sanity. Without another thought, I swing my fist into his jaw, the sickening crack of bone echoing in the silence between us. His head jerks to the side, but there's no grunt of pain, just another defiant spit of blood onto the deck.

"What did they do to her?" I take a step closer. My hands tremble, but not with fear. My fists are clenched, my breath coming harder with each word. "What *did you* do to her?"

"I did nothing," he sneers, his voice dripping with bitterness. "I tried to help her escape."

A mocking laugh escapes me before I can hold it in. "I don't believe a fucking word you say."

His jaw clenches. "Then why bother asking me? I'm telling you the truth. I wanted to help her."

"And you deserve my thanks for that?" My voice cracks with fury, and without thinking, I strike again. My fist slams into his face, and he reels back, this time with a grunt. The satisfaction of the punch lingers, but it does nothing to still the ache inside me. "You were the one who *stole* her from me. You sided with those Ithranor traitors. *You* are the reason I lost her."

His swollen lips twist into a grimace as he spits more blood, but his gaze remains unflinching. The spiteful glint in his eyes doesn't fade. "You lost her all by yourself," he sneers, voice thick with scorn. "You lost her when you married her, when you dragged her away from her own people. You made her leave everything she loved. You doomed her the moment you bound her to you. *You* destroyed her. How could you not see it? How could you, knowing what she was? How could you not see how the Fae would covet her, despise her, all at once?"

The words land like a dagger, sinking deep into the hollow pit of my chest. The accusation rings true, and I feel the weight of it crushing me. Reon and Orios, standing by, their silent questions heavy on me, their eyes too sharp. The quiet judgment presses against me.

"You don't know what you're talking about," I murmur, barely more than a growl, but the words taste bitter in my mouth. How can I defend myself against this, against him? Against the truth I cannot hide?

His laugh is soft, low, almost pitying. "Maybe I don't understand everything," he says. "But Anethesis, that bastard, loved the sound of his own voice. He told me what she is. What she's capable of. You married an *Awakened*. You put a child inside her." His eyes turn hard, cruel. "Did you really think you could have it all? You're just another Fae parasite, aren't you? Selfish, pathetic. You don't care what you destroy, as long as you have power over it."

Each word cuts through me, leaving a jagged wound, and though I want to fight it, deny it, I know in the deepest part of me that he is right. I wanted it all. Amara, our life, our daughter. And now, I see the cost. The price of it all. My fists tighten, nails biting into my palms, but I can't move, can't stop the storm of guilt and rage building inside me.

For the first time, I wonder if he's right. If I've destroyed everything I touched.

"Leave him, Daed."

Amara's voice cuts through the fury pulsing in my veins, and I turn to find her leaning against the doorframe. She is pale but standing, strong despite the exhaustion that must weigh on her limbs. My heart stammers, torn between relief and concern, and in an instant, I'm at her side.

"My love," I murmur, bracing her with my hands, steadying her before she can sway. "You need to rest."

She scowls, pushing me away with a stubborn frown that is so wholly her it makes my chest ache.

"I've had a baby, not lost a leg," she grumbles, and it takes every ounce of my restraint not to kiss the irritation right off her lips.

But there is no time for indulgence, no time for the way my body sings with the need to hold her, have her, keep her.

Her gaze flickers past me, landing on the bloodied, battered form of the Golden Son.

"He tried to help me escape Driftspire," she says, each word measured. "For that alone, he has saved himself from a death sentence."

I shake my head, waiting for the punchline, for the fire I know lurks beneath her steady voice. "Amara. After all he's done? After Arax?"

I regret saying his name the moment it leaves my mouth.

She wavers, like a candle caught in a draft, like a flower wilting beneath the weight of winter. And I see it, the memories flashing behind her eyes, shadows of the past curling their fingers around her. I can only imagine the depth of the pain lurking beneath her skin, the agony she keeps pressed beneath the surface.

But Amara is nothing if not unbreakable. She squares her shoulders, forces herself to breathe, and comes back to me, just like she always does.

"I said it saved him from death, not from punishment," she says, her voice iron.

My jaw tightens, and I drag my gaze back to him, to the blood dripping from his mouth, to the smug twist of his lips that makes my hands itch to rip his head clean from his shoulders.

But then Amara cups my face, her fingers a whisper of warmth against my skin, and gods, I have dreamed of this. Of her touch, of her scent, of the quiet way she soothes the rage inside me.

"You will not kill him on this ship, husband." Her voice is gentle, but there is no room for argument. "His fate will be decided when we reach the Sundered Kingdoms."

I inhale her scent and nod into her touch. "Yes, wife. If that is what you wish."

Then I flick a sharp glance to Reon and Orios. "Put him below deck."

They nod, their grip tightening around his arms, hauling him toward the heavy door that leads to the ship's underbelly. To the cages. To the dark. The Golden Son does not fight. He moves at his own pace, his head held high, smirking despite the blood smeared across his teeth.

And as he passes, he does not look at me.

No. His eyes, bright blue, gleaming, knowing... find her.

And she looks away.

But I see it.

The flicker of something.

A memory. A secret. A shard of *him* buried somewhere inside *her*.

It takes everything in me not to crush his skull beneath my hands, to pry open his mind and pick that memory free piece by bloody piece.

But then he is gone, dragged below by Reon and Orios, and my pulse is still roaring, pounding so hard I can hear it in my ears.

Amara tightens her grasp on my cheek, her touch pulling me back.

I place my hand over hers. "He cannot be trusted, Amara."

Her gaze sharpens. "Some would say the same about you."

The words crack against my ribs. My head jerks up, but she presses on.

"When Ronin discovered what Anethesis intended for me, he came to my cage, risked everything, to set me free. If not for his warning, I might already be dead."

There are a hundred things in her words that should seize my attention, but only one lodges itself in my skull. A name. One I have never heard before. A sound foreign to me, bitter on my tongue.

Through clenched teeth, I ask, "Is that what he is called? Ronin?"

Her eyes widen, startled. Then, a slow swallow, her lips parting as if to take it back, but it's too late.

"I'm sorry," she mutters, as if she knows she has lodged a knife in my heart. "I don't know why I called him that."

Something close to a smile pulls at my mouth, but it is a razor-thin thing. I force the words past my teeth, my mouth working hard to keep them soft. "You call him by his name now? This man who saved you when I could not. Tell me more of the bond you two share."

Amara's brown eyes narrow, her spine straightening like a drawn bowstring. "Husband. Is this really the path you want to take with me? After our time apart. After the birth of our daughter. You truly want to play the jealous husband now?"

Her reason claws at my insides, but the petty, bitter part of me wants to snap yes. Yes, I am jealous. Yes, I want to tear him apart with my bare hands for every moment he was near you. For every word he spoke to you. For every breath he stole in your presence, and if he touched you, gods help me, if he touched you, there would be nothing left of him to bury. I would grind his bones to dust in my fist.

But I cannot say these things. Because she is right.

There is nothing more important than us right now. Than our family. We are together, and I will not let my jealousy, my seething, insatiable, marrow-deep, gut-wrenching, soul-consuming jealousy ruin that.

So instead, I slide my hand around the soft curve of her waist and pull her against me. I feel the sharp hitch of her breath, hear the pounding of her heart, watch the rise and fall of her chest. The swell of her breasts beneath her nightgown would have me hard if I weren't such a gentleman.

I whisper against her lips, "No, wife. I want nothing but to bring you peace and ease."

Our mouths brush, a feather-light touch that sends a tremor through her breath as I feel the warmth of her beneath the thin fabric.

I crave her. I always have. The way she yields to my touch yet remains unbowed. And before I can feed my addiction to the way she tastes, the way she shatters under my hands, there is a soft cough behind us.

We pull apart slowly. Reluctantly. Frustratedly.

I turn, a growl forming at the back of my throat, until I see who it is.

Solena bows her head. "I am sorry to interrupt, but..."

"Solena!" Amara breathes, and just like that, I am forgotten. She pushes me aside, barely sparing me a glance, as she rushes to Solena, throwing her arms around her.

Solena's smile is tight with relief, her eyes slipping closed as she falls into Amara's embrace. Her fingers dig into Amara's back the same way mine had a moment ago, desperate, as if afraid she might slip away again.

They hold each other for a long while, and when they finally part, their fingers remain laced.

"Thank you, Solena," Amara murmurs. "Thank you so much."

Solena shakes her head. "Amara, no. You do not need to thank me for anything."

"But I do," Amara insists. "And I will thank you for the rest of my life. You brought my daughter into this world. You were the first pair of hands to hold her, and there is no one else I would rather share that with."

Despite Amara's words, Solena only looks away, her smile brittle, her voice strained.

"I was only doing what needed to be done."

Amara tilts her head, studying her. "Well, you and I have much to talk about. So much time to make up for."

Solena nods, but something flickers behind her eyes. "Yes. Of course. We have waited for this day for so long." Her gaze shifts to me. "But I need to check Rook's sigils. He went into the void to pull you free, and I fear they have weakened."

The warmth in Amara's expression dims as her attention drifts to me.

"Rook?" The word sits sourly on her tongue. She raises an eyebrow at me. "Sigils?"

I nod. "Runes that keep me hidden from Gygarth. They helped me keep control while I searched for you, but they are not permanent. Solena has been reapplying them often."

A silence settles between us, heavy and brimming with unspoken things. It makes my skin itch.

"She has?" Amara asks, her voice even, but the furrow of her brow betrays the curiosity threading through her words. Her gaze flickers between Solena and me, sharp and assessing, before finally settling on me. It burns like a brand against my skin, and I recognize that look. The same one I wore when she called that bastard by his name. *Ronin*.

"I have," Solena murmurs, dipping her chin.

"Well then, by all means," Amara says, and the clipped edge of her tone does not go unnoticed. "The last thing we want is for my husband to lose control." She exhales, then turns to Solena, squeezing her hands tighter. "I should be with my daughter, anyway. But we'll talk soon, please?"

"Yes, soon."

Neither of them lets go. Their hands remain clasped, fingers interlaced in a silent standoff, as if waiting for the other to be the first to break away. When they finally part, it is Amara who releases first, their fingers drifting apart like something reluctantly severed.

She returns to me then, rising onto her toes to press a kiss against my cheek.

"I will see you soon," she murmurs, softer now.

Then she slips into the cabin, the door clicking shut behind her, leaving only the whisper of her warmth in the space she's abandoned.

A stifling silence stretches between Solena and me.

"Well, that was fucking awkward," Zyphoro drawls from above.

Solena and I both glance up to where she's perched on the railing, her legs swinging lazily, expression entirely too entertained.

"Looks like everyone has some explaining to do."

I exhale sharply, running a hand down my face.

This ship suddenly feels far smaller than it did before.

CHAPTER 22

AMARA

None of this feels real. Not being free of Anethesis. Not being back in Daed's arms. Not staring down at this tiny, perfect being who curls her impossibly small fingers around mine, as if she already knows me, as if she belongs to me in a way no one else ever has.

She is flawless. And I should know, I have checked every inch of her. Ten fingers, ten toes. Two ears, their tips delicately pointed. Eyes gray as the storm. A head thick with dark hair, so much like her father's. She is more of him than me in features, and there is no doubt in my mind that she will grow into the same impossible beauty. But her skin... her skin belongs to the Grove. To the ancestors who know the forest as well as they know their own heartbeats.

And I will take her home.

I will lay her beneath the old trees and wait, and I will pray that the Souls will speak to her, that they will claim her as their own. She may be a child of two worlds, but I will make sure she knows mine first. The only one that ever loved me. The only one I still trust. Because the Fae... the Fae have given me nothing but pain, and I will not let them do the same to her. Even her father, for all the love I have for him, has not changed that.

She stirs, taking a deep breath, wriggling against her bed of soft furs in her barrel crib. Her grip on my finger slackens as sleep pulls her under, her tiny belly full and round with milk. Carefully, I tuck her in, smoothing my palm over her silken hair.

I shift, stretching to ease the stiffness in my back from being hunched over as I fed her. It's the only pain I have. I don't remember how I did it, or why, but I've healed myself. Somehow, I spared my body the agony most women endure after bringing life into the world.

It feels selfish.

I stole that suffering from myself, and part of me wonders if I should feel more grateful. Who wouldn't want to recover from childbirth in moments instead of days or weeks? Still, guilt lingers beneath the relief. A quiet whisper that says I didn't earn this the way others have.

With my daughter asleep, I wander across the cabin, taking a seat at a dresser in the corner. I let out a slow breath and reach for a comb, dragging it through my hair, untangling knots and thoughts alike. The ship rocks gently, the waves slapping against the hull in an endless, soothing rhythm. This quiet, this normalcy, it feels foreign. After Driftspire. After the torment. After *him*.

Ronin.

The name slithers into my mind, unbidden, unwelcome. When did I start calling him that?

The Golden Son was easier. A title steeped in hatred, something impersonal, something monstrous. Something undeserving of sympathy. But somewhere between freeing him and Daed pulling me from the void, the title lost its power. It no longer fit. He had shown me another face. And that face had a name.

It still feels strange on my tongue, and I spit it out as much as I speak it.

But he is not the stranger he once was.

It seems no one is.

I don't mean to dwell on the way Solena and Daed looked at each other. It was nothing. Or at least, it should be nothing. He is mine, and I am his. But still. The way she wouldn't meet my eyes. The way his name sounded on her lips.

The comb snags on a tangle, yanking me back from my spiraling thoughts. I tug sharply, as if I can pull the unease from me the same way.

Just as I have been with Ronin all this time, so has Daed been with Solena.

And where just a moment ago I'd brushed off Daed's jealousy as foolish, now I'd give anything to be a fly on the wall in the cabin next door.

I tell myself not to stand. Not to leave my cabin. Not to go next door. But I do.

I tell myself not to press my palm against the doorframe. Not to slip the door open just a crack, breath shallow, praying the wood doesn't creak. But I do.

Not to look inside.

But I do.

Daed lies stretched out on the table, his shirt discarded, a bottle of rum dangling from his fingers. Solena leans over him, one hand braced on his shoulder, the other carefully inking runes into his back.

I don't know how long I stand there, the wind pressing at my back. Maybe I'm waiting for something. No, I *am* waiting for something. A confirmation. A betrayal. The tilt of his head toward hers. The brush of her lips against his. *Something.*

And when nothing happens, when I feel something dangerously close to disappointment, I turn away.

But I do not return to my daughter.

Instead, my feet carry me below deck, to the dim, damp belly of the ship, where water sloshes in thin rivulets over old wood and the beams groan like restless spirits.

In the corner, shackled to a beam by his ankle, Ronin sits with his back against the wall, arms draped over his bent knees.

"I really wish you had just left me in Driftspire," he sighs at the sight of me. "I'm just chained up somewhere else. At least in the tower, my ass wasn't wet."

A smirk tugs at my mouth. "It could be worse. You could be dead."

His brow furrows. "You know what it smells like down here, right?" Then, more thoughtful, "Besides, you are only delaying the inevitable."

I raise a questioning eyebrow.

He exhales, the sound almost amused. "Your husband will kill me the moment I step on land."

I don't correct him because I cannot be sure he's wrong.

"I will talk to him," I say.

Ronin taps his boot against the wet floor, droplets splashing. "Why?"

I shake my head. "Because I have no desire to see you dead."

"Alright," he says with a shrug. "Then set me free, give me a sword, and I'll kill your husband instead."

"No," I breathe. "I have no desire to see him dead either."

Ronin sighs. "Then we're at an impasse." He lifts his gaze to mine, eyes shadowed beneath his brow. "Is that why you came down here? To tell me you want us both to live?"

My frown deepens, confusion tugging at my features. "No."

He shifts slightly, his eyes steady on mine. "Then why are you here? You've given me mercy, but you don't owe me your time. Why aren't you with your family?"

217

His question hits me harder than I expect as the water rises, soaking the hem of my nightgown. I exhale slowly, the breath catching somewhere in the middle.

"I... I don't know." My gaze flickers toward him, almost reluctantly. "I suppose... I'm used to talking to you."

A scoffing laugh escapes him. "Getting sentimental on me, Amara Tyne?" His smirk is laced with something far more biting as he leans back. "Should I fetch a chessboard for old times' sake?" He laughs again, but this time it's mocking, cutting through the silence. "I don't ask for mercy. Never have. But I'd prefer to contemplate my fate alone, if you don't mind."

His words catch me off guard, his coldness making me feel foolish. Like I've been reading far too much into every gesture. I nod quickly, eager to escape the sting of my own vulnerability.

"Very well." I turn, almost fleeing, my wet hem dragging behind me as I hurry up the stairs.

"Does she have a name?" His voice halts me just before I close the door.

I hesitate. "No. Not yet."

"She's a pretty little thing," he says softly. "What I saw of her anyway between the flashes of lightning. She deserves a name just as pretty."

I pause, then reply quietly, "I'll do my best."

And with that, I shut the door.

I make my way above deck, the salty air biting at my skin like a harsh slap, but somehow it's exactly what I need to shake me from the fog of my thoughts.

"Princess," Orios calls as he drops from the mast, landing with a quiet grace that contradicts the share size of him. "It's good to see you again."

"And you," I smile. "You look... bigger."

He grins, the movement quick and easy. "Perhaps."

"I'm grateful to you and Solena," I say. "It couldn't have been an easy choice to go on this journey with Daed."

"It was the easiest decision I've ever made," he replies without hesitation, his voice steady and sure. "I go where my prince goes," he gives a deep bow. "And where my princess needs me."

Before I can respond, Reon approaches, his copper hair glinting like fire.

"Princess Amara," he says with a wry smile. "I feel like we've never met under anything less than chaotic circumstances." He takes my hand, bows and then straightens.

"I'm thankful to you as well," I say, my voice sincere.

"Don't forget me," Zyphoro calls from across the deck, leaning casually against the railing. "I do enjoy the attention."

I smirk at her, knowing full well that she's not joking.

"I'm surprised you and Daed haven't torn each other apart," I remark.

"It's been touch and go," she sighs dramatically. "But I've returned him to you, mostly unspoiled."

Before I can form a response, she throws her arms around me in a bone-crushing hug that steals the air from my lungs. Then shakes me as though I'm little more than a ragdoll.

"I'm so glad you're not dead," she exclaims, her voice muffled against my shoulder.

I frown, catching my breath. "Me too."

When she finally lets go, I can still feel the pressure of her hands on my shoulders.

"So," she says, eyes twinkling with mischief. "Do I get to meet my niece yet? Can't wait to teach her how to use a dagger."

"Zyphoro," I sigh, but it's mostly in fond exasperation.

"No, no," she counters, shaking her head. "You're right. She shouldn't rely on a weapon. Throttling someone with her bare hands, now that's a true skill and Aunty Zyph is an excellent teacher."

I stifle a laugh. "Perhaps we wait until she can walk?"

Zyphoro frowns, disappointed. "Fine. But when she's attacked in her crib, you'll wish she'd learned to defend herself."

I can't help but glance toward the cabin where Solena and Daed are. I try to dismiss the thought, but Zyphoro notices immediately.

"They're doing it for his own good," she says with a knowing look, crossing her arms. "To keep him out of Gygarth's reach. But it won't work forever. Soon, it won't matter at all."

"Then I'll pull him back to me, like I've done before," I reply firmly.

"For the rest of your life?" Zyphoro's eyebrow arches, her tone skeptical. "Seems like a waste of a human lifespan."

"Do you have a better idea?" I ask, matching her tone. "One that doesn't involve cutting off my husband's head?"

Her expression flickers with disappointment. "In the end, it must be one or the other. For Daedalus to be truly free of him, Gygarth must die."

I scoff, the idea ludicrous. "You can't kill a god."

Zyphoro taps her chin thoughtfully. "That's only because no one's tried."

"Perhaps we let Princess Amara recover from childbirth before we discuss killing gods, Zyphoro?" Reon interjects, his tone light but enough to shift the conversation.

I'm grateful for the distraction.

"Are you hungry?" he asks. "We've got some cheese, I think, a few other bits and pieces. It's no feast, I'm afraid."

"No, I'm fine," I reply, giving a small shake of my head. "It's just... nice to walk around without feeling that collar around my neck."

"Collar?" He raises an eyebrow.

I nod, a faint bitterness lacing my words. "They put one on me to numb my powers. Ashen too."

The Fae exchange knowing, silent glances.

"Such tools are forbidden," Reon mutters.

"I'll be sure to mention that next time," I say.

"Anethesis truly had gone rogue," Zyphoro muses. "What did he want from you, Amara?"

Too many questions, and I have too few answers. But maybe, just maybe, they can make sense of all this.

Before I can speak, the cabin door creaks open on its hinges. Daed steps onto the deck, the wind immediately tugging at the loose fabric of his shirt as he slides his arms through the sleeves with a quiet wince. His gaze sweeps over the deck until it snags on me, those silver eyes narrowing, gleaming like storm light.

"You're out of bed... again."

"Our daughter sleeps, and I am restless," I reply.

A slow grin spreads across his face. "I would expect nothing less."

Sea air threads through his hair, salt clinging to his skin that is far bronzer than I've ever known it to be. He's nothing like the pale prince I left behind. The sun has kissed away his polish, leaving behind something rougher, more untamed. Every muscle is leaner, every sinew taut. My heart stumbles, my stomach tightens in a slow, curling heat. Souls, he is as beautiful as I remember, but this version of him, this hardened, wilder Daed, stirs something even deeper.

He closes the distance between us in a few long strides. His arm slips around my waist, pulling me flush against him, and his fingers comb through my hair before settling at the nape of my neck.

"I still can't believe you're here," he murmurs. The rasp of his voice, the weight of his stare. It knocks the air from my lungs. "I need you to myself. Now."

The words send a shiver through me, my mind momentarily blanking. His voice is all I hear, the shape of his mouth all I see. I forget, just for a moment, that we are not alone.

Then the cabin door opens again, and Solena steps onto the deck.

Her fingers are smudged black with ink. She's changed, too. Her skin bronzed from the sun, her once-waifish frame stronger. Her hair is longer now, left loose in a way she never allowed before, save for a few thin braids framing her sharp features. She has always been stunning, but suddenly I notice it far more than I once did.

She inclines her head. "Hello, Amara."

"Solena," I say, nodding in return, though the air between us feels strange. Tense. Like speaking to a ghost of someone I used to know.

Before I can dwell on it, Daed's fingers tighten in my hair, his lips brushing my temple as he leans close.

"Shall we go below?" he asks, voice dark with promise.

Reon chuckles. "Give the lass a moment to breathe, will you?"

"Besides," Zyphoro adds, arms crossed. "She was just about to tell us what happened in Driftspire."

Daed's hold on me eases, but his attention sharpens. "Is that true?" His voice is softer now, careful. "Are you sure you want to talk about it?"

I nod. "I must tell you everything. I don't fully understand what happened, but I fear it is far from over."

Daed exhales slowly. "Very well."

He keeps his arm draped around me as he guides me across the deck, back toward the door he came through. The others fall in behind us. When we reach it, he holds it open for me, but hesitates, his eyes flicking to the floor where the wet hem of my nightgown trails across the wooden boards.

His brow knits, gaze lifting to meet mine. He doesn't speak, though I can tell he wants to. He knows just as well as I do why my nightgown is in such a state. Instead, he tilts his head toward the cabin, wordless in his urging, and waits until I step inside before following.

The cabin is dimly lit, the scent of salt and rum thick in the air. Chairs scrape against the wooden floor as they pull them up around the same table where Daed had been lying only moments ago, Solena carving sigils into his skin. Reon strides forward, dropping two bottles of rum onto the table with a satisfying thud before sliding glasses toward each of us.

I take a moment, letting myself linger on the edges, watching the way they move around each other.

Reon kicks his boots onto the table as he pours himself a drink. Across from him, Zyphoro twirls a strand of raven-dark hair around her finger, gaze flicking between Orios and Solena. Solena pulls out a chair, but before she can sit, Orios catches her by the waist and pulls her onto his lap instead, holding her there with a firm, claiming grip.

I wonder how many times they've sat around this table. How many bottles of rum they've emptied while I was caged in the sky.

The talks they must have had. The battles. The adventures. The misfortunes.

I have never felt at home among the Fae, never truly belonged. But watching them now, the ease of their movements, the unspoken language between them, I feel it even more acutely.

I am an outsider here.

Daed's touch draws me from my thoughts as his fingers weave through mine, warm and steady. There is something in his smile, a quiet reassurance. A reminder that I am wanted.

"Go on then, wife," he says, his voice low. "Tell us everything."

I exhale, slow and measured, trying to find where to begin. "We sailed for days. I slept through most of it. They put a collar around my neck. Invisible, but I could feel it and when I tried to summon my power, it burned. It was bound to a chain, anchored deep in the floor. I spent every day and night locked in a tower high above Driftspire. Ashen..." my throat tightens, "they kept in a cage on the other side of the city."

Daed's expression darkens. His canines lengthen. "Anethesis." He says the name like a curse. "Did he hurt you?"

"Not at first." The words barely leave my lips before his grip tightens around my hand, his body tensing. "At first, he was kind. Then the trials began."

Zyphoro leans forward, her gaze sharp. "Trials? For what?"

"He said they were tests," I murmur. "And that if I passed, he would set me free. As soon as I opened the portal."

Daed stiffens. "A portal to where?"

I hesitate. The name feels dangerous, even here. "Meranor."

The silence that follows is absolute. Tension snaps through the room.

"Meranor?" Reon repeats, his voice eerily quiet. "You're certain he said Meranor?"

I nod.

"That's impossible." Daed shakes his head. "There is no going back to Meranor."

Zyphoro's lips curve into something resembling a smile. "Unless the legends are true. That an Awakened can tear the fabric of worlds and lead the way home."

"That's all they are," Daed snaps. "Legends."

Reon scoffs. "Only because they killed the last Awakened before she had the chance to prove them true."

Daed's head whips toward him, his glare so blistering the room seems to darken under the weight of his fury.

Reon clears his throat, shifting in his seat. "Apologies, friend. My words weren't well chosen."

But I cannot unhear them. My pulse pounds in my throat. "There was another Awakened? You... you knew her?"

Daed's storm-gray eyes meet mine. "Yes. But she wasn't human. She was Fae."

My chest tightens. "And she was killed? For being Awakened?"

Zyphoro answers before he can. "It is considered unnatural," she says, her voice lilting. "Strange, isn't it? That something so natural could be called unnatural? But the Fae believe that no one among them should possess power greater than a king or queen." Her gaze flickers to Daed. "Or even a prince. For all his cursed gifts, Daedalus can only void-walk. Even he cannot open a portal, or see through magic, or unravel the secrets of time and fate. The Fae fear what they cannot control." Her smirk fades, and her voice lowers. "And so they destroy it. As a human, you should know this better than anyone."

"I think you know it as well as I do, Zyphoro," I say, meeting her gaze.

Something shifts in her expression. "I suppose I do."

"The tests," Daed presses. "What were they?"

I draw a breath, steadying myself. It all feels like a nightmare now, but speaking of it brings it back. The panic, the pain, the suffocating dread. But I must endure. I always must endure.

"There was one where I had to mend a shattered mirror with only my mind. Another where I had to choose the correct door from many." My throat tightens. I try to steady the tremble in my voice. "They all had penalties if I wasn't fast enough."

Daed drags my chair closer with a sharp scrape. His hand cups my face, his touch warm despite the fire in his eyes. "Penalties?"

"Pain," I whisper.

The sound of Daed's fist slamming into the table is deafening. Wood cracks beneath his rage, splintering under his knuckles.

"And you passed the tests?" Zyphoro asks. When I nod, she exhales sharply, as if in disbelief. "The cost to open a portal is blood. Lots and lots of blood. You know that?"

"I didn't at first," I murmur. "Not until Ronin told me."

Zyphoro frowns. "Who is Ronin?"

"The Golden Son," Daed growls, the title heavy with disdain.

Solena shifts in Orios' lap. "So The Golden Son betrayed Anethesis to save you?"

I exhale. "I sort of saved him in the end."

Daed growls again, even lower, his teeth grinding so hard I expect them to chip.

Solena's brows knit together. "But why? Why would he do that?"

A silence stretches between us until Zyphoro lets out a wicked, knowing laugh.

"Oh, dear. Did someone get sweet on you?"

"Enough, Zyphoro," Daed snaps.

She only smirks. "I'll take that as a yes."

Daed ignores her, turning his attention back to me. "Where is Anethesis now?"

I let a slow smile creep across my lips. "I left most of him in Ashen's cage."

Reon's brow lifts. "Most of him?"

"Well, his hands are in Ashen's belly."

That earns me a round of approving grins. Fae humor is what it is.

"I should have just flown from Driftspire on Ashen's back," I admit, my voice dropping to a quiet murmur. "Instead, I told him to take us home. I never imagined his instincts would lead us to the void."

"He is a creature of that place. It is written into his bones," Daed answers, pausing as his boot taps once against the wooden floor. His jaw tightens, the muscle ticking as he weighs his next words. "Amara," he says slowly, "when I found you in the void, when I saw Emranth reaching for you... was it you who opened the portal to An'kel?"

A shiver creeps across my skin. I remember that wasteland. I remember the cold. I remember how close I came to releasing something I couldn't hope to control.

"I didn't mean to. I was thinking of the Grove, but that place appeared instead. An'kel."

"You used blood?" Zyphoro asks, her voice quieter now.

I nod. "Just a little."

Daed turns his head toward his sister. "Then the portal was too small. That's why Emranth couldn't get through."

"This Emranth," I repeat the name, its shape heavy on my tongue. "You know him?"

Daed's nod is reluctant. "He serves Gygarth. He is an envoy, a lieutenant, capable of walking between realms where the Father Below cannot."

"He's a lapdog," Zyphoro adds, her tone dry. "He scours the ground for his master's scraps."

"No," Daed says, shaking his head. "He is far more dangerous than that." His attention sharpens on me. "What did he say to you, wife?"

The memory rises, and with it comes the chill of that place. Endless dark. A silence that screamed.

"He wanted our daughter," I say, the words falling from my lips in a tremble.

Daed's shoulders sag. His grip on my hand grows fierce. "We must return to Baev'kalath. With the Blades and the thrall houses behind us, perhaps it will be enough. Perhaps we can protect you both."

Zyphoro hums, unbothered. "It will never be enough."

Daed moves before she finishes speaking. He is on his feet, shadows carved deep into his face.

"I tolerate your jabs because I owe you a century of debt. Because I failed to save you from that prison. But do not test me. Not on this. Not when it comes to my family."

The room goes quiet. Reon hides behind his cup, pretending to drink, while Solena and Orios suddenly find great interest in the walls and floor, unwilling to meet anyone's gaze.

Zyphoro reclines in her chair, arms folded. "Very well, brother," she says with a faint smile. "We will return to Baev'kalath." Her gaze finds mine, and for once, there is no mockery in her eyes. "To protect *our* family."

CHAPTER 23
DAED

*B*efore her. I storm the stone arteries of Baev'kalath, fury in my wake. Each footfall lands with the weight of judgment, louder than the thunder that shudders against the cliffs, more relentless than the sea battering the fortress walls. The very rock beneath my boots seem to flinch.

The Blades stationed in the halls lower their gazes, not from protocol, but fear. They sense it, the storm in my chest, the wrath thickening the air around me like smoke before the fire.

The doors to the throne room loom before me. I don't slow. Magic spills from my palms, dark and furious, curling like ribbons of night. With a thought, I loose it, smoke surging like a tide, slamming into the doors and blasting them from their hinges. They crash to the floor with a final, echoing thud.

At the end of the grand hall, my father rises to his feet and steps in front of her. Queen Lanneth. As if his flesh and bone could shield her from the fire he lit in me.

My lip curls. My vision narrows. Then I step into the void.

The shadows part for me, welcome me. I vanish from the ruined threshold and reappear in a burst of smoke and shadow at the base of the dais. The air cracks as the void closes behind me, and still they flinch. They gasp, startled by the violence I wear like a second skin.

"Daedalus," my father booms, though I hear the uncertainty beneath his voice. "What is the meaning of this?"

I lift a trembling hand, pointing straight at his chest. "You know why I'm here. Don't pretend you don't."

He straightens. "This day was always fated. Zema could not…"

"Do not say her name," I snarl. The sound that tears from my throat is strained. "How could you? And to give the task to Modok…"

"I asked you to do it," he says, calm as ever. "More than once. You could have ended her quickly. You refused."

Pain slices through me. I stagger back a step, breath catching. "She could have lived," I whisper. "She wasn't hurting anyone."

"She would have," Lanneth interjects, her voice like silk soaked in poison. Her hands curl around the throne's arms as she stands. "It was only a matter of time. The houses would have used her, twisted her. Or worse, she would have awakened on her own. And then..."

"You don't know that," I breathe, shaking my head. My voice cracks. "You don't know."

"We knew it was a risk we couldn't allow," she replies coolly.

My rage burns white. My lip trembles. "We. Who is we?" My eyes snap to her, and I spit the words like venom. "You are not my queen. You're just the body that keeps my father's bed warm. You wear my mother's crown like it was made for you, but you command nothing."

"Careful, Daedalus," my father warns. "You speak out of turn."

I look at him. Truly look. At the male who raised me, loved me once. At what he has become beneath her spell. A shadow of himself. A Fae undone by lust and lies.

"You were once a king," I say quietly. "Now you're just her puppet. She told you to do this, didn't she? She told you to have Zema killed."

"She was a distraction, Daedalus," Lanneth cuts in and there it is. Confirmation. The rot beneath the crown.

My fists curl at my sides, the bones aching with restraint.

"Now you can stop wasting time on that forsaken island," she continues, as though offering a kindness. "Focus on your future. A wife. A child. Your duty as the favored son of the Father Below."

I tear my gaze from her poisoned poise and lock eyes with the one I once called father. My jaw is clenched so tightly it aches.

"Do you make any decisions yourself, King Kaelus?" I snarl. "Or does she pull all your strings? What other betrayals have you swallowed to earn your reward between the legs of this poor imitation of my mother?"

"Daedalus! Enough!" Father roars, his voice shaking the stonework, and at that same instant, lightning splits the sky beyond the windows. The throne room is bathed in a sudden white light and in that breathless flash, I see it.

Not the queen.

Not the female.

But the thing beneath.

Where Lanneth should be is a corpse in silk. Sagging flesh over brittle bone, a mouth unhinged in a silent scream, hollow eyes like pits of night.

The light dies.

So do I.

I vanish into the void.

In a blink, I reappear before her, the shadow-slick magic still clinging to my skin. She looks the same, composed, porcelain, cruel, but I know. I see her now.

I seize her by the shoulders. My fingers bite into her flesh.

"What are you?" I roar. "What have you done to my family?"

It's the first time I've seen her break. Her mask fractures. She quivers in my grasp, lips parted, but no sound escapes. And then something cracks in me.

A vision floods my mind, spreading like oil across water. I stagger, disoriented, the world blotted out by what I see.

Endless stairs spiraling into nothing.

A room that shouldn't exist.

And within it, an enchanted cage.

Inside sits a Fae female. Around her neck hangs the other half of the moonstone that rests against my own chest.

A haze settles over me. My stomach lurches. I stumble again, trying to shake the image, to blink it away, but it remains.

She rises from a worn chair, a book in her hands. Then she sees me. She's looking directly at me.

Her hair is black as midnight. Her eyes, gray as the storm.

It's like looking into a mirror.

She steps forward, fingers curling around the bars of her prison. Her lips part, trembling with a single word.

"Brother?"

Then, darkness comes.

Not like sleep.

Like drowning.

It starts in my feet. Shadow coiling, climbing, threading into my veins until every drop of blood feels like smoke. I choke on it as it reaches my throat, my eyes, until the world blinks out in black.

She vanishes.

And with every heartbeat, I lose her. Her face. Her name. The stone. The voice that called me brother.

Gone.

Erased.

Like she never was.

All that remains now is the Father Below, his hand heavy on my shoulder, anchoring me in the dark.

My fingers slip from Lanneth's arms. My hands fall limp at my sides as she gasps for breath, trying to compose herself.

"Can you hear me, Daedalus?" she pants.

"Yes," I murmur, hollow. The world around me is distant, meaningless. There is no more defiance, no more resistance. I want neither. All I want is to serve the void.

She brushes a hand through my hair. I feel nothing.

"Good," she says softly, a cruel smile blooming on her lips.

"You won't hold him like this forever," my father says from somewhere far away, his voice echoing like a ghost in a cavern. "He'll break free. One day, he'll remember."

Lanneth's smile does not fade. She turns her gaze toward him, calm and cold.

"Not while our blessed Father Below holds him," she replies. "They are bound. One cannot live without the other."

***

After her. I stand at the prow of the ship, the sea stretching endlessly before me, cloaked in midnight's embrace. The wind stings my face, the salt clings to my skin, but for those small reminders, it could be the void itself, vast and unknowable.

I close my eyes and listen.

The wind sings, thin and high, carrying voices like echoes from another world.

"Lady Ilyra," I murmur. "Can you hear me?"

It doesn't take long. A whisper weaves through the air, a note of music no louder than a breath. Then moonlight and stardust scatter beside me, coalescing into the shape of a female. She bows low, her form flickering at the edges.

"My Prince," Ilyra says. "Are you well? Have you found her?"

"Yes." Just saying it aloud fills my chest with something close to peace.

Amara is here. She's safe. For now.

"That is wonderful news. Will you return to the Sundered Kingdoms?"

"We sail for the Untold Sea now. If all goes well, we'll reach you before the hunter's moon." My voice lowers. "Lady Ilyra... do we still hold our territories?"

"Yes, Prince Daedalus," she replies, her voice a shiver in the wind. "But we await your return. The days grow darker."

I nod. "Hold fast. I'm coming."

The wind rises, and her form dissolves, scattering like petals on a breeze until nothing remains.

I descend quietly to the cabin below. The room is dim, lit only by the warm orange flicker of a lone candle near the bed. Amara sits with our daughter in her arms, nursing her with tender focus. She looks up when she hears me enter.

"She's hungry again," she says softly.

I nod, letting the warmth of the moment ground me. "Good. She'll grow strong."

I move to sit at the edge of the bed, but before I can, Ashen hops up, small as an armful tonight, circling once before curling into a ball exactly where I would have sat.

He doesn't spare me so much as a glance. Still sulking, no doubt, over being banished back to the void. But as soon as Amara asked, I bought him right back. That doesn't seem to have changed anything.

I frown. "No room for me, then?"

It's almost a joke. Almost. But Amara doesn't laugh. Her gaze drops to the baby at her breast.

"There's a cot," she says, nodding toward the corner where a lonely hammock sways gently with the motion of the ship.

I wait for her to smirk, to glance at me sideways with teasing eyes. But there's no smile. No softness.

"You want me to sleep there?" I ask.

Still, she doesn't look at me. She watches our daughter instead, her fingers brushing a dark curl from the infant's brow while Ashen snores quietly at her feet.

"For tonight. If that's alright."

A dozen responses catch in my throat, none of them right. If my wife wants space, she shall have it. But I've faced war and monsters and the void itself, and nothing has ever cut as deep as this: knowing she doesn't want me beside her.

"Of course," I say, forcing the words past the sharp ache in my chest. "If that is what you wish."

Finally, her eyes lift to meet mine. For a moment, I think this is it, where she says she was joking, where she smiles and beckons me back to bed.

But instead, she just says, "Thank you," and looks down again at our daughter.

I nod, but my body stays frozen, dumb and stiff as stone. Only when the silence stretches long enough to bruise do I turn on my heel and cross to the sad little hammock in the corner.

I strip with more drama than necessary. Shrugging off my shirt and throwing it over the chair, yanking my belt free with a sharp snap. I kick off my boots louder than I need to, glancing at Amara between each move, but she doesn't look at me once. Not a flicker.

With a quiet curse, I pull off the last of my gear and stare down the hammock like it's an enemy formation. I've commanded fleets, conquered cities, survived the void, and yet climbing into this damn thing might be my undoing. I grip both sides, brace myself, and hurl my body at it.

It sways violently. My arms flail. My dignity dies a swift, merciless death.

Finally, it steadies.

A soft giggle escapes from Amara.

It's faint. But it's something. I cling to it like a lifeline.

Still, the words spill from me, uninvited and unforgivable.

"I noticed your nightgown was wet," I say. "Did you go below deck? To see *him*?"

I don't look at her. I can't. The shame of even asking knots my throat. But I hear her heavy, exasperated sigh.

"I did," she says flatly. "Am I not allowed?"

I shrug, the hammock groaning beneath me. "He's dangerous. Our prisoner. I'm just not sure why you'd want to see him."

She doesn't answer.

Only the sound of our daughter nursing, the soft rhythmic pull and swallow, fills the room between us.

I clear my throat, trying to pretend this doesn't matter to me. Trying and failing.

"Well," I say, with a cough. "Why *do* you want to see him?"

"Husband," she says at last, but it sounds more like a reprimand than a vow. "Does it matter?"

I shift in the netting, trying to get comfortable, but it's like curling into barbed wire.

It *does* matter. Gods, it matters more than anything. But I can't say that. Not if I want her to look at me again. Not if I want to be allowed within three feet of her heart.

"No," I lie. "You're right. It doesn't. I trust you."

That earns a dry, mocking scoff. "Oh, do you?" she mutters. "Well thank you so much for trusting me, considering *I'm* not the one who tried to sacrifice the other to a demon god. Goodnight, Daedalus."

And just like that, she blows out the candle. A soft *whoosh*, and the room is swallowed by shadow.

Silence creeps in. The hammock rocks with every breath I take, every regret I cradle in my chest.

I stare at the ceiling, wide awake.

I don't think that could have gone any worse.

I may be a prince. A commander. A legend in battle.

But when it comes to being her husband, I am endlessly, irreparably, *fucking lacking*.

The sea is fickle this far out. Some mornings break clear and blue, the sun gilding the waves with gold, so bright it almost blinds. Other days come in gray and low, with wind that claws through the sails and rain that drums like war on the deck. On those days, everything is soaked. Boots, mood, spirit.

We make steady progress, but each day stretches long.

Amara and I speak little. What we say is often about our daughter, nothing more. She keeps her voice soft when she hands me the child, keeps her hands from touching mine. I hold the baby close, trying to memorize her warmth, her smell, the small sounds she makes when she wakes in my arms.

I carry her on deck when the sun is gentle. Show her the sea. Point to gulls. Tell her stories of leviathans and cloud serpents and all the things that once lived out here. Her eyes, still too young to focus, seem to follow the sway of the sky.

Amara watches from a distance, sometimes. Sometimes she doesn't.

One night sleeping apart folds into several, without discussion or apology.

Each night, I return to the hammock.

Each morning, my back aches and my pride aches worse.

I bring her food. Fresh water. An extra blanket when the wind cuts cold. She accepts them all with polite nods, never cruelty, never warmth. I wonder if I should be grateful for the courtesy.

One afternoon, I find her lingering outside the door to the brig, where the Golden Son is chained like a dog.

She doesn't go in. Just... lingers. Her fingers curl and uncurl at her sides. Her hair whips in the wind, loose and wild, her back rigid and tense.

She turns before I can call out to her.

Later, I pass by again and see her there. Again.

She never speaks of it.

And I never ask.

Once, I try. I brush her shoulder gently as she passes me on the stairs.

"See him if you must," I say, reluctantly giving permission if that is what she needs. Anything to bring her some semblance of joy.

She looks at me then, not with anger, but with exhaustion. Like I am something she once loved, now worn threadbare, and then she's gone.

I throw myself into the rhythm of the ship. I spar with Zyphoro on the upper deck, play dice with Reon, watch Orios train Solena, oil my weapons, scrub the rust from my old gauntlets. Anything to move, to sweat, to keep from looking at that closed door to the brig.

Our daughter grows more alert each day, a miracle I do not deserve. I sing to her, quietly, at first, then louder when I realize Amara doesn't mind or maybe just doesn't hear me. I'm sure my daughter is smiling, but Solena is always quick to point out it's most likely just gas.

Still, I treasure those smiles like hoarded treasure.

Especially as each time I glance up, hoping to see Amara smiling, I find nothing but her turned back or worse, her empty absence.

The nights are the hardest. Not because of the hammock, not anymore.

But because I am beginning to understand something I didn't before.

That you can be on the same ship, breathing the same wind, caring for the same child and still be drifting apart in every way that matters.

That night, after Amara blows out the candle, I wait in silence, listening to her breath even out, slow and deep. Once I'm certain she's asleep, I slip from the hammock and onto the floor, moving quietly. When Ashen stirs at the foot of the bed, I shoot him a sharp look. He blinks but stays still, sensing this isn't a moment for mischief.

I don't go to my sister. I don't seek out my companions. I head straight to the door that's haunted me for days. The brig.

The wood creaks beneath my boots as I descend the narrow staircase. The air turns colder. A lantern swings from a hook overhead, casting weak gold light that sloshes back and forth like dirty water, revealing little but shadows and damp walls, barrels, crates. Then, in a sudden sway of light, I see him.

Ronin.

Asleep and slumped against the wall.

I step closer, the wet floor slapping under my boots. The ship groans around me, hiding the sound of my approach. My eyes catch a broken plank propped against a crate, and for a heartbeat, I consider it. One strike to the skull. Quick. Clean. Done.

But I leave it.

Because as much as I want him dead, he's still the only man who might understand what's happening to my wife. And right now, that makes him useful.

"Is this it?" His voice cuts the silence, hoarse but steady. "Is this how I die?"

He lifts his head and looks at me with one open eye. Calm. Curious.

"Sneaking up on a chained man. I thought you had more honor than that."

I step closer. "It's the best way to kill an enemy."

He cracks a grin. "I figured you'd want a fair fight."

"Chains or sword, the end's the same. Me standing over your dead body."

His grin widens. "So, we're doing this now?"

"I don't need you to bleed tonight. Just to talk."

The Golden Son groans. "I think I would prefer to bleed."

"Amara," I say, and that does it.

His whole body tenses. His gaze snaps to mine.

"What about her?" His voice is sharp. "Is she hurt? The baby...?"

"They're fine."

His shoulders ease, and he slumps back against the wall. "Then what?"

I hesitate.

The words are hard to find, or maybe it's just the pride I have to kill to say them. But if I can bleed for Amara, if I can kill for her, then I can damn well humble myself too.

"She won't speak to me," I say, flat and honest. "She barely looks at me. I don't know what I've done."

I pause, jaw tight, breath shallow.

"Tell me the truth." My voice drops. "Is there something between you? Has she... chosen you?"

The silence that follows crackles. His face is unreadable, maddeningly blank, and the longer he holds it, the more I want to take him up on his earlier offer. Make him bleed.

Just when I'm ready to snap, he speaks.

"No," the Golden Son says. "She hasn't chosen me."

Relief hits so hard my knees nearly give out, but doubt is a stubborn thing.

"How can you be sure?" I ask, hating how desperate I sound.

He dips his head, a slow grin spreading across his face.

"Because in the void, when we were alone in the dark, when she was shaking from pain and that thing reached for her from the shadows, it wasn't my name she screamed."

His words soothe something raw in me, like a balm over a wound I hadn't let myself touch. But there's a gentleness in them too, one he didn't owe me.

"Then why won't she fucking look at me?" I mutter, staggering back to lean against a barrel.

He snorts. "For someone who's lived centuries, you're dumb as shit."

I glare, but he's not done.

"Instead of skulking down here, why not just ask your wife what's wrong?"

The simplicity stuns me. I search for something, anything, to say.

He raises an eyebrow. "You did think of that, right?"

I jolt upright, squaring my shoulders like an idiot caught off guard.

"Of course I did."

He nods. "Good. Then maybe you can repay my wisdom with a bit more bread. I'm wasting away down here."

I consider it. Grudgingly.

I give a curt nod, then turn on my heel and leave him in the dark.

Tomorrow, I'll ask her. Tonight, I'll prepare for the answer.

CHAPTER 24

AMARA

The lantern burns low in the corner, its glow brushing soft gold across my daughter's sleeping face. She's so small. So impossibly perfect. I hold her close, barely daring to breathe, afraid that even my heartbeat might be too loud for her fragile world. I've cared for children before. Wiped their noses, filled their bellies, carried them laughing through the trees, but this is different. She is mine. Flesh of my flesh and the fear that coils in my chest is nothing like I've known. What if I'm not enough for her?

Being a mother is one thing, but being a mother with enemies at every door makes it something else entirely. I don't just need to meet her needs. I have to protect her from demons and Fae and men who would see her parents dead. Who might be cruel enough to hurt her just to get to us. A flare of guilt catches in my throat. I've brought her into a world wracked with danger. She deserves simpler things. Simpler parents. Not a Fae warrior and an Awakened Jewel tangled in a war that hasn't yet ended.

I lay her gently in her crib, onto the soft furs that brush against her tawny skin. Her lips curl. Her little nose twitches. I brush a single dark curl from her brow and breathe through the ache in my chest. There's no use drowning in what-ifs and maybes. Looking at her now, this beautiful, precious thing, I regret nothing.

Her mother will bring the forest. Her father will bring the storm. And she... she will be stronger than us both.

And I will do everything in my power to protect her.

There's a soft tap at the door, and I glance over my shoulder. "Come in," I whisper, barely louder than breath, nevertheless, Solena hears me.

The door creaks open just a sliver, and her face appears through the gap. I'm still adjusting to the changes in her. The wild tangles of her hair, the sunburnt edges of her skin, the sea-weathered look that's replaced the refined Solena I once knew.

"Am I disturbing you?" she asks quietly.

I shake my head. "No. She sleeps like a stone... though only because she drinks her weight in milk twice over."

Solena steps inside, gently closing the door behind her. Her movements are nearly silent as she crosses the cabin and stops behind me.

"She's beautiful, Amara," she says softly. "You've done well. Does she have a name yet?"

A laugh escapes me, dry and a little tired. "I haven't even had time to think of one. Everything happened so fast. She wasn't supposed to arrive for months yet."

"Does Daedalus have any suggestions?" she asks.

My eyes flick to the empty hammock in the corner. My throat tightens. "No," I murmur.

She hums gently. "Well... I'm sure when the right name comes, you'll know."

When I turn to look at her, I study her face. Soft smile, eyes kind despite the salt and sun. Her edges are rougher now. Her beauty hardened by the sea. But there's warmth there, too. The familiar warmth I once trusted.

And yet...

I blink once, then again. The thoughts that haunt me in the dark press at the edge of my tongue. Not in Driftspire. I never saw it then. But here, on this ship, I've watched them, her and my husband, standing too close, sharing too much silence. I thought I saw something. A glance. A breath held too long.

But looking at her now, there's none of it.

She tilts her head, catching me watching too long. "Amara? Are you alright?"

I hesitate. My pulse stutters. I wonder if I should say it. Spill the suspicion gnawing at my insides. But instead, my gaze falls to her fingers. Ink stains the tips, dark and fresh.

"Do you tattoo him often?" I ask, voice low, eyes following the dark marks up her leathers until they meet hers again.

Her brow creases in quiet confusion, but she nods. "As often as I need to. At first, the marks lasted a week. Sometimes two. But now... they fade faster. Melt off like wax in the sun. I redo them almost daily."

"That's... a lot of time alone together," I say, before I can stop myself. "Touching."

Solena's nose wrinkles. "Touching?" she repeats, like the word itself is offensive.

I don't want to say another word. I don't want to embarrass myself further, but when Solena's eyes widen with realization, I know I've already said too much.

"Amara," she says, her voice stern. "You don't think... you can't possibly believe..."

239

"I don't," I blurt, heat rushing up my neck, burning my cheeks. "Of course not." I wave my hands as if I can scatter the words hanging between us. "I'm not myself. My emotions are all over the place. I don't know if I'm coming or going."

The words pour out fast, unfiltered, desperate to fill the space before she can speak again. Before the silence turns thick enough to choke me. I'm rambling, trying to outrun the shame twisting in my gut, but then she grabs my wrists, firm and grounding, and my breath catches.

Her grip is steady. Her gaze, sharper than steel.

"Amara," she says again, quieter this time but no less intense. "Listen to me. There is nothing between Daedalus and me. I ink the sigils. That is all."

Her fingers tighten slightly.

"Not only would I never betray you like that, but my heart doesn't beat for him. It never could. Orios holds it, wholly."

I sag beneath the weight of her honesty. My shoulders collapse inward, my chin dropping to my chest. "Forgive me," I whisper, shame curling tight inside me. "I don't know what I was thinking."

She leans down until her face is level with mine, and I feel her eyes pull me back to her. I force myself to meet them.

"There's nothing to forgive," she says gently. "You've been kidnapped, tortured, dragged through the void, and given birth in the aftermath. You're standing in the ruins of everything you thought you understood."

She lets out a quiet breath, then adds with a faint smile, "Not to mention the part where you burst into green flames and walked away without so much as a scratch. But I imagine you'll tell me more about that when you're ready."

It's enough to pull a smile from me, but it withers just as fast.

"You and Orios," I say, worrying my lower lip, trying to bite back the nerves. "You trust him?"

Solena's head tilts, her brow knitting. "Of course I do. With my heart. With my life."

I nod, lips twitching toward a smile that doesn't quite reach my eyes. It's a cover, flimsy and transparent. She sees right through it.

"Daedalus," she says slowly. "You don't trust him?" A pause. "You think he'd be unfaithful?"

I let my head fall back, exhaling long and low. "No. It's not that." I glance at her, the ache tightening in my chest. "I know he loves me... fiercely. But there's so much I don't know about him. Parts of him locked behind doors he doesn't let anyone near. Secrets scratching at the inside of him like claws in the dark."

My voice drops. "He knew. About Lanneth. About the sacrifice. That it was his role to give me a child and then lead me to slaughter."

Her expression hardens. "But he stopped it. He chose you. He turned his back on his family, on his father, to save you."

"I know," I whisper. "And I've told myself that should be enough. That love like that should be everything."

Solena's gaze sharpens, searching. "I thought you forgave him. In the Grove."

"I thought so too," I murmur, eyes drifting to the wall, trying to blink away the sting. "Part of me did. The part that still aches for him. That needs him. That wants him, even now. But the rest of me..."

My voice falters.

"Ronin," I say. The name isn't as hard to say as it once was. "He told me there's no love without trust."

Her expression sours instantly, that familiar scowl, the one she always reserved just for me, sliding into place. "What does it matter what *he* thinks?"

"I don't know," I admit, shoulders tightening. "You're right. It doesn't."

But the way she keeps staring, eyes fixed and unrelenting, makes me wish I'd said nothing at all.

Then she asks, blunt as a blade: "Is there something between you and the Golden Son?"

"No," I snap, sharp and absolute. There's no lie in my voice. "But... being away from Daedalus for so long, away from his pull, his presence, the gravity of his eyes and the heat of his touch..."

I breathe in slowly.

"It's made things clearer. Like I can finally hear my own thoughts again."

She arches a brow. "You mean without him on top of you, you're capable of coherent reflection?"

A startled laugh bursts from me, half-guilty, half-relieved, my cheeks flushing. "Something like that."

241

The sound is enough to make my daughter stir. She murmurs softly in her crib, swaddled tight and warm. I bite down on my tongue, holding my breath, willing her back to sleep.

Ashen leaps onto the bed with the grace of a shadow. No sound, barely a ripple in the covers. He hisses at me, low and reprimanding, as if warning me to keep it down. Then he circles once and settles, curling beside the crib.

My daughter sighs herself back to sleep.

"There is nothing wrong with how you feel," Solena says, lowering her voice. "But perhaps you should speak to Daedalus."

"What if I can't?" I whisper.

She lifts an eyebrow. "You've stood against human armies. You've brought down a Fae queen with green fire spilling from your palms. I think you can manage a conversation with your husband." A pause. "Just try to keep your hands to yourself long enough to get the words out."

"But it's more than that," I say, my voice thin, as if pleading a case no one asked me to defend. "It's this... presence. This thing coiled in my belly. It fills me up, moves in my blood."

I glance down, my thumbs brushing the pads of my fingers, the memory of his touch blooming in my skin.

"There's a thread. Gold. Blinding when we touch. I know I must be imagining it, but..."

Solena freezes, eyes widening before she grabs my shoulders, hard enough to jolt me.

"What did you say?"

Her voice spikes louder than she intends. Ashen lifts his head with a low growl, eyes flashing as he checks the crib. My daughter sighs again, undisturbed.

"Golden threads?" Solena repeats, her voice tight with urgency. "Are you certain?"

I nod slowly. "They're strongest when we..." I don't finish, but the way my jaw locks says enough.

She nods once, understanding passing silently between us.

"Those are Binds of Fate," she says, her voice wrapped in reverence. "They're the threads of destiny that connect soul-bound mates, Amara."

"Mates?" The tiny hairs along my arms prickle. "That word is for the Fae only. Why would I see something like that?"

Solena's gaze flicks to the rune inked at the base of my neck. "You may be human, but Fae magic courses through you, rivers of it, pulsing beneath your skin. That word *is* yours now, and if you're truly searching for why you feel the way you do, why you're drawn to Daedalus like the moon pulls the tide, then the Binds of Fate explain everything. You two were matched. Meant for each other long before you ever met."

A scoff slips from my lips. "That can't possibly be true. How does that make sense? How can something as powerful as love leave you so helpless?"

Solena's eyes narrow slightly, as if I've missed something painfully obvious. "You say that like it's a flaw. Love, true love, is powerlessness. That's the point, Amara."

I hate how the words settle. How they fit like puzzle pieces I didn't even realize I'd been fumbling with. How, suddenly, everything makes sense. The gravity between us. The ache when he's not near. The madness when he is. It's ridiculous, absurd, even, to believe that before I ever laid eyes on him, some ancient force had already etched our story into the stars, or stone, or any other mystical artifact.

And yet... I feel a strange relief. A little less unhinged. As if the chaos inside me has been given a name, a reason. Permission to love him with no logic. To want him past sense, past reason, past self.

To need him in that breathless, tangled way that leaves me feeling more *whole* than I ever have in my life.

"Do you think Daed knows?" I ask softly.

Solena nods without hesitation. "If *you* see the threads, then he must too. I'm surprised he hasn't said anything."

Her eyes drift to my neck again, but not to the rune this time.

"Or," she adds, tone sharpening, "why he hasn't bitten you."

My brow shoots up. "Come again?"

A ghost of a smirk curls Solena's lip as she parts them, and I spy her canines, just slightly longer now.

"It's a remnant of the old ways," she says. "A primal trait, a mark of the Vornahl still buried in our blood. When we find our mate, we bite. Not out of cruelty, but instinct. It marks them. Claims them. The taste of their blood, the imprint of our teeth, it links us. Strengthens the threads. Affirms the bond. And it has... benefits."

"Benefits?" I echo.

"Your mate can track you. Sense you more clearly. Feel your distress across great distances and others, especially other Fae, will *know*. No one touches what's already claimed without consequences."

The words sink into me slowly, heavy and disorienting. "Daed never told me any of this."

My eyes flick to Solena's neck, and I lean slightly, curiosity catching hold. "Do you have one? The bite. Does it hurt?"

In a swift motion, she pulls her hair over her shoulder, concealing the place I'd looked. Her expression hardens.

"Orios hasn't bitten me."

"Why not?" I ask, the idea striking me as almost laughable. If any two people embodied the Binds of Fate, it was Solena and Orios.

But then I see the hard swallow in her throat, the way her eyes drop to the floor, the faint tremble in her shoulders.

"Orios is not my mate," she says quietly.

Well, now I'm confused. How does that make sense? She speaks again before I can voice it.

"He is my love. My heart. I would spend today, tomorrow, and every day after with him. I'd be his wife if he asked. I'd bear his children, if we were so lucky." Her voice catches. "But there are no threads that tie us. No binds carved by fate. We are in love, but not mated."

"I'm sorry," I murmur. "I shouldn't have assumed."

She waves away my awkward apology. "You didn't know. It's fine."

But the ache in her voice says it isn't.

A question rises unbidden. "What happens if... someday... you *do* meet your mate? What then?"

Solena lifts her chin, noble and proud as ever, and offers a smile, not bright, not full of joy, but steady. Resigned.

"I would hope our love would be enough to keep us to each other," she says.

But the words ring hollow. Her voice quivers at the edges. And when she finishes speaking, her lower lip trembles, betraying everything her pride tries to conceal.

I start to answer, to offer the comfort she so often gives me, but I don't get the chance.

The door crashes open.

Wind howls through the room, catching in my daughter's dark curls. Her face scrunches, her mouth opens, and a startled cry bursts from her throat.

Ashen is on his feet in a blink, a snarl erupting from his chest. His teeth flash, his eyes blaze white-hot, and his body shudders as it grows, larger, broader, a shadow-forged beast trembling with barely leashed fury. The bed groans under his sudden weight.

Zyphoro stands in the doorway, unbothered, her brows arched in mild annoyance. "Alright, I'm *sorry*," she says dryly, shoulders rising in a theatrical shrug. She steps inside and closes the door with exaggerated care, making a show of how softly it clicks shut. "Happy now?"

Ashen growls, a low sound that vibrates the floor. His lips curl back, glistening canines bared. Then, with a great exhale, he turns his head toward the crib. He lowers his massive snout and gently nudges my daughter's brow.

Solena instinctively moves forward, but I reach out, placing a hand on her arm to stop her.

With each soft, smoky touch of Ashen's nose, my daughter's cries ease. Her sobs grow quiet, until finally, she exhales a soft, shuddering breath and falls asleep once more.

Ashen lingers a moment longer, watching her. Then his form begins to shift, his smoke-drenched bulk curling inward, shrinking, softening. Within seconds, the monstrous guardian is gone, replaced by a tiny kitten, all fluff and soot, already curling into a ball beside her and purring as he dozes off.

Zyphoro clicks her tongue. "That pet of yours needs to learn his place."

I glance at the crib, then back at her. "I think he knows exactly where his place is. At my daughter's side."

Zyphoro considers this, then grins. "Hmm. You might be right. He'll serve her well."

I arch a brow, my voice dry as I address the unspoken question. "To what do I owe the pleasure of your visit?"

Zyphoro slumps lazily against the closed door, arms crossed. "I was wondering where you'd gone, is all. The males are drinking and singing, badly, I might add, and I'm bored to tears with their endless chatter about swordplay and muscle. So..." She shrugs. "I've come to collect you."

I shake my head. "I'm not in the mood for drinking or banter," I say. "Besides... my baby."

Zyphoro gestures lazily toward the crib. "Your baby sleeps soundly with a void-born demon curled at her side. She's safer than any of us."

Solena catches my gaze and offers a gentle smile. "The weather is fair," she murmurs. "The stars are bright, and the water carries us smooth and steady. Perhaps tonight is a good night to speak with your husband."

Her knuckles graze mine, warm and grounding. That subtle, steady touch eases something tight in my chest.

"Perhaps it is," I say with a slow smile.

"Speak to him about what?" Zyphoro cuts in. "Whatever it is, I hope it improves his mood. He's been more insufferable than usual these past few days."

"We'll find out soon enough," I reply.

Zyphoro grabs the door handle and twists it open with a long, exaggerated sigh. "Thank the stars. One more day of this tension and I might combust."

Her gaze slides to Solena, a teasing smile tugs at her lips.

"If only there were... other ways to burn it off."

Solena saunters to the door as Zyphoro swings it open, her hand braced above the frame. She ducks beneath Zyphoro's arm.

"We're surrounded by ocean," Solena says coolly. "Maybe a cold dip is in order?"

She slips past Zyphoro like a breeze. But from the way Zyphoro licks her lips, amused and undeterred, it feels less like rejection and more like the opening move of a game.

I glance at her, one brow raised. "Do I want to know what that was about?"

Zyphoro sighs dramatically. "Dearest sister, such details would curl your toes and corrupt that sweet little innocence of yours." She motions grandly. "After you."

I cast one last look at my daughter. She sleeps peacefully, one chubby hand curled beside her cheek. Ashen lifts his head, eyes half-lidded but watchful. Our gazes meet, and in that silent exchange, I feel it. The vow unspoken but unbreakable. While I'm gone, she is his to protect.

I cross the cabin, pass Zyphoro, and step out into the night.

Just as Solena promised, the weather is perfect. The ink-dark sky is scattered with stars, endless and glittering. Salt wind sweeps across the deck, and the waves crash gently against the hull, steering us onward toward the Sundered Kingdoms.

And then I hear it, Souls, the singing. Horrendous and heartfelt.

Up ahead, lantern light spills across the huddle of males. Their cups slosh with rum, their laughter spilling louder than their melody. The golden glow of the lamps casts halos around them, softening the edges of hardened faces.

As I near, Daed lifts his head.

His storm-colored eyes find me, and whatever smile he wore falters, replaced by something quieter. Something reverent. I watch them unfold, the Binds of Fate, golden and luminous, unfurling from his skin like ribbons caught on the wind.

And they drift toward me.

Drawn to me.

As if I were the way home.

CHAPTER 25
DAED

She steps into the lantern light, and for a moment, I forget how to breathe. The waves of her long hair catch the wind like silk. Her warm brown eyes sweep the deck, settling on me, and I feel the impact like a blow to the chest. Her skin, kissed bronze, glows against the dark, as though the stars themselves had conspired to shape her from light. There's a kind of beauty to her that slips through language, something not meant for the bluntness of words. And still, she is more than beautiful. She is mine, even when she tries not to be.

From my skin, the golden threads unravel, drifting toward her across the space between us. They move like ribbons through the dark, weaving their way toward her, seeking the place they belong.

I haven't touched her in so long. Not really. Not the way I remember. And yet her feel is carved into me, mapped into the hollows of my palms, the curve of my fingers, the ache in my chest. The ghost of her lingers on my skin, a memory too vivid to fade. I could live a thousand lifetimes and still not forget the shape of her in my arms, the way she fit there, like she was made to.

And though I pride myself on being a creature of strength, a Fae warrior with ice in his veins, a living nightmare to any who dare meet my gaze. In this moment, for her, I am coming undone.

Amara slips into the circle, and it's as though the fire itself bends toward her. The moment she sits, flanked by Zyphoro on one side and Solena on the other, the huddle shifts and the singing comes to an abrupt halt.

Reon, ever too quick to speak and too slow to think, grins and leans forward with a mug sloshing with rum. "Welcome, Amara. Have a drink with us."

Solena's hand snaps out. She swats his wrist just enough to send a few drops splashing onto his trousers. "She's breastfeeding, you idiot. The rum will taint her milk."

Reon blinks, confused. "How was I supposed to know that's how it works? I've never breastfed before."

"Please don't try," I mutter to him with a grin.

The silence that follows is brief, fractured by Orios's laughter, loud and shameless.

Solena glares at him like she's contemplating murder. "You find that funny?"

Orios doesn't answer with words. He just wraps an arm around her waist and pulls her into his lap like it's the most natural thing in the world. His mouth finds that tender spot at the base of her neck, and he kisses her there, slow and firm.

Solena stiffens for half a second, then exhales. Her fingers curl over his shoulder. His hand slides along her thigh in that way he always does when he's reminding the world she's his.

I watch them and I feel it like a bruise, the closeness, the unspoken understanding between them. I want that same feeling. I would give anything for it. If only my wife would let me.

Even now I can't look away from her. From Amara.

She lifts a hand in graceful refusal, her voice calm but firm. "I appreciate the offer, Reon, but Solena's right. I can't drink rum."

Reon grins, utterly unbothered. "No problem at all. I'll drink for the both of us."

With theatrical flair, he downs the entire cup in one long, exaggerated gulp. When he finishes, he smacks his lips together like he's just tasted the nectar of the gods and lets out a contented sigh.

Then he swivels toward me with a gleam in his eye. "Now, where were we?"

He thrusts his cup out expectantly. I top it off from the jug in my hand, but I've barely begun to pour when he launches into song again, loud, off-key, and with more enthusiasm than melody.

Raise your cup, all kin of light, To Vornahl's flame, our ancient might. From Meranor's golden halls we came, To claim new lands, to forge new names.

Orios slams his heel to the deck in time with the chant, the dull thud echoing like a war drum. Reon rises, lantern light catching in the copper of his hair, casting fire along his silhouette as his voice rises strong and sure.

The Old World lost, its whispers fade, Yet in our hearts, its debts are paid. Their fire burns in kin unborn, A legacy whispered, calling me home.

Zyphoro's foot taps once, twice, then finds rhythm with the beat. Her fist clenches and crashes against the mast beside her, and when she joins in, her voice is deeper than expected and gloriously off-key, matching Reon's with unrepentant boldness.

Drink deep, remember who we are, The shattered past, our guiding star. To those who walked before this night, We drink for them, and for the fight.

They sing louder, over and over, their voices rising like a tide, drowning the sea's roar beneath a chorus of memory and pride. The song doesn't echo, it commands the air, pushes back the dark, as if their voices alone could keep the stars in place.

Reon finishes a final swig and flings his cup aside, rum splashing across the deck, then bows low to Zyphoro. His hand extends toward her in dramatic invitation.

She grins, feral and bright. She takes his hand, and he yanks her up and into his arms, spinning her across the deck. There's no refinement, no choreographed elegance like the ballroom dances of Bellamar. This is untamed, tribal. A collision of movement and laughter, hips crashing, boots stomping. Zyphoro tosses her head back, hair flying like a raven's wing in flight, her laugh wild and loud as Reon pulls her into him again.

Then even Orios, stone-faced sentinel of restraint, gets to his feet. With the ease of a man thrice his size, or thrice as drunk, he lifts Solena clean off the deck, her legs hooking around his hips. He staggers under the rum's weight, but never loosens his grip. Her arms twine around his neck, and they lock eyes, lost in some private, sacred moment as if blissfully unaware that anyone else exists.

And across the chaos, beyond the sloshed bottles and overturned cups, I find Amara's gaze.

I rise slowly, each step toward her weighted with purpose as glittering golden threads unfurl from my chest to hers. They twist, they tangle, until there's no separating them. Until we are one.

I extend my hand.

Her fingers slide into mine, and the spark is immediate. A jolt, white-hot. The connection is more than skin deep. It is blood, breath, memory. *Need.*

I pull her up, steadying her as her body finds mine, her arm draping over my shoulder like she belongs there. My hand settles at her waist. Her warmth seeps through the fabric. I can't help the way my fingers flex, slow and claiming.

Then we begin to move.

This isn't the wild, reckless riot of Reon and Zyphoro, nor the fevered, shameless hunger of Orios and Solena. Ours is something older. Quieter. More dangerous.

This is the kind of dance that leaves marks.

A sway. A breath. A step that brings us closer than the last.

I don't hear the music anymore. Don't hear the stomp of boots or the clatter of cups. The world falls away until all that's left is her. Her body against mine, her scent in my lungs, her eyes on my lips.

"How is our daughter?" I manage, my voice low, rougher than it should be. My hand shifts slightly, thumb dragging against her waist where the fabric clings soft and worn. I can feel the shape of her, warm, real and mine.

Her breath shudders through her. "She's been fed. She sleeps now. Ashen watches over her."

I nod, brushing my knuckles higher along her spine. "Then she is well guarded."

She smells like the first breath of morning air. Like firelight and softness. Like things I never knew I needed until I lost them.

I lean in. I don't mean to. But the pull is magnetic, inescapable. I lower my head, slowly, giving her time to turn away.

She does.

But only just.

Only enough to bare the slender column of her neck.

My control frays.

I draw her closer, holding her hand over my heart while my other slides lower, to the small of her back, slipping beneath her shirt. My thumb brushes bare skin. She stiffens, but doesn't stop me.

That's when I know I'm done for.

I bury my face in that delicate stretch of throat, lips against her skin, breathing her in like a starving man.

She trembles.

I feel her pulse racing beneath my mouth, hear the blood quicken in her veins. My lips part. My canines lengthen. I graze them along her neck, just a whisper of contact.

Then she makes a sound, soft and involuntary. A gasp that blooms into a breathless moan.

It shatters me.

And I am hard in an instant.

Then she breathes the word.

"Wait."

It's strained. Weak. A sound born of conflict, not conviction. But still, I stop.

I ease my hand from her waist, pull my face back from that sweet spot in the hollow of her neck. My pulse thrashes. My body aches. But I let her go, as much as I can bear.

"What is it?" I ask, trying not to reach for her again. Trying not to kiss her when my whole soul is begging for it.

Her lashes flutter, and for a moment her eyes are hazy, like she's not entirely here. Then she meets my gaze.

"When were you going to tell me about the Binds of Fate?"

I go still. A windless hush sweeps between us. The golden threads curl tighter, pulsing in the space where we once touched.

"How did you know?" I ask, my voice unsteady.

Her gaze flicks to Solena, still straddling Orios, laughing breathlessly as he spins her like the world might end tomorrow.

Ah. Of course.

"I was going to tell you," I murmur, shame dragging across my tongue. "In Pariseth. That night... I didn't know it would be taken from us."

Amara studies me, eyes narrowing, voice certain. "Is it true what that means?"

Her lips part slightly before she speaks again, the word raw and unfamiliar in her mouth.

"That we're... mates?"

The sound of it makes my blood heat. A single word, and the bond between us hums like fire licking at dry wood.

"Yes," I say, no hesitation. "Our destinies are woven together. Irrevocably. You are mine, Amara. As I am yours."

She inhales sharply, but not in surrender. Her gaze flickers, her throat bobbing once as she looks away. The silence stretches and with it, dread coils in my gut.

"That... displeases you?" I ask, quieter now, bracing for the blow.

She doesn't answer.

Not with words.

She slips from my arms, and it feels like loss, like the cold rush of sea air where once there was warmth. But then her hand finds mine again, fingers twining gently.

"Can we walk?" She asks softly, like it's not a question about movement at all, but something else. Something harder to name.

At that moment, Reon and Zyphoro collapse in a heap on the deck, howling with laughter, legs tangled. Solena cheers them on from Orios's arms, his expression smug and smitten.

But all of it fades when Amara looks up at me.

I nod. "Of course."

She leads me away from the lantern light and laughter, up the narrow stairs toward the prow of the ship. The sounds behind us dim, until there is only the rhythmic creak of wood, the hush of the ocean below, and the ever-present thrum of the thread between us, pulling taut with every step.

We reach the front of the ship, where the sea stretches out before us like eternity painted in ink and silver. Stars ripple in the water. A full moon crowns the waves. The wind brushes her hair across her cheek and I tuck it behind her ear, unable to stop myself.

She doesn't pull away.

"I am human, Daed," she says into the wind, her voice brittle and breaking against it. "We do not have mates. Not the way Fae do. So tell me, what does it mean? What must I *do*?"

I lift my hand to her face, gently cupping her cheek, desperate to tether her to me. "Nothing," I whisper. "You do nothing but let me love you, Amara."

But still, she resists.

She always resists.

"What is it?" I ask, my voice raw. "What has changed in you? Why do you flinch from my touch? Why will you not let me share your bed?" I pause, then let the question that has gnawed at me for days fall from my lips like poison. "Is it him? The Golden Son? Has *he* changed you?"

Her head jerks toward me, eyes fierce.

"Do you... feel something for him?" The words burn. My chest aches, hollow and tight.

Her response is quick, almost furious. "Do not mistake asking you to spare him for having any feelings for that man. He threatened the Grove. He murdered Arax." Her voice catches like splinters in her throat. "I will never forgive him for that. Even if he's trying to make amends. But if I can't forgive *Ronin*, how in all the realms am I supposed to forgive *you*?"

I stare, the words crashing into me like a wave.

"Forgive me?" I echo, stunned. "For what?"

She gives a mocking gasp. "For what you *knew*. For what you *planned*." Her gaze cuts through me. "It wasn't until we were apart that I saw it clearly. What you put me through was not worthy of love. You lied to me, Daed."

I nod once, slowly, accepting the weight of what she lays before me. "I know I have wronged you, but you cannot imagine the grip they had on me. The power. The scars they carved deep, beneath the skin, into my very soul. I didn't know another way to survive." My voice wavers, pleading now. "But *you*... you freed me from that prison. You made me *want* to be different. You made me *better*. I was myself, Amara. Truly myself, for the first time, because of *you*."

I move toward her, step by careful step, drawn like the tide to the moon. My hands find her waist, gods, how I ache to touch her, and I draw her gently toward me, until the shape of her presses into mine.

"I'm sorry," I whisper, the words a vow etched into the dark. "I'll be sorry every day I breathe. Sorry until my final breath, and I will show you every day that I am sorry. Just... please, wife..." My voice breaks, trembling with the weight of it. "Let me lie beside you. Let me hold you. Let me kiss you. Let me give you everything you need... and everything you deserve."

I bend to her, lips hovering just above hers. I can feel her breath, sweet and uneven. Her chest rises with each inhale, desire clashing with defiance. My hands slide along the curve of her hips, the softness of her drawing a tremble from me, my thumb brushing across her skin like a man desperate for absolution.

"Amara," I whisper, her name a sacred thing. "My queen. My wife. My life. I love you."

I lean in, aching to claim her lips, her mouth, her surrender.

But her hand rises. Firm, cold, and unrelenting, and presses hard against my chest.

I freeze.

I look down at that hand. So delicate. So slender. Yet it holds me like iron.

"No," she says, the word immovable.

I blink, as if I must have imagined it. But then she says it again, lower this time.

"No... *husband*."

The title should bring closeness. Instead, it carves a canyon between us.

I flinch, staring at her in a haze of disbelief. "What must I do, then?" I ask, barely breathing. "How do I earn your forgiveness?"

Slowly, she pushes against my chest. I stagger back like a man struck.

"I don't know," she says, and there's sorrow in it. Sorrow and truth. "But you won't earn it tonight."

Even as she speaks, even as she denies me, my eyes are helplessly drawn to her neck. That warm, tawny flesh. The throb of her pulse. The rush of blood running just beneath the surface.

The urge to pull her to me, to make my mark, is almost as strong as the darkness inside me, always pressing closer, always waiting to take hold.

Just one bite.

That's all it would take to claim her.

To make her mine beneath the stars and moon and night. For now. For always.

She can keep denying me. Keep fighting. Pretending what's between us is anything less than an inevitable fate.

But if I bit her... if I marked her... I'd never lose her again. I'd find her anywhere and the world would know what she is.

Mine.

To protect.

To love.

Then her hand glides to that tender spot, and it's as if she senses where my thoughts have strayed. I force my eyes away.

I've already done enough. Given her enough reasons to despise me.

To take her now, to sink my teeth into her flesh without permission... it would only drive her further from me. Would only harden the fury already simmering in her gaze.

Instead, I lift my eyes to the sky, to the crescent moon against the stretch of black velvet. My Amara follows, tilting her head toward the stars.

Her brow furrows. "That's not the Lover's Moon, is it?"

I laugh, low and quiet, my chin dropping to my chest. "No, my love. There's no spell on us tonight. No Fae magic in the air. Just you and me."

She exhales slowly, relief softening the edge of her voice.

"Good. The last thing I need is to be under the sway of more Fae trickery."

She turns away then, toward the endless sea. The wind catches in her hair, and the moon spills across her skin like it worships her. And how could it not?

I don't need to bite her.

Maybe I just need to tell her.

Tell her about the first time I saw her in the Grove. How I knew, even then, that she was mine. How I tried to stay away, to protect her from the life that would follow. From me.

Because if I claimed her, I knew how it would end. I'd seen it before. I watched it kill my mother.

But Amara, my wild, fierce bride... she wouldn't care for words. Not now. Not after everything I've done.

So once again, I stay silent.

The great Prince of the Mordorin, brought low by the fear of his own wife's wrath.

No teeth then. No words. But I must make her see.

I let the glamor rise, magic sliding across my skin like water. My features shift, melt, settle into the face of the man she stumbled upon in the forest. The human she mistook for a poacher. The one cloaked in a shimmer she couldn't name.

When Daedalus fades, a shaky breath ripples through my chest.

I'm nervous.

My lips part. Her name trembles on the edge of my tongue, dry and clumsy. I hesitate.

She turns, slowly, her gaze moving toward me.

But just before her eyes can settle on my new face a cry splits the night.

At first, I don't believe the words.

Then the wind stirs. The air snaps to life.

"Rook! Ithranor!"

CHAPTER 26
DAED

Even under the blanket of midnight, the golden sails of the Ithranor ships are unmistakable.

They'd caught up so quickly. No sign of them through the day, not even a shadow at dusk.

But of course there wasn't.

They control the wind, carving through the waves like lightning, unseen until it's too late.

My glamor dissolves before Amara can see it. She takes a step forward, brushing past me, her eyes locked on the enemy ships drawing closer with every gust.

Before she can take another step, I reach out and wrap my fingers around her wrist, pulling her back firmly.

"Wife," I say. "Go to the cabin. Lock the door."

Her head snaps toward me. "No. I will not cower and hide before them. Not after what they did to me."

"I'm not asking you to cower," I say, sharper now, impatience threading through my tone as I glance toward the ships again. "I'm asking you to protect our daughter while I hack these bastards to pieces."

She jerks her wrist from my grip. I exhale through my nose, equal parts ire and desire. Of course she won't make this easy.

"She has Ashen for that," Amara bites out. Her eyes flash, green burning bright. "If what I did to Anethesis wasn't enough of a warning, then I'll give them all a matching lesson. They won't touch our child."

I tilt back my head, squaring my shoulders as I take in the full force of her fury. Proud. Noble.

And a fucking pain in my ass.

"They're not here for our child, wife," I say, voice dropping to a growl. "They're here for you."

Her eyes widen, but she barely has time to react before I scoop her into my arms in one smooth motion.

She thrashes, hissing and snarling like a wild thing caught in a trap.

"What are you doing?" she screams, kicking at me. "Put me down!"

I don't respond. Don't even flinch. Her fists beat at my chest, her skin flushed red with fury, but I don't feel it. Not really. I'm already moving.

Zyphoro watches silently as I stomp across the deck and kick open the cabin door.

Our daughter stirs in her crib, and Ashen lifts his head from the edge of the bed.

At first, his lip curls back and a low snarl vibrates in his throat. White flashes through his eyes.

But one commanding look and he stills.

"The Ithranor are here," I say.

He rises.

"Protect my family."

Without waiting for a reply, I toss Amara onto the bed. She lands with a bounce and an indignant squeak.

"How dare you!" she snaps, shoving herself upright, but then smoke ripples off Ashen's body. He swells, growing larger, twice his size, then three times. Until the bed groans beneath his weight.

He places one massive paw on Amara's chest and pins her down.

She gasps. "Ashen! What are you doing? Let me up!"

But he doesn't move. Instead, he gives me a single, grave nod.

I slam the door shut before Amara can spit another word.

The wind is fiercer now, tearing at the sails, lashing cold and sharp across my face. I step to Zyphoro's side as we stare out at the enemy almost upon us.

Ithranor Fae rise into the sky on spiraling discs of air. Dozens of them, maybe more.

We are horribly outnumbered.

But we didn't come this far to die. Not when we're so close to returning home. With Amara, with my daughter. The Ithranor will not take her from me again. Not while I still draw breath.I will be the end of their house.

"Got a plan?" Zyphoro asks.

I shrug. "I thought we might kill them all."

She barks a laugh, her hair whipping in the gale. "Fair enough. But I'm not sure how much help you'll be, brother. If you reach into the void, you'll doom us all. We can't fight the Ithranor *and* Gygarth."

"Then I won't call upon it," I say simply.

She arches a brow, grin curling at the corners of her mouth. "Oh, now this should be fun. Let's at least give you a fighting chance."

She pulls a dagger from the harness strapped to her thigh, flips it once in her hand, and offers it to me handle first.

It's almost offensive how small it is. I'm used to Death Singer's weight in my grip. But I can't summon it, not without stirring the void, and on that, Zyphoro is right.

Still, this little dagger is barely enough to poke out an eye, let alone dismember the traitors flying toward us.

She catches the disdain on my face and frowns. "It kills just fine. Actually, it's my favorite. And I *want it back*."

Reon, Orios, and Solena walk backward towards us, eyes trained on the sky as a wave of Ithranor descends upon *The Shattered Edge*.

Runes pulse. Wings snap wide into the night. Steel sings from its sheath.

Reon cracks his knuckles, sparks dancing across his fingers as he rolls his shoulders. "Typical Ithranor. Always know how to ruin a good time."

I glance over just as Orios leans down to kiss Solena's forehead. Her eyes are closed, serene, while he presses a sword, embarrassingly larger than my borrowed toothpick, into her hands. He has trained her near every day, and she has even managed to disarm him once or twice. Yet Orios is simple, easy to read, his heart worn plainly for all to see. He is proud of her, yes, proud that she can stand her ground, but he knows what every warrior does. A sword may give her strength, but it will never shield her from death. If anything, it draws her closer to it.

Then Orios looks at me.

The tension between us, riddled with doubt and anger, burns away like ash in wind.

"Do you need assistance, Rook?" he asks.

I grin, flicking my gaze upward. "Just a boost, if you don't mind."

He nods once, grabs a fistful of my shirt, bends his knees, and launches into the air.

The wind howls. His wings snap open as we surge skyward, and when we reach the height, when the cold sinks into my bones and the enemy encircles us like a noose, he hurls me straight into them.

I slice into the sky, arms tight to my sides, dagger ready. The wind screams past my ears, and for a brief heartbeat, I'm weightless, until I crash *into* the first Ithranor.

I hit hard, knees to chest, blade to throat, and ride the bastard down. His blood fans across my face as I rip the dagger free and use the collapsing body as a launch point. My feet strike his shoulders, and I push.

I vault upward, twisting mid-air as another surges toward me. They see me too late.

The blade sinks into the hollow of his stomach, his cry stolen by the wind. I yank sideways, spilling guts into the open air, then propel myself toward the next.

An Ithranor male slashes at me, but I fold backward, wind curling over my spine, and flip beneath his swing. I kick upward, catching him under the chin, and use the momentum to launch off his chest, again, again, climbing the sky one body at a time.

But my luck breaks. I miss a grab and suddenly there's nothing but cold air and the looming ocean below.

A hand grabs the back of my collar.

Zyphoro.

Her wings beat hard as she swings me once, twice, then hurls me higher into the fray.

I hit hard, blade first, plunging the dagger into an Ithranor's neck. Blood spurts across my arm as I wrench it free. Another charges. I catch his wrist mid-strike, twist, and drive my elbow into his throat. Bone cracks. He drops and this time, so do I.

We spiral downward, his body limp in my grip. I catch flashes as I fall. Orios blurring by, colliding with an enemy mid-air, steel screaming against steel. Zyphoro tangling with a female above me, throttling her with her bare hands. Solena crashes into the crow's nest, pins an Ithranor to the wood, and drives her sword straight through his chest.

No one sees me falling.

They're too busy trying to stay alive.

The deck rushes up fast. I grit my teeth, wondering how the fuck I got into this mess. *Just a boost*, I'd said. *Just a fucking boost.* I squint through half-lidded eyes, bracing for the splintering crack of my bones on timber.

But I don't hit.

The Ithranor I dragged down with me does, hitting the ground in a wet crack of bone and flesh.

I freeze midair.

Light sparks around me. I glance down.

Reon stands below, arms out, fingers lit up like kindling.

"Maybe try staying on the ground," he groans, sweat beading on his forehead.

He lowers me gently, and when I'm a few feet off the deck, he snaps his fingers. I drop with a soft thud.

I flip the dagger in my hand, wipe the blood off on my trousers. "Where's the fun in that when the enemy's up there?"

Reon stretches his back with a grimace. Copper wings flare out, the edges gleaming gold. He gives me a crooked grin.

"I'll throw some down for you to finish off."

With that, Reon soars upward, sword flashing free from its sheath. He crashes into another Ithranor mid-flight, and true to his word, kicks the bastard hard from the sky. He spirals down, heading straight for me.

I don't flinch. I just wait, blade poised and as he hits the deck with a sickening crunch, I slit his throat in one clean pull. Blood spurts across the boards. Reon nods once before vanishing into the fray, leaving a crimson trail in his wake.

But then I see it. A fresh wave rising from the Ithranor ship like a swarm of insects.

A sharp twist of pain in my chest signals a truth I cannot deny.

There are too many. Even for us.

A heavy thud lands beside me, splintering the deck. I twist around, dagger ready to finish off another of Reon's airborne gifts. But it's not an Ithranor.

It's Zyphoro.

She groans, blood streaking from her lip, feathers torn from her wings and scattered like ash around her.

"Sister," I say, reaching down.

She grabs my arm, hauls herself to her feet with a grimace.

"You alright?" I ask, eyeing the blood seeping through her leathers.

"It's not mine," she mutters, but she's cradling her left arm like it might not be working properly. "I have to get back up there."

She's barely spoken when a loud crack above makes us both look up.

Orios slides down the mast, one wing limp and dragging. He doesn't get a chance to breathe. Two Ithranor dive after him, blades flashing. He snarls and parries, but they come hard, fast.

Solena appears just in time, intercepting one of Orios' attackers, but a third closes in immediately.

"They're coming faster than we can slay them!" Reon shouts.

My hands twitch at my sides. Smoke curls from my fingers. The air turns cold.

The void hums.

It would be so easy to call it. So easy to give in, to let the darkness rise and devour them all. One breath, one whisper, and the Ithranor would fall screaming into nothing. Meat for the beast.

It is not only a want, but a need. A need to let go, to lose myself in the forsaken gift that is my birthright.

But before I can take the step over that edge, a hand finds mine.

I flinch, thinking it's Zyphoro, dragging me back.

But no, there's a softness in the touch. Gentle. Grounding.

Amara.

She's beside me, calm in the chaos, her smile lighting something in my chest.

"What..." I murmur. "You're supposed to..."

I glance toward the cabin.

Ashen is on the deck.

Far from where he should be.

I shoot him a glare, and he wilts slightly, shoulders slumping.

"He is mine, remember?" Amara says. She lifts her chin toward the sky.

Without hesitation, Ashen leaps into the air. With his teeth bare, he tears through the Ithranor like he's at a banquet, limbs and blood flying in every direction.

Zyphoro watches, jaw tight. "Who knows how many more are on those ships. Even with the demon kitty, we can't keep them back."

"You're right," Amara says softly. "We'll need something bigger."

She turns to the railing and places her hand against the wood.

I move to stop her, whatever madness she's considering, I know that look, but Zyphoro shakes her head.

I freeze, watching.

Amara closes her eyes.

A faint glow leaks from her skin, threading through the veins in her arms, green and pulsing like the roots of something ancient. Her hair lifts in the air, as though caught in a storm only she can feel. When she opens her eyes, they blaze a fierce green.

And on her brow... a mark carves itself in light.

This is power.

Real, old, wild and it's about to be unleashed.

From the depths, the ocean splits with a roar.

A massive shape rises, long as a warship, scales black as oil-slicked stone. Its jaws open wide, revealing rows upon rows of serrated teeth, and those *eyes*, massive, yellow, slitted, lock onto the Ithranor vessel.

Screams rise as the stormwyrm dives.

It rushes the ship like a harpoon loosed from the gods themselves. Wood shatters. The hull splinters. Ithranor Fae scatter in a frenzy, but not fast enough. The wyrm punches straight through the side of their ship, a wet, grinding crunch of bone and timber echoing across the sea before it disappears beneath the surface, leaving only chaos in its wake.

But it isn't alone.

Another stormwyrm bursts from the waves, scales glinting green-blue in the dim light, a hiss like steam escaping its throat. It coils mid-air before slamming down across the enemy deck, snapping its massive head down to pluck a screaming Ithranor clean from the ship. The Fae's sword clatters to the wood. Then silence, save for the gulp as the wyrm swallows him whole.

Then another rises and another.

The sea becomes teeth and scales and screaming. Stormwyrms tear through the enemy like vessels of vengeance, dragging Ithranor Fae from the skies, crashing onto the deck with impossible force. One leans over the railing and drags its fangs along the wood, shoveling soldiers into its mouth like meat swept from a cutting board.

"They answered her call," Zyphoro breathes beside me, her voice both reverent and terrified.

The Ithranor ship groans, tilts.

"They're sinking," Reon says as he touches down beside me, blood dripping from his blade, caught somewhere between awe and disbelief.

Amara turns toward us, toward *me,* and for a moment, there's nothing human in her face. Just raw, unrelenting power. Old as the deep. Cold as the grave.

The last of the Ithranor retreat, vanishing into the night, but I wonder how far their wind will carry them before their strength fails and they're swallowed by the black sea in the middle of nowhere.

Orios and Solena land beside us, saying nothing as we watch the enemy ship split clean down the middle, its hull groaning before it's slowly devoured by the waves. The stormwyrms circle once, then slip back beneath the surface, the ocean closing over them as if they were never there at all.

Amara watches a moment longer, then smiles, the glow of her power receding.

"Now," she says, voice calm and final, "to Baev'kalath."

None of us speak.

Ashen glides down in her wake, landing with a soundless thud. She doesn't look back as she walks toward the cabin. Just reaches out, fingers slipping through his shadowy mane as he shrinks beneath her touch, small enough to follow her inside.

I feel it again, the cold. But this time, it's not the void.

It's *her.*

And I don't know if I should fall to my knees... or run.

CHAPTER 27

AMARA

I see the way they look at me.

Never did I think I'd see fear in the eyes of the Fae. But I see it now.

They keep their distance on deck, stepping wide when they pass. They smile, polite, strained. Curious. I can feel the questions in their silence: *How did you do it? How did you call them?*

But it's not something words can explain.

Not since the Souls infused me with their power. Ever since then, I can *hear* the things that walk, crawl, or slither, and I think they can hear me, too. I asked for help, and the stormwyrms came.

I only hope their destruction marks the last I'll ever see of the Ithranor Fae.

It doesn't surprise me they came looking. Anethesis made it clear just how important I was to their cause. They couldn't return home without me. Even without him to lead them, still they came, his absence proof enough that he's dead, that he bled out in that cage.

But I am no longer their pawn. My life not theirs to gamble.

My family is returning to the Sundered Kingdoms. I have a life to build there. A future to claim. If this wind holds, we should arrive in a few days.

It can't come soon enough. The tension aboard this ship is thicker than the air itself. Harder to stomach than the stale scraps they dare call food from the galley.

"Are we almost there?" Ronin asks as I descend the stairs.

"So eager to get off this ship?" I say. "You're not worried Daed will kill you the second we hit land?"

He grins up at me. "I was never worried, Jewel. I'm just hoping to get some feeling back in my ass before then."

I pace. He watches me with narrowed eyes, the chain around his ankle rattling as he shifts.

"Please tell me you're not here to talk more about your marriage," he says. "If you are, I beg of you, kill me now."

"They're treating me differently," I say. "Since the night with the stormwyrms."

"Going by the way you described it, I'm not surprised," Ronin sighs. "Sounds like quite the night. Wish I could've been there. Does that kind of power come with being Awakened?"

I shake my head. "The Souls of the Forest gave me the gift to speak with beasts. But I thought it only worked on creatures of the earth. Maybe being Awakened made it stronger. Maybe that's why Ashen answers my thoughts the way he does."

"Let's not get ahead of ourselves," he mutters, tugging the iron loop around his ankle. "I watched that cat walk us straight into demon-infested land, no matter how much you begged him otherwise."

I snort. "Then perhaps the Father Below holds a stronger leash on him than I ever will."

Ronin tilts his head, studying me. "The Father Below. That's who that was? Some kind of Fae god?"

My stomach twists. My mind conjures the cloaked figure again. Tentacles writhing beneath a jawless face, fingers like bones stretched too long, like they were made to reach through nightmares. Whatever that thing was, it wasn't Gygarth. Gygarth is smoke and shadow. But this... this had form. It looked almost human. Which somehow made it worse.

"No," I murmur. "I don't know what that monster was. But I pray it stays caged in that place forever. I have enough to deal with in this world."

"What? The Fae up there giving you the cold shoulder?" he asks. "That's more concerning than a nine-foot demon from the void?"

"It's not coldness," I say. "It's fear."

"And that's a bad thing?"

"It is when I know what the Fae do to the Awakened. To what they fear."

His expression hardens. "You think they'll kill you?"

"I don't know," I admit, voice low, almost to keep them from hearing.

Ronin lets out a gruff laugh. "Because the Fae have *never* tried to kill you before?"

266

I shoot him a glare. "I'm not naïve. I know they can't be trusted. But now I've given them a reason. A reason to see me as a threat." A shiver ghosts over my skin. "Maybe even my daughter."

He's quiet for a moment. Then, with a sigh, he says, "I'd love to sit here and agree wholeheartedly with all your terrible choices, Jewel. But, tragically, I appear to be the voice of reason. You are the mother of Fae royalty and though I have a thousand unseemly words to describe your husband, 'coward' is not one of them. Only a coward would harm his own child."

I close my eyes and nod. His words, sharp-edged but true, anchor me.

"But if he's not the threat," I murmur, "then who is? Will I always be hunted? Watched? Used for what I am?" My voice drops to a whisper. "Will I ever know peace while I live among them?"

Ronin exhales, slumping back against the wall. He runs a hand through sweat-dampened blond hair, dulled by grime and salt. "Jewel," he says tiredly, "I'm just a human, chained to a post. What the fuck would I know?"

My chin drops. Shoulders fold. I dig my fingers into the roots of my hair, trying to ground myself. "You're right," I say, voice bitter. "Why am I even asking you?" I lift my gaze to his, the fire in me dimming to smoke. "Why am I even here?"

Ronin's chains creak as he shifts, the faintest smile playing at his lips. "Because when you're surrounded by monsters, the one with the human face doesn't seem so bad?"

I huff out a dry laugh, shaking my head. Souls, what was I thinking? What madness dragged me down here in the first place?

"You won't see me again, Ronin. Not until it's time for you to die for what you've done."

He doesn't wince. Doesn't blink. He watches me with the eerie calm of someone who's already made peace with the end. And maybe that's what makes my skin prickle, that he's the only one on this ship who isn't afraid of me. Instead, he brings his hands together slowly, bows his head with quiet reverence. "Until then."

I turn away, steps pounding up the stairs, each footfall a thunderous drumbeat of my own frustration.

"But instead of drowning in what they think of you," he calls after me, "why not embrace it? Why not become exactly what they fear?"

I stop.

"Be the Awakened they whisper about in terror. The human who defies them. In all our history, Jewel, they've never feared us. Never once. They crushed us beneath their boots and forgot our names before the blood dried."

His voice drops low. "But now... now they have something to fear."

I turn slowly, mouth dry.

"Leave the Fae," he says. "Join the Legion. Make the Sundered Kingdoms ours again. A haven for humankind." He tilts his head, and when he speaks next, it's softer. "For your daughter."

Something inside me cracks. My teeth press down hard on my lower lip, head shaking as fury and sorrow squeeze tight in my chest.

"You're no different from them," I breathe. "No different from Anethesis. You want to use me, use my power, for your own ends." I shake my head. "I will not be a soldier in your army, Ronin."

"I do not need a soldier," he says through gritted teeth. "I need a leader, Jewel. I would have you wear the mask."

My words fail. Stolen from my lips like breath torn by the wind.

I stare at him, and he stares back, eyes wide, unblinking, like he's already seen the future and is waiting for me to catch up.

But I can't. Not now. Not yet.

So I spin on my heel and climb, each step faster than the last, and I don't stop until the door slams behind me.

Wear the mask.

Is he insane?

After everything he's done. After Arax.

He thinks I would lead an army of humans who see foes in Fae and mortals alike. He speaks of righteousness and virtue with the tongue of a zealot, but I see the truth gleaming behind his teeth: he wishes to rule. Not serve. Not save. Rule us all.

Every creature in the Sundered Kingdoms would bend the knee under his vision of peace.

No.

My place is not with tyrants cloaked in ideals.

My place is with Daed.

The male who stood at the gates of my home and bled to keep it safe. Who defied Lanneth's grip, fought the curse of ancient power with nothing but raw will. Who searched the uncharted seas, shattered, crown cast aside, wings reaped from his back.

Who heard my call across the realms, dived into the void to brave the endless dark in search of me, and when he found me, he didn't flinch. He wrapped his arms around the broken thing I'd become and carried me back to the light.

Who begs for forgiveness each dawn. Who holds our child when she cries, walks her through the late hours while I sleep. Who slumbers in a threadbare hammock in the corner of the ship with no complaint. No pride.

Whose golden threads intertwine so perfectly with mine that time itself must have woven us together.

My husband. My love. My mate.

The truth slams into me like thunder on stone.

What am I doing? Why have I kept him at arm's length, tortured him with silence and distance? Why have I let Ronin worm into my thoughts, dig his claws beneath my skin and twist my love into something small and fragile and doubtable?

Daed.

I need to see him.

I step onto the deck, my breath shallow, heart hammering in my throat. The wind bites at my cheeks, tangles in my hair, and waiting above, perched on the railing like a crow, is Zyphoro.

Crouched, hands resting on her knees, raven curls flaring behind her in the wind.

"How is our guest?" she asks, voice casual, curious.

"He's alive," I reply. "And well enough."

"Luxuries I'm not sure he deserves," she says, lifting her hand and inspecting her nails. "He did kidnap you after all, sister. Held you hostage. Mother Moon, I can only hope he didn't defile you in any way."

The sly grin she flashes is pure provocation, all teeth and glittering mischief, like a cat batting at a bird.

"I appreciate your concern, Zyphoro," I say, steady, giving her nothing. "But nothing sordid happened."

She shrugs, pout forming. "Pity. What a scandal that would be."

I scan the deck, feigning indifference even as my eyes hunt. Where is he? That pull, that magnetic ache deep in my chest, seeks him.

"Where is Daedalus?" I ask idly.

Zyphoro's grin sharpens. "Speaking of scandals," she purrs, tongue sweeping over her teeth, "he's with Solena below deck. It's that time again."

My brows knit, a flicker of unease twisting in my gut.

She softens then, leans her elbow on her knee, and smiles with something almost like affection. "His sigils, of course. I believe she's inking him as we speak."

I glance over my shoulder, eyes lingering on the door that leads to them.

I imagine him stretched out on that table, shirt discarded, Solena's hands gliding over his skin. A flicker of something sharp catches in my chest. Not jealousy. Envy.

There's no bitterness toward Solena. I believe her when she says I have nothing to fear. But I want *my* hands on him. My fingers tracing the heat of his body, his firm flesh slick with sweat beneath my touch. Our breaths tangling, melting together in the humid haze of the cabin.

Something stirs low in my belly, hot and undeniable. A need. A hunger I've denied for far too long.

"You're still here?" Zyphoro asks, one brow arched as her gaze flicks to the door.

A slow smirk curves my lips. I say nothing.

I turn, stride to the door, grip the handle and push it open without hesitation.

Daed's eyes flick up from the table, a dark strand of hair falling over one half-lidded eye. Solena glances up too, standing beside him, a fine-tipped needle in one hand and a small cup of black ink in the other.

"Amara," she says gently. "Is everything alright?"

Daed lifts his head. "Is it our daughter...?"

I shake mine. "She's fine. Everything's fine." My gaze lingers on the ink. "I just thought... maybe you could show me how to do that."

Daed's brow draws together. "Really?"

I nod, swallowing the knot in my throat. "If that's alright."

Solena offers a soft smile. "There's a great deal that goes into runeweaving, but I'm nearly done. You can finish the last lines."

I step toward her, feeling Daed's gaze settle on me like heat. Solena steps aside, pressing the needle into my hand, her fingers stained black.

"Just trace the edges," she instructs, holding out the cup. I dip the tip of the needle into the ink, tapping it lightly against the rim.

Then I turn to him.

Daed's back is lean and taut, his skin glistening with sweat and streaked with dark sigils, some still seeping blood. My hand hovers, the ink dripping from the needle's tip. I can see the tremble in my fingers.

"Nothing to worry about," Solena murmurs. "The runes are marked. You can't change them now. It's just finishing."

I nod to steady myself. Then, I lower the needle.

"Good," she says. "Now, prick. Quick and steady."

I exhale, then press.

The needle resists. The sensation startles me, and for a heartbeat I falter. But I close my eyes, breathe deep.

No. I want this.

I press again.

Daed flinches barely, but I catch it. Another press. Then another. Sharp breaths hiss through his teeth.

I pause. "Am I doing it wrong?"

"You're fine," he mutters. "But you could be a little gentler."

My brow lifts. That only makes me press harder.

He hisses, eyes flashing as he glances over his shoulder. But when he meets my scowl, he doesn't speak, just turns back around and rests his head on the table again, missing the satisfied smirk that curls my lips.

"That's it," Solena encourages. "On to the next one."

I move from rune to rune, darkening each mark, watching the way his muscles shift and twitch beneath my touch. The way his breath stutters and falls into rhythm. My fingers glide over warm skin, and every time I touch him, truly touch him, he shivers.

"You'll need to sit him up to finish the neck," Solena says quietly.

"I can hear you," Daed groans, pushing himself upright and swinging his legs over the side of the table.

He throws back his head, sweeping the dark fall of hair from his eyes, and when he looks up, our faces are barely a breath apart.

He swallows hard, startled. "Sorry."

271

I shake my head, my cheeks warming with a sudden, helpless heat. Gods, how long had it been since my husband made me blush? "It's fine."

But it isn't fine. It's devastating.

The heat radiating off him rolls over me like a tide, thick and stifling, laced with the scent of him, deep, musky, familiar. I feel dizzy with it. Drunk on him.

Solena, oblivious, leans over my shoulder, peering at my hand.

"You're drifting off the line," she mutters, her tone clipped. "Focus."

I clear my throat and nod, noticing the smug curve of Daed's lips. "Right. Focus."

I press the needle again, quick and steady, darkening the edge of the rune. My eyes stay fixed on the pattern, but I can feel his gaze burning into me like the blaze of a molten sun. His legs shift, just enough that his knee brushes me, subtle yet deliberate. I don't move.

His fingers slide along the leather of his trousers, back and forth. Sometimes they skim over the seam where his thigh touches mine, casual, calculated.

"That's better," Solena says, approving. "Keep going like that."

"Yes," Daed murmurs. "Keep going like that."

His thumb presses gently into my thigh, just above the knee.

I gulp.

Then a knock.

The door creaks open before anyone gives leave. Orios leans in, ducking his massive frame.

"Solena," he says, scanning the room until he finds her. "I've made you something to eat."

She nods, still more interested in the runes than the interruption. "Thank you. I'll be there soon."

My heart thunders. "I can finish this," I say somehow. "It's nearly done."

"You're sure?" she asks, brows raised.

"If I need help, I'll find you."

Orios brightens, reaching out a broad hand. "Come then, my love."

Solena finally smiles as she steps away from me. "Very well."

She touches my shoulder as she passes, a brief reassurance, before ducking beneath Orios's arm. He holds the door open, impossibly gentle for a man his size, and she rises on her toes to kiss his cheek. He's carved from granite, but I swear, he melts under her touch.

The door clicks shut.

Only Daed and I remain and the heat, thick and consuming, growing heavier with each breath that stretches between us.

I try to hold my focus. I really do.

I trace the sigils along the curve of his neck, the lines steady and precise, even as ink drips and mingles with the sweat slicking his skin. Still, his eyes never leave me, dark, smoldering, relentless. The kind of stare that strips me bare.

Where his thumb once brushed my thigh, now his whole hand slides over it. Slow. Firm. Circling. Drawing me closer.

He inhales, growls in his throat, rumbles in his chest. His lashes flutter at whatever he scents in me.

And then he guides me between his legs.

Even when he settles me on his thigh, I keep going, determined to finish what I started. Even as he fists the fabric of my gown, dragging it higher inch by inch, until it pools at my knee. My breath shudders. I gulp.

His hand slips beneath the fabric.

At last, skin meets skin.

And he pauses.

His eyes locked on mine, asking a question without words.

I say nothing.

Not because I can't.

But because I don't want to.

The needle slips from my hand, forgotten, as my arm drapes over his shoulder. He pulls me into him, his lips hovering at my neck, his breath warm, heady, before his mouth finally presses to my skin.

I exhale, eyes fluttering shut, and thread my fingers through his hair, dragging my nails gently against his scalp. Daed kisses me slowly, each press of his mouth soft and sure, his tongue tasting the sweat beading along my neck.

My chest rises sharply, breath catching when his hand travels higher along my inner thigh, slow, slow, until he finds the heat of me. I gasp, unable to stop it, hips twitching at the first teasing stroke of his fingers.

The sound I make, a soft whimper, pulls a growl from deep in his throat.

I fist his hair tighter when his kiss deepens, hungrier now, tongue sweeping against my neck as he presses a finger into me. My spine arches against him, a moan escaping, desperate and shameless.

His other arm anchors me, wrapped tight around my waist, holding me flush against him, denying me even the smallest escape as I squirm in his grip. His touch is possessive, his mouth relentless, and the way he groans my name against my skin sends shivers down to my bones. I feel it everywhere. In my veins, my nerves, every trembling inch of me.

Then he slides another finger inside, and I can't help the way I grind against his palm, riding the pressure, the pace. I'm straddling his lap, gown rucked up around my hips, my breath ragged. His kisses trail down my neck, across my collarbone, lower, until his mouth finds my nipple through the thin fabric. His tongue laps at it, and when his teeth graze over me, a gasp bursts free from my lips.

His fingers work inside me, firm and coaxing, while his mouth toys with my breast, and the tension inside me coils tighter, higher. My hands tangle in his hair, gripping hard, pulling him closer. I roll my hips shamelessly, chasing the friction, the heat, the sweet ache.

The ship rocks beneath us, the floor groaning in rhythm with my gasps. I hear the ocean lapping at the hull, the creak of timber, everything outside us swallowed by the storm rising inside me. His fingers move with perfect purpose, his mouth devouring me, and then my body seizes, back arching as the wave crashes through me. I bite my lip, trying to muffle it, but the moan escapes anyway. Long, low, broken. My head falls back and I shake with the release, shivering against him, undone in his arms.

My hand falls back on the table, tipping the cup of ink, sending it spilling onto the floor.

"Oh no," I gasp, stumbling back from him as the inkwell tips. Black ink blooms across the floor, dark and slick, sliding between my toes like cold blood.

"It's fine," he says, voice rough with need. "I'll clean it up. But if you don't get back here right now, it will be the end of me."

The ink between my toes shocks me like a spell broken. I look at him, his chest rising and falling, eyes sharp with hunger, the outline of his thick cock beneath his leathers unmistakable.

I grin. "What do you want to do? Take me here, now, on this table?"

He nods, not missing a beat. "It's one of the things I plan to do, yes."

The haze of climax still hums through me, loosening my limbs, giving me a boldness I hadn't expected. I tug down the hem of my gown, slowly stepping toward the door, and watch his expression shift.

"That's enough," I murmur, teasing. "I think I hear our daughter."

He straightens from the table, slowly stalking after me. "You hear nothing. She's asleep."

"Still," I say, fingers curling around the door handle, "I should really check."

"Amara," he growls, head lowered, gaze burning up at me beneath his brow.

But I've already twisted the handle. The door creaks open.

"Another time."

I slip through the doorway, closing it firmly behind me, just as I feel the thud of his body against the other side and hear his low, agonized groan of frustration.

A laugh bubbles up and I smother it with my hand, pressing my palm to the wood, almost as if I can feel the heat of him radiating through it.

The aftershocks of him still spark across my skin. My lips part with the memory. His mouth, his fingers, the exquisite torment of his touch.

A cough breaks the moment.

I turn to find Zyphoro still there, watching me with a grin she doesn't bother to hide. Reon stands beside her, his brow pressed to her shoulder, laughter caught in the curve of his smile.

"Just a little something to take the edge off, sister?" Zyphoro asks.

Reon snorts, trying and failing to stifle another laugh.

For the first time in days, they're not wary. Not watching me like I might explode.

They're just... grinning.

"I have to check on my daughter," I say quickly, clearing my throat and dragging a hand down my flushed face.

"Oh, don't be embarrassed," Zyphoro calls after me. "We can smell it a mile away."

Reon bursts out laughing, louder this time, but I don't stop to fire back. I turn and hurry toward my cabin, leaving my mortification and the lingering scent of lust trailing behind me as I shut the door and seal myself inside.

CHAPTER 28
DAED

The wind claws at our sails, snarling through the rigging as the sea rears and bucks beneath us. Lightning rips across the sky, blinding and crooked, followed by a thunderclap that shakes the bones of the ship.

There's no doubt now. We're close. Baev'kalath is calling us home.

And still, my wife torments me.

She let me touch her. Taste her. She let my mouth worship her body, my hands draw sounds from her that haunt me even now. But since then, nothing. No kiss. No release. Only the cruel seduction of her nearness. Her body brushing past mine. Her scent in every breath I take.

She is ruthless in her restraint, and I am unraveling beneath it. Gods help me, I never knew I could want someone like this.

Another bolt of lightning flashes, and this time, in the distance, I see them.

The craggy spires of Baev'kalath, rising like black teeth from the ocean.

The storm lashes harder as we near, as if the sea itself is trying to tear us away from our destination.

Waves crash against the hull, spilling over the deck in surging sheets. Rain comes sideways, pelting the wood and soaking through cloaks and skin. *The Shattered Edge* groans under the strain, her masts swaying, ropes creaking in protest.

"Shorten the sails!" I bellow over the roar. "Don't give the wind more to tear."

Reon and Orios sprint, slick with spray, yanking wet canvas down and binding it tight against the yards. Zyphoro and Solena lash barrels to the rails so they won't become rolling battering rams while I haul at the wheel. It fights like an angry beast, trying to wrench from my grip whenever a wave strikes us broadside.

The ship bucks, corkscrews. Boards shriek. Another wave smashes across the deck, knee-deep and frigid, but the crew cling on, faces set, pulling lines tighter, hammering in fresh wedges, dumping water by the barrelful back into the roaring sea.

I plant both hands on the wheel. My shoulders burn, my palms slip, but I will not let the storm turn us aside. Not with home so close.

Amara is below deck with our daughter, under Ashen's constant, watchful gaze. I can only hope they're not being thrown around too violently down there until, of course, the gods decide to punish me further.

She appears.Soaked through in seconds, rain clinging to her like silk, her hair plastered to her face, her jaw set like iron.

Exactly where I want her least.

Exactly where I want her most.

I bare my teeth. "Amara. Below. Now."

She lifts her chin, blinking through the deluge. "I can help. What do you need?"

"I need you out of the damn way!" I snap. "Back to the cabin!"

But it's like throwing kindling on fire. Her eyes flash, a wildfire glare that could cut through steel, and she charges straight into the chaos, heading for Zyphoro as she fights the ropes.

"Amara!" I roar again, but the storm swallows her name.

My canines lengthen.

"Orios!" I bellow, turning toward the mast.

He hears me. Even through the thunder and the scream of the wind. His wings burst from his back, feathers buffeted by the gale as he pushes into the sky, lands hard at the wheel, and folds them away with a crackle of rune-light and for a brief second I'm reminded of how much I miss my own wings.

"Hold her steady," I bark. "Don't let her veer."

Orios nods and takes the wheel. I leap from the helm and charge across the slick deck. Water surges underfoot, thunder cracks overhead, and lightning casts her in stark flashes, head bowed, hands on rope, the line of her back tight with fury and defiance.

She doesn't see me coming.

I grab her around the waist and lift her, furious and writhing, hauling her back toward the cabin. Her voice shrieks over the rain.

"Put me down, Daedalus! Right now!"

I don't. I carry her as if she's nothing.

"You'll regret this, I swear it!" she screams, rage thick in her throat.

Still, I ignore her. She's taught me well.

I kick the cabin door open and slam it behind us. Inside, the lanterns flicker wildly, casting half-shadows across the ink-stained table and swinging maps. I set her down hard. She's still yelling, arms flailing, until she looks around and realizes we're not in her quarters.

Her voice falters. "What is this? What are we doing here?"

And then she sees the look on my face.Sees the way my eyes drag over her, every line, every soaked inch of her skin-tight gown, white fabric sheer now, clinging to her breasts, her curves, her thighs. Her nipples stand tight against the cold, and I feel my cock pulse beneath my leathers, already half undone.

She steps back toward the table, hands bracing on the edge, her breath catching.

"What are you doing?" she asks again, softer now, but not uncertain.

I say nothing.

Rain slicks over my skin as I rip my shirt open, the soaked fabric tearing under my hands. The runes across my chest flare bright, light carving over hard muscle, tracing the ridges of my abdomen. Water slides between each line, gathering at the sharp dip of my hips, where the deep V cuts down toward the buckle I shove open. I fling the belt aside. Her gaze follows, hungry, drawn to the strength in my stomach, the carved hollows that frame every breath. Power thrums beneath my skin, runes burning hot, alive, pulsing with restrained fire. Then I see it, her rune, glowing softly at her throat, alive with heat and want. It calls to mine. It calls to me.

Her pulse jumps beneath the skin. That perfect throat. A vein begging for teeth.

I close the space between us in a single step, her breath hitching as I loom over her. She's trembling, part fury, part anticipation. Her scent hits me like a punch to the gut, sweet and wild and storm-sharpened, and I don't even try to fight it.

"Say something!" she yells, hair dripping into her mouth, eyes alight. "Daedalus, answer me!"

I grip the edge of the table behind her, caging her between my arms, my body pressing hers, my lips brushing her ear.

"I know I have a lifetime of wrongs to make up for," I rasp, voice barely a whisper above the storm. "And I swear to every god still watching that I will earn your forgiveness."

My hand slips down, anchoring her hips to mine. She gasps, arching.

"I will worship you as my queen."

Her nails bite into my shoulders.

"But right now?" I growl, mouth grazing the shell of her ear. "Right now, I need to fuck my wife."

She trembles beneath me, her chest heaving. Her glare hasn't dulled, but her breath has changed, faster now, sharper. Anticipation and fury colliding in her eyes.

But then she lunges for me, her mouth crashing against mine. She gasps into the kiss, and I take it, drinking her in. My hand grips her chin, holding her mouth to mine, while my other hand roams down, gripping her hips, dragging her soaked body flush against mine. Her thighs part around me instinctively, and I lift her onto the table in one swift motion.

My fingers slide up under the clinging fabric of her gown, dragging it over her hips and baring her to me. She shudders when my hands find her. Hot, slick, already aching for me.

"Daedalus," she breathes, voice trembling on the edge of desperation.

"I told you," I mutter against her throat, "I need you."

Then I drop to my knees.

She stiffens in surprise, her hands bracing on the table behind her. But I hook one of her thighs over my shoulder, spreading her open with a firm grip as I drag my mouth along her inner thigh. Her breath catches when I kiss just beside where she wants me, and again when my tongue finally finds her, slow at first, savouring every taste, every twitch of her hips.

She lets out a strangled sound, thighs trembling around my head, her hands darting into my hair and fisting tight.

I groan into her, the sound vibrating against her, and her hips buck in response. I lick her again, firmer, deeper, letting her ride the rhythm of my tongue until she's writhing, panting, muttering broken curses in a voice I barely recognize. Her gown slips down her chest, baring one breast, and I reach up to cup it, thumb brushing over the hardened peak while I fuck her with my mouth like I'm starving.

Her cries rise higher with every flick of my tongue, her whole body clenching, desperate and close.

"Daedalus," she gasps, breath hitching.

I look up, lips slick with her, and rasp, "Cum for me."

She does.

Her thighs clamp tight, her back arches, and she cries out my name like a prayer as she breaks apart against my mouth.

I stand, catching her before she can slump fully back, and kiss her, messy, possessive, letting her taste herself on my tongue.

She's still trembling when her hands slide down, fingers deft and hungry, pushing at the edge of my trousers. When she finally frees me, her hand wraps around my cock, her fingers damp and chilled by rain, but the heat steaming off me warms them almost immediately. I grunt, hips twitching in response, but she doesn't rush. She strokes me with a teasing rhythm, slow at first, gliding from base to tip, her thumb brushing over the head with maddening lightness. My breath hitches when she tightens her grip just slightly, dragging her fist back down.

"You're going to make me lose my mind," I rasp, jaw clenched as I fight to stay still, to let her touch me like this.

Her eyes gleam with something wicked and knowing. "Good."

She strokes me again, longer this time, firmer, twisting her wrist at the end in a way that makes me groan low and dangerous. My hand finds her hip, fingers digging in, but still I wait. She leans in, brushing her lips against mine as her hand works me, wet and slick and mercilessly slow.

"You're so hard," she whispers. "All for me."

"All for you," I growl. "Always."

I can barely breathe, can barely think. She's reduced me to this, a trembling, pulsing ache in her palm. And still, she strokes, teasing just enough to make me twitch with the urge to take her, to pin her to the table and bury myself deep.

"Enough," I grit out.

And then, without waiting, I'm inside her in one hard thrust.

She cries out, head falling back as I fill her, her legs locking around me, drawing me in deeper. The table creaks beneath us, the storm battering the ship outside in a perfect, violent rhythm to our movements. Rain lashes the portholes, thunder booms, but all I hear is her moaning my name.

I fuck her hard, the way she's needed, the way I've dreamed of every damned night since she came back to me. My hips slam into hers, skin on skin, our soaked bodies sliding together with a feverish need that feels like it might consume us both. She clutches at my shoulders, nails scraping down my back, gasping with each thrust.

"You're mine," I growl, voice rough and shaking. "Mine, Amara. Do you hear me?"

She pants against my lips, eyes wide and blazing. "Yes...yes, Daed..."

"Say it."

"I'm yours," she gasps. "I'm yours."

I snarl, mouth dropping to the crook of her neck where her pulse throbs wild beneath her skin.

"And I am yours," I whisper, fangs bared, "forever."

Then I bite.

Her climax crashes through her like a wave, her body trembling violently beneath mine.

I hold her through it, my teeth still sunk deep in her throat, her taste flooding my senses, heady, intoxicating, unlike anything I've ever known. It's not just blood. It's *her*. Wild and sweet, threaded with magic and trust and something so fiercely tender it almost hurts to feel it.

The bond surges between us, alive now, burning gold-hot under my skin. Her scent deepens, thickens, coils around me like smoke. I can smell her pleasure, her desire. I can *feel* it in my mind, taste it behind my teeth.

Flashes of her thoughts rip through me, not words, not images, but raw feelings. The helpless wonder at the way I touch her. The hunger. The *joy*.

Gods.

I have never felt anything so purely, wildly happy. No conquest. No crown. Nothing in my life has ever tasted this right.

I ease my teeth from her neck, breath heaving, blood smeared warm across my lips. She looks up at me, dazed, her lashes fluttering. Her gaze dips to my mouth, to the blood, and her pupils flare with something darker.

Then she kisses me.

Hard. Desperate. Her blood on both our tongues. Her moan vibrates into my mouth, and when she pulls back, eyes blazing, she grips my jaw with trembling fingers and says, "Again. Bite me *again*."

She turns without waiting, bracing herself against the table, hips rocking back into me, her ass grinding against my cock. Her hair tumbles forward, exposing the curve of her neck as she sweeps it aside in offering.

I grip her hips, gather the folds of her dress and lift it over her ass, baring her to me completely. Her skin glows in the low light, flushed, glistening. I drag the head of my cock between her thighs, feel her tremble before I push inside her with one slow, possessive thrust. Her body takes me inch by inch, slick and hot, tightening around me until the air leaves my lungs.

She gasps, fingers curling against the edge of the table. Her back arches, hair tumbling forward, and I move, slow, deep, savoring the sound of her breath breaking with every stroke.

"You feel that?" I growl against her shoulder, the words rough, scraped from my chest. "That's what you do to me."

She clenches around me, and fuck she's tight, wet, perfect. I bend her over, my grip tightening on her waist as I drive into her harder, faster, the slap of our bodies filling the quiet room. Her breath turns to gasps, to broken sounds that shatter against the table's surface.

Then, I brace my hands beside her, muscles straining as I push deeper still. Her cry rips through the air, and I fist a hand in her hair, pulling her head back toward me. Her throat arches, bare and trembling beneath my lips, and I press a kiss there as I keep thrusting, lost in the heat, the sound, the feel of her breaking apart beneath me.

"You're mine," I whisper.

And then I bite her again.

Her skin parts for me like it's always been waiting, blood blooming warm and sweet against my tongue. The bond ignites, blazing to a blinding crescendo as she breaks apart beneath me, her release tearing through her in wild, unrestrained waves.

Her body trembles, convulsing against mine, and I hold her there, buried to the hilt, mouth sealed to her throat as her pulse flutters frantic and alive beneath my tongue.

And then I'm gone. The tension rips free from my body with a violent shudder, my release hitting hard, deep, spilling into her as my muscles seize and lock. A growl claws its way up my throat, breaking into her name, a rough, hoarse cry torn from somewhere primal. Every nerve burns, every heartbeat caught in the same inferno as the bond seizes us both. Two stars colliding, burning, drawn together in the same consuming orbit.

CHAPTER 29

AMARA

Though lightning still flickers in the clouds, and thunder murmurs faintly across the horizon, the worst of the storm has passed. The sea lies eerily still, black and gleaming. It feels as though the ship is gliding silently across the surface of a mirror, slipping toward Baev'kalath.

The gentle lapping of water against the hull stirs me. My eyes flutter open just as Daedalus shifts behind me. His arm tightens instinctively around my waist, pulling me against the warmth of his chest.

His lips find the back of my neck, and he exhales a slow, sleepy groan. "Go back to sleep, wife," he mutters at my ear, his voice gravelled with drowsy satisfaction. "There is no force in all the Sundered Kingdoms that will drag you from this bed."

"Not even your crown?" I murmur, smiling faintly. "We must be close now."

He groans again, louder this time, and buries his face in my hair. "Has time moved so quickly?"

"I hear that happens when you're happy," I whisper, stroking the forearm draped over me. He responds by curling tighter around me, his legs tangling with mine.

A soft chuckle stirs against my skin. He presses another kiss to my shoulder, reverent and lingering. "Let me enjoy this peace just a little longer," he murmurs, "before I'm dragged back to blood and steel."

"Does it have to be that way?" I ask, voice barely above a breath.

He goes quiet for a beat, and I know the answer before he gives it. "You know it does, my love. Some things are worth the fight. A kingdom for my wife and child is worth everything."

"We don't need a kingdom," I say gently. "We have each other. We could return to the Grove. Let the world tear itself apart if it wants to."

His silence is heavier this time. It stretches between us like a chasm, and I feel the truth settle like a stone in my chest. I am a creature of peace and earth. He is made for battle and fire.

I feel him shift behind me. The warmth of his arm slips away, and the bed creaks as he swings his legs over the edge and sits up. His back is to me. The silence says more than any words could.

He stretches, his joints cracking, a groan slipping from him that's just loud enough to disturb the bundle resting nearby. He winces. "I'm sorry, my sweetheart," he says as he leans over the cradle. "Your father is a clumsy oaf unworthy of something so perfect."

I turn onto my back and watch him gently stroke our daughter's cheek, the look on his face softening into something fragile.

"She's probably hungry," I say, voice quiet in the stillness.

He glances at me. "Want me to change her first?"

I shake my head. "No. You should get dressed. Go above deck. The others will be waiting."

He turns his head, gaze heavy with quiet certainty. "I'll keep you safe here, wife. Lady Ilyra has guarded Baev'kalath well. There is nothing to fear."

"I know," I reply, and though I nod, the smile that touches my lips feels paper-thin and unconvincing, even to myself. A lie dressed in softness, spoken only to reassure the man I love.

Daedalus rises, stretching to his full, towering height, the muscles in his back flexing before he reaches for the dark folds of his clothing. I trace his runes with my gaze and notice the red scars just above his shoulder blades where his wings once were, but he pulls on his shirt before I can linger. Before stepping out, he casts one final look over his shoulder. The smile he gives me nearly breaks me. Then he's gone, the door clicking softly behind him.

I cradle our daughter to my chest, her small body warm and familiar against my skin as she latches, her soft suckling the only sound in the dim cabin. Her tiny fingers curl instinctively around mine, holding me as if she senses the storm I try so hard to hide.

Time has moved too quickly. Her silver eyes, once cloudy and uncertain, are now bright and aware, watching everything. Her hair has grown longer, curling at the ends. Even the points at the tips of her ears seem sharper.

My poor daughter. She has already survived more than most children will ever have to, and she doesn't even understand what she has endured. She doesn't yet feel the looming dread and I fear... I fear the worst is still to come.

Daed believes Baev'kalath is safe. That within those impenetrable walls, with their ancient towers and old magic, no harm can touch us. But Baev'kalath has never been safe. Not for me. Not for his mother or sister. So how can it be for the child in my arms?

I long for the Grove. For the hush of wind through the branches, for the songs that echo through the trees like lullabies. I yearn to hide her there, deep within the embrace of the forest, beneath the protection of the Souls. She would be safe there. We all would.

But Daedalus will never agree. He cannot sever his crown from his soul, and though I once thought I could live beside that duty, now I wonder if I am strong enough to stay.

As my daughter feeds, my hand drifts to my throat, fingers brushing the two crescent wounds still raw on my skin. His bite lingers, bruised and burning. A mark of more than passion. More than marriage. The bond we sealed was deeper than blood, deeper than any vow whispered beneath stars.

I am his. He is mine. That is the truth of it.

But never did I think loving him would mean having to choose.

Between him... and everything else I hold dear.

Because never did I believe that the journey which began in chains would lead me here. That I would board that ship as a prisoner and find myself falling for the Fae male I was forced to marry. That the one I once resented, feared, would become the one I crave with every breath. That I would bear his child. That he would become my mate, my other half, written into my soul with blood.

Once, I would have fled him without hesitation.

But now... now the thought of running feels like the unraveling of everything I've built. Of everything we are. Of my family.

And it would destroy me.

My daughter dozes off, her lips still parted in sleep as I gently ease her back into the crib. I move quietly while Ashen stirs at the foot of the bed but does not rise. I dress in silence, brushing out my hair and weaving it into a loose braid that drapes over my shoulder.

Only when I'm fully clothed do I pause, drawing in a long, steadying breath.

Then I step out, leaving behind the warmth, the quiet, the safety, and climb above deck.

The air bites colder here. Through the misted light and slivers of cloud veiling the morning sun, I see it.

Baev'kalath.

Spires clawing toward the slate sky. A fortress of black stone and nightmares.

We have arrived.

I join Daedalus at the helm, flanked by his brethren. The silence between them is thick enough to raise gooseflesh on my arms as they stare out at the black rock ahead.

"It's quiet," Orios mutters, narrowing his eyes at the courtyard that should be crawling with Blades of the Ebon Flight. "Why is there no one to meet us?"

Reon plants one boot on the railing, his brow furrowed. "Something's wrong."

I step up behind Daed, slipping my fingers into his. He curls his hand around mine, firm but distracted, gaze locked on Baev'kalath.

"Lady Ilyra sent no warning," he says.

Zyphoro glances over her shoulder. "What if she didn't have time to?"

Daed draws in a heavy breath, then exhales just as heavily. When he finally turns to me, there's tension in his jaw.

"Wife. I need you to go back to the cabin."

I roll my eyes and yank my hand free. "I'm so tired of being told to go back to the cabin. Must I remind you I'm more than capable of protecting myself? Or shall I demonstrate with green fire? Or perhaps another stormwyrm?"

Zyphoro laughs quietly into her hand. Daed hears it. His frown deepens.

"Fine," he concedes. "Stay on deck if you must. But we're going ahead to make sure it's safe before you and our daughter set foot on that island."

I part my lips to argue, but he cuts me off with a look.

"I'm not debating this. I know exactly what you are and what you're capable of. Which is why I'm asking you to use that strength to protect her."

That lands. That makes sense. Protecting our daughter is the only thing that matters.

"Very well," I say, quieter now.

Around us, the others release a breath as surprised as relieved.

Daed's shoulders drop slightly as he takes my hand again, this time with reverence. He lifts it to his lips and presses a kiss to my knuckles.

"As soon as I know it's safe, I'll come back for you."

"With what?" Zyphoro asks, that cruel smile curving across her lips. "Have you forgotten your wing situation? I'm not sure the prince being *carried* into Baev'kalath is the grandest of entrances."

Daed doesn't flinch. He's already considered it clearly because within a heartbeat, he stretches out his hand.

A coil of smoke unfurls beside him, and Ashen appears, small and soft in his kitten form. He lets out a low mewl and curls around Daed's leg, his wispy tail flicking through the air like mist.

Daed kneels, fingers gliding through smoke-fur, and whispers something only Ashen can hear.

Ashen's form ripples.

What was once delicate begins to grow, tiny paws stretch into massive, padded feet. His sweet, pointed face shifts into that of a great lion, framed by a thick mane of swirling shadow. His small body expands into something enormous, muscled, powerful. He arches his back and with a low rumble, wings tear from his shoulders, curling out in an elegant, smoke-woven spread.

When the transformation settles, Daed places a steadying hand on Ashen's neck. The creature huffs, adjusting to his size.

Without hesitation, Daed mounts him, just as the sound of wings snapping open fills the air. One by one, the others shift, and I find myself surrounded by true Fae. Tall and commanding, with wings stretching wide, runes burning bright across skin that gleams like starlight. Power radiates from them in pulsing waves.

"I will see you soon," Daed says.

Ashen opens his jaws in a wide yawn or a complaint; with him it's always hard to tell. I smile despite myself, reaching up to cup his jaw, brushing my nose against his.

We've been through too much, he and I. And though the void may live inside him, he is no demon, not to me.

Sometimes, I think he would rather trade it all for the quiet of my Grove. Sleep all day. Roll in the grass. Chase birds and dream beneath the sun.

Daed gives the word, and Ashen unfurls his wings and leaps into the sky. The others follow in perfect formation, slicing through the dim shafts of sun, blotting out the pale light as they soar toward Baev'kalath.

I watch them go until they blur into shadows against the clouds, and then, until they vanish altogether.

I know they're right. I remember Baev'kalath well enough to know its walls should be lined with Blades, and if they are not... something is deeply wrong.

But there's no force more capable of facing it than the one I just watched disappear into the sky.

Still, I wait.

I stand there far too long, the silence growing heavier with every heartbeat. Daed does not return. No one does and nothing stirs on the wind but stillness. Ominous, choking stillness.

My eyes sweep the cliffs. There is no path to reach the fortress. You must fly. One thing I cannot do. But even if I could find a way, I could not take her with me and I will not leave her behind.

I begin to pace, the ship's timbers creaking beneath my feet, my thoughts spiraling with impossible plans. None of them work. Every one ends with the same truth: she must be protected.

And then, like lightning slicing through fog, a thought strikes.

It's absurd. Reckless. Infinitely foolish.

But it's the only option I have.

I turn from the helm, make my way across the deck, and descend into the ship's underbelly.

Ronin is still chained to the central beam.

When he looks up, I frown. "You look dreadful."

He arches a brow. "Your words wound me." He gives a theatrical sniff and grimaces. "But I assure you, the smell is fucking worse."

Then he lets his head fall back with a dramatic sigh. "I take it we've arrived? Do I die now?"

I tilt my head, considering him. "Not yet. There's something I need first."

He eyes me with cautious amusement. "You want a favor... from *me*?"

"They've been gone too long," I say quietly. "I need to go after them. But I can't take the baby."

His brows pull together. "So?"

"So," I breathe, "I need someone to stay with her."

The words feel even more foolish out loud. Like tossing a match into dry grass.

Ronin blinks. Stares. Then narrows his eyes like he's sure he misheard me.

"You want *me* to... babysit?"

I lift my chin, refusing to waver. "Yes."

He lets out a bark of a laugh. "You'd entrust your child to the prisoner in the brig?"

"If I believed you meant her harm, you'd be ash by now."

He studies me. "And what makes you so sure I won't take my chance and run?"

I meet his gaze, steady. "Because I think, just maybe, there's a sliver of something left in you that still understands what it means to protect something precious. And because," I add, softer, "there is a part of you that does not want my daughter to come to any harm."

Silence stretches between us.

Finally, he glances at the shackle on his ankle. "Well, then... you'll have to unchain me. Unless you want the little one nestled in filth beside me."

I nod, because he's right. Of course he's right. And yet, the weight of what I'm about to do twists low in my stomach. This could be the best decision I've ever made or the one that ruins everything. I'm not sure which yet.

My eyes fall on the chain.

Maybe I should just stay put. Do what my husband asked. Be safe. Be still.

"No key?" Ronin asks, mouth curving in a lazy pout. "They don't trust you that much?"

I frown. "I don't need a key."

I move toward him, kneel by his side, and wrap my fingers around the chain. It's cold beneath my skin, but not for long. My magic answers instantly, green light threading up through my veins, pulsing just beneath the surface. The metal begins to shimmer, glow, then burn. I keep my hold even as the heat grows unbearable, until the chain melts away in a hiss of smoke and light, leaving only the cuff around his ankle.

And then it hits me. I didn't do it for strategy or mercy. I did it to prove I could. That I wasn't afraid.

Too late, I realize what that kind of pride invites.

He's already on his feet, looming over me, chest heaving, fists clenched as if he's fighting something inside himself. The room seems to shrink beneath his presence, the air pulling tight around us.

The fire still simmers at my fingertips, humming with warning. This isn't what I wanted and I was a fool to ever believe this man could be anything but danger. My enemy.

But then, slowly, his hands ease open. He exhales through his nose, and lifts one toward me, not in anger, but in offering.

We don't speak. We just look at each other, the moment stretching quiet and long between us. His eyes, usually so sharp, so cold, have gone still, their blue softening to a summer sky. As if they're asking me to trust him. Just this once.

The fire fades. The light in my skin flickers and dies.

I place my hand in his.

His fingers close gently around mine, warm and sure, and he lifts me to my feet.

"So," he says once I'm upright, voice light, "where's the little bundle of joy?"

I nod toward the stairs, already moving. He follows without question, his footsteps trailing behind mine like a shadow I've willingly invited too close. I glance over my shoulder more than once, not out of fear, exactly, but disbelief. That I freed him. That I trusted him.

And yet... something deep within me whispers that no harm will come to her in his presence. He's had a hundred chances to kill me. To leave me broken and bleeding in the name of Anethesis' dream. But he didn't. He chose otherwise.

We leave the brig and step into the gray light of day, crossing the deck toward the cabin. I pause at the door, pressing my palms flat against the wood. If I'm going to change my mind, return to reason, to safety, this is the moment. This is the last breath of sense before the descent.

But then I lift my gaze to Baev'kalath, shrouded in unnatural stillness. The silence of it sings louder than any scream. There's no sign of Zyphoro. No flicker of Orios or Solena. No Reon. No husband.

I grip the handle and twist.

The door creaks open, and Ronin's heavy steps follow me inside.

"It's nice in here," he comments, gaze sweeping the space. "Much drier than my quarters."

I ignore him, walking straight to the crib where she sleeps, small and perfect and utterly unaware of the war outside her walls. My hand hovers above her chest for a moment, drawn by the rhythm of her breath. Then, I look back at him, standing just inside the threshold.

"If you harm her," I say, my jaw tight, "I will do to your limbs what I did to that chain. Burn them off, one by one and I'll make certain you stay conscious to watch every moment of it."

His brows rise. "What a visceral image," he murmurs. "But unnecessary, Jewel. You were right. I wish her no harm."

He pauses. A flicker of curiosity crosses his face as his gaze shifts to the sleeping child.

"Her," he says. "What is her name? I'd rather call her by that."

My throat tightens. I glance down at the crib again. The truth, thick and bitter, rises in my chest.

"You *really* haven't named her yet?"

I shoot him a look. "The last few weeks have not been generous. I've had other things occupying my mind."

Ronin exhales, not unkindly. "Well, she needs a name."

His eyes catch on the ribbon tied to the crib. A soft red, faded with time and memory.

"You used to wear that around your wrist," he says, almost gently.

I nod, surprised he remembers.

"It must mean something."

"It does," I say quietly. "It belonged to someone. A warrior. She died in the Betrayer's Battle. Her name was Estra."

"If the ribbon means that much... if she meant that much... why not give your daughter her name?"

Silence folds between us. I look up at him, my eyes darker now, the weight of memory rising like a tide.

"My friend, the one you killed that day in the fields. He was her father."

Ronin stills. A beat passes. Then I hear the thick swallow, the shift of his stance as if he's bracing against something that won't stay down.

He straightens, ready to mask it with indifference. But this time... the regret clings to him. Lingers. Presses against his skin like sweat on a sweltering summer's day. And unlike before, he doesn't reach for an excuse. Doesn't say *I did what I had to do.*

He just stands there.

Haunted.

"If things had been different," he says softly, so softly I almost miss it, like he's confessing to the wind. "Maybe I wouldn't have done what I did that day. Maybe you wouldn't

291

have either. But the past is stone, Jewel. Heavy, unmoving. It does not change, no matter how we wish it would. All we can do is carry it and hope, one day, we're worthy of forgiveness. Even if the only one who ever grants it is ourselves."

He drifts closer to the crib, hesitant. His eyes flick toward her, but never settle. The smile that tugs at his mouth is nervous, unsure, a far cry from the man who once wielded fear like a blade. Still, he keeps his distance.

"She looks like she'd wear the name *Estra* well," he murmurs. "There's a warrior spark in her already. I can see it."

I study him in silence, drinking in every shift of his posture, every flicker of expression, wondering how much of this is truth and how much is just another mask, another trick to earn my trust before the blade comes down.

"I'll consider it," I say at last, my voice cool but not unkind. "But for now…"

I untie the ribbon from her crib and instead gently loop it around her wrist, finishing it in a bow.

"To keep you safe, my darling," I say with a smile. She smiles back, and warmth swells in my chest. I notice Ronin watching over my shoulder. My eyes rake over him. "Wash up a little before you touch her." I raise a finger, voice clipped. "And only touch her if you need to."

Before he can open his mouth, I turn away, dragging a cloak off the wall and fastening it at my throat.

I'm halfway to the door when he speaks again.

"Jewel," he calls. "Are you sure? You don't know what's waiting in that place."

I glance back at him, fingers on the handle. "Whatever waits there," I say, "it can't be worse than where I've already been."

Then my eyes drift to my daughter, still curled in her sleep, and back to him once more. I fix him with a slow, pointed stare.

"Remember. A limb at a time."

He sighs, exasperated. "Yes, yes. And I'll be wide awake for every moment. You're very poetic when you're threatening."

A smile curls at the edges of my mouth, sharp, fleeting, and gone by the time the door shuts behind me.

CHAPTER 30
DAED

My shadow stretches across the courtyard, long, formless, more smoke than substance. It slithers into every crack and seam in the stone, a silent herald of what follows. Behind me, my brethren descend, their wings snapping in the howling wind like torn banners.

This place is darker than I remember. Colder. Hostile.

Rain lashes my face, soaking through my clothes, tangling in hair that still carries the warmth of distant, sun-scorched shores. The sting of it makes me flinch.

How long have I been gone, that even the rain of Baev'kalath feels foreign to me?

But it is not just the rain.

Baev'kalath may still rise like a fortress of nightmares, spires piercing the sky, obsidian stone swallowing the light, endless corridors and stairs that spiral into nothing, but something has shifted. The soul of this place has changed.

Where are the Blades? Where is Ilyra?

We should have been met the moment *The Shattered Edge* appeared on the horizon. But no watchmen stood on the towers. No horns. No movement. No sound.

Baev'kalath feels... empty. Abandoned.

My chest tightens. Have they fled? Or fallen? Have I returned not to a stronghold, but to a tomb?

I grip Ashen's mane, and with a command, guide him to the high balcony. His massive paws strike the stone with a heavy *thud*, sending muddy water rippling outward. I slide off his back, the leather of my boots hissing against wet stone. One by one, my warriors land beside me, their blades at their sides, wings folding in before vanishing with the soft flicker of rune-light.

Ashen bows his head. He will wait.

We press forward.

Still, even this close to the heart of the fortress, there is no sign of life. No torchbearers. No guards posted at the thresholds. Not even a whisper echoing off the walls.

I don't need to speak. The scrape of steel follows, blades drawn with silent precision. I nod once, then turn toward the nearest alcove, stepping beneath the overhang and out of the punishing rain. The torches here still burn low, their flames guttering in the damp, casting flickering shadows across the black stone.

But there is no line of Blades guarding the throne room passage.

I move soundlessly, hugging the darkness as we approach. My steps are deliberate, every inch of my body tuned to the silence.

I glance back. My eyes find Orios and narrow. He understands immediately, peeling away to stalk the far wall.

The massive doors of the throne room loom.

Memories assault me.

I have stood before these doors more times than I can count, summoned by my father, by Lanneth, by the cruel weight of bloodbound duty. Dread was always waiting on the other side. Orders I could not refuse. Betrayals I could not undo.

I wonder now if anything has truly changed.

We halt. I listen, straining through the thunder and the hiss of rain for the faintest sign of life.

Nothing.

My hands press to the cold wood, my heart a furious rhythm in my chest, skin prickling like something unseen brushes against it.

And then, the doors explode open before I can push.

Standing within the yawning threshold is Lady Ilyra.

She is illuminated by moonlight, a vision carved from ice and grace. Her gown is the color of glacier water, pale and flowing, caught in a wind that doesn't touch me. Her hair, fair and thick, is braided loosely and long over one shoulder, and her blue eyes are wide with shock.

"Your Highness," she breathes. "You've returned?"

My brow furrows, rain trailing down the side of my face and along the sharp line of my jaw. I swipe it away with the back of my sleeve, narrowing my gaze on her.

"Lady Ilyra," I say. My eyes flick past her, to the hall cloaked in shadows behind her. "Are you alright?"

She straightens. "Of course. Why wouldn't I be?"

I peer into the gloom again, eyes straining for movement in the corners. "Where are the Blades? The Reapers?"

"The hour is late, Your Highness," she replies smoothly. "They're in their quarters. Sleeping."

My brow furrows. "Blades rarely sleep. Reapers even less."

She lifts a delicate shoulder in a shrug. "Had I known you would return tonight, I would've roused them."

Something cold skitters down my spine. A slow, gnawing unease curls in my gut. I glance over my shoulder. Zyphoro's scowl matches the storm still thrashing beyond the walls. When I turn back, I study Ilyra again, her posture, her tone, her too-calm presence in an empty, echoing castle.

My gaze flicks past her once more, to the twin thrones at the end of the hall.

"How is my father?"

Ilyra inclines her head. "As well as a prisoner can be. Though his chambers are far more luxurious than most. Would you like to see him?"

I shake my head too quickly. "No. Not yet." A pause. "And Lanneth? Does her cage still hold?"

A faint smile ghosts across her lips. An expression rare for Ilyra. "It does. There are days I forget she's even there."

"Modok," Zyphoro calls behind me, loud and clipped.

I frown at the interruption, but gesture for her to speak.

"Has he crossed the sea?"

"Not yet," Ilyra replies. "The Blades still guard the coast, and my spies have eyes on his stronghold. For now, we hold the advantage. You return to order."

Order.

The word rings hollow.

I lower my head slightly. "You have my thanks, my lady."

She clasps her hands together. "You must be hungry. Or weary. Shall we see to your needs?"

I shake my head. "No."

She glances over my shoulder at my brethren behind me, drenched, silent, waiting. "What of the others?" Her eyes pause on the last of them. "What of your wife?"

"She will join us soon enough," I say, voice cool. "When I know it's safe."

Ilyra cocks her head, the movement almost birdlike. "But Your Highness... I've already told you. It is safe."

I offer a shallow dip of my head, the closest thing to a smile I can manage. "You have. But after what I've seen these past weeks, I no longer take things at face value. Let us sit. Talk. I would hear everything."

She nods slowly. "Of course. The dining hall, then. I'll have wine brought up."

"Wine," Reon mutters, stepping from the ranks with a dramatic sigh. "I never thought I'd grow sick of rum, but here we are."

Ilyra leads us to the dining hall, and it's colder than I remember.

Not just in temperature, though the fire at the far end does little to soften the stone, but in presence. In memory. In silence.

She strides ahead, confident and regal, and slips into the seat at the head of the table as though it's hers by right.

My brow arches. Zyphoro, mid-step, freezes beside me. Her eyes find mine, and there's a flicker of shared understanding between us.

Solena is the one to speak, her voice soft but unyielding. "Lady Ilyra. That is the prince's chair."

Ilyra's eyes narrow, like a blade being unsheathed. "I don't need lessons in etiquette from a maid."

The air stills. Solena's gaze drops at once, her spine stiff with quiet shame.

Chairs creak, shoulders tighten, jaws clench, eyes darken. One careless phrase, and the room turns against her.

A breath passes. Then another.

She glances down at the seat beneath her and lets out a soft, almost rueful laugh. "Apologies. Of course it is. I've been sitting here so long... I suppose I forgot what belonged to me, and what does not."

Her voice lingers on that last part a little too long. A little too wistful.

I nod once. "It's fine. The food tastes the same no matter which chair you sit in."

She dips her head and slides one seat to the side. I take my rightful place, but there's something hollow about it now. As if the weight of tradition feels trivial in a world where thrones fall and death waits at every turn.

The heavy doors creak open, breaking the moment.

Servants file in, quiet as ghosts.

I don't recognize a single one of them.

Then again, there was a time I didn't recognize Solena either.

They move with the precision of the well-trained, laying down the first courses in reverent silence. Goblets of deep red wine. A board of cheese and thick bread still warm from the ovens. Dried fruits, honeycomb, thin curls of salted meat.

Zyphoro slings her boots onto the edge of the table and rips into a hunk of bread like she hasn't eaten in days. Reon grunts his approval, already filling his goblet to the brim.

Ilyra leans back in her seat, eyes flicking across our ragged company. "There's more than enough food," she says lightly. "Are you sure your wife does not wish to join us?"

My fingers curl around the arms of my chair. One boot taps against the cold stone floor, steady and sharp.

"She's fine where she is," I say. "Tell me about Modok."

She meets my gaze without flinching.

"He's building," she says. "Quietly. Carefully. The longer you were gone, the more the houses of the Untold Sea turned to him. Some believe he's the only Fae strong enough to reclaim the Sundered Kingdoms."

I say nothing. I watch her instead.

She pours herself a goblet of wine. The jug lands back on the table with a soft slam, wine sloshing over the lip. Her fingers wrap around the stem in a grip too tight, too tense. Her knuckles go white.

I've seen Ilyra fierce. I've seen her cruel, clever, biting.

But not like this.

Not rough.

Not trembling.

She lifts the goblet to her lips and drinks. The wine stains her mouth like blood. Her eyes hold mine over the rim, darker than they were a moment ago.

"Your return is well-timed, Your Highness," she says softly. "He will strike soon and Baev'kalath must be ready."

"No rest for the wicked," Reon sighs, pouring himself another generous goblet. "If this is true, I should return to Eyr'Drogul at once, see what state my house is in. I will rally my warriors to fight at your side, as always, Rook."

Orios doesn't sit. Doesn't eat. Instead, he remains at the far end of the table, the firelight carving sharp edges into the line of his jaw. Then he bows his head and presses a closed fist to his chest in salute.

"My prince, if matters are truly this dire, we're wasting precious time. The Blades must be summoned now."

I had hoped, perhaps foolishly, for more time. For peace. For the warmth of Amara's skin beside mine and the hush of a kingdom untroubled by war. But I see now how naïve that hope was. The war had never ended. It had merely paused to draw breath.

And now it exhales.

I rise slowly, the gravity of the moment anchoring each movement. My hand flattens on the table, steadying myself. My kingdom. My family. My daughter's future. All of it teeters on the edge.

"You're both right. There's no time for rest. We must prepare for war."

My gaze cuts to Ilyra.

"I want full reports from your spies. Everything. I need to know which houses remain loyal to me and I want them summoned to Baev'kalath immediately. This war will not be won alone."

I pause, turning the thought on my tongue before letting it free.

"And I want to speak with my father."

Zyphoro lifts a brow, her goblet pausing halfway to her lips. "Why?"

"Because, for all his sins he has survived more centuries than any of us combined. He knows the houses. Their strengths, their fractures, the secrets they bury and the heirs they pretend don't exist. That knowledge might be the only edge we get."

She snorts, finishing her drink in one long pull before slamming the cup down. "Fine. But if he starts acting like a sanctimonious prick, we throw him in that cage with Lanneth. That alone is a fate worse than death."

A corner of my mouth lifts. "Agreed, sister."

I turn back to Ilyra. "Where is he?"

"The hour is late," she begins, voice softening as she bows her head. "Perhaps in the morning..."

The scrape of Zyphoro's chair splits the air. She stands, eyes hard as flint.

"My brother didn't ask for suggestions."

I raise a hand before it can escalate.

"Zyphoro," I say quietly, "we owe Lady Ilyra our thanks. Without her, we'd have no castle to return to."

Ilyra straightens. "No. The Princess Zyphoro is right."

She lowers herself into a shallow bow.

"I misspoke. My nerves are frayed, as I imagine all of ours are. These halls have known too much silence. Too much waiting. With the prince away and the houses circling like wolves, we've all been on edge."

She lifts her chin, eyes clearing.

"Come. I will take you to him."

We follow Ilyra through the silent halls of the fortress, the storm outside snarling low across the sky, thunder rolling like a warning too late. She walks ahead of us, unhurried, silent, her gaze cast downward, and I study her carefully, her every movement, every flicker of tension in her shoulders.

I lean toward Reon.

"None of this feels right, does it?"

He shrugs. "I've always thought Baev'kalath to be a peculiar place. I assumed this was normal."

I frown. "Well, it's not." My fingertips graze the pommel of the dagger at my waist, more out of instinct than threat, but it calms me to know it's there.

"I still want that back," Zyphoro mutters.

Reon glances sideways, speaking under his breath. "You doubt, Ilyra? I thought she was our ally."

"Are there such things among the Fae?" I whisper back. "I hope I'm wrong. I hope Modok hasn't gotten to her. But if I'm right... we're walking into a trap."

Ilyra halts suddenly before a pair of tall carved doors.

"He is in here," she says softly, stepping aside.

My jaw tightens. "Open it," and my voice is harsher than I mean it to be. She flinches, just slightly.

"Of course, Your Highness."

She reaches for the handle, but her fingers hesitate, brushing it as if it might bite.

I square my shoulders. "Now, Ilyra."

Her throat bobs with a swallow, and she pulls the door open. It creaks with protest, groaning under its own age. Beyond the threshold, there is nothing. No firelight, no hearth-glow, only blackness that swallows the room whole.

A flash of lightning forks the sky outside, and for a heartbeat the room blazes white, revealing the silhouette of a figure seated in a high-backed chair, unmoving, face cloaked in shadow.

"Kaelus," Ilyra says. "Your son has returned and wishes to speak to you."

I step forward, cautious, lingering at the edge of the darkness. Close enough to see, not close enough to fall.

"Father?" I call out.

No response. No movement.

Zyphoro scoffs behind me. "Enough of this," she says, stepping into the room.

"No!" I snatch at her arm, but she's faster than my grasp.

In a blink of steel and shadow, they descend, Fae cloaked in the dark, knives glinting, eyes hollow with fury. They crash into her, dragging her down. I surge forward, magic pulsing to life in my blood.

But then, impact.

A shield slams into me, flinging me back with a force that rattles through my skull. I stumble, brace myself against the doorframe, blinking hard. And then I feel it, the shimmer, the hum of something far older than mere wards.

Mor'Thravar magic.

A barrier, thin as gossamer but pressing down with the force of a mountain. My fingers twitch, smoke curling up from my palms, my power coiling at the edges of my control, begging to be unleashed. Ready to burn. Ready to destroy.

But I can't. Not here. Not now. Not when I'm this close. Not when summoning it could call something darker.

Something I might not be able to send back.

Instead, my companions fight in my stead.

Reon lunges toward Zyphoro, arm outstretched, golden sparks of his gift already beginning to shimmer across his fingers. But before time can bend to his will, a barrier flares around his hands, snuffing out the magic like a candle under glass. The light dies with a hiss. He grits his teeth, wrestling against it, but it's too late. A boot slams into the back of his knees and he collapses with a grunt, taken down hard.

Orios is next. He hurls himself into the shadows, fury made flesh. His sheer strength alone sends two, three of them flying, bodies hitting stone, crashing into tables, thrown like dolls. For a heartbeat, hope flares. For a heartbeat, I believe he might actually do it, tear through every coward in the dark, every fool who dares lay hands on us.

But even the fiercest champions have weaknesses.

"Enough!" Ilyra's voice cuts through the chaos like a whip crack.

Orios stills, his chest heaving. He turns toward her, and I see the way his rage falters. The way it dies.

Because she's holding a blade to Solena's throat.

A slow burn begins in my chest as the shield coils tighter around me, crushing me to my knees. It scalds my skin, dragging fire across my ribs, over my spine.

"You fucking traitor," I grit out, voice ragged with pain. "Ilyra."

"She is no traitor," says a voice from the dark.

The figure in the armchair has finally moved. He steps forward slowly, as if he has all the time in the world, and though I have not yet seen his face, I know the voice. I knew it the moment it curled from his lips.

Modok.

"She sees the truth," he continues. "Her eyes are open now. As all Fae eyes will be. She knows who should rule the Sundered Kingdoms."

He steps into the light. The same cruel grin, the beard like bramble, the jagged spikes of hair pointing skyward except for that single, braided strand hanging like a noose over his collarbone.

"I expected more surprise," he says, his smile widening. "Not even a blink?"

"I'm only surprised I let myself walk into this ambush," I reply, jaw clenched. "I *knew* it reeked of rot."

"Another reason I should be king," he says, his voice like gravel. "Any Fae who smells a trap and walks into it, anyway? That's a Fae unfit to rule. That's a Fae who deserves to die on his knees."

He gives a long sigh, moving about the room with casual ease. Then, with mock courtesy, "Now. Didn't you say you wanted to see your father?"

My pulse stalls. My fists clench against the burning barrier.

Modok tucks his fingers into his belt and throws back his head. "Who am I to deny a last wish?"

CHAPTER 31

AMARA

I step onto the deck. The boards slick beneath my feet, the rain a steady curtain that soaks through my cloak within moments. I pull the hood tighter around my neck, bracing against the wind that slices in from the sea, but it's no use. The cold clings to me like a second skin. Still, I lift my gaze to the cliffs above, to the fortress that waits beyond them, and wonder for the hundredth time how I'm supposed to scale that impossible wall of stone.

I don't have long to consider.

A shadow moves across the deck.

My heart lurches. I stumble back a step, hand flying up on instinct as green fire sparks to life across my skin.

Then I see him.

Tall. Strong. Beautiful in the way only he could be. My breath catches in my throat.

"Daed?" I whisper.

He takes one slow step toward me. "Yes, Amara. It's me."

My chest tightens. I blink hard, the rain stinging my eyes. "You're back. Does that mean it's safe?"

He nods. His hand lifts to brush my face, his fingertips skimming my jaw.

"Yes, it's safe. Come back with me. To the fortress."

Relief floods my chest, chasing out the icy cold. I don't think I could have borne one more shock, one more fight. It feels like I haven't had a single breath since I first set foot in Baev'kalath a lifetime ago. Souls, how everything has changed since then.

Just one stretch of time where we aren't fighting to survive is a blessing.

Now I only need to explain why my husband's sworn enemy is the one watching over our daughter.

But that can wait.

I sag into him, burying myself in his warmth. My arms wrap around his waist, fingers curling into him. It takes him longer than it should to respond.

Slowly, his arms fold around me. His hand slips into my hair.

"There's nothing to fear anymore," Daed murmurs against my temple. "I'm here now, my love."

I press closer and let my eyes fall shut, breathing him in.

Then, a thought slices through the quiet.

My head snaps up, gaze sweeping the deck.

"Where is Ashen?"

A pause.

"Ashen," he repeats, like he's tasting the name, like it's foreign on his tongue.

I pull back just enough to search his face. "Did he come back with you?"

Another pause, and this time the flicker of something wrong behind his eyes. Something... empty.

I step away, inch by inch. His gaze follows, unblinking. Unnervingly calm.

"Where's Zyphoro? Solena?" I ask, heart thudding now, faster and faster.

"In the castle," he says. "They're waiting for us."

He extends a hand. Rain slides down his fingers like blood. "Come."

But I don't move.

I shake my head slowly, biting the inside of my cheek so hard I taste copper. I reach inward, past the storm and the fear, past the noise in my head, and search for what should be there.

The threads. The bonds. The shimmer of fate that ties me to him.

I find nothing.

"I don't see them," I murmur.

His brow creases. "See what?"

"The threads," I say, louder now. "The Binds of Fate. I don't see them between us."

His jaw tightens.

"Amara," he says, a roughness threading through his voice. "Come to me. Now."

I stare at him, every inch of him perfect. His eyes, his mouth. The face I have traced with my hands, kissed beneath moonlight. The face I have loved.

But it isn't him.

There is no glamor. No Fae shimmer. No glittering edge of deception. Just a perfect replica of the male who owns my heart. But my soul does not answer his.

"Who are you?" I breathe. "Where is Daedalus?"

"You are confused," he says, tone taut with irritation. "But my patience grows thin."

I grit my teeth, refusing to flinch. "You're not him. So tell me, who are you? And how do you wear his face?"

Then... *thud*. Heavy paws slamming onto wet wood draws both our attention toward the helm.

Ashen.

His form prowls from the shadows, smoke made flesh, his white eyes glowing with unholy light. He snarls, teeth bared, every muscle coiled with threat as he pads closer, the rain slicking his fur, steam rising off him in ghostly curls. He stops inches from the impostor and sniffs the air. His jaw quivers.

"If I were you," I growl, "I would answer. I am not the only one who knows you lie."

Silence fractures the space between us. The male's silver eyes hold mine until they don't.

They shift.

A flicker of violet flashes in the depths, and I suck in a breath, stumbling a step back.

Then he lunges.

His hand snatches my wrist with bruising force, the other slamming around my throat. I cry out, thrashing, but he's strong. Stronger than me. The cabin door slams into my back with a crack. I don't know if it's the wood or me that splinters.

Stars burst behind my eyes. My vision dims. His breath is hot against my face, and in my panic, my power awakens. A swell of heat surges from my chest, and a bright burst of green fire explodes between us.

He screams as the flames lash his face, searing flesh and hair. He stumbles back with a howl, dropping to one knee, hands clawing at his scorched skin.

And then, right before my eyes, he changes.

Dark hair recedes into a shorn, rune-marked scalp. Silver eyes ignite violet. Leathers ripple, becoming furs. My husband is gone. In his place stands a Fae female, and I recognize her. One of the Lady Twins of Jor'Thalas, but I do not know whether it is Vashar or Vasheeth.

She lets out a shriek, high and furious, her face half-melted, skin peeled back in angry welts.

"Look what you've done!" she screeches.

No shimmer is visible. No glamor needed.

The Fae of Jor'Thalas are shapeshifters.

"Where is Daed?" I hiss, flames dancing in my palm.

The twin staggers upright, blood slicking her jaw. Her hand peels away from her cheek. Skin comes with it.

"You will return with me to the castle," she rasps. "Modok commands it."

I raise my hand, fire flaring brighter. "Take another step," I warn, "and I will reduce you to ash scattered to the winds."

She stills.

The rain falls in sheets now, drumming against the deck, washing her blood into the wood.

Then, from the cabin, comes an infant's wail.

The twin's eyes narrow, lips parting in curiosity.

"Is that…" she breathes, "a baby?"

I say nothing. But my throat bobs. A single tremble.

She sees it, and she smiles. A cold, wicked thing that exposes a mouth full of sharp, animal teeth.

"My, my," she croons. "You have been *very* busy, haven't you? Oh, Modok will be *thrilled*."

Her tongue darts across her teeth.

"He *loves* human babies."

Fury surges, blinding and absolute, a fire that ignites in the pit of my stomach and spreads like poison through my veins. My jaw clenches so tight my teeth grind together, my body trembling, not from sorrow, not from fear, but from the unrelenting, soul-scorching *hatred* that comes only when someone threatens what you love most.

I lift my hand, fingers trembling with the sheer effort of holding back the inferno I long to unleash. But the twin doesn't wait. She lunges.

Teeth bared. A snarl tearing from her throat. One arm lifted high as her fingers twist into talons, long, curved. Blades made of bone and malice.

I reach for the fire, my green flames coiling in answer, but I don't need them.

Ashen moves first.

He hurtles from the helm in a blur of smoke and muscle, slamming into her side with a bone-rattling crash. The impact sends them sprawling across the deck in a whirl of limbs and mist. Her form is swallowed by his shadow, their bodies locked in a brutal tangle.

I step forward, fire dancing at my fingertips, ready to end it. Burn her to cinders. But then...

Smoke surges.

Shapes shift.

And suddenly there are *two* Ashens.

Identical.

"Ashen!" I cry out.

Both heads whip toward me. Two pairs of white eyes.

But then they crash together again, savage and relentless, rolling across the rain-slick deck. Massive paws striking, claws scraping wood, teeth snapping like bone-cracking thunder. One pins the other, only to be hurled off with a snarl. Then teeth sink deep into flesh.

A roar splits the air.

No blood. Only thick, black tar oozing from the wound, slow and vile, dragging itself along the planks.

My breath catches.

Fae don't bleed black.

But... does their magic mimic even blood when they shift?

The other Ashen lunges and bites, ripping open a line along the first one's flank. The same foul tar spills, slick and inky.

No. No, no, this cannot be happening.

My thoughts race, but with every snap of their jaws, every brutal blow, more of Ashen is torn apart and every heartbeat I hesitate, I risk losing him.

I have to *choose*.

Then the cabin door creaks open.

I spin around, flames ready to devour anything in their path, but it's Ronin.

He stands in the doorway, my daughter cradled to his chest.

My eyes flash green, the color surging with barely leashed power. "Get back inside," I growl, and it's not my voice that answers. It's something older. Wilder. Unfamiliar even to me.

Ronin startles. His arms tighten around my daughter. "Right," he chokes, his eyes too wide. He obeys without hesitation, vanishing behind the door as it slams shut with finality.

I turn back to the chaos.

Two Ashens.

Beasts of shadow and smoke, locked in a savage clash. Tufts of that ghost-lit, vaporous fur tear loose and whirl through the air as they maul and rip each other to shreds. Each rake of claw, each brutal bite sends black ichor spattering across the deck. Still, they don't relent.

They will not stop. Not until one of them falls. Not until one of them is dead.

I have to end this. Now.

But which is he? Which is my Ashen?

I rake my gaze over them, desperate for some mark, some flaw, anything to tell him from the impostor. But it's like staring at twin reflections, each movement mirrored in perfect, terrible symmetry.

And then I remember.

The tether between us.

The way he hears me even when no sound leaves my mouth, a frequency tuned only to us.

So I reach, not with breath, but with will. With every piece of me that knows him.

Ashen.

Look at me.

And one of them goes still.

His head snaps toward me, those white-hot eyes locking on mine, wild, feral at the edges, but inside... inside they are soft. Gentle. The same trusting glow that has been my anchor through every storm.

It is my Ashen. Fool that I am for not seeing him sooner.

My hand lifts, green fire spilling across my palm, but before I can release it, the impostor lunges. Jaws gape, and then clamp down on Ashen's throat.

A strangled sound tears from him. Shock. Pain. But what breaks me is the way his eyes flare wide first, that kindness still there, shining through agony. His light pulses once, twice, like a star trying to fight the dark, and then dims.

"No..."

The impostor shakes him, vicious and merciless. Thick black blood spills. I can only stare as his smoke, his soul, unravels in soft curls, thinning, drifting, disappearing like breath into the cold. Until he's gone.

My chest caves. I clutch at my heart when it hammers so violently I can't breathe.

"Ashen," I choke, the name cracking out of me as tears spill hot down my cheeks.

The impostor. The twin, Vashar or Vasheeth, I don't give a fuck! It turns to me wearing his face. Wearing my Ashen's face!

I curl my fist. Emerald flame roars, devouring rain, turning it to steam in violent bursts. Magic crashes through me, furious and vengeful, and I loose it with a scream inside my bones.

A whip of green flame lashes out, striking the impostor square in the chest.

The twin screams, high and keening, as the fire engulfs her. The illusion peels away, fur dissolving, smoke vanishing until only her true form remains, writhing in a storm of green flame. She reaches to me through the blaze, begging for mercy, pleading for me to stop!

I make the fire hotter.

The noise she makes loses its horror after a while, so numb to it do I become. Her screams gutter out like dying coals, and then there's only rain-soaked silence and her blackened husk curled grotesquely on the deck. The stench of charred flesh crawls up my nose.

Then my knees hit the wood.

I fold, shaking, rain and tears blurring everything, thunder swallowing the ugly, broken sound that tears out of me. I can't hold him. I can't touch him one last time. Can't drag him into my arms, bury my face in his fur, whisper how sorry I am. He's gone and I don't even get the chance to mourn him properly. The way he deserves, because the twin came wearing Daed's face, to take me to the fortress. Which means Daed walked straight into a trap.

So, I force myself up. My legs buckle. My chest feels like it's split open, but I move. I have to. If I fall apart now, I lose more than Ashen.

I reach the cabin door, throw it open and then gasp as pain blooms in my abdomen.

I stagger back, blinking down at the hilt of a dinner knife lodged just beneath my ribs. I lift my eyes to Ronin's face.

"What are you doing?" I stammer, wincing through the ache.

His jaw clenches. "Stabbing you. Obviously." With infuriating calm, he withdraws the blade and tosses it onto the table with a dull clink.

"I didn't know who you were. Had to be ready." His gaze flicks to the wound. "You can heal that, right?"

I grit my teeth. It's nothing, barely a flesh wound. It was only a dull knife after all, but I am in no mood. I press my hand to my stomach, emerald light flooding under my fingers, sealing flesh in a heartbeat. I need pain to heal, and there's enough sorrow burning through me right now to heal an army.

He mumbles something, but I don't care. I push him aside as my gaze darts to the crib. My daughter reaches up with tiny hands, blinking at me with her father's eyes.

She's safe. That knowledge alone is enough to steady me.

"Daed is in danger," I tell him, breath catching as I swallow my sobs. "I need to go to him. You have to stay here with her."

Ronin bristles. "When did I become the damned wet nurse? I am a warrior. I command the Legion of Saints."

"Perhaps in the Sundered Kingdom," I snap. "But here, in this cabin, you're just the idiot who tried to stab me with cutlery, and right now, I need you to protect my child."

He doesn't budge. That scowl stays iron-flat.

I roll my eyes. "You're the only one who can," I bite out.

That does it. His face changes immediately, smugness blooming like a weed.

"Well, why didn't you lead with that?"

Souls. Male pride. So easily stroked, so pathetically delicate. For all their boasts of strength, I've never known creatures more desperate to be needed.

"You will take Ashen then?" he asks. "Did my eyes deceive me? There were two of them out there?"

My lips tremble as I struggle to find the words I need, but before I can speak, Ronin yells.

"Behind you!"

It's too late. I see the reflection first, the blur of motion in his wide, panicked eyes. A shadow moves behind me, and something heavy cracks across the back of my skull.

The world fractures. My legs give out, and the last thing I see is the wooden floor as I fall.

CHAPTER 32
DAED

The stone is cold as ice beneath my cheek, drenched with rain that pelts down like it means to drown the world. I lie sprawled on my stomach, hands bound tight behind my back, face turned just enough to catch a glimpse of the brilliant, full moon burning in the storm-wracked sky.

We're in the sparring courtyard. I'd know this stone anywhere, by its sharp edges, by the hollow sound of water striking its surface like a drumbeat of memory.

Boots march past my face, splashing in puddles gone black with blood. I track one pair, sluggishly, until my gaze finds Reon collapsed to my left, his mouth slack against the stone, unmoving. Orios lies next to him, then Solena. All of them soaked through. All of them bloody. Faces swollen and half-unrecognizable from the beating.

"Brother," Zyphoro murmurs, her voice raw beside me.

I force my head to turn. Even that small movement grinds pain through my skull. Look what they've done to her. Raven hair plastered to her face, soaked in blood. Her hands are bound like mine, the ropes biting into her wrists. Through the curtain of rain and the blur of my bruised, half-shut eye, I can barely see her.

"Can you hear me?" she asks.

I nod, or try to. "Do not show them fear. That's what they want."

She smiles, but it's a grim, crooked thing. "Fear was burned out of me long ago." Her gaze shifts upward then, mouth tightening, her expression draining of all color. "Let us hope our father found his courage before the end."

I follow her eyes and wish I hadn't.

The thick wooden pole rises into the night.

I see the lashed feet first, bruised and bare. Then legs flayed to the bone, and a chest carved open. His neck slashed so deep I see tendon. His arms limp at his sides like broken branches. Then his face. Or what remains of it. Once marble-smooth. A face that could

311

command a court with nothing but a single, frigid glance. Now it's a butchered mangle of torn flesh, unrecognisable to anyone else.

But I know him.

I would know him anywhere.

Even faceless.

Even dead.

Father.

I'd seen centuries with him. Fought by his side. Bled in his name.

And now the rain washes over his corpse as if it means to cleanse what's left. But no blood pours from his wounds. No color clings to his skin.

"How long?" I rasp, my voice hoarse and barely louder than the storm. "Ilyra! When did they..."

But the words die in my throat as my gaze shifts.

Another pole. Another body.

Long, pale limbs exposed to the elements. Blonde hair tangled and soaked red with blood. Lady Ilyra. Butchered like my father.

I freeze. Ice crawling down my spine.

Because just then, something brushes past. The shimmer of silk, the swish of a gown's hem dragging through puddles.

I look up and I see her.

Ilyra.

Alive.

Yet her body still hangs above, eyes wide and staring, and that's when realization hits me.

The pieces slide into place with a sickening click, and if I hadn't already had the shit beaten out of me, I'd do it myself for being so fucking blind.

"Which one are you?" I groan through cracked lips, the taste of blood thick on my tongue. "Vashar... or Vasheeth?"

The figure before me cocks her head. Slowly her form begins to ripple, silk and satin dissolving into worn leather and filthy furs, soft blonde waves receding until only a slick, bald scalp remains.

She drops into a crouch before me, leathers creaking, then she fists my hair and yanks my head up, forcing me to look her in the eye.

"I'm wounded you don't recognize me, Your Highness," she hisses, lips curling back to reveal rows of needle teeth. "I am Vasheeth. At your service."

And then she slams my head back toward the ground.

I catch myself inches before my face meets stone.

"How long have they been dead?" I spit, my voice gravel.

She rises slowly, letting her gaze drift to the poles looming behind her. "Days. Weeks. I stopped counting," she says with indifference, almost boredom. "There were so many to play with."

She steps back and lifts a hand in a sweeping arc and I realize there are dozens of poles. Maybe hundreds. Bodies strung up like trophies. Blades, Reapers, Servants. Anyone who had once served House Mordorin.

Their flesh hangs in ribbons. Eyes hollow. Necks twisted at impossible angles.

My warriors. My brethren. My house.

Butchered.

Lightning rips across the sky, casting the courtyard in a harsh, momentary glare, and there stand the Fae of House Mor'Thravar, lined in ranks.

Modok stands at their head, tall, wiry, and still, his shoulders hunched, his long, rust-colored leather coat flapping in the wind, eyes fixed on me with pure malice. Beside him is his sister, Nyraxes, her gaze no warmer.

She steps forward, rain dripping from the curve of her brow, her mouth forming a smile that doesn't reach her eyes.

"Welcome home, Daedalus."

The words are a blade, sinking slow.

"It's only fitting you hang on a pole of your own, don't you think? Your warriors will be comforted, I'm sure. With their commander beside them. It might please you to know they died well. Swore loyalty to their prince until I cut their tongues out."

Her smile widens.

"But loyalty," she whispers, "is just ash in the wind."

She turns, lifting her arms to the storm above.

"There is only one true power in this world," she says. "Us. The Fae. House Mor'Thravar. Fear is the fire that burns long after loyalty crumbles to dust."

Modok reaches for his sister's hand, fingers outstretched. Nyraxes gazes at him with reverence, as if he is something sacred and righteous. She clutches his hand with a reverent grace and he lifts it to his lips, brushing a kiss across her bloodstained knuckles.

"Well said, Nyraxes," he murmurs. She dips her chin, demure as a blushing bride, though there is nothing soft about her.

"Now," Modok continues, turning back to me with a grin that shows too many teeth, "all that remains is to show the Fae that House Mor'Thravar *is* the power in the Sundered Kingdoms. And to do that?" He spreads his arms wide, the rain slicking over his leathers, over his fury. "We hang the last heirs of House Mordorin. Then all will kneel."

"Fine," I rasp, blood sliding down my throat. "Do what you will with me. But let my companions go. They are nothing to you. They have no part in this."

Modok's smile vanishes. He lunges, storming forward, kicking water in my face as he closes the distance.

"Of course they do!" he roars. "They bore the mark, sword and wings, same as you and I do not doubt for a second they would die for you. That kind of loyalty, that kind of devotion to a failed line and a pathetic excuse for a monarch... it spreads like a sickness. I cannot, *will not*, let it fester in *my* Sundered Kingdoms."

His foot rises, pressing against the crown of my skull.

"I will burn your memory from this realm like rot from a dying tree," he breathes. "But not before I rip your heart out and squeeze the life from it in front of you."

Then he steps down.

My face smashes into the stone. Pain flares, and I hiss through clenched teeth.

"I'll have her soon," Modok says. "That mortal you chose. The human girl you defiled your bloodline for. I'll string her up first. Strip her to the bone. I'll peel her apart, layer by layer, scream by scream, until there's nothing left but meat and guts and you will watch. Every slice. Every tremble."

My chest heaves. Rage roars beneath my skin.

"If you're going to kill me," I grind out, "then do it now. Quickly. Because every second you delay is another I spend plotting how I'll escape this place. How I'll cut my way through your disgraced fucking house until your head rolls and your soul howls."

I look up at him through the blood in my eyes. "Your punishment is long overdue, Modok. You betrayed your Fae blood long before I ever did and I swear to every cursed star, I will see my people avenged." I swallow. "I will see Zema avenged."

His boot crashes into my face again, harder this time. My lip splits. I spit blood into the stones, vision tilting, a red haze swallowing the edges.

"That's always been your weakness, Daedalus," he sneers. "Sentiment. You never had the spine to do what was necessary. Never had the courage to watch the world bleed to make our kind strong. You let love soften you."

He crouches, his voice dropping to a hiss. "Zema haunted you, didn't she? All these years. Her death. Your guilt. Do you want to know the truth?"

He leans closer, his breath a hot whisper against my ear. "I barely remember her. But sometimes in my sweetest dreams, I'm reminded of how wondrous her face looked after I smashed it against the rocks."

A snarl claws from my throat as I writhe against my bindings, the cord biting into my wrists.

Modok laughs.

"Easy now. Be patient. Vashar should return any moment with your beloved in tow. And then," he straightens, his smile feral, "then the real fun begins."

My heart hammers against my ribs, each beat a brutal thud echoing through my chest.

No.

Not Amara.

I led her straight into this trap.

How long has it been since Modok took Baev'kalath? Since he murdered my father and Ilyra?

The last time I heard from her spies was just after I found Amara. She must have still been alive then. And I... I hadn't thought much of the silence that followed. I was too consumed with my wife. With our child. With foolish hopes of normality.

Why didn't I check in?

Did she call for me?

I look up at her body, and the thought rips through me. I left my ally isolated. Exposed. She is dead because of me.

My gaze drags across to my father's corpse.

He is truly gone and with him any hope of redemption.

He will never find the salvation I once, in my weakest moments, wished for him. Never atone for his ambition, for the carnage he wrought in the name of the Father Below, for the love he bore Lanneth, who murdered my mother and stole my sister into shadow.

And I... I will never know why he did the things he did.

I will never get to forgive him and I will never, not truly, get to hate him as I once swore I would.

But I will not hang beside him and my wife, my fierce, furious light, will not hang beside him.

Because it is not our time to die.

If Vashar is with Amara now, it will not take long for Modok to discover the truth. To find our daughter and I will not allow him to take one more thing from me. Not tonight. Not ever.

But then I hear her cry, splitting the storm open. The sound stills everything. I close my eyes, and for a moment I drift, weightless in dread.

No. How did I let this happen?

When I open them again, Modok's expression is one of disbelief, his face a mirror of the horror cracking me in two.

A Mor'Thravar Fae steps forward, holding my daughter. Rain streaks down her tiny body, pooling in the delicate curve of her neck. She wails into the night, limbs flailing, and then Modok takes her.

"What is this?" he mutters, his voice overwhelmed with disgust, shock. "A half-breed?"

He brushes a callused, vile hand over the pointed tips of her ears.

I thrash against my restraints with a roar, the sound torn from the deepest part of me. I snarl, teeth bared. But I don't know if he even hears me. He's too consumed by her. By *my* daughter.

Nyraxes lingers nearby, revulsion twisting her face.

"You couldn't just slake your lust with Fae, could you?" she sneers. "You had to pollute your bloodline with *that*."

She spits, the glob landing inches from me.

"Kill the baby first, brother," she screeches. "Every breath it takes is an offense. A stain. An abomination!"

I barely have time to process the words before I hear a heavy thud.

Amara.

Her body is dropped without care onto the stones.

I stop breathing.

My eyes lock on her. I scan every inch, searching, *begging* for a sign of life and then the Golden Son is hurled down beside her. He groans, drops to his knees, head bowed.

He glances my way, but only briefly before turning to her. Reaching out. Touching her arm like he has every right to know the feel of her skin.

Rage burns through my veins.

I would tear the flesh from his hand if I could.

But she stirs.

The smallest shift. A twitch of her fingers.

Relief crushes me like a tidal wave. She's alive.

Vasheeth paces nearby, her eyes scanning the Mor'Thravar ranks. Then she halts.

"Where is Vashar?"

Silence.

One male shakes his head, then nods once...toward Amara.

Realization takes a breath to land and when it does, I see it ripple across Vasheeth's face. Vashar is not coming back. Killed. By my wife.

That grief... that fury... that blood vow begins in her eyes.

Her hand drops to her hip. The dagger there is already whispering for vengeance.

She draws it, slow and sure, steel gleaming beneath the stormlight.

Modok and Nyraxes don't even glance her way.

They're still lost in their sick fascination with my daughter.

They don't see Vasheeth cross the stones toward Amara, dagger poised to strike.

"Modok!" I shout, the word ragged. "Nyraxes!"

But both ignore me.

All I can do is watch helplessly as Vasheeth reaches Amara and hovers over her.

The Golden Son lunges to intercept, but he's too slow. She kicks him hard, and he flies backward, skidding across the stone.

No.

Not like this.

Not when I've just gotten her back.

Not when my life had finally started to mean something.

Not when I had purpose.

When I'd started to believe I could have something pure, something perfect, something beautiful, even with the curse upon my soul.

317

I close my eyes. Shadows press against the edges of my vision. I try to blink them away.

But I can hear it now...the darkness. It sings to me.

It tells me I do not have to be helpless. That there is power waiting. Terrible, ancient, endless. All I need do is call to it. Summon it. Let it in, and I can make this all go away. I can make them *suffer*. I can make them *pay*. I can tear them into pieces and feed them to the void.

But I know what else it brings. What waits inside me. Something monstrous.

And still... I have no choice. Because I swore I'd only call on it if my life depended on it.

But this isn't about my life anymore.

This is *her* life.

Smoke slithers between my fingers. Shadows pour from the edges of the courtyard, rushing toward me like a dam breaking. They swarm me. Swirl in a furious, hungry vortex. The air hums with the echo of a thousand ancient voices, speaking in unison, welcoming me back.

I feel him. His hand presses on my shoulder, and when I open my eyes, they are black.

Death Singer manifests in my grip, inch by inch. As the blade finishes its descent, my bindings melt into smoke and then, with a roar of shadow, I walk the void.

It is cold, suffocating, endless, but I cannot deny the way my skin hums at its touch. White eyes flicker in the dark, demons watching from the depths. Then I walk again, tearing through space and shadow to appear at Vasheeth's side.

She gasps when she sees me. They all do. They realize too late what they've forced me to become, what they've unleashed. But I give her no time for regret. I drive my blade between her shoulder blades, the steel erupting through her chest. Vasheeth chokes, blood dripping from the corners of her mouth, her limbs trembling, her eyes wide and glassy with the knowledge of her death. I watch until the sounds she makes bore me, then yank Death Singer free. Her body is swallowed by smoke, devoured before it ever hits the ground.

But even in death, she leaves behind her dagger, slipped from her grip before the void claimed her. The blade spins slowly through the air, landing beside Amara's face with a sharp, ringing clang and her eyes flash open.

CHAPTER 33

AMARA

It's weightless where I am. Weightless and warm and untethered, like I've finally slipped beyond the grasp of all that ever hunted me. I'm floating, drifting somewhere soft and golden, suspended far away from the death and cruelty and endless hardship that's clung to me like a second skin since I left the Grove. There is no fear here. No pain. Just quiet, perfect stillness. For the first time in what feels like lifetimes, I am not afraid. Not for myself. Not for the ones I love. It's just peace. Soft and whole and final.

Am I dead?

Is this what waits for us after our light flickers out and the world lets us go?

But then, like a crack shattering across glass, a metallic clang rings in my ears, so loud and sudden I think my skull might split open from the sound alone. My eyes fly open on a gasp, and the weight of this world returns with cruel precision, rain slicing at my face like knives, my spine throbbing where stone juts against it. Lightning cracks across the sky above Baev'kalath, followed by the deep, rolling growl of thunder.

I'm back. Here. Alive. My journey far from over.

There is no peace. Not in this world and as the fog clears from my mind in tatters and wisps, it leaves only chaos in its wake and a blooming pain at the base of my skull that throbs with each passing second. I blink through the haze, through the sting of rain and blood in my eyes, and see them. Zyphoro and Orios. Reon and Solena. All of them bound and facedown on the courtyard stone like discarded scraps. Ronin lies sprawled opposite me, unmoving, and lining the courtyard walls are poles, too many to count, each one strung with a grotesque offering: bodies, slack and rain-slicked, their lifeless forms swaying in the storm.

Then I hear her.

A cry, high and terrified, slicing through the sound of the rain and my heart stops.

My daughter.

She's in Modok's arms, while his sister hovers too close.

I shove my palms against the stone, every muscle in my body screaming as I fight to rise, my stomach lurching with the effort, but I don't stop. I can't. Because then, then I hear it. The screeching drag of a blade against stone. That high-pitched shriek that sets my teeth on edge, makes my entire body recoil in instinctive horror. I turn and see him.

Daed.

He walks with slow, striding steps, stalking toward Modok, his hand wrapped around Death Singer, and though he is mine—my Daed, my husband, my mate—I can already feel the wrongness radiating from him. I see it in his eyes as they roll black. I feel it in the tether between us, stretched and fraying.

The rain carves rivers down his skin. The ink of his sigils, the ones that protect him, the ones that hide him from Gygarth, from the void itself, they begin to run. Thick, oily streaks of black bleeding from his body like tears.

He raises his sword, voice like smoke and thunder.

"Give me the child," he demands. "Or give me your head."

Modok's arms tighten around our daughter, pressing her closer. "One move, Daedalus, and I will crush the life from her body. You know I will."

But Daed doesn't stop.

He keeps coming.

His steps slow, unrelenting, deadly. The last of his sigils melts away, pooling around his feet. They're gone. All of them. The last protections he had, the only thing keeping him from being found. From being taken. From being consumed.

But Daed no longer looks like a male who cares about being found.

He walks like vengeance incarnate. Like a Fae who has surrendered everything that once tethered him to this world. He is what I was warned about. The cursed prince whose soul belonged not to me, not even to himself, but to the darkness that waits with outstretched hands and as the final drip of ink falls from his fingertip, splashing against the stone like a heartbeat, something stirs.

A speck of midnight and silver, flaring to life in the air before him. Small at first, a flicker, but it grows. Faster than I can breathe. A maw opens wide and infinite and full of screams, a gaping mouth of nothing.

The void.

He is here.

He has found us.

But it is not Gygarth who slithers through, descending on this world like a nightmare. No, it is the other. The one I glimpsed in the portal. The one who haunts the edge of dreams. A skeletal figure draped in black, flesh like dried leather stretched too thin over bones too long, claws that drag like blades through the air, and beneath his chin, a writhing beard of tentacles, slick and twitching and hungry.

Modok snarls, voice cracking with rage tainted with fear. "Save your pathetic Mordorin tricks! I will kill every fucking last one of..."

But he doesn't finish. The creature lifts one hand in a slow, languid motion, so casual, so cruel, and the air itself answers. Smoke, black and thick like spilled ink, erupts from his fingertips, soaring across the courtyard in serpent coils. It wraps around Modok in an instant, twining around his limbs, tightening. I scream. I *scream*, because I see her, my daughter, torn from his arms, flung skyward like a discarded doll.

The sound that rips from my chest is not human. It is pain and terror and fury forged into a single note that rends the very core of this world. Thunder silences. Lightning halts mid-strike. The world holds its breath as my daughter sails through the air, arms outstretched, her tiny mouth open in a cry I cannot hear over the roar of my heart.

The demon flicks its wrist.

Modok explodes.

His body tears apart in a vicious snap, limbs ripped in four directions, blood raining down in thick splatters. A scream shatters the air, not mine this time, but Nyraxes', her brother's blood hot on her skin. Her hands claw down her cheeks in horror, but I barely register her. I see only my daughter.

She's still falling.

I lunge, scrambling to my feet, legs numb, arms desperately reaching, but I am too far. The space between us is a chasm. My hands stretch through it anyway, begging the Souls, the void, the creature who brought this nightmare, *anyone*, to let me be fast enough, strong enough.

But then a blur of movement surges past me. A body, reckless and sure, hurls itself against the wet stone.

Ronin.

He hits the ground hard, the slap of his body making me flinch, but he never looks away from her. He reaches, catches, curls his body around hers just before she hits the ground.

A sob tears from my throat. My knees threaten to buckle.

"Thank you," I gasp, the words barely a breath. "Thank you, Ronin."

He nods once, the motion sharp, but there is no time for gratitude, no time for anything but survival.

"They have *murdered* your Lord!" Nyraxes shrieks, voice unhinged in its grief. "Kill them! Kill them *all!*"

The courtyard erupts.

The warriors of House Mor'Thravar descend like a tide of death, but before the first sword is drawn, the demon lifts his hands again, stretching them wide as if parting a curtain of reality itself. The portal behind him groans, widening, pulsing like a wound torn into the sky. Screams echo from its depths, high and thin, followed by the pounding of hooves and the screech of wings. A dark swarm surges forward, creatures of nightmare and smoke, twisted things with too many limbs and eyes that burn white.

They come and when they burst from the void, when they flood the courtyard like a dam broken loose, the demon merely watches. He does not fight. He does not command. He *invites*. His arms are outstretched like a prophet baptizing the world in horror, and his children—his *monsters*—gladly answer the call.

Steel clashes. Claws tear. Screams rise and fall in a symphony of pain and fury as blood and rain turn the stones into a river of crimson. The air tastes of steel and ash, of endings.

And in the center of it all, the demon turns his gaze on me.

He smiles, I think, and speaks with a voice made of a thousand others, layered like a chorus of blight and shadow.

"You," he says. "At last. The master will get his taste."

"No, Emranth!" Daed roars, voice breaking against the storm. "*Never!*"

Death Singer arcs through the air, fast and furious, singing a deadly hymn of steel and fury, but the demon catches it in one clawed, leather-bound hand, like it's nothing more than a toy sword carved from wood.

"Favored one," Emranth breathes, voice curling. "Welcome back to the darkness."

Daed snarls, his grip tightening on the hilt with both hands, muscles straining as he tries to wrench the blade free, but it doesn't move, not even an inch. It's as if the steel itself has bent to the will of the void.

Above, the sky becomes a writhing mass of wings and fangs, the winged horrors screeching down in relentless waves, crashing into the Fae with talons bared. On the ground, monsters thunder through the gates, shadows on all fours, jaws unhinged, tearing through warriors like parchment.

Daed turns to me. Not just to me. To Ronin, too. I see him fighting. I see that promise in his eyes that somehow, somehow, he will hold the darkness at bay.

"Free them," he growls. "Keep them safe."

And then he throws himself at Emranth, slamming the void-born creature back with the full force of his body. They crash onto the stone in a blur of shadows.

I don't waste a second.

With a grunt, I scramble across the courtyard, legs aching, blood roaring in my ears. I reach Solena first, and with a flicker of flame that dances from my fingertips like a serpent's tongue, I sear through the ropes binding her wrists. She gasps as they fall away, and I'm already moving.

Then Reon. His bonds hiss into ash.

Orios next, breath ragged, eyes wide with disbelief as the fire licks away his restraints.

Then Zyphoro.

She rises to her full height, shoulders squared, eyes of the storm blazing. With a flick of her wrists, smoke coils around her fingers, and twin daggers shimmer into being, forged from shadow and wrath.

"Go now, Amara," she commands. "Take your child and get to the castle."

"I will not hide!" I shout, fury blooming hot in my chest.

She whirls on me, eyes flashing. "You stay, and you'll die and then she will have no one. Is that what you want?"

The words catch on the edge of my tongue like thorns. I don't want to flee. I want to burn. I want to carve my rage into the bones of every creature that dares to threaten what is mine. But I want her to see the Grove more. I want her to run barefoot through its mossy trails, to laugh beneath the ancient trees. I want her to know green things, not this ruin of blood and nightmare and shadow.

"No," I whisper, voice catching as Ronin places my daughter into my arms. "No. That isn't what I want."

Zyphoro bares her teeth at me, something feral and desperate in the sound. "Then go. Now."

I don't wait. My grip tightens around my child, and I run, legs aching, lungs burning, as I press her small, warm body to my chest and barrel toward the castle in the distance.

"You," Zyphoro snaps, whirling on Ronin. "Keep her safe. If she dies, you better hope I find you already dead."

He gives a sharp nod and takes off at my heels.

"Wait!" Orios calls, and we all freeze, just for a heartbeat, amidst the howling chaos. Monsters screaming, wings slashing through the air, stone cracking beneath claw and fang.

He pulls Solena to him with both arms, lifting her like she weighs nothing, then kisses her, hard, desperate, like it might be the last time. When they part, breathless, I can't tell if the wetness on his cheeks is rain or grief.

"You too, my love," he says, voice raw. "Go with them. Please."

Solena shakes her head, her hands tangled in his tunic. "My place is with you."

"And mine with you," he murmurs, pressing his forehead to hers. "And when we survive this, I'll make it my place forever. I'll make you my wife, Solena. But give me something to fight for. If I know you're safe, I'll cut through a thousand armies to reach you again."

She closes her eyes, her whole body trembling as she kisses him once more, a soft sob caught between their lips. "I love you," she breathes.

"I love you," he echoes, his voice breaking.

He lowers her gently to the ground, and with one last glance that embodies all the words they don't have time to speak, she turns and runs after us.

We flee toward the fortress, toward the shadowed alcove not far beyond, with smoke and teeth and screams chasing at our heels.

I don't dare look back, not at the battle unraveling behind us, not at the slaughter we've barely outrun.

Or have we?

Because as I turn the corner, her laughter follows. Low. Crooked. Crawling like smoke along the walls, seeping into the cracks of the stone, chasing us like a starving dog who can scent its next meal.

"Amara," Nyraxes calls, voice gliding after us. "Where do you think you're going? I'm not finished with you or that half-breed wretch you clutch so tight."

She is not alone. A small cluster of warriors falls into step behind her, blades drawn. I remember their stink from the night they attacked me in my chambers, the unmistakable scent of Mor'Thravar Fae: musk and salt and damp.

We run for a while, but Ronin never stops glancing over his shoulder. His jaw clenches tight, brow furrows deep, and then suddenly his steps slow until he eases into a walk and finally turns to face our pursuers.

I stop. "What are you doing? Run!"

He shakes his head. "No. I'm not running. Not from Fae scum."

Solena scowls at him but holds her tongue.

"We have no choice!" I snap, cradling my daughter closer. "We're outnumbered."

"Those are my favorite odds," he says, the smug grin crawling across his face still sickening even now.

I roll my eyes. "You don't even have a blade."

Suddenly, a flash of silver streaks past my face and Ronin snatches the pommel midair. I turn to Solena, startled.

"If he wants to be a hero, let him," she says curtly, glancing at her blade in his hand. "We can protect ourselves, Amara."

Ronin tests the sword's weight, swings it, twirls it, getting a feel for the balance. A half-smile creeps up his scarred face, as if this meagre weapon will somehow be enough.

"You heard your friend," he says to me. "You don't need me. You never did."

Without hesitation, Ronin charges into the cluster of Fae, sword swinging wildly. All I see is a flash of his blonde hair before they engulf him.

I could stay, fight alongside him, who knows the power my flames could unleash? Maybe I could destroy them all. But with Daed battling demons and Fae in the courtyard, I might be all my daughter has left.

We of the Grove were never fighters. Why else would we choose a dense, tangled forest for home? Why else would we never cross our borders, never seek alliances or bargain at

325

tables of power? We valued preservation above all. The Tenders mend and grow. I will make sure my daughter knows that life. I will not risk losing her or risk her losing me.

We were never creatures of war. This is what the Fae have forced upon us.

Solena grabs my arm. "Come. I know exactly where we can hide."

I nod, knowing she's thinking of the same place I am. We tear through the winding halls, shadows dancing in the flickering lightning, the cold stone walls pressing in around us. Behind us, the clang of steel rings out, the roar of battle surges, and anguished cries pierce the air, but whether it's Ronin's sword striking true or his last breath escaping, I can't tell.

We climb the stairs, and my daughter grows restless, clawing at me, squirming in my arms. I press my hand gently against her mouth, muffling her cries; I cannot let them find us. I slip my pinky finger into her tiny hand, and she wraps her delicate grip around it, squeezing tight.

Each tapestry we pass, each burning torch, each blind turn, feels painfully familiar. I remember every crack, every cold surface, from when I first came to Baev'kalath and wandered these halls with Arax, lost in silence and sorrow, memorizing the stone and mourning my fate.

Solena and I move faster now, my breath ragged and sharp in my chest. The heavy doors come into view, the same doors that welcomed me the day I arrived, the ones Arax stormed through with that stubborn scowl, the ones Daed slammed shut in fury or closed softly before pulling me into his arms.

We're almost there. But then, that voice slices through the storm, unwelcome and relentless.

"Found you!" Nyraxes screams.

I glance back to see her in pursuit, half her face soaked in blood, clutching a wound in her stomach. Blood seeps between her fingers, slowing her body, but not her hunger to hunt me down.

I glance beyond her, searching for a familiar flash of blond hair or blue eyes, a scarred face, but there's nothing. If Nyraxes lives, he does not.

Solena reaches the door first and pushes it open, but I come to an abrupt halt.

She arches a questioning brow. "What are you doing? Come on!"

I shake my head, rocking my daughter as she stirs in my arms.

"Fine. Fight then," Solena snaps. "Just hand me the baby. I suppose I'll have to raise her and tell her every day how she had fools for parents."

When I do as she asks, she stares at me stunned, and a thick silence falls. She holds my baby close, rocking her gently against her chest.

"I wasn't serious," she finally murmurs.

"You're always serious," I reply, a faint smile tugging at my lips. My mind drifts, wondering what lies ahead, what fate awaits. I glance down, flickers of green flame stirring at my fingertips.

"Tell her some good things about me," I whisper.

Solena lifts her chin, defiant. "Tell her yourself after you've killed Nyraxes."

With that, she slips inside the room, the door slamming shut behind her.

I stand alone, as Nyraxes stalks toward me, her blade scraping the stone floor with a metallic rasp, her limp leg barely slowing her relentless advance.

"This will solve nothing," I say, voice steady though my heart pounds beneath my ribs. "Your brother is dead. You risk the annihilation of your house if you challenge me."

She laughs then, harsh and bitter, blood bubbling over her teeth like poison. "Challenge?" The word spits from her lips, cruel and mocking. "I doubt I'll break a sweat."

Still, I reach for the path of peace, for my daughter's sake. "It doesn't have to end this way. Let us talk."

"I do not negotiate with humans!" she shrieks, eyes blazing. "They are dogs and slaves, nothing more. I put them down all the same. This war is your fault. Can you not see it? Before you came, the thrall houses followed Mordorin. We were loyal. We held the Sundered Kingdoms. Now look at us. Depleted, broken, dead. All because of you."

Her gaze sweeps over me, revolted. "You're not even the prettiest human I've seen. But I've heard whispers...there's magic in you." She leers. "Do you keep it between your legs? An enchanted cunt, perhaps?"

The cruel laughter that follows cuts like shards of ice, but then she keels over mid-guffaw, coughing violently before spitting clots of blood onto the stone. She struggles to compose herself, breath ragged as she rises, half bent.

"Looks like you're bleeding from the inside," I say quietly. "That's a horrible way to go. Slow, painful. I wish I had the time to watch every moment." Flames flicker to life between my fingers, green and fierce. "But I've wasted enough time on your petty threats."

Her eyes widen, fixating on the fire. "What are you?"

I feel the heat pulsing through my veins, the ancient power thrumming beneath my skin, rising like a tide that refuses to be contained. For a moment, everything stills. The world narrows to the crackling fire, to the strength rising in my chest, to the unbreakable core of who I am. I breathe it in.

"I am Amara Tyne. Jewel of the Tenders. Sister of the Vine. Fury of the Forest." I watch the flames dance, reflecting in my gaze. "I am Awakened and scorned, and I am the earth itself and the Fae will not decide my fate."

I thrust my palm forward, unleashing a surge of green fire toward her. She raises her arms, summoning a shimmering barrier that flickers but holds, repelling the inferno. When I see not a single ember pierce her defense, I clench my fist, drawing the flames back, but in that breath, she collapses her shield, gasping as if it drained the very breath from her lungs.

I inhale deep and summon another bolt of fire, harder, hotter, pouring every ounce of myself into it. Again, she raises her barrier, gritting her teeth as she holds the flames at bay, but the strain is clear. Her legs tremble beneath her, and she drops to one knee, wobbles, and finally collapses, powerless against the blaze. Now she kneels.

"How are you doing this?" she screams, eyes wild. "You are nothing!"

"I am Awakened. Just like your sister. But I will not be erased from this world so easily."

I step forward, pressing the attack harder, sweat beading on Nyraxes's brow, streaming down her face. Centuries of Fae strength crumble beneath me. But I don't allow myself the luxury of satisfaction. If I have the advantage, I must end this swiftly.

Then, a chorus of high-pitched screeches tears through the night air. I whirl toward the balcony. The sky is a roiling canvas of pitch black, veined with star-white flashes of lightning. Wings fill the night, but they are not Mordorin. Beasts from the void surge forward, rain splattering off their leathery wings with a sickening flap as their bodies crash and jostle in flight.

They slam onto the balcony, tumbling and rolling, but rise again without hesitation. Their beady eyes lock on me as they charge.

My flames flicker and fade, granting Nyraxes the reprieve she desperately needed. Her shimmering barrier collapses in sync with her body, slumping onto the floor.

It's only as I race toward my old chambers that she comprehends the demon storm about to flood in behind us. She scrambles to her feet, dragging her bloody, battered form as fast as she can, but she is too slow.

I burst into the room, spin on my heels, and brace to slam the door shut in her face.

"Wait!" she calls out, hand raised in desperate plea. "You can't leave me to die like this! Let us talk!"

My words drip like ice water. "I do not negotiate with Fae."

The door crashes shut just as her hands pound against the wood, screams clawing from her throat. A mighty weight crashes into the door, shaking it on its hinges. I step back, eyes locked on the narrow gap beneath the door, watching shadows twist and writhe.

Silence falls, but it is brief. The gnawing and chewing begins, and then a dark pool of blood seeps towards my feet.

"Excellent," Solena's voice calls out. "Not so stupid after all."

She stands by the secret door hidden in the wall panel, halfway inside, holding it ajar for me.

"Hurry!"

I don't hesitate. I rush toward her, the endless tunnels of Baev'kalath sprawling before us.

But the weight of the void beasts is too great. The door shudders, splinters, and bursts open under a brutal push, flooding the room with shadows and gnashing teeth.

I sprint for the open door, but a long, clawed hand shoots out and snatches my ankle, dragging me down.

I grit my teeth, eyes locking with Solena's.

"Close the door! Get her away from here!"

The longer Solena hesitates, the hotter my fury burns.

"Do what you're told, maid," I hiss.

Her brow tightens, but she nods, turning away just as the demons overwhelm the room like a ravenous tide. But she's too slow, too slow to shut the door.

A leathery, clawed hand lashes out and holds the secret door open, its forked tongue flicking over slick, bloodied lips as it fixes its hunger-filled gaze on my daughter like she's a prize to be devoured.

I clench my fists, green flames licking along my arms, coiling beneath my skin just as sharp teeth sink into my leg.

Pain rips through me, but it only steels me harder. I scream, and the agony feeds my flame.

A burst of emerald light explodes from me, setting the demons closest ablaze. Flesh chars, smoke curls upward, and the one biting my leg howls in furious pain.

For a moment, I falter, my leg mangled and useless beneath me, but the muscle knits, skin smooths, and I'm back on my feet quicker than I thought possible.

I lunge for the door, hand reaching toward the demon still blocking Solena's escape, but more beasts fall on me, claws raking my back, teeth sinking into my shoulder.

I scream again as they drag me back, each inch feeling like a mile, drawing me farther from my daughter, farther from hope.

My flames falter, flickering like dying embers, as if the very fuel that feeds them, my strength, my will, is draining away. I've never pushed myself this far before, never tested the limits of my power and now, when my daughter's life hangs by a thread, I learn it's not endless.

Then, salvation, a fierce grip tears the demon from my back, wrenching it free. Red haze clouds my vision, but I focus through the pain and see Ronin, cutting, slashing, tearing through the swarm with savage precision. Claws, wings, limbs fly through the air like leaves caught in a storm.

But all I want is my daughter.

Trembling, I crawl toward Solena, still locked in a deadly fight with the demon blocking the door.

Finally, I grab hold of its leg, skin soft and sickly, as if my fingers could slip right through it.

It looks down at me, at the bloody, broken mess still fighting to survive.

Green light courses through my veins. My body heals again, but then another demon strikes, its fangs sinking into my throat, tearing through the rune etched there.

I gasp, eyes wide as blood wells and spills in thick, relentless waves.

A sword arcs downward, cleaving the demon's head from its body. Ronin lifts me onto his hip and drags me toward the secret door. With one last desperate surge of strength, I launch myself at the demon threatening my daughter, pinning it hard to the ground.

It hisses and shrieks, but I find the power within me, gripping its head between my hands and filling them with fire. Its flesh melts away from the bone, dripping onto the floor in steaming, bloody puddles until all that remains is a twisted skull with patches of sizzling meat.

Solena stumbles into the tunnel, and Ronin follows, bracing the door open as he reaches for me.

"Come on, Jewel. More are coming. We have to get inside."

I lift myself up, the stench and steam from the burning demon stinging my eyes. But I barely make it to one knee before my body betrays me, staggering forward. Hot, thick blood still pours from my neck. It isn't healing. None of my wounds are. With every passing second, I leave more and more blood staining the floor.

"Jewel!" Ronin shouts. I look over my shoulder at him, his face smeared with blood, his voice urgent. "Come here now!"

I nod and stumble toward him, bracing myself against the secret door as Ronin steps back, ready for the next wave of demons crashing into the room. I glance down at my fingers. There is still fire there. I feel it coursing, molten green lava pulsing through my veins.

As the life drains from me, I look at Solena. I look at my daughter.

"Tell her good things," I whisper.

The sudden understanding in Solena's eyes is the last thing I see before I slam the secret door shut. I press against it with every ounce of my strength. I won't hold it for long, not long enough to save myself, but I don't need to. Only a breath. Only a whisper. Only a blink in time.

The demons of the void scream as they surge toward me. The fire rises, bursting through my skin, lifting my hair, swirling around me like a hurricane of emerald flame. When I see my reflection in their glowing eyes, I know I am the terror they fear. I am glorious.

Then the room ignites.

CHAPTER 34
DAED

Rivers of blood run between the stones of the courtyard, thunder fading into the harsh clang of blades, the savage roar of battle, and the ragged screams of the dying. There are no allies here. Only enemies. The Mor'Thravar Fae clash violently with the demons of the void, bodies crashing and tearing into one another, wounding and maiming anything that dares to move. Reon fights fiercely against a ruthless Mor'Thravar warrior, blade flashing in a deadly dance, while Orios grapples on the ground with a snarling beast of teeth and claw. Above, Zyphoro cuts through the sky, locking talons with winged horrors, slicing through membranous wings and sending twisted forms spiraling earthward.

But there is no respite for my brethren. For every one who falls, two rise to take their place, and this endless night promises none of us will survive to see the dawn.

Yet all the battles raging around me pale beside the furious clash between the Prince of Mordorin and Emranth, Envoy of the Father Below, a violent storm unto itself, tearing through the darkness with devastating fury.

I can feel the weight of Death Singer in my hands, heavy with the blood and fury I've poured into it. Emranth stands before me, a nightmare in flesh and shadow, tentacles writhing beneath that hollow, grinning skull. He smells of death and smoke and decay.

I lunge, blade arcing like lightning, aiming for his exposed ribs. He catches it barehanded, fingers like iron bands closing around the steel. I wrench, twisting with all my might, trying to rip it free, but his grip tightens.

A tentacle lashes out, wrapping around my arm and squeezing so tight it feels like a band of fire. Pain lances up my arm, but I shove a fist into his snarling maw, smashing bone and teeth. He roars, a sound like a thousand screams warping into one.

I kick out, slamming my heel into his side, cracking ribs beneath my boot. He stumbles but recovers instantly, claws slicing across my face, a hot, ragged tear from cheek to jaw. Blood trickles, mixing with the rain, stinging my eyes.

I wipe it away, fury burning hotter than the wound. Death Singer hums in my hands, a howl of power begging to be unleashed. I plunge it again, deeper this time, slicing through slick, black leather skin and into something colder, void essence writhing beneath.

The blade shudders, my hands trembling from the force, but Emranth only laughs, that terrible noise that echoes inside my head. Then, with a sudden surge, he tears free, sending shards of dark smoke pouring from the wound like ink in water.

"Your effort is admirable, Prince, but pointless," he says, and I watch as his wound seals before my eyes. "I cannot be killed. I am smoke and shadow. The flesh and bone you see are an illusion. I am the essence of the void. Its lifeblood."

He takes a step toward me, eyes burning white but somehow devoid of all light. "You cannot destroy what was never alive. I am raw, vicious power to be wielded, in his name."

Suddenly I taste it, the power he boasts of, drifting from the wound, thick on the air, bitter and heady and intoxicating. I had always thought of Emranth as flesh and bone, not a well of shadow-magic. The thought slams into me. Maybe I don't need to kill him. Maybe I drink from that well instead. Take every drop of that darkness into myself until there is nothing left of Emranth but the echo of his last scream. He commands these void-spawned creatures, but if his power were mine... they would bow to me.

I lash out, knuckles cracking against his cheekbone. The blow should've sent any man reeling. He doesn't so much as blink. My teeth grind. I hit him again, harder and again. Every strike lands with a satisfying jolt through my bones, but still he turns back to me, unflinching. Mocking.

I don't stop. I can't.

With a thought, Death Singer dissolves into the void, the weight gone from my grip so my hands are free to ruin him. My elbow slams into the bridge of his nose. There's the crunch. A knee drives into his gut. My fist arcs up in a clean uppercut to his chin. He only laughs, the sound low and grating, but I'm past hearing it.

Because I see it, thin wisps of smoke curling from his skin every time I make contact. I inhale deep. The smoke shifts, slithering toward me, seeping my lungs. It burns in a way that makes me want more. With every breath, my fists land heavier, my strikes drive deeper.

Now he stumbles. His knees tremble. For the first time, a flicker of uncertainty mars his perfect arrogance.

"Favored one. Enough!" he roars, but there's a tremor beneath the bark, a fissure in his control. "Let me serve you. Together, we can burn away every soul that dares to stand against you. We can return these lands to their rightful heir. There is still time to undo your missteps." His voice drops, dark and coaxing. "The Father Below will give you everything you crave. All he asks is to be fed. Give him what he hungers for... and the void will be yours."

My vision tunnels, my eyes rolling black as the abyss.

"You've told me a thousand times," I hiss through my teeth. "I am the favored one. Where I walk, darkness follows. Where I call, the void answers. This is my birthright. My bloodline."

I drive my fist into his face again, and this time he drops. Blood-smoke pours from him in thick coils, rising off his weakening frame.

"I *am* the void," I snarl. "*I* control you."

My hand shoots out, fingers locking around the slick, twitching tentacles beneath his chin. They writhe against my palm, desperate to root themselves back into him, but I rip them free with a savage wrench. The sound is wet and tearing, and black, reeking ink bursts across the courtyard, splattering my chest, my face.

My other hand clamps around his throat. I squeeze until I feel the cartilage grind, until his pulse stutters beneath my thumb. His mouth falls open in a shuddering gasp and smoke gushes out in a torrent.

I inhale it. All of it.

His malice shreds into me, his hate scalds down my throat, his power threads itself through my blood until my body vibrates with it. It's agony, bliss, hunger, and satisfaction all at once. My vision swims black, my heartbeat becomes a drum older than the sun.

His eyes bulge. The leathery mask of his face pulls tight, skin drawn so taut I can hear it strain, stretching until it finally splits like soaked parchment.

I keep drinking him in until there's nothing left, until the smoke is mine and his body is a hollow, brittle shell.

Suddenly, pain detonates across my back. I hiss, teeth bared, as something forces its way through bone and muscle, ripping, splitting me open. The pressure builds until my spine arches and the air leaves my lungs in a roar that shakes the sky.

Two colossal wings of smoke tear free, unfurling wide enough to cast a shadow over the entire courtyard.

When I finally drag in a breath, I look down. What's left of Emranth crumbles in my grasp, flakes of blackened flesh lifting away on the wind. His bones collapse into dust, carried off by the storm.

Mine. All of it is mine.

My wings snap wide, stretching to their full span, and the song in my soul soars at their return. There are no words for it, no Fae or mortal tongue that could capture the rapture soaring through me. I want to launch into the skies, tear through the clouds, taste the wind rushing beneath me.

But not yet.

The portal still gapes wide, a hungry wound in the night. The void spills its horrors into my kingdom.

And I am the void.

I command it. I walk with the darkness, and it knows my name.

Daedalus Phaedren. The favored son.

They will heed me.

I raise my hand to the night and summon Death Singer back to me. The blade bleeds into existence, smoke curling like serpents along its edge. My voice rolls from me, thunder cracking across the dark.

"Return to the void. Your prince commands you."

The beating of leathered wings, the scrape of claws on stone, fall into silence.

They turn to me. Blazing eyes. Crooked mouths. Teeth like shards of a nightmare. They listen.

One by one, they obey.

Quietly, calmly, they step into the darkness, vanishing like shadows at dawn. The flying horrors wheel overhead, weaving, diving, gliding down into the abyss until only the Fae remain.

I lower Death Singer's tip toward the portal. Will it closed and it obeys. The tear seals shut, the last flicker of creation gone, as if it had never been.

The world exhales. Ragged breaths rasp through the air, followed by the clatter of steel striking stone. The Mor'Thravar Fae sink to their knees, heads bowed.

I accept their surrender.

Zyphoro lands lightly on the black stone, her gaze sharp as she circles me. Her hand comes to my cheek, her eyes searching mine as if she could sift through every shadow in my soul.

"You are not alone in there, brother," she murmurs.

I incline my head. "He is an aspect of me now. I feel him. But his soul is mine to wield."

Her chin lifts. "Then let us use it to take back the Sundered Kingdoms and burn An'kel to ash."

We clasp forearms.

I have never been the master of my curse. It has ruled me, driven me to horrors I can never erase, stolen the things I loved most. Zyphoro has hated me for it. Pitied me for it. She has never been shackled to the void's will. She wields it, yes, but it has never been her master. That was why they locked her away: because she could not be controlled.

Does that make her stronger than me? How can it not?

But now... the way she looks at me is not as she once did. Not as a slave. Not as a puppet. Not as some pathetic instrument of a demon god.

She looks at me as if, for the first time, her burden might finally be lifted.

Orios and Reon come forward, cautious, but they bow all the same.

"Baev'kalath is ours, but I don't for a moment believe all our Blades are lost. Tear through the fortress."

Orios slams a fist to his chest. "Yes, Rook."

I nod toward Zyphoro. "Round up the Mor'Thravar Fae. If they want to live, they'll wear the Mordorin mark."

Her eyes flicker, and she inclines her head. "As you command, brother."

I grip Reon's shoulder. "We need to find Amara. Tell her it's safe."

My wings spread wide, smoke and shadow unraveling like dark silk in the rain. Reon's gaze slides to them, a crooked grin tugging at his mouth.

"Well, aren't those impressive? Is this a pissing contest?"

He summons his wings, copper and gold burst from his back, feathers bright and fierce.

I leap into the storm, tearing through the sky, wind howling in my ears and the rain parting like a curtain. Reon follows, but he can't hold pace. I burn forward in black plumes, a tempest unleashed.

"Amara!" My voice cuts through the night, desperate and raw. Silence answers.

Every spire, every tower, empty. I close my eyes and breathe deep, sorting through scent and magic, through blood-memory and bond. For her pulse. For the place my teeth broke skin. For the mark that binds us. There. A spark. A pull. My eyes fly open, fixed on a flash of green flame curling over the eastern balcony stone.

I dive hard.

The balcony is littered with the charred remains of demons, embers still glowing faintly in the rain.

Only Amara could have left this trail. She must be close. Why does she not call to me?

My boots hit the stone as I weave through broken bodies. The doors ahead are shattered, splintered, scorched black from fire's kiss.

I slow, and an icy knot tightens in my gut and when I turn the corner and my world shatters.

Amara. My light, my fury, my heart.

Bloodied, broken, her skin blistered and torn, her hair burned away in ragged patches. Great wounds gape where flesh should be. More blood pools around her than flows within her veins and the cruelest cut of all, she is not healing.

I gulp, the sharp sting like shattered glass scraping down my throat as I drop to one knee beside her.

"Amara," I whisper, voice raw and brittle, as if saying her name too loud might shatter what little remains of her. But there is no answer.

My hands tremble as they reach for her, hesitating before brushing against her cheek. Her skin is hot, almost burning, melting beneath my touch.

"Amara," I breathe again, louder this time, desperate.

Tears burn behind my eyes, but I swallow them down, letting raw fury rise in their place. My jaw tightens until it aches, my skin flushes with heat. I cradle her fragile body in my arms.

"Amara! No!"

Before I can say more, the secret door's panel crashes open, slamming against the wall. The Golden Son stumbles through, breathless, eyes wild with urgency.

In one smooth motion, I summon Death Singer, blade humming with deadly intent, raising it toward him. He freezes, barely a step from impalement.

"Where is she?" I demand, voice sharp as the steel at his throat. "Where is our..."

Then Solena steps out from behind him. My daughter is nestled in her arms, un-harmed. Safe. The sight should loosen the knot in my chest, should wash me clean of the fear choking me. But relief cannot drown the agony.

My gaze drags back to Amara. To the ruin of her flesh. To the rune on her neck, shredded and almost unrecognizable.

"She's not healing," I murmur, drawing her closer. My arms lock around her, pulling her upright so I am closer to her mouth. "My love. You need to heal yourself. Amara."

Nothing. No words. No movement nevertheless, I refuse to believe she is anything other than alive. She is not gone. I will not accept that. Not until the sky bleeds and the seas turn to dust. When day becomes night and the end is the beginning. When every law of above and below collapses in on itself. Until then, she breathes. She is mine and if she is not living...

Heavy steps echo across the stone. What remains of the door splinters apart when Reon forces his way through. His eyes go wide with horror as he nears.

"Rook. Is she..."

"She just needs to heal," I roar, my voice booming until the walls quake.

Reon inclines his head, a cautious hand half-raised. "Of course, Rook."

I do not realize I am rocking her. Holding her close though the contact tears at her charred skin. The Golden Son staggers to the wall, sliding down until his shoulders slump forward, chin tucked.

My canines ache as they lengthen. My voice is a low growl. "This is your fault. If you had not stolen her from me..."

His head lifts. His gaze cuts like a blade. "There is no one to blame but you. She is here because of you. You put her in danger. You put the noose around her neck."

"I love her!" The words thunder out of me, and my vision blurs. I feel the tears fall, streaking down my face, but when they touch Amara's skin, they drip black as ink.

"You cannot love," the Golden Son says, pushing himself to his feet, squaring his shoulders. "You do not know how. So put her in the ground and go find your next plaything, your next innocent soul to corrupt and destroy."

My jaw locks. In my mind, I carve him apart piece by piece, imagining the thousand ways to make him suffer. Which limbs to take, what to leave, how to keep him breathing so I can begin again and again. For years if I wish.

But before I can rise, my daughter cries out.

Solena rocks her gently. "I... I think she's hungry."

I nod. "Yes. Amara will feed her. She just needs to heal." I turn back to my wife, smoothing a hand over her head, ignoring the strands that come away in my palm. "Amara. My love. You need to heal. Our daughter needs you. I need you."

Reon edges closer, his steps slow and cautious, like he's approaching an unchained beast. He lowers himself to one knee, exchanging a sharp, worried glance with Solena.

"Rook," he says, quiet, careful. "Come, my friend. We need to leave her."

"To heal?" I demand.

He nods once. "Yes. To heal. Will you come with me?"

The words scrape against my skull, senseless. Leave her? Why would I leave her? Why would I be anywhere but at her side?

Movement catches my eye. The Golden Son. He shakes his head, a mocking grunt slipping from his mouth. I don't hear the words. Don't need to. I know the tone. I know the loathing, the accusation. I know they doubt my love. Blame me for her death, and that alone is enough.

The void tears open for me, and in the next heartbeat, I am at his side. My hand clamps around his throat, lifting him from the ground as I slam him into the wall hard enough to rattle the stone. Solena gasps, stumbling back. The Golden Son claws at my grip, kicks against my legs, but it's useless. I will not release him. Not until I've wrung every last breath from his lungs.

I lock onto those bright blue eyes and watch the light dim. He gasps, spits broken words that barely register. I watch only until the flicker fades.

"Rook!"

Reon's voice cuts through, sharp, but I don't turn.

"Rook!" Louder this time. Harder. "She lives!"

My head snaps toward him.

The Golden Son drops from my grasp, crumpling to the ground in a choking heap. My focus is already gone from him, fixed on Reon where he crouches over Amara.

"But only barely, my friend," Reon says. "She does not have much time."

"She needs a healer," Solena blurts. Her brow furrows, lips trembling, then her eyes flare wide. "The Grove."

Reon's head shakes immediately. "We will never reach it before she..." He stops when my glare finds him, his jaw clenching. "It is too far. Unless..."

339

His gaze falls to his fingertips, where golden sparks crackle and dance. "I can slow time. Just for her. It could be enough."

"Can you do that?" Solena asks.

A shrug. "We're about to find out."

The void swallows me again, and I reappear at Amara's side, sweeping her into my arms.

"Then let's not waste anymore time."

I rise, but the moment I'm fully upright, the ground quakes beneath us. Stone groans. My back arches as my canines lengthen, every muscle coiled for attack. Ready to face whatever comes next.

The world splits. A wound in reality gapes wide, and from its unending blackness, something stirs. Something vast. A beast born of teeth and nightmares, its form too great to comprehend. Tentacles, thrashing and coiling, each ending in glinting, blade-sharp edges forged to rend not only flesh, but hope.

The Father Below.

His presence crushes the breath from my lungs, pins me to the trembling stone. I can command demons. I can devour them. But not him. Not Gygarth. Before him, I am an ant standing against the tide.

A voice rumbles from that fathomless dark, low and terrible.

"You are a disappointment."

The words seep into me, cold and absolute.

"No matter how many sigils you shroud yourself with, no matter how you twist and claw at the thread of fate, you cannot escape me. We are one, favored son. I dwell within you, as you dwell within me. There is no severing us. I am eternal and our bargain was struck in blood long ago."

His shadow deepens, swallowing every flicker of light. "So now," he says, voice curling into a snarl, "I take what is mine, Daedalus Phaedren."

My grip on Amara tightens until my arms ache, until my claws bite into my own flesh. I will not give her up. I will not...

But it is not Amara he reaches for.

Gygarth's attention shifts. His gaze falls on my daughter. A roll of black smoke unravels from the void, thick and clinging, snaring her small form. Her cry pierces me, high, panicked, before the smoke smothers it into silence.

"Meat for the beast," he hisses.

The temperature plummets. The world dims. It is as if night itself pours into the chamber, and the cold cuts through to my marrow. It happens in the span of a heartbeat.

Her cries vanish. The smoke fades. The light stutters back. The void is gone, Gygarth swallowed once more into the abyss.

I turn to where she had been, safe, I thought, in Solena's arms. But those arms are empty.

Solena's knees hit the floor. Her face crumples. "She's gone."

CHAPTER 35
DAED

Before her. I cut through the night sky, wings beating in slow, lazy arcs. The wind sings against my feathers, cool and damp, and now and then my eyes slip shut. My wings fold back. My body tips forward. I plummet toward the black roll of the ocean below.

Only the sting of rain wakes me, cold needles against my skin. I pull up at the last breath, boot heels scraping the water, laughter spilling out of me, wild and unrestrained, as the spires of Baev'kalath pierce the horizon.

I narrow my eyes, trying to anyway, intent on making a graceful landing on the balcony. Instead, my boot catches the railing. My momentum flips me head over heels, and I slam onto the stone. The roll doesn't stop until I crash against the fortress wall with a solid, skull-rattling thud.

I stay there for a moment, curled and groaning, pain blooming down my spine. Then, inevitably, I start laughing again.

Dragging myself upright, I clumsily limp down the halls, staggering toward the throne room, and when I finally arrive, I shove the great doors open with a dramatic flourish. The booming crack of them hitting their hinges echoes through the dark.

"My king and queen," I proclaim, arms spread wide. "I am home!"

Father sits slouched on his throne, fingers drumming against the armrest, his scowl cutting even through the dim candlelight.

"Where have you been, Daedalus?" he demands. "It's been weeks."

I shrug, dragging my sorry carcass closer. Even the flicker of the candles feels like blinding sunlight in my bleary eyes. "Enjoying the fine hospitality of Eyr'Drogul. Lord Reon had some... pressing thrall-house matters to discuss."

"All you've done is drink yourself into a stupor," Lanneth snaps from her seat beside him. "You shame yourself, Daedalus. You shame *us*."

I tilt my head toward her, grinning without warmth. "My queen, you wound me. That is simply not true. You hardly need me to embarrass you. You do well enough on your own. Do you know what they whisper about you?" I do not give her time to answer. "No? Then please allow me..."

"Silence, Daedalus!" Father roars, surging to his feet.

I halt mid-step, swaying, biting my lip as I glare at him. The pathetic excuse for a king. For a father.

"You will clean up and sober yourself immediately. We have important news."

I exhale, his severity dulling the pleasant burn in my veins. "What now?"

Lanneth's smile coils through me like poison.

"She is on her way, Daedalus."

I roll my eyes, weary of their riddles. "Who is on their way?"

"Your wife," Father says flatly.

For a beat, I just stare at him. "I'm aware I'm drunk, but I could have sworn you just said wife."

"I did. We told you we would not wait much longer. If you wouldn't choose, we would." His gaze drops to Lanneth, who lays her long fingers over his arm like she's claiming a prize. "And we have struck a bargain that will see our house flourish."

The wine in my blood feels as if it evaporates all at once. My shoulders square. My hand rakes through my damp hair, jaw tightening.

"Who is she, then? What Fae house have we bound ourselves to?"

Father shakes his head. "Not Fae. Human."

No. I must have misheard him. "A joke, then? Why would you marry me to a human? What possible advantage could that give us?"

"All you need do is your duty, Daedalus," he says, voice flat and cold and devoid of feeling. "Wed her. Bed her. Put an heir in her belly. Then do whatever you like with her. I couldn't care less. But until your task is complete, you will behave. Do you understand?"

"And if I don't want to marry this human?" My voice drops to a growl. "If I don't behave? If I cut off her head the moment I lay eyes on her just to spite you?"

Lanneth rises, skeletal fingers unfurling toward me. Her face twists, her voice turns shrill. "You will do as he commands you!"

And I feel it. The pull. The darkness. Creeping in, coiling around my mind like smoke. She doesn't mean my father when she says *he*. She means Gygarth. The Father Below. His

343

presence channels through her, dripping into me, inevitable as the tide. My mind screams *no*, but my body knows the truth: Gygarth is eternal. He dwells in me as I dwell in him. We are one.

I clench my fists until nails pierce skin. Bite my lip until I taste copper. Fight the void's pull with everything I have.

"At least tell me who she is," I snarl through my teeth.

My father and Lanneth lower themselves back into their thrones, all regal precision, clasping hands between them like they've already won.

"You know her," Father says. "The girl Eryndor feared was Awakened. The human in his forest. Amara, I think. I've already forgotten."

But I haven't. Not for a single day.

Amara Tyne, the woman whose golden threads twine perfectly with mine.

No, she cannot come here. If she comes, they will discover what she is. Discover I lied. And then... she will die.

"What if I take another wife instead?" I blurt, desperate. "A Fae one. It would be disgusting to pollute our bloodline."

Father laughs, low and cold. "You had your chance. Instead you've spent your nights drunk, rotting on the islands of the Untold Sea. Besides..." He leans back, sighing as though this conversation bores him. "She is already on her way."

The words land like a blade between my ribs. "She is?"

He nods. "Any day now. So clean yourself up and prepare to greet your wife."

I stare at him, waiting for him to come to his senses. But he's already turned to Lanneth, falling under her touch as she strokes his cheek like she's petting a prized hound.

I spin on my heel, bile burning my throat. "Keep your expectations low," I throw over my shoulder. "You may force me to marry her, but you cannot make me love her."

"Who said anything about love?" Kaelus calls after me. "I just want a wedding and an heir, Daedalus. You're too ruined for anything else."

My step falters. I half-turn, meet his eyes once more, but the words that crowd my mouth taste like ash. I swallow them whole, turn back toward the door, and leave.

***

After her. The void has never been so black, so devouring. Endless. Infinite. I walk its depths for hours, days, perhaps, treading on nothing but smoke and shadow, screaming until my throat is raw, my voice a withered husk on the windless air. No one answers. Not even the demons that haunt the farthest, foulest corners.

The void is empty.

They're hiding in An'kel. A place I cannot reach. He knows that.

For all the curses the Father Below shackled to my soul, opening a portal to his kingdom was not among them. But today... today I try again.

With Emranth's power now bound to mine, there must be hope. He could travel between realms. So perhaps... perhaps I can too.

What do I have to lose? Everything worth losing is already gone.

My father, for all his cruelty, was still my sire, my king. My mother, stolen before she could give me a name. My daughter, wrenched from my arms by the very thing I feared most. And my wife... my Amara. My heart. She dances between the worlds of life and death, and I do not know if we will reach the Grove before the music stops forever.

I stand in the dark, the silence a living, hollow thing, its thrum echoing in my skull. Emranth's power coils within me, threaded through my own magic, his wails a constant, desperate plea in the back of my mind. I shove them aside. Voices in my head are nothing new.

I reach deep. Past the smoke, past the shadow, hunting for that elusive thread of power, the one that will rip the wall between the void and An'kel to shreds. The one that will take me to my daughter. To Gygarth.

I will kill him when I find him. Kill him and be free at last.

How? I haven't dared think that far. I can barely think at all these days. But with a blade in my hand and hatred boiling in my blood, I will carve a way to make the god of death bleed for every piece of me he has stolen.

My body screams as I try to wrench the magic from Emranth's grasp. Veins throb, muscles burn, teeth grind. But no power answers my call.

I fall to my knees. Fists clenched so hard the skin over my knuckles feels paper-thin, ready to tear. I lift my gaze, lungs dragging for breath, heart desperate for even the smallest sliver of light in the dark.

There is none.

No whisper of An'kel beyond the layers of realms. Only the void and it is endless.

A breath rattles out of me, long, shuddering. There's sorrow in it, sharp as broken glass. A sound no one else will ever hear, because it comes from somewhere too deep, too fragile.

I do not breathe it into the shadows, for fear they might swallow it whole, for fear they might know the truth it carries:

That I am weak. That I am hopeless.

That after everything, I could not keep them safe.

That I have failed.

That I was never meant to hold anything good in my hands for long.

That death and pain are the only companions I will ever know.

When the last shred of breath leaves me, the void unravels like smoke in the wind.

The deck solidifies beneath my knees. Salt-laced air whips against my skin, carrying the roar of the distant waves. Above, the hunter's moon blazes, full and beaming in a stretch of midnight sky.

"No luck again?"

Zyphoro leans against the railing, the wind tugging her dark curls into a wild halo as moonlight gilds her cheekbones.

I drag my gaze to her, chest still heaving from the effort. Then I shake my head, chin bowing until I can't bear to meet her eyes.

"I cannot open the portal."

Silence falls so thick it smothers. For a heartbeat, I think she's gone. But when I look up again, she's still there. Her eyes pinned to mine, her jaw tight enough to crack.

"If you have something to say, say it," I bite out, sharper than I intend.

"You won't like it." Her voice is quiet, edged with a sigh.

"When has that ever stopped you?"

She straightens, shoulders rolling back. Nervous. That is never a good sign.

"If Anethesis was right... then Amara can open portals."

I laugh, harsh, mirthlessly. Born of exhaustion, frustration, and a grief that has long since rotted into something uglier.

"Amara barely breathes, yet you think she could open a portal to An'kel?"

"I can think of no other way."

I shove to my feet, raking a hand through my hair.

"Even if she could, you know the price. Blood. Every last drop." My heart thunders painfully. "If I haven't already lost her, opening a portal would take her from me for certain."

"But it could save your child."

346

My eyes snap to hers. "You would have me choose between one and the other?"

Her composure does not falter.

"Amara risked her life to protect your daughter. She didn't expect to survive. She was willing to pay the price. I have no doubt she would lay down her life again if it meant her child lived."

My jaw aches with the force of my clenched teeth. "That is not your decision to make. And what if…"

The words wedge in my throat. They burn like fire, tear like claws.

"What if?" Zyphoro presses, her voice low.

When I meet my sister's gaze, the sting of tears betrays me.

"What if my daughter is already dead? What if I lose them both?"

The warmth comes from the last place I expect. Her hand on my shoulder, firm and steady.

"Then at least we'll be in his temple," she says, her grip tightening. "Where Gygarth waits and we will kill him, brother. End him, once and for all."

"I dream of nothing more, sister. But he is no different from Emranth. He cannot be killed. He is not flesh and blood."

Her head tilts, moonlight catching the sharp line of her jaw. "But you destroyed Emranth."

My hand presses to my chest, deeper than fabric, deeper than flesh, seeking the shadowed place where that truth festers. "Not truly. Only contained him… in here."

"Yes," Zyphoro says, voice calm though her eyes storm. "And now he is your prisoner. You control him. There cannot be one without the other, but there can only be one master, Daedalus."

Her hand falls away, and then her wings burst from her back in a sweep of darkness, catching the wind.

I watch her silhouette rise against the moon, gliding into the crow's nest. She folds her wings, settling into the shadows, the wind whispering through her feathers as she bathes in silver light.

I watch her for a long moment, her words seeping into me like ink through cloth, sinking past skin, finding some quiet, dangerous place of reason.

She is my twin. The other half of my splintered soul.

Time and betrayal have stolen centuries from us, yet I know her as I know my own heartbeat and still, there are shadows in her I will never reach. Dark corners I will never fully see, never truly understand.

I trust her with my life, and I know without a doubt that she would end it if she had to.

Sometimes I wonder how different the world might have been if Gygarth had chosen a favored daughter over a favored son. If the curse had been hers, not mine. If I had been the one locked away in a room that does not exist, counting the years slip by while the world outside forgot my name.

There cannot be one without the other.

Does Zyphoro speak of the Father Below... or of us?

I leave Zyphoro in the moonlight and descend below deck.

The door groans open beneath my hand, and the first thing I see is the crib.

Empty.

Haunting.

I wrench my gaze away before the hollow ache in my chest can deepen, but there is no peace elsewhere.

Amara lies silent on the bed, arms still at her sides, her body a ruined statue. Char clings stubbornly to her skin, burned and blistered, red and raw, torn as though the world itself had tried to unmake her. I barely recognize her and yet golden threads, the Binds of Fate, still wind through the dark between us, reaching for me, reminding me that beneath the agony, she is still mine. My mate. My heart.

A faint golden halo wraps around her, holding her in place, freezing her in this single moment in time.

Hunched in a chair beside the bed is Reon. Exhaustion drips from every line of him. His hair has dulled, his eyes ringed in dark shadows, their usual glow snuffed out. His skin is ashen, his once sharp frame worn thin. One trembling arm stretches toward Amara, his fingers sparking with faint flickers of light as if they might gutter out at any second.

He's been holding the barrier since we departed Baev'kalath, pouring every scrap of his essence into keeping Amara suspended, so her body cannot slip further toward decay. The strain is eating him alive.

I do not know the full extent of his Fae gifts, only scraps from old texts, the kind of knowledge gathered in fragments over years. Each House's magic is bound to their bloodline. The Mordorin, with their void-walking. The Taramethos, masters of transmutation. The Maledannan, healers without peer and the Fae of Eyr'Drogul, manipulators of time itself.

I've seen Reon use it before, moments in battle where seconds meant survival, or in smaller moments, like plucking a boy from mid-fall. He's even been known to boast, with a roguish grin, how his gift serves him in the bedroom, stretching out pleasures far beyond what his own body could claim credit for.

But this... this I have never seen.

Holding her like this takes more than skill. More than will. It demands the very lifeblood of him and it could fail at any moment.

All Fae gifts have limits. No matter how infinite they may seem, magic is fickle. Wild. It has no master, only slaves and yet, I have never seen Reon so fixed, so unshakably devoted to a single purpose.

I know without question that he will hold this barrier for as long as he can, until his last breath if it comes to that, and for that, I am more grateful than I can ever say. More grateful than he will ever know.

I'm so fixed on Amara. On Reon. On the empty crib, I don't notice Solena at first. She moves quietly in the corner, leaning over a washbowl. Her hands twist a cloth, wringing water from it until droplets patter back into the basin.

She crosses to Reon without a word, pressing the cool fabric to his brow, wiping away the sheen of sweat that clings there. Then she reaches for a cup on the table, lifts it to his lips until he drinks. When he swallows, she returns it to its place.

All of it done in silence.

"How much longer until we reach land?" Solena asks finally, though her gaze does not meet mine, fixed instead on the tasks she vigilantly tends to.

"Not long. A day or two at most. Zyphoro and I can conjure more smoke to drive the winds." I exhale. "I can summon as much of the void as I wish, it seems. Gygarth doesn't care. He's not hunting me anymore. He has something else."

A small, sharp gulp from her. "What do you think he will do with her?"

"I do not know," I breathe.

Truth is, I don't want to know. My heart cannot bear the weight of what that answer might be, and to speak my fears aloud would give them teeth.

"What will happen when we reach the Grove? Will her people truly be able to heal her?"

I turn from her. From Reon. From the bed and drift toward the crib. My fingers graze its edge, and the chill of the wood startles me. The furs inside are just as cold, robbed of my daughter's warmth.

"You ask questions I cannot answer," I say quietly.

"They are questions that must be answered. Months, Rook. We have journeyed for months. We have bled and endured, and in that time our enemies have only multiplied. Their power has grown. And us? We have gained nothing. We have only lost more." Her voice sharpens. "You must give us something if you wish to keep hope alive."

I lift my gaze to hers at last, though my stare feels hollow. "If hope is what you seek, Solena, you're looking for it in the most hopeless of places. I have none to give you."

"Then what are we fighting for?" Her voice cracks on the words, and the moment they leave her lips, she flinches like they weren't meant to be spoken.

My eyes find the crib again. Still empty.

"I fight for Amara. For my daughter. For my family." My voice is low, steady. "That is the fire in me. The reason I will burn until nothing is left but ash. If you mean to stand beside me, then you must find your own fire. What would you burn for? What would you die for? I cannot give that to you, Solena. But if you choose to walk away. If you and Orios take to the skies to carve out your own peace, far from the torment I've brought upon you, I will not fault you. I would take that peace myself if I could."

I hear Solena's breath in the quiet, in the dark.

She has given so much to my cause. Inked sigils into my skin until her fingers bled. Transformed from a maid to a warrior, all for the human she once despised. From a servant to a trusted, beloved friend, both to Amara and to me.

I owe her everything. Granting her freedom is the least I can do.

"I stay for Amara, and for her daughter," Solena says at last, and the weight of those words carries a freedom for me that she does not realize. "I fight for the peace you speak of. For Orios and me, for our eternity together. But we will not know happiness until this is finished. Whatever shape that may take. However it may end. But you must give us hope, Rook. Without it, we have already lost this battle."

350

Her words drift on the wind, press against my skin, trap my breath. She demands something of me, something I have struggled to claim for my entire cursed life, let alone offer freely.

Then I notice, as my hand brushes over the crib, the absence of red. The ribbon. Arax's ribbon. His daughter's ribbon.

"Estra's ribbon is missing," I murmur.

Solena exhales, a note of frustration threaded with sadness. "Yes," she says, voice catching. "I think... I remember... it is with your daughter. Amara must have..."

I nod, sparing her the weight of recollection.

"She loved Arax," I say softly, my gaze settling on Amara, frozen in time. "She barely knew him, and yet her heart found a way, and I know Arax felt the same. He saw Estra in her, I do not doubt that for a second. Amara's heart mourned Estra even though she was nothing more than a memory."

A smile slips across my face, fragile and fleeting, yet it eases the ache just slightly. "Only Amara could carry such a heart."

And then the truth settles in me, warm and solid as the gold threads of the Binds of Fate. Hope is not gone. Hope lives in her. In this child. In the promise that no matter the darkness, there is something worth fighting for.

I kneel beside the crib, pressing my hand gently over the empty furs. "If it is hope you want, Solena, then it will have a name," I murmur, feeling the weight and the lightness all at once. "Our daughter... Estra. A name for hope. For love. For the pieces of us we refuse to lose. Estra will carry us forward. She will carry Amara, and she will carry all the light we have left. She is a new age for Fae and human. A binding. A reckoning. Estra."

Solena's eyes widen, and I can see the hope she's been demanding finally take root, warming her from the inside out. "Estra," she whispers, tasting it. "She is... our hope."

"Yes," I say, letting the word hang in the air, heavy with promise. "And if she is anything like her mother, she will never stop fighting. She is alive."

CHAPTER 36
DAED

The night bleeds into dawn, an orange haze gnawing at the infinite dark, chasing shadows from the edges of the world. I step up from the cabin to find a modest company of Blades, those that survived the horrors of Modok, working the ship. Meanwhile, Orios hauls the ropes, sails snapping against the brisk wind, and beside him, muscles straining, burning with every ounce of effort, is a figure I am still unaccustomed to seeing unshackled and unmasked.

The Golden Son pulls in time with Orios, grunting in unison until a final, hard thump secures the sail. They tie off the rope, and Orios, silent as ever, gives only the sharpest nod, a wordless acknowledgment, the closest this human will come to thanks from a Reaper. Above, Zyphoro stands watchful in the crow's nest, eyes fixed ahead, fingers weaving through the air as she summons smoke into waves that churn the water, joining the wind to carry us faster toward land.

I approach Orios, slapping him hard on the back. He straightens with a groan, towering, long hair matted and soaked with sweat, knotted atop his head.

"Solena is tired but refuses to sleep," I say.

He grunts, a sound that says he understands exactly what I mean.

"I'll take care of it," he murmurs. One last nod to the Golden Son, then he wipes the sweat from his neck and heads for the cabin.

The Golden Son wipes his hands on his trousers, wincing at the raw blisters and scratched skin. I spot a waterskin on deck and, in a rare moment of consideration, toss it to him. The leather strikes his blistered palms, and he winces again. I study the way his scarred face contorts and find the sight... interesting.

He nods at me, the same wordless gratitude Orios would offer, then lifts the waterskin to his lips and drinks long and deep. When he finishes, he exhales, wipes the last drops from his mouth, and looks up at me from beneath his shaggy blond hair.

"How is she?"

I hesitate, weighing the truth, but he has earned my honesty, even if I will never admit it aloud.

"She is no better. No worse. For now, Reon holds her in time."

His gaze drifts to the horizon, and both our ears prick at the distant cry of seabirds. "We're close. Then you will take her to the Grove?"

I nod.

"You must take me first to the Legion camp. They must know you mean no harm. If they see you unannounced, they will attack."

I bark a mocking laugh, the sound lost to the wind. "If they dare attack me, it will be the last thing they do. I will show no mercy. Amara must reach the Grove."

"What of the beast Ashen? I could ride him if you are not willing," he offers.

Another laugh bubbles inside me. Who does this human think he is that he could ride a demon of the void like it's a fucking pony? But that lunacy is least of my thoughts. I square my shoulders. "Ashen has not been seen since Baev'kalath."

The Golden Son narrows curious eyes at me. "Can you not summon him? Do you not control demons?"

I dislike the way this human presumes to know anything about me. Still, I answer.

"He does not answer me."

"Does that mean... but isn't he immortal?"

"Demons die as easily as humans do. As easily as Fae do. If he died protecting Amara, then he served her well. What do you care anyway? He was a demon, after all."

The Golden Son leans on the railing. "Demon or not, I saw bravery. I saw loyalty in the beast."

A flash of feathers and smoke, and Zyphoro descends from above, landing deftly between us. "Then you and Ashen are alike in that sense," she says with a grin. Her gaze sweeps over the ripples of his sweat-slicked muscles, and I roll my eyes, stomach churning.

"I will take him to his Legion," she says abruptly. "You do not need another pair of hands to get Amara to the Grove."

I eye her suspiciously. "And why are you so eager to escort this human, who hates us, to his army?"

Zyphoro shrugs. "Curiosity, insanity, boredom. Take your pick, Daedalus. Regardless, I'll be happy to see him delivered."

I shake my head. "I did not promise him safe passage." I inhale, letting the weight of it settle. "I promised him death. A promise already overdue."

Zyphoro laughs, sharp and wild, and both the Golden Son and I are caught off guard by it.

"Then stop going on about it and kill him already," she says.

Her taunts fuck me off to no end. I should kill him just to show her I'm not bluffing. But perhaps that's a little childish. So I do not. I stand there, brow furrowed, fingers twitching as if summoning Death Singer. Yet my sword does not come forth.

Zyphoro sighs, mocking my frayed patience. "He has done all you asked. He protected Amara and your daughter to the best of his ability."

"And he failed," I growl.

"So did you. So did we all," she retorts sharply, yet her words cut like a dull knife. Slow and agonizing.

I release a low rumble from my chest, grudging acknowledgment in my throat.

"I'm curious to see what he will do next," Zyphoro purrs, amusement threading every word.

The Golden Son bows his head as Zyphoro's gaze sweeps over him, then he straightens. "I appreciate your... kindness, and you need not fear me."

Zyphoro's laughter breaks loose again, louder. She slaps her knee, nearly tipping over. "Oh, darling, I am neither kind nor afraid. But how deliciously naïve of you to think so much of yourself... and of me."

She tilts her chin, eyes dragging over him, not just assessing, but devouring. A slow smile curves her mouth. "Perhaps I won't return you to your army of traitors after all. Perhaps I'll keep you for myself. Make you my pet."

Her finger taps against her chin. "You can crawl at my feet, lick the mud from my boots. Hmm... yes. I think I'll call you... Scratch."

"My name is Ronin," he replies. Calm. Unflinching. Not the usual reaction to Zyphoro's teasing.

My eyes flash, eager for chaos to follow.

He squares his shoulders as Zyphoro circles, smoke curling between her fingers, a dagger materializing from the shadows in her hand.

They stand off for what feels like eternity, neither yielding, neither breaking eye contact, every breath thick with the possibility of violence or fucking, it could go either way with my sister.

"Ronin," she says at last, voice a velvet whip. "Very well."

The smoke swirls, then the dagger vanishes as if it had never existed.

"Not long to go now."

Her wings snap from her back, catching the dawn light, and she ascends to the crow's nest.

I turn to him. He does not relax. His chest broadens, fists clenched, body taut as a drawn bow, ready for whatever I might do and he should prepare. He should anticipate. Gygarth is not hunting me, and I am free to call the void. I could rend him into so many pieces there wouldn't be enough for the birds to scavenge.

But Zyphoro is right. Somehow, impossibly, she is right. I will not kill him. It would bring me no pleasure.

"You've earned yourself a reprieve," I say, voice edged with gravel. "But if you enjoy your head attached to your neck, don't do anything stupid."

"I want the same things you do," he says, shoulders easing just enough to suggest a truce. "So, I will work with you until Amara is healed. But I will not bow. I am not yours to command. I have not forgotten."

My jaw ticks, teeth grinding. A whisper of smoke unfurls from my back, wings stretching wide enough to blot out the rising sun as it paints the horizon in fire and shadow.

"Neither have I," I rasp, each word heavy with warning and promise. "So on second thought, please... do something stupid."

He doesn't respond. Only takes a single step back, and the faintest sting of disappointment coils in my chest.

I lift from the deck, soaring upward before settling beside Zyphoro in the crow's nest.

"Calm yourself, brother," she says. "He has an army on land, which is more than we do. The thrall houses lie in ruins. Lords and ladies dead. The Blades' ranks shattered. There may still be a use for him."

I furrow my brow. "That is very fucking rational of you, sister."

She exhales, a soft huff laced with amusement despite herself. "I may have lost fragments of my mind over the centuries, but I'm not a fool, brother."

My gaze lingers on her, the eyes so like mine, the other half of the moonstone glinting at her throat, our mother's moonstone. A reminder of blood and bond, of a past neither of us can escape. "Of course you're not."

Her frown severs the brief warmth between us. "Don't get sentimental. Just help me move this ship faster, would you?"

I draw in a breath and let my fingers brush the frayed edges of the void. Smoke unfurls at my command, spilling into the waves until the sea itself blackens, alive with shadow. The ship surges forward, leaping as though the very currents bend to me.

My eyes cut to the horizon, the silhouette of the mainland sharpening with each beat of my heart. But the fate that awaits there is anything but clear.

***

It has been so long since I've worn my armor that it feels almost foreign now. The leathers and boots creak as they mold once more to my body, the harnesses biting into chest and thighs, blades nestled in their familiar sheaths. Iron plates rest on my shoulders, and the shrouded helm hangs heavy under my arm. Beside me, my sister conjures her own war-garb, boot braced on the railing, tapping her dagger against a bent knee while the rolling green of the mainland stretches before us.

"It's quiet," she mutters, scanning the shore.

Kale Harbor is unnervingly still. No sails on the water. No cries of children racing the tide. No bustle of dockhands cursing under their breath. The silence clings thick to everything.

A breath rumbles in my chest. "I won't walk into another ambush. Not with Amara's life in the balance. Not when time slips like sand between our fingers."

"Modok is dead. Nyraxes too. The Fae are finished here." Her eyes flick past me to the Golden Son, bent over a water barrel, washing salt and grime from his face. "The Legion will be the danger here."

My jaw locks, teeth grinding. "And you're certain you want to hand him over to them?"

"He's the only leverage we have. Their commander. They'll bend if he tells them to."

"And what if that command is to shred us to ribbons?" I say. "That human owes us no loyalty."

Zyphoro only gives a languid shrug, shrugs, as if the thought doesn't stir her blood in the slightest. "Then I'll take him apart. Piece by screaming piece. Until his little soldiers do as they're told. Makes no difference to me. So long as it spares us a battle."

A bitter laugh slips from me, low and humorless. "Never thought I'd see the day you'd speak of avoiding a fight."

The corner of her mouth lifts, but her gaze stays on the land. "Amara saved me," she says, her voice carried on the warm breeze curling over the waves. "I owe her a debt. Stilling my blade for a day is the least I can do." Then her eyes cut to mine, sharp as the dagger she toys with. "But the moment she is well..."

"Yes, yes." I roll my eyes and sigh. "Then the oceans will run red with the blood of your enemies."

Her hand snaps out, gripping my forearm. The unexpected weight of it startles me, but what unsettles me more is the sheen in her eyes.

"I will keep the Legion occupied while you get Amara to the Grove."

My shoulders sag, the truth unraveling itself between us. "That's what this is, isn't it? You're planning to be the distraction. The bait." I shake my head, voice dropping low. "Sister, I cannot let you. It should be me."

Her fingers shift, softness turning to steel, before she thumps my shoulder with a playful blow. I wince, though it's nothing more than a nudge.

"You can't be everywhere at once," she says, almost gently. "Amara. The Legion. All the wars you insist on fighting. Lucky for you, you've a twin who can stand where you cannot. Besides, it may not even come to that. Ronin may still control them."

Her words are meant as comfort, but they strike something deeper. A reminder of all the places I cannot be. Of all I've already failed. Estra's face rises unbidden in my mind, my daughter swallowed by the void, lost to me.

Without speaking, my sister steps closer, as if she can feel the dread gathering inside me, strangling me from within.

"What if this doesn't work, Zyphoro?" I murmur, hating the fracture in my voice. "What if I lose them both?"

She exhales, steady as ever. "We have never known defeat, brother. That truth will not change today."

And in that moment, I see her more clearly than ever. The other half of my coin. Where I am steel, she is fire. Where I falter, she stands unshaken. When the weight drags one of us down, the other rises to bear it. Together, we are unbreakable.

How many centuries have been stolen from us? Stolen from her, her name struck from memory, her face erased. Yet now, with Zyphoro Phaedren restored, what wonders, what terrors, might we unleash?

I will hold my wife and daughter again with my sister at my side.

Orios' heavy strides upon the deck shift my thoughts, the clang of his steel boots thunderous. He stands a mountain beside us, his armor so black its sheen reflects nothing, spiked pauldrons and flowing leather cloak at his back, his fists hidden beneath sharp gauntlets. Behind him, Solena appears, her dark hair slicked back and braided intricately down the middle of her head, trailing like a whip down her back, her fingertips stained now forever with black ink.

With one hand she carries Orios' helm, while her other nestles inside his.

"Rook," Orios says. "Reon is fading. We must move now."

My eyes flick to the cabin door, and a weight like iron pools in my gut. Nerves crawl through my veins, strange and unwelcome. I've longed for this moment, yet dreaded it all the same. There is no turning back. Not now.

The heavy tread of boots on timber reaches me before the Golden Son himself steps into view, wearing a mismatch of whatever scraps of armor we found lying around the ship. Our gazes collide, no words needed. Hatred and malice simmer there, stitched together by duty. Amara's fragile, stubborn threads the only thing binding us from bloodshed.

Zyphoro steps forward with a predatory smile. "It is time, darling." She reaches to brush a stray blond lock from his eye. He bats her hand away, glaring.

She laughs. "Oh, we'll have to get much closer than that if you want an escort to your army."

The runes carved into her skin flare to life, pulsing with light as her vast black wings unfurl in a thunderous snap. The wind catches their span before she folds them into a lethal, elegant bloom. She opens her arms.

"The only way you're getting there is in my embrace, lover," she smirks.

The Golden Son drops his head, shaking it as disbelief flickers over his face. Yet he doesn't resist. Instead, he steps forward, reluctant but resigned, as Zyphoro smiles victoriously. She seizes his waist, yanking him tight with a force that wrenches a gasp from his chest. He grumbles in frustration, but she only laughs and launches from the deck, their bodies swallowed by cloud, her cackle echoing like a banshee on the wind.

"I almost pity him," Solena muses with a sly grin. It draws the faintest curve of one from Orios and, despite myself, from me.

The levity dies quickly. Orios turns grave. "We cannot carry Reon and Amara as easily. We risk breaking the time loop…" His voice falters when he meets my eyes. "We could lose her."

"Gather the Blades. Meet me at the Grove. I will get Reon and Amara there."

They exchange a questioning glance, but I offer no explanation. There is no time, no strength for words.

"Go. Now," I order, clipped and final.

Solena's lips part, ready to spill concern, but Orios stills her. He tightens his grip on her hand, lifts it, and presses his lips to her knuckles with quiet reverence. It silences her doubts.

"Yes, Rook," he says.

He bends, allowing Solena to pull his helm into place. His face vanishes beneath its shroud, smoke curling over his armor until he is no longer just a male but a Reaper, born of shadow and war. Solena's runes flare, black wings bursting from her back in a sleek, deadly unfurl. Orios follows suit, his wings spanning so wide she is nearly swallowed whole in their shadow.

"We will meet you in the Grove," Solena says, and then they soar together, their forms climbing higher, two streaks of shadow slicing across the perfect blue sky.

I stand motionless, and though it lasts only a breath, in that breath lies an eternity, an eternity where doubt knots my limbs, where fear threatens to rip me apart. Before it can burrow deeper, I turn sharply, boots pounding across the deck. The cabin door groans under my hand as I throw it open so hard it nearly shatters against its hinges.

They are exactly as I left them. My friend. My love.Reon's skin is almost as pale as Amara's now, his very life bleeding away to feed the loop that holds her tethered to this world. Orios was right: I cannot carry them both. And I cannot risk pulling them apart, not when Amara clings to that fragile thread of existence.

So I must call on the only thing left to me.

My power. My curse.

The darkness that whispers in my blood.

With a flick of my hand, the air rends open. A jagged wound tears through the cabin, a slice of reality itself unspooling. Beyond it yawns the void, endless, silent, grave-dark.

Reon does not stir, too bound to the loop. Amara does not move, frozen in her fragile stasis, and from the void, something comes.

Two figures emerge. Insubstantial, smoke and shadow barely given form. Wisps trailing, they still carry the unmistakable shape of arms, of grasping fingers, of cowled heads and long, drifting robes. They glide in eerie unison, their gestures mirrored, their movements in perfect, unnatural accord.

They break from the void and stop before me, faceless heads bowed.

My heart thunders, but I force my steps toward the bed where Amara lies. My hand trembles as I reach for her, and sparks lash across my skin from the barrier that holds her. I hiss, withdrawing. No time to waste. No room for failure.

I turn to the specters and nod once.

They bow, still faceless, still insubstantial. Then their bodies unravel.

The edges of their shadowy robes shred into streamers of smoke, each strand twisting and lengthening as though caught on some unseen wind. Their arms contort, fingers elongating, fusing into skeletal limbs that snap and bend until they resemble legs, not Fae or human legs, but the spindly, bone-thin forelimbs of some nightmare beast. Their torsos split, stretching impossibly, their hoods collapsing inward as the shadow pours forward, reshaping into the outline of elongated skulls. Hollow sockets gape where eyes should be, burning faintly with ash-pale light.

A low, unnatural sound escapes them, not quite a neigh, not quite a scream, but both at once. The resonance vibrates through the cabin, rattling its beams. Their chests heave as ribs force themselves into existence, formed of shadow one moment, skeletal the next, then gone again in a swirl of smoke. Veins of darkness ripple down their sides, hardening into flanks that glisten like oil in starlight.

Their tails writhe first as tendrils, then snap into lashing whips of smoke. Their hooves take form last, slabs of black fire solidifying with a sound like cracking stone. Each stomp splinters the deck beneath them, though when I glance, the wood bears no mark, as though reality itself refuses to acknowledge their weight.

By the time their transformation is complete, the robed phantoms are gone, replaced by two massive steeds wrought entirely of shadow and despair. Their manes whip like storm-clouds, their mouths drip smoke instead of breath, and their eyes burn like pale dying stars.

I flick my wrist, and a swell of smoke surges to life, curling and twisting. It engulfs Reon and Amara, swallowing them whole, and for a moment they vanish in darkness. Then the smoke thins, revealing them wrapped within its writhing tendrils, lashes of shadow clinging to the spectral steeds.

"Go!"

The command rips from me, and they obey. The steeds rear, their hooves cracking like thunder, their haunting whinnies tearing the silence as they charge into the dark, taking Reon and Amara with them.

My wings snap open, each beat heavy with the cries of a thousand lost souls and then I surge forward, into the wound I carved, into the void itself, black lightning lancing through eternity.

Behind me, reality stitches closed.

I follow the steeds, my gaze locked on Amara through the shifting veil of smoke. From the edges of my vision, the demons of the void stir. Their pale eyes gleam like knives in the dark, their whispers scratching at the walls of my mind. They stalk the boundaries, watching, waiting, but they do not strike. Not with the power I wield now. Not with Emranth's blackened soul pulsing inside me.

There is only one they would obey above me. Yet he does not come. He skulks in An'kel like a coward.

Or perhaps he is simply bored with me. Perhaps he torments another now.

The thought guts me, tears raw lines across my heart.

It makes sense. Gygarth does not hunt me. His gaze, his fury, is fixed on Estra now, and that is enough to give me hope that she still lives. If she were dead, gods help me, he would already be in search of a new plaything.

My teeth grind, my fists clench so hard blood drips down my palms. Still, I keep my eyes fixed on Amara. For she is not only my redemption, she is my salvation.

Ours.

Mine and Estra's.

The void stretches forever, a prison without walls, but with a flick of my hand, I tear a wound in the fabric of night. A flash of green sears the dark. Then light, true light, erupts, blinding, glorious. The sun.

I rip the rift wider, and the void screams. The demons scatter, shrieking as they're cast back into their corners. The steeds explode forward, hooves hammering down on earth and grass as we break free.

They rear, manes of smoke thrashing, the sunlight stabbing through them like spears. Their forms buckle beneath it, the edges of their shadow-flesh tearing apart in ragged wisps. I raise my hand, and at my command they unravel, slow at first, like silk threads pulled loose, then faster, their bodies fraying into ribbons of darkness. Piece by piece they dissolve, their massive bodies folding inward until nothing remains but twisting streams of black mist.

The smoke coils toward me, wrapping around my arm like chains seeking a master, before streaking backward into the wound in the air from which they were born. The void hungrily drinks them in, swallowing every trace, and then seals itself shut with a final, shuddering snap.

The silence that follows is absolute.

When the haze clears, Amara lies upon the grass, just beyond the Grove's border. No shimmer of magic shields her now. No time-loop binds her. Beside her, Reon heaves ragged breaths, his chest rattling, his skin scorched raw, his fingers blackened where power burned through him.

I fall into shadow, void-walking the distance in a heartbeat. Smoke swirls as I reform at her side and sweep her into my arms.

Once, I feared her heat, feared the fire that blistered my skin. Now, the cold terrifies me more. She is ice in my embrace. Too cold. Too still.

"She doesn't have much time," Reon rasps, clawing at the grass, blood streaking his hands. "Go, Rook. Now."

I need no more reason to move. No more hesitation. I gather Amara into my arms, pressing her against my chest where her heartbeat trembles so faintly I can scarcely feel it. My wings flare wide, and I surge forward, tearing through the forest. Branches snap and splinter against the iron strength of my pinions, smoke streaming from me in thick waves that churn like a storm tide. The wind howls in my wake, a beast unchained, bowing the trees as though the forest itself fears my passing.

I race over lakes that shatter beneath the force of my wings, through tangles of vine and root, until the vine wall of the Grove looms ahead. But it is not the living fortress I remember. It is withered, scorched, torn open in places, its great heart wounded.

No guards. No sentries. Only silence.

I fling a lash of smoke forward, and the gate groans open under its weight. Screams erupt. The Tenders scatter like leaves before a gale as I descend upon them, my wings driving gusts that snuff their pyres and send tools clattering across the earth. Doors slam. Windows shutter. But I am not here for blood.

I strike the ground in a thundering landing, dirt exploding beneath me. They cower, but I spread my wings wide, and from the very pit of my chest I cry out, my voice breaking.

"Please! Help her!"

The plea rips the air apart. For a heartbeat there is only silence.

Then, a sudden whip across my throat. A vine coils hard around my neck, thorns biting, cutting deep. I choke but do not release her. I only clutch Amara tighter, even as more vines burst from the ground, ensnaring my legs, yanking me to my knees.

A figure cloaked in green steps from the shadows. She pulls back her hood, revealing a scar cleaving across what was once unmarred.

"You have killed her!" Mirael's scream splits the air, raw with fury and grief. The Tenders flood forward, their faces twisted in horror as their eyes fall on Amara, bloodied and broken in my arms.

"You have killed our Jewel!"

CHAPTER 37
DAED

Before her. The stone presses cold beneath my knees, hard enough to bite through the fabric of my leathers. My fists grind against my thighs as smoke drifts from me in restless wisps, curling with every inhale, every exhale, wreathing around me as the cobalt circle of symbols etched into the stone pulses faintly.

"Is this the debt to be paid?" I murmur. "Is it time?"

A hand brushes my shoulder, pale, skeletal, dripping with jewels.

"Yes, Daedalus," Lanneth says, her voice coiling like a pit of serpents. "Our master hungers, and our people weaken. When he feasts, so shall all Mordorin. Your house will rise again, reborn, stronger than ever."

I roll my shoulders, the weight in my chest refusing to lift. "Must I do it?"

She laughs lightly, but even a sound supposed to carry joy curdles when it comes from her. "Of course not, sweet boy. Leave that to me. I will not sully your hands. All you need do is take your wife to bed and provide an heir for House Mordorin. When all is done, you will have a precious child, and the Father Below will have his meal."

"And she does not know," I ask, teeth clenched.

Lanneth drifts beyond the circle, her shimmering gown dragging over the stone. "No. Better she remain blind, lost in the euphoria of you, my prince. No need for terror while she is our guest."

I shake my head, lips tight with anger and shame. "Why play games? Why not take her, rip what we need, then throw her aside until she's... ripe?"

Silence follows, stretching long enough to echo my own vile words. Words I cannot unsay.

"You could do that?" Lanneth asks, voice curling around me like a whip. "You could destroy her, take her against her will, forget her, slaughter her when the time comes?"

I do not answer. My silence earns a snigger from her.

"No. Not even the cursed prince of Baev'kalath could do that," she says. "She must be kept safe. Protected, and when the time comes, you must take her gently, with care and affection, even if you must feign it. A child conceived in kindness, a sacrifice given in love, will keep Gygarth's belly full for centuries."

Her heels tap against the stone. She comes to my back, hands pressing into my shoulders. "Just as it was with Queen Veloria."

The words should cut me deeper, yet the blade of Lanneth's voice shatters against the cold, black wall inside me, the barren place where love and hope come to die.

"What if I can't..." The words slip out before I can stop them, ragged and desperate.

Lanneth exhales, her breath misting in the cold air. Her fingers dig into my leathers, nails sharp as needles, yet her touch is less felt than her words, less cruel than the truth she delivers.

"You have no choice, Daedalus," she says. "You are his to command. Whether by your hand or his, the girl's fate is sealed. All you can do is make it swift... less painful than it could be. Do you understand?"

I say nothing, and that in itself is defiance. Her fingers tighten, harder, sharper, a strength no brittle frame should wield and then I feel the darkness within me, deep and hungry, responding to her call, a malevolent whisper ready to force my hands to commit things... unspeakable, horrid, in his name.

My vision rolls black. I yield. To the darkness. To my master. To Gygarth.

"Yes. I understand."

***

My vision tunnels as my throat cinches shut, vines grinding into flesh, thorns breaking skin until the taste of blood floods my mouth. My eyes bulge, pressure threatening to burst them from their sockets, my bones creaking as if they'll snap. Still, I cling to her. Still, I fight. My voice tears from me in a ragged shred, nothing but broken glass dragged across stone.

"She's... not dead," I rasp, each word costing me blood. "But she needs your help. Kill me if you want, but save her first!"

Mirael heaves a breath as if she's the one being strangled, rage pouring from her in waves. Her brown eyes blaze, glossy with fury, daring me to break my stare. I do not. I will not.

"Damn you," I choke, my voice nothing but gravel. "You are wasting time!"

Her gaze flickers, against her will, to Amara, and in that moment, the stone mask cracks. The rage falters. Her lips part as if the thought itself carves a wound in her.

"She's... alive?" Mirael whispers, her voice so faint it trembles.

I cannot answer. No air remains. My skin burns violet, stars exploding in my vision, and still I refuse to let her go. Tears leak from my eyes. Not weakness, not surrender, but defiance. Tears no one could ever drag from me but my love.

Mirael's fist loosens. The vines recoil. They slither back into the earth with a hiss, and I collapse forward, hacking, every breath agony as I clutch Amara tighter against me.

"Take her," Mirael commands.

The Tenders swarm me. Hands claw at my arms, prying, pleading, pulling, but my grip locks like iron.

Mirael looms above. "If you want her saved, you must let her go."

Her words strike deeper than thorns, deeper than steel. They carve into me, severing something vital. My fingers twitch. My chest caves and then, gods forgive me, Amara slips from my arms.

The Tenders catch her, their arms weaving beneath her broken body like the sacred creature she is. They lift her high, carrying her toward the vine wall. Mirael follows, her scarred face set like stone, her emerald cloak trailing behind her, its edges darkened with dirt and blood.

"Wait," I croak, clutching at my raw throat, stumbling forward. My breath scrapes, my vision veils in shadow, but I will not stop.

Through the blur I see Amara, her scorched skin, her fragile chest barely rising, her body swaying in the arms of those who bear her into the forest.

"Please..." My voice shreds itself on the word. "Use your rune."

Mirael casts a bitter glance over her shoulder, her scar stark in the dappled light.

"Only the earth can heal her now."

She turns away before I can respond, her cloak whispering over roots and stone. I stumble after her, dropping to a knee, dragging myself upright with a growl.

Just as I manage to find my footing, a rustle in the distance pulls my attention north. My head snaps toward the sound, senses sharpening in an instant, smoke crackling faintly at my fingertips. Through the lush green tangle of the forest, towering trees, hanging vines, and drifting mists, I see a swarm of darkness cutting through the wild beauty. Their heavy boots crush the moss beneath them, their armor clinks and hums, the sound sharp enough to startle birds from their branches.

"Quiet," I snap, voice low but commanding. Orios halts immediately, raising his fist to signal the Blades behind him to still themselves.

The only one who doesn't heed the silence is Solena. The moment her eyes find Amara, carried deeper into the forest in the arms of the Tenders, she surges forward.

"Where are they taking her?" she demands.

I catch her by the elbow before she can push past me. Her glare is sharper than shattered glass.

"I don't know," I mutter, not wanting the Tenders to hear my doubt. "She needs the earth now. Whatever that means. So leave them to their work, Solena."

She twists in my grip, a growl in her throat, but her strength is no match for mine.

"I said enough," I snarl, leaning close. "I will not earn the Tenders' wrath and risk Amara's life again. Stay with Orios. Guard the Grove. Stay out of their way. Understand?"

Solena's jaw tightens, but she nods. Beneath her fury, I see the same fear that coils like a noose around my own throat.

Ahead, Mirael pauses, glancing back at us before she turns away again to follow the procession. My chest tightens when I realize how far Amara has gotten from me. I let Solena go, and she steps back, stopping only when Orios catches her shoulder and draws her close. Together they watch as I push forward, following Mirael and the Tenders deeper into the forest.

The path winds endlessly, twisting through roots and rocks. My boots catch, my balance falters, exhaustion gnaws at my edges, but I force my body onward. I will not stumble. I will not fail.Not when the only purpose left to me is keeping Amara alive.

We walk for so long my legs feel they will give way beneath me. My vision blurs, but slowly the forest brightens. The canopy parts, spilling sunlight into a glade awash in lavender bloom. The air thickens with the perfume of a thousand blossoms, the scent so rich I feel it in my blood. The ground is impossibly soft beneath my boots, as though I tread upon clouds, and for a breath I think I might float away.

The Tenders carry Amara to the heart of the clearing. Their hands are gentle, reverent, as though she is not broken flesh and bone but something divine. They lay her upon the bed of lavender and step back as one, forming a circle. Knees press into earth. Heads bow. A hundred whispers rise, threads of prayer weaving with the sigh of the wind, with birdsong spiraling through the trees.

At her feet, Mirael stands. Waiting. Watching. Not reaching for her rune. Not summoning the power of the Vornahl.

My restraint wilts. My voice tears the reverence apart. "What are you doing?" The words hiss, earning incensed glares from the kneeling Tenders. I do not care. "She is dying!"

Mirael's eyes snap to mine, molten with fury. "And it is your fault!" Her voice rings through the glade. "I do not doubt that for a second. Yet even with all your infinite, ancient power, you brought her here because you cannot save her. So keep your mouth shut!"

My lip curls, rage trembling through me, fangs bared. But before I can retort, Amara sinks.

The flowers curl over her, the soil opening like a grave. She slides downward, slowly, her body cradled by earth. Panic seizes me. I surge forward, but Mirael's glare halts me like a blade to the chest.

"This is how we must heal her," she snarls. "The earth must take her in, mend her wounds. Only then will she rise."

I shake my head, muscles taut, horror twisting in my gut as the ground swallows her deeper, until only her face remains. Pale. Still.

"You're certain? This is the only way?" My voice cracks, betraying the terror I cannot cage.

Mirael does not answer.

And then... Amara is gone.

The soil closes over her, flowers swaying as though undisturbed, as though they hadn't just devoured the only woman I've ever loved.

I collapse onto the soil, sorrow, rage, exhaustion crushing me into the earth. My filthy hands clutch at my face, then rake through my tangled hair, tugging until my scalp burns. When I finally lift my head, my vision blurs on Mirael.

"What now?" My voice is cracked, hollow.

"Now we wait," Mirael says. Her hand sweeps toward the Tenders gathered in their circle. "We pray."

"Where are your sisters?" I demand, spitting the words through clenched teeth. "Together, you are stronger. Together, you could save her!"

Her chest trembles with a breath that nearly breaks her, but she steels herself, straightening. Slowly, she gestures to either side of Amara. It is only then I notice. The flowers there are wilted, their once-vibrant purple darkened and brittle, petals strewn like ashes across the grass.

"They did not wake," she says at last. There is no grief in her voice. Only the heavy weight of acceptance. "It is just me."

The truth hits me like a lash across the face, blinding, impossible to deny. In its wake, the fragments of what I've seen knit together in cruel clarity: the vine wall shattered, the village reduced to rubble, the Tenders cowering in their shattered homes and Mirael's face carved with scars, eyes veiled by the ghosts of what she's endured.

"Who did this?" I rasp, bile rising in my throat. "The Fae..."

She shakes her head, and the bitterness in her eyes is colder than any denial. "The Legion came for vengeance and they painted these beloved woods with Tender blood."

My eyes snap wide. The first ugly thought ripping through me is Zyphoro. She's with the Legion now. Who's to say the Golden Son still holds power over them? Heat crawls up my spine. The itch in my feet is a beast. My runes pulse under my skin, my shadow-wings ache to tear free, to lash the sky and rend whatever fools stand in my way. I can feel the dark answering me like a hound at the leash.

And then my gaze drags back, drawn like a hook, to the bed of lavender, to the hollow the earth made for her. The soil that swallowed Amara with the promise of returning her to me.

I cannot leave her.

Something in me breaks and hollows at once. The crack opens like a wound. The thought that she might never rise is a black stone in my throat. I swallow. If the fates decree she will not come back, then let that same earth have me too. Bury me beside her. Let me lie under the lavender so that when her soul goes wandering, she finds me there.

So for now, I take my place, to watch over her, to wait for her return. I lower myself into the grass, bones creaking, body aching, wincing as I roll to my side. My head sinks into the blossoms, the wind sweeping over me, lifting strands of my hair like phantom fingers. I wrench off my gloves and toss them aside, skin aching to feel something real. My hand drifts to the place where the earth swallowed her whole; I drag my fingers through the flowers as if they were her skin, her hair, before pressing my palm to the soil. My chest swells, and for one mad, desperate moment I'm certain I feel her there. Her heartbeat echoing through the earth, a tremor beneath my hand. Gods help me, I pray I'm not losing my mind, because I have never needed anything to be truer in my entire miserable, cursed life.

The Tenders murmur their prayers, though I feel their eyes like pinpricks on my back. Mirael's light footsteps press through the grass until she stands close enough to cast a shadow over me.

"I do not know how long it will take," she says quietly. "Hours. Days. Weeks."

"I'll not leave her side until she wakes," I mutter, eyes fixed on the earth as though sheer will might drag Amara back to me. "Or until I turn to dust and the wind carries me. Whichever comes first."

"So be it," Mirael replies. Then she turns away, her cloak brushing the blossoms as she walks into the forest, the sound of her steps fading until only the whisper of leaves remains.

As Mirael vanishes into the trees, the truth settles heavy in my chest. The Tenders their home reduced to ruin, still pray. Still believe. Their faith has not withered, even when every reason to do so has and I, who should have protected them, who swore to keep the Legion from their gates... I failed them. My kind failed them. The bargain was meant to keep them safe from the Legion, and yet their sisters lie buried, their walls burned, their peace stolen by the very war we promised to hold back and now I have returned their precious jewel to them just as broken and bloodied and still, they showed me mercy. They could have cast me out, let me choke on their vines or bleed in the dirt beside the fallen. But they didn't. They chose faith over vengeance, hope over hate.

Amara's life hangs in the balance, yet as I watch these remnants of grace, I think perhaps they are saving more than my wife. Perhaps they are saving what little remains of me.

Time folds in on itself. The hours creep past, and still Amara does not rise. The sunlight fades to a dull amber through the canopy, then thins to silver. Warmth slips from my skin, replaced by the chill of dusk. One by one, the Tenders climb to their feet and leave the clearing, their voices still threaded with prayer even as they vanish into the dark. Even in their absence, I hear them in the sighing of the wind, the cry of distant birds, the unseen scurrying beneath the soil. Their prayers seem to belong to the forest itself, a pulse that beats with the earth.

When night finally comes, the familiar kiss of darkness brushes my skin. Moonlight spears through the branches in slanted beams, washing me in its cold glow. The blossoms around me shift beneath it, their pale heads shimmering as though they've been dipped in starlight. I do not look up, afraid that if I glance away, she will rise in that instant and I will miss her first breath. But even without seeing it, I feel the Crone's moon above, its pull, its sway, the final phase before renewal. A time of cleansing. A time for endings and beginnings.

But just because the Crone's moon promises rebirth does not mean it grants new life. Ends are not always beginnings. Sometimes they are only ends.

Please, Pale Mother, let it be otherwise this time.

The air thickens and grows colder, the forest around me swallowing light. Darkness pools between the trees, almost as black as the void itself, and yet I do not move. I am a statue, rigid and eternal, my chest barely rising with breath, my eyes locked on the space where she will emerge when the earth finally releases her. Every thought, every heartbeat, every pulse of blood in me belongs to her.

In the village, my Blades wait, silent but poised for the command I cannot yet give. Beyond them, the threat of the Legion presses closer, relentless and merciless, hungering for war, a war they intend to finish, once and for all. My sister, my twin, Zyphoro, could be walking straight into their jaws, and the Golden Son, Ronin, still breathes when his life should have been mine to take. Each misstep, each hesitation, gnaws like a starving dog with a bone, and still I remain here, rooted in the one place that matters.

Even with the weight of the world pressing on my shoulders, with the chaos of all I have failed to protect swirling around me, there is no other place I wish to be. Not in any realm, any plane, any lifetime. All else must wait. She must rise. She must return.

Then together, we will reclaim what was stolen from us. Not this cursed kingdom. Let the wolves fight over those scraps. I speak of the piece torn from both our hearts. Our hope. Our Estra. Only when she is home, can we be made whole.

I bury my face deeper into the grass, tasting the cold dew on my lips, curling my fingers until my nails bite into the soil.

"Please, wife," I murmur into the shadowed hush of the forest, voice raw and trembling. "Please come back to me."

CHAPTER 38
DAED

"Daedalus."

I'm not sure if I hear my name or the wind through the trees. My mind has been a traitor these last days, making me see and hear things. Cruel enough to convince me Amara has risen. That she has returned to me. For a heartbeat, I feel her. Her hand on my cheek, breath at my neck, the warm tangle of the threads that bind us. I reach for her, pull her close, kiss her in the way my soul yearns to... then she melts away. My eyes snap open, and I'm still on the grass, alone, my shape pressed into the blossoms where the earth took her. The place that feels less like a promise now and more like a grave.

"Daedalus."

This time I stir. The voice is real, but it is not Amara.

"What is it, Solena?" I mutter, voice raw.

"It's been two days," she says. "You must eat."

I don't answer. My silence earns a scolding grunt.

"If you don't eat, you'll rot here in this patch of grass, and the worms will make a feast of you." She wrinkles her nose at the dirt, and it reminds me Mordorin were never meant for the earth, nor for the things that slither and crawl beneath it.

The blooms sway, and for a second they trick me again. Her scent flits through them like a lie. I swallow. "What if I'm not here when she wakes?" I rasp.

She kicks my boot. I grimace, dragging my eyes up to her. She hovers with a wooden bowl, shaking it at me like I'm anyone but the Prince of House Mordorin, if I'm even that anymore.

"Then eat here," she snaps. "I don't care."

The thought of leaving this spot feels like surrender, another failure stacked on the heap, but Solena kicks my boot again. "I've got better things to do than stand here all night. You're not the only one who needs tending. Reon barely survived, if you're interested. Mirael healed him some, but she's not as strong without the others. He needs time to heal on his own."

Reon. The name lands like a stone. I hadn't even...

"And there's still no sign of your sister," Solena adds, twisting the knife. "Or the Golden Son. Or the Legion."

"Why hasn't Orios sent scouts?" I ask, voice finding itself as I clear my throat.

She rolls her eyes. "Because he waits on your command. That's what a Blade does."

She kicks my boot once more, and I groan, finally hauling myself upright. Gods, my fucking back creaks like old timber, and a hot stab in my shoulder has me hiss. No sympathy from Solena. She shoves the bowl in my face.

"Hurry. Eat. I need to get back to the village."

The bowl is warm in my hands, steam curling up in ribbons that smell of herbs and salt and something faintly sweet. I don't bother to savor it. I tip it back and drink. The broth scalds my tongue, burns a path down my throat, but I don't care. I'm starving. I drink until the bowl is empty, until only the faint taste of wood remains, and still I want more.

"You'll be chewing splinters if you keep at it like that," Solena mutters, frowning.

I look up at her over the rim, the edges of the bowl biting into my fingers before I hand it back. Her grimace softens, if only a fraction.

"Come to the village," she says quietly. "There is more broth, and the Blades need your instruction."

I shake my head. "Orios can lead them. Tell him I give him command."

Her eyes flash. "Tell him yourself."

The words snap through the air between us. My patience, already thin as wire, frays. "You forget your place, Solena," I say, my voice a low growl. "Do as I say."

She doesn't flinch. Not this one. She takes only a half step back, chin lifting.

"You promised me hope," she says, voice trembling but unbroken. "But if all is lost. If we lose Amara, Zyphoro, Reon... and you, my prince, then who will bring back Estra? Do you entrust that too to Orios and the Blades?"

Her words cut through the armor I've built around the hollow inside me. I swallow hard, the ache settling deep. "No," I murmur, rolling my shoulders to loosen the knots that have fused there. "That is my duty."

It takes effort to stand. Every muscle protests, stiff and screaming from days of stillness. I stretch, arch my neck, and draw a slow, steady breath. Then I glance down, to the lavender blossoms that have become her shroud, and even though my body creaks and aches, I crouch down beside them.

"I will be back, wife," I whisper. My fingers brush the petals, trembling as if they might bruise beneath my touch. I kiss my fingertips and lay them upon the blooms. "Soon."

I feel Solena's eyes on me as I speak to my love, but I don't care for the pity in her gaze. Straightening, I rise to my full height, shoulders squaring, and as I tower over her, she bows her head, almost submissive, as if she finally recognizes the prince she demanded I become.

"Come then," I say, my voice steady, strength returning to my bones. "We must bring back Zyphoro."

She nods once, and a thunderous boom shakes the air before she steps into the void, vanishing in a curl of black smoke. I follow, slipping through shadow, the endless dark folding around me until a flash of light burns my vision. When the smoke fades, I'm standing in the village courtyard.

The cooking fires roar with my arrival, the sudden rush of wind snuffing some of them out. The Tenders gasp, startled with fright. They scatter, most back into their homes, but the children linger, wide-eyed, their faces lit with wonder rather than terror. To them, Fae magic must look like a story come to life. Their parents disagree. They snatch their children by their collars and drag them inside.

Solena takes longer to appear, her connection to the void not as attuned as mine. When she does, she tips her chin toward one of the great dwellings woven through the upper branches. Candlelight glows in the arched windows, silhouettes pacing within.

"They're up there," she says. "Waiting for you."

I nod, my shoulders tensing as I prepare to call my wings, but before I can, a woman approaches. Her cloak is woven from forest greens and fresh blooms, as if she carries the woods themselves on her back. A gnarled staff rests in her hand, her dark eyes fixed on me with a force that could cleave stone.

"Prince Daedalus," she says, her voice hard and cold as the walls of Baev'kalath.

I incline my head, not enough to break her gaze. "Keeper Erania."

Solena glances between us, then takes a careful step back. "I'll see if I'm needed else-where," she mutters, seizing the excuse to escape.

As the tension between us thickens, the Tenders reemerge, resuming their work under the soft glow of early twilight. Solena joins them, tossing herbs into simmering pots and barking instructions. Judging by their faces, none of the Tenders seem particularly grateful, but since when has that ever stopped Solena?

Erania steps closer, and I match her. Between us, shadow and light meet like opposing tides, an invisible wall neither of us dares to cross.

"I prayed to the Souls for the day our Jewel would return to us," she says, voice trembling beneath its steel. "How cruel the gods are, to bring her back so broken, hovering between life and death." Her gaze sharpens. "But what else should I expect when the Prince of Smoke and Shadow is involved? Tell me, how did this happen?"

"I'm not certain," I reply, breath tight in my chest. "When I found her, I was already too late. I brought her here as quickly as I could."

"But how?" Erania presses.

"There was a fire," I say quietly.

Her jaw hardens. "And who set it? Who did this to her?"

The words claw their way up my throat before I can stop them. "She did."

Silence falls, incredulous, as Erania stares at me, trying to grasp what she's heard.

"She set herself on fire?" Her voice rises, sharp with disbelief. Her fingers curl around her staff, wood creaking as the runes carved along it flare bright green. "Do you take me for a fool, Prince?"

"Never, Keeper Erania." My voice stays firm. "But you must understand. Amara is not as she was. Her power has changed. Grown. It is... something new. Something beyond anything the Sundered Kingdom has ever seen."

Her eyes narrow. "Explain."

"She still heals," I say, choosing my words carefully. "But that gift, her healing, it's twisted now, bound to another force. She wields green fire. It burns from her very skin, devouring everything in its path. It spares her only because she can command it, because she heals herself through it. But this time, her rune was damaged in battle. She couldn't control it. The fire consumed her."

Erania shakes her head. "The Sisters cannot heal themselves. They can only heal others."

I draw a slow breath. "Amara can. But only by inflicting pain on herself first."

Erania laughs then. A brittle, broken sound that scrapes the air raw. My chest tightens at the sound.

"Of course," she says, her voice trembling with fury and grief. "Since the day she left the Grove, since she met you, her life has been nothing but pain. What choice did she have but to make something of it? Turn suffering into salvation, as only our Jewel could." Her hands shake. The runes along the staff blaze so brightly now they nearly blind me. "You never should have had her."

"I agree," I say quickly, and the admission startles her. "I tell myself that every day. I wish I had never laid eyes on Amara Tyne. Never heard her voice. Never breathed her in. Never felt her touch." The words scrape my throat. "Even though she made me a better creature than I ever deserved to be. If it meant she could have stayed here, with her people, untouched by the horrors beyond these trees, I would take it all back. I would have gladly drowned in my own darkness, lived a thousand years in despair if it stopped her from boarding that ship. Before I could love her. Before I could ruin her. Before our fates were tangled, only to be sundered to ash."

I meet her burning gaze. "So yes, Keeper Erania. I never should have had her. Does that ease your ire?"

Her jaw tightens. The runes on her staff blaze bright. "No. It does not, Prince of Lies."

Smoke stirs under my skin, shadows whispering for release, but I hold them back.

She is owed her anger.

Slowly, her fury cools. The runes etched into her staff dim, fading to nothing. "But you brought her home," she says at last. "To her people. To the Souls and the earth, so she might once more feel the sunlight on her face and the soil between her toes. That is the everlasting wish of all Tenders before the end."

I stiffen. "This is not the end." My voice is low, hard. "Mirael said the earth will heal her."

Erania lifts her gaze to the treetops. I follow, finding Mirael high among the branches, staring toward the bruised sky and the pale moon rising between the leaves. Even from here, I can feel her sorrow, the shimmer of her tears, the heaviness of her thoughts.

"The Souls give the earth power," Erania says softly. "But Mirael knows, as do I, it is not guaranteed."

I bow my head. "She told me. About her sisters."

"Lira and Saren fought bravely," Erania replies, her voice threaded with strength and sorrow. A tapestry she weaves like no other. "Their sacrifice saved many lives. We laid them in the soil quickly, and we waited. But after a time, we knew they would not rise."

The question catches in my throat, barely a whisper. "When did you know?"

Her expression softens, the first trace of sympathy she's shown me. "When the flowers wilted, we knew they were gone."

Relief surges through me, fierce and bright. I remember the lavender blooms that blanket the earth where Amara lies. The blossoms are still sweet, still vibrant. Still alive.

My wife is not lost.

I clear my throat, masking the swell of solace in my chest. "Thank you, Keeper Erania, for allowing my people to remain here in the Grove."

Her frown deepens. "We weren't given much of a choice."

For a moment, I brace for the runes on her staff to flare again, but they stay dim. "Still," she concedes, "your people are proving useful. The Grove suffered greatly under the Legion's attacks, so we welcome your warriors' aid as we rebuild."

Her gaze drifts past me, toward Solena, who appears to be lecturing a group of villagers on the *proper* way to stack firewood. Erania sighs. "Even if that one is a little... overzealous."

I almost smile. "Do I need to post my Blades along the forest border?" I ask, straightening. "To intercept any further Legion strikes?"

Erania tilts her head, considering. "With our numbers so few, we would not refuse some scouts, especially ones with wings. The Souls do their best to protect us." A faint, wry smile tugs at her lips. "Those who dare venture too deep into the woods soon find themselves devoured by the forest. Swallowed by sinkholes, mauled by bears, gored by stags."

Her words shouldn't unsettle me, but the pleasant curve of her smile makes them far more chilling than they should be.

"Still," she continues, "enough have survived to leave their mark, but it's been quiet lately. We've neither seen nor heard anything from the Legion since your arrival." Her tone turns thoughtful. "Perhaps your presence keeps them away?"

I know better. This silence has nothing to do with me or my Blades.

Zyphoro and the Golden Son reached the Legion's encampment the same day we arrived here. Perhaps he holds them at bay, restrains them from inflicting more harm on these people. Perhaps he's done exactly what I asked of him.

But then why hasn't Zyphoro come to the Grove to tell me just this?

I must find her.

I bow low. "Thank you again, Keeper Erania. If you'll excuse me, I need to debrief with my Blades."

I step past her, careful to keep my distance. Smoke coils from my skin until my wings unfurl, vast and shadowed, wisps of dark vapor curling from their edges like breath.

Erania's eyes widen. "I have not seen wings like that before."

I glance back over my shoulder. "They're... new."

My boots grind into the soil as I ready myself to leap skyward.

"Wait," Erania says, her voice halting my ascent.

I pause mid-motion, wings half-spread.

"Why would Amara risk her life? What was she protecting?" Her mouth hardens. "Not you, I hope."

There's a glint beneath her scowl, a faint curve of a grin that doesn't quite reach her eyes. I find myself matching it.

"No. Not me."

Then the truth hits me like a blade through the ribs. She doesn't know.

Not about Estra. Not about Gygarth.

My breath falters. My face drains of all warmth. How do I tell her something so monstrous?

My wings fold back, then unravel into slow, curling wisps of black smoke that fade into the air.

"There was..." My voice cracks, splintering apart along with my heart, my soul, everything I am. "A child, Keeper. Our child. A daughter."

The air shifts. Cold. Sharp. Heavy as grief.

Erania's skin pales, her eyes shining with unshed tears. "You had a child together?" she manages.

Her hand trembles as she clutches her staff, as though it's the only thing keeping her upright. I reach out instinctively, but she flinches from my touch.

"Amara has a daughter? Half human." The words hang heavy between us, her voice softening only to harden a heartbeat later. "Half Fae."

I see the conflict ripple across her face, the shock, the disbelief, the flicker of joy at the thought of a child of the forest still breathing somewhere in this broken world. But that joy quickly fractures, fear seeping through the cracks. Fear that this child is not wholly human. That her blood carries the taint of the very beasts who've kept humankind beneath their heel for centuries.

I stay silent, letting her turn it over in her mind, letting her face what it truly means. Slowly, color returns to her cheeks, a faint warmth chasing away the pallor, and a whisper of a smile ghosts across her lips.

"A daughter," she breathes.

I nod once. "Her name is Estra."

Erania lifts her head, eyes wide, the hope fragile as a spider's web. "Where... where is she?"

The tremor in her voice cuts through me.

I swallow hard, pushing down the storm clawing its way up my throat. "Taken. By Gygarth. The Father..."

Her hand abruptly slices through the air. "I know who he is."

I still. "You do?"

Her gaze snaps to mine, so intense with anger and grief I can barely meet it. "Of course I do. I know all your gods. The good, the wicked, and the ones that should've stayed buried." Her lip curls. "And you're telling me that demon holds our child of the forest?"

"He does," I rasp. "Amara tried to save her."

"Of course she did." The words crack from her like thunder. "What else would our Jewel give her life for, if not her child?" Her spine straightens. "Then why, Prince, are you still standing here? Why are you wasting time in that clearing when you should be tearing that child back from the jaws of death itself?"

Her words hit their mark, sharp and clean. "I didn't want to leave Amara," I admit, voice low. "I wanted to be there when she woke."

Erania clicks her tongue, shaking her head. "I'm sure she'd rather you spend your energy saving her daughter than mourning her like she's already dead."

"Our daughter," I bite out, because she's left me out of this story one too many times.

She hums, the sound rough as gravel. "Then how do we do it? How do we bring her home?"

"We?" I arch a brow.

She mirrors the gesture, defiant as ever. "Your Blades might fend off the Legion, but against the god of death, you'll need all the help you can get. Besides," she exhales, the words almost breaking on her lips, "you're not just Amara's husband anymore. You are family."

The word strikes deep. Family. It burns as much as it soothes. I never knew my mother's touch. Spent my immortal life as my father's weapon and the crone's puppet. Even reuniting with my sister has done little to fill the hollow inside me. That guilt and emptiness runs deeper than the void itself.

Now, standing in this forest, so rich with life and song, so achingly alive, it feels impossible to breathe. The air hums with growth and warmth, so unlike the roaring frozen oceans of my homeland, the lightning-veined skies that crown my world, and yet here, surrounded by green and gold, being told *I am family* chokes me as tightly as Mirael's vines.

Do I say thank you? Or do I summon my wings and fly, far and fast, until the trees blur into nothing and this impossible kindness can't reach me?

But I don't. I stay. The wall between Erania and me crumbles, one brittle stone at a time.

"Even with the Blades and the Tenders united," I say quietly, "we'll need Amara if we're to reach Gygarth."

Erania tilts her head, eyes narrowing. "Because of her power," she finishes for me, fitting the pieces together. But she doesn't see the complete picture, not yet, and even if she could, I'm not sure I want her to. Her brow furrows. "There's more you're not telling me, isn't there?"

If only she knew. If only she understood what truths I've buried, what horrors I'd keep from her, just as I tried to shield Amara. Yet somehow, this woman sees right through me. Through the armor, through the centuries. Straight into whatever remains of my heart.

It must be something in their blood, these Tenders. They look past power and title, see through the divine and the monstrous alike. They care nothing for the ancient blood that thrums in my veins, blood born when the first winged creatures rose from the mist and drank from the old founts of magic that birthed gods.

I exhale slowly, shoulders easing for the first time in what feels like forever. "You know much about the Fae, Erania?"

She nods once, the motion slow but sure. The space between us seems to shrink.

I reach out, resting a hand on her shoulder. She doesn't flinch.

"Then tell me," I say, voice low, "do you know what an Awakened is?"

CHAPTER 39
DAED

It feels strange to stand so high without my wings flared, without the dark, cracked stone of Baev'kalath beneath my feet. No rain, no starless sky pressing down on my shoulders. Only green. Only gold.

The timber beneath my boots, the curved wooden walls, it all creaks and groans, breathing with life around me. Shafts of dappled sunlight spill through the arched windows, gilding the dust in the air. Outside, flashes of color dart past. Small birds with jewel-bright feathers, their songs threading through the constant hush of wind in the leaves. The trees murmur like an old god dreaming, and though I have not seen them, I know those lesser faeries, the creatures the Tenders call the Souls of the Forest, watch me with great interest.

Vines find their way between the floorboards and wall panels. Their leaves are broad, heart-shaped, mottled white and green. I crouch, tracing a finger along the edge of one. The serpentine vine.

I'd know it anywhere.

I remember it in Amara's hands when she first stepped into Baev'kalath. Then in her chambers, wilting a little more each night as she did. Its color fading, its spirit dimming, until she set it free in Pariseth. Something I could never do for her. I had caged her in my shadow and called it protection.

I rise, gaze shifting toward the clearing beyond the trees. I cannot see it from here, not even with my Fae sight, but I can *feel* her. Through my mark. Through the threads still binding us together. The blossoms still bloom where she sleeps and as long as they live, so does she.

"Rook."

Orios's voice snaps me back from the edge of memory. He's sprawled in a chair that looks far too small for his massive frame, legs wide, elbows resting on his knees. He studies me with a soldier's quiet patience, eyes sharp as the spikes along his gauntlets.

"Are the Blades ready?" I ask.

He nods. "We are few, but still a fine company of Ebon warriors. Disciplined, loyal, lethal and more than enough to handle those Legion sacks of shit." His mouth hardens, the hard set of him wavering. "Surely Zyphoro isn't..."

I cut him off with a glare. "After what my sister endured for centuries? She's too proud, too stubborn, to die at mortal hands." My teeth scrape my bottom lip. "But her silence gnaws at me."

Orios leans forward, eyes glinting. "A hostage, maybe. Perhaps the humans mean to strike a bargain."

The word *bargain* hits like a blow to the chest.

My jaw clenches until my fangs ache. "After what they've done to Amara, to the Grove?" Smoke curls from my skin. "The only bargain offered will be drowning in their own blood."

Orios's grin is feral as it pulls across his face.

I stare out the window again, to where sunlight drips through the canopy like molten gold.

"No more bargains," I murmur, the words a vow now, more than a warning.

"And what if the Golden Son leads them?"

I square my shoulders until my spine feels like forged iron beneath my skin.

"That changes nothing. There is no going back now. For what they did to my wife's people alone, they deserve smoke and wrath."

Orios gives a low, rumbling exhale as one huge hand rubs at his chest through the worn leather of his vest. "I don't need convincing, Rook. Just point me to the massacre."

His enthusiasm is contagious, a scent in the air that stirs the warrior in me, that puts heat in the runes of battle and berserking etched along my skin. The pulse of it hums in my blood, begging to be unleashed. But not yet. Not until the right moment.

"What news from your scouts?" I ask, crossing the room to lean against the wall near the window. The breeze that slips through carries warmth and the faint sweetness of blossoms. I've grown used to it, this strange softness in the air.

"They got as close as they could without drawing attention," Orios says, voice steady but edged. "Their encampment in the valley isn't as large as before, but still holds strength. Mostly ground troops. Some horses. Archers. But something new. Ballistas. Dozens of them."

My brow furrows. I fold my arms across my chest. "Not a favored human weapon."

"Not human," Orios replies, a shadow crossing his expression. "Even from a distance, they gleamed with gold. Fae craftsmanship, without question."

I exhale slowly. "A gift from House Ithranor then, to use against us."

"Seems likely. Why else aim for the skies?"

"Will they cause us trouble?"

A low sound rumbles from Orios' chest, reluctant, almost a growl. "We Mordorin are fast. Almost impossible to track when we void-walk. But if they land a lucky shot... one of those bolts would split us clean in half."

I grin, teeth flashing. "Then let's not get hit."

His shoulders ease, the faintest smirk touches his mouth. "Yes, Rook."

He glances toward the canopy, where sunlight filters through the leaves in golden shards. "Is it late afternoon?" he asks. Beneath this dense cover, it's always hard to tell. "We leave at dawn?"

I shake my head. "Do you remember, Orios, how the humans once called us the nightmare Fae? Of all our kind, they feared the Mordorin the most. Demons made flesh. The monsters that haunted their waking dreams."

"I remember," he says, quiet but firm.

"Then we will be those Fae to the Legion. We'll finish them. Rescue my sister. Avenge the Grove. Make this world something my Amara can look upon without sorrow when she rises." I pause, the air thick with the weight of it. "We'll strike when nightmares are strongest."

A sharp grin curls my lips. "Within the long, terrible dark."

***

As dusk approaches, the Blades fill their bellies with as much as they can fit. Battle is a beast, after all and the beast must be fed.

My warriors still struggle with the lack of meat. Never before have they eaten so much green. So many nuts and beans and things better suited to the small creatures that scurry through the branches than to Fae warriors. Yet even they, like me, will admit quietly, when no one's listening, that the food is not terrible. It fuels us as well as any spiced rack of meat. And the bread... gods, the bread. Warm and soft and light as air. I've never tasted such a thing.

And the way they cook it together. No servants scurrying through dark, crowded galleys. No barked orders or clanging trays. Just people gathered around a great fire, working side by side. Each offering something, a skill, a herb, a steady hand, to make the work faster, the food richer. Then they eat together, too. Around that same fire. Talking, laughing, singing. Sharing.

So different from the long, cold banquet tables of home, the silence between my father and the crone stretched on and on, while my warriors dined in the depths of the fortress.

The memory makes me ache for Pariseth. For the home Amara built for us there, brief, yes, fleeting as a dream, but real. She brought her world to ours, showed us what it could be if we simply *chose* to see each other.

Pale Mother, she is in everything now. Even with centuries of memories behind me, lifetimes before she ever drew breath, she eclipses them all. I can barely recall a world that did not have her in it.

I sit on a long bench, surrounded by Tenders and Mordorin alike, shoulder to shoulder, bowls cupped in our hands as we eat. I cannot remember a time when human and Fae sat this close without blades drawn, without hatred coiling between us.

And still, there is calm. A stillness before the storm, one that hums through us like a held breath. I can only credit it to the Tenders' influence, another thing we are not accustomed to. There has been no sparring, no taunting, none of the blood-hungry rituals that usually seize us before battle. No snarling, no frenzy, no dogs frothing at the mouth for war.

Only quiet. Only peace, the strangest omen of all.

But I know, despite the rituals and this unnatural calm, when the hour comes our ferocity will rear. Fangs bared, wings flared, smoke and shadow answering our call. Even now the thought prickles my skin; every nerve hums with it. My body aches for battle and I cannot deny my nature. War walks beside me as surely as the void does.

With my bowl empty, I lift my head and spot Solena by the great bubbling pot set over the fire, ladling another portion. She straightens, eyes drifting to a cottage below where a candle flares in the window, its light brightening with the dusk. Before she moves I rise, close the space between us, and take the bowl from her hands as gently as I can.

385

"I'll take it," I say. "I must speak to him, anyway."

"Good," she breathes, half a sigh, half a laugh. "He's as surly as you are at the moment."

"He wants to go to battle," I tell her.

"He can barely walk," Solena replies.

"A fact he refuses to accept," I say.

She frowns. "He is not the only one who wants to go."

"I need you here," I say, firm. I ignore her small huffs and the way she pouts as if I haven't already told her this a thousand times already. "The Grove needs protecting, and if Amara wakes, I want it to be you she sees."

Solena's jaw tightens. Reluctantly, she nods. "I know. I will do what you ask. That does not mean I'm happy about it."

I incline my head and turn toward the cottage, the bowl warm against my palms.

Each step grows heavier than the last, and my mind tangles with words that refuse to come. Gratitude wars with guilt, gratitude for his sacrifice, guilt for what it's cost him. He's fought beside me for centuries, through every tide of blood and fire. Since our youth, a youth I can barely recall beyond flashes of laughter, booze, and victory. There were battles against minotaurs, wraiths, harpies... even the occasional siren bold enough to test us. Never once did he falter. Never once too wounded to raise his blade. Not until now.

I reach the door, an evening breeze stirring the dust at my feet. It should be nothing, air and earth, but it feels like an iron wall, holding me back.

The bowl in my hands is cooling fast. Whatever words I cannot find, my friend at least deserves a hot meal. I tighten my grip to hide the tremor in my fingers, then reach for the handle and turn.

The door creaks open, groaning on its hinges. Twilight spills into a wide room divided by hanging curtains. The air tastes of sickness, scrubbed clean but still clinging to the walls. This is where they keep their ill and wounded.

Jars and vials fill a cabinet along the far side. Herbs and drying flowers sway gently from their hooks, and rows of potions and pungent-smelling balms line a long, worn table. Beyond one of the drawn curtains, I glimpse two bare feet, pale as moonlight, resting at the edge of a cot, a pair of weathered leather boots placed neatly at the foot of the bed.

The silence is deep enough to press against my ribs. When those pale toes twitch, I swallow hard.

"Who's there?" The voice is rough, weary. Before I can answer, it continues, harsher now. "Daedalus? That's you, isn't it? Are you just going to stand there like a pervert?"

I roll my eyes, a huff escaping me. "I was coming to you…if you'd give me a damned second."

A snap of fingers sounds behind the curtain, followed by a bark of laughter. Brittle, humorless. "I couldn't give you a second even if I tried, Rook."

I move closer, my steps careful, though each one crashes through my head like thunder. My fingers curl around the curtain's edge. I draw it back slowly.

Reon lies on his back, hands folded over his chest, a woven blanket pulled to his waist — not quite long enough to cover him.

He nods at the thing draped across him. "They're all so short here."

He tries to tease, tries to smile at his own expense, but his lips barely shift. His head turns toward me, limp hair falling across one eye. He's still Reon, the same sharp lines, the same roguish charm that sets mortals and Fae alike spinning, but the spark is gone.

His copper hair, once bright as torchlight, has dulled to tired rust. His skin hangs thin and ashen around the fierce angles of his face. Even his freckles have faded, and his eyes, those bright hazel flames that always held mischief, danger, life, whether seducing his next conquest or warning an enemy to run, are empty now. Burnt out like a dying star.

He lifts a hand from his chest and snaps his fingers.

Nothing. No gold spark, no shimmer of time bending to his will.

"It's all gone," he murmurs, voice barely more than air. "Every last drop."

"It will come back, Reon," I say.

A grin cuts across his mouth, sharp but without heat. "Huh. You're usually such an excellent liar."

I've never heard him sound like this. So hollow. So stripped of the assurance that once defined him. I should know how to comfort him. I remember what it was to lose my wings. To feel the empty ache where power should have been. Fae magic isn't some trick of light; it is *us*. In our blood. Our breath. Our very bones. When it's gone, we are never whole again. We are fragile, mortal in all the worst ways.

He's right to doubt me. I don't know if his power will return. I had to devour a void demon to reclaim what I'd lost, and Reon, the master of time himself, what would he have to do to restore his?

My throat tightens, but I keep my face composed. I hold the bowl out to him, steady despite the weight of everything between us.

"Broth," I say, keeping it short so I don't end up saying something stupid.

Reon groans as he props himself up on his elbows, peering into the bowl. His nose wrinkles.

"Is it good?"

I tip my head side to side, weighing my answer. "For a human concoction of weeds and flowers, it's not the worst thing I've ever had in my mouth."

That earns a rasping laugh from him. "Careful, Rook. Don't tempt me with such unworthy bait."

He reaches out, takes the bowl from my hand, and studies it like it might bite back. A cautious sniff, then a glance at me for reassurance. I nod once, and he drinks.

It's just a testing sip at first. Then he licks his lips.

"That's good weed," he mutters, before draining the rest in a few gulps.

When he's done, he wipes his mouth on his sleeve and lets out a small, satisfied sigh.

"How do you feel?" I ask, navigating the unfamiliar terrain of empathy.

"The same," he says, "but slightly fuller." His eyes narrow, glinting faintly with the ghost of his old mischief. "But enough about me. How are *you*, Rook?"

I wave him off, but he hisses, that sharp Reon tone still alive beneath the weariness.

"Please. I'd much rather hear about your misfortune than dwell on mine."

I smirk. "We go to battle soon. I couldn't be better."

He snorts. "I didn't mean the battle, though thank you for reminding me what I'll miss. I meant *Amara*. You know, that troublesome wife of yours I spent every drop of magic keeping alive?"

My chin dips. The smirk fades. "She sleeps still beneath the soil. All I can do is wait."

The words I've been swallowing for days finally claw their way free. "I am sorry this has happened to you, Reon. What you've given... I'll never be able to repay. I am so very thankful and so very sorry, my friend."

I brace for his sharp retort, the biting humor he wields when emotion runs too close. But none comes. He just looks at me, steady and quiet, knowing the truth when he hears it.

"There is nothing to be sorry for," he says softly. "Nothing to repay. I'd do it again, Daedalus, because you are my prince, and my friend, and my brother."

My lips part, words tearing loose to mirror his, to tell him I would do the same if ever asked. Before I can shape them, he jabs the bowl at my stomach, a mock shove that lands harder than it should.

"Now make yourself useful, will you, and get me a refill? But don't bring it back yourself. Ask that lovely, sweet girl who pops in to clean every now and then." He sighs, half-grin crooked. "She is stunning. Wears a yellow flower in her hair like some kind of forest fairy. Perhaps I'll take a Grove bride for myself."

I frown and snatch the bowl from him. "They're more trouble than either of us can handle."

He chuckles at last, and I can't help the small smile that answers it. It is a sound I needed to hear as much as he did. "Go well into battle, Rook," he says.

"Thank you, Reon." I glance down as his toes wiggle again. "That's progress."

Still propped on his elbows, he watches their movement with exaggerated solemnity. "Yes. Perhaps tomorrow I'll move the whole foot."

I straighten. "Be quick about it. Once I've finished with the Legion, when Amara has risen, I'll need you at Gygarth's doorstep. I'll need you when I take the battle to An'kel."

He nods, brow creased. "Then hurry with the broth. I need all the help I can get."

I incline my head, pocketing the weight of his words, and slip toward the door before sentiment can unravel us both. I close it behind me and find Solena waiting.

"How is he?" she asks, taking the bowl from my hand.

"Surprisingly himself," I reply.

"What do you mean?" she presses.

I sweep my gaze across the courtyard, Tenders moving between benches, Mordorin sharing the evening meal, and find the girl with the yellow flower in her hair stirring the dinner pot with a broad wooden spoon.

"He wants more broth," I say. "But he insists she bring it."

Solena's brow hardens, then she scowls. "Scoundrel. I'll take it to him myself with a side of face-punch." She glances up through the canopy at the deepening dusk. "You leave soon?"

I nod. "Just one last thing to do."

She nods back. She knows what I mean.

I draw a breath, roll my shoulders, and my wings unfurl with a snap, bursting into the twilight. The air shivers with the motion as they stretch wide, catching the fading light before I launch skyward. I cut through the village like a thrown spear, past the vine wall and beneath the tall, curved roots of the great trees until the forest breaks open around me.

The clearing glows ahead, a sea of lavender blossoms bathed in the soft, milky light. The breeze moves through them in waves, carrying that sweet, familiar scent. I angle my wings, glide low, then land without a sound beside her.

Warmth floods my chest. I can *feel* her, my wife, my love. Still sleeping, but still *there*. Still alive.

I drop into a crouch. "I will return soon, wife," I murmur, hoping my voice threads through the earth to reach her beneath. "Then together we will bring Estra home." My voice catches. The words break on a breath. "But for that to happen, you must wake, my love. Because I cannot do this without you."

My hand trails across the blossoms, impossibly soft, fragile things beneath the roughness of my palm. "I need your fire, Amara. Your fury. I need my queen."

Then something snags my attention, small, almost nothing. Among the vibrant blooms, one flower pales. Its edges shriveled, its color drained.

My jaw tightens. "Amara," I breathe. "Wife, can you hear me?"

No answer. The quiet stretches too long. I grit my teeth until my jaw aches.

"Don't you dare think of leaving me," I growl, voice rough with the threat of breaking. "This is not the time for rest. It's time to fight, and you..." My hand clamps around the withered stem, fingers closing until the brittle thing snaps free from the soil, because I will not stand for omens. "...you have never turned from a fight in all the time I've known you."

I bow my head, voice trembling between fury and prayer. "You will not start now."

I pause, waiting, foolishly, for something to happen.

For her to answer my defiance.

For the ground to tremble, for the blossoms to part, for her to rise like a phoenix from the earth, even if only to scold me for my insolence and strike me across the face.

But the world stays still.

Only the sharp crack of a twig disturbs the quiet.

I'm on my feet before I even think, the air shattering around me as smoke bursts from my skin in coiling, snaking tendrils. Death Singer solidifies in my grasp, the blade cloaked in shadow, whispering for release.

My burning white eyes lock on the trees ahead. "Show yourself," I snarl. "And perhaps I'll make it quick."

Silence answers, deep, waiting silence. Death Singer hums against my palm, whispering awful, hungry things. I take a step forward, and the shadows seem to hold their breath.

Then something moves. Heavy steps, unhurried, reverberate through the earth. A stag steps from the shadowed treeline, each stride filled with quiet power. Pale moonlight spills across its massive golden antlers, gilding them like the crowns of kings long dead. Vines wind around them in intricate spirals, blossoms blooming where they touch, unfurling petals that glow faintly against the dark.

More vines coil around its legs, threading through fur that shimmers deep emerald, each movement sending ripples of light through the clearing. Its breath clouds the air like mist, carrying the scent of earth and rain. When it lifts its head, the night itself seems to hold still and in its eyes, bright and green as cut gems, burns the ancient light of something old. Even older than me.

This is no mere creature.

When its gaze meets mine, a voice fills the air that does not leave its lips. A voice I hear in my soul. "Prince Daedalus of the Mordorin Fae. You are not welcome here. Your presence pollutes this place of peace."

My grip tightens on the hilt. Death Singer quivers, eager, but I hold her back.

"You dare speak to me that way, fairy?" I growl. "The Tenders may worship you and call you Soul, but I know what you are. You serve the Fae."

"Not anymore." The voice is calm, but beneath that serenity thrums long-held anger. "Not since we chose to stop serving. Not since we laid ourselves to rest here and woke reborn with new purpose."

"So what then?" I sneer. "You expect me to bow?"

"No, Prince." Its voice fills my head. "No one should bow. Not ever again."

I feel Death Singer grow lighter in my hand, the smoke thinning, the edge dulling, the shadows ebbing away like a tide.

My voice is low when I ask, "And in this world where no one bows... who will rule?"

The stag's jade eyes turn toward me. "That is the curse of our kind. To believe peace cannot exist without a throne. When there is no ruler, there is only balance and balance does not crave worship... or war."

It shifts its majestic head toward where Amara lies beneath the blossoms. "Our Jewel understands the balance. It is she who will show the world the path of peace. It always has been."

Something in my chest tightens until it feels like it might shatter. "Do you have the power to bring her back?" The demand in my voice strains into pleading.

"Yes." The single word carries like stone.

My fist tightens until my knuckles blanch. "Then do it." My chest convulses, the plea rips out of me. "Please. She's fading. I feel it."

The stag stamps the earth once, the sound deep and resonant. "The power to wake her may lie within us. But the will to wake is hers alone. She must want to return and there must be a world worth returning to. Go, fight your war, Prince Daedalus. Take your crown."

I grit my teeth, tempering the fire that wants to consume me. "I fight for the Grove," I say, each word dragged through my throat.

The stag regards me a long moment, then turns. Its hooves strike the ground in a slow rhythm. A heartbeat of the earth itself before the edges of its form come undone, vines and blossoms loosening into the air. Its voice softens, becoming almost mournful.

"Then you have already lost, Prince. For peace cannot be found through victory. Only through surrender."

The antlers dissolve next, their golden branches breaking apart into spiraling threads of light.

"The world does not need another crown," it whispers, as it scatters with the wind, "only someone willing to set one down."

The last of its leaves catch in a rising breeze, carried through the lavender field until even the echo of its presence fades. Only the rustle of petals remains and the hollow ache of its words inside my chest.

"Wait!" The word bursts from me like a command, my hand stretching toward the forest.

"Rook." The voice pulls me back. Orios stands behind me, his hand firm on my shoulder. I seize it, knuckles white, breath shuddering out in uneven gasps.

When I turn to him, his face is puzzled, eyes searching mine.

"Rook. It is time."

I force air into my lungs, each breath a battle. My grip loosens on his hand until he draws it away.

There's no point in explaining. There isn't time. There's never enough time.

My wings flare open, runes igniting across my chest in a blaze of violet heat. Orios mirrors the motion beside me, wind rushing between the ink black feathers.

Together, we take to the sky.

CHAPTER 40
DAED

Moonlight spills thinly over the forest canopy as we cut through the night sky, wings whispering against the wind. Below us, the Legion's encampment sprawls across the valley, a wound of fire and steel burning in the dark. It should be a warrior's moon guiding us, full and bright, the kind that blesses battle and blood. But it isn't. It's the new moon. The Silent Eye. A night of reflection and restraint. A night when Fae seek clarity, not carnage.

The omen sits wrong in my chest. I should welcome the darkness for the cover it gives us, yet the stag's words gnaw at me still: *Peace cannot be found through victory. Only through surrender.* The memory is a stone lodged in my throat. What if he was right? What if laying down my blade, staying my hand, would be enough to bring Amara back?

But the thought curdles as quickly as it comes. I look down at the glow of the enemy camp, the shadows shifting like teeth around the fires, and I know there can be no peace while they still breathe. Still march. Still kill.

Death Singer manifests, my fingers tightening around the hilt until the leather creaks. If surrender is the path to peace, then I was never meant for it. Because how can I save her... if I do not fight?

We fold into the ridge and drop like shadows behind the crest. The Blades settle around me, a circle of breathing steel and feathered silence, waiting for the word I haven't yet decided to give.

Orios lands beside me, breath barely a ghost. He leans close, voice a rasp only I can hear. "Patrols move the lines. Archers on the walls. Look." He jabs a thumb toward the encampment and my eyes find them, men pacing with lanterns, heads tilting to the sky, always watching. "And the ballistas." He nods toward a ring of gleaming machines near the center, their limbs heavy and cruel, gilded in filigree that catches the torchlight. Beautiful, deadly, without a doubt crafted by Fae hands

Around the camp, pyres burn in circles, threaded between tents. They carve the dark into pools of fire and shadow. From here we are nearly invisible, but any closer and the flames will bring us into the light. The men at those pyres will see movement long before our blades can silence them.

I weigh the options. Strike the ballistas first and risk exposure to the pyres and patrols. Slip a small band down to snuff the fires and disable the crew, then collapse the camp in one bite. Or burn everything to distraction and hope chaos hides us. None of them are clean. None of them promise Amara at the end.

Finally, I breathe out. "Hold," I tell them, and the word is a stone that drops into a still pool. "Orios. Take four. Quiet. Void-walk close to those pyres. Find the crews and silence the ballistas. Do it without bells." He nods once.

"The rest of you, archers on the walls."

The Blades incline their heads, no hesitation, only the silent promise of obedience.

My gaze sweeps the pyres burning bright across the camp, their flames turning night to false day. "I'll handle the fires. Even with their numbers, they don't stand a chance under darkness. We are Mordorin. The shadows bend to us."

"And then?" Orios asks.

"Then I find Zyphoro," I answer. "Then we return to the Grove."

My warriors need no further words. Each takes their helm in both hands and pulls it over their head. Faces vanish into shadowed hoods, eyes blaze white beneath the veil. Runes ignite across skin, pulsing like heartbeats, and wings unfurl with a hiss of smoke. They dissolve into the void one by one, curls of shadow and whispering air, until only Orios and I remain.

A low growl rumbles from his chest. "It has been too long since I've let my blade run wild. So many souls down there. So many sweet cries waiting to be ripped from their throats before I sever them."

"Only if you must," I cut in sharply.

His head snaps toward me, disbelief flickering in his eyes. "Rook?"

The stag's voice echoes in my skull, a whisper that gnaws at the edge of my resolve. *Peace cannot be found through victory. Only through surrender.* I war with the part of me that is born for killing and the part that wants to be worthy of her.

"If you can let them live," I say slowly, "then let them live." It's the closest I can come to mercy.

Orios bares his teeth, gaze flicking toward the encampment. "And if it comes down to my life…" He gestures toward the humans moving through the firelight. "…or theirs?"

I hesitate, only for a breath, before exhaling the answer that feels like a blade to my own chest.

"Then make it quick."

That earns a wolfish grin. "Yes, Rook."

He pulls on his helm, the shadows swallowing his face, but I can still hear that grin in his voice when he speaks again. "I always kill clean."

Then, with a ripple of smoke and a sharp crack of air, Orios steps into the void, leaving only the scent of ash and the promise of blood in his wake.

I watch them ghost through the camp, appear, vanish, reappear, void-walking along walls and through the shadows. My eyes bolt to the pyres. They are the threat that will betray us first. I must snuff them. Only if the fires die can we sift through the mess of tents, tear the camp open, find my sister. If she is not the same as when I last saw her, I take back my mercy. If they have harmed her, then kill them all, every last one, but leave the Golden Son for me.

I rise, full height to the highest crag. Smoke washes over me and my leathers unmake themselves into armor, black as starless night, etched with silver, runes seared into the steel until they hum under my skin. I flex my hands, the gauntlets sigh as the spikes kiss the leather. Smoke curls around my scaled pauldrons. A long black cloak unfurls behind me, catching the wind, and I settle the helm last, a shrouded hood that turns my face into a void. The last thing my enemies will see is the white storm of my eyes.

I arch my back and feel the muscles knit. My shadow-wings burst free, and my head falls back as I soak in their power. Then I hear him, the demon I keep caged beneath my ribs. He is always there, a low hunger I rarely feed. Emranth is a whisper compared to Gygarth, and if I could silence the Father of Below even for a flicker, then this thing is nothing I cannot bind.

When I call the wings, though, his voice comes clearer, slick and ravenous. "I hunger for blood," he murmurs in my head. "Is it time? Do we feast?"

I let a smirk cut across my face. "There may be a morsel for you, demon. But not yet. Back to the void."

He hisses and withdraws, folding into the dark.

My gaze hardens on the outer ring of pyres. They will fall first. That will give my Blades the sliver of shadow they need to move unseen and strike true.

I dangle a boot over the crag, feeling the valley yawn beneath. Few know the sensation of falling forever and never hearing the ground. Of tasting the end and then being hauled up into flight. I do.

It never dulls.

I step off and do exactly as I promised. Fall. The wind slams into me, hard enough to cut, stinging behind my eyes. Time fractures, everything accelerates beyond even Fae sight until the rocks below swell into a single, jagged mouth. For an instant I taste the end, before my wings fling themselves wide. The air catches me like a hand, hurling me back up. I pin them, shoulders burning, and drive forward, a shadow turned spear toward the camp.

It never dulls.

On any other night, I would send blades of smoke slicing through the throats of these humans, clean, silent deaths before they even knew I was there. But not tonight.

Tonight, I show restraint.

Seven coils of living shadow slip from my fingers, twisting like serpents through the air. They wind around fragile human necks, not to kill, but to silence. The coils tighten just enough to steal breath, to draw the light from their eyes until they crumple soundlessly to the ground. The air stirs, the wood creaks beneath me as I land on the wall.

The first pyre blazes below. I stretch out my hands and call to the smoke. It answers, swirling and writhing before me, alive and hungry. With a thought, I send it forth. The smoke lashes around the flames, devouring the fire whole until nothing remains but a bed of cooling embers.

I rise again. East wall. More Legion soldiers fall. More fires die. Each extinguished blaze paints the camp in deeper shadow, until the darkness itself begins to feel alive beneath my wings. The Blades strike with precision, but even in the frenzied heat of battle, they obey. No blood spills. Not yet. We will take this camp through cunning, not slaughter.

Orios and his contingent of Blades reach the ballistas, their forms ghosting through the shadows. He disarms the crews without a sound, without breaking a sweat, with a skill honed over centuries, and begins dismantling the gilded machines. Ithranor craftsmanship. Beautiful, terrible things. Like everything the Fae touch.

A parting gift from Anethesis. I snarl, canines sliding free. If only I had killed him myself. The bliss of feeling his light go out under my hands. Steel is quick but cold, impersonal. Hands on flesh are different. To close my fingers around a throat, to watch the fire in someone's eyes gutter and die. There is no greater satisfaction.

I smother the east wall, then the south. The last of the pyres collapses into smoke and ash. The archers and ballista crews lie still, unconscious, disarmed. Not a drop of blood spilled. The camp is ours.

But where is my sister?

I land hard in the center of the camp, boots striking earth beside the last burning pyre. Smoke coils up around me, wrapping my armor in shifting shadow. I wait, eyes sweeping over the maze of tents, expecting the Legion to flood from them in waves of steel and fury. But nothing moves. Nothing breathes.

My jaw tightens.

Across the clearing, I catch Orios's gaze, the same unease written on his face. We Mordorin are no strangers to victory, but this kind of surrender is not in our enemy's nature.

I storm toward the nearest tent and rip the canvas flap aside. Empty. No soldiers. No sound. Only a single candle burning low, its flame barely clinging to life. I move to the next tent, and the next. All the same.

"Rook!" Orios calls out as I step from another tent. "There is no one here."

My fists clench. I tear off my helm and suck in a ragged breath, smoke burning my throat.

"Zyphoro!" My voice cracks the night, raw and sharp, carrying all the guilt, all the grief I have buried for centuries, the thousand apologies I owe her for the life she lost. "Where are you?"

The wind steals the echo, and silence answers me again.

The Blades scour the camp, tearing through every corner, but the only sign of the Legion are our prisoners. The rest are gone. Vanished.

Orios finds me again, eyes cutting across the emptiness. "Why does she not answer? Why doesn't she void walk? What could these humans possibly do to contain her?"

He's right. Nothing in this realm could silence Zyphoro. Nothing mortal.

"I'll ask them myself," I snarl.

In a single bound I clear half the encampment, landing hard on the wall platform, wood splintering beneath me. I seize a Legion lookout by the collar and haul him into the air, his body limp, his head lolling.

"Wake up," I boom. When he doesn't stir, I shake him until his teeth rattle. "I said wake up!"

His eyes snap open and the moment he sees me, terror floods his face. His hands claw at my wrist as he realizes I'm holding him over the edge.

"Where is Zyphoro Phaedren?" I snarl, my voice cracking like thunder. My eyes blaze white, the shadows bending away from me. "Where is my sister?"

"I will tell you nothing," he hisses through gritted teeth, though fear threads every syllable. "I would rather die."

"Oh, you will die," I growl, my fist closing in the collar of his shirt until the weave groans. "But not soon. Not quick. It will be long and slow. I will cut through each layer of your soft flesh, pull out what should stay inside and lay it beside you so you can *see* the horror with your own eyes. Then I will sew you back and start again. Is that what you mean when you say you would rather die?"

His eyes brim, his lip trembles. Heat crawls up my throat as I watch piss soak dark through his trousers and drip onto the camp below.

"Where is Zyphoro?" I ask again.

Those horrified, watery eyes flick to the monstrous banner at the camp's center. I follow his gaze to the Legion of Saints flag, red cloth, golden crossed swords framed by praying hands and feel the bile rise.

I shake him. "You lie!" I snarl.

"No!" he keens. "Please. She's there, I swear it! Under the banner."

His words bring no comfort, only a fresh, blade-sharp ache. If she lies beneath that flag, why is she silent? Why is she still?

I fling him aside, not over the platform but hard enough that he slams into the wooden wall and collapses into a damp, pathetic ball of sobs.

My wings snap free, and I charge the banner, landing at its base. I crane my neck and stare up into the shadowed folds, every muscle coiled. Still, I cannot see her. The human's confession tastes like ash in my mouth. I will find his tongue, rip out his lies, and make him swallow them whole.

Then I see a thick mast of wood, rough and splintered, with a crossbeam nailed through its middle. The banner hangs from it, heavy and crimson. My heart goes still.

I reach out, grab a fistful of the fabric, twist it tight around my hand. For a breath, I can't move. Then I pull. The banner tears free with a rip, the red sheet catching the wind as it falls away.

Revealing Zyphoro.

Her arms are chained to the cross, her legs lashed to the post, and around her throat gleams a silver collar.

"No..." The word is a breath, a plea, a curse. "No."

My wings flare wide, and I rise to meet her. Her curls hang limp and matted, clotted with dirt and blood. The stench of filth and piss burns my throat. I bite my lip hard as I brush the hair from her face.

"Zyphoro," I whisper, the name splintering in my mouth. "Sister... do you hear me?"

She doesn't stir. Doesn't breathe. Her skin is ash-grey beneath the grime, her lips cracked and colorless. What hangs before me now is only the husk of her, the shadow left behind after light burns out.

"Zyphoro..." I try again, the sound barely more than breath. "Please."

The silence that answers is unbearable. It presses into my chest, fills the space where hope should live. My heart stutters, and I can feel that familiar, suffocating weight settling over me. Too late. I was too late again.

I rest my forehead against hers, closing my eyes against the sting. "I'm here," I whisper. "I'm here now."

And then a sound. Faint. Trembling.

A murmur so small it could have been the sigh of the wind, but I know it. I *feel* it.

Her lips part, and a thin, broken whisper escapes.

"Daedalus..."

Then, slowly, her head shifts, just enough for her to lift it a fraction, her breath shaking.

"Daedalus," she says again, her voice the rasp of torn glass. "It hurts."

She tilts her head, what little strength she has spent on the motion. The collar gleams, cruel and bright.

Fury scorches through me.

Fucking Anethesis. Fucking Ithranor.

I know this device. These collars were forged to choke Fae magic. They are outlawed. Ordered to be destroyed... or so I believed.

Another gift from Ithranor to their precious Legion. A chain made for the Mordorin.

I have no key for this collar, only fury, and no time.

I slip my fingers beneath the cold silver, jaw locking as I call the smoke. It coils around my wrist, then threads itself over the collar, loop after loop, hissing as it tightens. Power snarls through me, the runes along my arms ignite. One final pull...crack.

The collar shatters, falling in a rain of silver grains that glitter before vanishing into the dirt.

Zyphoro gasps, the sound sharp and broken, as if she's bursting through the surface of a black sea. Her eyes open, raw and red, and her breath trembles out of her. When she finally finds her voice, it's not gratitude that spills from her cracked lips.

"Where the fuck were you?"

Her words are a blade I deserve, but I'm too relieved to complain.

I send smoke to the chains that bind her. They twist, constrict, and splinter apart until she collapses forward, weightless in my arms. Her hands clutch at my neck, her head pressing weakly against my chest.

"Thank you, brother," she whispers, voice small and hoarse.

I hold her tighter, lowering us gently to the ground. When my boots touch the earth, Orios and the Blades are already there.

"The camp is abandoned, Rook," Orios says, anger trembling beneath his calm. "Where are they?"

I prop Zyphoro up, her body still slumped against me. "Sister," I murmur, "what happened here? Where is the Legion?"

She draws a breath, her chin lifting with visible effort. "It was a trap, brother. They knew you would come. They needed you away from the Grove."

"Why?" Orios demands. "Why not face us here?"

But I already know. The truth curdles cold in my gut.

"It's not *us* they want," I say softly. "It never was."

"They want the Grove," Zyphoro breathes. "They want Amara."

My voice lowers, heavy. "And the Golden Son. Did he do this to you?"

She shakes her head, weak but certain. "They threw us in shackles the moment we arrived. He was a prisoner, like me. I don't know where he is now."

401

I glimpse Orios.

He shakes his head. "He is not here, Rook."

I look down at Zyphoro, brushing a thumb against the bruises at her throat. "We're returning to the Grove. Can you fly?"

She nods faintly, rubbing at her neck. "I'm already stronger. Free of that collar, I can feel my magic stirring again."

"I haven't seen one of those in centuries," I mutter. "I can't believe the Legion dared use them." Then the memory strikes, sharp and sudden. "But only a Fae can enchant such a collar."

Zyphoro bites her bottom lip, a snarl bleeding through. "Yes, brother. That is true."

"Then who?"

"The Legion has a new leader. It was under his command we were imprisoned. He is the one who fastened the collar around my throat." Her gaze spears mine.

I shake my head, refusing the truth even as it settles like ice in my veins. "No. It cannot be."

But she nods, a harsh certainty in her eyes.

"Yes," she breathes. "Anethesis is here."

CHAPTER 41
DAED

What a fool I am to have underestimated the Legion. To have forgotten that even the great Fae Houses, eternal, unbending, ancient as the stars, fell to these humans in the blink of an eye. How easily I dismissed them, believing time itself had made me wiser. As if age alone could make me clever. As if centuries of watching the sun rise and set could teach me more than the desperation of a mortal soul.

My arrogance will cost me everything I swore to protect.

I thought I knew speed. Thought I'd felt the limit of my wings, the ache of air turned to fire against my face. But not until now. The wind lashes my skin, sharp as needles. My wings blaze through the night, and the sky screams around me.

Orios, Zyphoro, and the Blades are at my back, voices carried thin on the wind, shouting for me to slow, to wait. But I cannot. Every heartbeat, every mile between me and the Grove is another life lost to the Legion and if it's true, if Anethesis has returned, if he commands them now, then his hunger for Amara must be endless.

Does he know she sleeps beneath the earth? Does he understand what he's meddling with? Or will his impatience drive him to drag her from the soil before she is whole. Before magic can anchor her to life again?

And if he does... if his blasphemous presence defiles that sacred ground, if he provokes the faeries, the Souls who guard her, will they abandon their work and leave her to fade? What if Mirael and Erania, and the Tenders who remain, are swallowed into that same darkness? What if the Grove dies with them?

The forest rises on the horizon. The haze parts, and the silence I once called sacred is gone.

Now the night is alive with screams and the wind carries the stench of blood.

We break through the treeline into a cacophony of chaos, and it takes me a moment to be sure my eyes are not deceiving me. A golem of living stone towers above, its granite fists slamming through ranks of Legion soldiers. Each strike sends men flying, armor crumpling like paper. Their screams echo through the Grove, drowned by the thunder of the creature's roar. At its feet, mauling bears, beasts of vine and fur, hold the line. Their stone claws tear through human steel, powerful jaws rip flesh from bone.

I dive low, wings slicing the air. Legion soldiers scatter below me like startled insects.

"Hold the line!" one screams before a bear swats him into a tree so hard the bark splits.

The Blades fan out behind me, their armor singing with motion. I signal for some to break formation, dropping to join the defense alongside the forces of the Grove. The rest stay tight on my trail as I streak deeper into the forest.

The vine wall comes into view, and beyond it, I can see smoke rising from the village. My gut twists.

They've made it through.

Beside me, Orios's eyes widen, his face hard as stone.

"Solena," he breathes. Even through the noise, I hear her name on his lips.

I meet his gaze and nod once. That's all he needs. He banks left, wings flaring wide as he dives toward the village.

I force my eyes forward, toward the lavender blossoms in the distance. Toward the clearing where Amara sleeps. That is where I should be. Where I *need* to be.

But the screams rip through me. Fear. Terror. Pain. Each cry cleaving me down the middle.

I grit my teeth, then growl, turning sharply, wings pinned back as I spear towards the village with Zyphoro at my side.

The vine wall burns, flames devouring it whole as smoke billows skyward, smothering the village in a choking charcoal haze. Light dies beneath it.

Bodies lie everywhere. Too many to count, the ground slick with blood, rivers spilling past the benches where we once sat to eat, pooling beneath an overturned pot by the hearth.

Some Tenders still fight, swinging weapons with shaking hands. Others flee into the trees, praying the forest will shelter them.

I have seen war. I have seen carnage.

But this scene. This massacre, will haunt me forever.

So much hate.

So much death.

So much blood.

Orios tears through Legion soldiers, hurling them aside, cleaving bone and flesh without slowing.

He hunts for Solena, every unfortunate fool who crosses his path cut down before they even scream. But the black, stinging smoke blinds everything.

It rises from an inferno at the center of the village, a conflagration that roars, spitting flame in every direction, tossing sparks that leap and catch and spread.

I land hard, shielding my eyes as heat lashes my face. Zyphoro drops beside me, and her hushed gasp cuts through the mayhem.

"Gods," she breathes, hand flying to her mouth. I have never seen her look so horrified. "It's Ronin."

There he stands, bound to a pyre in the center of the flames. Engulfed. Burning.

He does not scream.

His silence is worse.

For a heartbeat, I think him already dead, but his eyes are open, jaw clenched, and when they meet mine I move.

Wings snap wide, blasting wind that smothers the flames. Then I hurl clouds of smoke, choking what remains of the fire. Zyphoro does the same, dousing burning beams as sparks hiss and die beneath our magic.

I rush to Ronin's side, tearing him from the pyre, hauling his charred weight over my shoulder. His skin, gods, his skin, but there is no time to think, no time to feel.

The healer's cottage still stands. Somehow untouched.

I slam my boot into the door, shattering it inward.

A scream pierces the room. Solena stands before Reon's bed, sword raised, eyes wild. When she sees me, she nearly collapses with relief.

I glance back over my shoulder.

"Orios!" I roar. "She is in here!"

It takes less than a breath for Orios to come barreling through the door, tossing his sword aside as he scoops her into his arms.

I carry Ronin onto the nearest cot while Reon fights and groans nearby, desperate to haul himself up.

"Stay there," I snap over my shoulder.

"Fuck you," Reon spits. "If I'm going to die, I'm doing it on my feet, not my fucking back."

I turn back to Ronin. His chest heaves in ragged stutters. There's almost nothing left of him, burned hollow like Amara when I found her in Baev'kalath. I know it's him only by scent, that stubborn human trace under the char.

"Ronin," I say. He gurgles. "Where is Anethesis?"

He convulses on the cot, limbs buckled and twitching, smoke curling off blackened skin. "Amara," he rasps.

That's all I need. I spin on my heel and storm past Orios, Solena still in his arms. I grip his shoulder as I pass. He looks up, eyes raw.

"Stay here," I command. "Bring these bastards to their knees. Every fucking one of them. Do you understand, Reaper?"

He nods. I don't wait.

Zyphoro steps aside when she arrives at the threshold. "Where are you going?"

I don't slow. I don't look back.

No more mercy. No more surrender.

"To kill Anethesis," I say, and take to the air.

I am a bolt of smoke and shadow as I tear past the vine wall toward the clearing. Even as I become a blur through night and wind, it is not fast enough. I rend open the void and spear through darkness in a plume of smoke, reemerging in the clearing to find Anethesis standing on the soil that holds Amara, Mirael on her knees before him, her hair wrapped in his fist. I hit the ground with a heavy thud.

"Anethesis! Stop!"

The hunched figure freezes. When he turns and the moonlight spills across his face, the creature that looks back at me is no longer the jade-eyed Fae I hunted across the Untold Sea. His features are a map of crevices and ridges carved deep into his once porcelain skin. One eye is fused shut by a thick scar, the other pale as fog. Half his mouth droops, slack and trembling, unable to close. What remains of his golden hair clings in uneven tufts to a ravaged scalp.

"My prince," he spits, his words slippery. A sound like something dying. "It is... so good to see you again."

"Let her go," I command, my voice sharp as steel, eyes flicking to Mirael. She thrashes in his grip, her breath short, defiant even through her pain.

Anethesis only tightens his hold, winding his fingers deeper into her hair until she hisses through her teeth. "I think not," he replies, that calm, precise tone still intact. "She has told me some interesting things, this one. That Amara is buried, but not dead." He glances around the clearing. "She will not tell me where though, and I see no disturbed earth."

I fight not to, but I cannot stop my gaze from flicking to the patch of blossoms at his feet. The place where the earth breathes and Amara sleeps. He notices. Of course he does, and when he stomps his boot on the soil, I hiss under my breath.

"She's down there, isn't she?" His voice slides into a purr, and he yanks Mirael's head back until she gasps. "At first, I thought the little Tender was lying. Why bury something that isn't dead? But it makes sense now. The Jewel of the Tenders, hidden beneath the earth like treasure. But it is time for her to come back to the light." He pulls harder on Mirael's hair, and she sobs. "I want to leave, Daedalus. Gods, how I want to leave. But I need sweet Amara to do it."

"She cannot open a portal, Anethesis," I say, forcing calm into my voice. "She doesn't know how."

He laughs, a broken, gurgling sound that dies in his throat. "No, perhaps not. But her blood remembers. Her *Awakened* blood. Once it's spilled, once she speaks the words I taught her, even if she doesn't understand them, the gate will open. Meranor will call me home." He meets my gaze, and for the briefest moment, there's a flicker of the Fae he once was. "And then, at last, I will be... at peace."

The irony stings.

For a heartbeat, I almost pity him. He has hunted, killed, and crossed worlds for what he's lost, as I have. He loves Meranor as I love Amara. His devotion is a mirror of my own obsession, warped and festering. We are two sides of the same broken coin. Two selfish fools clinging to the same dream, and there's no reasoning with Anethesis, just as there's no reasoning with me. I know deep down, one of us will not survive this.

"One last time," I say, breath burning in my chest. "Let her go."

He lifts his other hand, his fingers curl, and the air around us stirs. Leaves lift from the ground, caught in a whirl of power that gathers in his palm.

"Amara's death will not be in vain," he says softly, ignoring my threats. "I want you to remember that when you die, Daedalus. All of Meranor will know of Amara's sacrifice. For all eternity, they will weep her name."

The whirl at Anethesis's fingertips grows, slow at first, a small twist of air that hums against my skin. Inch by inch it widens, gathering speed until the clearing itself trembles. My cloak lashes my legs, my hair whips across my eyes. The funnel stretches skyward, cutting through the canopy until it punches a hole clean through the trees. Harsh white moonlight pours through, spilling across the grove like a wound torn open.

The wind surges in every direction, shoving the long grass flat, tearing at the vines that drape the trees. Lavender blossoms rip free, spinning into the air in a rush of purple and silver and then, one by one, the flowers above Amara's resting place rise. First the petals, delicate as breath, then the stalks, then the roots, until the very soil itself lifts in trembling layers.

My heart hammers. Beneath the roar, I see the thin golden threads weaving through the dirt, stretching between us, but they're fraying. Fractured. What was once unbreakable iron is now splintered and fading. My mark. My bite. The link between our souls. I reach for it, desperate, but her heartbeat beneath the earth is faint.

It's too soon. If she wakes now, she'll die.

"Anethesis!" I roar.

Smoke coils around my arm as Death Singer manifests in my grip, its blade gleaming like a captured star. I hurl myself into the wind, muscles burning as I fight the storm's pull. Each step is agony, each breath, a war against the air.

Anethesis only smiles. With one scarred hand, he lifts Mirael off her feet as easily as if she weighed nothing and flings her into the raging vortex.

Her scream splits the night.

She spirals upward, swallowed by the cyclone, her body flung higher and higher until she's a blur amid the storm of debris. Then, as the wind shifts, she drops, arms flailing, hair streaming, a mortal comet plummeting toward the earth.

I look to Anethesis. He watches me through the chaos, his face calm, almost serene. Another layer of earth tears free, dirt and roots ripped away.

Do I let Mirael fall? Do I trade her life to end Anethesis? To save Amara?

I'm sorry, Mirael.

A blur of motion cuts through the storm.

Zyphoro.

She bursts into the clearing like vengeance itself, wings cracking the air like thunder. Her hair is wild, her runes blazing. She climbs through the vortex with impossible speed and snatches Mirael from the air, just before she hits the ground.

Relief barely has time to register before I move. My wings explode from my back, black smoke spiraling outward, swallowing moonlight whole. I drive forward, hard, fast, colliding with Anethesis with all the force of a boulder. The impact cracks the world open.

We slam into a tree at the clearing's edge. The ancient trunk splinters under the force, groaning as bark and branches rain down.

The cyclone dies with a shuddering sigh, collapsing into silence as soil and blossoms fall like ash from the sky.

We hit the ground in a tangle of limbs. I'm on him before he can rise, my knee in his chest, Death Singer raised high. Smoke curls along its edge, hungry, alive.

"Now is the time?" Emranth hisses from the pit of my mind. "Yes, yes. Fae blood is sweetest. This one is old. Aged like wine."

But I couldn't care less about the demon's hunger.

Anethesis stares up at me, his one cloudy eye wide. The color long gone, but deep beneath that milky surface there's a flicker. Fear. That small, trembling glimmer when the soul finally sees death coming for it. And I *am* death.

"You're no better than them," he spits, his fingers, ringed with scars, scratching at my wrists, desperate, trembling. "A killer of Fae. You butcher your own kind, Daedalus. The last of us left!"

My jaw tightens. I bring both hands to Death Singer's hilt, and the blade hums with my fury. The runes across my chest ignite, flaring violet-bright. "Perhaps that's what this world needs," I mutter, and there is a clarity threaded through the words. "The time of the Fae is over, Anethesis. Let the humans have their turn. Let *her* lead them."

The sword trembles in my hands, the tip pressing closer to his throat. Emranth growls, a low, guttural plea for blood, but I don't need the encouragement. This is for everything Anethesis has done. For that night in Pariseth when my world changed forever. For the Grove. For Amara.

He wants peace? Then I'll give him the only kind he deserves. The kind found in silence and eternal dark.

Smoke whips from my back, serpentine and alive, lashing around his wrists and driving them into the dirt. He thrashes, chokes, the ground trembling beneath him as I raise Death Singer high, ready to end this once and for all.

And then his lips twist. "*Nael tir'an velthra.*"

The words slither through the air like a curse.

I roar. Something cold snaps tight around my throat then a click, final and cruel.

The blade dissolves in my hand. My fingers rake at my neck, scraping against polished metal. A collar. Smooth, seamless.

My wings falter, the shadow bleeding from them like smoke escaping a cracked vessel. I reach for the void, my power, my rage, but it slides through my grasp, slipping away like mist through fingers.

And then... nothing.

No smoke. No shadows. No void. Not even Emranth.

I feel the warmth drain from me. My veins turn to ice beneath my skin, the color leeching away until I'm the shade of ash. My lips move soundlessly, shaping half-formed words, the horror of what's been done stealing even the air from my lungs.

Before I can take another breath, Anethesis thrusts his hand forward.

The wind strikes like a hammer. It tears me from him, hurling me backward. My spine collides with the same ancient tree we shattered moments ago. The trunk groans under the impact, splitting wider, its age-old strength finally faltering. I drop to my knees, pulling at the collar, just as the tree gives a long, low creak and topples.

I have no wings to carry me. No smoke to shield me. Not even the void to vanish into.

I lurch to my feet and run, throwing myself clear just as the massive trunk crashes to the ground. The impact shakes the earth, throwing up a storm of dust and bark and leaves.

I gasp for air, lungs burning. As the dust clears, I catch a flash of movement above. Zyphoro with Mirael still in her arms.

"No!" I shout, arm stretched toward her. "Zyphoro, get away!"

Too late.

Anethesis's voice slices through the chaos. He whispers the curse again. His finger rises, and a streak of silver leaps from it like a lightning bolt. It catches her, coiling around her throat.

The collar locks with a sharp metallic click, my sister caged once again.

Her wings vanish mid-flight. She plummets.

In the fleeting time that follows, as she tumbles towards the earth, Zyphoro folds herself around Mirael, cocooning the human tight against her chest. The two of them spin through the air and, at the last instant, Zyphoro turns, her back crashing against the earth, taking the shattering impact.

I turn on Anethesis, voice breaking with rage. "You shame our ancestors by using this device!" I snarl. "You desecrate everything sacred! Even in desperation, the old covenants must be honored!"

He stares at me for a heartbeat, expressionless, then shakes his scarred head. "As you said, Daedalus," he murmurs, almost gently. "The time of the Fae is over. The old laws mean nothing now."

His gaze slides back to the churned soil, to where Amara lies beneath the broken earth. His lips curve in a small, terrible smile. "Now. Where was I?"

He stretches out his hand, and the air twists once more. The vortex roars to life, faster, stronger than before, clawing deeper into the ground.

I stagger to my feet, every muscle screaming. No wings, no magic, just fury and flesh and the promise I made her. I charge, but the air catches me mid-stride.

It wraps around me like iron bands, lifting me from the ground. My arms lock at my sides, ribs compressing under the pressure. I hang there, helpless, forced to watch as Anethesis digs deeper, closer to her.

Her heartbeat is a whisper now, barely a flutter against the pull of the cold creeping into my bones.

"You don't understand!" I shout, voice hoarse. "She will die!"

But Anethesis doesn't hear me. Or perhaps he does and simply doesn't care. He is far beyond reason, beyond redemption. There is nothing left in him but obsession. All he wants is Amara. All he craves is Meranor. Nothing else matters.

Then, through the roar of the vortex and the shatter of my pleas, the forest stirs.

The wind shifts. It hums. Voices rise from within the trees, low and resonant, their song threaded with age and power. The melody crawls under my skin, vibrating in my bones, until the whole world seems to thrum with it. The trees groan and bow as branches twist, and from the darkness, a thousand green eyes open, ancient and furious.

The first strike comes from the sky.

A flood of birds bursts from the canopy, their feathers flashing like shards of flame and gemstone as they dive, screaming, toward Anethesis. They fall upon him like a storm of arrows.

He snarls, throwing out his arm. A gust of wind tears through the air, scattering the flock in all directions. But in doing so, his concentration wavers, and I *feel* it. The invisible grip around my body loosens.

I drag in a breath, force my limbs to move, to fight.

Then the ground trembles.

The next wave comes on four legs. Wolves burst from the treeline, moving with inexplicable speed, blurs of motion, even to my eyes. Their howls split the air, a wild, ancient sound, as they descend upon the clearing. From the other side come the boars, muscled beasts, their tusks carved from stone, their hides thick and earthen. They crash through the undergrowth, charging headlong for Anethesis.

The Souls.

The forest itself rises to protect its Jewel.

Anethesis spits bitter curses, summoning wall after wall of wind to hold back the onslaught. The gale rips through the clearing, flattening grass and lavender alike, but the more he defends, the more his power splinters and then his hold on me breaks entirely.

I hit the ground hard, roll, and come up in a crouch. The collar still burns cold against my throat, but I no longer care. If I can't wield magic, I'll wield rage. If I can't summon smoke, I'll use my hands. I like using my hands.

I charge.

He doesn't see me at first, too busy battling nature's wrath. But before I reach him, fresh foes spill across the field. Legion soldiers pour in from the west, from the direction of the village. Their boots crush the lavender underfoot, dragging blood and muck through the grass as they surge forward, blades flashing.

Wolves meet steel, tusks meet shields, screams and howls fill the night. Flesh rends and metal shatters. Blood paints the earth, Fae, beast, and man alike, and still, through it all, the vortex rages. The earth continues to tear itself open.

I launch myself at Anethesis, fingers closing hot and merciless around his throat. The vortex stammers, wavers, loses a breath of power.

He slams his hands to mine, jaw a hard line, clawing at my grip. His skin is paper-thin beneath my fists. It splits under the pressure, warm wetness slicking my palms. He hisses, gurgles, a ragged plea. But the cyclone eats every scrap of his strength. He has nothing left to give me.

I squeeze. His eyes bulge wide, veins blackening beneath the sick, bruised purple of his skin as the air wheezes out of him in wet, rasping gasps. I don't stop. I squeeze harder.

Then, absurd and fragile against the slaughter, a rabbit appears. Tiny and white and utterly out of place. It hops through the crimson grass as if the world were still simple, as if it were still spring. It pauses at the edge of the vortex, lifts a paw to its nose, and is calm in a way that feels like a rebuke. For one impossible heartbeat I think the Souls have sent it as a sign, some small mercy in the madness.

An arrow snaps free. Sharp, sudden. Whether aimed true or stray, it finds the rabbit's chest. The shaft pierces through fur and flesh, its dark eyes gloss and close. It collapses like a dropped thing, the tiny body folding into the earth.

The pain that rips through me is not rational. It is something primal, hollow and vast, a raw wound clawing its way up from my gut, burning through my chest until it tears free of my throat in a sound I barely recognize as my own and then I understand.

It isn't just the rabbit I mourn.

It's the silence. The unbearable, suffocating silence where her heartbeat should be. The bond between us, those golden threads I have felt all my life, lies severed, lifeless.

I can't hear her. I can't feel her.

Amara... is gone.

CHAPTER 42
DAED

The world crumbles around me, but it means nothing.

Anethesis thrashes beneath my hands, his pulse fluttering like a trapped bird, his breath wet and broken against my knuckles. I should end him. But is vengeance when the only heartbeat that tethered me to this wretched world has gone still?

Our bond was never just magic. It was fate. A golden thread woven through every piece of me, binding my darkness to her light. I felt her in everything, in the pull of the void, the whisper of smoke, the rise and fall of my breath. She was my constant, the warmth beneath my ribs, the tether that kept me from becoming nothing.

And now she's gone. Torn away, leaving only this harrowing silence.

I want to fill it with her voice, the way my name sounded on her lips.

How can this be the end? How do I keep breathing?

My hands slip from Anethesis's throat, falling useless at my sides as I collapse to my knees. My head bows, breath ragged, the fight bleeding out of me until there's nothing left but the hollow thrum of loss.

Anethesis staggers backward, clutching at his neck, drawing in greedy, wheezing gulps of air. He watches me, wary and bewildered, waiting for the trick, for the snare I no longer have the will to spring.

"What are you doing?" he rasps.

"She's gone," I whisper, the words splintering on my tongue. "She was all that mattered. Now nothing matters. So kill me."

He frowns, uncomprehending. "What?"

"You heard me," I murmur. "Kill me."

Hope leaves me in pieces, thin wisps of smoke escaping through my chest. Amara was everything. With her gone, I have lost more than love. I have lost the future, the means to bring Estra back from An'kel, to restore what was stolen. The flame of another Awakened has gone dark, and with it, every possibility their magic could have given us. Just like Zema before her.

Anethesis glances toward the vortex still clawing at the earth. "What do you mean, she's gone?"

"The earth was healing her," I say through clenched teeth. "But you wouldn't listen."

He swallows hard. "No. She can't be gone. She's Awakened."

I snarl. "And since when has that made them immortal?"

"No..." His voice trembles, panic crawling through it like cracks in glass. "No, no, no. She can't be dead. I need her. I need the portal. I need to get to Meranor. I need to get *home!*"

He throws his arm toward the vortex, but instead of rising higher, it collapses. The wind dies, the soil settles, and my hair falls heavy against my face.

Anethesis stumbles forward, half crawling, half running. Twice he trips before reaching the upturned mound of dirt. He drops to his knees and digs, fists clawing at the dirt, hurling it aside in frantic handfuls. The sight of him, this once-proud lord reduced to a madman scrabbling in the mud, turns my stomach.

Through the fog of grief, I drag myself upright. My limbs shake beneath the weight of my despair, but still, I move. Step by step. Until I stand behind him, watching the soil fly.

"Enough, Anethesis," I say, voice breaking.

He doesn't listen. He continues to mindlessly dig.

"I said enough!"

But my plea comes too late. The dirt gives way to flesh, and my stomach lurches. Gods. It's her.

"Stop!" I seize his arm and wrench it back, but he tears free with a wild cry, throwing himself forward again. Nails rake through the soil, clawing deeper, unearthing her an inch at a time.

"Get away from her!" I roar, lunging. My hands hook beneath his arms, dragging him away.

Anethesis jolts in my grip, and when something slams into my ribs, I think he's driven an elbow into my chest. The pain is blinding, far too strong for the state he's in. I release him, then stumble and drop to one knee.

Then it strikes again.

Harder.

A violent pulse beneath my sternum.

I choke on a gasp, clutching my chest. Another impact follows. And another.

But Anethesis isn't touching me.

He isn't even close.

This isn't him.

It's my own heart, pounding like it's trying to tear free of me. Heat flares bright through my vision. I press both palms to my chest, gasping around the ache, the world tunneling to that merciless rhythm.

And then... a second heartbeat.

I go still.

Fear and hope collide inside me. I stagger toward the mound of disturbed earth. I hover there, trembling, suspended between terror and desperate belief. I don't want to see. I can't bear to, but I make myself look.

The soil cradles her face, the soft curve of her cheek, the slope of her nose, the mouth I have kissed and cursed and prayed for. She lies utterly still, burned and quiet and unbearably beautiful.

Something inside me breaks.

I stumble back, dragging my hands into my hair, pulling until pain shoots across my scalp. My heart riots, a frantic drum. I will tear it out of my chest before I let it lie to me again.

And then her eyes open, bright as the dawn and blazing.

A blinding shock of green light erupts from them, slamming into me with such force I'm thrown backward. I shield my face, but the radiance sears through my fingers, painting the world in emerald flame.

The beam bursts skyward, piercing through the canopy, shattering the night. The very air trembles. The battle halts. Legion soldiers stare, slack-jawed, blades falling from their hands. The beasts retreat, step by slow step, into the dark embrace of the forest.

"I told you!" Anethesis cries, voice shrill with wild ecstasy. "She cannot die!"

The earth heaves beneath us. The wind spirals, keening like the cry of gods, and the stars seem to shrink away, and then she rises, my Amara. Her arms outstretched, her chin dipped low, her body aglow with that same impossible light. The earth falls from her like dust shaken from a dream. The glow carries her upward, wrapping her in radiance and life.

Her wounds are gone. Every burn erased, leaving not even the faintest shadows of what had been. Her skin is even richer, smoother, bronzer than before, her hair longer, spilling in silken waves, tumbling past her knees.

A mantle of living moss and tiny blooms drapes over her body, clinging as though the forest itself had risen to claim her, to mark her as its own reborn queen.

And over her face rests a sheer emerald veil, the fabric is nearly transparent, a breath of green that barely softens the lines beneath: the curve of her cheek, the quiet shape of her lips, the rise of her breath that moves the gossamer like a sigh.

She looks untouched by death.

Untouched by anything but power.

"Amara!" Anethesis's voice shatters the moment. He staggers to his feet, arms outstretched, his face lit with manic devotion. "Look how glorious you have become! Allow me to ease the weight of that power, sweet Awakened."

My stomach twists. I see the hunger in his eyes, the same blasphemous greed that drove him to ruin. I know what he means to do before his lips even part. The collar. The curse.

"Don't..." I choke out, but it's too late.

Amara moves.

Her hands rise, palms facing outward, and she traces mirrored sigils in the air. I don't understand the gestures. I don't need to. The ground answers.

Vines burst from the earth beneath Anethesis's feet. They wind up his legs, his torso, his arms, binding him tight. He gasps before the vines coil around his throat. One vine pauses, hovering, almost curious and then drives forward, forcing itself between his lips.

His eyes bulge, his body convulsing as the vine burrows deeper. The sound is wet, terrible. I want to look away but cannot. His throat swells and pulses and then, impossibly, beauty blooms from the horror.

Golden blossoms spill from his mouth, delicate petals bursting open, followed by smaller vines studded with heart-shaped leaves. The growth spreads swiftly, mercilessly, devouring him whole. In moments, Anethesis is gone, consumed entirely, his body replaced by a towering sculpture of vines and flowers, swaying gently in the wind as though it had always been there.

The air stills. His magic vanishes with him. The collar around my throat loosens and fades to dust.

I rise slowly, circling the floral monument that was once the Lord of House Ithranor. My steps falter as I look to her. My wife.

I have never feared Amara. I have fought beside her, bled for her, loved her with the reckless arrogance of a warrior who thought himself unbreakable. I believed I was the stronger of us, the darker, the more dangerous. But as she hovers above me, silent and radiant, her emerald robes flowing like banners of the earth itself, I understand how foolish I have been.

"Wife," I say, my voice barely a breath. "Amara. My love."

She does not answer. The veil ripples faintly across her face, concealing whatever emotion might live beneath it.

Without a word, Amara turns from me, gliding through the air toward the fallen rabbit, the small, broken thing lying still in the grass with the arrow through its heart.

She descends in silence. Bare feet touch the ground like whispers. Her green robe parts as she kneels, the moss and blossoms pluming around her like breath. One slender hand slips from the long sleeve and hovers over the creature. She traces a single knuckle along its fur, matted and red.

I move closer anyway, my steps slow and careful, wanting her to know I am here, yet terrified she might look at me.

"Amara," I murmur.

No reply. She doesn't so much as flinch. Her touch remains tender, as if the rabbit might stir under her hand at any moment.

"Amara," I try again. "It's me. Daed."

Still nothing. It's as though she's elsewhere entirely, half here, half somewhere beyond my reach.

I stand close enough to feel the faint pull of her magic, the warmth of the bond that still ties us. Her scent drifts toward me, earth and rain and the faint sweetness of blossoms, and it breaks me open in quiet ache. I want to touch her, to fall to my knees and beg her to see me, but I wait. I've always waited. For her beneath the ground, above the clouds, across the sea. I could wait an eternity more if that's what she asked of me.

She lifts her hand, her fingers brushing the shaft of the arrow buried in the rabbit's chest. The wood is slick with blood, far too large for such a fragile creature. She studies it a moment, then closes her hand around it.

"We can bury it, if you wish," I say softly. My words sound foolish in the hush that follows.

Then, swift as the snap of a branch, she yanks the arrow free. The small body jerks with the motion before going still again. Amara tosses the arrow aside and gathers the rabbit in both hands.

The earth trembles beneath my boots.

A shiver ripples through the clearing, a breath through the bones of the world. I hear voices rising from the forest. Low. Ancient. The language of roots and wind. The trees stir as if remembering something long forgotten.

I turn toward the dark edge of the woods, and between the trunks, eyes gleam. Dozens of them. Watching. Waiting. The forest holds its breath.

Amara's robes lift in a wind that belongs only to her. The veil rises with it, and for the first time I see her eyes clearly, blazing green, alive with power. Veins of light thread through her skin, pulsing like the heartbeat of the earth itself, and that wild energy flows into the small, lifeless creature in her hands.

A sound. A faint sputter. A gasp. Then a delicate chitter.

The rabbit's eyes snap open, bright and black and shining. Its legs twitch, kicking weakly, and for a moment it simply sits there in her palms, uncertain.

Then, above it all, comes the sweetest sound I have ever heard.

Amara laughs.

Soft and easy. A sound of pure, effortless joy.

The green light fades from her skin. The veins dim. The forest exhales, and the Souls watching from the trees retreat, melting back into the dark. Amara strokes the rabbit's fur once more, her thumb brushing over its ear. The creature twitches its nose and leaps from her hands, bounding through the grass before vanishing into the trees.

I can't move. Can't think. My jaw hangs useless as I stare at her.

"Amara... how did you..." My voice fails. My mind spins. I saw that arrow. I saw it tear through the poor thing's chest. There was no life left in it. No magic that could restore what had been taken. Dead is dead. Dead cannot return.

Unless...

Slowly, she turns her head toward me, as if I'd spoken the thought aloud. Her gaze finds mine, then she rises and walks towards me. With every place her foot touches, the ground blossoms anew. Grass greening, tiny flowers unfurling, life blooming in her wake.

Gods, I am trembling. My bottom lip caught between my teeth, my breath trapped in my chest.

Her face, the face my heart could sketch in the dark, is alight with warmth and knowing. She inhales and when her lips curve, it almost undoes me.

"Husband," she says.

The word strikes through me like lightning, and I fall. My knees hit the earth before I even realize it. My arms wrap around her waist, pulling her close, clinging as if I could anchor her here by sheer will, and when her hands slip into my hair, fingers threading gently through the dark strands, I break completely.

The words tumble from my mouth like a sacred oath.

"My queen."

Chapter 43

Amara

I wake to a world that breathes with me.

The first thing I feel is *everything*.

The wind is no longer wind, it is breath, shared between leaf and sky, between beast and soil. I feel it flow through me, a gentle inhale that fills my lungs and roots itself deep into the marrow of the earth. The pulse of the land thrums beneath my skin, soft and unending. The heartbeat of the trees. The slow hum of stone. Even the smallest creature, a worm turning in the dark, sings its note into the symphony of life, and I hear it all.

No. *I am* it all.

The air is alive with threads of gold and green, shimmering like silk. I can see them, the tiny fibres that bind everything together, the luminous veins of existence itself. They weave through every blade of grass, every feather, every drop of dew, connecting all living things in a tapestry so intricate it takes my breath. When I blink, I see the magic beneath the world's skin. Raw, beautiful, endless.

Every root remembers the sun. Every stone remembers the rain.

And I remember *them*.

I am no longer what I was. Not princess, not priestess, not even Awakened. I am something more. The boundary between myself and the living world is gone.

Those who do not belong here scatter from the clearing, slipping into the trees.

In the tall grass, Mirael lifts her gaze to me, tears caught behind her lashes. She has her hands on Zyphoro, the healing rune around her neck glowing faintly, her magic working, but mine works faster.

I kneel beside them and brush my thumb across Zyphoro's brow. Sweat beads warm against my skin. The moment I touch her, emerald light blooms, soft at first, then surging.

My magic pours into her, mending what's broken, sealing what has been torn. Bones knit. Organs repair. Breath returns steady and sure.

Zyphoro exhales, color flooding her cheeks again. She pushes herself onto her elbows, wonder flickering across her face.

"Amara," she breathes. "Thank the gods you are alive."

"Not the gods," I say quietly, rising to my feet as the wind stirs around us. "The earth."

Mirael reaches for me, and our hands lock. "Welcome back, sister," she says softly.

My gaze wanders over her scars, and she turns away slightly. I draw her chin back.

"Mirael," I breathe. "Where are the others? Lira? Saren?"

Her silence falls heavy, and the cold rushes in, icy and cruel, as the truth seeps into my bones.

Mirael blinks rapidly, trying to hold back the tears.

"Shh," I whisper, brushing her cheek. My veins flare with light, green threads pulsing beneath my skin. The glow spills from my palms and into her, washing over her scars like sunlight melting frost.

Mirael gasps, her eyes wide as the warmth spreads. Her skin softens, the harsh lines fading, vanishing until only smooth, unbroken flesh remains. She touches her face with trembling fingers, her voice breaking. "Thank you, sister."

I smile, nod, then take Daed's hand and we walk toward the village, every blade of grass seeming to lean towards me, every flower bowing, every branch reaching, as it would for the sun.

Daed's hand is warm in mine, and I trace the jagged scar on his palm, the one the Archdruid carved the night we were married. His scar will never fade, but mine is gone. Yet I remember its sting. I remember every pain I have ever known. It is my curse now to carry them all. The ache of every wound, the echo of every death. The tremor of every creature's last breath lives somewhere inside me. It should crush me, this weight, but it doesn't. It humbles me. It reminds me of the cost of what I am.

A small price for what I have become.

For what I can do.

For the lives I can mend and now, it seems, the ones I can return.

I felt the rabbit's death while I was still beneath the earth. I wasn't dead. Not truly. But I wasn't alive either. I walked the narrow path between. A place of stillness and shadow and soft, endless light. I don't know if the Souls were testing me, weighing my worth or if the power to rise was always mine, sleeping quietly within, waiting for the moment I would finally listen.

But I remember that sound.

The soft thump of the rabbit's feet on the soil. The sharp whistle of the arrow slicing the air. The crack of its tiny bones, the puncture through flesh and lung and heart. Its final breath, a thread snapping in the fabric of life and in that instant, even while buried beneath the roots of the world, I knew.

I could hear the silence where life had stopped and I knew how to make it move again. So I woke.

But not into my beloved Grove as I remembered it. Not into peace or light or song.

I woke into war.

The scent of blood filled the air before I even opened my eyes. I felt the pain of every fallen beast, every dying man, every fading Fae. Hatred, sharp as iron, cutting through the song of the world I had just begun to hear.

I rose into a symphony of suffering.

When I was beneath the earth, there had been quiet. A stillness so pure it filled me with peace. No hunger. No hate. No grief. Only light.

I wanted to rest. I needed to rest. But I could not.

Something always pulled me back. His voice, maybe. His tears. Or perhaps it was simply my nature, this curse of always returning when I should fade.

I should have been grateful to breathe again, to see the stars. But I wasn't.

I wanted to close my eyes and sink back into that silence, where I could no longer feel the weight of a thousand living hearts beating inside me. Here, everything *hurts*. The earth hums with pain. The sky shudders with loss. Even the wind carries the sorrow of the dead, brushing cold fingers against my skin.

Daed walks beside me now, his thumb tracing circles over my hand as though grounding me, but even his touch feels distant, muffled beneath the roar of life. I want to tell him how the world sounds to me now. How it screams. How I can hear the roots mourning the trees cut from them, the rivers weeping for every drop of blood spilled in their waters.

I want to tell him that though I am alive, I do not feel *living*.

I was somewhere... better. Not heaven, not home, but peace.

And now I am here again, among men and monsters, where the soil is slick with blood and the stars turn away their faces.

The balance is broken. And I reborn, remade, unwilling, am the one who must fix it.

Even if I no longer know how to live in this world that I was never meant to return to.

When we reach the vine wall, the whispers of my people strike like thunder. Every breath, every heartbeat, every tremor of emotion surges through me too loud. I hear their joy, their disbelief, their fear. I *feel* it, every heartbeat like a note in the song of the living, and it drowns me. My gaze drifts over them, their faces a thousand stories etched in skin and in each I sense a lifetime of love and pain.

As we pass through, I lift my hand. A flick of my wrist, and the earth obeys. Fresh vines burst from the soil, climbing high, twining thick and strong as they rebuild the shattered wall. Leaves unfurl, blossoms bloom, life mending what death had torn apart. The wall stands again, vibrant and alive, stronger than before.

Gasps ripple through the gathered crowd, half awe, half unease.

Among the Tenders, the Fae stand apart, not just in height, but in the aura that clings to them. Their light is darker, more dangerous, flickering like smoke in sunlight. Solena watches me, wide-eyed and trembling, her hands twisted together. Behind her, Orios's heavy hand steadies her shoulder, though his own eyes betray a flicker of uncertainty.

All of them watch me, searching.

And I wonder what they see. Is it *me* they recognize? Or something reborn, remade? Am I better now... or something far worse?

"Amara. Jewel."

Erania's voice cuts through the quiet. She surges forward, tears streaking her cheeks, and throws her arms around me. That single act breaks the spell. The dam bursts. The Tenders rush forward as one, falling to their knees, hands grasping for me, for proof that I am real. Fingers tangle in my hair, brush the hem of my robe, trembling as if afraid I might vanish again.

"Jewel," they chant, voices trembling. "She has awoken!"

Awoken. Awakened. Two words, two meanings, yet in this moment, they are one.

Solena breaks through the crowd, her sobs shattering what little composure she has left. I reach for her, our fingers tangling as she presses herself close, clinging to me.

"Amara," she whispers, her voice shaking. "You're alive. You're *really* alive."

"Praise the Souls," Erania cries. "Praise the Souls, for they have returned our Jewel!"

"Praise the Souls!"

The chant builds. Hands crowd closer, reverent but suffocating. I can barely breathe beneath their devotion. Barely feel anything but their suffering, even those who try to hide it.

"There is so much pain here." The weight ripples through me.

Erania's voice cuts through the murmurs. "You cannot heal it all, Amara."

I lift my chin, ousting the weariness from my limbs. "Yes I can."

Time slips away. I do not count the minutes, only the pain I take. I move from Tender to Tender, from child to elder, pressing my palms to wounds both seen and unseen. Bones knit beneath my touch. Torn flesh seals. Fever fades. Each soul I mend leaves a weight within me, a shard of their hurt lodged deep beneath my ribs.

All the while, the Fae work on the other side of the village.

Zyphoro returns from the clearing, and she and Orios round up the remaining Legion, hunting them down, those too slow, too broken to flee. They've locked them in the underground den we built long ago, a sanctuary meant to protect the Tenders. Now it has become a cage.

I watch Daed huddled with the others, their heads bowed close in urgent conversation. There's something different about him now. He is reborn, as I am, his magic changed, tempered, heavier. It hums beneath his skin, and yet, beneath that new power, I sense something fragile. A man holding himself together by sheer will.

Every so often, he glances over his shoulder, as if my gaze tugs on the golden thread between us. When our eyes meet, he smiles, but only halfway. The kind of smile meant to reassure, though it never quite reaches his eyes. There is so much between us now, so many words left unsaid. But when in all this madness, will we find the time to speak them?

My thoughts scatter when a soft voice reaches me.

"Jewel?"

Malana, a young Tender mother, barely older than me, stands a few paces away, her arms wrapped around a small bundle. The baby inside coos, tiny hands reaching for the air, as if trying to grasp the sunlight itself. So pure. So untouched by all this pain.

"How can I help you or your child?" I ask, stepping closer.

Malana shakes her head quickly. "No, no, Jewel. We're well. I only..." She hesitates, cheeks pinking as she shifts her weight. "I hoped you might just hold her? Perhaps bless her?"

The request startles me. "Bless her?"

She nods, embarrassed. "A blessing from the Jewel of the Grove for a prosperous life."

"I don't know how to do that," I admit softly.

Her shoulders hunch. "Of course. Forgive me, Jewel. I didn't mean to…"

"Malana," I interrupt gently, reaching out to touch her arm. "It's Amara. Just Amara. We used to chase chickens through the village together, remember? We made poor Elder Varin faint once."

She laughs awkwardly, but fondly. "I remember."

I open my arms. "Then let me try."

Relief floods her face as she steps forward, carefully placing the baby into my waiting arms. I cradle the child close, breathing in that soft, powdery scent that belongs only to new life. I pull back the blanket to see her face. Warm brown skin, dark curls, a tiny, perfect mouth. A little girl. So small, so achingly beautiful.

She grips my finger with both her hands, giggling, a sound so pure it cuts straight through me. It's comforting. It's familiar. It's *too* familiar.

The world tilts.

A memory flares.

A baby in a crib, small mouth at my breast, tiny feet kicking against my palm. Black curls brushing her brow. Eyes the color of a gathering storm.

A girl.

My girl.

The haze in my mind fractures. My throat tightens, breath catching as a tremor racks me. My arms go slack, and the baby slips. Malana screams, but I clutch the child back to my chest, heart racing.

The baby wails now, startled by my shaking. Malana quickly takes her, whispering comfort, her eyes wide with concern.

"Amara? What's wrong?"

I can't answer. The ache blooming in my chest is a chasm. It devours my breath, my strength, my calm.

I rise unsteadily, legs trembling. "Daed," I call, my voice cracking like glass.

He turns immediately, eyes wide, alert.

My breath trembles as the truth claws its way out of me, raw and desperate.

"Where," I whisper, then louder, "Where is our daughter?"

I don't want his hand on my shoulder, comforting me.

I don't want to walk beside him, to leave the village, to be led somewhere quiet so he can make explain.

I want the truth. Now.

But still, I go.

Daed's hand wraps around mine, his grip so tight I can feel the thrum of his pulse. It matches my own.

We walk in silence until the sound of the river reaches us, the steady rush of water tripping over stone.

He leads me to the bank, the ground soft and cool beneath my bare feet. I sink down, and he crouches beside me, his hand still locked in mine as though letting go might shatter us both. His face, once carved from battle and rage, looks different now, frayed at the edges, fragile in ways I've never seen.

"First," he begins, voice low, "know that I love you, Amara. Because everything that follows breaks me to speak."

And so he tells me.

He tells me of my sacrifice. My bravery. My death and how even that was not enough. He tells me that when I thought I had saved our daughter, she was taken anyway, dragged into An'kel, into the hands of Gygarth.

The words tear through me. My knees give out and I fall against him, my body shaking as though the ground has opened beneath me. His arms wrap around me, but they bring no warmth, nothing could. The pain steals everything.

He tells me how Reon held me in a loop of time, trying to keep me alive, how they laid me beneath the earth to heal, to wait, to hope. But the only thing waiting was silence.

I cry until I am emptied of sound, until my grief has burned through me and what remains is fury.

I strike him. My fists find his chest and he does not move, does not defend himself. I hit him harder, desperate to make him feel.

"Why?" I choke out. "Why didn't you bring her back? Why didn't you do something?"

My strikes grow wilder, my voice hoarse with the effort of breaking him. He does not break.

So I call the vines.

They burst from the moss at our feet, curling up his legs and around his torso, tightening until they bite into his skin. But he summons his smoke, dark and violent, and the two collide, ash falling around us like snow.

"I wanted to," he says, his voice raw as his hand finds my cheek. "I tried, Amara. Every day, I walked the void searching for her. But I cannot open the gate to An'kel. Only you can."

Memories stir. Driftspire, the trials, the void, the demon at the threshold of An'kel.

I shake my head, my breath trembling. "The demon...he guards the gate."

Daed presses his palm to his chest. "That demon will not be waiting for us this time, but there will be others." He exhales, gathering me close until my ear rests over his heart. "This will be unlike anything we've faced, Amara. We may not come back."

My fingers slide into his. The warmth that left me begins to return.

"I've already died," I whisper, voice quiet but sure. "What more could the darkness possibly take from me that it hasn't already?"

Daed cups my face and draws me close, not to kiss me, not even to speak, but simply to look. His storm-lit eyes roam over me as though seeing me for the first time. They are wide and reverent, filled with wonder, and he studies me in silence for so long I begin to think he is mapping every line of my face to keep with him always.

"I thought I lost you," he murmurs at last, his thumb brushing slowly along my jaw. "Forever, this time."

"If our time together has taught me anything, husband," I say softly, "it is that we can be torn and broken, our destinies split, our fates sundered, but nothing in this life, or the next, will ever keep us apart."

I watch the golden threads shimmer faintly beneath his skin, swirling over the steady beat of his heart. They drift down his arm, tracing glowing lines where his skin touches mine, binding us in soft light.

"I should have known then," I whisper. "That day in the forest. The human who fell from a tree." His eyes widen with sudden recognition. "I saw the golden ribbons around you that day and didn't understand what they were. I saw them again when we made love in Pariseth. I should have known we were never strangers. That this..." I gesture between us, breath trembling "...was always meant to be. You and I."

He bites his bottom lip as if holding something fragile inside him, and his eyes sheen with feeling.

"Yes," he says quietly. "The fates always get their way, no matter how hard we fight them."

"What do the fates say about our daughter?" I ask, my voice barely a breath.

His expression falters, softens. "I wish I knew."

I exhale, steadying my heart. "Then we will make our own fate."

That earns me a small, crooked grin. "Will we?"

I nod. "We will find our daughter. Be a family again. Build a new world, one free of war and hate, where she, half human and half Fae, can guide the Sundered Kingdom into something whole."

Daed's eyes warm as my words sink in, as belief takes root. "I named her, you know," he says quietly.

I straighten, brows lifting. "You did? Seems like a discussion I should have been part of."

He shrugs lightly, the corner of his mouth twitching. "You were half dead. I didn't want to disturb you."

A laugh slips from me before I can stop it, small, but real. It startles even me, but it lifts something heavy from my chest, and suddenly I can breathe again.

"Well then, husband," I say, smiling. "What is her name?"

He smiles back, softer now. "Estra. I named her Estra."

The name carries with it a memory. Arax, brave, noble, infuriating Arax, my friend, my protector. A Fae who loved his daughter as fiercely as I love mine.

"That is a good name," I whisper, and I lay my hand over his, still cupping my cheek. "It's a warrior's name."

"With parents like us," he says, his smile deepening, "the child had no chance of being anything else."

"Then let us gather our forces, husband," I say, rising, my voice clear and sure. "Let us bring Estra home."

"Yes, wife," he breathes, lifting my hand to his lips and pressing a kiss to my palm, light as wind, eternal as promise.

His eyes drift to the dirt crusted beneath my fingernails, to the smudges of soil painting every inch of my skin. He kisses my wrist.

"Let me take care of you."

Before I can protest, Daed reaches over his shoulder, grips his shirt in one hand and pulls it off, casting it aside on the riverbank. His body is as I remember it. Every plane and line etched into my memory by touch and hunger. But now, those same planes are bruised and battered, the once-smooth skin streaked with blood and dust.

His hands find the edge of my robe, woven from vines and flowers, the garb of my rebirth, and slide beneath it. Slowly, reverently, he eases it from my shoulders. It slips away, falling soundlessly to the grass. I stand bare before him, heart pounding like war drums.

He dips his chin and kisses me, first the curve of my neck, then the hollow of my collarbone, then the space between my breasts. Each touch is a spark, each breath against my skin a promise. My nerves come alive, burning molten beneath his lips.

The river calls softly beside us, and when he takes my hand and leads me in, the water's cool caress feels like a baptism. His leathers creak as he lowers himself onto a submerged stone, the water reaching his waist. He pulls me down between his legs, my back pressed to the sculpted warmth of his chest. I feel his breath at my ear, his heartbeat steady against my spine, as he scoops handfuls of water and lets it run over me.

The dirt melts away beneath his touch. His hands move slowly, over my shoulders, down my arms, over my breasts and stomach, along the curve of my hips, down to my thighs and feather-light between my legs. His touch is tender, worshipful, and I feel myself unraveling with every pass of his fingers.

When he gathers water and runs it through my hair, his fingers massage my scalp until the river runs clear again. I close my eyes, lean into him, drowning in his gentleness.

But the need to touch him grows too sharp to ignore. I turn, kneeling between his legs, water swirling around us. Our eyes lock, his storm meeting my earth, and the air between us crackles. I cup water in my palms and pour it over his chest, watching the rivulets trace down his ribs and abs, washing away blood and battle.

He winces when my fingers graze a bruise, hisses softly when I near a wound. I dip my head and press a kiss to the bruised flesh, and his body shudders as the mark fades beneath my lips. His hands tighten at my hips, his breath deep and ragged as I slide my body against his cock, his leathers creaking. I move higher, my hands caress every inch of smooth skin, feeling the hard muscles flex beneath.

When my fingers reach his face, I wash away the grime, trace the lines I love so well. My hands tangle in his hair, slick and dark, gripping lightly at the roots and still, we do not break our gaze.

"I love you, Amara," he breathes, voice rough and trembling. "I have always loved you. I loved you without wanting to. Without trying to. I loved you because I had no choice. Because you were already written into my soul."

I smile through the ache in my chest, cradle his face between my hands, and kiss him, slow and deep and infinite, until time itself bends around us, and the world is nothing but the sound of our hearts finding each other again.

CHAPTER 44

AMARA

Daed and I return to the village, and I feel closer to him than I ever have before. Something in him has changed quietly, profoundly. It's as if he has finally found the key to his prison, the one forged of guilt and grief and wrath, and stepped free of it at last. The weight that once bent his shoulders has lifted. My dark prince, who once wore his sorrow like armor, now walks in the light.

There is color to his face. Warmth to his touch. When he looks at me, his gaze is not shadowed by regret or self-loathing, but filled with something brighter, gentler, something whole. His love feels pure now, stripped of the ghosts that haunted it.

Ronin once told me that love cannot exist without trust. I hadn't wanted to listen then. I hadn't wanted to admit that I, too, harbored doubt. But now, walking beside this beautiful Fae who has laid every scar, every sin bare before me, I understand.

Because I do trust him.

The vine wall parts for me with a whispering sigh, leaves brushing over one another like tongues of silk. It seals behind us with a soft groan. The Tenders bow as we pass, their eyes lowered to the ground, their reverence a weight I can feel pressing against my skin. None turn their backs until I am gone from sight.

Once, I was their Jewel of the Tenders. Their Sister of the Vine. A guide, a guardian. But this... this is something else entirely. I have only ever seen such reverence given to the Souls of the Forest themselves. Is that what they see when they look at me now? Something godlike? The thought makes me shudder.

I will not let them think of me as anything more than what I am. So I smile. I reach out. I touch their hands and speak their names, reminding them, and myself, that I am still Amara. I will always be Amara. Especially to my people.

We reach the courtyard, and Daed turns to me, his hands resting gently on my shoulders. He lifts my chin with a knuckle, and for a moment I'm caught by the way the sunlight breaks behind him, gilding the dark waves of his hair. It always looks strange to me when it's dry, untempered by rain or battle.

"I will gather the Fae," he says, his touch trailing along my neck as he brushes my hair over my shoulder, lingering on the two crescent-shaped marks.

I nod, but my thoughts have drifted elsewhere. He notices it. His gaze sharpens. "What is it?" he asks quietly. "What do you need?"

"There is more healing I need to do," I say at last, my head turning towards a cottage across the village.

He follows my gaze. His jaw tightens. "Reon will be grateful to see you, but Ronin..." Daed exhales. "Part of me wonders if I should've cut his throat instead of the ropes. Released him from the pain."

I shake my head. "No. Not when I can take the pain away."

"You're really going to heal him?" Daed asks.

"I must."

Daed's eyes narrow, searching mine. "After all that human has done to you? After everything he took from you, you would still bless him with your gift?"

He takes my hands gently, his thumbs tracing slow circles over the delicate skin of my wrists. I do not let him see what that touch does to me, the dizzying sweep of warmth that climbs up my arms and pools low in my stomach.

"You are one to talk," I murmur, lifting a brow. "You saved his life, did you not?"

His frown deepens, the realization dawning slowly across his face.

"Besides," I continue, voice softer now, "another warrior to face Gygarth is not something we can afford to waste. Especially one as skilled as Ronin."

Daed scoffs, the sound low and rough. "Let's not get too poetic. He's *adequate* at best."

I squeeze his fingers, smirking despite myself. "Estra deserves every soul brave enough to fight for her. Even the *adequate* ones."

He turns his head, reluctant as ever. "Of course she does," he mutters.

So I pinch his hand, a light reprimand. He winces dramatically, even though I know he felt nothing at all.

"Go then," I tell him, my voice softening. "Rally the Fae. I will join you soon."

He nods, chin tilted high, ever the proud prince. Still, there's a touch of sulk in the set of his jaw that makes me want to laugh.

I rise onto my toes, and though he doesn't meet me halfway, he dips his head just enough. I press my lips to his cheek, breathe him in, smoke and leather and the faint sweetness of rain. Even now, beneath the leather and the grit, there is tenderness in him he only lets me see and for all his brooding, my dark prince still melts against my touch like wax to flame.

"As you wish," he grumbles.

He walks away, our arms stretching between us, fingers clasping until they finally slip apart. The distance aches more than I expect. I stand there a moment, watching him go, before drawing a slow, steadying breath and turning toward the healer's cottage.

Vellis stands near the door, refilling a jug from a rain barrel. She looks older now, more sure of herself, with a yellow flower tucked behind her ear and her warm auburn hair tied half-up, half-down. Once, she dreamed of becoming a Sister of the Vine, but the Souls never called her name. So she found her own way to serve, healing not with runes, but with herbs and potions, and perhaps she's saved just as many lives as those of us who wear the marks.

She dips her head when she sees me approach, nearly dropping the jug in her haste. I step forward quickly and steady it in her hands.

Her cheeks flush. "Sorry, Amara."

"There's nothing to apologize for," I say gently, relieving her of the jug and setting it aside.

She wipes her damp hands on her crinkled apron, voice dropping to a whisper. "Which one were you coming to see? The poor soul with the burns..." she frowns. "Or the one who keeps asking me to marry him."

I stifle a laugh. "Both," I reply. "But the one with the burns I fear needs me most."

She nods. "I was just tending to his wounds again." She glances toward the door, worry clouding her eyes. "They're bad, Amara. Very bad. He won't let me help him."

"That sounds like him." My chest tightens, a familiar sting crawling down my spine. I close my eyes briefly. "But I'll help him, whether he wants it or not. He's suffered enough."

Vellis's brow furrows. "You can... feel it?"

"Yes," I murmur. "I feel everything."

Her lips part, hesitation flickering in her gaze. "Does it hurt?"

I offer her only a small, polite smile. She doesn't need to know the truth, that yes, it hurts. It burns. It claws through me like fire, tearing me apart from the inside out. But the pain always fades.

I gesture to the cottage door, and Vellis steps aside.

Inside, the air is heavy, thick with the scent of blood, char, and pain. The curtains are drawn tight, swallowing what little light remains, but even in the dim I can see the shape of him on the bed. Ronin. The Golden Son. The man who was once both my enemy and my ally and now something in between.

I move to Reon first, and when he sees me, his eyes flare with life.

"Gods, you're here to heal me, aren't you? Fucking fantastic!" He pauses, tongue pressing into his cheek. "I mean, don't get me wrong. I am thrilled you are alive, Amara. The healing is simply a delightful bonus."

A tired breath leaves me. Almost a sigh. "You do not have to explain anything, Reon. I know what you did for me. Thank you."

His face softens, and he discards the arrogance that he wears as well as his armor. I place my hand on his chest, and he closes his eyes. I feel his heartbeat, his warmth, the pulse beneath skin as my magic flows into his flesh. When I am done, he swings his legs over the bed and stands, under his own power, on his own two feet, and he weeps. Quietly. Stubbornly. He wipes the tears away before they can fall.

I leave him to his dignity and move to the next bed across the room.

From the shadows, his voice rasps. "Leave me the fuck alone, Jewel."

"Truly?" I arch a brow. "I have been welcomed by all with open arms. Showered with love and adoration. Worshiped as some sort of sacred being, and you tell me to fuck off?"

A pause. "I didn't say fuck off," he mutters. "But the sentiment is the same. Leave me alone."

"No," I say simply, stepping closer. "You have no power over me, Ronin. You're in my home now. Surrounded by my people. You make none of the rules here." I stop at his bedside. "I do."

He turns his head toward me with a low groan, every movement laced with pain. The effort alone steals his breath and for a moment, I understand Daed's words more clearly than I wish to. Perhaps death *would* have been a mercy.

I had known his scars before, those silver lines that carved across his cheek, trailed down his neck and shoulder. But these... these are worse.

435

The burns are cruel things. Angry, raw welts crawl across his chest and arms, blistered and blackened where the fire stole flesh entirely. Some still glisten, wet, red, weeping, while others have already hardened and cracked like scorched earth.

I follow the path of the flames up his throat, where they claimed the other side of his face. The skin there puckers and pulls, uneven and warped. His lips are split, lashes burned away, and his hair, once gold as sunlight, as bright as the mask he wore, is gone.

The smell of him is the worst part. Burnt skin. Dried blood. Ash and smoke. It clings to the air.

Every breath he takes is a tremor, shallow and rattling, and when his chest rises I see how the skin pulls taut and splits again at the seams, as if his body itself has forgotten how to heal.

For the first time, I wonder if even my gift will be enough.

"I know why you're here," he rasps. "Don't you dare. I've never once asked to be saved, and still you deny me the honor of dying on my own terms."

I don't answer him. The Souls whisper at the edges of my mind, soft and insistent, their murmurs like wind through leaves. Beneath my bare feet, I feel the pulse of the earth through the floorboards. I step closer.

"Don't, Amara!" he roars. The sound cracks the air... and then falters. His voice shatters into something small, broken. "Leave me," he pleads, the words trembling. "For fuck's sake, just leave me to die."

My hand stills above him.

He drags in a ragged breath, eyes glinting in the dim light. "I have nothing left. My army turned on me...my brother's army and of all the punishments they could've chosen... they chose fire." His throat works, the words scraping out raw. "I deserve this. I earned this. I'm glad you live, Amara. What we fought for wasn't in vain. But please... let me go."

"I cannot," I say quietly, and his chest rises hard with another breath. "I need you, Ronin."

He shakes his head weakly. "You need someone better."

"Estra needs you," I whisper, and his jaw trembles.

"This isn't over," I continue, voice steady now, the truth thrumming through me like a heartbeat. "It won't be over until Gygarth is dead and my daughter is cradled in my arms. I need you to stand beside me."

436

I place my hand upon his chest. His skin is searing to the touch. He flinches, but I do not pull away. The Souls hum in my blood, the glow rising beneath my skin like a dawn waiting to break.

"But first," I whisper, "I need you whole."

The glow builds between us, an emerald light blooming from my palm, spreading in delicate threads across his ruined flesh. His body trembles as the fire's legacy peels away: the cracked skin knitting, the blackened edges softening to pink, new life unfurling where death had claimed its hold. His breath catches, and though he tries to hide it, a single tear slips down the side of his face. My power moves through me like a current, washing him clean, mending him piece by piece.

But when my hand reaches the old scars, the ones carved deep across his chest from the flames of Rethmar long ago, his fingers, renewed, snap up, closing around my wrist.

"Stop," he says. The look in his eyes is something I've never seen before, defiance, yes, but also pride. The fire of a boy who survived what should have killed him. "Not these." He draws my hand away from the ridged skin. "These belong to me. They're what's left of the boy I was... the boy who learned what it means to live through fire. They're mine to keep."

For a long moment, I say nothing. The light at my fingertips flickers, then fades.

I nod softly and withdraw my hand. "Then keep them."

Ronin sits up, rolling his shoulders, testing his limbs. He rakes a hand through a head of thick blond hair, then he stands, and the sheet slips away, leaving him utterly bare. He doesn't seem to care, turning his attention to his healed body, flexing muscle and pinching skin in disbelief.

I turn away, though if I'm honest, not as fast as I should have.

"Do you have a blacksmith in this place?" he asks.

I nod, continuing to look the other way. "The Tenders are fine crafters. Metal, wood, stone, they shape them all."

He nods once, more to himself than to me. "Good." His fingers curl into a fist, testing it's strength. "I am in need of a new mask."

I clear my throat. "Well... perhaps put some pants on first."

He glances down, finally noticing. His hand flies to cover himself — not very successfully.

A laugh cracks the silence. We both turn. Reon is peeking out from behind his curtain.

437

"Not bad, human," he says, nodding in approval. "Not bad."

When we step out into the fading afternoon light, the murmurs ripple through the village like wind through reeds. The Tenders stop what they're doing. Their eyes widen, flicking between me and the man who walks beside me.

Ronin's transformation steals their breath. Whispers follow in our wake. *The Jewel has healed him... the Golden Son lives...* Their reverence presses like a tide, warm and suffocating all at once.

We move toward the great tree at the village's heart, its spiraling trunk hollowed into a staircase that winds upward, lined with glittering lanterns. Reon and Ronin climb behind me. The air grows cooler as we rise, the murmurs below fading into a hum.

At the top, the Fae await. What remains of the Blades. Daed, Orios, Solena and Zyphoro huddled together in hushed discussion, but when Zyphoro sets eyes on Ronin, she breaks away in an instant. For a heartbeat they simply look at each other, a silent exchange of something none of us will ever quite understand. A bond forged not by words, but by survival and the impossible things they must have endured together.

Then Zyphoro reaches for him, her arm sliding around his neck as she draws him in. Her cheek rests against his shoulder, and for the first time since I've known him, Ronin allows himself to lean back into someone's touch. His mouth twitches, the faintest ghost of a smile crossing it, and his hand comes to rest against the small of her back.

The tension in the room breaks like a wave. Shoulders ease. Eyes soften. The others look between one another, surprise first, then relief, and the tight circle loosens, opening as though granting Ronin space to stand among them.

Zyphoro's acceptance is enough.

If she, fiercest of the Blades, can stand beside the Golden Son, then the rest of them can too.

And thank the Souls for that, because the battles we have already fought will mean nothing if we turn on one another now.

Daed steps forward. "Do you wish to speak, wife?" he asks.

I shake my head. "I may be many things now," I answer, "but I am no tactician. War is your art, husband, and in that, you are unmatched. Lead us as you always have."

"I will not paint you a pretty picture," he begins, voice deep, echoing through the hollow trunk of the great tree. "An'kel is a place of nightmares. Its soil soaked in the blood of every soul who's dared trespass there. Its demons are ancient, their power boundless and upon his throne, within the temple of his making, sits Gygarth. We will be taking the fight to him, into his own dominion, where he holds every advantage."

Zyphoro exhales sharply, folding her arms. "Your pep talks are as bleak as ever, brother."

Daed's jaw tightens. "Would you rather I lied to you? We owe our people honesty. And the truth is, some of us will not make it back."

Silence settles like dust.

"But I would not ask any of you to face what I am unwilling to face myself."

Daed's gaze sweeps the room and finds mine, and the air between us tightens. "I will risk my life to bring back my daughter," he continues, voice low but certain. "Because I cannot imagine a world where she is gone. Where I must live knowing the sound of her laughter has faded. That I will never feel her in my arms, never hear her call me *father*."

Something inside him fractures then, so subtle I doubt anyone else sees it, but I do. I feel it, the sharp twist of grief and longing, the desperate hope holding him together by threads. My chest aches with the urge to go to him, to take his face in my hands and tell him that he will not face that pain alone. But he straightens before I can move, shoulders squaring, armor of command snapping back into place. Daedalus the warrior. Daedalus the prince. The male who does not break.

He draws a long breath. "But we are not without our strengths. We have Amara, Jewel of the Tenders, the Awakened. She will open the portal we need to cross into An'kel, and with the power she wields over the earth, with the green fire that burns in her veins, she will make even the horrors that await us tremble."

I bow my head slightly at his words, but my stomach knots. His faith in me is unwavering and that terrifies me more than any demon ever could.

Daed lifts his hand, thick tendrils of smoke twisting between his fingers. "And I," he says, his voice deepening, "now wield the void freely without fear of Gygarth's gaze. The smoke and shadow obey me."

The air ripples around him. His jaw tightens, his body seizes. The temperature in the room drops. Then, before anyone can react, a *second head* splits into being over his shoulder, shrouded in black, its eyes white and empty, its mouth a writhing pit of teeth and tentacles.

A collective gasp fills the room. Solena grips Orios' arm. Reon presses his back against the wall. Even Zyphoro's hand goes to her blade.

The demon head snarls, a wet, guttural growl, but as quickly as it appeared, it vanishes with a rush of smoke, making me wonder if it was ever there. Daed staggers, bracing himself on the table, chest heaving.

"And I have a passenger now," he says, his voice almost conversational. "Another weapon against Gygarth."

Zyphoro's voice cuts through the uneasy silence. "Are you sure you can control Emranth?" she demands. "How is he any different from Gygarth?"

It's the question lodged in all our throats.

Daed straightens, his expression cold as stone. "Because his soul belongs to me. I am the master now." His eyes blaze white, smoke coiling off his skin, and for a terrible heartbeat, I can't tell where Daed ends and the demon begins. "I will do the same to Gygarth. I will consume him, devour him, and end him forever."

The silence that follows is taut, until Zyphoro lets out a short, unexpected laugh. "He is death, brother," she says, shaking her head. "You cannot kill death."

Daed smiles faintly. "Perhaps you're right, sister. But I will try, and I will keep trying until Estra is home."

Daed's gaze sweeps over the room, lingering on each of his warriors.

"You are the finest, bravest, and noblest Fae I have ever had the honor of fighting beside," he says, each word steady as stone. "There is no one else I would trust at my side. No one else I would trust to fight for my daughter as fiercely as I will."

They do not speak, but they don't need to. The silence that follows is a sacred one, a wordless acknowledgment of the bond that has just been forged.

Then Daed turns his attention to Ronin.

"Never," Daed says at last, "in a thousand lifetimes, did I imagine I would stand beside *you* in battle... Ronin." His mouth hesitates around the name, as though it tastes strange, bitter and hard to swallow. "But you have proven more than once that you are a man of honor. A warrior who will fight to his last breath for what he believes in. And if we survive what comes, I would count you not only as an ally, but as a friend."

For a heartbeat, no one moves.

Then Ronin steps forward, meeting Daed in the center of the room. Their eyes lock, chests rising and falling, two creatures of immeasurable power, and inescapable rage. In another world, I have no doubt they would've been as close as brothers, had one not been born Fae and the other human.

But this world gives them something else. The chance to stand side by side and destroy something far worse than either of them could ever be.

Ronin offers his forearm, and the room falls still.

Daed exhales, lifts his chin, and clasps Ronin's arm in his own.

A pact sealed. A hatred buried... for now.

CHAPTER 45

AMARA

We spend hours more planning, until dusk bleeds into midnight and the night itself begins to tremble toward dawn. Yet no matter what scenario we prepare for, no matter how many outcomes we twist and turn in our minds, the beginning is always the same.

I must open the portal, and I must bleed to do it.

When all is said and every argument spent, when our voices have grown hoarse and raw, we fall into silence. It settles thickly over us, heavy and fragile all at once. No one speaks. Not for a long while. Each of us trapped in our own thoughts, our own fears and hopes, with the same aching hunger to see Estra again.

No one dares speak the truth that gnaws beneath it all.

We do not know if she still lives.

To say it aloud would be to give despair wings and none of us are ready to watch hope fly away.

It is Orios who finally breaks the silence, his voice graveled and rough.

"What about the Tenders?" He clears his throat. "Can they aid us in An'kel?"

Daed shakes his head before I can answer. "I told Keeper Erania we would accept their aid, but these people have suffered enough. I won't see them wiped from the earth."

"They are not afraid to fight," I say quietly.

Daed's hand finds my shoulder, gentle but firm. "I know, wife. I meant no slight. The Tenders have warrior blood, as fierce as any Fae. But I would not curse them with what we are about to face. What waits in An'kel will haunt those who survive." His jaw tightens, his voice falling low. "If any survive."

Zyphoro's voice cuts through the air. "What of the Legion dogs?" She jerks her chin toward the window, to the den where a few dozen prisoners are packed shoulder to shoulder.

"Yes," Ronin growls, his voice dark and hoarse. "Let them be fodder. Throw them in first."

Daed shakes his head again. "Leave them where they are. I will take care of them."

Zyphoro raises an eyebrow and stalks forward. She jabs a finger into Daed's stomach. He jerks back, scowling. "What was that for?"

"I was expecting to find your belly soft and pillowy," she replies sweetly, "with all the sappy drivel you've been spewing lately."

A ripple of restrained laughter circles the room. Even Ronin smirks.

"Because I won't slaughter prisoners?" Daed asks, incredulous.

"Exactly," Zyphoro snaps, arms crossed like a petulant child. "I was rather looking forward to it."

"As was I," Ronin mutters under his breath.

But the Fae hear him. Their ears are as sharp as their tempers.

"Leave our prince be," Solena interjects, her voice silken but commanding enough to quiet the room. She looks up at Orios, her hand sliding into his massive one. "He's given his orders. Now let us rest..." her eyes soften, "...and spend what precious time we have with those we love."

Zyphoro rolls her eyes, throwing her hands up. "If I'm going to war with a god, I need to loosen my wrists first. I'll be in the forest. Target practice."

My brow furrows, and she sighs dramatically.

"Not on your precious creatures, Jewel. Only trees. I promise."

"Trees have souls too, you know," I remind her.

She groans. "I imagine the rocks do as well?"

"They do," I say, fighting the smile tugging at my mouth.

Her glare sharpens. "Then I'll throw my daggers at the air. Surely that's not sacred?"

"Air should be fine," I reply, deadpan.

Zyphoro mutters something about sanctimonious nature-priests under her breath, then strides to the window. With one boot on the sill, she flashes us a sharp grin.

"Try not to die before I get back," she says just before she jumps.

Reon groans as he pushes himself to his feet. "Looks like everyone's pairing off. Guess that leaves me with the human."

Ronin doesn't even look up. "Touch me and I'll snap both your hands off at the wrists."

Reon lifts his hands in surrender. "Didn't mean it. Not entirely." He tucks his hands behind his back for good measure. "Maybe I'll go throw things at the air with Zyphoro instead."

He follows her lead literally by vaulting through the open window, his laughter echoing faintly as his wings catch the wind.

The Blades disperse, and Solena and Orios exchange a knowing glance, also deciding to take the long way down, hand in hand.

Ronin lingers behind me for a moment. "I'm going to find the blacksmith," he says. "I'll be ready when it's time."

I nod. He lifts his gaze to Daed, who's already watching him.

"Daedalus," Ronin says with an acknowledging dip of his head.

Daed straightens, shoulders squaring. "In battle," he replies, "you call me Rook."

Ronin doesn't understand the full meaning of what Daed has just offered him, few would, but the solemn look in his eyes says he feels the weight of it all the same.

"Rook, then," he says simply, before turning and following the others down the stairs.

When they're gone, Daed leans forward on the table, palms braced, shoulders heavy with thought. I step behind him, sliding my hands around his waist, pressing my nose against the warm line of his spine.

"Come, husband," I murmur. "Solena is right. We should rest. I would hold you a long while before the end."

He turns his head just enough that I catch his storm-gray eyes over his shoulder.

"I want that too," he says quietly, "forever and always."

His breath leaves him rough, uneven. "But I can't still my mind."

My hands trail up his chest, feeling the steady rhythm of his heartbeat beneath my palms.

"Do you need me to distract you?" I whisper.

He tips his head back, a rumbling moan slipping out as he laces my fingers over his chest.

"Fuck yes. I've been able to think of nothing else since you rubbed yourself all over me in the river."

He turns in one fluid motion, palms circling my wrists, pulling me flush against him. I smile, teeth catching my bottom lip as he leans in—only for him to freeze, breath stalling just as heat licks through me.

"What is it?" I ask, brow arching. "Am I not as enticing as I was a second ago?"

He gives a half-grin, a flimsy mask, then shakes his head as his gaze catches mine.

"You are all I want. All I think of."

"Then what?" I press.

He drags a finger along his cheek, pressing hard into his temple as if trying to burrow through bone.

"Even your heat wrapped around my cock would not stop the noise," he says. "Even as sweet as you taste on my tongue when you come," he leans close to my ear, voice a rasp, "and you will come... if I am to rid this world of Gygarth, and reunite us with Estra, I need the voices to quiet."

If he's trying to stop me from wanting him to take me on this table, he is doing a painfully poor job. I drag in a breath, steadying the ache curling low in my belly.

"Then how can I help you, husband? Tell me."

He goes still, thinking, chin lifting as I slide my nose along the sharp line of his jaw. He hums, deep in thought.

Then he stills completely, as if a notion has struck fast and clean.

"Zema," he says.

I nod. "Your friend who was Awakened?"

"She had the power to bring back memories so vivid, so real that I felt as if I were living them all over again. It took away the noise. Can you..." Then he shakes his head. "No, you have already given so much of yourself."

"And I will continue to give." I straighten my shoulders and clear my throat. "Now...how do I do it?"

"I'm not sure. Zema just...did it."

"Then kneel," I tell him.

His brow arches, a slow, teasing grin curving his lips. But he obeys, sinking to his knees before me, gaze burning as it drifts down my body like a touch. His hands find the backs of my thighs, strong fingers curling against my skin.

I cradle his face between my palms, my thumbs brushing the stubble along his jaw before sliding upward. My fingers sink into his hair, silken and damp against my hands. "Stay still," I whisper, though my voice wavers under the weight of his nearness. "And close your eyes."

He exhales, the sound a low, amused rumble that vibrates against my palms. But he does as he's told, lashes lowering, head tilting forward until his breath warms the inside of my wrist.

I focus, centering myself as the power stirs. My veins hum, threads of green light shimmering faintly beneath the surface. The moment my fingers touch his temples, it begins.

A prickling warmth races through me. Flashes of memory burst behind my eyes, blinding shards of Daed's life.

Fire. Screams. Steel and blood.

A child's cry cut short.

A kiss in a storm.

A battlefield of smoke.

Too violent. Too painful. I push them aside, weaving through the chaos until I hear a sound.

Soft and pure. A baby's soft breaths.

The vision steadies. A bed of furs, pale light spilling through a porthole, and a tiny hand reaching from the blankets, a red ribbon tied around a chubby wrist. My heart twists when I see her. Estra.

Daed kneels beside her. His smile trembles as he holds out a finger, and their hands meet, his massive and calloused, hers impossibly small as she curls her entire fist around him.

"Yes," I whisper. "This is the one."

Daed flinches beneath my touch, and his whole body shudders as the memory floods through him.

I watch as color warms his skin, as the furrow in his brow softens. The corner of his mouth lifts into something bright, something unguarded. A breathless laugh escapes him, quiet but full, like sunlight breaking through cloud.

I don't know how long we stay like that, lost in the memory, but when he at last opens his eyes and looks up at me, there's something different in his. The storm in his eyes has quieted to a calm tide, and in its reflection I see us both as we were, as we might still be.

His hands slide higher, tracing the shape of me, the warmth of me, until they find my hips. Gently, he pulls me down, guiding me into his lap. His breath catches; mine follows. His fingers trace the bite marks on my neck before sliding into my hair, threading deep until his palm cups the back of my head, just beneath my ear. His other hand finds the curve of my waist, resting there as he pulls me closer.

And then he kisses me. A kiss that tastes of sunlight and sorrow, of love that has survived too many endings. For a moment, there is no war, no gods, no fate, only us, and the fragile beauty of the last dawn we may ever see.

Daed surges to his feet, lifting me with him. My thighs lock around his hips as he devours my mouth, hungry and unrestrained. He stalks backward until the back of his legs hit the edge of the table, then drops to sit, lips still claiming mine like he'll starve if he stops.

I pull away for a moment. "I thought this isn't what you needed?"

His canines lengthen and gleam, and my breath hitches at the sight of them.

"Only a fucking fool would not want this," he says.

A low sound rumbles from him as he trails hot kisses down my throat, his tongue dragging along the center of my chest. His hands slide under my robe, grip tightening on the back of my thigh before climbing higher, palms claiming my ass, spreading me open to straddle him wider. His cock strains against leather, nudging my heat, cruel in its restraint.

I drag my hand down the curve of my neck, over my chest, tugging the fabric aside to bare my breast. His mouth is there instantly, lips closing around my nipple, tongue flicking, circling, teasing until I gasp. My fingers keep moving, lower, lower, sliding between my thighs before finding his lap. I rub him through the leather and he groans against my skin, breath hot, sending a violent shiver through me.

I fumble at his leathers, desperate, shaking with need, and the moment my hand closes around the perfect, smooth length of him, slickness pools between my legs. His gaze lifts to mine, ravenous, worshipful. As if I am sunrise and sunset and every night he's ever wished for.

His mouth breaks from my breast, parted in awe as I sink down on him. The first stretch steals both our breath. He shudders, a sharp gasp punched from him as I begin to move, slow at first, savoring every inch, sliding from the swollen head down to the exquisite base, riding him with purpose.

At first he lets me set the rhythm, hands firm on my ass, holding me steady but not controlling the pace.

"Gods, Amara," he groans into my chest, voice wrecked. "Don't fucking stop."

I don't. I can't. I move faster, grinding, circling, chasing the heat blooming hot and desperate inside me.

Then his grip changes. Tightens.

He snarls softly, fingers digging into my ass as he thrusts up, hard and deep, stealing the breath right from my lungs. I bite my lip to keep quiet, but when he drives into me again, deep, brutal, perfect, I can't hold back.

I slap a hand over my mouth but he won't have it. He pulls it away, twists my arm behind me, pinning it there as he fucks up into me, relentless, hungry, each thrust a command.

My breath breaks. My body shakes. The heat becomes unbearable, sweet, scorching, splitting me apart.

I cry out as I come, trembling around him, and he catches my mouth with his, tongue claiming mine as he follows, thrusts stuttering, voice rough and undone against my lips as he spills inside me, the two of us breaking together.

We lie together on the floor for hours, resting in each other's arms, dozing in and out of sleep. It takes all my strength to stand up. To kiss him goodbye, but I know I must see Mirael and Keeper Erania one final time. Reluctantly, he lets me go, though his fingers linger against mine before he reminds me that we will meet again at dusk.

Solena and Orios do not emerge from their cottage. Ronin spends the day with the blacksmith, the steady clang of hammer striking steel ringing through the village, while Reon and Zyphoro spar in the forest. Their laughter drifts faintly on the wind, and for a moment, I remember Daed and Zyphoro doing the same the last time we stood together in the Grove. The memory warms me, until it brings with it another ache. Ashen.

Guilt tugs at me like thorns beneath my skin. In the chaos of all that has happened, I have not given his spirit the mourning it deserves. I miss him. The way he'd climb along my shoulder, get tangled in my hair, his deep purrs vibrating through my bones and the way he'd transform into the beast he truly was: fierce, beautiful, loyal beyond measure. I can still feel the phantom brush of his smoky mane between my fingers.

I never thought I could love a Fae prince, and I never thought I could love a creature born of the void. Yet I love them both. I wish Ashen were here now, that I could ride into battle with him one last time. But that fate was never meant for us.

"Will the Souls aid you?" Keeper Erania asks as we sit in the field. Mirael perches on a nearby rock, staring absently into the distance.

"I cannot ask that of them," I say. "Besides, they are needed here. They are the heart of this forest."

"So are you, Amara," Mirael murmurs, finally meeting my gaze.

"Someone else must carry that mantle while I'm gone," I tell her gently. "It needs to be you, Mirael."

She shakes her head, her dark hair flowing like ink in the wind. "I am not you. I don't have your power."

"You have something greater," I say. "You've kept our people alive by your will alone."

Her jaw trembles. "I couldn't keep our sisters alive. Lira and Saren are gone because of me."

I reach for her hand. "They are not gone, sister." I place one hand over my heart. "They are here." Then I press my palm to the earth. "And here. They walk with us always."

Where my fingers touch the soil, tiny buds unfurl, stretching toward the light, soft green and trembling with life.

"I know little of the void," Keeper Erania says quietly. "But it is a place where nothing grows. If your power is rooted in life, Jewel, how will you wield it in a realm of death?"

I watch the vines coil around my fingers, winding up my arms like veins of living light, flowering even as they fade beneath my sleeve.

"Life will always find a way to endure," I whisper. "Even in the heart of darkness."

The sun drifts lazily across the sky, its light spilling through the canopy in flickering ribbons that dance across my skin. Birds sing soft, lilting songs through the trees, and I close my eyes, breathing it all in. The Grove. My home. Where it all began and where, perhaps, it will all end. I am grateful that I came back. That I've felt the sun on my face one last time, the soil cool between my toes.

Keeper Erania leans on her staff and rises to her feet, her joints creaking like old branches. "Come, Jewel," she says, her voice warm but heavy. "Let us share food and words before you go. The Tenders wish to bid you farewell."

I nod and rise, brushing the earth from my palms. Erania gestures me closer, then cups my face in both hands. She kisses my cheek, her thumb lingering on my jaw.

"I will see you again, Amara Tyne," she murmurs. "And when I do, I will welcome your daughter to the Grove beside you."

Her words settle in me like sunlight, the reassurance I hadn't known I was still searching for. She smiles, then turns back toward the village, her staff pressing deep into the soil with each step.

I wait for Mirael to climb down from the rock. She moves slowly, as if every motion weighs something. When she reaches me, her hand disappears into the folds of her robe and returns holding a small wooden rune, threaded with a black leather cord.

"This is yours," she says, holding it out to me. "The one we made for you when you left." Her eyes flick to my neck, to where the tattoo once marked me. "But it seems you've no need of tokens now."

"No," I say softly, taking it from her hand. "This I need."

I tie it around my neck, letting the familiar weight settle against my collarbone. Mirael is right, my power no longer depends on carved runes or whispered words. But this piece of wood carries more than magic. It carries home. The memory of my sisters. The strength of the Souls. It is not a charm. I wear it for comfort, for courage. For the girl I used to be.

Mirael steps forward and pulls me into an embrace, firm, reluctant, but strong and steady as she has always been. The eldest of us. The fiercest. The one who bore the heaviest burdens without complaint. It was she who taught me, guided me, broke me down and built me back stronger.

"You must bring new sisters into the fold," I murmur against her ear. "Teach them as you taught me."

She exhales, pulling back with a small, crooked smile. "I suppose you're right. I did train an Awakened, after all."

Together, we return to the village. The Grove hums with twilight song, a low, lilting melody that drifts through the trees. The fire crackles, its smoke curling into the darkening sky, and bowls of roasted grain and sweetroot are passed from hand to hand. Laughter ripples softly, though there is a heaviness beneath it.

I smile where I can. Speak where I must. The warmth of the fire paints the faces of my people in gold, and for a time, I let myself believe this moment could stretch forever.

But there is one absence that gnaws at me.

I glance toward the shadows beyond the firelight, where the path winds toward the underground den. The others have all returned. Orios and Solena. Zyphoro and Reon. Even Ronin, standing quietly by the treeline, his new mask glinting faintly in the dusk. Yet Daed is nowhere to be seen.

My gaze searches for that familiar silhouette, the way the shadows gather where he stands. But there is nothing. Not even the whisper of his power in the air.

A quiet unease coils in my chest.

"Have you seen Daedalus?" I ask Solena as she passes me a bowl.

She shakes her head. "Not since the council ended."

The fire blurs before my eyes, its crackle too loud all of a sudden. I set the bowl down and rise, brushing my palms on my robes. "Excuse me," I murmur, though no one stops me.

The night air meets me cool and damp as I step beyond the firelight, the sound of the feast fading behind me. Then the air changes, thick, acrid, choking. The stench of smoke and ash hits first, then something far worse. Burnt flesh.

I lift a hand to cover my nose and press forward, eyes narrowing against the sting of it. The trail leads me toward the den. My pulse hammers as I draw closer. The door hangs open, its hinges groaning softly in the wind. Then I hear it, the wet, obscene sound of tearing flesh and the snap of bone between teeth.

"Daed," I whisper.

My feet move on their own, closer, until I reach the threshold. I reach for the handle and recoil when my fingers come away slick with blood. Still warm.

"Daed... what have you done?"

Inside, he kneels in the dark. His head is thrown back, body shuddering as if caught between pain and ecstasy, and there, above the corpse of a Legion soldier, hovers the creature bound to him. Emranth. Cloaked in smoke and shadow, his form is translucent, a nightmare half-born of the void. I can see right through him as he feeds, his fanged mouth buried in the flesh, tethered to my husband by a swirling thread of darkness.

Then Daed convulses, and his head jerks toward me. His eyes, wild and unfocused, meet mine. Emranth looks too, his hollow gaze burning before he lets out a piercing hiss that rattles the walls.

The apparition retreats, slipping back into Daed's chest. As he vanishes, so do the shadows, leaving only the dim shafts of light seeping through cracks in the ceiling. It's enough to see the horror laid bare, dozens of Legion bodies scattered across the floor, their blood pooling around my husband's knees.

Daed staggers upright, breath ragged, sweat running down his temples.

451

"I thought you weren't going to execute the prisoners," I say. My voice trembles, part fear, part fury, but beneath it all, something worse. Understanding.

"I said I'd *take care* of them," he rasps. He drags a hand through his hair, slick with sweat and smoke. "And I have." He swallows hard, his jaw tight. "I am not perfect, Amara."

I stare at him, at the man I love, the monster he can't escape.

I whisper. "I know, husband."

He steps forward, his hands gripping my shoulders.

"Now that Emranth is fed," he says quietly, "he is stronger and so am I."

The night wind brushes past us, cool and sharp, carrying the scent of smoke and death away with it.

I lift my chin, meeting his gaze.

"Then now is the time."

Chapter 46

Amara

The dawn breaks not with birdsong, but with silence.

The kind that hums beneath the skin and sets the heart to trembling.

The Tenders line the path, their heads bowed, hands clasped over their chests. Mirael stands among them, her face streaked with tears she doesn't bother to hide. Keeper Erania holds her staff high, offering final blessing as Daed and I pass.

They murmur prayers to the Souls, soft and reverent. *For the Jewel. For the Awakened. For Estra.*

I touch their hands as I pass, each one a goodbye, each one a promise that I will return.Then I look back one last time at my home, my heart, the Grove that gave me life and light.

"This is it," Daed says quietly. "Once the gate is open, there's no turning back."

"I know."

He extends his hand, and I take it. The earth stirs beneath my bare feet.

His jaw tightens. "You don't need to…"

"I do." I meet his gaze, steady and sure. "You know I do."

For a moment, the storm in his eyes breaks, not with fury, but sorrow. Then, with a breath that sounds too much like a prayer, he raises his other hand. The air splits open with a sound like the world tearing. Within the wound, there is only darkness, endless and ancient. The rift widens until it becomes a doorway, a mouth yawning toward eternity.

One by one, they step through. The last of the Blades of Baev'kalath, then Zyphoro, Orios and Solena, Reon close behind, Ronin last of them until only Daed and I remain.

He squeezes my hand, steadying me, the pounding heart, the rushing blood, the swirl of fear and faith. A breeze sweeps through the village, brushing a strand of hair across my face, and he tucks it back behind my ear with a tenderness that hurts.

I manage a breathless smile. "Maybe I should've braided my hair before going to battle."

He studies me, the corner of his mouth lifting. "No. I prefer you like this," he murmurs. "This is how I want to remember you."

For a heartbeat, we simply look at each other, the golden threads between us glowing faintly, dusting the twilight like fireflies only we can see. Then, we turn together to face the void.

The rift seals behind us as we step through, the world stitching its wound closed until all light vanishes. Darkness folds around us, thick and absolute. The Fae move with ease, their eyes keen in shadow, but Ronin and I are not so blessed. I refuse to stumble blindly, so I lift my palm.

A single green flame blossoms to life, small, but it burns bright enough to guide us through the dark.

It does not improve the view.

There is only infinite darkness, an unbroken sea of shadow, but at least now I can see it with my own eyes.

Ronin falls into step beside me, the two of us human among gods, our breaths shallow in the thick, cold air. Together, we walk deeper into the abyss.

Zyphoro's sharp eyes rake the dark, fingers twitching above the daggers strapped to her thighs, while Orios' gloved hand never strays from the hilt of his sword.

"No demons," Zyphoro mutters.

Daed's reply is low, edged with unease. "It's been this way since they took Estra. They've sealed themselves in An'kel where they know I cannot follow."

Zyphoro's mouth twists. "She must be precious to Gygarth. To surrender so much territory. To let us walk his shadow unchallenged."

A tremor catches in my chest, and the sound that escapes me, half gasp, half sob, turns every gaze toward me. I shake my head, turning from their concern, unwilling to speak my fear aloud.

Because I know Estra is precious.

She was precious from the moment she stirred in my womb to the moment she came screaming into this world.

But Gygarth cannot love, and the thought that she might be precious to him only as the finest morsel in his eternal hunger shreds what's left of my composure.

454

"How far must we go, Rook?" Orios rumbles.

Daed comes to a halt, the smoke curling faintly from his armor as he turns. "Here. The void is only the veil between our world and An'kel. No matter where the portal opens, it will lead to the same place."

All eyes shift to me.

Now is the moment I've dreaded. The one I've been walking toward since the day I woke beneath the earth.

"The blood of the Awakened opens the gate," I whisper, more to myself than anyone else. "The earth will drink it... and the void will answer."

The green flame in my palm extinguishes with a soft hiss.

I push my sleeves to my elbows, baring my wrists to the still air. The pulse beneath my skin beats in time with the trembling of the ground.

I lift my gaze to Daed.

"I need you to cut me."

He doesn't argue. He doesn't plead. We are far beyond the comfort of hesitation.

He exhales once and extends his hand. The shadows at his fingertips coil and twist, shaping themselves into a blade, a weapon both beautiful and terrible. Death Singer. The silver hilt gleams faintly, the purple stone at its center burning like a star as smoke drifts from its edge.

He holds me in his gaze, unblinking. His jaw is clenched, his whole body drawn tight as a bowstring.

"Tell me to stop," he murmurs. "And I will."

"I won't."

For a heartbeat, silence. Then a tremor of breath, and he draws the blade across my wrist.

Steel kisses flesh. The bite is deep but clean. Pain blooms white-hot, a flower opening in my veins, and still I do not flinch. The darkness beneath my feet quivers, hungry, drinking each drop that falls.

My voice cuts through the void, low and steady, carrying the weight of something ancient.

"Véthari lios an'thera. Véthari lios an'thera. Véthari lios an'thera."

The words strike the air like lightning. The earth shudders. Then, with a roar that seems to come from the marrow of the world, a gate erupts in fire before us.

Flames spiral upward in violent columns, heat slamming through the air hard enough to drive the others back, but not me. My feet stay rooted. My blood runs in twin rivers down my arms, pooling around my toes before the earth swallows it whole.

The portal widens. Its edges blacken and crack, spitting embers as smoke of silver and shadow spills through like breath from another realm.

And beyond it, An'kel.

I see the city through the rippling haze. Towering spires of jagged obsidian thrust into a sunless sky. A wasteland of ash and ruin stretched to every horizon. Winged horrors circle high above, shrieking like broken angels. The air itself seems to bleed light, gray and cold and endless.

At the center stands his temple. A fortress of death, its stairways climbing into infinity, its pyres burning with ghostly flame. Demons writhe in the carvings along its pillars, their twisted faces frozen mid-scream and I know. I know without question. She's there. Estra.

Hidden within those walls, within the heart of the void and within the grasp of the Father Below.

The more I think of her, the fainter the world becomes. My vision blurs, my head swims, my limbs turn heavy as stone. I can barely lift my arms. My brown skin fades toward the pallor of the Fae around me, every heartbeat a distant echo, slow, uneven, thunder in my ears. My life spills out in waves, feeding the gate that roars before us.

Death Singer dissolves into smoke. Daed's hands replace it, pressing hard against my wounds.

"That's enough, wife," he says. "It's open. You've done it. Now heal yourself."

His voice sounds far away, like a memory drowned beneath water. Even his face wavers before me, a blur of shadow. All I can see is Estra. My daughter. My little girl.

"Amara," he snarls through clenched teeth, his voice breaking through the haze. His grip tightens around my wrists, blood slicking his palms. "Heal yourself. Now."

When I don't respond, his control fractures. "Amara Tyne!" he roars. "Do as you're told, just one fucking time!"

I blink up at him, eyes half-lidded, and whisper, "If I heal... the portal will close."

His jaw hardens. "Then I'll throw your stubborn ass through it myself."

He swings his head toward the others. "Go!" he commands, voice booming like thunder through the void. They obey without hesitation, leaping through the portal into the unknown, their figures swallowed by the scorched horizon of An'kel.

When the last of them are gone, Daed looks back at me. "There. They're through. Now your turn."

But then he sees it, the blood slowing, thick and dark as wine, the streams reduced to trembling drops. His eyes widen, disbelief warring with fear.

"You can't die on me again," he says, his voice trembling in its fury. "Do you hear me, Amara? You can't. Do what you must, but you will heal."

It's not that I want to refuse him. I do not wish to die. It's that I don't yet know how. Keeper Erania's voice returns to me, a whisper in the dark. How can you bring life where only death dwells?

And then I remember my answer.

The one I have always carried.

Life endures.

Warmth blooms beneath my skin, slow at first, then bright enough to chase back the darkness. My veins flood with green light, pulsing in time with my heartbeat until it spills from me.

From the folds of my sleeves, vines unfurl, winding down my arms in slow, serpentine curls. Heart-shaped leaves burst to life along their length, trembling as though drawing breath for the first time. The vines loop and twist, finding my wrists. I gasp when they slip into the open wounds, a brief, searing sting, then release and where blood once flowed, blossoms bloom.

They fall in a cascade, a waterfall of petals and light spilling into the void. Wherever they land, the dark recoils. The blossoms spread, climbing the fractured walls of the gate, threading through black stone and shadow. Life surges wild and uncontained, vines racing up the scorched surface until a scattering of green and color blooms where only ash once lived.

The air hums. The earth itself seems to breathe again. I feel it fill me, life, raw and endless, mending every fracture within me. My veins blaze like dawn and the first breath I draw feels like drawing the world itself into my lungs.

Daed's hands find my face. He looks at me as if it kills him to love me this much, and then he does what he always does when he feels too much. He kisses me hard and desperately.

When he pulls away, his voice cracks through the hush, sharp as a whip.

"Stop doing that," he growls before he snatches my hand and pulls me through the gate where the others wait for us.

The moment we cross the threshold, the air changes. It thickens, the scent of sulfur and decay floods my lungs. The sky above us bleeds grey and black, split by streaks of crimson lightning.

Then the darkness moves.

Shapes crawl from it, too many to count. Limbs where no limbs should be, eyes burning white within faces that twist and reform with every breath. They shriek, the sound so shrill it makes the bones in my skull hum. The demons of the void have come to greet us.

Zyphoro takes to the skies in a flash of silver, her wings igniting like burning steel. She dives through the swarm, twin daggers slicing clean arcs that trail fire while below her, Orios wades through the fray, his sword cleaving through flesh and shadow, his armor already slick with black blood. Beside him, Ronin's blade hums, precise and merciless.

The ground beneath my feet trembles, whispering my name. I drop to one knee and press my palm to the ashen soil. "Rise," I whisper, and the land obeys.

From the cracks and scars of An'kel's wasteland, vines burst through, blackened roots turned green by my touch, sprouting thorns sharp as blades. They lash outward, wrapping around the demons, impaling them, dragging their shrieking bodies down into the earth that birthed them.

For every one that falls, three more rise. But I am no longer afraid. The Grove lives within me now, even here, where life was never meant to be.

And through it all, Daed.

He is death incarnate, a storm of shadow and smoke. Death Singer gleams in his hand, cutting through the void with every swing. The smoke around him takes form, tendrils and wings, the echoes of Emranth's power surging through him. Shadows bend at his will, wrapping around the enemy like chains.

The great doors of the temple groan open, and from the depths emerges a gargantuan demon, black armor fused to molten flesh, each breath a furnace roar. Reon turns toward it, cutting down the last of the creatures between them. His blade hums, his gaze locked on the oncoming goliath.

He darts left, too fast to follow, but the demon's claw catches him mid-stride. It hurls him like a rag doll across the field, his body slamming against jagged rock. He crumples to the ground, blood dark against the ash. The demon closes in, forming a spike of hardened bone in its smoky hand. Reon lifts his head, eyes widening as the spike plunges toward him and then time stops.

The air stills. The demon freezes, spike suspended inches from his chest, golden sparks dancing from Reon's trembling fingers. His lips part in disbelief, then curve into a slow, feral smile.

He pushes to his feet, the power blazing gold around him. In one bound he scales the demon's arm, boots striking sparks against its armor. He vaults onto its shoulder, then onto its head, his sword raised high and drives his blade straight through its skull.

Light bursts from the wound. The demon convulses, fractures, and collapses into a storm of ash. When the dust settles, Reon lands lightly on his feet, hair wild, sword gleaming, eyes alight and behind him, the battle roars on.

"Get to the temple!" Reon bellows, his voice cracking like thunder over the battlefield. "We'll take care of these pitiful demons!"

I nod once, breathless, and Daed and I push forward, shoulder to shoulder through the carnage.

We reach the base of the temple steps just as fresh horrors pour forth. Demons wrapped in smoke and sinew, claws like hooked blades, their fangs dripping trails of venom. They surge toward us in a tide of shrieks and gnashing teeth.

Daed and I exchange a single glance. No words, only the grim understanding that this is what we were made for.

I draw in a breath and let the power build. My veins blaze with light, throbbing with living fire until the energy burns behind my eyes. When I raise my hands, they are wreathed in emerald flame. The nearest demon lunges, too slow. I hurl a blazing sphere into its chest, and it detonates, bursting the creature into ash. The explosion ripples outward, catching the others in its wake. Those who survive stagger, burning, their shrieks echoing up the black steps. The stone runs slick with their blood, thick, oily, and dark as tar.

Out of the corner of my eye, I catch Daed. He's not moving, just watching. Still as a statue in the storm.

"Daed?" I call.

He doesn't answer. He lifts Death Singer high, both hands wrapped tight around the hilt. Then, with a roar, he drives it down.

The blade strikes stone with the force of a quake. Sparks burst out, white-hot, and the ground cracks in spiderwebs beneath our feet.

Then the world inhales.

Smoke floods upward, coiling around him, cloaking him. When it clears, wings of shadow erupt from his back, unfurling banners of night that stretch wide enough to blot out the dim light of An'kel's sky. The wind howls as they snap open, the sound like a scream torn from the void.

And then Emranth.

The demon tears free of Daed's chest in a torrent of shadow and smoke. His form is monstrous, tattered cloak whipping like a storm as his tentacles writhe, his white eyes gleaming with hunger. He swoops upon the oncoming horde, a specter of horror, swallowing everything in his path. Screams cut short. Bodies vanish into his gaping maw.

We push forward, side by side. The steps climb and climb, each one a drumbeat in my chest, each corpse a promise that we are closer. Estra hangs at the edge of every breath I take, a name like a prayer on my lips.

The horde crumbles. Demons shriek and unmake beneath green fire and void, bodies unspooling into smoke. For a moment, the world settles. Then, at the top of the stairs, new danger lays itself bare.

The creature is not like any demon we've faced, but something other. I've never seen such armor. Heavy plates etched with impossible filigree, ribs and runes carved into black steel that seems to swallow the light. The helm is forged into a snarling maw, a demon's face twisted in eternal hunger, and within the hollow sockets burn two white, furious eyes.

Daed's mouth quirks. "Is this all that's left?" he calls.

Emranth laughs. He vaults from Daed in a column of smoke, a ravenous silhouette that plunges toward the armored figure.

The demon reaches to the sheath at its back and draws a blade slender and silver, a line of moonlight forged in steel. Emranth slashes. The demon meets him in midair.

The cut is obscene in its elegance. One clean diagonal of silver that cleaves the shadow. Emranth howls. His monstrous shape unravels, unpicking itself into drifting smoke. He is gone in a single breath. A ripple runs through Daed as the shadow recoils, folding into him like a returning tide.

For a heartbeat he keels, shoulders collapsing as he sucks in air. I fear, for an instant, that the fight has left him. Then he steadies, rolls his shoulders, flings hair from his eyes and hauls Death Singer free from the stone.

"Good," he breathes. "A challenge. I will enjoy taking your head, demon, and shoving it down your master's throat."

He plants his feet, shoulders squared, Death Singer held high. Around us the ruined city listens, and the grin on his face is a promise that will not be broken.

Daed launches himself upward, wings of smoke and shadow snapping wide, the night folding beneath their span. He rises with impossible speed, the force of it cracking the stone at his feet. Death Singer burns in his grip, the blade alive with the void's hum. The armored demon tilts its head as if in mockery, unmoving and with ice-veined patience.

When Daed descends, he brings the blade down in a strike that could cleave mountains. Only then does the demon move, raising its silver weapon in a single, lazy arc.

Steel meets steel.

The sound is cataclysmic. Sparks burst like dying stars, their light scattering over the blackened temple steps. The impact drives a shockwave through the air, rippling the smoke around them in concentric waves.

They break apart, then crash together again.

The fight becomes a storm. Blades whistle and shriek as they meet, each strike a flash of light against the dark. Daed's wings beat once, propelling him forward. The demon pivots effortlessly, its cloak swirling like liquid night. There is rhythm in the violence, an ancient, dreadful grace. Each movement echoes the other, as if they were mirror images born from the same void.

I watch, breath trapped in my chest, unable to look away. For all Daed's ferocity, this thing meets him without strain, without fear.

Daed's blade howls through the air again, a deadly arc of shadow. The demon sidesteps, the blow missing by a breath. Then it counters, spinning, slashing upward, and Daed blocks, the force of it sending cracks through the landing.

It's not a battle. It's a dance between gods.

I can feel the earth tremble with every clash, the air split with their fury. Still, Daed doesn't call for me, but I know he needs me. His strength cannot match this creature alone.

I summon my power, a flare igniting in my palm. The flame builds and builds until it roars to life, searing green, my veins burning. I thrust my hand forward and the fire tears through the air.

But the demon doesn't even glance my way.

It lifts its free hand, and from the air itself, a wall of smoke materializes. My flame crashes into it, shattering. The embers scatter harmlessly into the dark and still, the warrior fights Daed with its other hand, unbothered.

How?

Smoke and vine. Death and life. Both subdued by a single foe.

My stomach twists with dread, my heartbeat stuttering as the truth takes shape in my mind. This is no mere servant of Gygarth.

This is his champion.

Emranth's successor.

And as its burning white eyes finally shift to me, I feel the weight of eternity in their gaze.

I will not be undone by this monster.

I will not fall to a servant before I've even set eyes on its master.

I have not come this far to fail now.

My fingers curl, power surging through my veins like wildfire. With a cry, I throw my hands forward and the earth answers. Vines burst through the stone in a thunderous crack, shards scattering as they spiral upward toward the demon.

It reacts instantly. Tendrils of smoke unravel from its armor, meeting the vines midair. They crash together, smoke and root, twisting and strangling as they fight for dominance, life and death locked in a furious embrace. But my power is older. Wilder. Some vines break through, snapping around the demon's leg and wrenching it to one knee with a groan that echoes like thunder.

"Now!" I shout.

Daed surges forward, wings flaring, raising Death Singer high. The void hums as he brings the blade down, but the demon catches the strike, its silver weapon raised above its head, steel locking against steel. The impact throws sparks, and for a heartbeat they are frozen, equals in strength and fury.

Daed grits his teeth, pressing down with all the power left in his battered body. Shadows rise from his skin, coiling around the demon's arm, trying to drag it lower. The stone beneath them cracks.

"Yield, damn you!" he snarls through clenched teeth.

I summon another surge. More vines spear through the fractured floor, wrapping the creature's other leg, dragging it down. The demon is forced onto both knees, armor screeching against stone. Death Singer's tip inches closer to its neck. The creature trembles, resisting, but I can feel it breaking.

So close. So very close.

Then, with a metallic cry, the demon's sword slips from its grasp and clatters to the ground. Victory flares in my chest until, in a blur of motion, it twists aside, Daed's killing blow slicing down and shearing through its arm instead. The cut is clean, armor and flesh giving way like paper. Black smoke spills from the wound, thick and writhing.

The creature makes no sound of pain. Not even a hiss.

It crouches low, and in one swift motion, draws a dagger from its boot, slicing through the vines at its feet. In a blink, it's up, retreating, limping toward the temple steps.

"No, you don't!" Daed bellows, fury ripping through the air. "Coward!"

He grips Death Singer in both hands, draws back, and hurls it with all his strength. The blade spins through the darkness, trailing smoke like comet tails.

It should have struck. It should have ended this.

But before the blade can pierce the fleeing demon's back, a massive tendril of smoke lashes from the temple's doorway, snapping through the air like a whip. It coils around Death Singer, tightens, and with a sickening crack, shatters it in two.

Daed staggers as if struck himself, his whole body jolting with the pain of it. His connection to the weapon breaks in that instant. He falls to one knee, gasping, as the shattered blade clatters to the stone beside the fallen purple gem, its light dying.

"Daed," I breathe, rushing to him.

He pulls me into his arms, holding me tight as we both lift our eyes to the temple's towering entrance.

The air ripples. The shadows bend, and then he comes.

Smoke bleeds from the shadows, thick and sentient, coiling upward until it blocks the sky. It gathers and swells, a towering mass of writhing tentacles and gnashing void-teeth, a gaping maw large enough to swallow a world. And above it all, a single white eye opens, the eye that sees all, staring down as if we are insects beneath its heel.

The temple groans. Stone cracks. The city trembles around us.

Gygarth.

The Father Below.

The God of Death.

His roar shakes the foundations of this forsaken world, and while the demons that still live answer with cries of devotion, the few of our own who yet breathe stare in terror.

But I do not bow.

I stand unbroken where I was always meant to. At Daed's side.

CHAPTER 47
DAED

B *efore her.* The storm is alive.

It screams as it tears across the cliffs, battering the black fortress of Baev'kalath until even the stones tremble beneath its fury. Waves crash against the sheer walls, spray bursting high enough to soak the battlements. The rain is relentless. It pours down my hair, over my eyes, through the seams of my leathers, filling my boots until the cold is bone-deep.

Before me, a Fae warrior kneels. Filth and rain streak his face, his hands clasp together in supplication. His shoulders tremble, not from the cold, but from the weight of his shame.

"Forgive me, Rook," he pleads, voice hoarse against the wind. "I was weak. I should not have been tempted."

I tighten my grip on Death Singer. The storm hisses across the blade, rain running down the steel like blood. My reflection wavers in the violet jewel at its hilt.

"You want forgiveness?" My voice cuts through the tempest. "You should have saved me the trouble and done this yourself. You've brought shame to your House, to your king... to yourself."

His chin lifts, just enough for me to see his eyes. "I can't fight this war anymore. I'm tired, Rook. Of the bloodshed. Of the screams. They haunt me." His breath shudders. "Forgive me."

I step closer, Death Singer angled toward the ground. The rain stings my cheeks like needles.

"I can't give you forgiveness," I tell him quietly. "But I can give you peace. From the voices. From the pain."

He closes his eyes, lips parting in something between a prayer and a sob.

"Go well into the void, Blade."

465

Death Singer sings once. The blade cleaves through rain and flesh alike. His head strikes the stone. His body topples over the railing, vanishing into the churning sea below.

Then, from above me, a gasp breaks the silence.

My head snaps upward. Through the storm, through the torrent, she stands on the balcony. The wind tangles her brown hair around her face, rain clinging to her lashes. Her eyes meet mine, wide as the dawn.

Amara Tyne.

The world stills. The roar of the storm fades into nothing. And then I see it, the shimmer of golden threads spinning through the air, weaving from my chest to hers. The Binds of Fate.

They glimmer like sunlight through rain and I feel them tighten around my ribs until I can barely draw breath.

I never wanted it to come to this.

You were never supposed to be here.

I tried to stay away. Harder than I've ever tried for anything. But I am nothing before the will of fate.

We are its puppets, you and I. Our story was etched into our souls long before this world was born.

And still, I will try to save you.

From this place. From me.

I will make you hate me, Amara Tyne. Hate me until the mere sound of my name burns your throat.

Hate me until you turn and never look back.

Because that is the only way you will live.

So when I am cruel, when I taunt you and break you, when I become every monster whispered about in frightened tongues, know this.

That I love you.

With every cursed breath.

With every damned heartbeat.

Until the end of this life and all others.

I love you, Amara Tyne.

***

After her. The temple trembles as Gygarth moves. A god of smoke and bone and shadow, his form fills the world, every writhing tentacle a mountain, every breath a hurricane. The air is poison, thick and burning in my lungs, and still I charge.

"Together!" I shout.

Amara's hand finds mine for a heartbeat, a spark of life that burns even in this place of death. Then she tears away, green fire erupting from her palms. It arcs through the darkness, slamming into Gygarth's chest, the explosion blinding, shaking the foundations of this world. Vines burst from the scorched stone, coiling up the monster's limbs, thorns digging deep.

He laughs.

The sound is hollow thunder that crawls inside my skull. The vines shrivel to ash before they even finish blooming, their life devoured, absorbed. Amara stumbles, clutching her chest, as if he's drinking straight from her veins.

The ground splinters. A dozen tentacles surge upward like towers, lashing through the battlefield.

Zyphoro is the first to answer, wings bursting as she soars high, twin daggers gleaming. She dives, slicing through tendons and shadow, each strike a blur of light.

Below her, Orios bellows, charging through the ash. He grips two tentacles in his massive hands, veins bulging, muscles straining, and rips them apart with a wet, shuddering crack. Black ichor spills across his armor, burning through the metal, but he doesn't stop. Solena fights at his side, her blade hacking at tendrils of smoke, weaving as they slam against the ground, too slow to catch her, until luck runs out. A tentacle whips through the air and catches her full across the face. Blood sprays. She screams just before another strike sends her tumbling down the stairs.

Orios roars. His wings explode as he launches himself into the air. He dives, catches her mid-fall, folding his body around hers as they hit the stone. The impact shakes the stairs, and still he takes the brunt of it, shielding her with his wings.

Reon rushes forward, fury burning bright in his hazel eyes. His sword flares gold as he thrusts it toward the advancing tentacles. Time shudders, the world flickering and stalling, freezing one, two, three of the monstrous limbs mid-strike.

But Gygarth is too vast, too ancient to be slowed. His other limbs surge through the cracks of time, moving faster than Reon can draw breath. A spike of shadow pierces his abdomen, lifting him from the ground before flinging him aside. He crashes against the temple wall, leaving a smear of blood as he slides to the floor.

"Reon!" Amara cries, but there's no time.

Another tentacle whips toward her, faster than I can move.

Ronin moves instead.

He lunges between her and the strike, sword flashing, deflecting one blow before another coils around him. The pressure is immediate and unbearable. His armor creaks, then cracks, the sound a sickening symphony of breaking bone and splintering steel.

He gasps, blood spraying from his lips as the demon crushes him. Then Gygarth drops him like refuse, his body slamming against the stone with a thud that silences even the storm.

Zyphoro drops beside me, one wing dragging, feathers torn and dripping shadow. Amara stumbles to my other side, green fire guttering weakly in her trembling hands. Together we stand amid ruin. Our friends broken, our strength bleeding from us as Gygarth looms above, his writhing limbs blotting out what remains of the sky.

Zyphoro spits blood. "This is impossible. He is death itself. He has no weakness. He cannot be killed." Her eyes flicker, mind grasping at anything. "Emranth. He could not die either, but you caged him."

I shake my head. "Emranth was not a god," I say quietly. "He was not pure death." I force Zyphoro to meet my eyes. "To consume Gygarth is to die, sister."

Her gaze cuts between Gygarth, then me, then Amara.

"Did you not hear me?" I snap.

"I heard you," she whispers. "To consume Gygarth is to die."

Then she punches me hard, stars bursting behind my eyes as I stumble. "But a cage does not need to live," she snarls, "it only needs to hold."

And then she launches herself into the sky, faster than I have ever seen her fly, even with one broken wing. A streak of black hair, a comet of fury and sacrifice, arrowing toward the monster that destroyed our world.

Amara grips my hand, voice shaking. "She won't survive."

"I know." My voice is ash. "It's suicide."

I look at my wife. At the woman I bled for, burned for, would kill gods for. I memorize her one last time.

She catches my stare. "What?" confusion tightening her brow.

"I love you," I murmur.

Realization hits her. "Daedalus... no."

"Zyphoro is right. He cannot be killed. This is the only way we save Estra. The only way we end him."

"There has to be another way," she begs, voice cracking, tears streaking dirt and blood on her cheeks.

"No." My voice is steady now. "I will not let my sister suffer for me. Not again."

Before she can scream another word, I cup her face and kiss her, leaving every breath I won't get to take, every word I'll never speak, every future I will not see, upon her lips.

She trembles against me. I let her go.

The void rips open at my call. Darkness claws across my skin as I step through, reappearing in the air before Zyphoro. Her eyes widen in shock, wings flaring as she jerks to stop before colliding.

"What are you doing?" she roars. "Move!"

"No." I plant myself in her path. "You cannot do this."

"I didn't ask you!" she snaps, rage shaking her frame. "Don't you see? This is the only way. Then you will be free. Your family will be free."

I meet her gaze. Twin storms, twin sacrifices and finally, softly.

"I know."

I draw in a long breath. A strange lightness fills me, like air before dawn.

"Zyphoro." Her name trembles on my tongue. My fingers move to the moonstone at my neck. I tear the cord free and fling it toward her. She catches it on instinct, confusion flashing across her face.

"Now we are even."

Her brow tightens. "Daed..."

I do not let her finish. Shadow rises at my call, a whip of smoke snapping toward her. It coils around her body, binding her arms, winding again and again until she cannot lift a finger. Her wings falter, and she plummets toward the earth screaming my name.

I watch as she falls, as the ground rushes up to claim her. At the last breath I catch her descent, slowing it so she crumples rather than breaks. But I do not free her. If I release her now she will rise again, furious and relentless. Infuriating, stubborn sister of mine.

She would follow me into death without hesitation.

So I must leave her behind to live.

For a moment I hover, breath shaking, fingers tingling like they are waking or dying. I do not know which.

Then I turn away.

I spread my wings, pin them back tight against the wind, and take the path my sister meant to fly.

The one she will not die for.

The one I will.

I turn to face Gygarth, his vast, smoke-wreathed form blotting out what little light remains. All my life he has haunted me. Controlled me. Made me his weapon. His shadow. His mirror and yet, now that I stand before him, ready to end this, ready to take him into the dark with me. I feel no hatred.

Because when I fall, I will take the Father Below with me, and the world, and everyone I love will finally be free.

I soar high, wings cutting through smoke. Gygarth lashes his tentacles at me, the air screaming with every strike. I summon a shard of shadow. It spears through one tendril and pins it to a crumbling column of the temple. Another comes. Then another.

I throw more shards of darkness forged from my will alone, each one sharper, more lethal than the last. They sear through Gygarth's flesh until the god howls, black ichor spilling across the stone like spilled night.

His voice follows, not from his mouth, but inside my skull, a thousand whispers layered as one.

"Favored son. Little prince. I command you. Kneel and serve me!"

My jaw tightens. Wings flare wide. Every muscle in me trembles with the pressure of his command. But I do not kneel. I do not bow. I hurl another shard and another until the air fills with them.

He roars once more, summoning the remnants of his army, the twisted demons still crawling through the ruins, but below me, Amara and Zyphoro meet them. Green fire and daggers of smoke and shadow.

"Kneel!" he booms.

But he cannot control me. Not anymore.

Because I have given myself to her completely.

To the light that burns brighter than death.

To the only soul I will ever kneel before.

She is my queen, and I will love her until the stars burn out.

I open my mouth, close my eyes, and inhale.

At first, it's only smoke, thin tendrils curling down my throat. But then it grows heavier, darker, thicker, until it's pouring into me in torrents. I drag Gygarth into myself one wisp at a time, swallowing his essence, his power. I feel him inside me.

The god. The void. The death that was never meant to be contained.

He floods my veins, burns through my skull, claws at my insides. His poison spreads, his rot devouring what's left of me. I glance at my hands and watch my veins turn black, branching beneath my skin like roots in dead soil. The corruption creeps higher, painting me in shadow.

Tears spill from my eyes, hot and stinging and when I touch them, they come away thick and dark as demon's blood.

My wings falter. The shadow in them flickers, thinning, fraying at the edges. My body is breaking under the weight of the god I've consumed, but I don't stop. I cannot stop.

I draw the last of him in. Every drop of unholy power until Gygarth is gone. Vanished. Devoured.

The voice in my head finally silenced. Meat for the beast.

My mouth closes with a snap that echoes through the ruin.

I feel so cold.

My wings collapse, my body plummets. I fall through the stillness, through the ash and the smoke, through the fading echoes of a god's death.

When I hit the temple floor, the sound cracks the air.

Pain surges, then nothing and just before darkness claims me, I swear I hear her. Estra.

Her laughter, soft and bright.

Then darkness.

CHAPTER 48

AMARA

"D^{aed!}"

His name rips from my throat before I even reach him. I stumble over broken stone and ash, my legs barely holding beneath me.

He lies still in the center of the ruin, the shadows around him gone quiet, the air hollow in his absence. I fall to my knees beside his body, gather him into my arms, the weight of him both familiar and unbearable. His head lolls against my shoulder, his hair matted with soot and blood. His skin is cold and when I press my palm to his chest, there's nothing. No heartbeat. No spark. No golden thread.

The bond that once hummed between us, that constant pulse of life and magic, is gone. Torn.

Zyphoro folds in on herself, knees tight to her chest, arms cinched around her ribs as though she's afraid she'll split apart. She rocks, breath hitching, sobs tearing out of her in ragged bursts. Daed's moonstone gleams in her fist, gripped so fiercely her knuckles bleed.

My fingers trace his face, his jaw, his mouth. I press my forehead to his.

"I love you," I whisper, again and again, like a prayer, like a curse. "And I will not live without you."

My tears fall through the cracks in the stone, vanishing into the dark beneath us. The earth stirs. A low hum begins in my bones.

Zyphoro sniffs, then gulps, then slowly rises to her feet, one trembling hand pressed to her heart. "Amara..."

The light comes first as a flicker, a single pulse of green beneath my skin. Then another. Then it spreads, winding across my arms, my throat, my face, until the air around me shimmers. The glow thickens, radiant and wild, spinning in a slow spiral around Daed's body.

"Amara, stop!" Zyphoro calls, shielding her eyes. She remembers the fire. "You'll burn yourself alive!"

But the power is beyond stopping. My grief is beyond stopping.

It builds, pulsing, swelling, until the entire temple trembles with it. The light engulfs us both, wrapping Daed in its embrace. I scream, my voice breaking with pain and power as the ground splits beneath us and a beam of green light erupts skyward, spearing through the heavy clouds above.

The brilliance blinds even the gods. Demons still crawling through the ruins crumble to ash, their bodies disintegrating in the wake of that holy fire.

And I feel it. A tearing, a ripping through bone and blood, something ancient and wild clawing its way out from beneath my skin. Heat sears down my spine, bright and unbearable, and then wings burst from my back. They tear into existence in a spray of emerald and gold light, feathers unfurling like shards of dawn.

The pain is exquisite. Pure. Endless. It is agony that remakes. Fire that cleanses. My body trembles, reshaping around power I did not know I carried. The world narrows to the raw, brutal beauty of it, to the sound of muscle splitting and magic stitching me into something new.

And through the torment, a terror and wonder fill me. I am not what I was. I can never be what I was.

When it finally ends, when the light fades and the world grows still again, I collapse. Exhausted. My hands tremble where they cradle him. Daed, motionless in my arms.

His face is pale beneath the soot, his lips are parted, but no breath escapes them. The golden threads that once connected us, that sang through my soul, remain dark.

"No..." The word breaks from me like glass. "No, please."

I press trembling fingers to his throat. Nothing.

To his chest. Still nothing.

I curl over him, the sob tearing through me so hard it steals my breath. My wings unfurl, curling around us both like a cocoon. Blossoms spill from them in a cascade of emerald and white, drifting over his body, over the stones, over my hands shaking against his heart.

The petals gather in his hair, on his shoulders, on the curve of his jaw. A thousand tiny goodbyes.

"I tried," I whisper into the hollow of his throat. "I tried to bring you back."

I press my lips to his skin.

Something shifts.

So faint I almost miss it.

A tremor beneath my palm.

I freeze, breath held, heart hammering, and then another. Stronger this time. A flutter. A heartbeat.

My head snaps up, tears still spilling freely down my cheeks.

"Daed?"

Then his chest rises. A ragged, shuddering breath breaks the silence, followed by another, and another, until he gasps, sharp and desperate, as though the world is rushing back into him.

His eyes open, unfocused at first, then burning.

The petals fall faster, the blossoms shiver on my wings, and I laugh through the tears still streaming down my face.

"Welcome back, my love," I whisper, cradling his face as he blinks up at me, confusion and awe mingling in those eyes I thought I'd never see again.

As the brilliance dims, glittering ashes of light drift down like slow-falling stars. They touch the wounded earth, the shattered stones and the fallen. The shimmering dust settles upon Solena and Orios, upon Reon and Ronin, seeping into their wounds, their blood, their bones.

I cradle Daed's face and lift his chin so he has to look at me.

"You brought me back," he whispers, voice thin as breath. His eyes focus, and when he notices my wings, his brows lift. "And now you can fly?"

I shrug. "I don't know. I haven't tried yet."

He manages a crooked smile, stubborn and bright as ever. "Then I will teach you, wife."

A laugh slips from me, small and soft, something I thought I had lost forever. "I look forward to it, husband."

He lifts his chin and I lean in, ready to kiss him.

Zyphoro barrels into me, shoving me aside. My wings vanish in shock as she wraps Daed up and squeezes him so hard his eyes bulge.

"I thought you were dead!" she shrieks.

"I was," he croaks.

She loosens her grip. He drags in a wheezing breath.

"Do not ever do that again," she orders, voice cracking.

Daed steadies his breathing. When he can speak, he reaches for her shoulder, squeezing it with what strength he has.

"You either," he breathes.

Zyphoro and I haul Daed to his feet. He sways, then steadies.

"Gygarth," I say quietly. "Is he truly gone?"

Daed brushes his knuckle against his chest. "I feel him," he murmurs. "Writhing like snakes inside me. But he is imprisoned for now."

I nod slowly. "For now. But what if..."

He cuts me off. "No buts. No what ifs. For now he is silent. and our daughter is waiting for us. Nothing else matters."

Suddenly he lets out a low groan and lurches forward.

"Is this what it feels like?" he rasps, breath shaky. "Being resurrected?"

"I'm not sure," I say softly. "How do you feel?"

He grimaces, rubbing the back of his neck. "Like shit."

"Then yes," I tell him. "That's what it feels like."

Ronin and the others climb the stairs toward us, healed and renewed, weapons drawn and ready to face whatever waits beyond the temple's doors.

But Daed lifts a hand, his voice low but certain. "The battle is won," he says. "What comes next, Amara and I must do alone."

I lace my fingers through his and nod in agreement. Then I take Zyphoro's dagger from her belt, draw it across my palm, and let my blood spill into the air. Each drop burns like molten emerald, and when they fall, the air shatters, splitting open in a shimmering rift. Through the veil, I glimpse the Grove.

"Go," I tell them. "We will follow soon."

"Are you sure?" Solena asks, worry shadowing her face. "You do not know what still lurks within."

I glance at Daed, my heart steady, a small smile finding its way to my lips. "There is nothing left in this world that can stand against us."

Solena exhales, nods once, then takes Orios' arm. Together they step through the rift. Reon follows with a wry grin and a bow of his copper head, then Ronin with a quiet nod.

Zyphoro lingers. She approaches Daed, holding his moonstone necklace between her fingers, but instead of returning it, she unclasps her own. With deft hands, she braids the two leather cords together before dropping the newly woven strand into Daed's waiting palm.

"Give that to my niece," Zyphoro says, her voice trembling just slightly. "Tell her it belonged to her grandmother. Queen Veloria."

Daed shivers. For a heartbeat, brother and sister mirror each other perfectly. The same storm flickering in their eyes, the same weight of legacy in their bones.

"As you wish, sister," he replies.

She steps to me then, presses a kiss to my cheek, her breath soft against my ear.

"Thank you, Amara," she whispers. "For saving my brother and for saving me from my oath to kill him."

Before I can answer, she turns, a blur of motion, and twirls into the portal. The veil closes behind her, and the blood on my palm blossoms into a spill of flowers that scatter across the temple stairs.

Then it is only Daed and I, standing before the mouth of the temple. The heart of Gygarth's kingdom. Darkness still lurks here, yet I feel no fear. Only resolve. Only faith that what waits inside will end with our family whole again.

We step forward. Once. Twice.

The temple looms ahead, columns scorched black where Gygarth fell, idols of bone and stone staring down from the walls. Demons, carved in the forms of beasts, a bat, a serpent, a lion, leer from every alcove.

We move deeper, our footsteps echoing against stone, until a single candle flickers in the distance. A trembling flame in a sea of dark. We follow it. The light grows, revealing a hall with open arches that gape toward the wasteland beyond and in the center of the chamber stands a crib.

My heart seizes, beating so hard I swear it might burst from my chest. Each step toward it feels like walking on a blade, thin and sharp and merciless.

We reach it together.

We peer inside.

Nothing.

Empty.

No... not empty.

I reach into the cradle, fingers brushing the furs within, and come away with a handful of pale ash that runs like dust through my trembling hand.

The sound that leaves me is not human. A scream, a sob, a breaking of the soul. I collapse against the edge of the crib.

"She's gone," I choke. "Daed. She's gone!"

He stands beside me, trembling. His fangs bared, biting down on his lip so hard his mouth drips blood as his chest heaves with breath. Then, with a roar that shakes the pillars, Daed loses control.

Tentacles of smoke and shadow lash from his back, cracking against the walls, splintering the ancient stone as if it were nothing. Columns shatter. Statues crumble. His grief is ruin given form.

Then, whether by fury or fate, one strike hits the cradle and it explodes into shards of bone, scattering Estra's ashes into the air.

Daed catches me as I fall, pulling me against his chest. He doesn't weep, but I feel his body quake beneath my hands, the ragged shudder of a warrior who cannot bear to stand and in that moment, I realize it is me holding him up, my hands, my body, keeping him from falling apart entirely.

A howl rips through our mourning. From the dark the demon warrior we thought dead edge-steps into the torchlight, blade already bared. Daed shoves me aside, arm up, bracing. The sword slams into his gauntlet. Metal screams, and though his armor takes most of it, a line of blood opens along his forearm.

Daed growls, clamps onto the creature's wrist and boots it in the gut until it folds. It spits and scrambles, refusing to be finished. Grief hollows me out, and rage fills the space. I want... I need to tear this thing apart for what it took. The thought is a small, terrible pleasure that steels my hands.

I curl my fingers. Green flame coils in my palm, hot with promise.

The demon lunges again, but no void-beast can stand against parents who have lost their child. Daed drives it back, again and again, pounding it down, forcing it up, his movements almost cruel with restraint. I have no patience for restraint. I want it burned. I want it to feel the same emptiness it left in me.

Daed takes the advantage once more, landing another hard blow that sends the demon reeling backwards. Its sword drops, clanging across the ground. The creature reaches blindly for its blade, but Daed's foot pins it. He yanks the weapon free, spins it, and levels the point, but before he can strike, I cry out.

"Husband."

The sword halts mid-arc. Daed's arms lock, then slacken.

"Look." I point. There's a smear of blood across the stone, a thin line that leaks from the demon.

But it is not black. This blood is red. Bright. Ordinary.

Daed blinks. The sword tip scrapes the stone. His hands go slack.

I step forward, and the demon drags itself on blood-slick elbows, desperate to get away. I don't let it. I seize its arm, fingers digging in. It cries out, but the sound is wrong. Not the guttural, hollow snarl from before, but something thinner, frayed.

It fights, and so do I. I wrench hard, refusing to release, until a gauntlet slips free. A ribbon lies beneath, worn and frayed, its color nearly lost to time and filth, but my heart knows it instantly.

Once, it was red.

"Where did you get this?" I breathe, and the room narrows to those words.

The demon does not answer. It still tries to crawl away. It lashes out, boots my abdomen, and I stagger back, breath punched from me, enough time for it to scramble upright and make its escape.

"Daed, stop it!" I scream.

He does. Smoke explodes from him in a shockwave that knocks the creature flat onto its belly, a black tendril lashes out and tangles its leg, dragging it back. It thrashes, fists battering stone, feet kicking blindly, but the magic holds. The howl cuts the air like a knife, but it changes now. Less a triumphant roar than the panic of something caught.

"Hold it," I tell him. Daed does as I ask, gripping the thing by the shoulders and holding so I can see.

Up close, it is smaller, no longer the hulking nightmare we fought on the temple stairs, its edges blunted as if its terror is being peeled away. The smoke that once cloaked it is gone, whatever ferocity fed it has dwindled. It stands barely taller than me, not much broader. The thing that frightened me two breaths ago is nowhere to be seen.

My hand trembles when I reach for its helm. Behind that hideous mask lie the answers I have been searching for. How my daughter died. What hands took her. What shape her end wore.

I need that truth even if it will splinter the last of me.

I pull.

The mask comes away with a wet, soft sound. I lose my grip, and it falls from my fingers and rolls across the stone, the echo like a bell tolling inside my chest.

This is not a demon. Not at all.

Soft brown skin. Dark curls escaping a careless braid. Pointed ears. Eyes of the storm... just like her father.

"Estra..." The name slips out of me before reason can catch it. The sound is lost to the temple, but it lands in the air between us. "It...it can't be..."

Daed goes still at the look on my face, at the way bewilderment and a terrible hope war there.

"What is it?" he asks, because he hasn't seen what I have.

"How?" I murmur. "You were only a baby. It's been weeks, weeks for us, not years..." My voice fractures. I look to Daed and know he reads every question on my face.

She screams. "Let me go, human! I will cut you down! In his name!"

Daed spins her, his hands clamping onto her shoulders, harder than they should. I reach to soften his grip, but he is stone beneath my touch, unmovable. He holds her there, breath shaking, staring into her face as though sheer will might rewrite what he sees... as if, by looking long enough, he can force the truth to change.

He exhales, a sound that carries more grief than I can bear. "Time moves strangely in the void. For us, it has been weeks. For Estra...her entire childhood has passed here."

I swallow hard, my throat raw. Daed cannot truly measure human years. Fae time passes differently, though not as severe as in the void. But I can, and looking at her now, at the young woman before me, I know. She can be no older than nineteen.

Then she spits in her father's face and before I can move, she drives her knee into Daed's groin.

He hisses, teeth bared, pain flashing across his face, but he does not let go.

"Filthy Fae," she snarls. "My father was right. You're a traitor and a coward. How dare you refuse the gifts he so graciously gave you! I'll carve his name into your flesh so he's with you forever!"

Her voice is pure venom, but beneath it trembles conviction, the kind taught, not born.

"Why is she saying these things?" My voice breaks as tears sting my eyes.

Daed's jaw tightens. "She doesn't know who we are," he says through gritted teeth. "Don't you see, Amara? She's been here too long. Under Gygarth's thrall. He's raised her as his own." His voice fractures, low and bitter. "She doesn't remember us."

No. No, that cannot be.

We came to An'kel to bring our child home, not to find a grown woman who calls our enemy *father*.

Who looks at us and sees monsters.

She doesn't remember. Souls, she doesn't remember.

How could she not know me? Her mother? How could she not see him? Her father? How could she not feel, even now, that we love her enough to face the dark and defy death itself to reach her?

Remember.

The words burns through me, cutting through the fog of grief. My spine straightens, my tears dry to salt on my skin.

"Hold her," I say quietly.

Daed's brow creases, but he obeys without question. He turns her in his arms to face me, even as she thrashes and kicks, a feral cry tearing from her throat. I would expect nothing less from my daughter. But I will not lose her again.

I reach for her face. She snaps at my hand, snarling, but I catch her anyway, threading my fingers through her dark curls, cradling the head that once fit in my palm. She fights me still, even when I press my thumbs gently against her temples.

Then she jolts. A shudder runs through her body, and she gasps.

I open my mind and I pour everything into her. Every memory. Every heartbeat. The moment her father and I stood as enemies. The moment we became something else. The battles. The loss. The rebuilding. The first flutter in my belly. Her tiny hands. Her laugh.

Every joy. Every heartbreak. Every shred of the love that forged her.

Light flickers behind her eyes, and a single tear slips free.

When the last thread of memory passes, I drop my hands, trembling with what might come next. We wait for another strike, another insult, another scream.

But none comes.

Instead, she looks at me. Really *looks* and in that moment, I see my child.

"Mother?" she whispers.

My heart fractures.

Slowly, she turns to Daed. He releases her, his hands shaking as if afraid to believe.

Her lips part, trembling on the word that unravels us both.

"Father?"

Then he breaks, sweeping her into his arms.

"Estra," he breathes, voice cracking on her name. "My daughter."

The words unravel me.

I watch as she hesitates, then her hands lift until they find his waist, and when she finally clings to him, something inside me shatters. I fall into them both, arms encircling them, holding tight, as if my body alone could keep the world from taking her again.

We weep together—father, mother, daughter—our tears mingling, our breaths uneven. I do not know how long we stand like that. In the void, time has no meaning.

But even if eternity were ours, it would not be long enough.

When there are no more tears left to cry, when our arms ache from holding one another, when the weight of what we've survived finally settles into our bones, the silence after the storm feels almost unbearable. My body trembles, every wound screaming now that the battle's fever has burned away. Still, I lift my hand and open a portal.

The air parts like a sigh, and through the tear, the Grove unfurls. The scent of earth and sunlight drifts through, and beyond it stand our friends, waiting.

Estra stands between Daed and me, our hands clasped around hers, a bond of flesh and blood and steel, forged in grief and fire. Our baby may be gone, but our daughter lives. The warmth of her skin, the steady beat of her heart, it's everything. Proof that we did not fight in vain.

Together, we step through the portal.

Into a world broken, but ours.

A world our blood has scarred, but our love will mend. A world where a cursed Fae prince and his Awakened bride can teach shadow and light to coexist, where our child can grow without fear, and the wounds of gods and mortals alike might finally heal.

The world we bargained for.

A world bound by shadows and souls and a love eternal, born of smoke and vine.

Epilogue
Amara

I stand on the balcony of the white marble castle, my hands resting against the railing. Vines curl along every wall and column, flowers bursting through cracks, and as I look out across Pariseth, I see that all this beautiful growth stems from a single vine in the garden below. The serpentine vine I planted so long ago has grown wild and spread.

In the garden, Daed works beneath the warm afternoon sun, his shirt discarded, his skin bronzed and gleaming with sweat, hands buried in the soil as he pulls up roots for dinner. Once, those hands wielded blades and shadows. Now they tend seedlings. His hair falls over his face, and for a moment I simply watch him, this Fae prince who once commanded armies and now hums softly while he gardens.

Footsteps sound behind me.

"You've made a farmer out of a Fae prince," Estra says, amusement lacing her tone as she joins me on the balcony.

I smile, turning to take her in. My daughter, my miracle. Her skin glows fair in the sun, her dark curls tied high in a loose ponytail. She wears leathers and boots, a linen shirt beneath a fitted vest, and around her wrist, as always, Arax's red ribbon.

"It keeps him busy," I say, warmth threading through my voice. "With no war, no demons, no crown to weigh him down, he barely knows what to do with himself."

Estra leans her elbows on the railing beside me, gazing down at her father. "It still surprises me, how easily he gave up the crown to Aunt Zyphoro."

"It shouldn't," I reply, my eyes following Daed as he straightens, wiping sweat from his brow. "He never wanted to rule, and once he realized the Sundered Kingdoms didn't need a king, he was glad to let it go. Zyphoro has the strength and vision to lead our world forward. After centuries of isolation, she's determined to rebuild what was lost."

A small grin tugs at my lips. "Though with Lord Reon as her counsel, we may see more chaos than diplomacy. He promises the debauchery will be kept to a minimum."

Estra laughs, and I close my eyes for a heartbeat, just to listen.

The laughter. The creak of the vines as they grow. The sound of Daed's hands in the soil.

The world has changed. So have we, and for the first time in my life, change does not frighten me.

"Speaking of which. Your father and I have been summoned to a great banquet in Baev'kalath."

Estra smirks, her silver eyes glinting. "And you're dreading it?"

"Absolutely," I say without hesitation, exhaling a weary sigh. "I've not had the best history with Baev'kalath or its banquets. But for your aunt and for Reon, I'll do my best to endure. It will be strange, though, not seeing Orios and Solena across the table."

Estra's expression softens. "Where do you think they are now?"

"Somewhere quiet," I answer, leaning against the balcony rail. "Somewhere far away, where their only care in the world is each other. They fought hard for that peace, defied every rule that tried to keep them apart. I imagine we might never see them again."

She goes silent, so I reach across the railing, my hand sliding over hers.

"Just promise me," I say softly, "that you will not vanish forever."

Estra turns to me, her face open, earnest. "I spent most of my life without you, Mother. I would never put any of us through that pain again. But I can't stay here forever. I need to see the world. I've known only the barren lands of An'kel and Gygarth's darkness. I want to know what else there is."

I nod, though her words twist something deep inside me. "I understand," I say, even if the ache of it nearly undoes me. "When you return, you know where to find your father and me. Wherever you are, whenever you call, we'll answer."

Movement catches my eye below. Through the tall grass, a figure walks toward the castle, the gold shimmer of his mask catching the afternoon light. Ronin. Dressed simply, no armor, no cloak, only worn travel clothes and a sword strapped to his back.

Daed sees him too. He straightens from where he's working in the garden, tosses the shovel aside a little too forcefully, and claps his hands together to rid them of dirt. His scowl is immediate, fangs flashing as the sunlight strikes his face.

Estra groans. "I'd hoped he'd be used to it by now."

A laugh slips from me before I can stop it. "Used to it? To his daughter riding off with the Golden Son? My love, you ask too much of him."

"His name is Ronin," she says pointedly. "And he wants the same thing I do."

I lift my chin, the faintest edge to my smile. "It's what Ronin wants that worries your father most."

Estra makes a sound halfway between a groan and a laugh. "Mother. It isn't like that."

I smirk, folding my arms. "Say what you will, but I'd keep your farewells short before your father beats him to death with that shovel."

She sighs. "You're probably right."

Estra rolls her shoulders, and the collar of her linen shirt shifts, just enough to reveal the bright blue moonstone resting at her collarbone. It glimmers like captured sky against the dark runes etched into her skin. They blaze, not the soft violet of old, but a wild, living green, and a heartbeat later, her wings burst free. They unfurl with a sharp sweep, feathers glossy as spilled ink and tipped with silver light. Smaller than most, yes, and she still hides her self-consciousness beneath bravado, but they are beautiful all the same.

She steps onto the balcony rail, her boots finding balance with effortless grace, sunlight gilding her curls. She glances back over her shoulder, eyes gleaming. "Are you coming?"

I smile. "After you."

Her grin flashes and then she falls backward into the open air, wings snapping wide to catch the wind. The rush lifts her into a sweeping arc that makes my heart ache with pride.

With a flick of my wrist, vines unfurl from the balcony's edge, weaving themselves into a ramp of living green. Leaves shimmer in the sunlight as I lift my skirts, stepping barefoot along its length until I reach the railing.

I summon my wings. They bloom from my back in a whisper of vines and petals, the scent of spring filling the air. Then, like Estra, I leap.

The wind rushes against my skin as I glide downward, landing lightly in the garden below. I barely touch the ground before Daed's arm curls around my waist, pulling me close, his lips pressing against the side of my neck.

"Wife," he murmurs, voice dark and velvet.

"Husband," I breathe, and I don't mind the sweat on his skin or the dirt on his hands. They are proof of life, of peace.

Estra groans, rolling her eyes. "Honestly. Do you ever stop?"

I do not get the chance to answer. Ronin lingers at the garden's edge, scratching the back of his neck and looking anywhere but at us.

"Do you even know what you're doing?" Daed snaps, folding his arms.

Ronin exhales. "I'm not a child, Rook. I've led armies."

Daed's brows lift. "The same army that set you on fire? I wouldn't lead with that."

I tap his chest, failing to hide my grin. "Be kind," I chide softly, but the laughter in my voice betrays me.

Ronin turns to me instead, wisely seeking refuge. "She'll be safe, Amara. You have my word."

Estra scoffs before I can answer. "I'll be safe because of me, not because of you, Ronin."

He mutters something under his breath, and I swear it's in perfect imitation of Daed's usual curses.

Estra turns to us, her face softening, caught between longing and resolve. I see everything she wants to say written across her expression, the pride, the fear, the love, and I lift my hand to her cheek before she can speak.

"I hope you find what you're searching for, daughter," I whisper.

Her eyes sheen, and the tension melts from her shoulders. She steps forward and presses a kiss to my cheek, warm and trembling and full of promise.

Her father, however, is silent. His gaze lingers somewhere far beyond the horizon, but I feel the faint twitch of his leg beside me, the only betrayal of his calm.

"Father," Estra says softly at first, then again, firmer this time, commanding, as if *he* were the child.

"Father."

Reluctantly, Daed drags his eyes from the distance to meet hers.

"I'll see you soon," she says. "I promise."

For a heartbeat, he holds on to that proud Fae stoicism, the hardness that's protected him for centuries, but it crumbles the moment she starts to turn away. He reaches out, catching her by the elbow.

Estra stops mid-step, a knowing smile curving her mouth before she steps closer. She rises onto her toes and presses a kiss to his cheek.

"I love you, Father," she whispers against his skin.

And just like that, the fearsome Fae prince, the one who has faced gods and demons without flinching melts.

"I love you too," he says, voice thick. "Be careful."

But we both know the truth. She does not need protection. It is the world that should be weary of her.

"I'll open a portal back to Baev'kalath," I say, stepping forward.

Estra and Ronin exchange a wary look.

"Unless," I add, lips twitching, "you'd rather she scoop you up and fly you through the tidal wall?"

Ronin grimaces. "A portal would be appreciated."

I smile faintly and extend my arm. From beneath my sleeve, a vine unfurls, curling around my wrist until thorns bloom and pierce my skin. Blood wells and drips to the earth, each drop shimmering before a rift tears open before us.

Through it, Baev'kalath glimmers, the black fortress beneath its eternal storm, waves crashing against its cliffs. Yet for the first time in centuries, the clouds seem thinner, the darkness not so absolute. There is hope there now, where once there was none.

"Goodbye," Estra says, her voice steady despite the tremor beneath it.

Daed and I only nod, holding each other close as we watch her step through just as lightning strikes the sky. Ronin follows, glancing over his shoulder to farewell us a last time before the portal seals behind them, my blood healing into a scatter of red petals that drift down to rest upon the grass.

For a moment, we stand there, quiet. The air hums with the ache of parting, but also with something deeper. Our daughter is free, the world remade, and if we can survive the God of Death, nothing will ever part us again.

"What do we do now?" I ask, voice soft against the hush of the wind.

Daed sweeps my hair over my shoulder, his fingers tracing the curve of my neck before gliding lazily down my skin. His touch sends a ripple of heat through me, slow and familiar.

"I need to rinse this sweat off," Daed says, gesturing to the slick sheen running down the hard lines of his body, over the carved planes of muscle, tracing the inked runes across his chest and abdomen, vanishing beneath the low hang of his leather trousers. His mouth curves, half-smirk, half-invitation. "What do you say to a walk in the forest? A soak in the river?"

I smile, unable to resist him even after all these years. "Sounds wonderful. What do you think, Ashen?"

From within the tumble of my hair, a faint curl of smoke unfurls before coalescing into the form of a bright-eyed kitten perched on my shoulder. Ashen purrs, a sound like a sighing ember, then leaps. Midair, his shape unravels, expanding, reforming, until a full-grown lion of shadow and smoke lands before us. His paws strike the earth with a reverberating thud, his mane rippling like stormclouds.

Daed exhales a long-suffering breath. "I wasn't hoping for an audience," he mutters.

I grin, running a hand along Ashen's massive jaw, the air humming where our skin meets. He rumbles a deep purr, pressing his head into my palm before lowering himself to the ground in silent invitation.

"Now, now," I tease, climbing onto his back and clutching his smoky mane, "we have eternity for that. Besides, the more he is with us, the sooner he will remember. Right?"

Daed's lips quirk, though his eyes soften, and he nods. "Right." His eyes narrow on me. "You wear your newfound immortality well, wife."

His words kindle something warm in my chest. The thought that I'll never have to watch him fade, that time, for once, is on our side. That Estra's journeying will last only a heartbeat compared to the endless life waiting for us here. That we have all the tomorrows the world can give.

"Then let's enjoy it together, husband," I say, reaching for him.

Our fingers brush, and golden threads, our bond, our promise, spiral between us, pulsing with light. The glow lingers, wrapping around our joined hands before fading into the air.

Ashen yawns, smoke curling from his jaws, then takes a heavy step toward the forest.

Daed walks beside us, his hand trailing along my leg, eyes gleaming with that familiar stormlight as we cross into the woods together. Into peace, into forever.

About the Author

Here there be dragons and starships

J.L. Tomlinson is a science fiction and fantasy writer hailing from New Zealand.
When not lost in worlds of magic and interstellar adventures, she enjoys reading, exploring spooky things that aren't too scary, and indulging in her love for fried chicken and eavesdropping on people arguing in malls.
Her stories blend the fantastical with the familiar, delivering tales as thrilling as they are heartfelt.
Find her online and keep up to date with all things booky.

www.ingramcontent.com/pod-product-compliance
Lightning Source LLC
Chambersburg PA
CBHW020824030726
47496CB00001B/83